THE BEST OF
JOE HALDEMAN

THE BEST OF
JOE HALDEMAN

JOE HALDEMAN

EDITED BY JONATHAN STRAHAN
AND GARY K. WOLFE

SUBTERRANEAN PRESS 2013

First Edition

ISBN
978-1-59606-526-0

Subterranean Press
PO Box 190106
Burton, MI 48519

www.subterraneanpress.com

TABLE OF CONTENTS

INTRODUCTION

It was an entertaining exercise in nostalgia to put together this collection, spanning as it does over forty years of writing. The importance of short stories to my daily life and my writing career has waxed and waned over those years, but writing them is always interesting. They pack surprises in a way that novels do not.

That career didn't begin until the late 1960s, so it barely brushed the "Golden Age" of magazine science fiction, when an energetic writer could make a living pounding out stories for the pulp magazines, for pennies a word, or less. In the sixties there were still as many as a dozen science fiction magazines on the newsstands—paper was still cheap, and magazines didn't have to compete with the barrage of media that now tries to grab the reader's attention and wallet. (Even then, though, oldsters were bemoaning the loss of the "real" pulps, the large-format 'zines with ragged edges that carried science fiction from the 'twenties through my childhood 'fifties.)

I wrote my first two short stories in a writing class, the last semester before finishing my bachelor's degree. Then I was drafted, and for a couple of years my only literary activity, except for a little poetry, was writing home.

When I returned from Vietnam I spent thirty days as a temporary civilian. During that time I rewrote those two undergraduate stories (both science fiction) and sent them out to magazines, and they both sold before I got out of the army, a few months later.

I knew from reading writers' magazines that this kind of success was unusual. I'd planned to go back to college when I was out of the army, to study for a Ph.D. in computer science, and so I sort of did that— I registered for half-time and took two required math courses while I wrote "on the side." But after a couple of weeks I sold my first novel.

9

I dropped out of graduate school quickly enough to get half of my tuition back. Bought a fresh typewriter ribbon and sailed off into a new life.

My wife Gay and I were living in the Washington suburbs then, going to the University of Maryland—but if I was going to be a writer, we could live anywhere, so we packed everything into an ancient Ford van and fled the Washington traffic and noise and snow for sunny Florida.

We went down to Brooksville, where fellow SF writer Keith Laumer lived—he'd said you could practically live for free there, picking oranges off the trees and catching fish for protein. It wasn't quite that easy, but it was doable. Our rent on a three-bedroom cottage was $100 a month, which came to about 2500 words at my average rate, four cents. I could do that in two good days—make it three—and then start paying for the groceries, to supplement those free oranges and fishes, which anyhow had lost their charm.

My first novel, *War Year*, came out, and was a critical success, although it never made much money. But Gay had a job, teaching Spanish at the local high school, and along with my regular-if-sporadic writing income, we were doing pretty well.

The science fiction novels I was working on were both episodic; I could sell their chapters to the magazines as stand-alone novellas. One was *The Forever War*, which I was calling *Hero*, and the other became *All My Sins Remembered* (its working title was "the spy story").

The conventional wisdom at the time was that there was no real money in magazine fiction, and no future; you had to write novels if you were going to write full time. But the magazines paid our rent and took us to Europe on a shoestring. They also gave me exposure for stories that ran the gamut from New Age surrealism to *Analog*-style hard science fiction.

In retrospect I can see that they gave the writing life a kind of continuity and rhythm. I've never been a prolific writer, by science fiction standards, but writing and selling a couple of short stories a month made me feel like a pro. I might not have known it then, but I'm certain of it now: a beginning writer needs confidence and validation. You can get it from your pals and relatives and teachers telling you how good you are, but trust me: all that is vapor compared to the reality of a check with an editor's signature. Somebody you don't know actually parted with his money for a chunk of your imagination.

That can become routine, but the first time makes you giddy with possibilities. (Giddy enough to rent a van and flee for the Sunshine State.)

INTRODUCTION

The writing itself never does become routine, because you don't know where it comes from, and you can't know how long it will last. Forever, you hope, whatever finite number of years that turns out to be. Meanwhile, you hope to keep surprising yourself and pleasing others.

I've often wished it were still possible to make a living writing just short stories. I came close to doing it for a year or two, around 1970 and 1971, when there were markets galore and short work paid more per word, and per day, than novels were bringing in. I tried to write a thousand words a day (which became 500 words of final copy), and I kept track on a clipboard beside my typewriter. There was a special charm to that kind of writing. I'd always have several stories in some stage of incompletion; while I showered in the morning I'd either come up with a new idea or decide which in-progress story I'd work on. Then get the coffee percolating and sit down with a fresh stack of paper, and have at it.

One thing that a novelist misses, that a short story writer has all the time, is the satisfaction of being near completion. And though finishing a novel that you've spent a year or more on is a special satisfaction, well, you do only get it once a year or so.

I don't know much about Charles Dickens, but they say that when he was writing short stories and came to the end of one, he inscribed a little flourish of a curlicue, and set down his pen. I do know how that feels, even though now it physically may be pulling a piece of paper out of the machine, or just hitting Command-S and sitting back. A job well done, or at least done as well as you can.

Here are some I'm still satisfied with.

INTRODUCTION TO "HERO"

I remember the day I started "Hero"—probably the most important day in my writing life, since that turned out to be the beginning of *The Forever War*. At the time, though, I was just idly typing.

My wife and I had driven down to Florida, to visit fellow writer Keith Laumer and escape the snows of Washington, D.C. The second day we were at his place—a modernist mansion on a wild island in the middle of nowhere—she and Keith drove into town for groceries, and I sat down at the dining room table with my manual typewriter and absolutely no idea of what to write.

I had been out of the Army for a year and a half, and had a vague ambition to write a science-fiction war story. So I remembered an absurd day in Basic Training, slogging through midnight snow supposedly training for jungle warfare, when they herded us into a frigid Quonset Hut where a young lieutenant stepped up onto a podium and intoned "Tonight we're going to show you eight silent ways to kill a man."

None of the methods articulated in the speech was particularly useful, as it turned out. But a couple of years later, I started a career with it.

HERO

I

"Tonight we're going to show you eight silent ways to kill a man." The guy who said that was a sergeant who didn't look five years older than me. So if he'd ever killed a man in combat, silently or otherwise, he'd done it as an infant.

I already knew eighty ways to kill people, but most of them were pretty noisy. I sat up straight in my chair and assumed a look of polite attention and fell asleep with my eyes open. So did most everybody else. We'd learned that they never scheduled anything important for these after-chop classes.

The projector woke me up and I sat through a short tape showing the "eight silent ways." Some of the actors must have been brainwipes, since they were actually killed.

After the tape a girl in the front row raised her hand. The sergeant nodded at her and she rose to parade rest. Not bad looking, but kind of chunky about the neck and shoulders. Everybody gets that way after carrying a heavy pack around for a couple of months.

"Sir"—we had to call sergeants "sir" until graduation—"Most of those methods, really, they looked...kind of silly."

"For instance?"

"Like killing a man with a blow to the kidneys, from an entrenching tool. I mean, when would you *actually* have only an entrenching tool, and no gun or knife? And why not just bash him over the head with it?"

"He might have a helmet on," he said reasonably.

"Besides, Taurans probably don't even *have* kidneys!"

He shrugged. "Probably they don't." This was 1997, and nobody had ever seen a Tauran; hadn't even found any pieces of Taurans bigger than a

13

scorched chromosome. "But their body chemistry is similar to ours, and we have to assume they're similarly complex creatures. They *must* have weaknesses, vulnerable spots. You have to find out where they are.

"That's the important thing." He stabbed a finger at the screen. "Those eight convicts got caulked for your benefit because you've got to find out how to kill Taurans, and be able to do it whether you have a megawatt laser or an emery board."

She sat back down, not looking too convinced.

"Any more questions?" Nobody raised a hand.

"Okay Tench-hut!" We staggered upright and he looked at us expectantly.

"Fuck you, sir," came the familiar tired chorus.

"Louder!"

"FUCK YOU, SIR!" One of the army's less-inspired morale devices.

"That's better. Don't forget, pre-dawn maneuvers tomorrow. Chop at 0330, first formation, 0400. Anybody sacked after 0340 owes one stripe. Dismissed."

I zipped up my coverall and went across the snow to the lounge for a cup of soya and a joint. I'd always been able to get by on five or six hours of sleep, and this was the only time I could be by myself, out of the army for a while. Looked at the newsfax for a few minutes. Another ship got caulked, out by Aldebaran sector. That was four years ago. They were mounting a reprisal fleet, but it'll take four years more for them to get out there. By then, the Taurans would have every portal planet sewed up tight.

Back at the billet, everybody else was sacked and the main lights were out. The whole company'd been dragging ever since we got back from the two-week lunar training. I dumped my clothes in the locker, checked the roster and found out I was in bunk 31. Goddammit, right under the heater.

I slipped through the curtain as quietly as possible so as not to wake up the person next to me. Couldn't see who it was, but I couldn't have cared less. I slipped under the blanket.

"You're late, Mandella," a voice yawned. It was Rogers.

"Sorry I woke you up," I whispered.

"'Sallright." She snuggled over and clasped me spoon-fashion. She was warm and reasonably soft.

I patted her hip in what I hoped was a brotherly fashion. "Night, Rogers."

"G'night, Stallion." She returned the gesture more pointedly.

Why do you always get the tired ones when you're ready and the randy ones when you're tired? I bowed to the inevitable.

II

"Awright, let's get some goddamn *back* inta that! Stringer team! Move it up—move your ass up!"

A warm front had come in about midnight and the snow had turned to sleet. The permaplast stringer weighed five hundred pounds and was a bitch to handle, even when it wasn't covered with ice. There were four of us, two at each end, carrying the plastic girder with frozen fingertips. Rogers was my partner.

"Steel!" the guy behind me yelled, meaning that he was losing his hold. It wasn't steel, but it was heavy enough to break your foot. Everybody let go and hopped away. It splashed slush and mud all over us.

"Goddammit, Petrov," Rogers said, "why didn't you go out for the Red Cross or something? This fucken thing's not that fucken heavy." Most of the girls were a little more circumspect in their speech. Rogers was a little butch.

"Awright, get a fucken *move* on, stringers—epoxy team! Dog 'em! Dog 'em!"

Our two epoxy people ran up, swinging their buckets. "Let's go, Mandella. I'm freezin' my balls off."

"Me, too," the girl said with more feeling than logic.

"One—two—heave!" We got the thing up again and staggered toward the bridge. It was about three-quarters completed. Looked as if the second platoon was going to beat us. I wouldn't give a damn, but the platoon that got their bridge built first got to fly home. Four miles of muck for the rest of us, and no rest before chop.

We got the stringer in place, dropped it with a clank, and fitted the static clamps that held it to the rise-beam. The female half of the epoxy team started slopping glue on it before we even had it secured. Her partner was waiting for the stringer on the other side. The floor team was waiting at the foot of the bridge, each one holding a piece of the light, stressed permaplast over his head like an umbrella. They were dry and clean. I wondered aloud what they had done to deserve it, and Rogers suggested a couple of colorful, but unlikely, possibilities.

We were going back to stand by the next stringer when the field first (name of Dougelstein, but we called him "Awright") blew a whistle and bellowed, "Awright, soldier boys and girls, ten minutes. Smoke 'em if you got 'em." He reached into his pocket and turned on the control that heated our coveralls.

Rogers and I sat down on our end of the stringer and I took out my weed box. I had lots of joints, but we were ordered not to smoke them until after night-chop. The only tobacco I had was a cigarro butt about three inches long. I lit it on the side of the box; it wasn't too bad after the first couple of puffs. Rogers took a puff, just to be sociable, but made a face and gave it back.

"Were you in school when you got drafted?" she asked.

"Yeah. Just got a degree in physics. Was going after a teacher's certificate."

She nodded soberly. "I was in biology..."

"Figures." I ducked a handful of slush. "How far?"

"Six years, bachelor's and technical." She slid her boot along the ground, turning up a ridge of mud and slush the consistency of freezing ice milk. "Why the fuck did this have to happen?"

I shrugged. It didn't call for an answer, least of all the answer that the UNEF kept giving us. Intellectual and physical elite of the planet, going out to guard humanity against the Tauran menace. Soyashit. It was all just a big experiment. See whether we could goad the Taurans into ground action.

Awright blew the whistle two minutes early, as expected, but Rogers and I and the other two stringers got to sit for a minute while the epoxy and floor teams finished covering our stringer. It got cold fast, sitting there with our suits turned off, but we remained inactive on principle.

There really wasn't any sense in having us train in the cold. Typical army half-logic. Sure, it was going to be cold where we were going, but not ice-cold or snow-cold. Almost by definition, a portal planet remained within a degree or two of absolute zero all the time—since collapsars don't shine—and the first chill you felt would mean that you were a dead man.

Twelve years before, when I was ten years old, they had discovered the collapsar jump. Just fling an object at a collapsar with sufficient speed, and out it pops in some other part of the galaxy. It didn't take long to figure out the formula that predicted where it would come out: it travels along the same "line" (actually an Einsteinian geodesic) it would have followed if the collapsar hadn't been in the way—until it reaches another collapsar field, whereupon it reappears, repelled with the same speed at which it approached the original collapsar. Travel time between the two collapsars...exactly zero.

It made a lot of work for mathematical physicists, who had to redefine simultaneity, then tear down general relativity and build it back up again. And it made the politicians very happy, because now they could send a shipload of colonists to Fomalhaut for less than it had once cost to put a brace of men on the moon. There were a lot of people the politicians would love to see on Fomalhaut, implementing a glorious adventure rather than stirring up trouble at home.

The ships were always accompanied by an automated probe that followed a couple of million miles behind. We knew about the portal planets, little bits of flotsam that whirled around the collapsars; the purpose of the drone was to come back and tell us in the event that a ship had smacked into a portal planet at .999 of the speed of light.

That particular catastrophe never happened, but one day a drone limped back alone. Its data were analyzed, and it turned out that the colonists' ship had been pursued by another vessel and destroyed. This happened near Aldebaran, in the constellation Taurus, but since "Aldebaranian" is a little hard to handle, they named the enemy "Tauran."

Colonizing vessels thenceforth went out protected by an armed guard. Often the armed guard went out alone, and finally the colonization group got shortened to UNEF, United Nations Exploratory Force. Emphasis on the "force."

Then some bright lad in the General Assembly decided that we ought to field an army of footsoldiers to guard the portal planets of the nearer collapsars. This led to the Elite Conscription Act of 1996 and the most elitely conscripted army in the history of warfare.

So here we were, fifty men and fifty women, with IQs over 150 and bodies of unusual health and strength, slogging elitely through the mud and slush of central Missouri, reflecting on the usefulness of our skill in building bridges on worlds where the only fluid is an occasional standing pool of liquid helium.

III

About a month later, we left for our final training exercise, maneuvers on the planet Charon. Though nearing perihelion, it was still more than twice as far from the sun as Pluto.

The troopship was a converted "cattlewagon" made to carry two hundred colonists and assorted bushes and beasts. Don't think it was roomy, though, just because there were half that many of us. Most of the excess space was taken up with extra reaction mass and ordnance.

The whole trip took three weeks, accelerating at two gees halfway, decelerating the other half. Our top speed, as we roared by the orbit of Pluto, was around one-twentieth of the speed of light—not quite enough for relativity to rear its complicated head.

Three weeks of carrying around twice as much weight as normal...it's no picnic. We did some cautious exercises three times a day and remained horizontal as much as possible. Still, we got several broken bones and serious dislocations. The men had to wear special supporters to keep from littering the floor with loose organs. It was almost impossible to sleep; nightmares of choking and being crushed, rolling over periodically to prevent blood pooling and bedsores. One girl got so fatigued that she almost slept through the experience of having a rib push out into the open air.

I'd been in space several times before, so when we finally stopped decelerating and went into free fall, it was nothing but relief. But some people had never been out, except for our training on the moon, and succumbed to the sudden vertigo and disorientation. The rest of us cleaned up after them, floating through the quarters with sponges and inspirators to suck up the globules of partly digested "Concentrate, High-protein, Low-residue, Beef Flavor (Soya)."

We had a good view of Charon, coming down from orbit. There wasn't much to see, though. It was just a dim, off-white sphere with a few smudges on it. We landed about two hundred meters from the base. A pressurized crawler came out and mated with the ferry, so we didn't have to suit up. We clanked and squeaked up to the main building, a featureless box of grayish plastic.

Inside, the walls were the same drab color. The rest of the company was sitting at desks, chattering away. There was a seat next to Freeland.

"Jeff—feeling better?" He still looked a little pale.

"If the gods had meant for man to survive in free fall, they would have given him a castiron glottis." He sighed heavily. "A little better. Dying for a smoke."

"Yeah."

"*You* seemed to take it all right. Went up in school, didn't you?"

"Senior thesis in vacuum welding, yeah. Three weeks in Earth orbit." I sat back and reached for my weed box for the thousandth time. It still wasn't there. The life-support unit didn't want to handle nicotine and THC.

"Training was bad enough," Jeff groused, "but *this* shit—"

"Tench-hut!" We stood up in a raggety-ass fashion, by twos and threes. The door opened and a full major came in. I stiffened a little. He was the highest-ranking officer I'd ever seen. He had a row of ribbons stitched into his coveralls, including a purple strip meaning he'd been wounded in combat, fighting in the old American army. Must have been that Indochina thing, but it had fizzled out before I was born. He didn't look that old.

"Sit, sit." He made a patting motion with his hand. Then he put his hands on his hips and scanned the company, a small smile on his face. "Welcome to Charon. You picked a lovely day to land; the temperature outside is a summery eight point one five degrees Absolute. We expect little change for the next two centuries or so." Some of them laughed halfheartedly.

"Best you enjoy the tropical climate here at Miami base; enjoy it while you can. We're on the center of sunside here, and most of your training will be on darkside. Over there, the temperature stays a chilly two point zero eight.

"You might as well regard all the training you got on Earth and the moon as just an elementary exercise, designed to give you a fair chance of surviving Charon. You'll have to go through your whole repertory here: tools, weapons, maneuvers. And you'll find that, at these temperatures, tools don't work the way they should; weapons don't want to fire. And people move v-e-r-y cautiously."

He studied the clipboard in his hand. "Right now, you have forty-nine women and forty-eight men. Two deaths on Earth, one psychiatric release. Having read an outline of your training program, I'm frankly surprised that so many of you pulled through.

"But you might as well know that I won't be displeased if as few as fifty of you, half, graduate from this final phase. And the only way not to graduate is to die. Here. The only way anybody gets back to Earth—including me—is after a combat tour.

"You will complete your training in one month. From here you go to Stargate collapsar, half a light away. You will stay at the settlement on Stargate 1, the largest portal planet, until replacements arrive. Hopefully, that will be no more than a month; another group is due here as soon as you leave.

"When you leave Stargate, you will go to some strategically important collapsar, set up a military base there, and fight the enemy, if attacked. Otherwise, you will maintain the base until further orders.

"The last two weeks of your training will consist of constructing exactly that kind of a base, on darkside. There you will be totally iso-lated from Miami base: no communication, no medical evacuation, no resupply. Sometime before the two weeks are up, your defense facilities will be evaluated in an attack by guided drones. They will be armed."

They had spent all that money on us just to kill us in training?

"All of the permanent personnel here on Charon are combat veterans. Thus, all of us are forty to fifty years of age. But I think we can keep up with you. Two of us will be with you at all times and will accompany you at least as far as Stargate. They are Captain Sherman Stott, your company commander, and Sergeant Octavio Cortez, your first sergeant. Gentlemen?"

Two men in the front row stood easily and turned to face us. Captain Stott was a little smaller than the major, but cut from the same mold: face hard and smooth as porcelain, cynical half-smile, a precise centimeter of beard framing a large chin, looking thirty at the most. He wore a large, gunpowder-type pistol on his hip.

Sergeant Cortez was another story, a horror story. His head was shaved and the wrong shape, flattened out on one side, where a large piece of skull had obviously been taken out. His face was very dark and seamed with wrinkles and scars. Half his left ear was missing, and his eyes were as expressive as buttons on a machine. He had a moustache-and-beard combination that looked like a skinny white caterpillar taking a lap around his mouth. On anybody else, his schoolboy smile might look pleasant, but he was about the ugliest, meanest-looking creature I'd ever seen. Still, if you didn't look at his head and considered the lower six feet or so, he could have posed as the "after" advertisement for a body-building spa. Neither Stott nor Cortez wore any ribbons. Cortez had a small pocket-laser suspended in a magnetic rig, sideways, under his left armpit. It had wooden grips that were worn smooth.

"Now, before I turn you over to the tender mercies of these two gentlemen, let me caution you again:

"Two months ago there was not a living soul on this planet, just some leftover equipment from an expedition of 1991. A working force of forty-five men struggled for a month to erect this base. Twenty-four of them, more than half, died in the construction of it. This is the most dangerous planet men have ever tried to live on, but the places you'll be going will be this bad and worse. Your cadre will try to keep you alive for the next month. Listen to them…and follow their example; all of them have survived here much longer than you'll have to. Captain?" The captain stood up as the major went out the door.

"Tench-*hut*!" The last syllable was like an explosion and we all jerked to our feet.

"Now I'm only gonna say this *once*, so you better listen," he growled. "We *are* in a combat situation here, and in a combat situation there is only *one* penalty for disobedience or insubordination." He jerked the pistol from his hip and held it by the barrel, like a club. "This is an army model 1911 automatic *pistol*, caliber .45, and it is a primitive but effective weapon. The sergeant and I are authorized to use our weapons to kill to enforce discipline. Don't make us do it, because we will. We *will*." He put the pistol back. The holster snap made a loud crack in the dead quiet.

"Sergeant Cortez and I between us have killed more people than are sitting in this room. Both of us fought in Vietnam on the American side and both of us joined the United Nations International Guard more than ten years ago. I took a break in grade from major for the privilege of commanding this company, and First Sergeant Cortez took a break from sub-major, because we are both *combat* soldiers and this is the first *combat* situation since 1987.

"Keep in mind what I've said while the first sergeant instructs you more specifically in what your duties will be under this command. Take over, Sergeant." He turned on his heel and strode out of the room. The expression on his face hadn't changed one millimeter during the whole harangue.

The first sergeant moved like a heavy machine with lots of ball bearings. When the door hissed shut, he swiveled ponderously to face us and said, "At ease, siddown," in a surprisingly gentle voice. He sat on a table in the front of the room. It creaked, but held.

"Now the captain talks scary and I look scary, but we both mean well. You'll be working pretty closely with me, so you better get used to this thing I've got hanging in front of my brain. You probably won't see the captain much, except on maneuvers."

He touched the flat part of his head. "And speaking of brains, I still have just about all of mine, in spite of Chinese efforts to the contrary. All of us old vets who mustered into UNEF had to pass the same criteria that got you drafted by the Elite Conscription Act. So I suspect all of you are smart and tough—but just keep in mind that the captain and I are smart and tough *and* experienced."

He flipped through the roster without really looking at it. "Now, as the captain said, there'll be only one kind of disciplinary action on maneuvers. Capital punishment. But normally *we* won't have to kill you for disobeying; Charon'll save us the trouble.

"Back in the billeting area, it'll be another story. We don't much care what you do inside. Grab-ass all day and fuck all night, makes no difference.... But once you suit up and go outside, you've gotta have discipline that would shame a Centurian. There will be situations where one stupid act could kill us all.

"Anyhow, the first thing we've gotta do is get you fitted to your fighting suits. The armorer's waiting at your billet; he'll take you one at a time. Let's go."

IV

"Now I know you got lectured back on Earth on what a fighting suit can do." The armorer was a small man, partially bald, with no insignia or rank on his coveralls. Sergeant Cortez had told us to call him "sir," since he was a lieutenant.

"But I'd like to reinforce a couple of points, maybe add some things your instructors Earthside weren't clear about or couldn't know. Your first sergeant was kind enough to consent to being my visual aid. Sergeant?"

Cortez slipped out of his coveralls and came up to the little raised platform where a fighting suit was standing, popped open like a man-shaped clam. He backed into it and slipped his arms into the rigid sleeves. There was a click and the thing swung shut with a sigh. It was bright green with CORTEZ stenciled in white letters on the helmet.

"Camouflage, Sergeant." The green faded to white, then dirty gray. "This is good camouflage for Charon and most of your portal planets," said Cortez, as if from a deep well. "But there are several other combinations available." The gray dappled and brightened to a combination of greens and browns: "Jungle." Then smoothed out to a hard light ochre: "Desert." Dark brown, darker, to a deep flat black: "Night or space."

"Very good, Sergeant. To my knowledge, this is the only feature of the suit that was perfected after your training. The control is around your left wrist and is admittedly awkward. But once you find the right combination, it's easy to lock in.

"Now, you didn't get much in-suit training Earthside. We didn't want you to get used to using the thing in a friendly environment. The fighting suit is the deadliest personal weapon ever built, and with no weapon is it easier for the user to kill himself through carelessness. Turn around, Sergeant.

"Case in point." He tapped a large square protuberance between the shoulders. "Exhaust fins. As you know, the suit tries to keep you at a comfortable temperature no matter what the weather's like outside. The material of the suit is as near to a perfect insulator as we could get, consistent with mechanical demands. Therefore, these fins get *hot*—especially hot, compared to darkside temperatures—as they bleed off the body's heat.

"All you have to do is lean up against a boulder of frozen gas; there's lots of it around. The gas will sublime off faster than it can escape from the fins; in escaping, it will push against the surrounding 'ice' and fracture it…and in about one-hundredth of a second, you have the equivalent of a hand grenade going off right below your neck. You'll never feel a thing.

"Variations on this theme have killed eleven people in the past two months. And they were just building a bunch of huts.

"I assume you know how easily the waldo capabilities can kill you or your companions. Anybody want to shake hands with the sergeant?" He paused, then stepped over and clasped his glove. "He's had lots of practice. Until *you* have, be extremely careful. You might scratch an itch and wind up breaking your back. Remember, semi-logarithmic response: two pounds' pressure exerts five pounds' force; three pounds' gives ten; four pounds', twenty-three; five pounds', forty-seven. Most of you can muster up a grip of well over a hundred pounds. Theoretically, you could rip a steel girder in two with that, amplified. Actually, you'd destroy the material of your gloves and, at least on Charon, die very quickly. It'd be a race between decompression and flash-freezing. You'd die no matter which won.

"The leg waldos are also dangerous, even though the amplification is less extreme. Until you're really skilled, don't try to run, or jump. You're likely to trip, and that means you're likely to die.

"Charon's gravity is three-fourths of Earth normal, so it's not too bad. But on a really small world, like Luna, you could take a running jump and not come down for twenty minutes, just keep sailing over the horizon. Maybe bash into a mountain at eighty meters per second. On a small asteroid, it'd be no trick at all to run up to escape velocity and be off on an informal tour of intergalactic space. It's a slow way to travel.

"Tomorrow morning, we'll start teaching you how to stay alive inside this infernal machine. The rest of the afternoon and evening, I'll call you one at a time to be fitted. That's all, Sergeant."

Cortez went to the door and turned the stopcock that let air into the airlock. A bank of infrared lamps went on to keep the air from freezing inside it. When the pressures were equalized, he shut the stopcock, unclamped the door and stepped in, clamping it shut behind him. A pump hummed for about a minute, evacuating the airlock; then he stepped out and sealed the outside door.

It was pretty much like the ones on Luna.

"First I want Private Omar Almizar. The rest of you can go find your bunks. I'll call you over the squawker."

"Alphabetical order, sir?"

"Yep. About ten minutes apiece. If your name begins with Z, you might as well get sacked."

That was Rogers. She probably was thinking about getting sacked.

V

The sun was a hard white point directly overhead. It was a lot brighter than I had expected it to be; since we were eighty AUs out, it was only one-6400th as bright as it is on Earth. Still, it was putting out about as much light as a powerful streetlamp.

"This is considerably more light than you'll have on a portal planet." Captain Stott's voice crackled in our collective ear. "Be glad that you'll be able to watch your step."

We were lined up, single file, on the permaplast sidewalk that connected the billet and the supply hut. We'd practiced walking inside, all morning, and this wasn't any different except for the exotic scenery. Though the light was rather dim, you could see all the way to the horizon quite clearly, with no atmosphere in the way. A black cliff that looked too regular to be natural stretched from one horizon to the other, passing within a kilometer of us. The ground was obsidian-black, mottled with patches of white or bluish ice. Next to the supply hut was a small mountain of snow in a bin marked OXYGEN.

The suit was fairly comfortable, but it gave you the odd feeling of simultaneously being a marionette and a puppeteer. You apply the impulse to move your leg and the suit picks it up and magnifies it and moves your leg *for* you.

"Today we're only going to walk around the company area, and nobody will *leave* the company area." The captain wasn't wearing his .45—unless he carried it as a good luck charm, under his suit—but he had a laser-finger like the rest of us. And his was probably hooked up.

Keeping an interval of at least two meters between each person, we stepped off the permaplast and followed the captain over smooth rock. We walked carefully for about an hour, spiraling out, and finally stopped at the far edge of the perimeter.

"Now everybody pay close attention. I'm going out to that blue slab of ice"—it was a big one, about twenty meters away—"and show you something that you'd better know if you want to stay alive."

He walked out in a dozen confident steps. "First I have to heat up a rock—filters down." I squeezed the stud under my armpit and the filter slid into place over my image converter. The captain pointed his finger at a black rock the size of a basketball, and gave it a short burst. The glare rolled a long shadow of the captain over us and beyond. The rock shattered into a pile of hazy splinters.

"It doesn't take long for these to cool down." He stooped and picked up a piece. "This one is probably twenty or twenty-five degrees. Watch." He tossed the "warm" rock onto the ice slab. It skittered around in a crazy pattern and shot off the side. He tossed another one, and it did the same.

"As you know, you are not quite *perfectly* insulated. These rocks are about the temperature of the soles of your boots. If you try to stand on a slab of hydrogen, the same thing will happen to you. Except that the rock is *already* dead.

"The reason for this behavior is that the rock makes a slick interface with the ice—a little puddle of liquid hydrogen—and rides a few molecules above the liquid on a cushion of hydrogen vapor. This makes the rock or *you* a frictionless bearing as far as the ice is concerned, and you *can't* stand up without any friction under your boots.

"After you have lived in your suit for a month or so you *should* be able to survive falling down, but right *now* you just don't know enough. Watch."

The captain flexed and hopped up onto the slab. His feet shot out from under him and he twisted around in midair, landing on hands and knees. He slipped off and stood on the ground.

"The idea is to keep your exhaust fins from making contact with the frozen gas. Compared to the ice they are as hot as a blast furnace, and contact with any weight behind it will result in an explosion."

After that demonstration, we walked around for another hour or so and returned to the billet. Once through the airlock, we had to mill around for a while, letting the suits get up to something like room temperature. Somebody came up and touched helmets with me.

"William?" She had MCCOY stenciled above her faceplate.

"Hi, Sean. Anything special?"

"I just wondered if you had anyone to sleep with tonight."

That's right; I'd forgotten. There wasn't any sleeping roster here. Everybody chose his own partner. "Sure, I mean, uh, no...no, I haven't asked anybody. Sure, if you want to..."

"Thanks, William. See you later." I watched her walk away and thought that if anybody could make a fighting suit look sexy, it'd be Sean. But even she couldn't.

Cortez decided we were warm enough and led us to the suit room, where we backed the things into place and hooked them up to the charging plates. (Each suit had a little chunk of plutonium that would power it for several years, but we were supposed to run on fuel cells as much as possible.) After a lot of shuffling around, everybody finally got plugged in and we were allowed to unsuit—ninety-seven naked chickens squirming out of bright green eggs. It was *cold*—the air, the floor and especially the suits—and we made a pretty disorderly exit toward the lockers.

I slipped on tunic, trousers and sandals and was still cold. I took my cup and joined the line for soya. Everybody was jumping up and down to keep warm.

"How c-cold, do you think, it is, M-Mandella?" That was McCoy.

"I don't, even want, to think, about it." I stopped jumping and rubbed myself as briskly as possible, while holding a cup in one hand. "At least as cold as Missouri was."

"Ung...wish they'd, get some, fucken, heat in, this place." It always affects the small women more than anybody else. McCoy was the littlest one in the company, a waspwaist doll barely five feet high.

"They've got the airco going. It can't be long now."

"I wish I, was a big, slab of, meat like, you."

I was glad she wasn't.

VI

We had our first casualty on the third day, learning how to dig holes.

With such large amounts of energy stored in a soldier's weapons, it wouldn't be practical for him to hack out a hole in the frozen ground with the conventional pick and shovel. Still, you can launch grenades all day and get nothing but shallow depressions—so the usual method is to bore a hole in the ground with the hand laser, drop a timed charge in after it's cooled down and, ideally, fill the hole with stuff. Of course, there's not much loose rock on Charon, unless you've already blown a hole nearby.

The only difficult thing about the procedure is in getting away. To be safe, we were told, you've got to either be behind something really solid, or be at least a hundred meters away. You've got about three minutes after setting the charge, but you can't just sprint away. Not safely, not on Charon.

The accident happened when we were making a really deep hole, the kind you want for a large underground bunker. For this, we had to blow a hole, then climb down to the bottom of the crater and repeat the procedure again and again until the hole was deep enough. Inside the crater we used charges with a five-minute delay, but it hardly seemed enough time—you really had to go it slow, picking your way up the crater's edge.

Just about everybody had blown a double hole; everybody but me and three others. I guess we were the only ones paying really close attention when Bovanovitch got into trouble. All of us were a good two hundred meters away. With my image converter tuned up to about forty power, I watched her disappear over the rim of the crater. After that, I could only listen in on her conversation with Cortez.

"I'm on the bottom, Sergeant." Normal radio procedure was suspended for maneuvers like this; nobody but the trainee and Cortez was allowed to broadcast.

"Okay, move to the center and clear out the rubble. Take your time. No rush until you pull the pin."

"Sure, Sergeant." We could hear small echoes of rocks clattering, sound conduction through her boots. She didn't say anything for several minutes.

"Found bottom." She sounded a little out of breath.

"Ice or rock?"

"Oh, it's rock, Sergeant. The greenish stuff."

"Use a low setting, then. One point two, dispersion four."

"God darn it, Sergeant, that'll take forever."

"Yeah, but that stuff's got hydrated crystals in it—heat it up too fast and you might make it fracture. And we'd just have to leave you there, girl. Dead and bloody."

"Okay, one point two dee four." The inside edge of the crater flickered red with reflected laser light.

"When you get about a half a meter deep, squeeze it up to dee two."

"Roger." It took her exactly seventeen minutes, three of them at dispersion two. I could imagine how tired her shooting arm was.

"Now rest for a few minutes. When the bottom of the hole stops glowing, arm the charge and drop it in. Then *walk* out, understand? You'll have plenty of time."

"I understand, Sergeant. Walk out." She sounded nervous. Well, you don't often have to tiptoe away from a twenty-microton tachyon bomb. We listened to her breathing for a few minutes.

"Here goes." Faint slithering sound, the bomb sliding down.

"Slow and easy now. You've got five minutes."

"Y-yeah. Five." Her footsteps started out slow and regular. Then, after she started climbing the side, the sounds were less regular, maybe a little frantic. And with four minutes to go—

"Shit!" A loud scraping noise, then clatters and bumps. "Shit—shit."

"What's wrong, Private?"

"Oh, shit." Silence. "Shit!"

"Private, you don't wanna get shot, you *tell me what's wrong!*"

"I...shit, I'm stuck. Fucken rockslide...shit.... DO SOMETHING! I can't move, shit I can't move, I, I—"

"Shut up! How deep?"

"Can't move my, shit, my fucken legs. HELP ME—"

"Then goddammit use your arms—push! You can move a ton with each hand." Three minutes.

She stopped cussing and started to mumble, in Russian, I guess, a low monotone. She was panting, and you could hear rocks tumbling away.

"I'm free." Two minutes.

"Go as fast as you can." Cortez's voice was flat, emotionless.

At ninety seconds she appeared, crawling over the rim. "Run, girl.... You better run." She ran five or six steps and fell, skidded a few meters and got back up, running; fell again, got up again—

It looked as though she was going pretty fast, but she had only covered about thirty meters when Cortez said, "All right, Bovanovitch, get down on your stomach and lie still." Ten seconds, but she didn't hear or she wanted to get just a little more distance, and she kept running, careless leaping strides, and at the high point of one leap there was a flash and a rumble, and something big hit her below the neck, and her headless body spun off end over end through space, trailing a red-black spiral of flash-frozen blood that settled gracefully to the ground, a path of crystal powder that nobody disturbed while we gathered rocks to cover the juiceless thing at the end of it.

That night Cortez didn't lecture us, didn't even show up for night-chop. We were all very polite to each other and nobody was afraid to talk about it.

I sacked with Rogers—everybody sacked with a good friend—but all she wanted to do was cry, and she cried so long and so hard that she got me doing it, too.

VII

"Fire team *A*—move out!" The twelve of us advanced in a ragged line toward the simulated bunker. It was about a kilometer away, across a carefully prepared obstacle course. We could move pretty fast, since all of the ice had been cleared from the field, but even with ten days' experience we weren't ready to do more than an easy jog.

I carried a grenade launcher loaded with tenth-microton practice grenades. Everybody had their laser-fingers set at point oh eight dee one, not much more than a flashlight. This was a *simulated* attack—the bunker and its robot defender cost too much to use once and be thrown away.

"Team *B*, follow. Team leaders, take over."

We approached a clump of boulders at about the halfway mark, and Potter, my team leader, said, "Stop and cover." We clustered behind the rocks and waited for team *B*.

Barely visible in their blackened suits, the dozen men and women whispered by us. As soon as they were clear, they jogged left, out of our line of sight.

"Fire!" Red circles of light danced a half-klick downrange, where the bunker was just visible. Five hundred meters was the limit for these practice grenades; but I might luck out, so I lined the launcher up on the image of the bunker, held it at a forty-five degree angle and popped off a salvo of three.

Return fire from the bunker started before my grenades even landed. Its automatic lasers were no more powerful than the ones we were using, but a direct hit would deactivate your image converter, leaving you blind. It was setting down a random field of fire, not even coming close to the boulders we were hiding behind.

Three magnesium-bright flashes blinked simultaneously about thirty meters short of the bunker. "Mandella! I thought you were supposed to be *good* with that thing."

"Damn it, Potter—it only throws half a klick. Once we get closer, I'll lay 'em right on top, every time."

"Sure you will." I didn't say anything. She wouldn't be team leader forever. Besides, she hadn't been such a bad girl before the power went to her head.

Since the grenadier is the assistant team leader, I was slaved into Potter's radio and could hear *B* team talk to her.

"Potter, this is Freeman. Losses?"

"Potter here—no, looks like they were concentrating on you."

"Yeah, we lost three. Right now we're in a depression about eighty, a hundred meters down from you. We can give cover whenever you're ready."

"Okay, start." Soft click: "*A* team, follow me." She slid out from behind the rock and turned on the faint pink beacon beneath her powerpack. I turned on mine and moved out to run alongside of her, and the rest of the team fanned out in a trailing wedge. Nobody fired while *A* team laid down a cover for us.

All I could hear was Potter's breathing and the soft *crunch-crunch* of my boots. Couldn't see much of anything, so I tongued the image converter up to a log-two intensification. That made the image kind of blurry but adequately bright. Looked like the bunker had *B* team pretty well pinned down; they were getting quite a roasting. All of their return fire was laser. They must have lost their grenadier.

"Potter, this is Mandella. Shouldn't we take some of the heat off *B* team?"

"Soon as I can find us good enough cover. Is that all right with you? Private?" She'd been promoted to corporal for the duration of the exercise.

We angled to the right and lay down behind a slab of rock. Most of the others found cover nearby, but a few had to hug the ground.

"Freeman, this is Potter."

"Potter, this is Smithy. Freeman's out; Samuels is out. We only have five men left. Give us some cover so we can get—"

"Roger, Smithy." *Click.* "Open up, *A* team. The *B*'s are really hurtin'."

I peeked out over the edge of the rock. My rangefinder said that the bunker was about three hundred fifty meters away, still pretty far. I aimed a smidgeon high and popped three, then down a couple of degrees, three more. The first ones overshot by about twenty meters; then the second salvo flared up directly in front of the bunker. I tried to hold on that angle and popped fifteen, the rest of the magazine, in the same direction.

I should have ducked down behind the rock to reload, but I wanted to see where the fifteen would land, so I kept my eyes on the bunker while I reached back to unclip another magazine—

When the laser hit my image converter, there was a red glare so intense it seemed to go right through my eyes and bounce off the back of my skull. It must have been only a few milliseconds before the converter overloaded and went blind, but the bright green afterimage hurt my eyes for several seconds.

Since I was officially "dead," my radio automatically cut off, and I had to remain where I was until the mock battle was over. With no sensory input besides the feel of my own skin (and it ached where the image converter had shone on it) and the ringing in my ears, it seemed like an awfully long time. Finally, a helmet clanked against mine.

"You okay, Mandella?" Potter's voice.

"Sorry, I died of boredom twenty minutes ago."

"Stand up and take my hand." I did so and we shuffled back to the billet. It must have taken over an hour. She didn't say anything more, all the way back—it's a pretty awkward way to communicate—but after we'd cycled through the airlock and warmed up, she helped me undo my suit. I got ready for a mild tongue-lashing, but when the suit popped open, before I could even get my eyes adjusted to the light, she grabbed me around the neck and planted a wet kiss on my mouth.

"Nice shooting, Mandella."

"Huh?"

"Didn't you see? Of course not.… The last salvo before you got hit— four direct hits. The bunker decided it was knocked out, and all we had to do was walk the rest of the way."

"Great." I scratched my face under the eyes, and some dry skin flaked off. She giggled.

"You should see yourself. You look like…"

"All personnel, report to the assembly area." That was the captain's voice. Bad news, usually.

She handed me a tunic and sandals. "Let's go." The assembly area-chop hall was just down the corridor. There was a row of roll-call buttons at the door; I pressed the one beside my name. Four of the names were covered with black tape. That was good, only four. We hadn't lost anybody during today's maneuvers.

The captain was sitting on the raised dais, which at least meant we didn't have to go through the tench-hut bullshit. The place filled up in less than a minute; a soft chime indicated the roll was complete.

Captain Stott didn't stand up. "You did *fairly* well today. Nobody killed, and I expected some to be. In that respect you exceeded my expectations but in *every* other respect you did a poor job.

"I am glad you're taking good care of yourselves, because each of you represents an investment of over a million dollars and one-fourth of a human life.

"But in this simulated battle against a *very* stupid robot enemy, thirty-seven of you managed to walk into laser fire and be killed in a *simulated* way, and since dead people require no food, *you* will require no food, for the next three days. Each person who was a casualty in this battle will be allowed only two liters of water and a vitamin ration each day."

We knew enough not to groan or anything, but there were some pretty disgusted looks, especially on the faces that had singed eyebrows and a pink rectangle of sunburn framing their eyes.

"Mandella."

"Sir?"

"You are far and away the worst-burned casualty. Was your image converter set on normal?"

Oh, shit. "No, sir. Log two."

"I see. Who was your team leader for the exercises?"

"Acting Corporal Potter, sir."

"Private Potter, did you order him to use image intensification?"

"Sir, I…I don't remember."

"You don't. Well, as a memory exercise you may join the dead people. Is that satisfactory?"

"Yes, sir."

"Good. Dead people get one last meal tonight and go on no rations starting tomorrow. Are there any questions?" He must have been kidding. "All right. Dismissed."

I selected the meal that looked as if it had the most calories and took my tray over to sit by Potter.

"That was a quixotic damn thing to do. But thanks."

"Nothing. I've been wanting to lose a few pounds anyway." I couldn't see where she was carrying any extra.

"I know a good exercise," I said. She smiled without looking up from her tray. "Have anybody for tonight?"

"Kind of thought I'd ask Jeff…."

"Better hurry, then. He's lusting after Maejima." Well, that was mostly true. Everybody did.

"I don't know. Maybe we ought to save our strength. That third day…."

"Come on." I scratched the back of her hand lightly with a fingernail. "We haven't sacked since Missouri. Maybe I've learned something new."

"Maybe you have." She tilted her head up at me in a sly way. "Okay."

Actually, she was the one with the new trick. The French corkscrew, she called it. She wouldn't tell me who taught it to her, though. I'd like to shake his hand. Once I got my strength back.

VIII

The two weeks' training around Miami base eventually cost us eleven lives. Twelve, if you count Dahlquist. I guess having to spend the rest of your life on Charon with a hand and both legs missing is close enough to dying.

Foster was crushed in a landslide and Freeland had a suit malfunction that froze him solid before we could carry him inside. Most of the other deaders were people I didn't know all that well. But they all hurt. And they seemed to make us more scared rather than more cautious.

Now darkside. A flyer brought us over in groups of twenty and set us down beside a pile of building materials thoughtfully immersed in a pool of helium II.

We used grapples to haul the stuff out of the pool. It's not safe to go wading, since the stuff crawls all over you and it's hard to tell what's underneath; you could walk out onto a slab of hydrogen and be out of luck.

I'd suggested that we try to boil away the pool with our lasers, but ten minutes of concentrated fire didn't drop the helium level appreciably. It didn't boil, either; helium II is a "superfluid," so what evaporation there was had to take place evenly, all over the surface. No hot spots, so no bubbling.

We weren't supposed to use lights, to "avoid detection." There was plenty of starlight with your image converter cranked up to log three or four, but each stage of amplification meant some loss of detail. By log four the landscape looked like a crude monochrome painting, and you couldn't read the names on people's helmets unless they were right in front of you.

The landscape wasn't all that interesting, anyhow. There were half a dozen medium-sized meteor craters (all with exactly the same level of helium II in them) and the suggestion of some puny mountains just over the horizon. The uneven ground was the consistency of frozen spiderwebs; every time you put your foot down, you'd sink half an inch with a squeaking crunch. It could get on your nerves.

It took most of a day to pull all the stuff out of the pool. We took shifts napping, which you could do either standing up, sitting or lying on your stomach. I didn't do well in any of those positions, so I was anxious to get the bunker built and pressurized.

We couldn't build the thing underground—it'd just fill up with helium II—so the first thing to do was to build an insulating platform, a permaplast-vacuum sandwich three layers thick.

I was acting corporal, with a crew of ten people. We were carrying the permaplast layers to the building site—two people can carry one easily—when one of "my" men slipped and fell on his back.

"Damn it, Singer, watch your step." We'd had a couple of deaders that way.

"Sorry, Corporal. I'm bushed. Just got my feet tangled up."

"Yeah, just watch it." He got back up all right, and he and his partner placed the sheet and went back to get another.

I kept my eye on Singer. In a few minutes he was practically staggering, not easy to do in that suit of cybernetic armor.

"Singer! After you set that plank, I want to see you."

"Okay." He labored through the task and mooched over.

"Let me check your readout." I opened the door on his chest to expose the medical monitor. His temperature was at two degrees high; blood pressure and heart rate both elevated. Not up to the red line, though.

"You sick or something?"

"Hell, Mandella, I feel okay, just tired. Since I fell I been a little dizzy."

I chinned the medic's combination. "Doc, this is Mandella. You wanna come over here for a minute?"

"Sure, where are you?" I waved and he walked over from poolside.

"What's the problem?" I showed him Singer's readout.

He knew what all the other little dials and things meant, so it took him a while. "As far as I can tell, Mandella...he's just hot."

"Hell, I coulda told you that," said Singer.

"Maybe you better have the armorer take a look at his suit." We had two people who'd taken a crash course in suit maintenance; they were our "armorers."

I chinned Sanchez and asked him to come over with his tool kit.

"Be a couple of minutes, Corporal. Carryin' a plank."

"Well, put it down and get over here." I was getting an uneasy feeling. Waiting for him, the medic and I looked over Singer's suit.

34

"Uh-oh," Doc Jones said. "Look at this." I went around to the back and looked where he was pointing. Two of the fins on the heat exchanger were bent out of shape.

"What's wrong?" Singer asked.

"You fell on your heat exchanger, right?"

"Sure, Corporal—that's it. It must not be working right."

"I don't think it's working at *all*," said Doc.

Sanchez came over with his diagnostic kit and we told him what had happened. He looked at the heat exchanger, then plugged a couple of jacks into it and got a digital readout from a little monitor in his kit. I didn't know what it was measuring, but it came out zero to eight decimal places.

Heard a soft click, Sanchez chinning my private frequency. "Corporal, this guy's a deader."

"What? Can't you fix the goddamn thing?"

"Maybe…maybe I could, if I could take it apart. But there's no way—"

"Hey! Sanchez?" Singer was talking on the general freak. "Find out what's wrong?" He was panting.

Click. "Keep your pants on, man, we're working on it." *Click.* "He won't last long enough for us to get the bunker pressurized. And I can't work on the heat exchanger from outside of the suit."

"You've got a spare suit, haven't you?"

"Two of 'em, the fit-anybody kind. But there's no place…say…"

"Right. Go get one of the suits warmed up." I chinned the general freak. "Listen, Singer, we've gotta get you out of that thing. Sanchez has a spare suit, but to make the switch, we're gonna have to build a house around you. Understand?"

"Huh-uh."

"Look, we'll make a box with you inside, and hook it up to the life-support unit. That way you can breathe while you make the switch."

"Soun's pretty compis…compil…cated t'me."

"Look, just come along—"

"I'll be all right, man, jus' lemme res'…."

I grabbed his arm and led him to the building site. He was really weaving. Doc took his other arm, and between us, we kept him from falling over.

"Corporal Ho, this is Corporal Mandella." Ho was in charge of the life-support unit.

"Go away, Mandella. I'm busy."

"You're going to be busier." I outlined the problem to her. While her group hurried to adapt the LSU—for this purpose, it need only be an air hose and heater—I got my crew to bring around six slabs of permaplast, so we could build a big box around Singer and the extra suit. It would look like a huge coffin, a meter square and six meters long.

We set the suit down on the slab that would be the floor of the coffin. "Okay, Singer, let's go."

No answer.

"Singer!" He was just standing there. Doc Jones checked his readout. "He's out, man, unconscious."

My mind raced. There might just be room for another person in the box. "Give me a hand here." I took Singer's shoulders and Doc took his feet, and we carefully laid him out at the feet of the empty suit.

Then I lay down myself, above the suit. "Okay, close 'er up."

"Look, Mandella, if anybody goes in there, it oughta be me."

"Fuck you, Doc. *My* job. *My* man." That sounded all wrong. William Mandella, boy hero.

They stood a slab up on edge—it had two openings for the LSU input and exhaust—and proceeded to weld it to the bottom plank with a narrow laser beam. On Earth, we'd just use glue, but here the only fluid was helium, which has lots of interesting properties, but is definitely not sticky.

After about ten minutes we were completely walled up. I could feel the LSU humming. I switched on my suit light—the first time since we landed on darkside—and the glare made purple blotches dance in front of my eyes.

"Mandella, this is Ho. Stay in your suit at least two or three minutes. We're putting hot air in, but it's coming back just this side of liquid." I watched the purple fade for a while.

"Okay, it's still cold, but you can make it." I popped my suit. It wouldn't open all the way, but I didn't have too much trouble getting out. The suit was still cold enough to take some skin off my fingers and butt as I wiggled out.

I had to crawl feet-first down the coffin to get to Singer. It got darker fast, moving away from my light. When I popped his suit a rush of hot stink hit me in the face. In the dim light his skin was dark red and splotchy. His breathing was very shallow and I could see his heart palpitating.

First I unhooked the relief tubes—an unpleasant business—then the biosensors; and then I had the problem of getting his arms out of their sleeves.

It's pretty easy to do for yourself. You twist this way and turn that way and the arm pops out. Doing it from the outside is a different matter: I had to twist his arm and then reach under and move the suit's arm to match— it takes muscle to move a suit around from the outside.

Once I had one arm out it was pretty easy; I just crawled forward, putting my feet on the suit's shoulders, and pulled on his free arm. He slid out of the suit like an oyster slipping out of its shell.

I popped the spare suit and, after a lot of pulling and pushing, managed to get his legs in. Hooked up the biosensors and the front relief tube. He'd have to do the other one himself; it's too complicated. For the nth time I was glad not to have been born female; they have to have two of those damned plumber's friends, instead of just one and a simple hose.

I left his arms out of the sleeves. The suit would be useless for any kind of work, anyhow; waldos have to be tailored to the individual.

His eyelids fluttered. "Man…della. Where…the fuck…"

I explained, slowly, and he seemed to get most of it. "Now I'm gonna close you up and go get into my suit. I'll have the crew cut the end off this thing and I'll haul you out. Got it?"

He nodded. Strange to see that—when you nod or shrug inside a suit, it doesn't communicate anything.

I crawled into my suit, hooked up the attachments and chinned the general freak. "Doc, I think he's gonna be okay. Get us out of here now."

"Will do." Ho's voice. The LSU hum was replaced by a chatter, then a throb. Evacuating the box to prevent an explosion.

One corner of the seam grew red, then white, and a bright crimson beam lanced through, not a foot away from my head. I scrunched back as far as I could. The beam slid up the seam and around three corners, back to where it started. The end of the box fell away slowly, trailing filaments of melted 'plast.

"Wait for the stuff to harden, Mandella."

"Sanchez, I'm not that stupid."

"Here you go." Somebody tossed a line to me. That *would* be smarter than dragging him out by myself. I threaded a long bight under his arms and tied it behind his neck. Then I scrambled out to help them pull, which was silly—they had a dozen people already lined up to haul.

Singer got out all right and was actually sitting up while Doc Jones checked his readout. People were asking me about it and congratulating me, when suddenly Ho said, "Look!" and pointed toward the horizon.

It was a black ship, coming in fast. I just had time to think it wasn't fair, they weren't supposed to attack until the last few days, and then the ship was right on top of us.

IX

We all flopped to the ground instinctively, but the ship didn't attack. It blasted braking rockets and dropped to land on skids. Then it skied around to come to a rest beside the building site.

Everybody had it figured out and was standing around sheepishly when the two suited figures stepped out of the ship.

A familiar voice crackled over the general freak. "Every *one* of you saw us coming in and not *one* of you responded with laser fire. It wouldn't have done any good but it would have indicated a certain amount of fighting spirit. You have a week or less before the real thing and since the sergeant and I will be here I will insist that you show a little more will to live. Acting Sergeant Potter."

"Here, sir."

"Get me a detail of twelve people to unload cargo. We brought a hundred small robot drones for *target* practice so that you might have at least a fighting chance when a live target comes over.

"Move *now*. We only have thirty minutes before the ship returns to Miami."

I checked, and it was actually more like forty minutes.

Having the captain and sergeant there didn't really make much difference. We were still on our own; they were just observing.

Once we got the floor down, it only took one day to complete the bunker. It was a gray oblong, featureless except for the airlock blister and four windows. On top was a swivel-mounted bevawatt laser. The operator—you couldn't call him a "gunner"—sat in a chair holding dead-man switches in both hands. The laser wouldn't fire as long as he was holding one of those switches. If he let go, it would automatically aim for any moving aerial object and fire at will. Primary detection and aiming was by means of a kilometer-high antenna mounted beside the bunker.

It was the only arrangement that could really be expected to work, with the horizon so close and human reflexes so slow. You couldn't have the thing fully automatic, because in theory, friendly ships might also approach.

The aiming computer could choose among up to twelve targets appearing simultaneously (firing at the largest ones first). And it would get all twelve in the space of half a second.

The installation was partly protected from enemy fire by an efficient ablative layer that covered everything except the human operator. But then, they *were* dead-man switches. One man above guarding eighty inside. The army's good at that kind of arithmetic.

Once the bunker was finished, half of us stayed inside at all times—feeling very much like targets—taking turns operating the laser, while the other half went on maneuvers.

About four klicks from the base was a large "lake" of frozen hydrogen; one of our most important maneuvers was to learn how to get around on the treacherous stuff.

It wasn't too difficult. You couldn't stand up on it, so you had to belly down and sled.

If you had somebody to push you from the edge, getting started was no problem. Otherwise, you had to scrabble with your hands and feet, pushing down as hard as was practical, until you started moving, in a series of little jumps. Once started, you'd keep going until you ran out of ice. You could steer a little bit by digging in, hand and foot, on the appropriate side, but you couldn't slow to a stop that way. So it was a good idea not to go too fast and wind up positioned in such a way that your helmet didn't absorb the shock of stopping.

We went through all the things we'd done on the Miami side: weapons practice, demolition, attack patterns. We also launched drones at irregular intervals, toward the bunker. Thus, ten or fifteen times a day, the operators got to demonstrate their skill in letting go of the handles as soon as the proximity light went on.

I had four hours of that, like everybody else. I was nervous until the first "attack," when I saw how little there was to it. The light went on, I let go, the gun aimed, and when the drone peeped over the horizon—*zzt!* Nice touch of color, the molten metal spraying through space. Otherwise not too exciting.

So none of us were worried about the upcoming "graduation exercise," thinking it would be just more of the same.

Miami base attacked on the thirteenth day with two simultaneous missiles streaking over opposite sides of the horizon at some forty kilometers per second. The laser vaporized the first one with no trouble, but the second got within eight klicks of the bunker before it was hit.

We were coming back from maneuvers, about a klick away from the bunker. I wouldn't have seen it happen if I hadn't been looking directly at the bunker the moment of the attack.

The second missile sent a shower of molten debris straight toward the bunker. Eleven pieces hit, and, as we later reconstructed it, this is what happened:

The first casualty was Maejima, so well-loved Maejima, inside the bunker, who was hit in the back and the head and died instantly. With the drop in pressure, the LSU went into high gear. Friedman was standing in front of the main airco outlet and was blown into the opposite wall hard enough to knock him unconscious; he died of decompression before the others could get him to his suit.

Everybody else managed to stagger through the gale and get into their suits, but Garcia's suit had been holed and didn't do him any good.

By the time we got there, they had turned off the LSU and were welding up the holes in the wall. One man was trying to scrape up the recognizable mess that had been Maejima. I could hear him sobbing and retching. They had already taken Garcia and Friedman outside for burial. The captain took over the repair detail from Potter. Sergeant Cortez led the sobbing man over to a corner and came back to work on cleaning up Maejima's remains, alone. He didn't order anybody to help and nobody volunteered.

X

As a graduation exercise, we were unceremoniously stuffed into a ship—*Earth's Hope*, the same one we rode to Charon—and bundled off to Stargate at a little more than one gee.

The trip seemed endless, about six months subjective time, and boring, but not as hard on the carcass as going to Charon had been. Captain Stott made us review our training orally, day by day, and we did exercises every day until we were worn to a collective frazzle.

Stargate 1 was like Charon's darkside, only more so. The base on Stargate 1 was smaller than Miami base—only a little bigger than the one we constructed on darkside—and we were due to lay over a week to help expand the facilities. The crew there was very glad to see us, especially the two females, who looked a little worn around the edges.

We all crowded into the small dining hall, where Submajor Williamson, the man in charge of Stargate 1, gave us some disconcerting news:

"Everybody get comfortable. Get off the tables, though, there's plenty of floor.

"I have some idea of what you just went through, training on Charon. I won't say it's all been wasted. But where you're headed, things will be quite different. Warmer."

He paused to let that soak in.

"Aleph Aurigae, the first collapsar ever detected, revolves around the normal star Epsilon Aurigae in a twenty-seven-year orbit. The enemy has a base of operations, not on a regular portal planet of Aleph, but on a planet in orbit around Epsilon. We don't know much about the planet, just that it goes around Epsilon once every 745 days, is about three-fourths the size of Earth, and has an albedo of 0.8, meaning it's probably covered with clouds. We can't say precisely how hot it will be, but judging from its distance from Epsilon, it's probably rather hotter than Earth. Of course, we don't know whether you'll be working…fighting on lightside or darkside, equator or poles. It's highly unlikely that the atmosphere will be breathable—at any rate, you'll stay inside your suits.

"Now you know exactly as much about where you're going as I do. Questions?"

"Sir," Stein drawled, "now we know where we're goin'…anybody know what we're goin' to do when we get there?"

Williamson shrugged. "That's up to your captain—and your sergeant, and the captain of *Earth's Hope*, and *Hope*'s logistic computer. We just don't have enough data yet to project a course of action for you. It may be a long and bloody battle; it may be just a case of walking in to pick up the pieces. Conceivably, the Taurans might want to make a peace offer,"—Cortez snorted—"in which case you would simply be part of our muscle, our bargaining power." He looked at Cortez mildly. "No one can say for sure."

The orgy that night was amusing, but it was like trying to sleep in the middle of a raucous beach party. The only area big enough to sleep all of us was the dining hall; they draped a few bedsheets here and there for privacy, then unleashed Stargate's eighteen sex-starved men on our women, compliant and promiscuous by military custom (and law), but desiring nothing so much as sleep on solid ground.

The eighteen men acted as if they were compelled to try as many permutations as possible, and their performance was impressive (in a strictly quantitative sense, that is). Those of us who were keeping count led a cheering section for some of the more gifted members. I think that's the right word.

The next morning—and every other morning we were on Stargate 1—we staggered out of bed and into our suits, to go outside and work on the "new wing." Eventually, Stargate would be tactical and logistic headquarters for the war, with thousands of permanent personnel, guarded by half a dozen heavy cruisers in *Hope*'s class. When we started, it was two shacks and twenty people; when we left, it was four shacks and twenty people. The work was hardly work at all, compared to darkside, since we had plenty of light and got sixteen hours inside for every eight hours' work. And no drone attack for a final exam.

When we shuttled back up to the *Hope*, nobody was too happy about leaving (though some of the more popular females declared it'd be good to get some rest). Stargate was the last easy, safe assignment we'd have before taking up arms against the Taurans. And as Williamson had pointed out the first day, there was no way of predicting what *that* would be like.

Most of us didn't feel too enthusiastic about making a collapsar jump, either. We'd been assured that we wouldn't even feel it happen, just free fall all the way.

I wasn't convinced. As a physics student, I'd had the usual courses in general relativity and theories of gravitation. We only had a little direct data at that time—Stargate was discovered when I was in grade school—but the mathematical model seemed clear enough.

The collapsar Stargate was a perfect sphere about three kilometers in radius. It was suspended forever in a state of gravitational collapse that should have meant its surface was dropping toward its center at nearly the speed of light. Relativity propped it up, at least gave it the illusion of being there...the way all reality becomes illusory and observer-oriented when you study general relativity. Or Buddhism. Or get drafted.

At any rate, there would be a theoretical point in spacetime when one end of our ship was just above the surface of the collapsar, and the other end was a kilometer away (in our frame of reference). In any sane universe, this would set up tidal stresses and tear the ship apart, and we would be just another million kilograms of degenerate matter on a theoretical surface, rushing headlong to nowhere for the rest of eternity or dropping to the center in the next trillionth of a second. You pays your money and you takes your frame of reference.

But they were right. We blasted away from Stargate 1, made a few course corrections and then just dropped, for about an hour.

Then a bell rang and we sank into our cushions under a steady two gravities of deceleration. We were in enemy territory.

XI

We'd been decelerating at two gravities for almost nine days when the battle began. Lying on our couches being miserable, all we felt were two soft bumps, missiles being released. Some eight hours later, the squawk-box crackled: "Attention, all crew. This is the captain." Quinsana, the pilot, was only a lieutenant, but was allowed to call himself captain aboard the vessel, where he outranked all of us, even Captain Stott. "You grunts in the cargo hold can listen, too.

"We just engaged the enemy with two fifty-bevaton tachyon missiles and have destroyed both the enemy vessel and another object which it had launched approximately three microseconds before.

"The enemy has been trying to overtake us for the past 179 hours, ship time. At the time of the engagement, the enemy was moving at a little over half the speed of light, relative to Aleph, and was only about thirty AUs from *Earth's Hope*. It was moving at .47c relative to us, and thus we would have been coincident in space-time"—rammed!—"in a little more than nine hours. The missiles were launched at 0719 ship's time, and destroyed the enemy at 1540, both tachyon bombs detonating within a thousand klicks of the enemy objects."

The two missiles were a type whose propulsion system was itself only a barely controlled tachyon bomb. They accelerated at a constant rate of one hundred gees, and were traveling at a relativistic speed by the time the nearby mass of the enemy ship detonated them.

"We expect no further interference from enemy vessels. Our velocity with respect to Aleph will be zero in another five hours; we will then begin to journey back. The return will take twenty-seven days." General moans and dejected cussing. Everybody knew all that already, of course; but we didn't care to be reminded of it.

So after another month of logy calisthenics and drill, at a constant two gravities, we got our first look at the planet we were going to attack. Invaders from outer space, yes sir.

It was a blinding white crescent waiting for us two AUs out from Epsilon. The captain had pinned down the location of the enemy base from fifty AUs out, and we had jockeyed in on a wide arc, keeping the bulk of the planet between them and us. That didn't mean we were sneaking up on them—quite the contrary; they launched three abortive attacks—but it put us in a stronger defensive position. Until we had to go to the surface, that is. Then only the ship and its Star Fleet crew would be reasonably safe.

Since the planet rotated rather slowly—once every ten and one-half days—a "stationary" orbit for the ship had to be 150,000 klicks out. This made the people in the ship feel quite secure, with 6,000 miles of rock and 90,000 miles of space between them and the enemy. But it meant a whole second's time lag in communication between us on the ground and the ship's battle computer. A person could get awful dead while that neutrino pulse crawled up and back.

Our vague orders were to attack the base and gain control, while damaging a minimum of enemy equipment. We were to take at least one enemy alive. We were under no circumstances to allow ourselves to be taken alive, however. And the decision wasn't up to us; one special pulse from the battle computer, and that speck of plutonium in your power plant would fiss with all of .01% efficiency, and you'd be nothing but rapidly expanding, very hot plasma.

They strapped us into six scoutships—one platoon of twelve people in each—and we blasted away from *Earth's Hope* at eight gees. Each scoutship was supposed to follow its own carefully random path to our rendezvous point, 108 klicks from the base. Fourteen drone ships were launched at the same time, to confound the enemy's antispacecraft system.

The landing went off almost perfectly. One ship suffered minor damage, a near miss boiling away some of the ablative material on one side of the hull, but it'd still be able to make it and return, keeping its speed down while in the atmosphere.

We zigged and zagged and wound up first ship at the rendezvous point. There was only one trouble. It was under four kilometers of water.

I could almost hear that machine, 90,000 miles away, grinding its mental gears, adding this new bit of data. We proceeded just as if we were landing on solid ground: braking rockets, falling, skids out, hit the water, skip, hit the water, skip, hit the water, sink.

It would have made sense to go ahead and land on the bottom—we were streamlined, after all, and water just another fluid—but the hull wasn't strong enough to hold up a four-kilometer column of water. Sergeant Cortez was in the scoutship with us.

"Sarge, tell that computer to *do* something! We're gonna get—"

"Oh, shut up, Mandella. Trust in th' lord." "Lord" was definitely lower-case when Cortez said it.

There was a loud bubbly sigh, then another, and a slight increase in pressure on my back that meant the ship was rising. "Flotation bags?" Cortez didn't deign to answer, or didn't know.

That was it. We rose to within ten or fifteen meters of the surface and stopped, suspended there. Through the port I could see the surface above, shimmering like a mirror of hammered silver. I wondered what it would be like to be a fish and have a definite roof over your world.

I watched another ship splash in. It made a great cloud of bubbles and turbulence, then fell—slightly tail-first—for a short distance before large bags popped out under each delta wing. Then it bobbed up to about our level and stayed.

"This is Captain Stott. Now listen carefully. There is a beach some twenty-eight klicks from your present position, in the direction of the enemy. You will be proceeding to this beach by scoutship and from there will mount your assault on the Tauran position." That was *some* improvement; we'd only have to walk eighty klicks.

We deflated the bags, blasted to the surface and flew in a slow, spread-out formation to the beach. It took several minutes. As the ship scraped to a halt, I could hear pumps humming, making the cabin pressure equal to the air pressure outside. Before it had quite stopped moving, the escape slot beside my couch slid open. I rolled out onto the wing of the craft and jumped to the ground. Ten seconds to find cover—I sprinted across loose gravel to the "treeline," a twisty bramble of tall sparse bluish-green shrubs. I dove into the briar patch and turned to watch the ships leave. The drones that were left rose slowly to about a hundred meters, then took off in all directions with a bone-jarring roar. The real scoutships slid slowly back into the water. Maybe that was a good idea.

It wasn't a terribly attractive world but certainly would be easier to get around in than the cryogenic nightmare we were trained for. The sky was a uniform dull silver brightness that merged with the mist over the ocean so completely it was impossible to tell where water ended and air began. Small wavelets licked at the black gravel shore, much too slow and graceful in the three-quarters Earth-normal gravity. Even from fifty meters away, the rattle of billions of pebbles rolling with the tide was loud in my ears.

The air temperature was 79 degrees Centigrade, not quite hot enough for the sea to boil, even though the air pressure was low compared to Earth's. Wisps of steam drifted quickly upward from the line where water met land. I wondered how long a man would survive exposed here without a suit. Would the heat or the low oxygen (partial pressure one-eighth Earth normal) kill him first? Or was there some deadly microorganism that would beat them both? ...

"This is Cortez. Everybody come over and assemble on me." He was standing on the beach a little to the left of me, waving his hand in a circle over his head. I walked toward him through the shrubs. They were brittle, unsubstantial, seemed paradoxically dried-out in the steamy air. They wouldn't offer much in the way of cover.

"We'll be advancing on a heading .05 radians east of north. I want Platoon One to take point. Two and Three follow about twenty meters behind, to the left and right. Seven, command platoon, is in the middle, twenty meters behind Two and Three. Five and Six, bring up the rear, in a semicircular closed flank. Everybody straight?" Sure, we could do that "arrowhead" maneuver in our sleep. "Okay, let's move out."

I was in Platoon Seven, the "command group." Captain Stott put me there not because I was expected to give any commands, but because of my training in physics.

The command group was supposedly the safest place, buffered by six platoons: people were assigned to it because there was some tactical reason for them to survive at least a little longer than the rest. Cortez was there to give orders. Chavez was there to correct suit malfunctions. The senior medic, Doc Wilson (the only medic who actually had an M.D.) was there, and so was Theodopolis, the radio engineer, our link with the captain, who had elected to stay in orbit.

The rest of us were assigned to the command group by dint of special training or aptitude that wouldn't normally be considered of a "tactical" nature. Facing a totally unknown enemy, there was no way of telling what might prove important. Thus I was there because I was the closest the company had to a physicist. Rogers was biology. Tate was chemistry. Ho could crank out a perfect score on the Rhine extrasensory perception test, every time. Bohrs was a polyglot, able to speak twenty-one languages fluently, idiomatically. Petrov's talent was that he had tested out to have not one molecule of xenophobia in his psyche. Keating was a skilled acrobat. Debby Hollister—"Lucky" Hollister—showed a remarkable aptitude for making money, and also had a consistently high Rhine potential.

XII

When we first set out, we were using the "jungle" camouflage combination on our suits. But what passed for jungle in these anemic tropics was too sparse; we looked like a band of conspicuous harlequins trooping through the woods. Cortez had us switch to black, but that was just as bad, as the light of Epsilon came evenly from all parts of the sky, and there were no shadows except ours. We finally settled on the dun-colored desert camouflage.

The nature of the countryside changed slowly as we walked north, away from the sea. The thorned stalks—I guess you could call them trees—came in fewer numbers but were bigger around and less brittle; at the base of each was a tangled mass of vine with the same blue-green color, which spread out in a flattened cone some ten meters in diameter. There was a delicate green flower the size of a man's head near the top of each tree.

Grass began to appear some five klicks from the sea. It seemed to respect the trees' "property rights," leaving a strip of bare earth around each cone of vine. At the edge of such a clearing, it would grow as timid blue-green stubble, then, moving away from the tree, would get thicker and taller until it reached shoulder high in some places, where the separation between two trees was unusually large. The grass was a lighter, greener shade than the trees and vines. We changed the color of our suits to the bright green we had used for maximum visibility on Charon. Keeping to the thickest part of the grass, we were fairly inconspicuous.

We covered over twenty klicks each day, buoyant after months under two gees. Until the second day, the only form of animal life we saw was a kind of black worm, finger-sized, with hundreds of cilium legs like the bristles of a brush. Rogers said that there obviously had to be some larger creature around, or there would be no reason for the trees to have thorns.

So we were doubly on guard, expecting trouble both from the Taurans and the unidentified "large creature."

Potter's second platoon was on point; the general freak was reserved for her, since her platoon would likely be the first to spot any trouble.

"Sarge, this is Potter," we all heard. "Movement ahead."

"Get down, then!"

"We are. Don't think they see us."

"First platoon, go up to the right of point. Keep down. Fourth, get up to the left. Tell me when you get in position. Sixth platoon, stay back and guard the rear. Fifth and third, close with the command group."

Two dozen people whispered out of the grass to join us. Cortez must have heard from the fourth platoon.

"Good. How about you, first? ... Okay, fine. How many are there?"

"Eight we can see." Potter's voice.

"Good. When I give the word, open fire. Shoot to kill."

"Sarge,...they're just animals."

"Potter—if you've known all this time what a Tauran looks like, you should've told us. Shoot to kill."

"But we need..."

"We need a prisoner, but we don't need to escort him forty klicks to his home base and keep an eye on him while we fight. Clear?"

"Yes. Sergeant."

"Okay. Seventh, all you brains and weirds, we're going up and watch. Fifth and third, come along to guard."

We crawled through the meter-high grass to where the second platoon had stretched out in a firing line.

"I don't see anything," Cortez said.

"Ahead and just to the left. Dark green."

They were only a shade darker than the grass. But after you saw the first one, you could see them all, moving slowly around some thirty meters ahead.

"Fire!" Cortez fired first; then twelve streaks of crimson leaped out and the grass wilted black, disappeared, and the creatures convulsed and died trying to scatter.

"Hold fire, hold it!" Cortez stood up. "We want to have something left—second platoon, follow me." He strode out toward the smoldering corpses, laser-finger pointed out front, obscene divining rod pulling him toward the carnage.... I felt my gorge rising and knew that all the lurid training tapes, all the horrible deaths in training accidents, hadn't prepared me for this sudden reality...that I had a magic wand that I could point at a life and make it a smoking piece of half-raw meat; I wasn't a soldier nor ever wanted to be one nor ever would want—

"Okay, seventh, come on up." While we were walking toward them, one of the creatures moved, a tiny shudder, and Cortez flicked the beam of his laser over it with an almost negligent gesture. It made a hand-deep gash across the creature's middle. It died, like the others, without emitting a sound.

They were not quite as tall as humans, but wider in girth. They were covered with dark green, almost black, fur—white curls where the laser had singed. They appeared to have three legs and an arm. The only ornament to their shaggy heads was a mouth, a wet black orifice filled with flat black teeth. They were thoroughly repulsive, but their worst feature was not a difference from human beings, but a similarity.... Whenever the laser had opened a body cavity, milk-white glistening veined globes and coils of organs spilled out, and their blood was dark clotting red.

"Rogers, take a look. Taurans or not?"

Rogers knelt by one of the disemboweled creatures and opened a flat plastic box, filled with glittering dissecting tools. She selected a scalpel. "One way we might be able to find out." Doc Wilson watched over her shoulder as she methodically slit the membrane covering several organs.

"Here." She held up a blackish fibrous mass between two fingers, a parody of daintiness through all that armor.

"So?"

"It's grass, Sergeant. If the Taurans can eat the grass and breathe the air, they certainly found a planet remarkably like their home." She tossed it away. "They're animals, Sergeant, just fucken animals."

"I don't know," Doc Wilson said. "Just because they walk around on all fours, threes maybe, and eat grass..."

"Well, let's check out the brain." She found one that had been hit in the head and scraped the superficial black char from the wound. "Look at that."

It was almost solid bone. She tugged and ruffled the hair all over the head of another one. "What the hell does it use for sensory organs? No eyes, or ears, or..." She stood up.

"Nothing in that fucken head but a mouth and ten centimeters of skull. To protect nothing, not a fucken thing."

"If I could shrug, I'd shrug," the doctor said. "It doesn't prove anything—a brain doesn't have to look like a mushy walnut and it doesn't have to be in the head. Maybe that skull isn't bone, maybe *that's* the brain, some crystal lattice…"

"Yeah, but the fucken stomach's in the right place, and if those aren't intestines I'll eat—"

"Look," Cortez said, "this is real interesting, but all we need to know is whether that thing's dangerous, then we've gotta move on; we don't have all—"

"They aren't dangerous," Rogers began. "They don't—"

"Medic! DOC!" Somebody back at the firing line was waving his arms. Doc sprinted back to him, the rest of us following.

"What's wrong?" He had reached back and unclipped his medical kit on the run.

"It's Ho. She's out."

Doc swung open the door on Ho's biomedical monitor. He didn't have to look far. "She's dead."

"Dead?" Cortez said. "What the hell—"

"Just a minute." Doc plugged a jack into the monitor and fiddled with some dials on his kit. "Everybody's biomed readout is stored for twelve hours. I'm running it backwards, should be able to—there!"

"What?"

"Four and a half minutes ago—must have been when you opened fire—Jesus!"

"Well?"

"Massive cerebral hemorrhage. No…" He watched the dials. "No… warning, no indications of anything out of the ordinary; blood pressure up, pulse up, but normal under the circumstances…nothing to…indicate—" He reached down and popped her suit. Her fine oriental features were distorted in a horrible grimace, both gums showing. Sticky fluid ran from under her collapsed eyelids, and a trickle of blood still dripped from each ear. Doc Wilson closed the suit back up.

"I've never seen anything like it. It's as if a bomb went off in her skull."

"Oh fuck," Rogers said, "she was Rhine-sensitive, wasn't she?"

"That's right." Cortez sounded thoughtful. "All right, everybody listen up. Platoon leaders, check your platoons and see if anybody's missing, or hurt. Anybody else in seventh?"

"I…I've got a splitting headache, Sarge," Lucky said.

Four others had bad headaches. One of them affirmed that he was slightly Rhine-sensitive. The others didn't know.

"Cortez, I think it's obvious," Doc Wilson said, "that we should give these...monsters wide berth, especially shouldn't harm any more of them. Not with five people susceptible to whatever apparently killed Ho."

"Of course, God damn it, I don't need anybody to tell me that. We'd better get moving. I just filled the captain in on what happened; he agrees that we'd better get as far away from here as we can before we stop for the night.

"Let's get back in formation and continue on the same bearing. Fifth platoon, take over point; second, come back to the rear. Everybody else, same as before."

"What about Ho?" Lucky asked.

"She'll be taken care of. From the ship."

After we'd gone half a klick, there was a flash and rolling thunder. Where Ho had been came a wispy luminous mushroom cloud boiling up to disappear against the gray sky.

XIII

We stopped for the "night"—actually, the sun wouldn't set for another seventy hours—atop a slight rise some ten klicks from where we had killed the aliens. But they weren't aliens, I had to remind myself—*we* were.

Two platoons deployed in a ring around the rest of us, and we flopped down exhausted. Everybody was allowed four hours' sleep and had two hours' guard duty.

Potter came over and sat next to me. I chinned her frequency.

"Hi, Marygay."

"Oh, William," her voice over the radio was hoarse and cracking. "God, it's so horrible."

"It's over now—"

"I killed one of them, the first instant, I shot it right in the, in the..."

I put my hand on her knee. The contact made a plastic click and I jerked it back, visions of machines embracing, copulating. "Don't feel singled out, Marygay; whatever guilt there is, is...belongs evenly to all of us,...but a triple portion for Cor—"

"You privates quit jawin' and get some sleep. You both pull guard in two hours."

"Okay, Sarge." Her voice was so sad and tired I couldn't bear it. I felt if I could only touch her, I could drain off the sadness like ground wire draining current, but we were each trapped in our own plastic world—

"G'night, William."

"Night." It's almost impossible to get sexually excited inside a suit, with the relief tube and all the silver chloride sensors poking you, but somehow this was my body's response to the emotional impotence, maybe remembering more pleasant sleeps with Marygay, maybe feeling that in the midst of all this death, personal death could be soon, cranking up the procreative derrick for one last try...lovely thoughts like this. I fell asleep and dreamed that I was a machine, mimicking the functions of life, creaking and clanking my clumsy way through the world, people too polite to say anything but giggling behind my back, and the little man who sat inside my head pulling the levers and clutches and watching the dials, he was hopelessly mad and was storing up hurts for the day—

"Mandella—wake up, goddammit, your shift!"

I shuffled over to my place on the perimeter to watch for God knows what...but I was so weary I couldn't keep my eyes open. Finally I tongued a stimtab, knowing I'd pay for it later.

For over an hour I sat there, scanning my sector left, right, near, far, the scene never changing, not even a breath of wind to stir the grass.

Then suddenly the grass parted and one of the three-legged creatures was right in front of me. I raised my finger but didn't squeeze.

"Movement!"

"Movement!"

"Jesus Chri—there's one right—"

"HOLD YOUR FIRE! f' shit's sake don't shoot!"

"Movement."

"Movement." I looked left and right, and as far as I could see, every perimeter guard had one of the blind, dumb creatures standing right in front of him.

Maybe the drug I'd taken to stay awake made me more sensitive to whatever they did. My scalp crawled and I felt a formless *thing* in my mind, the feeling you get when somebody has said something and you didn't quite hear it, want to respond, but the opportunity to ask him to repeat it is gone.

The creature sat back on its haunches, leaning forward on the one front leg. Big green bear with a withered arm. Its power threaded through my mind, spiderwebs, echo of night terrors, trying to communicate, trying to destroy me, I couldn't know.

"All right, everybody on the perimeter, fall back, slow. Don't make any quick gestures.... Anybody got a headache or anything?"

"Sergeant, this is Hollister." Lucky.

"They're trying to say something...I can almost...no, just..."

"All I can get is that they think we're, think we're...well, *funny*. They're not afraid."

"You mean the one in front of you isn't—"

"No, the feeling comes from all of them, they're all thinking the same thing. Don't ask me how I know, I just do."

"Maybe they thought it was funny, what they did to Ho."

"Maybe. I don't feel they're dangerous. Just curious about us."

"Sergeant, this is Bohrs."

"Yeah."

"The Taurans've been here at least a year—maybe they've learned how to communicate with these...overgrown teddybears. They might be spying on us, might be sending back—"

"I don't think they'd show themselves if that were the case," Lucky said. "They can obviously hide from us pretty well when they want to."

"Anyhow," Cortez said, "if they're spies, the damage has been done. Don't think it'd be smart to take any action against them. I know you'd all like to see 'em dead for what they did to Ho, so would I, but we'd better be careful."

I didn't want to see them dead, but I'd just as soon not have seen them in any condition. I was walking backwards slowly, toward the middle of camp. The creature didn't seem disposed to follow. Maybe he just knew we were surrounded. He was pulling up grass with his arm and munching.

"Okay, all of you platoon leaders, wake everybody up, get a roll count. Let me know if anybody's been hurt. Tell your people we're moving out in one minute."

I don't know what Cortez had expected, but of course the creatures followed right along. They didn't keep us surrounded; just had twenty or thirty following us all the time. Not the same ones, either. Individuals would saunter away, new ones would join the parade. It was pretty obvious *they* weren't going to tire out.

We were each allowed one stimtab. Without it, no one could have marched an hour. A second pill would have been welcome after the edge started to wear off, but the mathematics of the situation forbade it; we were still thirty klicks from the enemy base, fifteen hours' marching at the least. And though you could stay awake and energetic for a hundred hours on the tabs, aberrations of judgment and perception snowballed after the second one, until *in extremis* the most bizarre hallucinations would be taken at face value, and a person could fidget for hours deciding whether to have breakfast.

Under artificial stimulation, the company traveled with great energy for the first six hours, was slowing by the seventh, and ground to an exhausted halt after nine hours and nineteen kilometers. The teddybears had never lost sight of us and, according to Lucky, had never stopped "broadcasting." Cortez's decision was that we would stop for seven hours, each platoon taking one hour of perimeter guard. I was never so glad to have been in the seventh platoon, as we stood guard the last shift and thus were able to get six hours of uninterrupted sleep.

In the few moments I lay awake after finally lying down, the thought came to me that the next time I closed my eyes could well be the last. And partly because of the drug hangover, mostly because of the past day's horrors, I found that I really didn't give a shit.

XIV

Our first contact with the Taurans came during my shift.

The teddybears were still there when I woke up and replaced Doc Jones on guard. They'd gone back to their original formation, one in front of each guard position. The one who was waiting for me seemed a little larger than normal, but otherwise looked just like all the others. All the grass had been cropped where he was sitting, so he occasionally made forays to the left or right. But he always returned to sit right in front of me, you would say *staring* if he had had anything to stare with.

We had been facing each other for about fifteen minutes when Cortez's voice rumbled:

"Awright everybody, wake up and get hid!"

I followed instinct and flopped to the ground and rolled into a tall stand of grass.

"Enemy vessel overhead." His voice was almost laconic.

Strictly speaking, it wasn't really overhead, but rather passing somewhat east of us. It was moving slowly, maybe a hundred klicks per hour, and looked like a broomstick surrounded by a dirty soap bubble. The creature riding it was a little more human-looking than the teddybears, but still no prize. I cranked my image amplifier up to forty log two for a closer look.

He had two arms and two legs, but his waist was so small you could encompass it with both hands. Under the tiny waist was a large horse-shoe-shaped pelvic structure nearly a meter wide, from which dangled two long skinny legs with no apparent knee joint. Above that waist his body swelled out again, to a chest no smaller than the huge pelvis. His arms looked surprisingly human, except that they were too long and undermuscled. There were too many fingers on his hands. Shoulderless, neckless. His head was a nightmarish growth that swelled like a goiter from his massive chest. Two eyes that looked like clusters of fish eggs, a bundle of tassles instead of a nose, and a rigidly open hole that might have been a mouth sitting low down where his adam's apple should have been. Evidently the soap bubble contained an amenable environment, as he was wearing absolutely nothing except his ridged hide, that looked like skin submerged too long in hot water, then dyed a pale orange. "He" had no external genitalia, but nothing that might hint of mammary glands. So we opted for the male pronoun by default.

Obviously, he either didn't see us or thought we were part of the herd of teddybears. He never looked back at us, but just continued in the same direction we were headed, .05 rad east of north.

"Might as well go back to sleep now, if you can sleep after looking at *that* thing. We move out at 0435." Forty minutes.

Because of the planet's opaque cloud cover, there had been no way to tell, from space, what the enemy base looked like or how big it was. We only knew its position, the same way we knew the position the scoutships were supposed to land on. So it too could easily have been underwater, or underground.

But some of the drones were reconnaissance ships as well as decoys: and in their mock attacks on the base, one managed to get close enough to take a picture. Captain Stott beamed down a diagram of the place to Cortez—the only one with a visor in his suit—when we were five klicks from the base's "radio" position. We stopped and he called all the platoon leaders in with the seventh platoon to confer. Two teddybears loped in, too. We tried to ignore them.

"Okay, the captain sent down some pictures of our objective. I'm going to draw a map; you platoon leaders copy." They took pads and styli out of their leg pockets, while Cortez unrolled a large plastic mat. He gave it a shake to randomize any residual charge, and turned on his stylus.

"Now we're coming from this direction." He put an arrow at the bottom of the sheet. "First thing we'll hit is this row of huts, probably billets or bunkers, but who the hell knows…. Our initial objective is to destroy these buildings—the whole base is on a flat plain; there's no way we could really sneak by them."

"Potter here. Why can't we jump over them?"

"Yeah, we could do that, and wind up completely surrounded, cut to ribbons. We take the buildings.

"After we do that…all I can say is that we'll have to think on our feet. From the aerial reconnaissance, we can figure out the function of only a couple of buildings—and that stinks. We might wind up wasting a lot of time demolishing the equivalent of an enlisted-men's bar, ignoring a huge logistic computer because it looks like…a garbage dump or something."

"Mandella here," I said. "Isn't there a spaceport of some kind—seems to me we ought to…"

"I'll *get* to that, damn it. There's a ring of these huts all around the camp, so we've got to break through somewhere. This place'll be closest, less chance of giving away our position before we attack.

"There's nothing in the whole place that actually looks like a weapon. That doesn't mean anything, though; you could hide a bevawatt laser in each of those huts.

"Now, about five hundred meters from the huts, in the middle of the base, we'll come to this big flower-shaped structure." Cortez drew a large symmetrical shape that looked like the outline of a flower with seven petals. "What the hell this is, your guess is as good as mine. There's only one of them, though, so we don't damage it any more than we have to. Which means…we blast it to splinters if I think it's dangerous.

"Now, as far as your spaceport, Mandella, is concerned—there just isn't one. Nothing.

"That cruiser the *Hope* caulked had probably been left in orbit, like ours has to be. If they have any equivalent of a scoutship, or drone missiles, they're either not kept here or they're well hidden."

"Bohrs here. Then what did they attack with, while we were coming down from orbit?"

"I wish we knew, Private.

"Obviously, we don't have any way of estimating their numbers, not directly. Recon pictures failed to show a single Tauran on the grounds of the base. Meaning nothing, because it *is* an alien environment. Indirectly, though…we count the number of broomsticks, those flying things.

"There are fifty-one huts, and each has at most one broomstick. Four don't have any parked outside, but we located three at various other parts of the base. Maybe this indicates that there are fifty-one Taurans, one of whom was outside the base when the picture was taken."

"Keating here. Or fifty-one officers."

"That's right—maybe fifty thousand infantrymen stacked in one of these buildings. No way to tell. Maybe ten Taurans, each with five broomsticks, to use according to his mood.

"We've got one thing in our favor, and that's communications. They evidently use a frequency modulation of megahertz electromagnetic radiation."

"Radio!"

"That's right, whoever you are. Identify yourself when you speak. So it's quite possible that they can't detect our phased–neutrino communications. Also, just prior to the attack, the *Hope* is going to deliver a nice dirty fission bomb; detonate it in the upper atmosphere right over the base. That'll restrict them to line-of-sight communications for some time; even those will be full of static."

"Why don't...Tate here...why don't they just drop the bomb right in their laps? Save us a lot of—"

"That doesn't even deserve an answer, Private. But the answer is, they might. And you better hope they don't. If they caulk the base, it'll be for the safety of the *Hope*. *After* we've attacked, and probably before we're far enough away for it to make much difference.

"We keep that from happening by doing a good job. We have to reduce the base to where it can no longer function; at the same time, leave as much intact as possible. And take one prisoner."

"Potter here. You mean, at least one prisoner."

"I mean what I say. One only. Potter...you're relieved of your platoon. Send Chavez up."

"All right, Sergeant." The relief in her voice was unmistakable.

Cortez continued with his map and instructions. There was one other building whose function was pretty obvious; it had a large steerable dish antenna on top. We were to destroy it as soon as the grenadiers got in range.

The attack plan was very loose. Our signal to begin would be the flash of the fission bomb. At the same time, several drones would converge on the base, so we could see what their antispacecraft defenses were. We would try to reduce the effectiveness of those defenses without destroying them completely.

Immediately after the bomb and the drones, the grenadiers would vaporize a line of seven huts. Everybody would break through the hole into the base...and what would happen after that was anybody's guess.

Ideally, we'd sweep from that end of the base to the other, destroying certain targets, caulking all but one Tauran. But that was unlikely to happen, as it depended on the Taurans' offering very little resistance.

On the other hand, if the Taurans showed obvious superiority from the beginning, Cortez would give the order to scatter. Everybody had a different compass bearing for retreat—we'd blossom out in all directions, the survivors to rendezvous in a valley some forty klicks east of the base. Then we'd see about a return engagement, after the *Hope* softened the base up a bit.

"One last thing," Cortez rasped. "Maybe some of you feel the way Potter evidently does, maybe some of your men feel that way...that we ought to go easy, not make this so much of a bloodbath. Mercy is a luxury, a weakness we can't afford to indulge in at this stage of the war. *All* we know about the enemy is that they have killed seven hundred and ninety-eight humans. They haven't shown any restraint in attacking our cruisers, and it'd be foolish to expect any this time, this first ground action.

"They are responsible for the lives of all of your comrades who died in training, and for Ho, and for all the others who are surely going to die today. I can't *understand* anybody who wants to spare them. But that doesn't make any difference. You have your orders and, what the hell, you might as well know, all of you have a post-hypnotic suggestion that I will trigger by a phrase, just before the battle. It will make your job easier."

"Sergeant..."

"Shut up. We're short on time; get back to your platoons and brief them. We move out in five minutes."

The platoon leaders returned to their men, leaving Cortez and ten of us—plus three teddybears, milling around, getting in the way.

XV

We took the last five klicks very carefully, sticking to the highest grass, running across occasional clearings. When we were five hundred meters from where the base was supposed to be, Cortez took the third platoon forward to scout, while the rest of us laid low.

Cortez's voice came over the general freak: "Looks pretty much like we expected. Advance in a file, crawling. When you get to the third platoon, follow your squad leader to the left or right."

We did that and wound up with a string of eighty-three people in a line roughly perpendicular to the direction of attack. We were pretty well hidden, except for the dozen or so teddybears that mooched along the line munching grass.

There was no sign of life inside the base. All of the buildings were windowless and a uniform shiny white. The huts that were our first objective were large featureless half-buried eggs some sixty meters apart. Cortez assigned one to each grenadier.

We were broken into three fire teams: team *A* consisted of Platoons Two, Four, and Six; team *B* was One, Three, and Five; the command platoon was team *C*.

"Less than a minute now—filters down!—when I say 'fire,' grenadiers, take out your targets. God help you if you miss."

There was a sound like a giant's belch, and a stream of five or six iridescent bubbles floated up from the flower-shaped building. They rose with increasing speed until they were almost out of sight, then shot off to the south, over our heads. The ground was suddenly bright, and for the first time in a long time, I saw my shadow, a long one pointed north. The bomb had gone off prematurely. I just had time to think that it didn't make too much difference; it'd still make alphabet soup out of their communications—

"Drones!" A ship came screaming in just above tree level, and a bubble was in the air to meet it. When they contacted, the bubble popped and the drone exploded into a million tiny fragments. Another one came from the opposite side and suffered the same fate.

"FIRE!" Seven bright glares of 500-microton grenades and a sustained concussion that surely would have killed an unprotected man.

"Filters up." Gray haze of smoke and dust. Clods of dirt falling with a sound like heavy raindrops.

"Listen up:

> *"Scots, wha hae wi' Wallace bled;*
> *Scots, wham Bruce has aften led,*
> *Welcome to your gory bed,*
> *Or to victory!"*

I hardly heard him for trying to keep track of what was going on in my skull. I knew it was just post-hypnotic suggestion, even remembered the session in Missouri when they'd implanted it, but that didn't make it any less compelling. My mind reeled under the strong pseudo-memories: shaggy hulks that were Taurans (not at all what we now knew they looked like) boarding a colonists' vessel, eating babies while mothers watched in screaming terror (the colonists never took babies; they wouldn't stand the acceleration), then raping the women to death with huge veined purple members (ridiculous that they would feel desire for humans), holding the men down while they plucked flesh from their living bodies and gobbled it (as if they could assimilate the alien protein)…a hundred grisly details as sharply remembered as the events of a minute ago, ridiculously over-done and logically absurd. But while my conscious mind was rejecting the silliness, somewhere much deeper, down in that sleeping animal where we keep our real motives and morals, something was thirsting for alien blood, secure in the conviction that the noblest thing a man could do would be to die killing one of those horrible monsters.…

I knew it was all purest soyashit, and I hated the men who had taken such obscene liberties with my mind, but I could even *hear* my teeth grinding, feel my cheeks frozen in a spastic grin, bloodlust…A teddybear walked in front of me, looking dazed. I started to raise my laser-finger, but somebody beat me to it and the creature's head exploded in a cloud of gray splinters and blood.

Lucky groaned, half-whining, "Dirty…filthy fucken bastards." Lasers flared and crisscrossed, and all of the teddybears fell dead.

"*Watch* it, goddammit," Cortez screamed. "*Aim* those fucken things—they aren't toys!

"Team *A*, move out—into the craters to cover *B*."

Somebody was laughing and sobbing. "What the fuck is wrong with *you*, Petrov?" Strange to hear Cortez cussing.

I twisted around and saw Petrov, behind and to my left, lying in a shallow hole, digging frantically with both hands crying and gurgling.

"Fuck," Cortez said. "Team *B*! Ten meters past the craters, get down in a line. Team *C*—into the craters with *A*."

I scrambled up and covered the hundred meters in twelve amplified strides. The craters were practically large enough to hide a scoutship, some ten meters in diameter. I jumped to the opposite side of the hole and landed next to a fellow named Chin. He didn't even look around when I landed, just kept scanning the base for signs of life.

"Team *A*—ten meters, past team *B*, down in line." Just as he finished, the building in front of us burped, and a salvo of the bubbles fanned out toward our lines. Most people saw it coming and got down, but Chin was just getting up to make his rush and stepped right into one.

It grazed the top of his helmet and disappeared with a faint pop. He took one step backwards and toppled over the edge of the crater, trailing an arc of blood and brains. Lifeless, spreadeagled, he slid halfway to the bottom, shoveling dirt into the perfectly symmetrical hole where the bubble had chewed indiscriminately through plastic, hair, skin, bone and brain.

"Everybody hold it. Platoon leaders, casualty report...check...check, check...check, check, check...check. We have three deaders. Wouldn't be *any* if you'd have kept low. So everybody grab dirt when you hear that thing go off. Team *A*, complete the rush."

They completed the maneuver without incident. "Okay. Team *C*, rush to where *B*...hold it! Down!"

Everybody was already hugging the ground. The bubbles slid by in a smooth arc about two meters off the ground. They went serenely over our heads and, except for one that made toothpicks out of a tree, disappeared in the distance.

"*B*, rush past *A* ten meters. *C*, take over *B*'s place. You *B* grenadiers, see if you can reach the Flower."

Two grenades tore up the ground thirty or forty meters from the structure. In a good imitation of panic, it started belching out a continuous stream of bubbles—still, none coming lower than two meters off the ground. We kept hunched down and continued to advance.

Suddenly, a seam appeared in the building and widened to the size of a large door. Taurans came swarming out.

"Grenadiers, hold your fire. *B* team, laser fire to the left and right—keep'm bunched up. *A* and *C*, rush down the center."

One Tauran died trying to run through a laser beam. The others stayed where they were.

In a suit, it's pretty awkward to run and keep your head down at the same time. You have to go from side to side, like a skater getting started; otherwise you'll be airborne. At least one person, somebody in *A* team, bounced too high and suffered the same fate as Chin.

I was feeling pretty fenced-in and trapped, with a wall of laser fire on each side and a low ceiling that meant death to touch. But in spite of myself, I felt happy, euphoric, finally getting the chance to kill some of those villainous baby-eaters. Knowing it was soyashit.

They weren't fighting back, except for the rather ineffective bubbles (obviously not designed as an antipersonnel weapon), and they didn't retreat back into the building, either. They milled around, about a hundred of them, and watched us get closer. A couple of grenades would caulk them all, but I guess Cortez was thinking about the prisoner.

"Okay, when I say 'go,' we're going to flank 'em. *B* team will hold fire.... Second and fourth platoons to the right, sixth and seventh to the left. *B* team will move forward in line to box them in.

"Go!" We peeled off to the left. As soon as the lasers stopped, the Taurans bolted, running in a group on a collision course with our flank.

"*A* team, down and fire! Don't shoot until you're sure of your aim—if you miss you might hit a friendly. And fer Chris' sake save me one!"

It was a horrifying sight, that herd of monsters bearing down on us. They were running in great leaps—the bubble avoiding them—and they all looked like the one we saw earlier, riding the broomstick; naked except for an almost transparent sphere around their whole bodies, that moved along with them. The right flank started firing, picking off individuals in the rear of the pack.

Suddenly a laser flared through the Taurans from the other side, somebody missing his mark. There was a horrible scream, and I looked down the line to see someone—I think it was Perry—writhing on the ground, right hand over the smoldering stump of his left arm, seared off just below the elbow. Blood sprayed through his fingers, and the suit, its camouflage circuits scrambled, flickered black-white-jungle-desert-green-gray. I don't know how long I stared—long enough for the medic to run over and start giving aid—but when I looked up the Taurans were almost on top of me.

My first shot was wild and high, but it grazed the top of the leading Tauran's protective bubble. The bubble disappeared and the monster stumbled and fell to the ground, jerking spasmodically. Foam gushed out of his mouth-hole, first white, then streaked red. With one last jerk he became rigid and twisted backwards, almost to the shape of a horseshoe. His long scream, a high-pitched whistle, stopped just as his comrades trampled over him. I hated myself for smiling.

It was slaughter, even though our flank was outnumbered five to one. They kept coming without faltering, even when they had to climb over the drift of bodies and parts of bodies that piled up high, parallel to our flank. The ground between us was slick red with Tauran blood—all God's children got hemoglobin—and like the teddybears, their guts looked pretty much like guts to my untrained eye. My helmet reverberated with hysterical laughter while we slashed them to gory chunks, and I almost didn't hear Cortez:

"Hold your fire—I said HOLD IT, goddammit! Catch a couple of the bastards, they won't hurt you."

I stopped shooting and eventually so did everybody else. When the next Tauran jumped over the smoking pile of meat in front of me, I dove to try to tackle him around those spindly legs.

It was like hugging a big, slippery balloon. When I tried to drag him down, he popped out of my arms and kept running.

We managed to stop one of them by the simple expedient of piling half a dozen people on top of him. By that time the others had run through our line and were headed for the row of large cylindrical tanks that Cortez had said were probably for storage. A little door had opened in the base of each one.

"We've *got* our prisoner," Cortez shouted. *"Kill!"*

They were fifty meters away and running hard, difficult targets. Lasers slashed around them, bobbing high and low. One fell, sliced in two, but the others, about ten of them, kept going and were almost to the doors when the grenadiers started firing.

They were still loaded with 500-mike bombs, but a near miss wasn't enough—the concussion would just send them flying, unhurt in their bubbles.

"The buildings! Get the fucken buildings!" The grenadiers raised their aim and let fly, but the bombs only seemed to scorch the white outside of the structures until, by chance, one landed in a door. That split the building just as if it had a seam; the two halves popped away and a cloud of machinery flew into the air, accompanied by a huge pale flame that rolled up and disappeared in an instant. Then the others all concentrated on the doors, except for potshots at some of the Taurans, not so much to get them as to blow them away before they could get inside. They seemed awfully eager.

All this time, we were trying to get the Taurans with laser fire, while they weaved and bounced around trying to get into the structures. We moved in as close to them as we could without putting ourselves in danger from the grenade blasts, yet too far away for good aim.

Still, we were getting them one by one and managed to destroy four of the seven buildings. Then, when there were only two aliens left, a nearby grenade blast flung one of them to within a few meters of a door. He dove in and several grenadiers fired salvos after him, but they all fell short or detonated harmlessly on the side. Bombs were falling all around, making an awful racket, but the sound was suddenly drowned out by a great sigh, like a giant's intake of breath, and where the building had been was a thick cylindrical cloud of smoke, solid-looking, dwindling away into the stratosphere, straight as if laid down by a ruler. The other Tauran had been right at the base of the cylinder; I could see pieces of him flying. A second later, a shock wave hit us and I rolled helplessly, pinwheeling, to smash into the pile of Tauran bodies and roll beyond.

I picked myself up and panicked for a second when I saw there was blood all over my suit—when I realized it was only alien blood, I relaxed but felt unclean.

"*Catch* the bastard! Catch him!" In the confusion, the Tauran had gotten free and was running for the grass. One platoon was chasing after him, losing ground, but then all of B team ran over and cut him off. I jogged over to join in the fun.

There were four people on top of him, and a ring around them of about fifty people, watching the struggle.

"Spread out, dammit! There might be a thousand more of them waiting to get us in one place." We dispersed, grumbling. By unspoken agreement we were all sure that there were no more live Taurans on the face of the planet.

Cortez was walking toward the prisoner while I backed away. Suddenly the four men collapsed in a pile on top of the creature.... Even from my distance I could see the foam spouting from his mouth-hole. His bubble had popped. Suicide.

"Damn!" Cortez was right there. "Get off that bastard." The four men got off and Cortez used his laser to slice the monster into a dozen quivering chunks. Heartwarming sight.

"That's all right, though, we'll find another one—everybody! Back in the arrowhead formation. Combat assault, on the Flower."

Well, we assaulted the Flower, which had evidently run out of ammunition (it was still belching, but no bubbles), and it was empty. We scurried up ramps and through corridors, fingers at the ready, like kids playing soldier. There was nobody home.

The same lack of response at the antenna installation, the "Salami," and twenty other major buildings, as well as the forty-four perimeter huts still intact. So we had "captured" dozens of buildings, mostly of incomprehensible purpose, but failed in our main mission, capturing a Tauran for the xenologists to experiment with. Oh well, they could have all the bits and pieces they'd ever want. That was something.

HERO

After we'd combed every last square centimeter of the base, a scout-ship came in with the real exploration crew, the scientists. Cortez said, "All right, snap out of it," and the hypnotic compulsion fell away.

At first it was pretty grim. A lot of the people, like Lucky and Marygay, almost went crazy with the memories of bloody murder multiplied a hundred times. Cortez ordered everybody to take a sed-tab, two for the ones most upset. I took two without being specifically ordered to do so.

Because it *was* murder, unadorned butchery—once we had the anti-spacecraft weapon doped out, we hadn't been in any danger. The Taurans hadn't seemed to have any conception of person-to-person fighting. We had just herded them up and slaughtered them, the first encounter between mankind and another intelligent species. Maybe it was the second encounter, counting the teddybears. What might have happened if we had sat down and tried to communicate? But they got the same treatment.

I spent a long time after that telling myself over and over that it hadn't been *me* who so gleefully carved up those frightened, stampeding creatures. Back in the twentieth century, they had established to everybody's satisfaction that "I was just following orders" was an inadequate excuse for inhuman conduct...but what can you do when the orders come from deep down in that puppet master of the unconscious?

Worst of all was the feeling that perhaps my actions weren't all that inhuman. Ancestors only a few generations back would have done the same thing, even to their fellow men, without any hypnotic conditioning.

I was disgusted with the human race, disgusted with the army and horrified at the prospect of living with myself for another century or so.... Well, there was always brainwipe.

A ship with a lone Tauran survivor had escaped and had gotten away clean, the bulk of the planet shielding it from *Earth's Hope* while it dropped into Aleph's collapsar field. Escaped home, I guessed, wherever that was, to report what twenty men with hand-weapons could do to a hundred fleeing on foot, unarmed.

I suspected that the next time humans met Taurans in ground combat, we would be more evenly matched. And I was right.

* * *

INTRODUCTION TO
"ANNIVERSARY PROJECT"

Harry Harrison asked me to do a story for an anthology of science fiction set one million years in the future. I wrote the first three pages of this one and ran into a wall. Started over, stopped again. Tried several angles and kept getting stuck.

Finally I wrote Harry and said I couldn't make the deadline, and those pages went into the "maybe someday" file.

Several years later, I came across the fragment in the proper mood, I guess, and immediately saw what was wrong—it was hamstrung by success. I wanted these "people" a million years in the future to have evolved into something totally alien, and in fact they were so alien they didn't have certain interesting attributes: love, hate, fear, death, birth, sex, appetites, politics. They did have ontological disagreements, but that's pretty dry stuff.

But in fact *as aliens* they did work pretty well. Most aliens in science fiction, it says here, aren't truly alien, because the purpose of an alien in a story is to provide some sort of refraction of human nature. But I wasn't really aiming that high. My aliens were there as unwitting vehicles for absurdist humor. All the story needed was a couple of bewildered humans, to act as foils for *alien* nature. Once I saw that, the story practically wrote itself.

* * *

ANNIVERSARY PROJECT

His name is Three-phasing and he is bald and wrinkled, slightly over one meter tall, large-eyed, toothless and all bones and skin, sagging pale skin shot through with traceries of delicate blue and red. He is considered very beautiful but most of his beauty is in his hands and is due to his extreme youth. He is over two hundred years old and is learning how to talk. He has become reasonably fluent in sixty-three languages, all dead ones, and has only ten to go.

The book he is reading is a facsimile of an early edition of Goethe's *Faust*. The nervous angular Fraktur letters goose-step across pages of paper-thin platinum.

The *Faust* had been printed electrolytically and, with several thousand similarly worthwhile books, sealed in an argon-filled chamber and carefully lost, in 2012 A.D.; a very wealthy man's legacy to the distant future.

In 2012 A.D., Polaris had been the pole star. Men eventually got to Polaris and built a small city on a frosty planet there. By that time, they weren't dating by prophets' births any more, but it would have been around 4900 A.D. The pole star by then, because of precession of the equinoxes, was a dim thing once called Gamma Cephei. The celestial pole kept reeling around, past Deneb and Vega and through barren patches of sky around Hercules and Draco; a patient clock but not the slowest one of use, and when it came back to the region of Polaris, then 26,000 years had passed and men had come back from the stars, to stay, and the book-filled chamber had shifted 130 meters on the floor of the

Pacific, had rolled into a shallow trench, and eventually was buried in an underwater landslide.

The thirty-seventh time this slow clock ticked, men had moved the Pacific, not because they had to, and had found the chamber, opened it up, identified the books and carefully sealed them up again. Some things by then were more important to men than the accumulation of knowledge: in half of one more circle of the poles would come the millionth anniversary of the written word. They could wait a few millennia.

As the anniversary, as nearly as they could reckon it, approached, they caused to be born two individuals: Ninehover (nominally female) and Three-phasing (nominally male). Three-phasing was born to learn how to read and speak. He was the first human being to study these skills in more than a quarter of a million years.

Three-phasing has read the first half of *Faust* forwards and, for amusement and exercise, is reading the second half backwards. He is singing as he reads, lisping.

"Fain' Looee w'mun…wif all'r die-mun ringf…" He has not put in his teeth because they make his gums hurt.

Because he is a child of two hundred, he is polite when his father interrupts his reading and singing. His father's "voice" is an arrangement of logic and aesthetic that appears in Three-phasing's mind. The flavor is lost by translating into words:

"Three-phasing my son-ly atavism of tooth and vocal cord," sarcastically in the reverent mode, "couldst tear thyself from objects of manifest symbol, and visit to share/help/learn, me?"

"?" he responds, meaning "with/with/of what?"

Withholding mode: "Concerning thee: past, future."

He shuts the book without marking his place. It would never occur to him to mark his place, since he remembers perfectly the page he stops on, as well as every word preceding, as well as every event, no matter how trivial, that he has observed from the precise age of one year. In this respect, at least, he is normal.

He thinks the proper coordinates as he steps over the mover-transom, through a microsecond of black, and onto his father's mover-transom, about four thousand kilometers away on a straight line through the crust and mantle of the earth.

Ritual mode: "As ever, father." The symbol he uses for "father" is purposefully wrong, chiding. Crude biological connotation.

His father looks cadaverous and has in fact been dead twice. In the infant's small-talk mode he asks, "From crude babblings of what sort have I torn your interest?"

"The tale called *Faust*, of a man so named, never satisfied with { symbol for slow but continuous accretion } of his knowledge and power; written in the language of Prussia."

"Also depended-ing on this strange word of immediacy, your Prussian language?"

"As most, yes. The word of 'to be': *sein*. Very important illusion in this and related languages/cultures; that events happen at the 'time' of perception, infinitesimal midpoint between past and future."

"Convenient illusion but retarding."

"As we discussed 129 years ago, yes." Three-phasing is impatient to get back to his reading, but adds:

"Obvious that to-be-ness
$$\left\{ \begin{array}{l} \text{same order of illusion as three-} \\ \text{dimensionality of external world.} \\[1em] \text{thrust upon observer by geomet-} \\ \text{ric limitation of synaptic degrees} \\ \text{of freedom.} \end{array} \right\}$$ "

"You always stick up for them."

"I have great regard for what they accomplished with limited faculties and so short lives." Stop beatin' around the bush, Dad. *Tempus fugit*, eight to the bar. Did Mr. Handy Moves-dat-man-around-by-her-apron-strings, 20th-century American poet, intend cultural translation of *Lysistrata*? If so, inept. African were-beast legendry, yes.

Withholding mode (coy): "Your father stood with Nine-hover all morning."

"," broadcasts Three-phasing: well?

"The machine functions, perhaps inadequately."

The young polyglot tries to radiate calm patience.

"Details I perceive you want; the idea yet excites you. You can never have satisfaction with your knowledge, either. What happened-s to the man in your Prussian book?"

"He lived-s one hundred years and died-s knowing that a man can never achieve true happiness, despite the appearance of success."

"For an infant, a reasonable perception."

Respectful chiding mode: "One hundred years makes-ed Faust a very old man, for a Dawn man."

"As I stand," same mode, less respect, "yet an infant." They trade silent symbols of laughter.

After a polite tenth-second interval, Three-phasing uses the light interrogation mode: "The machine of Nine-hover...?"

"It begins to work but so far not perfectly." This is not news.

Mild impatience: "As before, then, it brings back only rocks and earth and water and plants?"

"Negative, beloved atavism." Offhand: "This morning she caught two animals that look as man may once have looked."

"!" Strong impatience, "I go?"

"." His father ends the conversation just two seconds after it began.

Three-phasing stops off to pick up his teeth, then goes directly to Nine-hover.

A quick exchange of greeting-symbols and Nine-hover presents her prizes. "Thinking I have two different species," she stands: uncertainty, query.

Three-phasing is amused. "Negative, time-caster. The male and female took very dissimilar forms in the Dawn times." He touches one of them. "The round organs, here, served-ing to feed infants, in the female."

The female screams.

"She manipulates spoken symbols now," observes Nine-hover.

Before the woman has finished her startled yelp, Three-phasing explains: "Not manipulating concrete symbols; rather, she communicates in a way called 'non-verbal,' the use of such communication predating even speech." Slipping into the pedantic mode: "My reading indicates that such a loud noise occurs either $\left\{\begin{array}{l}\text{following a stimulus under}\\\text{conditions of}\end{array}\right.$

$\left.\begin{array}{l}\text{that produces pain}\\\text{extreme agitation}\end{array}\right\}$ since she seems not in pain, then she must fear me or you or both of us."

"Or the machine," Nine-hover adds.

Symbol for continuing. "We have no symbol for it but in Dawn days most humans observed 'xenophobia,' reacting to the strange with fear instead of delight. We stand as strange to them as they do to us, thus they register fear. In their era this attitude encouraged-s survival.

"Our silence must seem strange to them, as well as our appearance and the speed with which we move. I will attempt to speak to them, so they will know they need not fear us."

Bob and Sarah Graham were having a desperately good time. It was September of 1951 and the papers were full of news about the brilliant landing of U.S. Marines at Inchon. Bob was a Marine private with two days left of the thirty days' leave they had given him, between boot camp and disembarkation for Korea. Sarah had been Mrs. Graham for three weeks.

Sarah poured some more bourbon into her Coke. She wiped the sand off her thumb and stoppered the Coke bottle, then shook it gently. "What if you just don't show up?" she said softly.

Bob was staring out over the ocean and part of what Sarah said was lost in the crash of breakers rolling in. "What if I what?"

"Don't show up." She took a swig and offered the bottle. "Just stay here with me. With us." Sarah was sure she was pregnant. It was too early to tell, of course; her calendar was off but there could be other reasons.

He gave the Coke back to her and sipped directly from the bourbon bottle. "I suppose they'd go on without me. And I'd still be in jail when they came back."

"Not if—"

"Honey, don't even talk like that. It's a just cause."

She picked up a small shell and threw it toward the water.

"Besides, you read the *Examiner* yesterday."

"I'm cold. Let's go up." She stood and stretched and delicately brushed sand away. Bob admired her long naked dancer's body. He shook out the blanket and draped it over her shoulders.

"It'll all be over by the time I get there. We'll push those bastards—"

"Let's not talk about Korea. Let's not talk."

He put his arm around her and they started walking back toward the cabin. Halfway there, she stopped and enfolded the blanket around both of them, drawing him toward her. He always closed his eyes when they kissed, but she always kept hers open. She saw it: the air turning luminous, the seascape fading to be replaced by bare metal walls. The sand turns hard under her feet.

At her sharp intake of breath, Bob opens his eyes. He sees a grotesque dwarf, eyes and skull too large, body small and wrinkled. They stare at one another for a fraction of a second. Then the dwarf spins around and speeds across the room to what looks like a black square painted on the floor. When he gets there, he disappears.

"What the hell?" Bob says in a hoarse whisper.

Sarah turns around just a bit too late to catch a glimpse of Three-phasing's father. She does see Nine-hover before Bob does. The nominally female time-caster is a flurry of movement, sitting at the console of her time net, clicking switches and adjusting various dials. All of the motions are unnecessary, as is the console. It was built at Three-phasing's suggestion, since humans from the era into which they could cast would feel more comfortable in the presence of a machine that looked like a machine. The actual time net was roughly the size and shape of an asparagus stalk, was controlled completely by thought, and had no moving parts. It does not exist any more, but can still be used, once understood. Nine-hover has been trained from birth for this special understanding.

Sarah nudges Bob and points to Nine-hover. She can't find her voice. Bob stares open-mouthed.

In a few seconds, Three-phasing appears. He looks at Nine-hover for a moment, then scurries over to the Dawn couple and reaches up to touch Sarah on the left nipple. His body temperature is considerably higher than hers, and the unexpected warm moistness, as much as the suddenness of the motion, makes her jump back and squeal.

Three-phasing correctly classified both Dawn people as Caucasian, and so assumes that they speak some Indo-European language.

"GutenTagsprechensieDeutsch?" he says in a rapid soprano.

"Huh?" Bob says.

"Guten-Tag-sprechen-sie-Deutsch?" Three-phasing clears his throat and drops his voice down to the alto he uses to sing about the St. Louis woman. *"Guten Tag,"* he says, counting to a hundred between each word. *"Sprechen sie Deutsch?"*

"That's Kraut," says Bob, having grown up on jingoistic comic books. "Don't tell me you're a—"

Three-phasing analyzes the first five words and knows that Bob is an American from the period 1935-1955. "Yes, yes—and no, no—to wit, how very very clever of you to have identified this phrase as having come from the language of Prussia, Germany as you say; but I am, no, not a German person; at least, I no more belong to the German nationality than I do to any other, but I suppose that is not too clear and perhaps I should fully elucidate the particulars of your own situation at this, as you say, 'time' and 'place.'"

The last English-language author Three-phasing studied was Henry James.

"Huh?" Bob says again.

"Ah. I should simplify." He thinks for a half-second and drops his voice down another third. "Yeah, simple. Listen. Mac. First thing I gotta know's whatcher name. Whatcher broad's name."

"Well…I'm Bob Graham. This is my wife, Sarah Graham."

"Pleasta meetcha, Bob. Likewise, Sarah. Call me, uh…" The only twentieth-century language in which Three-phasing's name makes sense is propositional calculus. "George. George Boole.

"I 'poligize for bumpin' into ya, Sarah. That broad in the corner, she don't know what a tit is, so I was just usin' one of yours. Uh, lack of immediate culchural perspective, I shoulda knowed better."

Sarah feels a little dizzy, shakes her head slowly. "That's all right. I know you didn't mean anything by it."

"I'm dreaming," Bob says. "Shouldn't have—"

"No you aren't," says Three-phasing, adjusting his diction again. "You're in the future. Almost a million years. Pardon me." He scurries to the mover-transom, is gone for a second, reappears with a bedsheet, which he hands to Bob. "I'm sorry, we don't wear clothing. This is the best I can do, for now." The bedsheet is too small for Bob to wear the way Sarah is using the blanket. He folds it over and tucks it around his waist, in a kilt. "Why us?" he asks.

"You were taken at random. We've been time-casting"—he checks with Nine-hover—"for twenty-two years, and have never before caught a human being. Let alone two. You must have been in close contact with one another when you intersected the time-caster beam. I assume you were copulating."

"What-ing?" Bob says.

"No we weren't!" Sarah says indignantly.

"Ah, quite so." Three-phasing doesn't pursue the topic. He knows that humans of this culture were reticent about their sexual activity. But from their literature he knows they spent most of their "time" thinking about, arranging for, enjoying, and recovering from a variety of sexual contacts.

"Then that must be a time machine over there," Bob says, indicating the fake console.

"In a sense, yes." Three-phasing decides to be partly honest. "But the actual machine no longer exists. People did a lot of time-travelling about a quarter of a million years ago. Shuffled history around. Changed it back. The fact that the machine once existed, well, that enables us to use it, if you see what I mean."

"Uh, no. I don't." Not with synapses limited to three degrees of freedom.

"Well, never mind. It's not really important." He senses the next question. "You will be going back...I don't know exactly when. It depends on a lot of things. You see, time is like a rubber band." No, it isn't. "Or a spring." No, it isn't. "At any rate, within a few days, weeks at most, you will leave this present and return to the moment you were experiencing when the time-caster beam picked you up."

"I've read stories like that," Sarah says. "Will we remember the future, after we go back?"

"Probably not," he says charitably. Not until your brains evolve. "But you can do us a great service."

Bob shrugs. "Sure, long as we're here. Anyhow, you did us a favor." He puts his arm around Sarah. "I've gotta leave Sarah in a couple of days; don't know for how long. So you're giving us more time together."

"Whether we remember it or not," Sarah says.

"Good, fine. Come with me." They follow Three-phasing to the mover-transom, where he takes their hands and transports them to his home. It is as unadorned as the time-caster room, except for bookshelves along one wall, and a low podium upon which the volume of *Faust* rests. All of the books are bound identically, in shiny metal with flat black letters along the spines.

Bob looks around. "Don't you people ever sit down?"

"Oh," Three-phasing says. "Thoughtless of me." With his mind he shifts the room from utility mood to comfort mood. Intricate tapestries now hang on the walls; soft cushions that look like silk are strewn around in pleasant disorder. Chiming music, not quite discordant, hovers at the edge of audibility, and there is a faint odor of something like jasmine. The metal floor has become a kind of soft leather, and the room has somehow lost its corners.

"How did that happen?" Sarah asks.

"I don't know." Three-phasing tries to copy Bob's shrug, but only manages a spasmodic jerk. "Can't remember not being able to do it."

Bob drops into a cushion and experimentally pushes at the floor with a finger. "What is it you want us to do?"

Trying to move slowly, Three-phasing lowers himself into a cushion and gestures at a nearby one, for Sarah. "It's very simple, really. Your being here is most of it.

"We're celebrating the millionth anniversary of the written word." How to phrase it? "Everyone is interested in this anniversary, but... nobody reads any more."

Bob nods sympathetically. "Never have time for it myself."

"Yes, uh...you *do* know how to read, though?"

"He knows," Sarah says. "He's just lazy."

"Well, yeah." Bob shifts uncomfortably in the cushion. "Sarah's the one you want. I kind of, uh, prefer to listen to the radio."

"I read all the time," Sarah says with a little pride. "Mostly mysteries. But sometimes I read good books, too."

"Good, good." It was indeed fortunate to have found this pair, Three-phasing realizes. They had used the metal of the ancient books to "tune" the time-caster, so potential subjects were limited to those living some eighty years before and after 2021 A.D. Internal evidence in the books indicated that most of the Earth's population was illiterate during this period.

"Allow me to explain. Anyone of us can learn how to read. But to us it is like a code; an unnatural way of communicating. Because we are all natural telepaths. We can read each other's minds from the age of one year."

"Golly!" Sarah says. "Read minds?" And Three-phasing sees in her mind a fuzzy kind of longing, much of which is love for Bob and frustration that she knows him only imperfectly. He dips into Bob's mind and finds things she is better off not knowing.

"That's right. So what we want is for you to read some of these books, and allow us to go into your minds while you're doing it. This way we will be able to recapture an experience that has been lost to the race for over a half-million years."

"I don't know," Bob says slowly. "Will we have time for anything else? I mean, the world must be pretty strange. Like to see some of it."

"Of course; sure. But the rest of the world is pretty much like my place here. Nobody goes outside any more. There isn't any air." He doesn't want to tell them how the air was lost, which might disturb them, but they seem to accept that as part of the distant future.

"Uh, George." Sarah is blushing. "We'd also like, uh, some time to ourselves. Without anybody...inside our minds."

"Yes, I understand perfectly. You will have your own room, and plenty of time to yourselves." Three-phasing neglects to say that there is no such thing as privacy in a telepathic society.

But sex is another thing they don't have any more. They're almost as curious about that as they are about books.

So the kindly men of the future gave Bob and Sarah Graham plenty of time to themselves: Bob and Sarah reciprocated. Through the Dawn couple's eyes and brains, humanity shared again the visions of Fielding and Melville and Dickens and Shakespeare and almost a dozen others. And as for the 98% more, that they didn't have time to read or that were in foreign languages—Three-phasing got the hang of it and would spend several millennia entertaining those who were amused by this central illusion of literature: that there could be order, that there could be beginnings and endings and logical workings-out in between; that you could count on the third act or the last chapter to tie things up. They knew how profound an illusion this was because each of them knew every other living human with an intimacy and accuracy far superior to that which even Shakespeare could bring to the study of even himself. And as for Sarah and as for Bob:

Anxiety can throw a person's ovaries 'way off schedule. On that beach in California, Sarah was no more pregnant than Bob was. But up there in the future, some somatic tension finally built up to the breaking point, and an egg went sliding down the left Fallopian tube, to be met by a wiggling intruder approximately halfway; together they were the first manifestation of the organism that nine months later, or a million years earlier, would be christened Douglas MacArthur Graham.

This made a problem for time, or Time, which is neither like a rubber band nor like a spring; nor even like a river nor a carrier wave—but which, like all of these things, can be deformed by certain stresses. For instance, two people going into the future and three coming back, on the same time-casting beam.

In an earlier age, when time travel was more common, time-casters would have made sure that the baby, or at least its aborted embryo, would stay in the future when the mother returned to her present. Or they could arrange for the mother to stay in the future. But these subtleties had long been forgotten when Nine-hover relearned the dead art. So Sarah went back to her present with a hitch-hiker, an interloper, firmly imbedded in the lining of her womb. And its dim sense of life set up a kind of eddy in the flow of time, that Sarah had to share.

The mathematical explanation is subtle, and can't be comprehended by those of us who synapse with fewer than four degrees of freedom. But the end effect is clear: Sarah had to experience all of her own life backwards, all the way back to that embrace on the beach. Some highlights were:

In 1992, slowly dying of cancer, in a mental hospital.

In 1979, seeing Bob finally succeed at suicide on the American Plan, not quite finishing his 9,527th bottle of liquor.

In 1970, having her only son returned in a sealed casket from a country she'd never heard of.

In the 1960s, helplessly watching her son become more and more neurotic because of something that no one could name.

In 1953, Bob coming home with one foot, the other having been lost to frostbite; never having fired a shot in anger.

In 1952, the agonizing breech presentation.

Like her son, Sarah would remember no details of the backward voyage through her life. But the scars of it would haunt her forever.

They were kissing on the beach.

Sarah dropped the blanket and made a little noise. She started crying and slapped Bob as hard as she could, then ran on alone, up to the cabin.

Bob watched her progress up the hill with mixed feelings. He took a healthy slug from the bourbon bottle, to give him an excuse to wipe his own eyes.

He could go sit on the beach and finish the bottle; let her get over it by herself. Or he could go comfort her.

He tossed the bottle away, the gesture immediately making him feel stupid, and followed her. Later that night she apologized, saying she didn't know what had gotten into her.

* * *

INTRODUCTION TO "TRICENTENNIAL"

In 1976, when everybody was doing bicentennial stuff, *Analog* editor Ben Bova was planning a special July edition to think about what things might be like a hundred years in our future—America's three-hundredth anniversary. He commissioned a cover painting from Rick Sternbach that had a "Tricentennial" American theme, and then asked me to write a story that went along with it.

The painting was marvelous, but I had to go through all kinds of hoops to make the story fit the picture and yet be scientifically plausible—but the constraints that art and science put on the story didn't seem to hurt it. It won the Hugo for Best Short Story of the Year.

I think that art loves restrictions, or craft does, anyhow.

* * *

TRICENTENNIAL

DECEMBER 1975

Scientists pointed out that the Sun could be part of a double star system. For its companion to have gone undetected, of course, it would have to be small and dim, and thousands of astronomical units distant.

They would find it eventually; "it" would turn out to be "them"; they would come in handy.

JANUARY 2075

The office was opulent even by the extravagant standards of 21st century Washington. Senator Connors had a passion for antiques. One wall was lined with leatherbound books; a large brass telescope symbolized his role as Liaison to the Science Guild. An intricately woven Navajo rug from his home state covered most of the parquet floor. A grandfather clock. Paintings, old maps.

The computer terminal was discreetly hidden in the top drawer of his heavy teak desk. On the desk: a blotter, a precisely centered fountain pen set, and a century-old sound-only black Bell telephone. It chimed.

His secretary said that Dr. Leventhal was waiting to see him. "Keep answering me for thirty seconds," the Senator said. "Then hang it and send him right in."

He cradled the phone and went to a wall mirror. Straightened his tie and cape; then with a fingernail evened out the bottom line of his lip pomade. Ran a hand through long, thinning white hair and returned to stand by the desk, one hand on the phone.

The heavy door whispered open. A short thin man bowed slightly. "Sire."

The Senator crossed to him with both hands out. "Oh, blow that, Charlie. Give ten." The man took both his hands, only for an instant. "When was I ever 'Sire' to you, heyfool?"

"Since last week," Leventhal said. "Guild members have been calling you worse names than 'Sire.'"

The Senator bobbed his head twice. "True, and true. And I sympathize. Will of the people, though."

"Sure." Leventhal pronounced it as one word: "Willathapeeble."

Connors went to the bookcase and opened a chased panel. "Drink?"

"Yeah, Bo." Charlie sighed and lowered himself into a deep sofa. "Hit me. Sherry or something."

The Senator brought the drinks and sat down beside Charlie. "You shoulda listened to me. Shoulda got the Ad Guild to write your proposal."

"We have good writers."

"Begging to differ. Less than two percent of the electorate bothered to vote; most of them for the administration advocate. Now you take the Engineering Guild—"

"*You* take the engineers. And—"

"They used the Ad Guild," Connors shrugged. "They got their budget."

"It's easy to sell bridges and power plants and shuttles. Hard to sell pure science."

"The more reason for you to—"

"Yeah, sure. Ask for double and give half to the Ad boys. Maybe next year. That's not what I came to talk about."

"That radio stuff?"

"Right. Did you read the report?"

Connors looked into his glass. "Charlie, you know I don't have time to—"

"Somebody read it, though."

"Oh, righty-o. Good astronomy boy on my staff; he gave me a boil-down. Mighty interesting, that."

"There's an intelligent civilization eleven light-years away—that's 'mighty interesting'?"

"Sure. Real breakthrough." Uncomfortable silence. "Uh, what are you going to do about it?"

"Two things. First, we're trying to figure out what they're saying. That's hard. Second, we want to send a message back. That's easy. And that's where you come in."

The Senator nodded and looked somewhat wary.

"Let me explain. We've sent messages to this star, 61 Cygni, before. It's a double star, actually, with a dark companion."

"Like us."

"Sort of. Anyhow, they never answered. They aren't listening, evidently; they aren't sending."

"But we got—"

"What we're picking up is about what you'd pick up eleven light-years from Earth. A confused jumble of broadcasts, eleven years old. Very faint. But obviously not generated by any sort of natural source."

"Then we're already sending a message back. The same kind they're sending us."

"That's right, but—"

"So what does all this have to do with me?"

"Bo, we don't want to whisper at them—we want to *shout*! Get their attention." Leventhal sipped his wine and leaned back. "For that we'll need one hell of a lot of power."

"Uh, righty-o. Charlie, power's money. How much are you talking about?"

"The whole show. I want to shut down Death Valley for twelve hours."

The Senator's mouth made a silent O. "Charlie, you've been working too hard. Another Blackout? On purpose?"

"There won't be any Blackout. Death Valley has emergency storage for fourteen hours."

"At half capacity." He drained his glass and walked back to the bar, shaking his head. "First you say you want power. Then you say you want to turn off the power." He came back with the burlap-covered bottle. "You aren't making sense, boy."

"Not turn it off, really. Turn it around."

"Is that a riddle?"

"No, look. You know the power doesn't really come from the Death Valley grid; it's just a way station and accumulator. Power comes from the orbital—"

"I know all that, Charlie. I've got a Science Certificate."

"Sure. So what we've got is a big microwave laser in orbit, that shoots down a tight beam of power. Enough to keep North America running. Enough—"

"That's what I mean. You can't just—"

"So we turn it around and shoot it at a power grid on the Moon. Relay the power around to the big radio dish at Farside. Turn it into radio waves and point it at 61 Cygni. Give 'em a blast that'll fry their fillings."

"Doesn't sound neighborly."

"It wouldn't actually be that powerful—but it would be a hell of a lot more powerful than any natural 21-centimeter source."

"I don't know, boy." He rubbed his eyes and grimaced. "I could maybe do it on the sly, only tell a few people what's on. But that'd only work for a few minutes...what do you need twelve hours for, anyway?"

"Well, the thing won't aim itself at the Moon automatically, the way it does at Death Valley. Figure as much as an hour to get the thing turned around and aimed.

"Then, we don't want to just send a blast of radio waves at them. We've got a five-hour program, that first builds up a mutual language, then tells them about us, and finally asks them some questions. We want to send it twice."

Connors refilled both glasses. "How old were you in '47, Charlie?"

"I was born in '45."

"You don't remember the Blackout. Ten thousand people died...and you want me to suggest—"

"Come on, Bo, it's not the same thing. We know the accumulators work now—besides, the ones who died, most of them had faulty fail-safes on their cars. If we warn them the power's going to drop, they'll check their fail-safes or damn well stay out of the air."

"And the media? They'd have to take turns broadcasting. Are you going to tell the People what they can watch?"

"Fuzz the media. They'll be getting the biggest story since the Crucifixion."

"Maybe." Connors took a cigarette and pushed the box toward Charlie. "You don't remember what happened to the Senators from California in '47, do you?"

"Nothing good, I suppose."

"No, indeed. They were impeached. Lucky they weren't lynched. Even though the real trouble was 'way up in orbit.

"Like you say; people pay a grid tax to California. They think the power comes from California. If something fuzzes up, they get pissed at California.

I'm the Lib Senator from California, Charlie; ask me for the Moon, maybe I can do something. Don't ask me to fuzz around with Death Valley."

"All right, all right. It's not like I was asking you to wire it for me, Bo. Just get it on the ballot. We'll do everything we can to educate—"

"Won't work. You barely got the Scylla probe voted in—and that was no skin off nobody, not with L-5 picking up the tab."

"Just get it on the ballot."

"We'll see. I've got a quota, you know that. And the Tricentennial coming up, hell, everybody wants on the ballot."

"Please, Bo. This is bigger than that. This is bigger than anything. Get it on the ballot."

"Maybe as a rider. No promises."

MARCH 1992

From *Fax & Pix*, 12 March 1992:
ANTIQUE SPACEPROBE
ZAPPED BY NEW STARS

1. Pioneer 10 sent first Jupiter pix Earthward in 1973 (see pix upleft, upright).
2. Left solar system 1987. First man-made thing to leave solar system.
3. Yesterday, reports NSA, Pioneer 10 begins AM to pick up heavy radiation, Gets more and more to max about 3 PM. Then goes back down. Radiation has to come from outside solar system.
4. NSA and Hawaii scientists say Pioneer 10 went through disk of synchrotron (sin-kro-tron) radiation that comes from two stars we didn't know about before.
   A. The stars are small "black dwarfs."
   B. They are going round each other once every 40 seconds, and take 350,000 years to go around the Sun.
   C. One of the stars is made of *antimatter*. This is stuff that blows up if it touches real matter. What the Hawaii scientists saw was a dim circle of invisible (infrared) light, that blinks on and off every twenty seconds. This light comes from where the atmospheres of the two stars touch (see pic downleft).
   D. The stars have a big magnetic field. Radiation comes from stuff spinning off the stars and trying to get through the field.

E. The stars are about 5000 times as far away from the Sun as we are. They sit at the wrong angle, compared to the rest of the solar system (see pic downright).

5. NSA says we aren't in any danger from the stars. They're too far away, and besides, nothing in the solar system ever goes through the radiation.

6. The woman who discovered the stars wants to call them Scylla (*skill*-a) and Charybdis (ku-*rib*-dus).

7. Scientists say they don't know where the hell those two stars came from. Everything else in the solar system makes sense.

FEBRUARY 2075

When the docking phase started, Charlie thought, that was when it was easy to tell the scientists from the baggage. The scientists were the ones who looked nervous.

Superficially, it seemed very tranquil—nothing like the bonehurting skinstretching acceleration when the shuttle lifted off. The glittering transparent cylinder of L-5 simply grew larger, slowly, then wheeled around to point at them.

The problem was that a space colony big enough to hold 4000 people has more inertia than God. If the shuttle hit the mating dimple too fast, it would fold up like an accordion. A spaceship is made to take stress in the *other* direction.

Charlie hadn't paid first class, but they let him up into the observation dome anyhow; professional courtesy. There were only two other people there, standing on the Velcro rug, strapped to one bar and hanging on to another.

They were a young man and woman, probably new colonists. The man was talking excitedly. The woman stared straight ahead, not listening. Her knuckles were white on the bar and her teeth were clenched. Charlie wanted to say something in sympathy, but it's hard to talk while you're holding your breath.

The last few meters are the worst. You can't see over the curve of the ship's hull, and the steering jets make a constant stutter of little bumps: left, right, forward, back. If the shuttle folded, would the dome shatter? Or just pop off?

It was all controlled by computers, of course. The pilot just sat up there in a mist of weightless sweat.

Then the low moan, almost subsonic shuddering as the shuttle's smooth hull complained against the friction pads. Charlie waited for the ringing *spang* that would mean they were a little too fast: friable alloy plates under the friction pads, crumbling to absorb the energy of their forward motion; last-ditch stand.

If that didn't stop them, they would hit a two-meter wall of solid steel, which would. It had happened once. But not this time.

"Please remain seated until pressure is equalized," a recorded voice said. "It's been a pleasure having you aboard."

Charlie crawled down the pole, back to the passenger area. He walked rip, rip, rip back to his seat and obediently waited for his ears to pop. Then the side door opened and he went with the other passengers through the tube that led to the elevator. They stood on the ceiling. Someone had laboriously scratched a graffito on the metal wall:

> Stuck on this lift for hours, perforce;
> This lift that cost a million bucks.
> There's no such thing as centrifugal force;
> L-5 sucks.

Thirty more weightless seconds as they slid to the ground. There were a couple of dozen people waiting on the loading platform.

Charlie stepped out into the smell of orange blossoms and newly-mown grass. He was home.

"Charlie! Hey, over here." Young man standing by a tandem bicycle. Charlie squeezed both his hands and then jumped on the back seat. "Drink."

"Did you get—"

"Drink. Then talk." They glided down the smooth macadam road toward town. The bar was just a rain canopy over some tables and chairs, overlooking the lake in the center of town. No bartender; you went to the service table and punched in your credit number, then chose wine or fruit juice; with or without vacuum-distilled raw alcohol. They talked about shuttle nerves awhile, then:

"What you get from Connors?"

"Words, not much. I'll give a full report at the meeting tonight. Looks like we won't even get on the ballot, though."

"Now isn't that what we said was going to happen? We shoulda gone with Francois Petain's idea."

"Too risky." Petain's plan had been to tell Death Valley they had to shut down the laser for repairs. Not tell the groundhogs about the signal at all, just answer it. "If they found out they'd sue us down to our teeth."

The man shook his head. "I'll never understand groundhogs."

"Not your job." Charlie was an Earth-born, Earth-trained psychologist. "Nobody born here ever could."

"Maybe so." He stood up. "Thanks for the drink; I've gotta get back to work. You know to call Dr. Bemis before the meeting?"

"Yeah. There was a message at the Cape."

"She has a surprise for you."

"Doesn't she always? You clowns never do anything around here until I leave."

All Abigail Bemis would say over the phone was that Charlie should come to her place for dinner; she'd prep him for the meeting.

"That was good, Ab. Can't afford real food on Earth."

She laughed and stacked the plates in the cleaner, then drew two cups of coffee. She laughed again when she sat down. Stocky, white-haired woman with bright eyes in a sea of wrinkles.

"You're in a jolly mood tonight."

"Yep. It's expectation."

"Johnny said you had a surprise."

"Hooboy, he doesn't know half. So you didn't get anywhere with the Senator."

"No. Even less than I expected. What's the secret?"

"Connors is a nice-hearted boy. He's done a lot for us."

"Come on, Ab. What is it?"

"He's right. Shut off the groundhogs' TV for twenty minutes and they'd have another Revolution on their hands."

"Ab..."

"We're going to send the message."

"Sure. I figured we would. Using Farside at whatever wattage we've got. If we're lucky—"

"Nope. Not enough power."

Charlie stirred a half-spoon of sugar into his coffee. "You plan to... defy Connors?"

"Fuzz Connors. We're not going to use radio at all."

"Visible light? Infra?"

"We're going to hand-carry it. In Daedalus."

Charlie's coffee cup was halfway to his mouth. He spilled a great deal.

"Here, have a napkin."

JUNE 2040

From *A Short History of the Old Order* (Freeman Press, 2040):

"...and if you think *that* was a waste, consider Project Daedalus.

"This was the first big space thing after L-5. Now L-5 worked out all right, because it was practical. But Daedalus (named from a Greek god who could fly)—that was a clear-cut case of throwing money down the rat-hole.

"These scientists in 2016 talked the bourgeoisie into paying for a trip to another *star*! It was going to take over a hundred years—but the scientists were going to have babies along the way, and train *them* to be scientists (whether they wanted to or not!).

"They were going to use all the old H-bombs for fuel—as if we might not need the fuel some day right here on Earth. What if L-5 decided they didn't like us and shut off the power beam?

"Daedalus was supposed to be a spaceship almost a kilometer long! Most of it was manufactured in space, from Moon stuff, but a lot of it—the most expensive part, you bet—had to be boosted from Earth.

"They almost got it built, but then came the Breakup and the People's Revolution. No way in hell the People were going to let them have those H-bombs, not sitting right over our heads like that.

"So we left the H-bombs in Helsinki and the space freeks went back to doing what they're supposed to do. Every year they petition to get those H-bombs, but every year the Will of the People says no.

"That spaceship is still up there, a skytrillion-dollar boondoggle. As a monument to bourgeois folly, it's worse than the Pyramids!!"

FEBRUARY 2075

"So the Scylla probe is just a ruse, to get the fuel—"

"Oh no, not really." She slid a blue-covered folder to him. "We're still going to Scylla. Scoop up a few megatons of degenerate antimatter. And a similar amount of degenerate matter from Charybdis.

"We don't plan a generation ship, Charlie. The hydrogen fuel will get us out there; once there, it'll power the magnetic bottles to hold the real fuel."

"Total annihilation of matter," Charlie said.

"That's right. Em-cee-squared to the ninth decimal place. We aren't talking about centuries to get to 61 Cygni. Nine years, there and back."

"The groundhogs aren't going to like it. All the bad feeling about the original Daedalus—"

"Fuzz the groundhogs. We'll do everything we said we'd do with their precious H-bombs: go out to Scylla, get some antimatter, and bring it back. Just taking a long way back."

"You don't want to just tell them that's what we're going to do? No skin off..."

She shook her head and laughed again, this time a little bitterly. "You didn't read the editorial in *Peoplepost* this morning, did you?"

"I was busy."

"So am I, boy; too busy for that drik. One of my staff brought it in, though."

"It's about Daedalus?"

"No...it concerns 61 Cygni. How the crazy scientists want to let those boogers know there's life on Earth.

"They'll come make people-burgers out of us."

"Something like that."

Over three thousand people sat on the hillside, a "natural" amphitheatre fashioned of moon dirt and Earth grass. There was an incredible din, everyone talking at once: Dr. Bemis had just told them about the 61 Cygni expedition.

On about the tenth "Quiet, please," Bemis was able to continue. "So you can see why we didn't simply broadcast this meeting. Earth would pick it up. Likewise, there are no groundhog media on L-5 right now. They were rotated back to Earth and the shuttle with their replacements needed repairs at the Cape. The other two shuttles are here.

"So I'm asking all of you—and all of your brethren who had to stay at their jobs—to keep secret the biggest thing since Isabella hocked her jewels. Until we lift.

"Now Dr. Leventhal, who's chief of our social sciences section, wants to talk to you about selecting the crew."

Charlie hated public speaking. In this setting, he felt like a Christian on the way to being catfood. He smoothed out his damp notes on the podium.

"Uh, basic problem." A thousand people asked him to speak up. He adjusted the microphone.

"The basic problem is, we have space for about a thousand people. Probably more than one out of four want to go."

Loud murmur of assent. "And we don't want to be despotic about choosing…but I've set up certain guidelines, and Dr. Bemis agrees with them."

"Nobody should plan on going if he or she needs sophisticated medical care, obviously. Same toke, few very old people will be considered."

Almost inaudibly, Abigail said, "Sixty-four isn't very old, Charlie. I'm going." She hadn't said anything earlier.

He continued, looking at Bemis. "Second, we must leave behind those people who are absolutely necessary for the maintenance of L-5. Including the power station." She smiled at him.

"We don't want to split up mating pairs, not for, well, nine years plus…but neither will we take children." He waited for the commotion to die down. "On this mission, children are baggage. You'll have to find foster parents for them. Maybe they'll go on the next trip.

"Because we can't afford baggage. We don't know what's waiting for us at 61 Cygni—a thousand people sounds like a lot, but it isn't. Not when you consider that we need a cross-section of all human knowledge, all human abilities. It may turn out that a person who can sing madrigals will be more important than a plasma physicist. No way of knowing ahead of time."

The 4,000 people did manage to keep it secret, not so much out of strength of character as from a deep-seated paranoia about Earth and Earthlings.

And Senator Connors' Tricentennial actually came to their aid.

Although there was "One World," ruled by "The Will of the People," some regions had more clout than others, and nationalism was by no means dead. This was one factor.

Another factor was the way the groundhogs felt about the thermonuclear bombs stockpiled in Helsinki. All antiques; mostly a century or more old. The scientists said they were perfectly safe, but you know how that goes.

The bombs still technically belonged to the countries that had surrendered them, nine out of ten split between North America and Russia. The tenth remaining was divided among 42 other countries. They all got together every few years to argue about what to do with the damned things. Everybody wanted to get rid of them in some useful way, but nobody wanted to put up the capital.

Charlie Leventhal's proposal was simple. L-5 would provide bankroll, materials, and personnel. On a barren rock in the Norwegian Sea they would take apart the old bombs, one at a time, and turn them into uniform fuel capsules for the Daedalus craft.

The Scylla/Charybdis probe would be timed to honor both the major spacefaring countries. Renamed the *John F. Kennedy*, it would leave Earth orbit on America's Tricentennial. The craft would accelerate halfway to the double star system at one gee, then flip and slow down at the same rate. It would use a magnetic scoop to gather antimatter from Scylla. On May Day, 2077, It would again be renamed, being the *Leonid I. Brezhnev* for the return trip. For safety's sake, the antimatter would be delivered to a lunar research station, near Farside. L-5 scientists claimed that harnessing the energy from total annihilation of matter would make a heaven on Earth.

Most people doubted that, but looked forward to the fireworks.

JANUARY 2076

"The *hell* with that!" Charlie was livid. "I—I just won't do it. Won't!"

"You're the only one—"

"That's not true. Ab, you know it." Charlie paced from wall to wall of her office cubicle. "There are dozens of people who can run L-5. Better than I can."

"Not better, Charlie."

He stopped in front of her desk, leaned over. "Come on, Ab. There's only one logical person to stay behind and run things. Not only has she proven herself in the position, but she's too old to—"

"That kind of drik I don't have to listen to."

"Now, Ab…"

"No, you listen to me. I was an infant when we started building Daedalus; worked on it as a girl and a young woman.

"I could take you out there in a shuttle and show you the rivets that I put in, myself. A half-century ago."

"That's my—"

"I earned my ticket, Charlie." Her voice softened. "Age is a factor, yes. This is only the first trip of many—and when it comes back, I *will* be too old. You'll just be in your prime…and with over twenty years of experience as Coordinator, I don't doubt they'll make you captain of the next—"

"I don't want to be captain. I don't want to be Coordinator. I just want to *go!*"

"You and three thousand other people."

"And of the thousand that don't want to go, or can't, there isn't one person who could serve as Coordinator? I could name you—"

"That's not the point. There's no one on L-5 who has anywhere near the influence, the connections, you have on Earth. No one who understands groundhogs as well."

"That's racism, Ab. Groundhogs are just like you and me."

"Some of them. I don't see you going Earthside every chance you can get…what, you like the view up here? You like living in a can?"

He didn't have a ready answer for that. Ab continued: "Whoever's Coordinator is going to have to do some tall explaining, trying to keep things smooth between L-5 and Earth. That's been your life's work, Charlie. And you're also known and respected here. You're the only logical choice."

"I'm not arguing with your logic."

"I know." Neither of them had to mention the document, signed by Charlie, among others, that gave Dr. Bemis final authority in selecting the crew for Daedalus/Kennedy/Brezhnev. "Try not to hate me too much, Charlie. I have to do what's best for my people. All of my people."

Charlie glared at her for a long moment and left.

JUNE 2076

From *Fax & Pix*, 4 June 2076:
SPACE FARM LEAVES FOR
STARS NEXT MONTH

1. The *John F. Kennedy*, that goes to Scylla/Charybdis next month, is like a little L-5 with bombs up its tail (see pix upleft, upright).
   A. The trip's twenty months. They could either take a few people and fill the thing up with food, air, and water—or take a lot of people inside a closed ecology, like L-5.

    B. They could've gotten by with only a couple hundred people, to run the farms and stuff. But almost all the space freeks wanted to go. They're used to living that way, anyhow (and they never get to go anyplace).

    C. When they get back, the farms will be used as a starter for L-4, like L-5 but smaller at first, and on the other side of the Moon (pic downleft).

2. For other Tricentennial fax & pix, see bacover.

JULY 2076

Charlie was just finishing up a week on Earth the day the *John F. Kennedy* was launched. Tired of being interviewed, he slipped away from the media lounge at the Cape shuttleport. His white clearance card got him out onto the landing strip, alone.

The midnight shuttle was being fueled at the far end of the strip, gleaming pink-white in the last light from the setting sun. Its image twisted and danced in the shimmering heat that radiated from the tarmac. The smell of the soft tar was indelibly associated in his mind with leave-taking, relief.

He walked to the middle of the strip and checked his watch. Five minutes. He lit a cigarette and threw it away. He rechecked his mental calculations; the flight would start low in the southwest. He blocked out the sun with a raised hand. What would 150 bombs per second look like? For the media they were called fuel capsules. The people who had carefully assembled them and gently lifted them to orbit and installed them in the tanks, they called them bombs. Ten times the brightness of a full moon, they had said. On L-5 you weren't supposed to look toward it without a dark filter.

No warm-up: it suddenly appeared, impossibly brilliant rainbow speck just over the horizon. It gleamed for several minutes, then dimmed slightly with the haze, and slipped away.

Most of the United States wouldn't see it until it came around again, some two hours later, turning night into day, competing with local pyrotechnic displays. Then every couple of hours after that. Charlie would see it once more, then get on the shuttle. And finally stop having to call it by the name of a dead politician.

SEPTEMBER 2076

There was a quiet celebration on L-5 when *Daedalus* reached the mid-point of its journey, flipped, and started decelerating. The progress report from its crew characterized the journey as "uneventful." At that time they were going nearly two-tenths of the speed of light. The laser beam that carried communications was red-shifted from blue light down to orange; the message that turnaround had been successful took two weeks to travel from *Daedalus* to L-5.

They announced a slight course change. They had analyzed the polarization of light from Scylla/Charybdis as their phase angle increased, and were pretty sure the system was surrounded by flat rings of debris, like Saturn. They would "come in low" to avoid collision.

JANUARY 2077

Daedalus had been sending back recognizable pictures of the Scylla/Charybdis system for three weeks. They finally had one that was dramatic enough for groundhog consumption.

Charlie set the holo cube on his desk and pushed it around with his finger, marvelling.

"This is incredible. How did they do it?"

"It's a montage, of course." Johnny had been one of the youngest adults left behind: heart murmur, trick knees, a surfeit of astrophysicists.

"The two stars are a strobe snapshot in infrared. Sort of. Some ten or twenty thousand exposures taken as the ship orbited around the system, then sorted out and enhanced." He pointed, but it wasn't much help, since Charlie was looking at the cube from a different angle.

"The lamina of fire where the atmospheres touch, that was taken in ultraviolet. Shows more fine structure that way.

"The rings were easy. Fairly long exposures in visible light. Gives the star background, too."

A light tap on the door and an assistant stuck his head in. "Have a second, Doctor?"

"Sure."

"Somebody from a Russian May Day committee is on the phone. She wants to know whether they've changed the name of the ship to *Brezhnev* yet."

"Yeah. Tell her we decided on 'Leon Trotsky' instead, though."

He nodded seriously. "Okay." He started to close the door.

"*Wait!*" Charlie rubbed his eyes. "Tell her, uh…the ship doesn't have a commemorative name while it's in orbit there. They'll rechristen it just before the start of the return trip!"

"Is that true?" Johnny asked.

"I don't know. Who cares? In another couple of months they won't *want* it named after anybody." He and Ab had worked out a plan—admittedly rather shaky—to protect L-S from the groundhogs' wrath; nobody on the satellite knew ahead of time that the ship was headed for 61 Cygni. It was a decision the crew arrived at on the way to Scylla/Charybdis; they modified the drive system to accept matter-antimatter destruction while they were orbiting the double star. L-5 would first hear of the mutinous plan via a transmission sent as *Daedalus* left Scylla/Charybdis. They'd be a month on their way by the time the message got to Earth.

It was pretty transparent, but at least they had been careful that no record of *Daedalus'* true mission be left on L-5. Three thousand people did know the truth, though, and any competent engineer or physical scientist would suspect it.

Ab had felt that, although there was a better than even chance they would be exposed, surely the groundhogs couldn't stay angry for 23 years—even if they were unimpressed by the antimatter and other wonders…

Besides, Charlie thought, it's not their worry anymore.

As it turned out, the crew of *Daedalus* would have bigger things to worry about.

JUNE 2077

The Russians had their May Day celebration—Charlie watched it on TV and winced every time they mentioned the good ship *Leonid I. Brezhnev*—and then things settled back down to normal. Charlie and three thousand others waited nervously for the "surprise" message. It came in early June, as expected, scrambled in a data channel. But it didn't say what it was supposed to:

> This is Abigail Bemis, to Charles Leventhal.
> Charlie, we have real trouble. The ship has been damaged, hit in the stern by a good chunk of something. It punched right through the main drive reflector. Destroyed a set of control sensors and one attitude jet.

As far as we can tell, the situation is stable. We're maintaining acceleration at just a tiny fraction under one gee. But we can't steer, and we can't shut off the main drive.

We didn't have any trouble with ring debris when we were orbiting, since we were inside Roche's limit. Coming in, as you know, we'd managed to take advantage of natural divisions in the rings. We tried the same going back, but it was a slower, more complicated process, since we mass so goddamn much now. We must have picked up a piece from the fringe of one of the outer rings.

If we could turn off the drive, we might have a chance at fixing it. But the work pods can't keep up with the ship, not at one gee. The radiation down there would fry the operator in seconds, anyway.

We're working on it. If you have any ideas, let us know. It occurs to me that this puts you in the clear—we were headed back to Earth, but got clobbered. Will send a transmission to that effect on the regular comm channel. This message is strictly burn-before-reading.

Endit.

It worked perfectly, as far as getting Charlie and L-5 off the hook— and the drama of the situation precipitated a level of interest in space travel unheard-of since the 1960s.

They even had a hero. A volunteer had gone down in a heavily-shielded work pod, lowered on a cable, to take a look at the situation. She'd sent back clear pictures of the damage, before the cable snapped.

DAEDALUS: A.D. 2081
EARTH: A.D. 2101

The following news item was killed from *Fax & Pix*, because it was too hard to translate into the "plain English" that made the paper so popular:

SPACESHIP PASSES 61 CYGNI—SORT OF

(L-5 Stringer)

A message received today from the spaceship *Daedalus* said that it had just passed within 400 astronomical units of 61 Cygni. That's about ten times as far as the planet Pluto is from the Sun.

Actually, the spaceship passed the star some eleven years ago. It's taken all that time for the message to get back to us.

We don't know for sure where the spaceship actually is, now. If they still haven't repaired the runaway drive, they're about eleven light-years past the 61 Cygni system (their speed when they passed the double star was better than 99% the speed of light).

The situation is more complicated if you look at it from the point of view of a passenger on the spaceship. Because of relativity, time seems to pass more slowly as you approach the speed of light. So only about four years passed for them, on the eleven-light-year journey.

L-5 Coordinator Charles Leventhal points out that the spaceship has enough antimatter fuel to keep accelerating to the edge of the Galaxy. The crew then would be only some twenty years older—but it would be twenty *thousand* years before we heard from them....

(Kill this one. There's more stuff about what the ship looked like to the people at 61 Cygni, and howcum we could talk to them all the time even though time was slower there, but its all as stupid as this.)

DAEDALUS: A.D. 2083
EARTH: A.D. 2144

Charlie Leventhal died at the age of 99, bitter. Almost a decade earlier it had been revealed that they'd planned all along for *Daedalus* to be a starship. Few people had paid much attention to the news. Among those who did, the consensus was that anything that got rid of a thousand scientists at once, was a good thing. Look at the mess they got us in.

Daedalus: 67 light-years out, and still accelerating.

DAEDALUS: A.D. 2085
EARTH: A.D. 3578

After over seven years of shipboard research and development—and some 1500 light-years of travel—they managed to shut down the engine. With sophisticated telemetry, the job was done without endangering another life.

Every life was precious now. They were no longer simply explorers; almost half their fuel was gone. They were colonists, with no ticket back.

The message of their success would reach Earth in fifteen centuries. Whether there would be an infrared telescope around to detect it, that was a matter of some conjecture.

DAEDALUS: A.D. 2093
EARTH: CA. A.D. 5000

While decelerating, they had investigated several systems in their line of flight. They found one with an Earth-type planet around a Sun-type sun, and aimed for it.

The season they began landing colonists, the dominant feature in the planet's night sky was a beautiful blooming cloud of gas that astronomers had named the North American Nebula.

Which was an irony that didn't occur to any of these colonists from L-5—give or take a few years, it was America's Trimillennial.

America itself was a little the worse for wear, this three-thousandth anniversary. The seas that lapped its shores were heavy with crimson crust of anaerobic life; the mighty cities had fallen and their remains, nearly ground away by the never-ceasing sand-storms.

No fireworks were planned, for lack of an audience, for lack of planners; bacteria just don't care. May Day too would be ignored.

The only humans in the Solar System lived in a glass and metal tube. They tended their automatic machinery, and turned their backs on the dead Earth, and worshiped the constellation Cygnus, and had forgotten why.

* * *

INTRODUCTION TO "BLOOD SISTERS"

This story was written with a sense of relief, having ground through nine months of writing a novel I really didn't want to do (but there was a contract and a deadline and I'd spent half of the money). I wanted to do something fun, and a private eye story set in the future sounded appealing.

I'd just read an article in *Esquire* about how real-life private investigators worked, and it was not appealing story material. Law books, searching for technicalities. Finding obscure contract violations, jurisprudential loopholes. They didn't even carry guns!

Of course the future would be a lot more interesting. There would be huge powerful computers and clones. Beautiful girl clones! If the beautiful girl clones were naked, maybe the story would sell to *Playboy*! They were and it did.

* * *

BLOOD SISTERS

So I used to carry two different business cards: J. Michael Loomis, Data Concentration, and Jack Loomis, Private Investigator. They mean the same thing, nine cases out of ten. You have to size up a potential customer, decide whether he'd feel better hiring a shamus or a clerk.

Some people still have these romantic notions about private detectives and get into a happy sweat at the thought of using one. But it is the twenty-first century and, endless Bogart reruns notwithstanding, most of my work consisted of sitting at my office console and using it to subvert the privacy laws of various states and countries—finding out embarrassing things about people, so other people can divorce them or fire them or get a piece of the slickery.

Not to say I didn't go out on the street sometimes; not to say I didn't have a gun and a ticket for it. There are Forces of Evil out there, friends, although most of them would probably rather be thought of as businessmen who use the law rather than fear it. Same as me. I was always happy, though, to stay on this side of murder, treason, kidnapping—any lobo offense. This brain may not be much, but it's all I have.

I should have used it when the woman walked into my office. She had a funny way of saying hello:

"Are you licensed to carry a gun?"

Various retorts came to mind, most of them having to do with her expulsion, but after a period of silence I said yes and asked who had referred her to me. Asked politely, too, to make up for staring. She was a little more beautiful than anyone I'd ever seen before.

"My lawyer," she said. "Don't ask who he is."

With that, I was pretty sure this was some sort of elaborate joke. Story detectives always have beautiful mysterious customers. My female customers tend to be dowdy and too talkative, and much more interested in alimony than romance.

"What's your name, then? Or am I not supposed to ask that either?"

She hesitated. "Ghentlee Arden."

I turned the console on and typed in her name, then a seven-digit code. "Your legal firm is Lee, Chu, and Rosenstein. And your real name is Maribelle Four Ghentlee: fourth clone of Maribelle Ghentlee."

"Arden is my professional name. I dance." She had a nice blush.

I typed in another string of digits. Sometimes this sort of thing would lose a customer. "Says here you're a registered hooker."

"Call girl," she said frostily. "Class One courtesan. I was getting to that."

I'm a liberal-minded man; I don't have anything against hookers *or* clones. But I like my customers to be frank with me. Again, I should have shown her the door—then followed her through it.

Instead: "So. You have a problem?"

"Some men are bothering me, one man in particular. I need some protection."

That gave me pause. "Your union has a Pinkerton contract for that sort of thing."

"*My* union." Her face trembled a little. "They don't let clones in the union. I'm an associate, for classification. No protection, no medical, no *anything*."

"Sorry, I didn't know that. Pretty old-fashioned." I could see the reasoning, though. Dump a thousand Maribelle Ghentlees on the market, and a merely ravishing girl wouldn't have a chance.

"Sit down." She was on the verge of tears. "Let me explain to you what I can't do.

"I can't hurt anyone physically. I can't trace this cod down and wave a gun on his face, tell him to back off."

"I know," she sobbed. I took a box of Kleenex out of my drawer, passed it over.

"Listen, there are laws about harassment. If he's really bothering you, the cops'll be glad to freeze him."

"I can't go to the police." She blew her nose. "I'm not a citizen."

I turned off the console. "Let me see if I can fill in some blanks without using the machine. You're an unauthorized clone."

She nodded.

"With bought papers."

"Of course I have papers. I wouldn't be in your *machine* if I didn't."

Well, she wasn't dumb, either. "This cod. He isn't just a disgruntled customer."

"No." She didn't elaborate.

"One more guess," I said, "and then you do the talking for a while. He knows you're not legal."

"He should. He's the one who pulled me."

"Your own daddy. Any other surprises?"

She looked at the floor. "Mafia."

"Not the legal one, I assume."

"Both."

The desk drawer was still open; the sight of my own gun gave me a bad chill. "There are two reasonable courses open to me. I could handcuff you to the doorknob and call the police. Or I could knock you over the head and call the Mafia. That would probably be safer."

She reached into her purse; my hand was halfway to the gun when she took out a credit flash, thumbed it, and passed it over the desk. She easily had five times as much money as I make in a good year, and I'm in a comfortable seventy percent bracket.

"You must have one hell of a case of bedsores."

"Don't be stupid," she said, suddenly hard. "You can't make that kind of money on your back. If you take me on as a client, I'll explain."

I erased the flash and gave it back to her. "Miz Ghentlee. You've already told me a great deal more than I want to know. I don't want the police to put me in jail, I don't want the courts to scramble my brains with a spoon. I don't want the Mafia to take bolt cutters to my appendages."

"I could make it worth your while."

"I've got all the money I can use. I'm only in this profession because I'm a snoopy bastard." It suddenly occurred to me that was more or less true.

"That wasn't completely what I meant."

"I assumed that. And you tempt me, as much as any woman's beauty has ever tempted me."

She turned on the waterworks again.

"Christ. Go ahead and tell your story. But I don't think you can convince me to do anything for you."

"My real clone-mother wasn't named Maribelle Ghentlee."

"I could have guessed that."

"She was Maxine Kraus." She paused. "Maxine…Kraus."

"Is that supposed to mean something to me?"

"Maybe not. What about *Werner* Kraus?"

"Yeah." Swiss industrialist, probably the richest man in Europe. "Some relation?"

"She's his daughter and only heir."

I whistled. "Why would she want to be cloned, then?"

"She didn't know she was being cloned. She thought she was having a Pap test." She smiled a little. "Ironic posture."

"And they pulled you from the scraping."

She nodded. "The Mafia bought her physician. Then killed him."

"You mean the real Mafia?" I said.

"That depends on what you call real. Mafia Incorporated comes into it too, in a more or less legitimate way. I was supposedly one of six Maribelle Ghentlee clones that they had purchased to set up as courtesans in New Orleans, to provoke a test case. They claimed that the Sisterhood's prohibition against clone prostitutes constituted unfair restraint of trade."

"Never heard of the case. I guess they lost."

"Of course. They wouldn't have done it in the South if they'd wanted to win."

"Wait a minute. Jumping ahead. Obviously, they plan ultimately to use you as a substitute for the real Maxine Kraus."

"When the old man dies, which will be soon."

"Then why would they parade you around in public?"

"Just to give me an interim identity. They chose Ghentlee as a clone-mother because she was the closest one available to Maxine Kraus's physical appearance. I had good makeup; none of the real Ghentlee clones suspected I wasn't one of them."

"Still…what happens if you run into someone who knows what the real Kraus looks like? With your face and figure, she must be all over the gossip sheets in Europe."

"You're sweet." Her smile could make me do almost anything. Short of taking on the Mafia. "She's a total recluse, though, for fear of kidnappers. She probably hasn't seen twenty people in her entire life.

"And she isn't beautiful, though she has the raw materials for it. Her mother died when she was still a baby—killed by kidnappers."

"I remember that."

"So she's never had a woman around to model herself after. No one ever taught her how to do her hair properly, or use makeup. A man buys all her clothes. She doesn't have anyone to be beautiful *for*."

"You feel sorry for her."

"More than that." She looked at me with an expression that somehow held both defiance and hopelessness. "Can you understand? She's my mother. I was force-grown so we're the same apparent age, but she's still my only parent. I love her. I won't be part of a plan to kill her."

"You'd rather die?" I said softly. She was going to.

"Yes. But that wouldn't accomplish anything, not if the Mafia does it. They'd take a few cells and make another clone. Or a dozen, or a hundred, until one came along with a personality to go along with matricide."

"Once they know you feel this way—"

"They do know. I'm running."

That galvanized me. "They know who your lawyer is?"

"My lawyer?" She gasped when I took the gun out of the drawer. People who only see guns on the cube are usually surprised at how solid and heavy they actually look.

"Could they trace you here, is what I mean." I crossed the room and slid open the door. No one in the corridor. I twisted a knob and twelve heavy magnetic bolts slammed home.

"I don't think so. The lawyers gave me a list of names, and I just picked one I liked."

I wondered whether it was Jack or J. Michael. I pushed a button on the wall and steel shutters rolled down over the view of Central Park. "Did you take a cab here?"

"No, subway. And I went up to One hundred and twenty-fifth and back."

"Smart." She was staring at the gun. "It's a .48 Magnum Recoilless. Biggest handgun a civilian can buy."

"You need one so big?"

"Yes." I used to carry a .25 Beretta, small enough to conceal in a bathing suit. I used to have a partner, too. It was a long story, and I didn't like to tell it. "Look," I said. "I have a deal with the Mafia. They don't do divorce work and I don't drop bodies into the East River. Understand?" I put the gun back in the drawer and slammed it shut.

"I don't blame you for being afraid—"

"Afraid? Miz Four Ghentlee, I'm not afraid. I'm *terrified*! How old do you think I am?"

"Call me Belle. You're thirty-five, maybe forty. Why?"

"You're kind—and I'm rich. Rich enough to buy youth: I've been in this *business* almost forty years. I take lots of vitamins and try not to fuck with the Mafia."

She smiled and then was suddenly somber. Like a baby. "Try to understand me. You've lived sixty years?"

I nodded. "Next year."

"Well, I've been alive barely sixty *days*. After four years in a tank, growing and learning.

"Learning isn't *being*, though. Everything is new to me. When I walk down a street, the sights and sounds and smells, it's...it's like a great flower opening to the sun. Just to sit alone in the dark—"

Her voice broke.

"You can't even *know* how much I want to live—and that's not condescending; it's a statement of fact. Yet I want you to kill me."

I could only shake my head.

"If you can't hide me you have to kill me." She was crying now, and wiped the tears savagely from her cheeks. "Kill me and make sure every cell in my body is destroyed."

She took out her credit card flash and set it on the desk.

"You can have all my money, whether you save me or kill me."

She started walking around the desk. Along the way she did something with a clasp and her dress slithered to the floor. The sudden naked beauty was like an electric shock.

"If you save me, you can have me. Friend, lover, wife...slave. Forever." She held a posture of supplication for a moment, then eased toward me. Watching the muscles of her body work made my mouth go dry. She reached down and started unbuttoning my shirt.

I cleared my throat. "I didn't know clones had navels."

"Only special ones. I have other special qualities."

Idiot, something reminded me, every woman you've ever loved has sucked you dry and left you for dead. I clasped her hips with my big hands and drew her warmth to me. Close up, the navel wasn't very convincing; nobody's perfect.

I'd done drycleaning jobs before, but never so cautiously or thoroughly. That she was a clone made the business a little more delicate than usual, since clones' lives are more rigidly supervised by the government than ours are. But the fact that her identity was false to begin with made it easier; I could second-guess the people who had originally drycleaned her.

I hated to meddle with her beauty, and that beauty made plastic surgery out of the question. Any legitimate doctor would be suspicious, and going to an underworld doctor would be suicidal. So we dyed her hair black and bobbed it. She stopped wearing makeup and bought some truly froppy clothes. She kept a length of tape stuck across her buttocks to give her a virgin-schoolgirl kind of walk. For everyone but me.

The Mafia had given her a small fortune—birdseed to them—both to ensure her loyalty and to accustom her to having money, for impersonating Kraus. We used about half of it for the drycleaning.

A month or so later there was a terrible accident on a city bus. Most of the bodies were burned beyond recognition; I did some routine bribery, and two of them were identified as the clone Maribelle Four Ghentlee and John Michael Loomis, private eye. When we learned the supposed clone's body had disappeared from the morgue, we packed up our money—long since converted into currency—and a couple of toothbrushes and pulled out.

I had a funny twinge when I closed the door on that console. There couldn't be more than a half-dozen people in the world who were my equals at using that instrument to fish information out of the System. But I had to either give it up or send Belle off on her own.

We flew to the West Indies and looked around. Decided to settle on the island of St. Thomas. I'd been sailing all my life, so we bought a fifty-foot boat and set up a charter service for tourists. Some days we took parties out to skin-dive or fish. Other days we anchored in a quiet cove and made love like happy animals.

After about a year, we read in the little St. Thomas paper that Werner Kraus had died. They mentioned Maxine but didn't print a picture of her. Neither did the San Juan paper. We watched all the news programs for a couple of days (had to check into a hotel to get access to a video cube) and collected magazines for a month. No pictures, to our relief, and the news stories remarked that Fraulein Kraus went to great pains to stay out of the public eye.

Sooner or later, we figured, some *paparazzo* would find her, and there would be pictures. But by then it shouldn't make any difference. Belle had let her hair grow out to its natural chestnut, but we kept it cropped boyishly short. The sun and wind had darkened her skin and roughened it, and a year of fighting the big boat's rigging had put visible muscle under her sleekness.

The marina office was about two broom closets wide. It was a beautiful spring morning, and I'd come in to put my name on the list of boats available for charter. I was reading the weather printout when Belle sidled through the door and squeezed in next to me at the counter. I patted her on the fanny. "With you in a second, honey."

A vise grabbed my shoulder and spun me around.

He was over two meters tall and so wide at the shoulders that he literally couldn't get through the door without turning sideways. Long white hair and pale blue eyes. White sport coat with a familiar cut: tailored to deemphasize the bulge of a shoulder holster.

"You don't do that, friend," he said with a German accent.

I looked at the woman, who was regarding me with aristocratic amusement. I felt the blood drain from my face and damned near said her name out loud.

She frowned. "Helmuth," she said to the guard, "*Sie sind ihm erschrocken.* I'm sorry," she said to me, "but my friend has quite a temper." She had a perfect North Atlantic accent, and her voice sent a shiver of recognition down my back.

"I am sorry," he said heavily. Sorry he hadn't had a chance to throw me into the water, he was.

"I must look like someone you know," she said. "Someone you know rather well."

"My wife. The similarity is…quite remarkable."

"Really? I should like to meet her." She turned to the woman behind the counter. "We'd like to charter a sailing boat for the day."

The clerk pointed at me. "He has a nice fifty-foot one."

"That's fine! Will your wife be aboard?"

"Yes…yes, she helps me. But you'll have to pay the full rate," I said rapidly. "The boat normally takes six passengers."

"No matter. Besides, we have two others."

"And you'll have to help me with the rigging."

"I should hope so. We love to sail." That was pretty obvious. We had been wrong about the wind and sun, thinking that Maxine would have led a sheltered life; she was almost as weathered as Belle. Her hair was probably long, but she had it rolled up in a bun and tied back with a handkerchief.

We exchanged false names: Jack Jackson and Lisa von Hollerin. The bodyguard's name was Helmuth Zwei Kastor. She paid the clerk and called her friends at the marina hotel, telling them to meet her at the *Abora*, slip 39.

I didn't have any chance to warn Belle. She came up from the galley as we were swinging aboard. She stared open-mouthed and staggered, almost fainting. I took her by the arm and made introductions, everybody staring.

After a few moments of strange silence, Helmuth Two whispered, *"Du bist ein Klon."*

"She can't be a clone, silly man," Lisa said. "When did you ever see a clone with a navel?" Belle was wearing shorts and a halter. "But we could be twin sisters. That *is* remarkable."

Helmuth Two shook his head solemnly. Belle had told me that a clone can always recognize a fellow clone, by the eyes. Never be fooled by a man-made navel.

The other two came aboard. Helmuth One was, of course, a Xerox of Helmuth Two. Lisa introduced Maria Salamanca as her lover: a small olive-skinned Basque woman, no stunning beauty, but having an attractive air of friendly mystery about her.

Before we cast off, Lisa came to me and apologized. "We are a passing strange group of people. You deserve something extra for putting up with us." She pressed a gold Krugerrand into my palm—worth at least triple the charter fare—and I tried to act suitably impressed. We had over a thousand of them in the keel, for ballast.

The *Abora* didn't have an engine; getting it in and out of the crowded marina was something of an accomplishment. Belle and Lisa handled the sails expertly, while I manned the wheel. They kept looking at each other, then touching. When we were in the harbor, they sat together at the prow, holding hands. Once we were in the open water, they went below together. Maria went into a sulk, but the two clones jollied her out of it.

I couldn't be jealous of her. An angel can't sin. But I did wonder what you would call what they were doing. Was it a weird kind of incest? Transcendental masturbation? I only hoped Belle would keep her mouth shut, at least figuratively.

After about an hour, Lisa came up and sat beside me at the wheel. Her hair was long and full, and flowed like dark liquid in the wind, and she was naked. I tentatively rested my hand on her thigh. She had been crying.

"She told me. She had to tell me." Lisa shook her head in wonder. "Maxine One Kraus. She had to stay below for a while. Said she couldn't trust her legs." She squeezed my hand and moved it back to the wheel.

"Later, maybe," she said. "And don't worry; your secret is safe with us." She went forward and put an arm around Maria, speaking rapid German to her and the two Helmuths. One of the guards laughed and they took off their incongruous jackets, then carefully wrapped up their weapons and holsters. The sight of a .48 Magnum Recoilless didn't arouse any nostalgia in me. Maria slipped out of her clothes and stretched happily. The guards did the same. They didn't have navels but were otherwise adequately punctuated.

Belle came up then, clothed and flushed, and sat quietly next to me. She stroked my bicep and I ruffled her hair. Then I heard Lisa's throaty laugh and suddenly turned cold.

"Hold on a second," I whispered. "We haven't been using our heads."

"Speak for yourself." She giggled.

"Oh, be serious. This stinks of coincidence. That she should turn up here, that she should wander into the office just as—"

"Don't worry about it."

"Listen. She's no more Maxine Kraus than you are. They've found us. She's another clone, one that's going to—"

"She's Maxine. If she were a clone, I could tell immediately."

"Spare me the mystical claptrap and take the wheel. I'm going below." In the otherwise empty engine compartment, I'd stored an interesting assortment of weapons and ammunition.

She grabbed my arm and pulled me back down to the seat. "You spare *me* the private eye claptrap and listen—you're right, it's no coincidence. Remember that old foreigner who came by last week?"

"No."

"You were up on the stern, folding sail. He was just at the slip for a second, to ask directions. He seemed flustered—"

"I remember. Frenchman."

"I thought so too. He was Swiss, though."

"And that was no coincidence, either."

"No, it wasn't. He's on the board of directors of one of the banks we used to liquify our credit. When the annual audit came up, they'd managed to put together all our separate transactions—"

"Bullshit. That's impossible."

She shook her head and laughed. "You're good, but they're good, too. They were curious about what we were trying to hide, using their money, and traced us here. Found we'd started a business with only one percent of our capital.

"Nothing wrong with that, but they were curious. This director was headed for a Caribbean vacation anyhow; he said he'd come by and poke around."

I didn't know how much of this to believe. I gauged the distance between where the Helmuths were sunning and the prow, where they had carefully stowed their guns against the boat's heeling.

"He'd been a lifelong friend of Werner Kraus. That's why he was so rattled. One look at me and he had to rush to the phone."

"And we're supposed to believe," I said, "that the wealthiest woman in the world would come down to see what sort of innocent game we were playing. With only two bodyguards."

"Five. There are two other Helmuths, and Maria is...versatile."

"Still can't believe it. After a lifetime of being protected from her own shadow—"

"That's just it. She's tired of it. She turned twenty-five last month, and came into full control of the fortune. Now she wants to take control of her own life."

"Damned foolish. If it were me, I would've sent my giants down alone." I had to admit that I essentially did believe the tale. We'd been alone in open water for more than an hour, and would've long been shark bait if that had been their intent. Getting sloppy in your old age, Loomis.

"I probably would have too," Belle said. "Maxine and I are the same woman in some ways, but you and the Mafia taught me caution. She's been in a cage all her life, and just wanted out. Wanted to sail someplace besides her own lake, too."

"It was still a crazy chance to take."

"So she's a little crazy. Romantic, too, in case you haven't noticed."

"Really? When I peeked in you were playing checkers."

"Bastard." She knew the one place I was ticklish. Trying to get away, I jerked the wheel and nearly tipped us all into the drink.

We anchored in a small cove where I knew there was a good reef. Helmuth One stayed aboard to guard while the rest of us went diving.

The fish and coral were beautiful as ever, but I could only watch Maxine and Belle. They swam slowly hand-in-hand, kicking with uncon- scious synchrony, totally absorbed. Though the breathers kept their hair wrapped up identically, it was easy to tell them apart, since Maxine had an all-over tan. Still, it was an eerie kind of ballet, like a mirror that didn't quite work. Maria and Helmuth Two were also hypnotized by the sight.

I went aboard early, to start lunch. I'd just finished slicing ham when I heard the drone of a boat, rather far away. Large siphon-jet, by the rushing sound of it.

The guard shouted, "Zwei—komm' herauf!"

Hoisted myself up out of the galley. The boat was about two kilometers away, and coming roughly in our direction, fast.

"Trouble coming?" I asked him.

"Cannot tell yet, sir. I suggest you remain below." He had a gun in each hand, behind his back.

Below, good idea. I slid the hatch off the engine compartment and tipped over the cases of beer that hid the weaponry. Fished out two heavy plastic bags, left the others in place for the time being: It was all up-to-date American Coast Guard issue, and had cost more than the boat.

I had rehearsed this a thousand times in my mind, but I hadn't realized the bags would be slippery with condensation and oil and be impossible to tear with your hands. I stood up to get a knife from the galley, and it was almost the last thing I ever did.

I looked up at a loud succession of splintering sounds and saw a line of holes marching toward me from the bow, letting in blue light and lead. I dropped and heard bullets hissing over my head; heard the regular cough-cough-cough of Helmuth One's return fire. At the stern there was a cry of pain and then a splash; they must have caught the other guard coming up the ladder.

Also not in the rehearsals was the effect of absolute death-panic on bladder control; some formal corner of my mind was glad I hadn't yet dressed. I controlled my trembling well enough to cut open the bag that held the small-caliber spitter, and it only took three tries to get the cassette of ammunition fastened to the receiver. I jerked back the arming lever and hurried back to the galley hatch, carrying an armload of cassettes.

The spitter was made for sinking boats, quickly. It fired small flechettes, the size of old-fashioned metal stereo needles, fifty rounds per second. The flechettes moved at supersonic speed and each carried a small explosive charge. In ten seconds, they could do more damage to a boat than a man with a chainsaw could, with determination and leisure.

I resisted the urge to blast away and get back under cover (not that the hull afforded much real protection). We had clamped traversing mounts for the gun on three sides of the galley hatch—nautically inclined customers usually asked what they were; I always shrugged and said they'd come with the boat—because the spitter is most effective if you can hold the point of aim precisely on the waterline.

They were concentrating fire on the bow, most of it going high. Helmuth One was evidently shooting from a prone position, difficult target. I slid the spitter onto its mount and cranked up its scope to maximum power.

When I looked through the scope, a lifetime of target-shooting reflexes took over: deep breath, half let out, do the Zen thing. Their boat moved toward the center of the scope's field, and I waited. It was a Whaler Unsinkable. One man crouched at the bow, firing what looked like a .20-mm. recoilless, clamped on the rail above a steel plate. They were less than a hundred meters away.

The Whaler executed a sharp starboard turn, evidently to give the gunner a better angle on our bow. Good boatmanship, good tactics, but bad luck. Their prow touched on the junction of my crosshairs right at the waterline, and I didn't even have to track. I just pressed the trigger and watched a cloud of black smoke and steam zip from prow to stern. Not even an Unsinkable can stay upright with its keel sliced off. The boat slewed sideways into the water, spilling people, and turned turtle. Didn't sink, though.

I snapped a fresh cassette into place and tried to remember where the hydrogen tank was on that model. Second burst found it, and the boat dutifully exploded. The force of the blast was enough to ram the scope's eyepiece back into my eye, painfully.

Helmuth One peered down at me. "What is that?"

"Coast Guard weapon, a spitter."

"May I try it?"

"Sure." I traded places with him, glad to be up in the breeze. My boat was a mess. The mainmast had been shattered by a direct hit, waist high. The starboard rail was splinters, forward, and near misses had gouged up my nice teak foredeck. My eye throbbed, and for some reason my ears were ringing.

I remembered why the next second, as Helmuth fired. The spitter makes a sound like a cat dying, but louder. I had been too preoccupied to hear it.

I unshipped a pair of binoculars to check his marksmanship. He was shooting at the floating bodies. What a spitter did to one was terrible to see.

"Jesus, Helmuth…"

"Some of them may yet live," he said apologetically.

At least one did. Wearing a life jacket, she had been floating face down but suddenly began treading water. She was holding an automatic pistol in both hands. She looked exactly like Belle and Maxine.

I couldn't say anything; couldn't take my eyes off her. She fired two rounds, and I felt them slap into the hull beneath me. I heard Helmuth curse, and suddenly her shoulders dissolved in a spray of meat and bone and her head fell into the water.

My gorge rose and I didn't quite make it to the railing. Deck was a mess anyhow.

Helmuth Two, it turned out, had been hit in the side of the neck, but it was a big neck and he survived. Maxine called a helicopter, which came out piloted by Helmuth Three.

After an hour or so, Helmuth Four joined us in a large speedboat loaded down with gasoline, thermite, and shark chum. By that time, we had transferred the gold and a few more important things from my boat onto the helicopter. We chummed the area thoroughly and, as sharks began to gather, towed both hulks out to deep water, where they burned brightly and sank.

The Helmuths spent the next day sprinkling the island with money and threats, while Maxine got to know Belle and me better, behind the heavily guarded door of the honeymoon suite of the quaint old Sheraton that overlooked the marina. She made us a job offer—a life offer, actually—and we accepted without hesitation. That was six years ago.

Sometimes I do miss our old life—the sea, the freedom, the friendly island, the lazy idylls with Belle. Sometimes I even miss New York's hustle and excitement, and the fierce independence of my life there.

We do travel on occasion, but with extreme caution. The clone that Helmuth killed in that lovely cove might have been Belle's sister, pulled from Maxine, or Belle's own daughter, since the Mafia had had plenty of opportunities to collect cells from her body. It's immaterial. What's important is that if they could make one, they could make an army of them.

Like our private army of Helmuths and Lamberts and Delias. I'm chief of security, and the work is interesting, most of it at a console as good as the one I had in Manhattan. No violence since that one afternoon six years ago, not yet. I did have to learn German, though, which was an outrage to a brain as old as mine.

We haven't made any secret of the fact that Belle is Maxine's clone. The official story is that Fraulein Kraus had a clone made of herself, for "companionship." This started a fad among the wealthy, being the first new sexual wrinkle since the invention of the vibrator.

Belle and Maxine take pains to dress alike and speak alike and even have unconsciously assimilated one another's mannerisms. Most of the non-clone employees can't tell which is which, and even I sometimes confuse them, at a distance.

Close up, which happens with gratifying frequency, there's no problem. Belle has a way of looking at me that Maxine could never duplicate. And Maxine is literally a trifle prettier: you can't beat a real navel.

INTRODUCTION TO
"LINDSAY AND THE RED CITY BLUES"

Marrakesh is about the most exotic and romantic place I've ever been, still, and thirty years ago it absolutely blew me away. I wrote a story about it immediately, while it was still fresh, and thought it was one of the best I'd ever done.

My agent agreed, but had no luck in placing it with any of the slick or literary markets. After a year or so he sent it back and asked whether I could put an element of weirdness in, so he could sell it to a fantasy or horror market.

I grumbled about that but didn't dispute his wisdom, and in fact the injection of horror did serve to amplify the alienation and isolation of the main character. So I decided to use that version here.

LINDSAY AND
THE RED CITY BLUES

The ancient red city of Marrakesh," his guidebook said, "is the last large
oasis for travelers moving south into the Sahara. It is the most exotic
of Moroccan cities, where Arab Africa and Black Africa meet in a setting
that has changed but little in the past thousand years."

In midafternoon, the book did not mention, it becomes so hot that
even the flies stop moving.

The air conditioner in his window hummed impressively but neither
moved nor cooled the air. He had complained three times, and the desk
clerk responded with two shrugs and a blank stare. By two o'clock his
little warren was unbearable. He fled to the street, where it was hotter.

Scott Lindsay was a salesman who demonstrated chemical glassware for a large scientific-supply house in the suburbs of Washington,
D.C. Like all Washingtonians, Lindsay thought that a person who could
survive summer on the banks of the Potomac could survive it anywhere. He saved up six weeks of vacation time and flew to Europe in
late July. Paris was pleasant enough, and the Pyrenees were even cool,
but nobody had told him that on August first all of Europe goes on
vacation; every good hotel room has been sewed up for six months,
restaurants are jammed or closed, and you spend all your time making
bad travel connections to cities where only the most expensive hotels
have accommodations.

In Nice a Canadian said he had just come from Morocco, where it was hotter than hell but there were practically no tourists this time of year. Scott looked wistfully over the poisoned but still blue Mediterranean, felt the pressure of twenty million fellow travelers at his back, remembered Bogie, and booked the next flight to Casablanca.

Casablanca combined the charm of Pittsburgh with the climate of Dallas. The still air was thick with dust from high-rise construction. He picked up a guidebook and riffled through it and, on the basis of a few paragraphs, took the predawn train to Marrakesh.

"The Red City," it went on, "takes its name from the color of the local sandstone from which the city and its ramparts were built." It would be more accurate, Scott reflected, though less alluring, to call it the Pink City. The Dirty Pink City. He stumbled along the sidewalk on the shady side of the street. The twelve-inch strip of shade at the edge of the sidewalk was crowded with sleeping beggars. The heat was so dry he couldn't even sweat.

He passed two bars that were closed and stepped gratefully into a third. It was a Moslem bar, a milk bar, no booze, but at least it was shade. Two young men slumped at the bar, arguing in guttural whispers, and a pair of ancients in burnooses sat at a table playing a static game of checkers. An oscillating fan pushed the hot air and dust around. He raised a finger at the bartender, who regarded him with stolid hostility, and ordered in schoolboy French a small bottle of Vichy water, carbonated, without ice, and, out of deference to the guidebook, a glass of hot mint tea. The bartender brought the mint tea and a liter bottle of Sidi Harazim water, not carbonated, with a glass of ice. Scott tried to argue with the man but he only stared and kept repeating the price. He finally paid and dumped the ice (which the guidebook had warned him about) into the ashtray. The young men at the bar watched the transaction with sleepy indifference.

The mint tea was an aromatic infusion of mint leaves in hot sugar water. He sipped and was surprised, and perversely annoyed, to find it quite pleasant. He took a paperback novel out of his pocket and read the same two paragraphs over and over, feeling his eyes track, unable to concentrate in the heat.

He put the book down and looked around with slow deliberation, trying to be impressed by the alienness of the place. Through the open front of the bar he could see across the street, where a small park shaded the outskirts of the Djemaa El Fna, the largest open-air market in Morocco and, according to the guidebook, the most exciting and colorful; which itself was the gateway to the mysterious labyrinthine medina, where even this moment someone was being murdered for his pocket change, goats were being used in ways of which Allah did not approve, men were smoking a mixture of camel dung and opium, children were merchandised like groceries; where dark men and women would do anything for a price, and the price would not be high. Scott touched his pocket unconsciously, and the hard bulge of the condom was still there.

The best condoms in the world are packaged in a blue plastic cylinder, squared off along the prolate axis, about the size of a small matchbox. The package is a marvel of technology, held fast by a combination of geometry and sticky tape, and a cool-headed man, under good lighting conditions, can open it in less than a minute. Scott had bought six of them in the drugstore in Dulles International, and had opened only one. He hadn't opened it for the Parisian woman who had looked like a prostitute but had returned his polite proposition with a storm of outrage. He opened it for the fat customs inspector at the Casablanca airport, who had to have its function explained to him, who held it between two dainty fingers like a dead sea thing and called his compatriots over for a look.

The Djemaa El Fna was closed against the heat, pale-orange dusty tents slack and pallid in the stillness. And the trees through which he stared at the open-air market, the souk, were also covered with pale dust; the sky was so pale as to be almost white, and the street and sidewalk were the color of dirty chalk. It was like a faded watercolor displayed under too strong a light.

"Hey, mister." A slim Arab boy, evidently in early teens, had slipped into the place and was standing beside Lindsay. He was well scrubbed and wore Western-style clothing, discreetly patched.

"Hey, mister," he repeated. "You American?"

"Nu. Eeg bin Jugoslav."

The boy nodded. "You from New York? I got four friends New York."

"Jugoslav."

"You from Chicago? I got four friends Chicago. No, five. Five friends Chicago."

"Jugoslav," he said.

"Where in U.S. you from?" He took a melting ice cube from the ashtray, buffed it on his sleeve, popped it into his mouth, crunched.

"New Caledonia," Scott said.

"Don't like ice? Ice is good this time day." He repeated the process with another cube. "New what?" he mumbled.

"New Caledonia. Little place in the Rockies, between Georgia and Wisconsin. I don't like polluted ice."

"No, mister, this ice okay. Bottle-water ice." He rattled off a stream of Arabic at the bartender, who answered with a single harsh syllable. "Come on, I guide you through medina."

"No."

"I guide you free. Student, English student, I take you free, take you my father's factory."

"You'll take me, all right."

"Okay, we go now. No touris' shit, make good deal."

Well, Lindsay, you wanted experiences. How about being knocked over the head and raped by a goat? "All right, I'll go. But no pay."

"Sure, no pay." He took Scott by the hand and dragged him out of the bar, into the park.

"Is there any place in the medina where you can buy cold beer?"

"Sure, lots of place. Ice beer. You got cigarette?"

"Don't smoke."

"That's okay, you buy pack up here." He pointed at a gazebo-shaped concession on the edge of the park.

"Hell, no. You find me a beer and I might buy you some cigarettes." They came out of the shady park and crossed the packed-earth plaza of the Djemaa El Fna. Dust stung his throat and nostrils, but it wasn't quite as hot as it had been earlier; a slight breeze had come up. One industrious merchant was rolling up the front flap of his tent, exposing racks of leather goods. He called out, "Hey, you buy!" but Scott ignored him, and the boy made a fist gesture, thumb erect between the two first fingers.

Scott had missed one section of the guidebook: "Never visit the medina without a guide; the streets are laid out in crazy, unpredictable angles and someone who doesn't live there will be hopelessly lost in minutes. The best guides are the older men or young Americans who live there for the cheap narcotics; with them you can arrange the price ahead of time; usually about 5 dirham ($1.10). *Under no circumstances* hire one of the street urchins who pose as students and offer to guide you for free; you will be cheated or even beaten up and robbed."

They passed behind the long double row of tents and entered the medina through the Bab Agnou gateway. The main street of the place was a dirt alley some eight feet wide, flanked on both sides by small shops and stalls, most of which were closed, either with curtains or steel shutters or with the proprietor dozing on the stoop. None of the shops had a wall on the side fronting the alley, but the ones that served food usually had chest-high counters. If they passed an open shop the merchant would block their way and importune them in urgent simple French or English, plucking at Scott's sleeve as they passed.

It was surprisingly cool in the medina, the sun's rays partially blocked by wooden lattices suspended over the alleyway. There was a roast-chestnut smell of semolina being parched, with accents of garlic and strange herbs smoldering. Slight tang of exhaust fumes and sickly-sweet hint of garbage and sewage hidden from the sun. The boy led him down a side street, and then another. Scott couldn't tell the position of the sun and was quickly disoriented.

"Where the hell are we going?"

"Cold beer. You see." He plunged down an even smaller alley, dark and sinister, and Lindsay followed, feeling unarmed.

They huddled against a damp wall while a white-haired man on an antique one-cylinder motor scooter hammered by. "How much farther is this place? I'm not going to—"

"Here, one corner." The boy dragged him around the corner and into a musty-smelling dark shop. The shopkeeper, small and round, smiled gold teeth and greeted the boy by name, Abdul. "The word for beer is 'bera,'" he said. Scott repeated the word to the fat little man and Abdul added something. The man opened two beers and set them down on the counter, along with a pack of cigarettes.

It's a new little Arab, Lindsay, but I think you'll be amused by its presumption. He paid and gave Abdul his cigarettes and beer. "Aren't you Moslem? I thought Moslems didn't drink."

"Hell yes, man." He stuck his finger down the neck of the bottle and flicked away a drop of beer, then tilted the bottle up and drained half of it in one gulp. Lindsay sipped at his. It was warm and sour.

"What you do in the States, man?" He lit a cigarette and held it awkwardly.

Chemical glassware salesman? "I drive a truck." The acrid Turkish tobacco smoke stung his eyes.

"Make lots of money."

"No, I don't." He felt foolish saying it. World traveler, Lindsay, you spent more on your ticket than this boy will see in his life.

"Let's go my father's factory."

"What does your father make?"

"All kinds of things. Rugs."

"I wouldn't know what to do with a rug."

"We wrap it, mail to New Caledonia."

"No. Let's go back to—"

"I take you my uncle's factory. Brass, very pretty."

"No. Back to the plaza, you got your cig—"

"Sure, let's go." He gulped down the rest of his beer and stepped back into the alley, Scott following. After a couple of twists and turns they passed an antique weapons shop that Scott knew he would have noticed, if they'd come by it before. He stopped.

"Where are you taking me now?"

He looked hurt. "Back to Djemaa El Fna. Like you say."

"The hell you are. Get lost, Abdul. I'll find my own way back." He turned and started retracing their path. The boy followed about ten paces behind him, smoking.

He walked for twenty minutes or so, trying to find the relatively broad alleyway that would lead back to the gate. The character of the medina changed: there were fewer and fewer places selling souvenirs, and then none; only residences and little general-merchandise stores, and some small-craft factories, where one or two men, working at a feverish pace, cranked out the items that were sold in the shops. No one tried to sell him anything, and when a little girl held out her hand to beg, an old woman shuffled over and slapped her. Everybody stared when he passed.

Finally he stopped and let Abdul catch up with him. "All right, you win. How much to lead me out?"

"Ten dirham."

"Stuff it. I'll give you two."

Abdul looked at him for a long time, hands in pockets. "Nine dirham." They haggled for a while and finally settled on seven dirham, about $1.50, half now and half at the gate.

They walked through yet another part of the medina, single file through narrow streets, Abdul smoking silently in the lead. Suddenly he stopped.

Scott almost ran into him. "Say, you want girl?"

"Uh…I'm not sure," Scott said, startled into honesty.

He laughed, surprisingly deep and lewd. "A boy, then?"

"No, no." Composure, Lindsay. "Your sister, no doubt."

"*What?*" Wrong thing to say.

"American joke. She a friend of yours?"

"Good friend, good fuck. Fifty dirham."

Scott sighed. "Ten." Eventually they settled on thirty-two, Abdul to wait outside until Scott needed his services as a guide again.

Abdul took him to a caftan shop, where he spoke in whispers with the fat owner and gave him part of the money. They led Lindsay to the rear of the place, behind a curtain. A woman sat on her heels beside the bed, patiently crocheting. She stood up gracelessly. She was short and slight, the top of her head barely reaching Scott's shoulders, and was dressed in traditional costume: lower part of the face veiled, dark blue caftan reaching her ankles. At a command from the owner, she hiked the caftan up around her hips and sat down on the bed with her legs spread apart.

"You see, very clean," Abdul said. She was the skinniest woman Scott had ever seen naked, partially naked, her pelvic girdle prominent under smooth brown skin. She had very little pubic hair and the lips of her vulva were dry and gray. But she was only in her early teens, Scott estimated; that, and the bizarre prospect of screwing a fully clothed masked stranger, stimulated him instantly, urgently.

"All right," he said, hoarse. "I'll meet you outside."

She watched with alert curiosity as he fumbled with the condom package, and the only sound she made throughout their encounter was to giggle when he fitted the device over his penis. It was manufactured to accommodate the complete range of possible sizes, and on Scott it had a couple of inches to spare.

This wonder condom, first-class special-delivery French letter is coated with a fluid so similar to natural female secretions, so perfectly intermiscible and isotonic, that it could fool the inside of a vagina. But Scott's ran out of juice in seconds, and the aloof lady's physiology didn't supply any replacement, so he had to fall back on saliva and an old familiar fantasy. It was a long dry haul, the bedding straw crunching monotonously under them, she constantly shifting to more comfortable positions as he angrily pressed his weight into her, finally a draining that was more hydrostatics than passion, which left him jumpy rather than satisfied. When he rolled off her the condom stayed put, there being more lubrication inside it than out. The woman extracted it and, out of some obscure motive, twisted a knot in the end and dropped it behind the bed.

When he'd finished dressing, she held out her hand for a tip. He laughed and told her in English that he was the one who ought to be paid, he'd done all the work, but gave her five dirham anyhow, for the first rush of excitement and her vulnerable eyes.

Abdul was not waiting for him. He tried to interrogate the caftan
dealer in French, but got only an interesting spectrum of shrugs. He
stepped out onto the street, saw no trace of the little scoundrel, went
back inside, and gave the dealer a five while asking the way to Djemaa
El Fna. He nodded once and wrote it down on a slip of paper in clear,
copybook English.

"You speak English?"

"No," he said with an Oxford vowel.

Scott threaded his way through the maze of narrow streets, carefully
memorizing the appearance of each corner in case he had to back track.
No street was identified by name. The sun was down far enough for the
medina to be completely in shadow, and it was getting cooler. He stopped
at a counter to drink a bottle of beer, and a pleasant lassitude fell over
him, the first time he had not felt keyed up since the Casablanca airport.
He strolled on, taking a left at the corner of dye shop and motor scooter.

Halfway down the road, Abdul stood with seven or eight other boys,
chattering away, laughing.

Scott half ran toward the group and Abdul looked up, startled, when
he roared "You little bastard!"—but Abdul only smiled and muttered
something to his companions, and all of them rushed him.

Not a violent man by any means, Scott had nevertheless suffered
enough at the hands of this boy, and he planted his feet, balled his fists,
bared his teeth, and listened with his whole body to the sweet singing
adrenaline. He'd had twelve hours of hand-to-hand combat instruction
in basic training, the first rule of which (*If you're outnumbered, run*) he
ignored; the second rule of which (*Kick, don't punch*) he forgot, and swung a
satisfying roundhouse into the first face that came within reach, breaking
lips and teeth and one knuckle (he would realize later); then assayed a
side-kick to the groin, which only hit a hip but did put the victim out of
the fray; touched the ground for balance and bounced up, shaking a child
off his right arm while swinging his left at Abdul's neck, and missing;
another side-kick, this time straight to a kidney, producing a good loud
shriek; Abdul hanging out of reach, boys all over him, kicking, punching,
finally dragging him to his knees; Abdul stepping forward and kicking
him in the chest, then the solar plexus; the taste of dust as someone
keeps kicking his head; losing it, losing it, fading out as someone takes
his wallet, then from the other pocket, his traveler's checks, Lindsay, tell
them to leave the checks, they can't, nobody will, just doing it to annoy
me, fuck them.

It was raining and singing. He opened one eye and saw dark brown. His tongue was flat on the dirt, interesting crunchy dirt-taste in his mouth. Lindsay, reel in your tongue, this is stupid, people piss in this street. Raining and singing. I have died and gone to Marrakesh. He slid forearm and elbow under his chest and pushed up a few inches. An irregular stain of blood caked the dust in front of him, and blood was why he couldn't open the other eye. He wiped the mud off his tongue with his sleeve, then used the other sleeve to unstick his eyelid.

The rain was a wrinkled old woman without a veil, patiently sprinkling water on his head, from a pitcher, looking very old and sad. When he sat up, she offered him two white tablets with the letter "A" impressed on them, and a glass of the same water. He took them gratefully, gagged on them, used another glass of water to wash them farther down. Thanked the impassive woman in three languages, hoped it was bottled water, stood up shakily, sledgehammer headache. The slip of paper with directions lay crumpled in the dust, scuffed but still legible. He continued on his way.

The singing was a muezzin, calling the faithful to prayer. He could hear others singing, in more distant parts of the city. Should he take off his hat? No hat. Some natives were simply walking around, going about their business. An old man was prostrate on a prayer rug in the middle of the street. Scott tiptoed around him.

He came out of the medina through a different gate, and the Djemaa El Fna was spread out in front of him in all its early-evening frenzy. A troupe of black dancers did amazing things to machine-gun drum rhythms: acrobats formed high shaky pyramids, dropped, reformed; people sang, shouted, laughed.

He watched a snake handler for a long time, going through a creepy repertoire of cobras, vipers, scorpions, tarantulas. He dropped a half-dirham in the man's cup and went on. A large loud group was crowded around a bedsheet-sized game board where roosters strutted from one chalked area to another, pecking at a vase of plastic flowers here, a broken doll there, a painted tin can or torn deck of playing cards elsewhere; men laying down incomprehensible bets, collecting money, shouting at the roosters, baby needs a new pair of sandals.

Then a quiet, patient line, men and women squatting, waiting for the services of a healer. The woman being treated had her dress tucked modestly between her thighs, back bared from shoulders to buttocks, while the healer burned angry welts in a symmetrical pattern with the smoldering end of a length of clothesline, and Scott walked on, charmed in the old sense of the word: hypnotized.

People shrank from his bloody face and he laughed at them, feeling like part of the show, then feeling like something apart, a visitation. Drifting down the rows of merchants: leather, brass, ceramics, carvings, textiles, books, junk, blankets, weapons, hardware, jewelry, food. Stopping to buy a bag of green pistachio nuts, the vendor gives him the bag and then waves him away, flapping; no pay, just leave.

Gathering darkness and most of the merchants closed their tents, but the thousands of people didn't leave the square. They moved in around men, perhaps a dozen of them, who sat on blankets scattered around the square, in the flickering light of kerosene lanterns, droning the same singsong words over and over. Scott moved to the closest and shouldered his way to the edge of the blanket and squatted there, an American gargoyle, staring. Most of the people gave him room but light fingers tested his hip pocket; he swatted the hand away without looking back. The man in the center of the blanket fixed on his bloody stare and smiled back a tight smile, eyes bright with excitement. He raised both arms and the crowd fell silent, switched off.

A hundred people breathed in at once when he whispered the first words, barely audible words that must have been the Arabic equivalent of "Once upon a time." And then the storyteller shouted and began to pace back and forth, playing out his tale in a dramatic staccato voice, waving his arms, hugging himself, whispering, moaning—and Lindsay followed it perfectly, laughing on cue, crying when the storyteller cried, understanding nothing and everything. When it was over, the man held out his cap first to the big American with the bloody face, and Scott emptied his left pocket into the cap: dirham and half-dirham pieces and leftover francs and one rogue dime.

And he stood up and turned around and watched his long broad shadow dance over the crowd as the storyteller with his lantern moved on around the blanket, and he spotted his hotel and pushed toward it through the mob.

It was worth it. The magic was worth the pain and humiliation.

He forced himself to think of practical things, as he approached the hotel. He had no money, no credit cards, no traveler's checks, no identification. Should he go to the police? Probably it would be best to go to American Express first. Collect phone call to the office. Have some money wired. Identity established, he could have the checks replaced. Police here unlikely to help unless "tipped."

Ah, simplicity. He did have identification: his passport, that he'd left at the hotel desk. That had been annoying, now a lifesaver. Numbers of traveler's checks in his suitcase.

There was a woman in the dusty dim lobby of the hotel. He walked right by her and she whispered "Lin—say."

He remembered the eyes and stopped. "What do you want?"

"I have something of yours." Absurdly, he thought of the knotted condom. But what she held up was a fifty-dollar traveler's check. He snatched it from her; she didn't attempt to stop him.

"You sign that to me," she said. "I bring you everything else the boys took."

"Even the money?" He had had over five hundred dirhams in cash.

"What they gave me, I bring you."

"Well, you bring it here, and we'll see."

She shook her head angrily. "No, I bring *you*. I bring you...*to* it. Right now. You sign that to me."

He was tempted. "At the caftan shop?"

"That's right. Wallet and 'merican 'spress check. You come."

The medina at night. A little sense emerged. "Not now. I'll come with you in the morning."

"Come now."

"I'll see you here in the morning." He turned and walked up the stairs.

Well, he had fifty out of the twelve hundred dollars. He checked the suitcase, and the list of numbers was where he'd remembered. If she wasn't there in the morning, he would be able to survive the loss. He caressed the dry leather sheath of the antique dagger he'd bought in the Paris flea market. If she was waiting, he would go into the medina armed. It would simplify things to have the credit cards. He fell asleep and had violent dreams.

He woke at dawn. Washed up and shaved. The apparition that peered back from the mirror looked worse than he felt; he was still more exhilarated than otherwise. He took a healing drink of brandy and stuck the dagger in his belt, in the back so he wouldn't have to button his sport coat. The muezzin's morning wail stopped.

She was sitting in the lobby's only chair, and stood when he came down the stairs.

"No tricks," he said. "If you have what you say, you get the fifty dollars."

They went out of the hotel and the air was almost cool, damp smell of garbage. "Why did the boys give this to you?"

"Not *give*. Business deal, I get half."

There was no magic in the Djemaa El Fna in the morning, just dozens of people walking through the dust. They entered the medina, and it was likewise bereft of mystery and danger. Sleepy collection of closed-off shopfronts, everything beaded with dew, quiet and stinking. She led him back the way he had come yesterday afternoon. Passing the alley where he had encountered the boys, he noticed there was no sign of blood. Had the old woman neatly cleaned up, or was it simply scuffed away on the sandals of negligent passersby? Thinking about the fight, he touched the dagger, loosening it in its sheath. Not for the first time, he wondered whether he was walking into a trap. He almost hoped so. But all he had left of value was his signature.

Lindsay had gotten combat pay in Vietnam, but the closest he'd come to fighting was to sit in a bunker while mortars and rockets slammed around in the night. He'd never fired a shot in anger, never seen a dead man, never this, never that, and he vaguely felt unproven. The press of the knife both comforted and frightened him.

They entered the caftan shop, Lindsay careful to leave the door open behind them. The fat caftan dealer was seated behind a table. On the table were Lindsay's wallet and a china plate with a small pile of dried mud.

The dealer watched impassively while Lindsay snatched up his wallet. "The checks."

The dealer nodded. "I have a proposition for you."

"You've learned English."

"I believe I have something you would like to buy with those checks."

Lindsay jerked out the dagger and pointed it at the man's neck. His hand and voice shook with rage. "I'll cut your throat first. Honest to God, I will."

There was a childish giggle and the curtain to the "bedroom" parted, revealing Abdul with a pistol. The pistol was so large he had to hold it with both hands, but he held it steadily, aimed at Lindsay's chest.

"Drop the knife," the dealer said.

Lindsay didn't. "This won't work. Not even here."

"A merchant has a right to protect himself."

"That's not what I mean. You can kill me, I know, but you can't force me to sign those checks at gunpoint. *I will not do it!*"

He chuckled. "That is not what I had in mind, not at all. I truly do have something to sell you, something beyond worth. The gun is only for my protection; I assumed you were wise enough to come armed. Relinquish the knife and Abdul will leave."

Lindsay hesitated, weighing obscure odds, balancing the will to live against his newly born passion. He dropped the dagger.

The merchant said something in Arabic while the prostitute picked up the knife and set it on the table. Abdul emerged from the room with no gun and two straight wooden chairs. He set one next to the table and one behind Lindsay, and left, slamming the door.

"Please sign the check you have and give it to the woman. You promised."

He signed it and asked in a shaking voice, "What do you have that you think I'll pay twelve hundred dollars for?"

The woman reached into her skirts and pulled out the tied-up condom. She dropped it on the plate.

"This," he said, "your blood and seed." With the point of the dagger he opened the condom and its contents spilled into the dirt. He stirred them into mud.

"You are a modern man—"

"What kind of mumbo-jumbo—"

"—a modern man who certainly doesn't believe in magic. Are you Christian?"

"Yes. No." He was born Baptist but hadn't gone inside a church since he was eighteen.

He nodded. "I was confident the boys could bring back some of your blood last night. More than I needed, really." He dipped his thumb in the vile mud and smeared a rough cross on the woman's forehead.

"I can't believe this."

"But you can." He held out a small piece of string. "This is a symbolic restraint." He laid it over the glob of mud and pressed down on it.

Lindsay felt himself being pushed back into the chair. Cold sweat peppered his back and palms.

"Try to get up."

"Why should I?" Lindsay said, trying to control his voice. "I find this fascinating." Insane, Lindsay, voodoo only works on people who believe in it. Psychosomatic.

"It gets even better." He reached into a drawer and pulled out Lindsay's checkbook, opened it, and set it in front of Lindsay with a pen. "Sign."

Get up get up. "No."

He took four long sharp needles out of the drawer and began talking in a low monotone, mostly Arabic but some nonsense English. The woman's eyes drooped half shut and she slumped in the chair.

"Now," he said in a normal voice, "I can do anything to this woman, and she won't feel it. You will." He pulled up her left sleeve and pinched her arm. "Do you feel like writing your name?"

Lindsay tried to ignore the feeling. You can't hypnotize an unwilling subject. Get up get up get up.

The man ran a needle into the woman's left triceps. Lindsay flinched and cried out. Deny him, get up.

He murmured something and the woman lifted her veil and stuck out her tongue, which was long and stained blue. He drove a needle through it and Lindsay's chin jerked back onto his chest, tongue on fire, bile foaming up in his throat. His right hand scrabbled for the pen, and the man withdrew the needles.

He scrawled his name on the fifties and hundreds. The merchant took them wordlessly and went to the door. He came back with Abdul, armed again.

"I am going to the bank. When I return, you will be free to go." He lifted the piece of string out of the mud. "In the meantime, you may do as you wish with this woman; she is being paid well. I advise you not to hurt her, of course."

Lindsay pushed her into the back room. It wasn't proper rape, since she didn't resist, but whatever it was he did it twice, and was sore for a week. He left her there and sat at the merchant's table, glaring at Abdul. When he came back, the merchant told Lindsay to gather up the mud and hold it in his hand for at least a half-hour. And get out of Marrakesh.

Out in the bright sun he felt silly with the handful of crud, and ineffably angry with himself, and he flung it away and rubbed the offended hand in the dirt. He got a couple of hundred dollars on his credit cards, at an outrageous rate of exchange, and got the first train back to Casablanca and the first plane back to the United States.

Where he found himself to be infected with gonorrhea.

And over the next few months paid a psychotherapist and a hypnotist over two thousand dollars, and nevertheless felt rotten for no organic reason.

And nine months later lay on an examining table in the emergency room of Suburban Hospital, with terrible abdominal pains of apparently psychogenic origin, not responding to muscle relaxants or tranquilizers, while a doctor and two aides watched in helpless horror as his own muscles cracked his pelvic girdle into sharp knives of bone, and his child was born without pain four thousand miles away.

INTRODUCTION TO "MANIFEST DESTINY"

This story had a dual genesis, travel and library books. My wife and I have spent several summers in Mexico, and I have a special interest in nineteenth century Mexico and its relationship with my native American west.

In a Florida library I found a fascinating account of everyday life in Mexico written by the wife of the American ambassador just after our Civil War. I devoured it in two hungry days and had to use her observations in a story. For authenticity I spent another couple of days verifying the slang that an American roughneck would have used in that time.

That was interesting. I made a list five pages long of slang and cant phrases that were common in America just before the Gadsden Purchase. Pretty easy to do nowadays, with powerful search engines eager to serve you, but then, I had to go through armloads of dictionaries to find out what nonstandard words and usages were common at that time.

Research isn't the whole story, either. For instance, you could have somebody "take a back seat to" somebody else, because they had back seats in landaus a long time before there were cars, and used the phrase exactly as we do. But it would still look like an anachronism.

Almost too much fun, and too much labor, you might think, to justify a few words in a short story. But it came in very handy a few years later, when I set most of the novel *Guardian* in that period. The schoolmarm protagonist would never use that kind of language. But she did have to hear it, if the writer was impolite enough to type it in.

MANIFEST DESTINY

This is the story of John Leroy Harris, but I doubt that name means much to you unless you're pretty old, especially an old lawman. He's dead anyhow, thirty years now, and nobody left around that could get hurt with this story. The fact is, I would've told it a long time ago, but when I was younger it would have bothered me, worrying about what people would think. Now I just don't care. The hell with it.

I've been on the move ever since I was a lad. At thirteen I put a knife in another boy and didn't wait around to see if he lived, just went down to the river and worked my way to St. Louis, got in some trouble there and wound up in New Orleans a few years later. That's where I came to meet John Harris.

Now you wouldn't tell from his name (he'd changed it a few times) but John was pure Spanish blood, as his folks had come from Spain before the Purchase. John was born in Natchitoches in 1815, the year of the Battle of New Orleans. That put him thirteen years older than me, so I guess he was about thirty when we met.

I was working as a greeter, what we called a "bouncer," in Mrs. Carranza's whorehouse down by the docks. Mostly I just sat around and looked big, which I was then and no fat, but sometimes I did have to calm down a customer or maybe throw him out, and I kept under my weskit a Starr pepperbox derringer in case of real trouble. It was by using this weapon that I made the acquaintance of John Harris.

Harris had been in the bar a few times, often enough for me to notice him, but to my knowledge he never put the boots to any of the women.

Didn't have to pay for it, I guess; he was a handsome cuss, more than six feet tall, slender, with this kind of tragic look that women seem to like. Anyhow it was a raw rainy night in November, cold the way noplace else quite gets cold, and this customer comes downstairs complaining that the girl didn't do what he had asked her to, and he wasn't going to pay the extra. The kate came down right behind him and told me what it was, and that she had too done it, and he hadn't said nothing about it when they started, and you can take my word for it that it was something nasty.

Well, we had some words about that and he tried to walk out without paying, so I sort of brought him back in and emptied out his pockets. He didn't even have the price of a drink on him (he'd given Mrs. Carranza the two dollars but that didn't get you anything fancy). He did have a nice overcoat, though, so I took that from him and escorted him out into the rain head first.

What happened was about ten or fifteen minutes later he barges back in, looking like a drowned dog but with a Navy Colt in each hand. He got off two shots before I blew his brains out (pepperbox isn't much of a pistol but he wasn't four yards away) and a split second later another bullet takes him in the lungs. I turned around and everybody was on the floor or behind the bar but John Harris, who was still perched on a stool looking sort of interested and putting some kind of foreign revolver back into his pocket.

The cops came soon enough but there was no trouble, not with forty witnesses, except for what to do with the dead meat. He didn't have any papers and Mrs. Carranza didn't want to pay the city for the burial. I was for just taking it out back and dropping it in the water, but they said that was against the law and unsanitary. John Harris said he had a wagon and come morning he'd take care of the matter. He signed a paper and that satisfied them.

First light, Harris showed up in a fancy landau. Me and the driver, an old black, we wrestled the wrapped-up corpse into the back of the carriage. Harris asked me to come along and I did.

We just went east a little ways and rolled the damned thing into a bayou, let the gators take it. Then the driver smoked a pipe while Harris and me talked for a while.

Now he did have the damnedest way of talking. His English was like nothing you ever heard—Spanish his mother tongue and then he learned most of his English in Australia—but that's not what I really mean. I mean that if he wanted you to do something and you didn't want to do it, you had best put your fingers in your ears and start walking away. That son of a gun could sell water to a drowning man.

He started out asking me questions about myself, and eventually we got to talking about politics. Turns out we both felt about the same way towards the U.S. government, which is to say the hell with it. Harris wasn't even really a citizen, and I myself didn't exist. For good reasons there was a death certificate on me in St. Louis, and I had a couple of different sets of papers a fellow on Bourbon Street printed up for me.

Harris had noticed that I spoke some Spanish—Mrs. Carranza was Mexican and so were most of her kates—and he got around to asking whether I'd like to take a little trip to Mexico. I told him that sounded like a really bad idea.

This was late 1844, and that damned Polk had just been elected promising to annex Texas. The Mexicans had been skirmishing with Texas for years, and they said it would be war if they got statehood. The man in charge was that one-legged crazy greaser Santa Anna, who'd been such a gentleman at the Alamo some years before. I didn't fancy being a gringo stuck in that country when the shooting started.

Well, Harris said I hadn't thought it through. It was true there was going to be a war, he said, but the trick was to get in there early enough to profit from it. He asked whether I'd be interested in getting ten percent of ten thousand dollars. I told him I could feel my courage returning.

Turns out Harris had joined the army a couple of years before and got himself into the quartermaster business, the ones who shuffle supplies back and forth. He had managed to slide five hundred rifles and a big batch of ammunition into a warehouse in New Orleans. The army thought they were stored in Kentucky and the man who rented out the warehouse thought they were farming tools. Harris got himself discharged from the army and eventually got in touch with one General Parrodi, in Tampico. Parrodi agreed to buy the weapons and pay for them in gold.

The catch was that Parrodi also wanted the services of three Americans, not to fight but to serve as "interpreters"—that is to say, spies—for as long as the war lasted. We would be given Mexican citizenship if we wanted it, and a land grant, but for our own protection we'd be treated as prisoners while the war was going on. (Part of the deal was that we would eavesdrop on other prisoners.) Harris showed me a contract that spelled all of this out, but I couldn't read Spanish back then. Anyhow I was no more inclined to trust Mexicans in such matters than I was Americans, but as I say Harris could sell booze to a Baptist.

The third American was none other than the old buck who was driving, a runaway slave from Florida name of Washington. He had grown up with Spanish masters, and not as a field hand but as some kind of a butler. He had more learning than I did and could speak Spanish like a grandee. In Mexico, of course, there wasn't any slavery, and he reckoned a nigger with gold and land was just as good as anybody else with gold and land.

Looking back I can see why Washington was willing to take the risk, but I was a damned fool to do it. I was no rough neck but I'd seen some violence in my seventeen years; that citizen we'd dumped in the bayou wasn't the first man I had to kill. You'd think I'd know better than to put myself in the middle of a war. Guess I was too young to take dying seriously—and a thousand dollars was real money back then.

We went back into town and Harris took me to the warehouse. What he had was fifty long blue boxes stenciled with the name of a hardware outfit, and each one had ten Hall rifles, brand new in a mixture of grease and sawdust.

(This is why the Mexicans were right enthusiastic. The Hall was a flintlock, at least these were, but it was also a breech-loader. The old muzzle-loaders that most soldiers used, Mexican and American, took thirteen separate steps to reload. Miss one step and it can take your face off. Also, the Hall used interchangeable parts, which meant you didn't have to find a smith when it needed repairing.)

Back at the house I told Mrs. Carranza I had to quit and would get a new boy for her. Then Harris and me had a steak and put ourselves outside of a bottle of sherry, while he filled me in on the details of the operation. He'd put considerable money into buying discretion from a dockmaster and a Brit packet captain. This packet was about the only boat that put into Tampico from New Orleans on anything like a regular basis, and Harris had the idea that smuggling guns wasn't too much of a novelty to the captain. The next Friday night we were going to load the stuff onto the packet, bound south the next morning.

The loading went smooth as cream, and the next day we boarded the boat as paying passengers, Washington supposedly belonging to Harris and coming along as his manservant. At first it was right pleasant, slipping through a hundred or so miles of bayou country. But the Gulf of Mexico ain't the Mississippi, and after a couple of hours of that I was sick from my teeth to my toenails, and stayed that way for days. Captain gave me a mixture of brandy and seawater, which like to killed me. Harris thought that was funny, but the humor wore off some when we put into Tampico and him and Washington had to off-load the cargo without much help from me.

We went on up to Parrodi's villa and found we might be out of a job. While we were on that boat there had been a revolution. Santa Anna got kicked out, having pretty much emptied the treasury, and now the *moderado* Herrera was in charge. Parrodi and Harris argued for a long time. The Mexican was willing to pay for the rifles, but he figured that half the money was for our service as spies.

They finally settled on eight thousand, but only if we would stay in Tampico for the next eighteen months, in case a war did start. Washington and I would get fifty dollars a month for walking-around money.

The next year was the most boring year of my life. After New Orleans, there's just not much you could say about Tampico. It's an old city but also brand new. Pirates burnt it to the ground a couple of hundred years ago. Santa Anna had it rebuilt in the twenties, and it was still not much more than a garrison town when we were there. Most of the houses were wood, imported in pieces from the States and nailed together. Couple of whorehouses and cantinas downtown, and you can bet I spent a lot of time and fifty bucks a month down there.

Elsewhere, things started to happen in the spring. The U.S. Congress went along with Polk and voted to annex Texas, and Mexico broke off diplomatic relations and declared war, but Washington didn't seem to take notice. Herrera must have had his hands full with the Carmelite Revolution, though things were quiet in Tampico for the rest of the year.

I got to know Harris pretty well. He spent a lot of time teaching me to read and write Spanish—though I never could talk it without sounding like a gringo—and I can tell you he was hellfire as a teacher. The schoolmaster used to whip me when I was a kid, but that was easier to take than Harris's tongue. He could make you feel about six inches tall. Then a few minutes later you get a verb right and you're a hero.

We'd also go into the woods outside of town and practice with the pistol and rifle. He could do some awesome things with a Colt. He taught me how to throw a knife and I taught him how to use a lasso.

We got into a kind of routine. I had a room with the Galvez family downtown. I'd get up pretty late mornings and peg away at my Spanish books. About midday Harris would come down (he was staying up at the General's place) and give me my daily dose of sarcasm. Then we'd go down to a cantina and have lunch, usually with Washington. Afternoons, when most of the town napped, we might go riding or shooting in the woods south of town. We kept the Galvez family in meat that way, getting a boar or a deer every now and then. Since I was once a farm boy I knew how to dress out animals and how to smoke or salt meat to keep it. Sra. Galvez always deducted the value of the meat from my rent.

Harris spent most evenings up at the villa with the officers, but sometimes he'd come down to the cantinas with me and drink pulque with the off-duty soldiers, or sometimes just sit around the kitchen table with the Galvez family. They took a shine to him.

He was really taken with old Doña Dolores, who claimed to be over a hundred years old and from Spain. She wasn't a relative but had been a friend of Sra. Galvez's grandmother. Anyhow she also claimed to be a witch, a white witch who could heal and predict things and so forth.

If Harris had a weakness it was superstition. He always wore a lucky gold piece on a thong around his neck and carried an Indian finger bone in his pocket. And though he could swear the bark off a tree he never used the names of God or Jesus, and when somebody else did he always crossed the fingers of his left hand. Even though he laughed at religion and I never saw him go in a church. So he was always asking Dolores about this or that, and always ready to listen to her stories. She only had a couple dozen but they kept changing.

Now I never thought that Dolores wasn't straight. If she wasn't a witch she sure as hell *thought* she was. And she did heal, with her hands and with herbs she picked in the woods. She healed me of the grippe and a rash I picked up from one of the girls. But I didn't believe in spells or fortune-telling, not then. When anybody's eighteen he's a smart Alec and knows just how the world works. I'm not so sure anymore, especially with what happened to Harris.

Every week or so we got a newspaper from Monterrey. By January I could read it pretty well, and looking back I guess you could say it was that month the war really started, though it would be spring before any shots were fired. What happened was that Polk sent some four thousand troops into what he claimed was part of Texas. The general was Zach Taylor, who was going to be such a crackajack president a few years later. Herrera seemed about to make a deal with the States, so he got booted out and they put Paredes in office. The Mexicans started building up an army in Monterrey, and it looked like we were going to earn our money after all.

I was starting to get a little nervous. You didn't have to look too hard at the map to see that Tampico was going to get trouble. If the U.S. wanted to take Mexico City they had the choice of marching over a couple thousand miles of mountains and desert, or taking a Gulf port and only marching a couple hundred miles. Tampico and Vera Cruz were about the same distance from Mexico City, but Vera Cruz had a fort protecting it. All we had was us.

Since the Civil War, nobody remembers much about the Mexican one. Well, the Mexicans were in such bad shape even Taylor could beat them. The country was flat broke. Their regular army had more officers than men. They drafted illiterate Indians and *mestizos* and herded them by the thousands into certain death from American artillery and cavalry—some of them had never even fired a shot before they got into battle. That was Santa Anna economizing. He could've lost that war even if Mexico had all the armies of Europe combined.

Now we thought we'd heard the last of that one-legged son of a bitch. When we got to Tampico he'd just barely got out of Mexico with his skin, exiled to Cuba. But he got back, and he damn near killed me and Harris with his stupidity. And he did kill Washington, just as sure as if he pulled the trigger.

In May of that year Taylor had a show-down up by Matamoros, and Polk got around to declaring war. We started seeing American boats all the time, going back and forth out of cannon range, blockading the port. It was nervous-making. The soldiers were fit to be tied—but old Dolores said there was nothing to worry about. Said she'd be able to "see" if there was going to be fighting, and she didn't see anything. This gave Harris considerable more comfort than it gave me.

What we didn't find out until after the war was that Santa Anna got in touch with the United States and said he could get Mexico to end the war, give up Texas and California and for all I know the moon. Polk, who must have been one fine judge of character, gave Santa Anna safe passage through the American blockade.

Well, in the meantime the people in Mexico City had gotten a belly full of Paredes, who had a way of getting people he disagreed with shot, and they kicked him out. Santa Anna limped in and they made him president. He doublecrossed Polk, got together another twenty thousand soldiers, and got ready to head north and kick the stuffing out of the gringos.

Now you figure this one out. The Mexicans intercepted a message to the American naval commander, telling him to take Tampico. What did Santa Anna do? He ordered Parrodi to desert the place.

I was all for the idea myself, and so were a lot of the soldiers, but the General was considerable upset. It was bad enough that he couldn't stand

and fight, but on top of that he didn't have near enough mules and horses to move out all the supplies they had stockpiled there.

Well, we sure as hell were going to take care of *our* supplies. Harris had a buckboard and we'd put a false bottom under the seat. Put our money in there and the papers that identified us as loyal Americans. In another place we put our Mexican citizenship papers and the deeds to our land grant, up in the Mesilla Valley. Then we drew weapons from the armory and got ready to go up to San Luis Potosí with a detachment that was leaving in the morning.

I was glad we wouldn't be in Tampico when the American fleet rolled in, but then San Luis Potosí didn't sound like any picnic either. Santa Anna was going to be getting his army together there, and it was only a few hundred miles from Taylor's army. One or the other of them would probably want to do something with all those soldiers.

Harris was jumpy. He kept putting his hand in his pocket to rub that Indian bone. That night, before he went up to the villa, he came to the hacienda with me, and told Dolores he'd had a bad premonition about going to San Luis Potosí. He asked her to tell his fortune and tell him flat out if he was going to die. She said she couldn't tell a man when he was going to die, even when she saw it. If she did her powers would go away. But she would tell his fortune.

She studied his hands for a long time, without saying anything. Then she took out a shabby old deck of cards and dealt some out in front of him, face up. (They weren't regular cards. They had faded pictures of devils and skeletons and so forth.)

Finally she told him not to worry. He was not going to die in San Luis. In fact, he would not die in Mexico at all. That was plain.

Now I wish I had Harris's talent for shucking off worries. He laughed and gave her a gold real, and then he dragged me down to the cantina, where we proceeded to get more than half corned on that damned pulque, on his money. We carried out four big jars of the stuff, which was a good thing. I had to drink half one in the morning before I could see through the agony. That stuff is not good for white men. Ten cents a jug, though.

The trek from Tampico to San Luis took more than a week, with Washington riding in the back of the buckboard and Harris and me taking turns riding and walking. There was about two hundred soldiers in our group, no more used to walking than us, and sometimes they eyed that buckboard. It was hilly country and mostly dry. General Parrodi went on ahead, and we never saw him again. Later on we learned that

Santa Anna court-martialed him for desertion, for letting the gringos take Tampico. Fits.

San Luis Potosí looked like a nice little town, but we didn't see too damned much of it. We went to the big camp outside of town. Couldn't find Parrodi, so Harris sniffed around and got us attached to General Pacheco's division. General looked at the contract and more or less told us to pitch a tent and stay out of the way.

You never seen so many greasers in your life. Four thousand who Taylor'd kicked out of Monterrey, and about twenty thousand more who might or might not have known which end the bullet comes out of.

We got a good taste of what they call *santanismo* now. Santa Anna had all these raw boys, and what did he do to get them in shape for a fight? He had them dress up and do parades, while he rode back and forth on his God damned horse. Week after week. A lot of the boys ran away, and I can't say I blame them. They didn't have a thousand dollars and a ranch to hang around for.

We weren't the only Americans there. A whole bunch of Taylor's men, more than 200, had absquatulated before he took Monterrey. The Mexicans gave them land grants too. They were called the "San Pats," the San Patricio battalion. We were told not to go near them, so that none of them would know we weren't actually prisoners.

After a couple of months of this, we found out what the deal was going to be. Taylor'd had most of his men taken away from him, sent down to Tampico to join up with another bunch that was headed for Mexico City. What Santa Anna said we were going to do was go north and wipe out Taylor, then come back and defend the city. The first part did look possible, since we had four or five men for every one of Taylor's. Me and Harris and Washington decided we'd wait and see how the first battle went. We might want to keep going north.

It took three days to get all those men on the road. Not just men, either; a lot of them had their wives and children along, carrying food and water and firewood. It was going to be three hundred miles, most of it barren. We saw Santa Anna go by, in a carriage drawn by eight white mules, followed by a couple carriages of whores. If I'd had the second sight Dolores claimed to have, I might've spent a pill on that son of a bitch. I still wonder why nobody ever did.

It wasn't easy going even for us, with plenty of water and food. Then the twelfth day a norther came in, the temperature dropped way below freezing and a God damned blizzard came up. We started passing dead people by the side of the road. Then Washington lost his voice, coughed blood for a while, and died. We carried him till night and then buried him. Had to get a pick from the engineers to get through the frozen ground. I never cried over a nigger before or since. Nor a white man, now I think of it. Could be it was the wind. Harris and me split his share of the gold and burnt his papers.

It warmed up just enough for the snow to turn to cold drizzle, and it rained for two days straight. Then it stopped and the desert sucked up the water, and we marched the rest of the way through dust and heat. Probably a fourth of Santa Anna's men died or deserted before we got to where Zach Taylor was waiting, outside of Saltillo in a gulch called Buena Vista. Still, we had them so outnumbered we should've run them into the ground. Instead, Santa Anna spent the first whole day fiddling, shuffling troops around. He didn't even do that right. Any shavetail would've outflanked and surrounded Taylor's men. He left all their right flank open, as well as the road to Saltillo. I heard a little shooting, but nothing much happened.

It turned cold and windy that night. Seemed like I just got to sleep when drums woke me up—American drums, sounding reveille; that's how close we were. Then a God damned band, playing "Hail Columbia." Both Taylor and Santa Anna belonged on a God damned parade ground.

A private came around with chains and leg irons, said he was supposed to lock us to the buckboard. For twenty dollars he accidentally dropped the key. I wonder if he ever lived to spend it. It was going to be a bad bloody day for the Mexicans.

We settled in behind the buckboard and watched about a thousand cavalrymen charge by, lances and machetes and blood in their eye, going around behind the hills to our right. Then the shooting started, and it didn't let up for a long time.

To our left, they ordered General Blanco's division to march into the gulch column-style, where the Americans were set up with field artillery. Canister and grapeshot cut them to bloody rags. Then Santa Anna rode over and ordered Pacheco's division to go for the gulch. I was just as glad to be chained to a buckboard. They walked right into it, balls but no brains, and I guess maybe half of them eventually made it back. Said they'd killed a lot of gringos, but I didn't notice it getting any quieter.

I watched all this from well behind the buckboard. Every now and then a stray bullet would spray up dirt or plow into the wood. Harris just stood out in the open, as far from cover as the chain would let him, standing there with his hands in his pockets. A bullet or a piece of grape knocked off his hat. He dusted it off and wiggled his finger at me through the hole, put it back on his head, and put his hands back in his pockets. I reminded him that if he got killed I'd take all the gold. He just smiled. He was absolutely not going to die in Mexico. I told him even if I *believed* in that bunkum I'd want to give it a little help. A God damned cannon-ball whooshed by and he didn't blink, just kept smiling. It exploded some ways behind us and I got a little piece in the part that goes over the fence last, which isn't as funny as it might sound, since it was going to be a month before I could sit proper.

Harris did leave off being a target long enough to do some doctoring on me. While he was doing that a whole bunch of troops went by behind us, following the way the cavalry went earlier, and they had some nice comments for me. I even got to show my bare butt to Santa Anna, which I guess not too many people do and live.

We heard a lot of noise from their direction but couldn't see anything because of the hills. We also stopped getting shot at, which was all right by me, though Harris seemed bored.

Since then I've read everything I could get my hands on about that battle. The Mexicans had 1,500 to 2,000 men killed and wounded at Buena Vista, thanks to Santa Anna's generaling. The Americans were unprepared and outnumbered, and some of them actually broke and ran—where even the American accounts admit that the greasers were all-fired brave. If we'd had a real general, a real battle plan, we would've walked right over the gringos.

And you can't help but wonder what would've happened. What if Zach Taylor'd been killed, or even just lost the battle? Who would the Whigs have run for president; who would have been elected? Maybe somebody who didn't want a war between the states.

Anyhow the noise died down and the soldiers straggled back. It's a funny thing about soldiering. After all that bloody fighting, once it was clear who had won the Americans came out on the battlefield and shared their food and water with us, and gave some medical help. But that night was terrible with the sounds of the dying, and the retreat was pure hell. I was for heading north, forget the land grant, but of course Harris knew that he was going to make it through no matter what.

Well, we were lucky. When we got to San Luis an aide to Pacheco decided we weren't being too useful as spies, so we got assigned to a hospital detail, and stayed there while others went on south with Santa Anna to get blown apart at Cerro Gordo and Chapultepec. A few months later the war was over and Santa Anna was back in exile—which was temporary, as usual. That son of a bitch was president eleven times.

Now this is where the story gets strange, and if somebody else was telling it I might call him a liar. You're welcome to that opinion, but anyhow it's true.

We had more than a thousand acres up in Mesilla, too much to farm by ourselves, so we passed out some handbills and got a couple dozen ex-soldiers to come along with their families, to be sort of tenant farmers. It was to be a fifty-fifty split, which looked pretty good on the surface, because although it wasn't exactly Kansas the soil was supposedly good enough for maize and agave, the plant that pulque was made from. What they didn't tell us about was the Apaches. But that comes later.

Now the Mesilla Valley looked really good on the map. It had a good river and it was close to the new American border. I still had my American citizenship papers and sort of liked the idea of being only a couple of days away in case trouble started. Anyhow we got outfitted in San Luis and headed our little wagon train north by northwest. More than a thousand miles, through Durango and Chihuahua. It was rough going, just as dry as hell, but we knew that ahead of time and at least there was nobody shooting at us. All we lost was a few mules and one wagon, no people.

Our grants were outside of the little town of Tubac, near the silver mines at Cerro Colorado. There was some irrigation but not nearly enough, so we planted a small crop and worked like beavers digging ditches so the next crop could be big enough for profit.

Or I should say the greasers and me worked like beavers. Harris turned out not to have too much appetite for that kind of thing. Well, if I had eight thousand in gold I'd probably take a couple years' vacation myself. He didn't even stay on the grant, though. Rented a little house in town and proceeded to make himself a reputation.

Of course Harris had always been handy with a pistol and a knife, but he also used to have a healthy respect for what they could do to you. Now he took to picking fights—or actually, getting people so riled that they picked fights with him. With his tongue that was easy.

And it did look like he was charmed. I don't know how many people he shot and stabbed, without himself getting a scratch. I don't know because I stopped keeping regular company with him after I got myself a nasty stab wound in the thigh, because of his big mouth. We didn't seek each other out after that, but it wasn't such a big town and I did see him every now and then. And I was with him the night he died.

There was this cantina in the south part of town where I liked to go, because a couple of Americans, engineers at the mine, did their drinking there. I walked down to it one night and almost went right back out when I heard Harris's voice. He was talking at the bar, fairly quiet but in that sarcastic way of his, in English. Suddenly the big engineer next to him stands up and kicks his stool halfway across the room, and at the top of his voice calls Harris something I wouldn't say to the devil himself. By this time anybody with horse sense was grabbing a piece of the floor, and I got behind the doorjamb myself, but I did see everything that happened.

The big guy reaches into his coat and suddenly Harris has his Navy Colt in his hand. He has that little smile I saw too often. I hear the Colt's hammer snap down and this little "puff" sound. Harris's jaw drops because he knows as well as I do what's happened: bad round, and now there's a bullet jammed in the barrel. He couldn't shoot again even if he had time.

Then the big guy laughs, almost good natured, and takes careful aim with this little ladies' gun, a .32 I think. He shoots Harris in the arm, evidently to teach him a lesson. Just a graze, doesn't even break a bone. But Harris takes one look at it and his face goes blank and he drops to the floor. Even if you'd never seen a man die, you'd know he was dead by the way he fell.

Now I've told this story to men who were in the Civil War, beside which the Mexican War looks like a Sunday outing, and some of them say that's not hard to believe. You see enough men die and you see everything. One fellow'll get both legs blown off and sit and joke while they sew him up; the next'll get a little scratch and die of the shock. But that one just doesn't sound like Harris, not before or after Doña Dolores's prediction made him reckless. What signifies to me is the date that Harris died: December 30th, 1853.

Earlier that year, Santa Anna had managed to get back into office, for the last time. He did his usual trick of spending all the money he could find. Railroad fellow named James Gadsden showed up and offered to buy a little chunk of northern Mexico, to get the right-of-way for a transcontinental railroad. It was the Mesilla Valley, and Santa Anna signed it over on the thirtieth of December. We didn't know it for a couple of weeks, and the haggling went on until June—but when Harris picked a fight that night, he wasn't on Mexican soil. And you can make of that what you want.

As for me, I only kept farming for a few more years. Around about '57 the Apaches started to get rambunctious, Cochise's gang of murderers.

Even if I'd wanted to stay I couldn't've kept any help. Went to California but didn't pan out. Been on the move since, and it suits me. Reckon I'll go almost anyplace except Mexico.

Because old Dolores liked me and she told my fortune many times. I never paid too much attention, but I know if she'd seen the sign that said I wasn't going to die in Mexico, she would've told me, and I would've remembered. Maybe it's all silliness. But I ain't going to be the one to test it.

INTRODUCTION TO "MORE THAN THE SUM OF HIS PARTS"

This story came directly from an assignment I made to my science-fiction writing class at MIT. (When I make a specific assignment I first write a couple of pages to use as an example; in this case I went ahead and finished the story.)

For this assignment, I gave each student a random number between 8 and 188, which corresponded to page numbers in the excellent source book *The Science in Science Fiction*, by Peter Nicholls, with David Langford and Brian Stableford. They had to come up with a story using that scientific device or principle. I further restricted them by saying they had to use a story structure from one of the stories in our textbook *The Science Fiction Hall of Fame*, edited by Robert Silverberg. The point of the assignment was partly to demonstrate that art thrives under restrictions. (It was also to give them a starting point; many had never written fiction before, and a blank page or screen is a terrible thing.) Then I gave them some time to confer, and give me a page number.

The students chose for me the non-random number 142, which came up "cyborg," a topic they decided was not a winner. (The editors of *Playboy* disagreed.) The beginning I chose to emulate was the masterful start of Daniel Keyes's classic "Flowers for Algernon."

MORE THAN THE
SUM OF HIS PARTS

21 AUGUST 2058

They say I am to keep a detailed record of my feelings, my perceptions, as I grow accustomed to the new parts. To that end, they gave me an apparatus that blind people use for writing, like a tablet with guide wires. It is somewhat awkward. But a recorder would be useless, since I will not have a mouth for some time, and I can't type blind with only one hand.

Woke up free from pain. Interesting. Surprising to find that it has only been five days since the accident. For the record, I am, or was, Dr. Wilson Cheetham, Senior Engineer (Quality Control) for U.S. Steel's Skyfac station, a high-orbit facility that produces foamsteel and vapor deposition materials for use in the cislunar community. But if you are reading this, you must know all that.

Five days ago I was inspecting the aluminum deposition facility and had a bad accident. There was a glitch in my jetseat controls, and I flew suddenly straight into the wide beam of charged aluminum vapor. Very hot. They turned it off in a second, but there was still plenty of time for the beam to breach the suit and thoroughly roast three quarters of my body.

Apparently there was a rescue bubble right there. I was unconscious, of course. They tell me that my heart stopped with the shock, but they managed to save me. My left leg and arm are gone, as is my face. I have no lower jaw, nose, or external ears. I can hear after a fashion, though, and will have eyes in a week or so. They claim they will craft for me testicles and a penis.

I must be pumped full of mood drugs. I feel too calm. If I were myself, whatever fraction of myself is left, perhaps I would resist the insult of being turned into a sexless half-machine.

Ah well. This will be a machine that can turn itself off.

22 AUGUST 2058

For many days there was only sleep or pain. This was in the weight-less ward at Mercy. They stripped the dead skin off me bit by bit. There are limits to anesthesia, unfortunately. I tried to scream but found I had no vocal cords. They finally decided not to try to salvage the arm and leg, which saved some pain.

When I was able to listen, they explained that U.S. Steel valued my services so much that they were willing to underwrite a state-of-the-art cyborg transformation. Half the cost will be absorbed by Interface Biotech on the Moon. Everybody will deduct me from their taxes.

This, then, is the catalog. First, new arm and leg. That's fairly stan-dard. (I once worked with a woman who had two cyborg arms. It took weeks before I could look at her without feeling pity and revulsion.) Then they will attempt to build me a working jaw and mouth, which has been done only rarely and imperfectly, and rebuild the trachea, vocal cords, esophagus. I will be able to speak and drink, though except for certain soft foods, I won't eat in a normal way; salivary glands are beyond their art. No mucous membranes of any kind. A drastic cure for my chronic sinusitis.

Surprisingly, to me at least, the reconstruction of a penis is a fairly straightforward procedure, for which they've had lots of practice. Men are forever sticking them into places where they don't belong. They are particularly excited about my case because of the challenge in restoring sensation as well as function. The prostate is intact, and they seem confident that they can hook up the complicated plumbing involved in ejaculation. Restoring the ability to urinate is trivially easy, they say.

(The biotechnician in charge of the urogenital phase of the project talked at me for more than an hour, going into unnecessarily grisly detail. It seems that this replacement was done occasionally even before they had any kind of mechanical substitute, by sawing off a short rib and transplanting it, covering it with a skin graft from elsewhere on the body.

The recipient thus was blessed with a permanent erection, unfortunately rather strange-looking and short on sensation. My own prosthesis will look very much like the real, shall we say, thing, and new developments in tractor-field mechanics and bionic interfacing should give it realistic response patterns.)

I don't know how to feel about all this. I wish they would leave my blood chemistry alone, so I could have some honest grief or horror, whatever. Instead of this placid waiting.

4 SEPTEMBER 2058

Out cold for thirteen days and I wake up with eyes. The arm and leg are in place but not powered up yet. I wonder what the eyes look like. (They won't give me a mirror until I have a face.) They feel like wet glass.

Very fancy eyes. I have a box with two dials that I can use to override the "default mode"—that is, the ability to see only normally. One of them gives me conscious control over pupil dilation, so I can see in almost total darkness or, if for some reason I wanted to, look directly at the sun without discomfort. The other changes the frequency response, so I can see either in the infrared or the ultraviolet. This hospital room looks pretty much the same in ultraviolet, but in infrared it takes on a whole new aspect. Most of the room's illumination then comes from bright bars on the walls, radiant heating. My real arm shows a pulsing tracery of arteries and veins. The other is of course not visible except by reflection and is dark blue.

(Later) Strange I didn't realize I was on the Moon. I thought it was a low-gravity ward in Mercy. While I was sleeping they sent me down to Biotech. Should have figured that out.

5 SEPTEMBER 2058

They turned on the "social" arm and leg and began patterning exercises. I am told to think of a certain movement and do its mirror image with my right arm or leg while attempting to execute it with my left. The trainer helps the cyborg unit along, which generates something like pain, though actually it doesn't resemble any real muscular ache. Maybe it's the way circuits feel when they're overloaded.

By the end of the session I was able to make a fist without help, though there is hardly enough grip to hold a pencil. I can't raise the leg yet, but can make the toes move.

They removed some of the bandages today, from shoulder to hip, and the test-tube skin looks much more real than I had prepared myself for. Hairless and somewhat glossy, but the color match is perfect. In infrared it looks quite different, more uniform in color than the "real" side. I suppose that's because it hasn't aged forty years.

While putting me through my paces, the technician waxed rhapsodic about how good this arm is going to be—this set of arms, actually. I'm exercising with the "social" one, which looks much more convincing than the ones my coworker displayed ten years ago. (No doubt more a matter of money than of advancing technology.) The "working" arm, which I haven't seen yet, will be all metal, capable of being worn on the outside of a spacesuit. Besides having the two arms, I'll be able to interface with various waldos, tailored to specific functions.

I am fortunately more ambidextrous than the average person. I broke my right wrist in the second grade and kept re-breaking it through the third, and so learned to write with both hands. All my life I have been able to print more clearly with the left.

They claim to be cutting down on my medication. If that's the truth, I seem to be adjusting fairly well. Then again, I have nothing in my past experience to use as a basis for comparison. Perhaps this calmness is only a mask for hysteria.

6 SEPTEMBER 2058

Today I was able to tie a simple knot. I can lightly sketch out the letters of the alphabet. A large and childish scrawl but recognizably my own.

I've begun walking after a fashion, supporting myself between parallel bars. (The lack of hand strength is a neural problem, not a muscular one; when rigid, the arm and leg are as strong as metal crutches.) As I practice, it's amusing to watch the reactions of people who walk into the room, people who aren't paid to mask their horror at being studied by two cold lenses embedded in a swath of bandages formed over a shape that is not a head.

Tomorrow they start building my face. I will be essentially unconscious for more than a week. The limb patterning will continue as I sleep, they say.

14 SEPTEMBER 2058

When I was a child my mother, always careful to have me do "normal" things, dressed me in costume each Halloween and escorted me around the high-rise, so I could beg for candy I did not want and money I did not need. On one occasion I had to wear the mask of a child star then popular on the cube, a tightly fitting plastic affair that covered the entire head, squeezing my pudgy features into something more in line with some Platonic ideal of childish beauty. That was my last Halloween. I embarrassed her.

This face is like that. It is undeniably my face, but the skin is taut and unresponsive. Any attempt at expression produces a grimace.

I have almost normal grip in the hand now, though it is still clumsy. As they hoped, the sensory feedback from the fingertips and palms seems to be more finely tuned than in my "good" hand. Tracing my new forefinger across my right wrist, I can sense the individual pores, and there is a marked temperature gradient as I pass over tendon or vein. And yet the hand and arm will eventually be capable of superhuman strength.

Touching my new face I do not feel pores. They have improved on nature in the business of heat exchange.

22 SEPTEMBER 2058

Another week of sleep while they installed the new plumbing. When the anesthetic wore off I felt a definite *something*, not pain, but neither was it the normal somatic heft of genitalia. Everything was bedded in gauze and bandage, though, and catheterized, so it would feel strange even to a normal person.

(Later) An aide came in and gingerly snipped away the bandages. He blushed; I don't think fondling was in his job description. When the catheter came out there was a small sting of pain and relief.

It's not much of a copy. To reconstruct the face, they could consult hundreds of pictures and cubes, but it had never occurred to me that one day it might be useful to have a gallery of pictures of my private parts in various stages of repose. The technicians had approached the problem by bringing me a stack of photos culled from urological texts and pornography, and having me sort through them as to "closeness of fit."

It was not a task for which I was well trained, by experience or disposition. Strange as it may seem in this age of unfettered hedonism, I haven't seen another man naked, let alone rampant, since leaving high school, twenty-five years ago. (I was stationed on Farside for eighteen months and never went near a sex bar, preferring an audience of one. Even if I had to hire her, as was usually the case.)

So this one is rather longer and thicker than its predecessor—would all men unconsciously exaggerate?—and has only approximately the same aspect when erect. A young man's rakish angle.

Distasteful but necessary to write about the matter of masturbation. At first it didn't work. With my right hand, it felt like holding another man, which I have never had any desire to do. With the new hand, though, the process proceeded in the normal way, though I must admit to a voyeuristic aspect. The sensations were extremely acute. Ejaculation more forceful than I can remember from youth.

It makes me wonder. In a book I recently read, about brain chemistry, the author made a major point of the notion that it's a mistake to completely equate "mind" with "brain." The brain, he said, is in a way only the thickest and most complex segment of the nervous system; it coordinates our consciousness, but the actual mind suffuses through the body in a network of ganglia. In fact, he used sexuality as an example. When a man ruefully observes that his penis has a mind of its own, he is stating part of a larger truth.

But I in fact do have actual brains imbedded in my new parts: the biochips that process sensory data coming in and action commands going back. Are these brains part of my consciousness the way the rest of my nervous system is? The masturbation experience indicates they might be in business for themselves.

This is premature speculation, so to speak. We'll see how it feels when I move into a more complex environment, where I'm not so self-absorbed.

23 SEPTEMBER 2058

During the night something evidently clicked. I woke up this morning with full strength in my cyborg limbs. One rail of the bed was twisted out of shape where I must have unconsciously gripped it. I bent it back quite easily.

Some obscure impulse makes me want to keep this talent secret for the time being. The technicians thought I would be able to exert three or four times the normal person's grip; this is obviously much more than that.

But why keep it a secret? I don't know. Eventually they will read this diary and I will stand exposed. There's no harm in that, though; this is supposed to be a record of my psychological adjustment or maladjustment. Let *them* tell *me* why I've done it.

(Later) The techs were astonished, ecstatic. I demonstrated a pull of 90 kilograms. I know if I'd actually given it a good yank, I could have pulled the stress machine out of the wall. I'll give them 110 tomorrow and inch my way up to 125.

Obviously I must be careful with force vectors. If I put too much stress on the normal parts of my body I could do permanent injury. With my metal fist I could certainly punch a hole through an airlock door, but it would probably tear the prosthesis out of its socket. Newton's laws still apply.

Other laws will have to be rewritten.

24 SEPTEMBER 2058

I got to work out with three waldos today. A fantastic experience!

The first one was a disembodied hand and arm attached to a stand, the setup they use to train normal people in the use of waldos. The difference is that I don't need a waldo sleeve to imperfectly transmit my wishes to the mechanical double. I can plug into it directly.

I've been using waldos in my work ever since graduate school, but it was never anything like this. Inside the waldo sleeve you get a clumsy kind of feedback from striated pressor field generators embedded in the plastic. With my setup the feedback is exactly the kind a normal person feels when he touches an object, but much more sensitive. The first time they asked me to pick up an egg, I tossed it up and caught it (no great feat of coordination in lunar gravity, admittedly, but I could have done it as easily in Earth-normal).

The next waldo was a large earthmover that Western Mining uses over at Grimaldi Station. That was interesting, not only because of its size but because of the slight communications lag. Grimaldi is only a few dozens of kilometers away, but there aren't enough unused data channels between here and there for me to use the land-line to communicate with the earthmover hand. I had to relay via comsat, so there was about a tenth-second delay between the thought and the action. It was a fine feeling of power, but a little confusing: I would cup my hand and scoop downward, and then a split-second too late would feel the resistance of the regolith. And then casually hold in my palm several tonnes of rock and dirt. People standing around watching; with a flick of my wrist I could have buried them. Instead I dutifully dumped it on the belt to the converter.

But the waldo that most fascinated me was the micro. It had been in use for only a few months; I had heard of it, but hadn't had a chance to see it in action. It is a fully articulated hand barely a tenth of a millimeter long. I used it in conjunction with a low-power scanning electron microscope, moving around on the surface of a microcircuit. At that magnification it looked like a hand on a long stick wandering through the corridors of a building, whose walls varied from rough stucco to brushed metal to blistered gray paint, all laced over with thick cables of gold. When necessary, I could bring in another hand, manipulated by my right from inside a waldo sleeve, to help with simple carpenter and machinest tasks that, in the real world, translated into fundamental changes in the quantum-electrodynamic properties of the circuit.

This was the real power: not crushing metal tubes or lifting tonnes of rock, but pushing electrons around to do my bidding. My first doctorate was in electrical engineering; in a sudden epiphany I realize that I am the first *actual* electrical engineer in history.

After two hours they made me stop; said I was showing signs of strain. They put me in a wheelchair, and I did fall asleep on the way back to my room. Dreaming dreams of microcosmic and infinite power.

25 SEPTEMBER 2058

The metal arm. I expected it to feel fundamentally different from the "social" one, but of course it doesn't, most of the time. Circuits are circuits. The difference comes under conditions of extreme exertion: the soft hand gives me signals like pain if I come close to the level of stress that would harm the fleshlike material. With the metal hand I can rip off a chunk of steel plate a centimeter thick and feel nothing beyond "muscular" strain. If I had two of them I could work marvels.

The mechanical leg is not so gifted. It has governors to restrict its strength and range of motion to that of a normal leg, which is reasonable. Even a normal person finds himself brushing the ceiling occasionally in lunar gravity. I could stand up sharply and find myself with a concussion, or worse.

I like the metal arm, though. When I'm stronger (hah!) they say they'll let me go outside and try it with a spacesuit. Throw something over the horizon.

Starting today, I'm easing back into a semblance of normal life. I'll be staying at Biotech for another six or eight weeks, but I'm patched into my Skyfac office and have started clearing out the backlog of paperwork. Two hours in the morning and two in the afternoon. It's diverting, but I have to admit my heart isn't really in it. Rather be playing with the micro. (Have booked three hours on it tomorrow.)

26 SEPTEMBER 2058

They threaded an optical fiber through the micro's little finger, so I can watch its progress on a screen without being limited to the field of an electron microscope. The picture is fuzzy while the waldo is in motion, but if I hold it still for a few seconds, the computer assist builds up quite a sharp image. I used it to roam all over my right arm and hand, which was fascinating. Hairs a tangle of stiff black stalks, the pores small damp craters. And everywhere the evidence of the skin's slow death; translucent sheafs of desquamated cells.

I've taken to wearing the metal arm rather than the social one. People's stares don't bother me. The metal one will be more useful in my actual work, and I want to get as much practice as possible. There is also an undeniable feeling of power.

27 SEPTEMBER 2058

Today I went outside. It was clumsy getting around at first. For the past eleven years I've used a suit only in zerogee, so all my reflexes are wrong. Still, not much serious can go wrong at a sixth of a gee.

It was exhilarating but at the same time frustrating, since I couldn't reveal all my strength. I did almost overdo it once, starting to tip over a large boulder. Before it tipped, I realized that my left boot had crunched through about ten centimeters of regolith, in reaction to the amount of force I was applying. So I backed off and discreetly shuffled my foot to fill the telltale hole.

I could indeed throw a rock over the horizon. With a sling, I might be able to put a small one into orbit. Rent myself out as a lunar launching facility.

(Later) Most interesting. A pretty nurse who has been on this project since the beginning came into my room after dinner and proposed the obvious experiment. It was wildly successful.

Although my new body starts out with the normal pattern of excitation-plateau-orgasm, the resemblance stops there. I have no refractory period; the process of erection is completely under conscious control. This could make me the most popular man on the Moon.

The artificial skin of the penis is as sensitive to tactile differentiation as that of the cyborg fingers: suddenly I know more about a woman's internal topography than any man who ever lived—more than any *woman*!

I think tomorrow I'll take a trip to Farside.

28 SEPTEMBER 2058

Farside has nine sex bars. I read the guidebook descriptions, and then asked a few locals for their recommendations, and wound up going to a place cleverly called the Juice Bar.

In fact, the name was not just an expression of coy eroticism. They served nothing but fruit and juices there, most of them fantastically expensive Earth imports. I spent a day's pay on a glass of pear nectar and sought out the most attractive woman in the room.

That in itself was a mistake. I was not physically attractive even before the accident, and the mechanics have faithfully restored my coarse features and slight paunch. I was rebuffed.

So I went to the opposite extreme and looked for the plainest woman. That would be a better test, anyway: before the accident I always demanded, and paid for, physical perfection. If I could duplicate the performance of last night with a woman to whom I was not sexually attracted—and do it in public, with no pressure from having gone without—then my independence from the autonomic nervous system would be proven beyond doubt.

Second mistake. I was never good at small talk, and when I located my paragon of plainness I began talking about the accident and the singular talent that had resulted from it. She suddenly remembered an appointment elsewhere.

I was not so open with the next woman, also plain. She asked whether there was something wrong with my face, and I told her half of the truth. She was sweetly sympathetic, motherly, which did not endear her to me.

It did make her a good subject for the experiment. We left the socializing section of the bar and went back to the so-called "love room."

There was an acrid quality to the air that I suppose was compounded of incense and sweat, but of course my dry nose was not capable of identifying actual smells. For the first time, I was grateful for that disability; the place probably had the aroma of a well-used locker room. Plus pheromones.

Under the muted lights, red and blue as well as white, more than a dozen couples were engaged more or less actively in various aspects of amorous behavior. A few were frankly staring at others, but most were either absorbed with their own affairs or furtive in their voyeurism. Most of them were on the floor, which was a warm soft mat, but some were using tables and chairs in fairly ingenious ways. Several of the permutations would no doubt have been impossible or dangerous in Earth's gravity.

We undressed and she complimented me on my evident spryness. A nearby spectator made a jealous observation. Her own body was rather flaccid, doughy, and under previous circumstances I doubt that I would have been able to maintain enthusiasm. There was no problem, how-ever; in fact, I rather enjoyed it. She required very little foreplay, and I was soon repeating the odd sensation of hypersensitized exploration. Gynecological spelunking.

She was quite voluble in her pleasure, and although she lasted less than an hour, we did attract a certain amount of attention. When she, panting, regretfully declined further exercise, a woman who had been watching, a rather attractive young blonde, offered to share her various openings. I obliged her for a while; although the well was dry the pump handle was unaffected.

During that performance I became aware that the pleasure involved was not a sexual one in any normal sense. Sensual, yes, in the way that a fine meal is a sensual experience, but with a remote subtlety that I find dif-ficult to describe. Perhaps there is a relation to epicurism that is more than metaphorical. Since I can no longer taste food, a large area of my brain is available for the evaluation of other experience. It may be that the brain is reorganizing itself in order to take fullest advantage of my new abilities.

By the time the blonde's energy began to flag, several other women had taken an interest in my satyriasis. I resisted the temptation to find what this organ's limit was, if indeed a limit exists. My back ached and the right knee was protesting. So I threw the mental switch and deflated. I left with a minimum of socializing. (The first woman insisted on buying me something at the bar. I opted for a banana.)

29 SEPTEMBER 2058

Now that I have eyes and both hands, there's no reason to scratch this diary out with a pen. So I'm entering it into the computer. But I'm keeping two versions.

I recopied everything up to this point and then went back and edited the version that I will show to Biotech. It's very polite, and will remain so. For instance, it does not contain the following:

After writing last night's entry, I found myself still full of energy, and so I decided to put into action a plan that has been forming in my mind.

About two in the morning I went downstairs and broke into the waldo lab. The entrance is protected by a five-digit combination lock, but of course that was no obstacle. My hypersensitive fingers could feel the tumblers rattling into place.

I got the micro-waldo set up and then detached my leg. I guided the waldo through the leg's circuitry and easily disabled the governors. The whole operation took less than twenty minutes.

I did have to use a certain amount of care walking, at first. There was a tendency to rise into the air or to limpingly overcompensate. It was under control by the time I got back to my room. So once more they proved to have been mistaken as to the limits of my abilities. Testing the strength of the leg, with a halfhearted kick I put a deep dent in the metal wall at the rear of my closet. I'll have to wait until I can be outside, alone, to see what full force can do.

A comparison kick with my flesh leg left no dent, but did hurt my great toe.

30 SEPTEMBER 2058

It occurs to me that I feel better about my body than I have in the past twenty years. Who wouldn't? Literally eternal youth in these new limbs and organs; if a part shows signs of wear, it can simply be replaced.

I was angry at the Biotech evaluation board this morning. When I simply inquired as to the practicality of replacing the right arm and leg as well, all but one were horrified. One was amused. I will remember him.

I think the fools are going to order me to leave Nearside in a day or two and go back to Mercy for psychiatric "help." I will leave when I want to, on my own terms.

1 OCTOBER 2058

This is being voice-recorded in the Environmental Control Center at Nearside. It is 10:32; they have less than ninety minutes to accede to my demands. Let me backtrack.

After writing last night's entry I felt a sudden access of sexual desire. I took the shuttle to Farside and went back to the Juice Bar.

The plain woman from the previous night was waiting, hoping that I would show up. She was delighted when I suggested that we save money (and whatever residue of modesty we had left) by keeping ourselves to one another, back at my room.

I didn't mean to murder her. That was not in my mind at all. But I suppose in my passion, or abandon, I carelessly propped my strong leg against the wall and then thrust with too much strength. At any rate there was a snap and a tearing sound. She gave a small cry and the lower half of my body was suddenly awash in blood. I had snapped her spine and evidently at the same time caused considerable internal damage. She must have lost consciousness very quickly, though her heart did not stop beating for nearly a minute.

Disposing of the body was no great problem, conceptually. In the laundry room I found a bag large enough to hold her comfortably. Then I went back to the room and put her and the sheet she had besmirched into the bag.

Getting her to the recycler would have been a problem if it had been a normal hour. She looked like nothing so much as a body in a laundry bag. Fortunately, the corridor was deserted.

The lock on the recycler room was child's play. The furnace door was a problem, though; it was easy to unlock but its effective diameter was only 25 centimeters.

So I had to disassemble her. To save cleaning up, I did the job inside the laundry bag, which was clumsy, and made it difficult to see the fascinating process.

I was so absorbed in watching that I didn't hear the door slide open. But the man who walked in made a slight gurgling sound, which somehow I did hear over the cracking of bones. I stepped over to him and killed him with one kick.

At this point I have to admit to a lapse in judgment. I relocked the door and went back to the chore at hand. After the woman was completely recycled, I repeated the process with the man—which was, incidentally, much easier. The female's layer of subcutaneous fat made disassembly of the torso a more slippery business.

It really was wasted time (though I did spend part of the time thinking out the final touches of the plan I am now engaged upon). I might as well have left both bodies there on the floor. I had kicked the man with great force—enough to throw me to the ground in reaction and badly bruise my right hip—and had split him open from crotch to heart. This made a bad enough mess, even if he hadn't compounded the problem by striking the ceiling. I would never be able to clean that up, and it's not the sort of thing that would escape notice for long.

At any rate, it was only twenty minutes wasted, and I gained more time than that by disabling the recycler room lock. I cleaned up, changed clothes, stopped by the waldo lab for a few minutes, and then took the slidewalk to the Environmental Control Center.

There was only one young man on duty at the ECC at that hour. I exchanged a few pleasantries with him and then punched him in the heart, softly enough not to make a mess. I put his body where it wouldn't distract me and then attended to the problem of the "door."

There's no actual door on the ECC, but there is an emergency wall that slides into place if there's a drop in pressure. I typed up a test program simulating an emergency, and the wall obeyed. Then I walked over and twisted a few flanges around. Nobody would be able to get into the Center with anything short of a cutting torch.

Sitting was uncomfortable with the bruised hip, but I managed to ease into the console and spend an hour or so studying logic and wiring diagrams. Then I popped off an access plate and moved the micro-waldo down the corridors of electronic thought. The intercom began buzzing incessantly, but I didn't let it interfere with my concentration.

Nearside is protected from meteorite strike or (far more likely) structural failure by a series of 128 bulkheads that, like the emergency wall here, can slide into place and isolate any area where there's a pressure drop. It's done automatically, of course, but can also be controlled from here.

What I did, in essence, was to tell each bulkhead that it was under repair, and should not close under any circumstance. Then I moved the waldo over to the circuits that controlled the city's eight airlocks. With some rather elegant microsurgery, I transferred control of all eight solely to the pressure switch I now hold in my left hand.

It is a negative-pressure button, a dead-man switch taken from a power saw. So long as I hold it down, the inner doors of the airlocks will remain locked. If I let go, they will all iris open. The outer doors are already open, as are the ones that connect the airlock chambers to the suiting-up rooms. No one will be able to make it to a spacesuit in time. Within thirty seconds, every corridor will be full of vacuum. People behind airtight doors may choose between slow asphyxiation and explosive decompression.

My initial plan had been to wire the dead-man switch to my pulse, which would free my good hand and allow me to sleep. That will have to wait. The wiring completed, I turned on the intercom and announced that I would speak to the Coordinator, and no one else.

When I finally got to talk to him, I told him what I had done and invited him to verify it. That didn't take long. Then I presented my demands:

Surgery to replace the rest of my limbs, of course. The surgery would have to be done while I was conscious (a heartbeart dead-man switch could be subverted by a heart machine) and it would have to be done here, so that I could be assured that nobody fooled with my circuit changes.

The doctors were called in, and they objected that such profound surgery couldn't be done under local anesthetic. I knew they were lying, of course; amputation was a fairly routine procedure even before anesthetics were invented. Yes, but I would faint, they said. I told them that I would not, and at any rate I was willing to take the chance, and no one else had any choice in the matter.

(I have not yet mentioned that the ultimate totality of my plan involves replacing all my internal organs as well as all of the limbs—or at least those organs whose failure could cause untimely death. I will be a true cyborg then, a human brain in an "artificial" body, with the prospect of thousands of years of life. With a few decades—or centuries!—of research, I could even do something about the brain's shortcomings. I would wind up interfaced to EarthNet, with all of human knowledge at my disposal, and with my faculties for logic and memory no longer fettered by the slow pace of electrochemical synapse.)

A psychiatrist, talking from Earth, tried to convince me of the error of my ways. He said that the dreadful trauma had "obviously" unhinged me, and the cyborg augmentation, far from effecting a cure, had made my mental derangement worse. He demonstrated, at least to his own satisfaction, that my behavior followed some classical pattern of madness. All this had been taken into consideration, he said, and if I were to give myself up, I would be forgiven my crimes and manumitted into the loving arms of the psychiatric establishment.

I did take time to explain the fundamental errors in his way of thinking. He felt that I had quite literally lost my identity by losing my face and genitalia, and that I was at bottom a "good" person whose essential humanity had been perverted by physical and existential estrangement. Totally wrong. By his terms, what I actually *am* is an "evil" person whose true nature was revealed to himself by the lucky accident that released him from existential propinquity with the common herd.

And "evil" is the accurate word, not maladjusted or amoral or even criminal. I am as evil by human standards as a human is evil by the standards of an animal raised for food, and the analogy is accurate. I will sacrifice humans not only for my survival but for comfort, curiosity, or entertainment. I will allow to live anyone who doesn't bother me, and reward generously those who help.

Now they have only forty minutes. They know I am

—end of recording

25 SEPTEMBER 2058

Excerpt from Summary Report

I am Dr. Henry Janovski, head of the surgical team that worked on the ill-fated cyborg augmentation of Dr. Wilson Cheetham.

We were fortunate that Dr. Cheetham's insanity did interfere with his normally painstaking, precise nature. If he had spent more time in preparation, I have no doubt that he would have put us in a very difficult fix.

He should have realized that the protecting wall that shut him off from the rest of Nearside was made of steel, an excellent conductor of electricity. If he had insulated himself behind a good dielectric, he could have escaped his fate.

Cheetham's waldo was a marvelous instrument, but basically it was only a pseudo-intelligent servomechanism that obeyed well-defined radio-frequency commands. All we had to do was override the signals that were coming from his own nervous system.

We hooked a powerful amplifier up to the steel wall, making it in effect a huge radio transmitter. To generate the signal we wanted amplified, I had a technician put on a waldo sleeve that was holding a box similar to Cheetham's dead-man switch. We wired the hand closed, turned up the power, and had the technician strike himself on the chin as hard as he could.

162

The technician struck himself so hard he blacked out for a few seconds. Cheetham's resonant action, perhaps a hundred times more powerful, drove the bones of his chin up through the top of his skull.

Fortunately, the expensive arm itself was not damaged. It is not evil or insane by itself, of course. Which I shall prove.

The experiments will continue, though of course we will be more selective as to subjects. It seems obvious in retrospect that we should not use as subjects people who have gone through the kind of trauma that Cheetham suffered. We must use willing volunteers. Such as myself.

I am not young, and weakness and an occasional tremor in my hands limits the amount of surgery I can do—much less than my knowledge would allow, or my nature desire. My failing left arm I shall have replaced with Cheetham's mechanical marvel, and I will go through training similar to his—but for the good of humanity, not for ill.

What miracles I will perform with the knife!

INTRODUCTION TO "SEASONS"

This story was the result of two independent coincidences. I don't often write novellas; they take as much work as the equivalent part of a novel, but pay less per word than a short story—often a lot less.

So it was with some reluctance that I agreed to teach a course in "Writing Longer Fiction" at MIT. The woman who taught it had suddenly retired, and I was a reasonable replacement, since I'd written several of the pesky little rascals. Normally, though, I write along with my students, and I didn't want to tie up a month or more of writing time. Certainly not for pennies a word.

I was quite literally sitting at my new desk at MIT when my first phone call came in. It was New York. The editor Betsy Mitchell wondered whether I would write a novella for her, for the collection *Alien Stars*. I recovered from synchronistic shock just long enough to ask for more money.

She said she'd check and call back—and then I realized I may have blown a truly unique opportunity. If there is a goddess for freelancers, she had just dropped a freebie in my lap, and I spurned her gift. But Betsy did call back with a yes, and I started in.

Most novellas don't work. They're either bloated short stories or shrunken novels. I tried to figure out why, and write a novella that didn't fail.

Most readers don't want to bother with all that theoretical stuff. For the few who do—or the unfortunate fewer who have to teach a course in Writing Longer Fiction—I'll append it as a "technical note" at the end of the story.

SEASONS

Transcripts edited from the last few hundred hours of recordings:

MARIA

Forty-one is too young to die. I was never trained to be a soldier. Trained to survive, yes, but not to kill or be killed.

That's the wrong way to start. Let me start this way.

As near as I can reckon, it's mid-noviembre, AC 238. I am Maria Rubera, chief xenologist for the second Confederación expedition to Sanchrist IV. I am currently standing guard in the mouth of a cave while my five comrades try to sleep. I am armed with a stone axe and flint spear and a pile of rocks for throwing. A cold rain is misting down, and I am wearing only a stiff kilt and vest of wet rank fur. I am cold to the very heart but we dare not risk a fire. The Plathys have too acute a sense of smell.

I am subvocalizing, recording this into my artificial bicuspid, one of which each of us has; the only post-Stone Age artifacts in this cave. It may survive even if, as is probable, I do not. Or it may not survive. The Plathys have a way of eating animals head first, crunching up skull and brain while the decapitated body writhes at their feet or staggers around, which to them is high humor. Innocent humor but ghastly. I almost came to love them. Which is not to say I understand them.

Let me try to make this document as complete as possible. It gives me something to do. I trust you have a machine that can filter out the sound of my teeth chattering. For a while I could do the Zen trick to keep my teeth still. But I'm too cold now. And too certain of death, and afraid.

165

My specialty is xenology but I do have a doctorate in historicultural anthropology, which is essentially the study of dead cultures through the writings of dead anthropologists. In the nineteenth and twentieth centuries, old style, there were dozens of isolated cultures still existing without metals or writing or even, in some cases, agriculture or social organization beyond the family. None of them survived more than a couple of generations beyond their contact with civilization, but civilization by then could afford the luxury of science, and so there are fairly complete records. The records are fascinating not only for the information about the primitives, but also for what they reveal of the investigating cultures' unconscious prejudices. My own specialties were the Maori and Eskimo tribes, and (by necessary association) the European and American cultures that investigated and more or less benignly destroyed them.

I will try not to stray from the point. That training is what led to my appointment as leader of this band of cold, half-naked, probably doomed, pseudo-primitive scientists. We do not repeat the errors of our forebears. We come to the primitives on equal terms, now, so as not to contaminate their habit patterns by superior example. No more than is necessary. Most of us do not bite the heads off living animals or exchange greetings by the tasting of excrement.

Saying that and thinking of it goads me to go down the hill again. We designated a latrine rock a few hundred meters away, in sight of the cave entrance but with no obvious path leading here, to throw them off our scent at least temporarily. I will not talk while going there. They also have acute hearing.

Back. Going too often and with too little result. Diet mostly raw meat in small amounts. Only warm place on my body is the hot and itching anus. No proper hygiene in the Stone Age. Just find a smooth rock. I can feel my digestive tract flourishing with worms and bugs. No evidence yet, though, nor blood. Carlos Fleming started passing blood, and two days later something burst and he died in a rush of it. We covered his body with stones. Ground too frozen for grave-digging. He was probably uncovered and eaten.

It can't be the diet. On Earth I paid high prices for raw meat and fish and never suffered except in the wallet. I'm afraid it may be a virus. We all are, and we indulge in discreet copromancy, the divining of future events through the inspection of stools. If there is blood your future will be short.

Perhaps it was stress. We are under unusual stress. But I stray.

It was specifically my study of Eskimos that impressed the assigning committee. Eskimos were small bands of hearty folk who lived in the polar regions of North America. Like the Plathys, they were anagricultural carnivores, preying on herds of large animals, sometimes fishing. The Plathys have no need for the Eskimos' fishing skills, since the sea teems with life edible and stupid. But they prefer red meat and the crunch of bone, the chewy liver and long suck of intestinal contents, the warm mush of brains. They are likable but not fastidious. And not predictable, we learned to our grief.

Like the Eskimos, the Plathys relish the cold and become rather dull and listless during the warm season. Sanchrist IV has no axial tilt, thus no "seasons" in the Terran sense, but its orbit is highly elongated, so more than two thirds of its year (three and a half Terran years) is spent in cold. We identified six discrete seasons: spring, summer, fall, winter, dead winter, and thaw. The placid sea gets ice skim in mid-fall.

If you are less than totally ignorant of science, you know that Sanchrist IV is one of the very few planets with not only earthlike conditions but with life forms that mimic our own patterns of DNA. There are various theories explaining this coincidence, which cannot be coincidence, but you can find them elsewhere. What this meant in terms of our conduct as xenologists was that we could function with minimal ecological impact, living off the fat of the land—and the blood and flesh and marrow, which did require a certain amount of desensitization training. (Less for me than for some of the others, as I've said, since I've always had an atavistic leaning toward dishes like steak tartare and sushi.)

Satellite observation has located 119 bands, or families, of Plathys, and there is no sign of other humanoid life on the planet. All of them live on islands in a southern subtropical sea—at least it would be subtropical on Earth—a shallow sea that freezes solid in dead winter and can be walked over from late fall to early thaw. During the warm months, on those occasions when they actually stir their bones to go someplace, they pole rafts from island to island. During low tide, they can wade most of the way.

We set up our base in the tropics, well beyond their normal range, and hiked south during the late summer. We made contact with a few individuals and small packs during our month-long trek but didn't join a family until we reached the southern mountains.

The Plathys aren't too interesting during the warm months, except for the short mating season. Mostly they loll around, conserving energy, living off the meat killed during the thaw, which they smoke and store in covered holes. When the meat gets too old, or starts running out, they do bestir themselves to fish, which takes little enough energy. The tides are rather high in summer and fall, and all they have to do is stake down nets in the right spots during high tide. The tide recedes and leaves behind flopping silver bounty. They grumble and joke about the taste of it, though.

They accepted our presence without question, placidly sharing their food and shelter as they would with any wayfaring member of another native family. They couldn't have mistaken us for natives, though. The smallest adult Plathy weighs twice as much as our largest. They stand about two and a half meters high and span about a meter and a half across the shoulders. Their heads are more conical than square, with huge powerful jaws: a mouth that runs almost ear to ear. Their eyes are set low, and they have mucous-membrane slits in place of external ears and noses. They are covered with sparse silky fur, which coarsens into thick hair on their heads, shoulders, armpits, and groins (and on the males' backs). The females have four teats defining the corners of a rectangular slab of lactiferous fatty tissue. The openings we thought were their vaginas are almost dorsal, with the cloacal openings toward the front. The male genitals are completely ventral, normally hidden under a mat of hair. (This took a bit of snooping. In all but the hottest times and mating season, both genders wear a "modest" kilt of skin.)

We had been observing them about three weeks when the females went into estrus—every mature female, all the same day. Their sexuality was prodigious.

Everybody shed their kilts and went into a weeklong unrelenting spasm of sexual activity. There is nothing like it among any of the sentient cultures—or animal species!—that I have studied. To call it an orgy would be misleading and, I think, demeaning to the Plathys. The phenomenon was more like a tropism, in plants, than any animal or human instinct. They quite simply did not do anything else for six days.

The adults in our family numbered eighty-two males and nineteen females (the terrible reason for the disparity would become clear in a later season), so the females were engaged all the time, even while they slept. While one male copulated, two or three others would be waiting their turn, prancing impatiently, masturbating, sometimes indulging in homosexual coupling. ("Indulging" is the wrong word. There was no sense that they took pleasure in any sexual activity; it was more like the temporary relief of a terrible pressure that quickly built up again.) They attempted coupling with children and with the humans of my expedition. Fortunately, for all their huge strength they are rather slow and, for all the pressure of their "desire," easily deflected. A kick in the knee was enough to send them stumping off toward someone else.

No Plathys ate during the six days. They slept more and more toward the end of the period, the males sometimes falling asleep in the middle of copulation. (Conversely, we saw several instances of involuntary erection and ejaculation while sleeping.) When it was finally over, everyone sat around dazed for a while, and then the females retired to the storage holes and came back with armloads of dried and smoked meat and fish. Each one ate a mountain of food and fell into a coma.

There are interesting synchronies involved. At other times of the year, this long period of vulnerability would mean extinction of the family or of the whole species, since they evidently all copulate at the same time. But the large predators from the north do not swim down at that time of year. And when the litters were dropped, about 500 days later, it would be not long after the time of easiest food gathering, as herds of small animals migrated north for warmth.

Of course we never had a chance to dissect a Plathy. It would have been fascinating to investigate the internal makeup that impels the bizarre sexual behavior. External observation gives some hint as to the strangeness. The vulva is a small opening, a little over a centimeter in extent, that stays sealed closed except when the female is in estrus. The penis, normally an almost invisible nub, becomes a prehensile purple worm about twenty centimeters long. No external testicles; there must be an internal reservoir (quite large) for seminal fluid.

The anatomical particulars of pregnancy and birth are even more strange. The females become almost immobilized, gaining perhaps fifty percent in weight. When it comes time to give birth, the female makes an actual skeletal accommodation, evidently similar to the way a snake unhinges its jaw when ingesting large prey. It is obviously quite painful. The vulva (or whatever new name applies to that opening) is not involved; instead, a slit opens along the entire perineal area, nearly half a meter long, exposing a milky white membrane. The female claws the membrane open and expels the litter in a series of shuddering contractions. Then she pushes her pelvic bones back into shape with a painful grinding sound. She remains immobile and insensate for several days, nursing. The males bring females food and clean them during this period.

None of the data from the first expedition had prepared us for this. They had come during dead winter and stayed one (terran) year, so they missed the entire birth cycle. They had noted that there were evidently strong taboos against discussing sexual matters and birth. I think "taboo" is the wrong word. It's not as if there were guilt or shame associated with the processes. Rather, they appear to enter a different state of consciousness when the females are in heat and giving birth, a state that seems to blank out their verbal intelligence. They can no more discuss their sexuality than you or I could sit and chat about how our pancreas was doing.

There was an amusing, and revealing, episode after we had been with the family for several months. I had been getting along well with Tybru, a female elder with unusual linguistic ability. She was perplexed at what one of the children had told her.

The Plathys have no concept of privacy; they wander in and out of each other's *maffas* (the yurtlike tents of hide they use as shelter) at any time of the day or night, or random whim. It was inevitable that sooner or later they would observe humans having sex. The child had described what she'd seen fairly accurately. I had tried to explain human sexuality to Tybru earlier, as a way to get her to talk about that aspect of her own life. She would smile and nod diagonally through the whole thing, an infuriating gesture they normally use only with children prattling nonsense.

This time I was going to be blunt. I opened the *maffa* flap so there was plenty of light, then shed my kilt and got up on a table. I lay down on my back and tried to explain with simple words and gestures what went where and who did what to whom, and what might or might not happen nine months later.

She was more inclined to take me seriously this time. (The child who had witnessed copulation was four, pubescent, and thus too old to have fantasies.) After I explained she explored me herself, which was not pleasant, since her four-fingered hand was larger than a human foot, quite filthy, and equipped with deadly nails.

She admitted that all she really understood was the breasts. She could remember some weeks of nursing after the blackout period the female language calls "(big) pain-in-hips." (Their phrase for the other blackout period is literally "pain-in-the-ass.") She asked, logically enough, whether I could find a male and demonstrate.

Actually, I'm an objective enough person to have gone along with it, if I could have found a man able and willing to rise to the occasion. If it had been near the end of our stay, I probably would have done it. But leadership is a ticklish thing, even when you're leading a dozen highly educated, professionally detached people, and we still had three years to go.

I explained that the most-elder doesn't do this with the men she's in charge of, and Tybru accepted that. They don't have much of a handle on discipline, but they do understand policy and social form. She said she would ask the other human females.

Perhaps it should have been me who did the asking, but I didn't suggest it. I was glad to get off the hook, and also curious as to my people's reactions.

The couple who volunteered were the last ones I would have predicted. Both of them were shy, almost diffident, with the rest of us. Good field workers but not the sort of people you would let your hair down with. I suppose they had better "anthropological perspective" on their own behavior than the rest of us.

At any rate, they retired to the *maffa* that was nominally Tybru's, and she let out the ululation that means "All free females come here." I wondered whether our couple could actually perform in a cramped little yurt filled with sweaty giants asking questions in a weird language.

All the females did crowd into the tent, and after a couple of minutes a strange sound began to emanate from them. At first it puzzled me, but then I recognized it as laughter! I had heard individual Plathys laugh, a sort of inhaled croak—but nineteen of them at once was an unearthly din.

The couple was in there a long time, but I never did find out whether the demonstration was actually consummated. They came out of the *maffa* beet-red and staring at the ground, the laughter behind them not abating. I never talked to either of them about it, and whenever I asked Tybru or the others, all I got was choked laughter. I think we invented the dirty joke. (In exchange, I'm sure that Plathy sexuality will eventually see service in the ribald metaphor of human culture.)

But let me go back to the beginning.

We came to Sanchrist IV armed with a small vocabulary and a great deal of misinformation. I don't mean to denigrate my colleagues' skill or application. But the Garcia expedition just came at the wrong time and didn't stay long enough.

Most of their experience with the Plathys was during deep winter, which is their most lively and civilized season. They spend their indoor time creating the complex sculptures that so impressed the art world ten years ago and performing improvisational music and dance that is delightful in its alien grace. Outdoors, they indulge in complicated games and athletic exhibitions. The larders are full, the time of birthing and nursing is well over, and the family exudes happiness, well into the thaw.

171

We experienced this euphoria ourselves. I can't blame Garcia's people for their enthusiastic report.

We still don't know what happened. Or why it happened. Perhaps if these data survive, the next researchers...

Trouble.

GABRIEL

I was having a strange dream of food—real food, cooked—when suddenly there was Maria, tugging on my arm, keeping me away from the table. She was whispering "Gab, wake up!" and so I did, cold and aching and hungry.

"What's—" She put her hand on my mouth, lightly.

"There's one outside. Mylab, I think." He had just turned three this winter, and been given his name. We crept together back to the mouth of the cave and both jumped when my ankle gave a loud pop.

It was Mylab, all right; the fur around one earhole was almost white against the blond. I was glad it wasn't an adult. He was only about a head taller than me. Stronger, though, and well fed.

We watched from the cave's darkness as he investigated the latrine rock, sniffing and licking, circling.

"Maybe he's a scout for a hunting party," I whispered. "Hunting us."

"Too young, I think." She passed me a stone axe. "Hope we don't have to kill him."

"Should we wake the others?"

"Not yet. Make us easier to scent." As if on cue, the Plathy walked directly away from the rock and stood, hands on hips, sniffing the air. His head wagged back and forth slowly, as if he were triangulating. He shuffled in a half-circle and stood looking in our direction.

"Stay still."

"He can't see us in the shadow."

"Maybe not." Their eyesight was more acute than ours, but they didn't have good night vision.

Behind us, someone woke up and sneezed. Mylab gave a little start and then began loping toward the cave.

"Damn it," Maria whispered. She stood up and huddled into the side of the cave entrance. "You get over there." I stationed myself opposite her, somewhat better hidden because of a projecting lip of rock.

Mylab slowed down a few meters from the cave entrance and walked warily forward, sniffing and blinking. Maria crouched, gripping her spear with both hands, for thrusting.

It was over in a couple of seconds, but my memory of it goes in slow motion: he saw Maria, or sensed her, and lumbered straight for her, claws out, growling. She thrust twice into his chest while I stepped forward and delivered a two-handed blow to the top of his head.

That axe would have cracked a human head from crown to jaw. Instead, it glanced off his thick skull and hit his shoulder, then spun out of my grip.

Shaking his head, he stepped around and swung a long arm at me. I was just out of range, staggering back; one claw opened up my cheek and the tip of my nose. Blood was spouting from two wounds in his chest. He stepped forward to finish me off and Maria plunged the spear into the back of his neck. The flint blade burst out under his chin in a spray of blood.

He stood staggering between us for a moment, trying to reach the spear shaft behind him. Two stones flew up from the rear of the cave; one missed, but the other hit his cheek with a loud crack. He turned and stumbled away down the slope, the spear bouncing grotesquely behind him.

The other four joined us at the cave entrance. Brenda, our doctor, looked at my wound and regretted her lack of equipment. So did I.

"Have to go after him," Derek said. "Kill him."

Maria shook her head. "He's still dangerous. Wait a few minutes; then we can follow the blood trail."

"He's dead," Brenda said. "His body just doesn't know it yet."

"Maybe so," Maria said, her shoulders slumping sadly. "Anyhow, we can't stay here. Hate to move during daylight, but we don't have any choice."

"We're not the only ones who can follow a blood trail," Herb said. He had a talent for stating the obvious.

We had gathered up our few weapons, the water bladders, and the food sack, to which we had just added five small batlike creatures, mostly fur and bone. None of us looked forward to being hungry enough to eat them.

The trail was easy to follow, several bright red spatters per meter. He had gone about three hundred meters before collapsing.

We found him lying behind a rock in a widening pool of blood, the spear sticking straight up. When I pulled it out he made a terrible gurgling sound. Brenda made sure he was dead.

Maria looked very upset, biting her lip, I think to keep tears away. She is a strange woman. Hard and soft. She treats the Plathys by the book but obviously has a sentimental streak toward them. I sort of like them too, but don't think I'd want to take one home with me.

Brenda's upset too, retching now. My fault; I should have offered to do the knife. But she didn't ask.

I'd better take point position. Stop recording now. Concentrate on not getting surprised.

MARIA

Back to the beginning. Quite hot when we were set down on the tropical mainland. It was the middle of the night and we worked quickly, with no lights (what I'd give for night glasses now), to set up our domed base.

In a way it's a misnomer to call it a "base," since we left it the next night, not to return for three and a half years. We thought. It was really just a staging area and a place where we would wait for pickup after our mission was ended. We really didn't foresee having to run back to it to hide from the Plathys.

It was halfheartedly camouflaged, looking like a dome of rock in the middle of a jungle terrain that featured no other domes of rock. To our knowledge at the time, no Plathy ever ventured that far north, so even that gesture toward noninterference was a matter of form rather than of actual caution. Now we know that some Plathys do go that far, on their rite-of-passage wanderings. So it's a good thing we didn't simply up a force field.

I think the closest terrestrial match to the biome there would be the jungles of the Amazon basin. Plus volcanoes, for a little extra heat and interest. Sort of a steam bath with a whiff of sulfur dioxide added to the rich smell of decaying vegetable matter. In the clearings, riots of extravagant flowers, most of which gave off the aroma of rotting meat.

For the first leg of our journey, we had modern energy weapons hidden inside conventional-looking spears and axes. It would have been more sporting to face the Mesozoic fauna with primitive weapons, but of course we had no interest in that sort of adventure. We often did run into creatures resembling the Deinonychus (Lower Cretaceous period)—about the size of a human but fast, and all claws and teeth. They travel in packs, evidently preying on the large placid herbivores. We never saw fewer than six in a group, and once were cornered by a pack of twenty. We had to kill all of them, our beams silently slashing them into steaming chunks of meat. None paid any attention to what was happening to his comrades but just kept advancing, bent low to the ground, claws out, teeth bared, roaring. Their meat tasted like chicken, but very tough.

It took us nine days to reach the coast, following a river. (Did I mention that days here are twenty-eight hours long? Our circadian rhythms had been adjusted accordingly, but there are other physiological factors. Mostly having to do with fatigue.) We found a conspicuous rock formation and buried our modern weapons a hundred meters to the north of it. Then we buried their power sources another hundred paces north. We kept one crazer for group defense, to be discarded before we reached the first island, but otherwise all we had was flint and stone and bicuspids with amazing memories.

We had built several boats with these tools during our training on Selva, but of course it was rather different here. The long day, and no comfortable cot to retire to at night. No tent to keep out the flying insects, no clean soft clothes in the morning, no this, no that. Terrible heat and a pervasive moldy smell that kept us all sniffling in spite of the antiallergenic drugs that our modified endocrine systems fed us. We did manage to get a fire going, which gave us security and roast fish and greatly simplified the boat-building. We felled two large trees and used fire to hollow them out, making outrigger canoes similar to the ones the Maori used to populate the sparse South Pacific. We weren't able to raise sails, though, since the Plathys don't have that technology. They wouldn't have helped much, anyway; summer was usually dead calm. We didn't look forward to rowing 250 kilometers in the subtropical heat. But we would do it systematically.

Herb was good at pottery, so I exempted him from boat-building in exchange for the fascinating job of crafting and firing dozens of water jugs. That was going to be our main survival problem, since it was not likely to rain during the couple of weeks we'd be at sea. Food was no problem; we could spear fish and probably birds (though eating a raw bird was not an experiment even I could look forward to) and also had a supply of smoked dinosaur.

I designed the boats so that either one would be big enough to carry all twelve of us, in case of trouble. As a further safeguard, we took a shake-down cruise, a night and a day of paddling and staying anchored near shore. We took our last fresh-water bath, topped off the jugs, loaded our gear, and cast off at sundown.

The idea had been to row all night, with ten minutes' rest each hour, and keep going for a couple of hours after sunup, for as long as we could reliably gauge our direction from the angle of the sun. Then anchor (the sea was nowhere more than ten or twelve meters deep) and hide from the sun all day under woven shades, fishing and sleeping and engaging in elevated discourse. Start paddling again when the sun was low enough to tell us where north was. It did go that way for several days, until the weather changed.

It was just a thin haze, but it was enough to stop us dead. We had no navigational instruments, relying on the dim triangle of stars that marked the south celestial pole. No stars, no progress.

This was when I found out that I had chosen my party well. When the sky cleared two nights later, there was no talk of turning back, though everyone was capable of counting the water jugs and doing long division. A few more days becalmed and we would be in real danger of dying from dehydration, unable to make landfall in either direction.

I figured we had been making about 25 kilometers per night. We rowed harder and cut the break time down to five minutes, and kept rowing an extra hour or so after dawn, taking a chance on dead reckoning.

Daytime became a period of grim silence. People who were not sleeping spent the time fishing the way I had taught them, Eskimo style (though those folks did it through a hole in the ice): arm cocked, spear raised, staring at one point slightly under the surface; when a fish approaches a handspan above that point, let fly the spear. No Eskimo ever applied greater concentration to the task; none of them was ever fishing for water as well as food. Over the course of days we learned which kinds of fish had flesh that could be sucked for moisture, and which had to be avoided for the salty blood that suffused their tissues.

We rationed water fairly severely, doling it out in measures that would allow us to lose one night out of three to haze. As it turned out, that never happened again, and when we sighted land, finally, there was water enough for another four days of short rations. We stifled the impulse to drink it all in celebration; we still had to find a stream.

I'd memorized maps and satellite photos, but terrain looks much different seen horizontally. It took several hours of hugging the shore before I could figure out where we were; fortunately, the landmark was a broad shallow river.

Before we threw away the crazer and its power source, we used it to light a torch. When the Plathys traveled, they carried hot coals from the previous night's fire, insulated in ash inside a basket of tough fiber. We would do the same, rather than spend an hour each day resolutely sawing two pieces of dry wood together. We beached the canoes and hauled them a couple of hundred meters inland, to a stand of bushes where they could be reasonably well camouflaged. Perhaps not much chance they would still be there after a full year, but it was better than simply abandoning them.

We walked inland far enough for there to be no trace of salt in the muddy river water, and cavorted in it like school children. Then Brenda and I built a fire while the others stalked out in search of food.

Game was fairly plentiful near the river, but we were not yet skilled hunters. There was no way to move quietly through the grass, which was shoulder-high and stiff. So the hunters who had the best luck were the ones who tiptoed up the bank of the stream. They came back with five good-sized snakes, which we skinned and cleaned and roasted on sticks. After two weeks of raw fish, the sizzling fatty meat was delicious, though for most of us it went through the gut like a dropped rock.

We made pallets of soft grass, and most of us slept well, though I didn't. Combination of worry and indigestion. I was awake enough to notice that various couples took advantage of the relative privacy of the riverbank, which made me feel vaguely jealous and deprived. I toyed with the idea of asking somebody, but instead waited for somebody to ask me, and wound up listening to contented snores half the night.

A personal note, to be edited out if this tooth survives for publication. Gabriel. All of us women had been studying his naked body for the past two weeks, quite remarkable in proportion and endowment, and I suppose the younger women had been even more imaginative than me in theorizing about it. So I was a little dismayed when he went off to the riverbank with a male, his Selvan crony Marcus. I didn't know at the time that their generation on Selva is very casual about such things, and at any rate I should have been anthropologist enough to be objective about it. But I have my own cultural biases, too, and (perhaps more to the point) so do the Terran males in the party. As a scientist, I can appreciate the fact that homosexuality is common and natural and only attitudes about it change. That attitude is not currently very enlightened on Earth; I resolved to warn them the next day to be discreet. (Neither of them is exclusively homosexual, as it turned out; they both left their pallets with women later in the night, Gabriel at least twice.)

We had rolled two large and fairly dry logs over the fire before bedding down, orienting them so as to take advantage of the slight breeze, and the fire burned brightly all night without attention. That probably saved our lives. When we broke camp in the morning and headed south, we found hundreds of tracks just downwind, the footpads of large catlike creatures. What an idiot I had been, not to post guards! Everyone else was sheepish at not having thought of it themselves. The numb routine and hard labor of the past two weeks had dulled us; now we were properly galvanized by fear. We realized that for all our survival training, we still had the instincts of city folk, and those instincts could kill us all.

This island is roughly circular, about a hundred kilometers in diameter, with a central crater lake. We would follow this river to the lake and then go counter-clockwise to the third stream and follow it to the southern shore. Then we would hop down an archipelago of small islands, another 80 kilometers, to the large island that was our final destination.

The scrub of the coastal lowland soon gave way to tangled forest, dominated by trees like Earth's banyan—a large central trunk with dozens or hundreds of subsidiary trunks holding up an extensive canopy of branches. It was impossible to tell where one tree's territory ended and another's began, but some of the largest must have commanded one or two ares of ground. Their bark was ashen white, relieved by splotches of rainbow lichen. No direct sunlight reached the ground through their dense foliage; only a few spindly bushes with pale yellow leaves pushed out of the rotting humus. Hard for anything to sneak up on us at ground level, but we could hear creatures moving overhead. I wondered whether the branches were strong enough to support the animals that had watched us the night before, and felt unseen cats' eyes everywhere.

We stopped to eat in a weird clearing. Something had killed one of the huge trees; its rotting stump dominated the clearing, and the remnants of its smaller trunks stood around like ghostly guardians, most of them dead but some of them starting to sprout green. I supposed one would eventually take over the space. After feasting on cold snake, we practiced spear-throwing, using the punky old stump as a target. I was the least competent, both in range and accuracy, which had also been the case on Selva. As a girl I'd shown no talent for athletics beyond jacks and playing doctor.

Suddenly all hell broke loose. Three cat-beasts leaped down from the forest canopy behind us and bounded in for the kill. I thrust out my spear and got one in the shoulder, the force of the impact knocking me over. Brenda killed it with a well-aimed throw. The other two checked their advance and circled warily. They dodged thrown spears; I shouted for everyone to hold their fire.

Brenda and I retrieved our weapons and, along with Gabriel and Martin, closed in on the beasts, moving them away from where the thrown spears lay. In a few seconds the twelve of us had them encircled, and I suddenly remembered the old English expression "having a tiger by the tail." The beasts were only about half the size of a human, but all muscle and teeth. They growled and snapped at us, heads wagging, saliva drooling.

I shouted "Now, Gab!"—he was the best shot—and he flung his spear at the closer one. It sank deep in the animal's side and it fell over, mewling and pawing the air. The other beast saw its chance and leaped straight at Gab, who instinctively ducked under it. It bounded off his back and sprang for the safety of the trees. Six or seven spears showered after it, but missed.

Gabriel had four puncture wounds under each shoulder blade from the cat's claws. Brenda washed them out thoroughly but decided against improvising a dressing out of leaf and vine. Just stay clean, always good advice.

We skinned and gutted the two cats and laboriously sliced their flesh into long thin strips for jerky. The old stump made a good smoky fire for the purpose. As darkness fell, we built another bright fire next to it.

I set up a guard schedule, with teams of three each standing three-hour shifts while the rest slept, but none of us slept too soundly. Over the crackle of the fires I was sure I could hear things moving restlessly in the woods. If they were there, though, they weren't bold enough to attack. During my watch a couple of dog-sized animals with large eyes came to the periphery of the clearing, to feast on the cat-beasts' entrails. We threw sticks at them but they just looked at us, and left after they had eaten their fill.

If my estimate of our progress was correct, we had about 30 kilometers of deep woods to go, until the topography opened up into rolling hills of grassland. Everyone agreed that we should try to make it in one push. There was no guarantee we could find another clearing, and nobody wanted to spend a night under the canopy. So at first light, we bundled the jerky up inside a stiff catskin and headed south.

As we moved along the river the nature of the trees changed, the banyans eventually being replaced by a variety of smaller trees—damn! Two of them!

BRENDA

I wasn't paying close attention, still grieving over Mylab—actually, grieving for myself, for having committed murder. I've had patients die under my care, but the feeling isn't even remotely similar. His eyes, when I drew the flint across his throat—they went bright with pain and then immediately dull.

We'd been walking for about an hour after leaving the cave, picking our way down the north slope of the mountain, when Maria, in the lead, suddenly squatted down and made a silent gesture. We all crouched and moved forward.

Ahead of us on the trail, two adult Plathys sat together with their backs to us, talking quietly while they ate. They were armed with spear and broadaxe and knives. I doubted that the six of us could take even one of them in a face-to-face combat.

Maria stared, probably considering ambush, and then motioned for us to go back up the trail. I kept looking over my shoulder, every small scuff and scrape terribly amplified in my mind, expecting at any moment to see the two huge brutes charging after us. But their eating noise must have masked the sound of our retreat.

We crept back a couple of hundred meters to a fork in the trail and cautiously made our way down a roughly parallel track, going as fast as silence would allow. The light breeze was coming from behind us; we wanted to be past the Plathys—downwind of them—before they finished eating. We passed close enough to hear their talking, but didn't see them.

After about a kilometer the trail disappeared. We had to pick our way down a steep defile and couldn't help making noise, dislodging pebbles that often cascaded into small rattling avalanches. We were only a few meters from the bottom of the cliff when the two Plathys appeared above us. They discussed the situation loudly for a few moments—using the hunting language, which none of us had been allowed to learn—and then set aside their weapons in favor of rocks.

When I saw what they were doing I slid right to the bottom, willing to take a few abrasions rather than present too tempting a target. Most of the others did the same. Herb took a glancing blow to the head and fell backward, landing roughly. I ran over to him, afraid he was unconscious. Gab beat me to him and hauled him roughly to his feet; he was dazed but awake. We each took an arm and staggered away as fast as we could, zigzagging as Gab muttered "go left" and "right," so as to present a more difficult target. I sustained one hard blow to the left buttock, which knocked me down. It was going to make sitting uncomfortable, but we wouldn't have to worry about that for a while.

SEASONS

We were lucky the Plathys hadn't brought rope, as a larger hunting party in the mountains would have done. They are rather clumsy rock climbers (though with their long arms they can run up a steep slope very fast). One of them started down after us, but after a nearly fatal slip he scrambled back up.

We pressed our advantage, such as it was. To pursue us they would have to make a detour of a couple of kilometers, and at any rate we could go downhill faster than they could. It seemed likely that they would instead go back to their main group to report our whereabouts, and then all of them try to catch us in the veldt. On level ground they could easily run us down, once they caught our scent.

Maria, xenologist to the end, remarked how lucky we were that they had never developed the idea of signal drums. It is strange, since they use such a variety of percussion instruments in their music and dancing.

Such music and dancing. They seemed so human.

Our only chance for survival was to try to confuse them by splitting up. Maria breathlessly outlined a plan as we hurried down the slope. When we reached the valley we would get a bearing on the stream we'd followed here, then go six different ways, rendezvousing at the stream's outlet to the sea three days later; at nightfall, whoever was there would cross to the next island. Even at high tide it should be possible to wade most of the way.

I suggested we make it three pairs rather than six loners, but Maria pointed out that two of us really didn't stand a much better chance against an armed Plathy than one; in either case, the only way we could kill them would be by stealth. Murder. I told her I didn't think I would be able to do it, and she nodded. Probably thinking that she would have said the same thing a few days ago.

We stopped for a few minutes to rest on a plateau overlooking the veldt, where Maria pointed out the paths she wanted each of us to take. Herb and Derek would go the most direct route, more or less north, but twining in and out of each other's path so as to throw off the scent. Gab, being the fastest, would run halfway around the mountain, then make a broad arc north. She would go straight northeast for about half the distance and then cut back; Martin would do the opposite. I was to head due west, straight for the stream, and follow it down, in and out of the water. All of us were to "leave scent" at the places where our paths diverged the most from straight north.

A compass would have been nice. At night we'd be okay if it didn't cloud up again, but during the day we'd just have to follow our direction bump through the tall grass. I was glad I had an easy path.

Not all that easy. The three water bladders went to the ones who would be farthest from the stream, of course. So, I had to go a good half day without water. Assuming I didn't get lost. We divided the food and scrambled down in six different directions.

MARIA

Where was I? Coming here, we got around the crater lake without incident, but the descent to the shore was more difficult than I had anticipated. It was not terribly steep, but the dense undergrowth of vines and bushes impeded our progress. After two days we emerged on the shore, covered with scratches and bruises. At least we'd encountered no large fauna.

(By this time I had a great deal of sympathy for the lazybones minority on the Planning Committee who'd contended that we were being overly cautious in putting the base so far from the Plathy island. They'd recommended we put it on this island, with only 80 kilometers of shallow sea separating us from our destination. I'd voted, along with the majority, for the northern mainland, partly out of a boneheaded desire for adventure.)

What we faced was a chain of six small islands and countless sandbars, in a puddle of a sea that rarely was more than a meter deep. We knew from Garcia's experience that a boat would be useless. With vine and driftwood we lashed together a raft to carry our weapons and provisions, filled the water jugs, and splashed south.

It was tiring. The sand underfoot was firm, but sloshing through the shallow water was like walking with heavy weights attached to your ankles. We had to make good progress, though; the only island we were sure had fresh water was 40 kilometers south, halfway.

We made a good 25 kilometers the first day, dragging our weary bones up onto an island that actually had trees. Marcus and Gab went off in search of water, finding none, while the rest of us gathered driftwood for a fire or tried lackadaisically to fish. Nanci speared a gruesome thing that no one would touch, including her, and nobody else caught anything. Susan and Brenda dug up a couple of dozen shellfish, though, which obediently popped open when roasted. They tasted like abalone with sulfur sauce.

As we were settling in for the night, we met our first Plathy. She walked silently up to the fire, as if it were the most normal thing in the world to happen upon a dozen creatures from another planet. She was young, only a little larger than me (now, of course, we know she was on her Walk North). When I stood up and tried to say "Welcome, sister" in the female language, she screamed and ran. We heard her splashing away for some time, headed for the next county.

The next day was harder, though we didn't have as far to go. Some geological gremlin had raked channels across our path, new features since Garcia's mission, and several times we had to swim as much as 200 meters before slogging again. (Thank the gods for Gab, who would gamely paddle out toward the horizon in search of solid ground, and for Marcus, who could swim strongly enough one-handed to tow the raft.)

It was dark by the time we got to the water hole island, and we had lost our coals to an inopportune wave. We were cold and terminally wrinkled, but so parched from sucking salt water that we staggered around like maniacs, even laughing like maniacs, searching blindly for the artesian well that Garcia's records said was there. Finally Joanna found it, stumbling in headfirst and coming up choking and laughing. We all gorged ourselves, wallowing. In my case the relief was more than mouth and throat and stomach. At sundown I'd squatted in the shallows and squeezed out piss dark with stringy blood. That scared me. But the fresh water evidently cleared it up.

There were no more surprises the next two days of island-hopping, except the pleasant one of finding another water source. We couldn't find any wood dry enough to start a fire with, but it didn't get all that cold at night.

Late afternoon of the second day we slogged into the swamp that was the northern edge of the Plathy island. The dominant form of life was a kind of bilious spotted serpent that would swim heavily away as we approached. We were out of food but didn't go after them. Before nightfall the swamp had given way to rather damp forest, but we found dry dead wood suspended in the branches and spun up a bright fire. We dug up a kind of tuber that Garcia's group had identified as edible and roasted them. Then tried to sleep in spite of the noises in the darkness. At first light we moved out fast, knowing that in 30 or so kilometers the forest would give way to open grassland.

The change from forest to veldt was abrupt. We were so happy to be out of the shadow of it—funny that in my present situation I feel exactly the opposite; I feel exposed, and hurry toward the concealment of the thick underbrush and close-spaced heavy trunks. I feel so visible, so vulnerable. And I probably won't find water until I get there. I'm going to turn off this tooth for a few minutes and try not to scream.

All right. Let me see. On our way to the Plathys, we walked across the veldt for two days. Food was plentiful; the *zamri* are like rabbits, but slow. For some reason they like to cluster around the *ecivrel* bush, a thorny maloderous plant, and all we would have to do to bag several of them was form a loose circle around the bush and move in, clubbing them as they tried to escape. I would like to find one now. Their blood is sweet.

There's a Plathy song:

> *Sim garlish a sim garlish farla tob—!ka.*
> *Soo pan du mairly garlish ezda tob—!ka.*
> *Oe vairly tem se garlish mizga mer—!ka.*
> *Garlish—!ka. Tem se garlish—!ka.*

Translating it into my own language doesn't work well:

> *Sacar sangre y sacar sangre para vivir—sí.*
> *En sangre damos muerte y sacamos vida—sí.*
> *Alabamos la sangre de vida que usted nos da—sí.*
> *Sangre—sí. Sangre de vida—sí.*

Herb, who's a linguist, did a more accurate rendering in English:

> *Take blood and take blood for living—yes.*
> *In blood we give death and take living—yes.*
> *We worship the blood of life you give us—yes.*
> *Blood—yes. Blood of life—yes!*

But there is really no translation. Except in the love of sweet blood.

I've become too much like them. My human instinct is to keep running and, when I can't run, to hide. But a strong Plathy feeling is to stand in a clearing and shout for them. Let them come for me; let me die in a terrible ecstasy of tearing flesh and cracking bone. Let them suck my soft guts so I can live in them—

God. I have to stop. You'll think I'm crazy. Maybe I'm getting there. Why won't it rain?

SEASONS

GABRIEL

Turned on the tooth while I sit by the water and rest. Maria wants us to record as much as we can, in case. Just in case.

Why the hell did I sign up for this? I was going to switch out of xenology and work for an advanced degree in business. But she came on campus recruiting, with all those exotic Earth women. They're just like women anywhere, big surprise. Except her. She is truly weird. Listen to this, tooth: I want her. She is such a mystery. Maybe if we live through this I'll get up the courage to ask. Plumb her, so to speak; make her open up to me, so to speak; get to the bottom of her, so to speak. A nice bottom for a woman of her advanced years.

How can I think of sex at a time like this? With a woman twice my age. If somebody on a follow-up expedition finds this tooth in a fossilized pile of Plathy shit, please excuse my digression. If I live to have the tooth extracted and played back, I don't think it will make much difference to my professional reputation. I'll be writing poetry and clerking for my father's export firm.

I ran around the mountain. Collapsed once and slept for I don't know how long. Got up and ran to the river. Drank too much. Here I sit, too bloated to move. If a Plathy finds me I won't be a fun meal.

I was really getting to like them, before they turned on us. They seemed like such vegetables until it started to get cold. Then it was as if they had turned into a different species. With hindsight, it's no big surprise that they should change again. Or that they should be capable of such terrible violence. We were lulled by their tenderness toward each other and their friendliness toward us, and the subtle alien grace of their dancing and music and sculpture. We should have been cautious, having witnessed the two other changes: the overnight transformation into completely sexual creatures and the slower evolution from lumpish primitives to charming creators, when the snow started to fall.

The change was obvious after the first heavy snowfall, which left about half a meter of the stuff on the ground. The Plathys started singing and laughing spontaneously. They rolled up their *maffas* and stored them in a cave and began playing in the snow—or at least it seemed like play, they were so carefree and childlike about it. Actually, they were building a city of snow.

The individual buildings, *lacules*, were uniform domes built up from blocks of snow. Maria called them igloos, after a similar primitive structure on Earth, and the name stuck. Even some of the Plathys used it.

There were twenty-nine domes arranged in a circle, eventually connected by tunnels as the snow deepened. The inside of the circle was kept clear, the snow being constantly shoveled into the spaces between the domes. The net result was a high circular wall that kept the wind out. Later we learned it would also keep people *in*.

They had a fire going most of the time in the middle of the circle, which served as a center for their daytime activities: music, dance, tumbling, athletic competition, and storytelling (which seemed to be a kind of fanciful history combined with moral instruction). Even with the sun up, the temperature rarely got above freezing, but the Plathys thrived in the cold. They would sit for hours on the ice, watching the performances, wearing only their kilts. We wore leggings and boots, jackets, and hats. The Plathys would only dress up if they had to go out at night (which they often did, for reasons they couldn't or wouldn't explain to us), when the temperature dropped to forty or fifty below.

I went out at night a couple of times, but I didn't go far. Too easy to get lost. If it was clear you could see the ring of igloos ghostly in the starlight, but if there was any weather you couldn't see your own hand in front of your face.

The igloos were surprisingly warm, though the only source of heat was one or two small oil lamps, plus metabolism. That metabolism also permeated everything with the weird smell of Plathy sweat, which resembled rotten bananas. Our own dome got pretty high with the aroma of unwashed humans; Plathys would rarely visit for more than a minute or two.

Seems odd to me that the Plathys didn't continue some of their activities, like music and storytelling, during the long nights. Some of them did routine housekeeping chores, mending and straightening, while others concentrated on sculpture. The sculptors seemed to go into a kind of trance, scraping patiently away at their rock or wood with teeth and claws. I never saw one use a tool, though they did carve and whittle when making everyday objects. I once watched an elder through the whole process. He sorted through a pile of rocks and logs until he found a rock he liked. Then he sat back and studied it from every angle, staring for more than an hour before beginning. Then he closed his eyes and started gnawing and scratching. I don't think he opened his eyes until he was done working. When I asked him if he had opened his eyes, he said, "Of course not."

Over the course of six nights he must have spent about sixty hours on the stone. When he finished, it was a delicate lacy abstraction. The other Plathys came by, one at a tune, to compliment him on it—the older ones offering gentle criticism—and after everyone had seen it, he threw it outside for the children to play with. I retrieved it and kept it, which he thought was funny. It had served its purpose, as he had served his purpose for it: finding its soul (its "face inside") and releasing it.

I shouldn't talk about sculpture; that's Herb's area of expertise. The assignment Maria gave me was to memorize the patterns of the athletic competitions. (I was an athlete in school, twice winning the Hombre de Hierro award for my district.) There's not much to say about it, though. How high can you jump, how fast can you run, how far can you spit. That was an interesting one. They can spit with great force. Another interesting one was wood-eating. Two contestants are given similar pieces of wood—kindling, a few centimeters wide by half a meter long—and they crunch away until one has consumed the whole thing. Since the other doesn't have to continue eating afterward, it's hard to say which one is the actual winner. (When I first saw the contest, I thought they must derive some pleasure from eating wood. When I asked one about it, though, he said it tastes terrible and hurts at both ends. I can imagine.)

Another painful sport is hitting. It's unlike boxing in that there's no aggression, no real sense of a fight. One contestant hits the other on the head or body with a club. Then he (or she) hands the club to the opponent who returns the blow precisely. The contest goes on until one of them drops, which can take several hours.

You ask them why they do this and most of them will not understand—"why" is a really difficult concept for Plathys; they have no word for it—but when you do get a response it's on the order of "This is part of life." Which is uninformative but not so alien. Why do humans lift heavy weights or run till they drop or beat each other senseless in a ring?

Oh my God. Here comes one.

MARIA

Finally, water. I wish there were some way to play back this tooth and edit it. I must have raved for some time, before I fell unconscious a few kilometers from here. I woke up with a curious *zamri* licking my face. I broke its neck and tore open its throat and drank deeply. That gave me the strength to get here. I drank my fill and then moved one thousands steps downstream, through the cold water, where I now sit concealed behind a bush, picking morsels from the *zamri's* carcass. When I get back to Earth I think I'll become a vegetarian.

This is very close to the place where we met our first cooperative Plathy. There were three of them, young; two ran away when they spotted us, but the third clapped a greeting, and when we clapped back he cautiously joined us. We talked for an hour or so, the other two watching from behind trees.

They were from the Tumlil family, providentially; the family that had hosted Garcia's expedition. This male was too young to actually remember the humans, but he had heard stories about them. He explained about the Walk North. In their third or fourth year, every Plathy goes off on his own, going far enough north to get to where "things are different." He brings back something odd. The elders then rule on how powerful the oddness of the thing is, and according to that power, the youngster is assigned his preliminary rank in the tribe.

(They know that this can eventually make the difference between life and death. The higher up you start, the more likely you are to wind up an elder. Those who aren't elders are allowed to die when they can no longer provide for themselves; elders are fed and protected indefinitely.)

Most of them travel as far as the crater lake island, but a few go all the way to the northern mainland. That was the ambition of the one we were talking to. I interrogated him as to his preparations for a boat, food, and water, and he said a boat would be nice but not necessary, and the sea was full of food and water. He figured he could swim it in three hands of days, twelve. Unless he was chaffing me, they can evidently sleep floating and drink salt water. That will complicate our escape, if they keep pursuing.

I take it that the three of them were cheating a bit by banding together. He repeatedly stressed that they would be going their separate ways as soon as they got to the archipelago. I hope they stayed together the whole way. I'd hate to face that forest alone. Maybe I'll have to, though.

Before he left he gave us directions to his family, but we'd decided to at least start out with a different one from Garcia's, in the interests of objectivity and to see how much information traveled from family to family. Little or none, it turned out. Our Camchai family knew about the Tumlils, since they shared the same area of veldt during the late summer, but none of the Tumlils had mentioned that ten hairless dwarfs had spent one winter with them.

After two days of relatively easy travel, we found the Camchais in their late-summer habitat, the almost treeless grassland at the foot of the southern mountains. Duplicating the experience of Garcia's group, we found ourselves unexcitedly welcomed into the tribe: we were shown where the food was, and various Plathys scrounged up the framework and hides to cobble together a *maffa* for us. Then we joined the family in their typical summertime activity, sitting around.

After a few weeks of trying to cajole information out of them, we witnessed the sudden explosion of sexual activity described earlier. Then they rested some more, five or six days, and began to pull up stakes.

Their supply of stored food was getting low and there was no easy hunting left in that part of the veldt, so they had to move around the mountains to the seashore and a wretched diet of fish.

The trek was organized and led by Kalyym, who by virtue of being the youngest elder was considered chief for such practical matters. She was one of the few Plathys we met who wore ornaments; hers was a necklace of dinosaur teeth she'd brought back from her Walk North, the teeth of a large carnivore. She claimed to have killed it, but everyone knew that was a lie, and respected her for being capable of lying past puberty.

It was significantly cooler on the other side of the mountains, with a chilly south wind in the evening warning that fall had begun and frost was near. The Plathys still lazed through midday, but in the mornings and evenings they fished with some energy and prepared for the stampede. They stockpiled driftwood and salt and sat around the fire chipping extra flints, complaining about eating fish and looking forward to bounty.

We spent several months in this transitional state, until one morning a lookout shouted a happy cry and the whole family went down to the shore with clubs. Each adult took about three meters of shoreline, the children standing behind them with knives.

We could hear them before we could see them—the *tolliws*, rabbit-sized mammals that chirped like birds. They sounded like what I imagine a distant cloud of locusts sounded like, in old times. The Plathys laughed excitedly.

Then they were visible, one whirring mass from horizon to horizon, like an island-sized mat of wriggling wet fur. Mammals schooling like fish. They spilled on to dry land and staggered into the line of waiting Plathys.

At first there was more enthusiasm than result. Everybody had to pick up his first *tolliw* and bite off its head and extol its gustatory virtues to the others, in as gruesome a display of bad table manners as you could find anywhere in the Confederación. Then, after a few too-energetic smashings, they settled into a productive routine: with the little animals milling around their ankles in an almost continuous stream, the adult would choose a large and healthy-looking one and club it with a backhand swipe that lofted the stunted animal in an arc, back to where the child waited with the knife. The child would slit the animal's throat and set it on a large hide to bleed, and then wait happily for the next one. When the carcass had bled itself nearly dry, the child would give it a squeeze and transfer it to a stack on the sand, eventually working in a smooth assemblyline fashion. The purpose of the systematic bleeding was to build up on the hide layers of coagulated blood that, when dry, would be cut up into squares and used for snacks.

Large predators were scattered here and there through the swimming herd, fawn-colored animals resembling terrestrial kangaroos, but with fingerlong fangs overhanging the lower jaw. Most of them successfully evaded the Plathys, but occasionally one would be surrounded and clubbed to death amid jubilant screeching and singing.

This went on for what seemed to be a little less than two hours, during which time the oldest elders busied themselves filling a long trench with wood and collecting wet seaweed. When the last stragglers of the school crawled out of the water and followed the others down the beach, there were sixty pyramidal stacks of furry bodies, each stack nearly as tall as a Plathy, ranged down the beach. We could hear the family west of us laughing and clubbing away.

(The statistics of the process bothered me. They seemed to have killed about one out of a hundred of the beasts and then sent the remainder on down the beach, where the next family would presumably do the same, and so on. There were more than a hundred families, we knew. Why didn't they run out of *tolliws*? For once, Tybru gave me a straightforward answer: they take turns. Only sixteen families "gather" the creatures during each migration, alternating in a rotating order that had been fixed since the dawn of time. The other families took advantage of the migrations of other animals; she was looking forward to two years hence, when it would be their turn for the *jukha* slaughter. They were the tastiest, and kept well.)

By this time it was getting dark. I had been helping the elders set up the long trench of bonfires; now we lit them, and with the evening chill coming in over the sea I was grateful for the snapping flames.

Tybru demonstrated the butchering process so we could lend a hand. Selected internal organs went into hides of brine for pickling; then the skin was torn off and the yellow layer of fat that clung to it was scraped

190

into clay jars for reducing to oil. More fat was flensed from the body, and then the meat was cut off in thin strips, which were draped over green sticks for smoking. Alas, they had no way to preserve the brains, so most of the Plathys crunched and sucked all night while they worked.

We weren't strong enough or experienced enough to keep up with even the children, but we gamely butchered through the night, trying not to cut ourselves on the slippery flint razors, working in the light of guttering torches. The seaweed produced an acrid halogen-smelling smoke that Tybru claimed was good for the lungs. Maybe because of its preservative effect.

The sun came up on a scene out of Hieronymus Bosch: smoke swirling over bloody sands littered with bones and heaps of entrails, Plathys and people bloodsmeared and haggard with fatigue. We splashed into the icy water and scrubbed off dried blood with handfuls of sand, then stood in the stinging smoke trying to thaw out.

It was time to pack up and go. Already the rich smell of fresh blood was underlaid with a whiff of rot; insects were buzzing, and hardshell scavengers were scuttling up onto the beach. When the sun got high the place would become unlivable, even by Plathy standards.

We rolled up the smoked meat and blood squares into the raw scraped hides, which would later be pegged out and dried in the sun, and followed a trail up into the mountains. We set up our *maffas* on a plateau about a thousand meters up and waited placidly for the snow.

Someone coming.

DEREK

I can no longer view them as other than dangerous animals. They mimic humanity—no, what I mean is that *we* interpret in human terms the things they do. The animal things they do. Maria, I'm sorry. I can't be a scientist about this, not any more. Not after what I just saw.

Herb and I were supposed to crisscross, going northeast a thousand steps, then northwest a thousand, and so forth. That was supposed to confuse them. They caught Herb.

I heard the scream. Maybe half a kilometer away. I should have run, knowing there was nothing I could do, but Herb and I've been close since school. Undergraduate. Were close. And there he—

Two of them had run him down in a small clearing, killed him and taken off his head. They were, one of them was...I can't.

I hid in the underbrush. All I had was a club there was nothing I could do. One of them was eating his, his private parts. The other was scooping him out, curious, dissecting him. I ran away. It's a wonder they didn't—

Oh shit. Here they come.

GABRIEL

I think my wrist is broken. Maybe just sprained. But I killed the son of a bitch. He came around a bend in the river and I was on him with the spear. Element of surprise. I got him two good ones in the thorax before he grabbed me—where are their goddamned vital organs? A human would've dropped dead. He grabbed me by the wrist and slammed me to the ground. I rolled away, retrieved the spear, and impaled him as he jumped on me. He made a lot of noise and finally decided to die, after scraping my arm pretty well. For some reason he wasn't armed. Thank God. He was Embrek, the one who taught me how to fish. We got along so well. What the hell happened?

It was the first time it rained instead of snowing. All the music and everything stopped. They moped around all day and wouldn't talk. When it got dark they went wild.

They burst into our igloo, four of them, and started ripping off our clothes. Nanci, Susan, and Marcus resisted and were killed right there. One bite each. The rest of us were stripped and led or carried out into the cold, into the center of the compound. The cheerful fire was black mud now, starting to glaze with ice.

All the family except the oldest elders were there, standing around like zombies. No one spoke; no one took notice of anybody else. We all stood naked in the darkness. Kalyym eventually brought out a single oil candle, so we could be mocked by its flickering warm light.

The nature of the rite became clear after a couple of hours. It was a winnowing process. If you lost consciousness the Plathys would gather around you and try to poke and kick you awake. If you stood up they would go back to ignoring you. If you stayed down, you would die. After a certain number of pokes and kicks, Kalyym or some other elder would tear open the thorax in a single rip. Even worse than the blood was the sudden rush of steam into the cold air. Like life escaping the body.

Then they would feed.

We knew we wouldn't last the night. But the slippery walls were impossible to scale, and the largest Plathys stood guard at every entrance to the ring of igloos.

After some whispered discussion, we agreed we had to do the obvious: rush the Plathy who stood guard in front of our own igloo. The ones who survived would rush in, quickly gather weapons and clothing, and try to make it out the back entrance before the Plathys could react. Then run for the caves.

We were lucky. We rushed the guard from six different directions. Crouching to slash at Derek, he turned his back to me, and I leaped, striking him between the shoulders with both feet. He sprawled face down in the mud, and didn't get up. We scrambled into the igloo and I stood guard with a spear while the others gathered up things. A couple of Plathys stuck their heads in the entrance and snarled, but they evidently didn't want to risk the spear.

We weren't immediately followed, and for the first hour or so we made good time. Then it started to rain again, which slowed us down to a crawl. With no stars, we had to rely on Maria's sense of direction, which is pretty good. We found the caves just at dawn, and got a few hours' sleep before Mylab found us and we had to kill him.

How long is this phase going to last? If it goes as long as the summer or winter phases, they're sure to track us down. We may be safe inside the dome, if we can get that far—

Noise...Maria!

MARIA

I might as well say it. It might be of some interest. None of us is going to live anyhow. I'm beyond embarrassment, beyond dignity. Nothing to be embarrassed about anyhow, not really.

The thing that was splashing up the stream turned out to be Gabriel. I ran out of hiding and grabbed him, hugged him; we were both a little hysterical about it. Anyhow he got hard and we took care of it, and then we went back to my hiding place and took care of it again. It was the first happy thing that's happened to me in a long time. Now I'm watching him sleep fighting the impulse to wake him up to try for thirds. One more time before we die.

It's a strange state, feeling like a girl again, all tickled and excited inside, and at the same time feeling doomed. Like a patient with a terminal disease, high on medicine and mortality. There's no way we can outrun them. They'll sniff us down and tear us apart, maybe today, maybe tomorrow. They'll get us. Oh, wake up, Gab.

Be rational. This ferocity is just another change of state. They don't know what they're doing. Like the sex and birth phases. Tomorrow they may go back to being bovine sweet things. Or artisans again. Or maybe they'll discover the wheel for a week. What a weird, fucked-up bunch of...

There must be some survival value in it. Certainly it serves to cull the weakest members out. And killing most of the females before puberty compensates for the size of the litters—or could the size of the litters be a response to the scarcity of females? Lamarckism either way. Can't think straight.

At any rate it certainly can't be instinctive behavior in regard to us, since we aren't part of their normal environment. Maybe we've unknowingly triggered aberrant behavior. Stress response. Olfactory catalyst. Violent displacement activity. Who knows? Maybe whoever reads this tooth will be able to make some sense of it. You will excuse me for the time being. I have to wake him up.

BRENDA

Maria and Gab were waiting for me when I got to the mouth of the river. Gab has a badly sprained wrist; I splinted and bound it. His grip is still good, and fortunately he's left-handed. Maria's okay physically, just a little weak, but I wonder about her psychological state. Almost euphoric, which hardly seems appropriate.

We waited an extra half day, but the others are either dead or lost. They can catch up with us at the dome. We have axe, spear, and two knives. Gab turned one of the knives into a spear for me. Two water bladders. We filled the bladders, drank to saturation, and waded out into the sea.

The water seems icy cold, probably more than ten degrees colder than when we walked through it before. Numb from the waist down after a few minutes. When the water is shallow or you get to walk along a sandbar, sensation returns, deep stinging pain. It was a good thing we'd found that second water island; only 10 kilometers of wading and limping along the wet sand.

We'd rolled up our furs and shouldered them, so they were fairly dry. Couldn't risk a fire (and probably couldn't have found enough dry stuff to make one), so we just huddled together for warmth. We whispered, mapping out our strategy, such as it was, and kept an eye out to the south. Though if we'd been followed by even one Plathy we'd be pretty helpless.

Thirty kilometers to the next water hole. We decided to stay here for a couple of days, eating the sulfurous oysters and regaining strength. It would have to be a fast push, going all the way on less than five liters of water.

In fact we stayed four days. Gab came down with bad diarrhea, and we couldn't push on until his body could hold fluid. It was just as well. We were all bone-tired and stressed to the limit.

The first night we just collapsed in a hamster pile and slept like the dead. The next day we gathered enough soft dry grass to make a kind of mattress, and spread our furs into a piecemeal blanket. We still huddled for warmth and reassurance, and after a certain amount of nonverbal discussion, Gab unleashed his singular talent on both of us impartially.

That was interesting. Something Maria said indicated that Gab was new to her. I'd thought that nothing—male, female, or Plathy—was safe around him. Maybe Maria's strength intimidated him, or her age. Or being the authority figure. That must be why she was in such a strange mood when I caught up with them. Anyhow, I'm glad for her.

Gab entertained us with poetry and songs in three languages. It's odd that all three of us know English. Maria had to learn it for her study of the Eskimos, and I did a residency in Massachusetts. Gab picked it up just for the hell of it, along with a couple of other Earth languages, besides Spanish and Pan-Swahili, and all three Selvan dialects. He's quite a boy. Maria was the only one who could speak Plathy better than he. They tried duets on the blood songs and shit songs, but it doesn't sound too convincing. The consonants !ka and !ko you just can't do unless you have teeth like beartraps.

The stress triggered my period a week early. When we fled the igloo I hadn't had time to gather up my moss pads and leather strap contraption, so I just sort of dripped all over the island. It obviously upset Gab, but I'm not going to waddle around with a handful of grass for his precious male sensibilities. (His rather gruesome sickness didn't do much for *my* sensibilities, either, doctor or no.)

We spent the last day in futile basket weaving, trying to craft something that would hold water for more than a few minutes. We all knew that it could be done, but it couldn't be done by us, not with the grass on the island. Maria did manage to cobble together a bucket out of her kilt by working a framework of sticks around it. That will double our amount of water, but she'll have to cradle it with both arms.

Thirty kilometers. I hope we make it.

MARIA

We were almost dead from thirst and exposure by the time we got to the water hole island. We had long since lost track of our progress, since the vegetation on the islands was radically different from summer's, and some of the shorelines had changed. We just hoped each large island would be the one, and finally one was.

Alongside the water hole we found the fresh remains of a fire. At first that gave us a little hope, since it was possible that the rest of our team had leapfrogged us while Gab was convalescing. But then we found the dropping place, and the excrement was Plathy. Three or four of them, by the looks of it. A day or so ahead of us.

We didn't know what to do. Were they hunters searching us out, or a group on their Walk North? If the latter, it would probably be smartest to stay here for a couple of days; let them get way ahead. If they were hunters, though, they might still be on the island, and it would be smarter for us to move on.

Gab didn't think they were hunters, since they would've overtaken us earlier and made lunchmeat out of us. I wasn't sure. There were at least three logical paths through the archipelago; they might have taken one of the others. Since they could drink salt water, they didn't have to go out of their way to get to the island we first stopped at.

None of us felt up to pushing on. The going would be easier, but it would still be at least ten hours of sloshing through cold water on small rations. So we compromised.

In case there were hunters on the island, we made camp on the southern tip (the wind was from the north) in a small clearing almost completely surrounded by thick brambles. If we had to stand and fight, there was really only one direction they could approach us from. We didn't risk a fire and sent only one person out at a time for water or shellfish. One stayed awake while the other two slept.

Our precautions wouldn't amount to much if there actually were three or four of them and they all came after us. But they might be split up, and both Gab and I had proved they could be killed, at least one at a time.

We spent two uneventful days regaining our strength. About midday on the third, Gab went out for water and came back with Derek.

He was half dead from exposure and hunger. We fed him tiny bits of shellfish in water, and after a day of intermittent sleeping and raving, he came around enough to talk.

He'd seen two Plathys in the process of eating Herb. They ran after him, but he plunged blindly into brambles (his arms and lower legs were covered with festering scratches), and they evidently didn't follow him very far. He'd found the river and run out to sea in a blind panic. Got to the first water island and lay there for days. He couldn't remember whether he'd eaten.

Then he heard Plathys, or thought he did, and took off north as fast as he could manage. He didn't remember getting here. Gab found him unconscious at the water's edge.

So now the plan is to wait here two or three more days, until Derek feels strong enough for the next push.

Hardest part still ahead. Even if we don't run into Plathys. What if the boats are gone?

GABRIEL

We didn't see any further signs of the Plathys. After four days Derek was ready to go. For a full day we drank all the water we could hold, and then at sundown set out.

There was only one place so deep we had to swim. I tried to carry Maria's water basket, sidestroking, but it didn't work. So the last 20 or 25 kilometers we were racing against the dwindling supply of water in the two bladders.

At first light there was still no sight of land, and we had to proceed by dead reckoning. (The Plathys evidently don't have this problem; they're somehow sensitive to the planet's magnetic field, like some Selvan migrating birds.) We saved a few spoonfuls of water to drink when we finally sighted land.

We went along in silence for an hour or so, and then Derek had a brainstorm. We were scanning the horizon from only a meter or so above sea level; if someone stood on my shoulders, he could see twice as far. Derek was the tallest. I ducked under and hoisted him up. He could stay balanced only for a second, but it did work; he saw a green smudge off to the left. We adjusted our course and slogged on with new energy. When all of us could see the smudge, we celebrated with a last sip of water.

Of course the stream that would be our guide uphill was nowhere to be seen. We stumbled ashore and did manage to lick enough moisture from foliage to partly allay our terrible thirst, though the bitter flavor soured my stomach.

We marked the spot with a large X in the sand and split into pairs, Brenda and I going one direction and Maria and Derek going the other, each with a water bladder to fill when one pair found the river. We agreed to turn back after no more than ten thousand steps. If neither pair found the river within 10 kilometers of our starting place, we'd just work our way uphill toward the crater lake. It would be slower going than following the stream's course, but we could probably manage it, licking leaves and splitting some kinds of stalks for water. And we'd be less likely to run into an ambush, if there were hunters waiting ahead. I wasn't looking forward to it, though. Coming down had been enough trouble.

We were lucky. In a sense. Brenda and I stumbled on the stream less than two kilometers from where we started. We drank deeply and jogged back to catch up with Maria and Derek.

We made an overnight camp some distance from the stream and foraged for food. There were no fish in the shallows, and none of the sulfurous oysters. There were small crabs, but they were hard to catch and had only a pinch of meat. We wound up digging tubers, which were not very palatable raw but would sustain us until we got to the lake, where fish were plentiful.

It might have been a little safer to travel by night, but we remembered how the brambles had flayed us before, and decided to take the chance. It was a mistake.

As we had hoped, progress was a lot faster and easier going up than it had been coming down. Less slipping. It was obvious that Plathys had preceded us, though, from footprints and freshly broken vegetation, so we climbed as quietly as possible.

Not quietly enough, perhaps, or maybe our luck just ran out. Damn it, we lost Derek. He had to be the one in front.

MARIA

We couldn't see the sun because of the forest canopy, but it was obvious from the reddening of the light that we would soon have to decide whether to make camp or push on through the darkness. Gab and I were discussing this, whispering, when the Plathy attacked.

Derek was in front. The spear hit him in the center of the chest and passed almost completely through his body. I think it killed him instantly. The Plathy, a lone young female, came charging down the stream bed toward us, roaring. She tripped and fell almost at our feet. Probably stunned. Gab and I killed her with spear and axe. After she was dead, Gab hacked off her head and threw it into the bush.

We waited for the rest of them, but she evidently had been alone. Gab had a hard time controlling his grief.

When it got dark we pushed on. The stream was lightly phosphorescent, but we relied mainly on feeling our way. A kind of fungus on the forest floor always grew in pairs, and glowed dull red, like pairs of sullen eyes watching us.

We made more noise than we had during the daytime, but there was probably little risk. Plathys sleep like dead things, and in this kind of terrain they don't post guard at night, since none of the predators here is big enough to bother them. Big enough to give us trouble, though. Three times we moved to the middle of the stream, when we thought we heard something stalking us.

The slope began to level off before it got light, and by dawn we were moving through the marshy grassland that bordered the crater lake.

We had unbelievable luck with the lake fish. Hundreds of large females lay almost immobile in the shallows. They were full of delicious roe. We gorged ourselves and then cut strips of flesh to dry in the sun. Not as effective as smoking, but we couldn't risk a fire.

We decided it would be safest to sleep separately, in case someone had picked up our trail. Like Gab, I found a tree to drape myself in. Brenda just found a patch of sunlight, arranged her furs on the wet ground, and collapsed. I thought I was too jangled to sleep, after Derek, but in fact I barely had time to find a reasonably secure set of branches before my body turned itself off.

Our survival reflexes have improved. A few hours later—it was not quite noon—I woke up suddenly in response to a slight vibration. One of the cat creatures was creeping toward me along another branch.

I didn't want to throw the spear, of course. So I took the offensive, crawling closer to the beast. He snarled and backed up warily. When I was a couple of spear lengths from him I started poking toward his face. Eventually I forced him onto too small a limb, and he crashed to the ground. He lay there a moment, then heaved himself up, growled at the world, and limped away. I went back to my branch and slept a few more hours unmolested.

Gab woke me up with the bad news that Brenda was gone. There was no sign of violence at the spot where she'd settled down, though, and we eventually found her hiding in a tree as we had. She'd heard a noise.

We gathered up our dried fish—that it hadn't been disturbed was encouraging—and killed a few fresh ones to carry along for dinner. Then we moved with some haste down along the river we had followed up so long ago. If all goes well we will be able to duplicate in reverse the earlier sequence: rest tonight on this side of the banyan forest, then push through to the large clearing; spend the night there, and at first light press on to the sea.

GABRIEL

The sea. I was never so glad to see water.

The first boat we found was beyond use, burned in two, but the water jugs nearby were unharmed, curiously enough. It's possible some immature Plathys had come upon it and not recognized that it was a boat, just a hollow log that had burned partway through. So they may have innocently used it for fuel.

The other boat, farther away from the river, was untouched. If anything, it might be in better shape now than when we left it, since it had been propped up on two logs, hollow side down. It was dryer and harder, and apparently had no insect damage.

Unfortunately, it was too heavy for three people to lift; it had been something of a struggle for all twelve of us. We went back upstream a couple of kilometers to where Maria remembered having seen a stand of saplings. Stripped of branches, they looked like they would make good rollers. We each took an armload. It was dark by the time we got back to the boat.

It might have been prudent to try to launch it in the darkness, and paddle out to comparative safety. But there hadn't been any sign of Plathys on this side of the island, and we were exhausted. I stood first watch, and had to trudge around in circles to stay awake. A couple of times I heard something out in the grass, but it never came close. Maria and Brenda heard it on their shifts, but it left before dawn.

At first light we started rolling the boat. A good three hours of hard labor, since when the saplings got into sand they forgot how to be wheels. We dragged it the last hundred meters, one bonecracking centimeter after another. Once it was floating free, we anchored it and sat in the shallow water for a long time, poleaxed by fatigue. It was amazing how much warmer the water was here, just a hundred or so kilometers north of the Plathy island: volcanic activity, coupled with distance from the continental shelf drop-off.

We dragged ourselves back to the place we'd slept and found that all our food was gone. Animals; the weapons were still there. Rather than start off with no reserve food, we spent the rest of the morning hunting. A dozen large snakes and seven small animals like *zamri*, but with six legs. We risked a fire to smoke them, which perhaps was not wise. One person guarded the fire while the other two loaded all the jars and then arranged a makeshift vessel in the stern, pegging the largest fur out in a cup shape.

Finally we loaded all the food and weapons aboard and swung up over the side (the outriggers kept us from losing too much water from the stern). We paddled almost hysterically for an hour or so, and then, with the island just a whisper of dark on the horizon, anchored to sleep until the guide stars came out.

BRENDA

It was smart of Maria to pick a beefy young athlete as one of her graduate assistants. I don't think she and I would have stood a chance alone, pushing this heavy old log 250 kilometers. We're all pretty tough and stringy after months of playing caveman, but the forced march has drained us. Last night I paddled more and more feebly until, just before dawn, I simply passed out. It's a good thing Gab was in the rear position. He heard me slump over and grabbed the paddle as it floated by. When the sun got too high to continue, he massaged the knots out of my arms and shoulders, and when I fell asleep again he was doing the same for Maria.

Perhaps we should have delayed our launch long enough to weave a sunshield. It isn't all that hot but it must have some dehydrating effect. And it would be easier to sleep. But Martin was the only one who could weave very well, and he—

Oh my God. My God, we left him for dead and I haven't even thought about him since, since we met up at the river mouth. Now we've left him behind with no boat. He could have been just a day or an hour behind us, and if he was we've murdered him.

MARIA

Brenda suddenly burst into tears and started going on about Martin. I gave him up before we left the Plathy island. His route was a mirror image of mine and he was a much faster runner. They must have caught him.

I pointed out to Brenda that if Martin did make it to the coast of the crater lake island, he could probably survive indefinitely with his primitive skills, since it would be fairly easy for one man alone to stay away from the Plathys who occasionally passed through there. Surely he would be intelligent enough to stamp out a regular marking in the sand, easily visible from the satellite. Then the next expedition could rescue him. That fantasy calmed her down a bit. Now she's sleeping.

I'm starting to think we might make it. We have water enough for twenty days and food for half that time, even if we don't catch any fish. Admittedly it's harder to keep a straight course when the guiding stars are behind you, but it shouldn't take us twice as long as the trip south, especially if there are no clouds.

Once we get to the mainland and retrieve the modern weapons, the trek back to the base will be simple. And the year waiting inside the dome will be sybaritic luxury. Real food. Chairs. No bugs. Books. Wonder if I can still read?

GABRIEL

Seven days of uneventful routine. On the eighth day I woke up in the afternoon and took a spear up to the bow to stare at the water. I stood up to piss overboard, which sometimes attracts fish, and saw a Plathy swimming straight toward us.

He stopped and treaded water about eight meters away, staring at me and the spear. I called out to him but he didn't answer. Just stared for several minutes in what seemed to be a calculating way. Then he turned his back and swam on, powerful strokes that gave him more speed than we could ever muster.

Could he tip us over? Probably not, with nothing to stand on. Once in the water, though, we'd be no match for one of them. My brain started to run away with fear, after a week of the luxury and novelty of not being afraid. He could approach underwater and pull us overboard one by one. He could grab an outrigger while we were sleeping and rock us out. He could for God's sake bite a *hole* in the boat!

When the women woke up I told them, and we made the obvious decision to maintain a rotating watch. I wondered privately how much good it would do. I suspected that a Plathy could hold his breath for a long time; if he approached underwater we might not be able to see him until he was right by the boat. Or one might overtake us in darkness. I didn't give voice to any of these specific fears. Neither of them lacks imagination, and they didn't need my scenarios to add to their own private apprehensions.

How much farther? I suspect we'll be making better time from now on.

MARIA

I began to have a recurrent dream that we'd somehow got turned around, and were paddling furiously back to the waiting Plathys. This daymare even began invading my waking hours, especially toward dawn, when I was in that vulnerable, suggestible mental state that extreme fatigue and undirected anxiety can bring on.

So when in the first light I saw land, the emotion I felt was speechless apprehension. We'd been paddling eleven days. We *must* have gotten turned around; we couldn't have covered the distance in that time. I stared at it for half a minute before Brenda mumbled something about it being too early to take a break.

Then Gab also saw the faint green line on the horizon, and we chattered on about it for a while, drifting. As it got lighter we could see the purple cones of distant volcanoes, which put my subconscious to rest.

The volcanoes simplified navigation, since I could remember what their relative positions had been on the way out. It looked as if we were going to land 10 or 15 kilometers west of the mouth of the river that led to the base. The question was whether to alter our course off to the right, so as to land closer to the river, or go straight in and walk along the beach. We were safer on the water but terminally tired of paddling, so we opted for the short approach.

It was little more than an hour before the canoe landed with a solid crunch. We jumped out and immediately fell down. No land legs. I could stand up, but the ground seemed to teeter. For some reason it was a lot worse than it had been on the outward trip. There had been a little more wave action this time, which could account for that. It might also account for the good time we made: some sort of seasonal current.

Using the spears as canes, we practiced walking for a while. When we could stagger pretty well unsupported, we gathered our stuff and started down the beach as quickly as possible. It would be a good idea to find the weapons and dig them up before dark.

Eventually we were making pretty good progress (though when we stopped the ground would still rock back and forth). The musty jungle actually smelled good, reassuring. We ate the last of the smoked snake while hungrily discussing the culinary miracles waiting for us at the base. There was enough food there to last twelve people for more than a year, a precaution against disaster.

We reached the mouth of the river before midday. But when we paced off from the rock to where the weapons were supposed to be buried, we got a nasty surprise: someone had already dug them up. Humus had filled the hole, but there was a definite depression there, and the ground was soft.

Dejected and frightened, we paced on to the next site, and it had also been dug up—but we found three of the exhumed fuel cells lying in the brush. The Plathys wouldn't know how to install them, of course. Even if, as now seemed likely, they had been watching us when we first buried them, they wouldn't have been able to find the hidden studs that had to be pushed simultaneously to open the camouflaged weapons. Even if they somehow got one open, they wouldn't know how to screw in the fuel cell and unsafe it.

We went back to the first site on the off-chance that they might have discarded the weapons, too, since ours weren't superior, in conventional capabilities, to what they would normally carry. That turned out to be a smart move: we found a club and a spear snarled in the undergrowth, still in good working order. (They'd been crafted of Bruuchian ironwood, and so were impervious to moisture and mold.)

We armed the two and confirmed that they worked. There were probably others hidden more deeply in the brush, but we were too tired to continue the search. We'd been pushing for most of a day, burning adrenaline. The two weapons would be enough to protect us while we slept.

SEASONS

GABRIEL

Brenda woke me up delightfully. I was having an interesting dream, and then it wasn't a dream.

I had the last guard shift before dawn. Scouting the perimeter of our site for firewood, I almost stumbled over a slow lizard, about a meter long, and fat. Skinned and cleaned him and had him roasting on a spit by the time the women woke up.

After breakfast, we spent a good two hours searching the area around the weapons pit, spiraling out systematically, but didn't find anything further. Well, it was good luck we even had the two weapons. We were considerably better with spear, knife, and club than we had been when we landed, but probably not good enough for an extended trek through the mainland. Packs of hungry carnivores, even if no Plathys waited in ambush.

Combing the other site did find us two more fuel cells, which should be plenty. Each one is good for more than an hour of continuous firing when new, and none of them was half used up. We could even afford to use the weapons to light fires.

So we started off in pretty high spirits. By noon we weren't quite so springy. One long sleep isn't enough to turn night creatures into day creatures, and though walking is easier than paddling, our leg muscles were weak from disuse. There was a bare rock island in the middle of the broad river; we waded out to it and made camp. That consisted of laying down our furs and collapsing.

Brenda usually takes the first watch, but she couldn't keep her eyes open, so I did odds-and-evens with Maria, and lost. And so I was the one to see the first Plathy.

I was gathering driftwood for the night's fire. I'd been concentrating my watch on the nearer bank, the one we'd come from. No telling how long the Plathy had been looking at me, standing quietly on the other side.

Our side was relatively open; compact stands of bamboolike grass every 20 or 30 meters, with only low bushes in between. The other bank was dense jungle, which was why we avoided it. The Plathy was making no special effort to conceal himself but was hard to see in the dappled shade. I continued picking up wood, studying him out of the corner of my eye.

He was an adult male, carrying a spear. That was bad. If he had been a child he might have been on his Walk North, accidentally stumbling on us. An adult had no reason to be here except us, and he wouldn't be here alone.

I didn't recognize him. If he wasn't from the Camchai family, that probably meant they had enlisted the aid of other families, so we might be up against any number. But I couldn't be sure; even in social situations I often got individuals mixed up. Maria was good at telling them apart. I took an armload of wood back to the camp and quietly woke her up and explained what was happening. She walked over to the other side of the island, casually picking up sticks, and took a look. But he was gone.

We had a whispered conference and decided to stay on the island. They would have a hard time rushing us; the river bottom was too muddy for running. And their spears couldn't reach us from either bank.

She's taken over the watch now. Enough talking. Try to sleep.

BRENDA

What a terrible night. Nobody woke me for my afternoon watch turn, so I slept almost until dark. Maria said she hadn't awakened me because she was too nervous to sleep anyhow, and explained about Gab seeing the Plathy.

When the sun went down we lit the fire, and Gab joined us. We decided to double the watch—two on, one off, one person with a crazer watching each bank. Maria curled up by the fire and tried to sleep.

They hit us about an hour before midnight, coming from Gab's side, the near bank. He called out and I ran over.

Spears falling out of the darkness. We had the fire behind us, and so were pretty good targets. Crazers don't make much light; we had to fan them and hope we hit someone. All the time running back and forth sideways, trying to spoil their aim. Maria woke up and I gave her the club crazer, then retired to the other side of the island, under Gab's orders: watch for an "envelopment." But they weren't that sophisticated.

No way to tell how many we killed. The spears came less and less frequently, and then there were rocks, and then nothing. When dawn came, pieces of four or five sliced-up Plathy bodies lay on the shore, any number having been washed downstream.

I wish I could feel guilty about it. Two weeks ago, I would have. Instead, I have to admit to a kind of manic glee. We beat them. They snuck up on us and we beat them.

SEASONS

MARIA

We burned both crazers down to quarter charge. A little more than half charge on the two backup cells. But I don't expect any more attacks like last night. They aren't dumb.

So much for the First Commandment. We've demonstrated high technology. Some of them must have survived, to go back and tell others about the magic. But we had no choice.

From now on we'll have to assume we're being followed, of course, and be triply careful about ambush setups. That won't be a real problem until the last day or two, traveling with thick jungle on both sides of the river. Why did we have to be so cautious in siting the dome?

Well, it may turn out that we'll be glad it's where it is. What if they follow us all the way there? If they try to encircle the clearing and wait us out, the jungle will get them; we won't have to do a thing. Plathy skills work fine down on their friendly island, but up where the dome is situated a hunting party armed with clubs and spears wouldn't last a week. Free lunch for the fauna.

We have to push on fast. Islands like this one will be common while the river is wide and slow. We'll be fairly safe. When the jungle closes in on both sides, though, the river will become a narrow twisting cataract. No island protection but its noise might confound Plathy hearing, make it harder for them to ambush us.

At any rate, this is the plan: each day on the plain, cover as much ground as possible, consistent with getting a few hours of sleep each night. Rest up just south of the jungle and then make a forced march, two days to the dome.

Maybe this haste is unnecessary. If the Plathys were their normal, rather sensible selves, they'd cut their losses and go home. But now we have no idea of what's normal. They may harry us until we kill them all. That would be good for the race, leaving it relatively uncontaminated culturally. Bad for us. A few more engagements like last night and we won't have enough power in the crazers to make it through the jungle. Might as well stand by the river and sing blood songs to the hungry lizards.

GABRIEL

Five days of no contact, but I can't shake the feeling we're being watched. Have been watched all the way. Now an afternoon and night of rest on this last island, and Maria wants us to push all the way to the dome.

Physically, I suppose we can do it. The terrain isn't difficult, since a game trail parallels the water all the way up. But the game that made the trail are formidable. They gave us plenty of trouble when there were twelve of us. And theoretically no Plathys.

(I wonder about that now, though. Surely someone was watching us back when we buried the weapons. How long had they been following us? They claimed that they never go to the mainland, except for a few brave Walkers, and of course they always tell the truth. About what they remember, anyhow.)

I haven't recorded anything for a long time. Waiting for my state of mind to improve. After the night of the attack I ran out of hope. Things haven't improved but I'm talking to myself to stay awake for the rest of this watch. I think Brenda's doing the same thing. Sitting on the other side of the island staring at the water, mumbling. I should go remind her to pay attention. But I can cover both banks from this side.

Besides, if they're going to hit us, I wish they'd hit us here. Clear fields of fire all around. Of course they won't; they learn from their mistakes, Maria says.

I'm being paranoiac. They're gone. The being-watched feeling, I don't know. Ever since Derek got it I've been a—I've been...loose in the head. Trying to control this—this panic. They look to me for strength, even Maria does, but all I have is muscle, jaw muscle to keep the screams in. When that one swam by us headed for the mainland I knew we were deep in shit.

Derek had religion. We argued long nights about that. What would he be doing now, praying? *"Nuestro Señor que vives en el cielo, alabado sea tu nombre...."* Good spear repellent. I miss him so.

Nobody will ever find this tooth with its feeble beep transmitter. When they come back and find the dome empty, that will be the end of it. Not enough budget for a search through obviously hostile territory. Not enough resources on this planet for anybody to want to exploit it, so no new money to find our teeth. We'll pass into Plathy legend and be forgotten, or distorted beyond recognition.

A good thing for them. If there was anything of use here, we'd be like the Eskimo anthropologists Maria talks about, recording the ways of a race doomed by the fact of recording. So maybe the Plathys will have another million years of untroubled evolution. Maybe they'll learn table manners.

I'm afraid of them but can't be mad at them. Even after Derek. They are what they are and we should have been more careful. Maybe I'm become a real xenologist, at this late date. Derek would say I'm trying to compose myself into a state of grace. Before dying.

It infuriated me that he always had answers. All I ever had was questions.

So two days' push and we're safe inside the dome. Food and cube and books and spears bounce off. Maybe I've read too much, written too much; the pattern seems inescapable. We're at death's door. Capital Death's Door. If we make it to the dome we'll break the rules.

Cálmate. Calm. Maybe I'm projecting, making patterns. Here there's only real things: cause, effect, randomness, entropy—your death is like the falling of a leaf, Derek said; like the leaf falling, it's a small tragedy, but necessary. If everything lived forever the universe would fill up in short order.

Mustn't blather. Reality, not philosophy. We rest so we can be alert. If we're alert enough we'll beat the jungle. Beat the Plathys that aren't there. It's all in my head. For the next two days take the head out of the circuit. Only reflex. Smell, listen, watch: react. React fast enough, you live.

Only I keep thinking about Derek. He never knew what hit him.

BRENDA

Gab asked me to watch both banks for a while so he could give love to Maria before it got dark. Hard to watch both banks when I want to watch him. Men look so vulnerable from this angle, bouncing; a new perspective for me. I've never been an audience except for watching on the cube. It's different.

Admit I'm jealous of her. She's fifteen years older than I and shows it. But he wants her for his last one. That was obvious in his tone of voice. At some level I think he's as scared as I am.

If he thinks this is his last one he doesn't know much about women. Maria will let me wake him up when our shift is over. If I can wait that long. I've watched him sleeping; he has the refractory period of a twelve-year-old. To be exact, I know from observation that he can do it twice and still get an erection in his sleep. No privacy under our circumstances.

Funny friendly sound, don't hear it like that while you're doing it—what was that? Something move?

Just a lizard, I guess. Nothing new. We've been seeing them the last two days on the jungle side, around dusk and in the firelight. They don't come in the water. What's going to happen tomorrow night, no island, no fire? Don't want to die that way, jumped by a pack of dinosaurs. Nor have my head bitten off by a sentient primitive. I was going to be a grandmother and sit on the porch and tell doctor stories and die with no fuss.

Why won't they attack? I know they're out there, waiting. If they would only come now, I could die that way. I remember the feeling, fifty or a hundred of them against the three of us and our two crazers. Not a fair fight, perhaps, but God it did feel good, holding our own, epinephrine from head to toe. This waiting and worrying. Light the fire.

Stack the wet wood around to dry. Gives me something to do while they're finishing up. Being quiet for the sake of my sensibilities, or theirs. Just heavier breathing and a faster rhythm of liquid sounds. I've followed that unspoken code, too; we haven't been all three together since the water hole. She's had him seven times since, to my four. To my knowledge. Why am I keeping score? They were made for each other. Iron man, iron woman.

I was in love once or twice and know this is something else. Not just sex; I've been that way before, too. Hysteria is part of it, but not in the old-fashioned womanish sense, the womb taking over. This is a certainty-of-death hysteria, to coin a category. It's different from just fear. It's like, it's like—I don't know. As if you had never tasted water before, or seen colors, and suddenly here is a cold spring or a rainbow. Minus the joy. Just something primal and unlike anything before. Does that make sense? We've been in danger God knows constantly for how long? Not the same. There was always hope. Now we're two days away from total sanctuary and for some reason I know we won't make it.

I remember from psych class a lesson about people who seemed to know they were going to die. Not sick people; soldiers, adventurers, whose sudden violent death seemed to resonate backward in time—they told their friends that somehow they felt that this was it, and by God it was. You can call it coincidence or invoke pragmatic causality—they were nervous and therefore careless and therefore died—but here and now I think there's more to it. Once I'm safe inside the dome I'll publish a retraction. Right now I feel my death as strongly as I feel the need for that man inside of me.

MARIA

Somehow we lived through that one.

We'd been in the jungle for perhaps twelve hours, dusk approaching, when a lizard pack hit us, or two packs, from in front and behind. The trail is scarcely two meters wide, which saved us. The carcasses piled up and impeded their charge. We must have killed forty of them, man-sized or slightly smaller. Not a type we'd seen on the way down.

Were they intelligent enough to coordinate their charge, or is it some kind of instinctive attack pattern? Scary either way. Used up a lot of energy. If it happens a few more times...it happens. No use thinking about it.

At least the action seems to have been good for morale. Both of them have been radiating depression and fear since we started out this morning. Reinforcing each other's premonitions of doom. I shouldn't have let her go to him at watch change, or I should have admonished her to fuck, don't talk. It was too much like saying goodbye. I got that feeling from Gab too, last night, but I tried to reassure him. Words.

By my reckoning we have fourteen to eighteen hours to go, depending on how much ground we can cover without light. Decided against torches, of course. The Plathys don't normally hunt at night, but they sure as hell attacked us in the dark.

Natural impulse is to climb a tree and wait for dawn. That would be suicidal. The jungle canopy is thick and supports its own very active ecology. We can't take to the water because the current's too swift, even if we wanted to chance the snakes.

We'll stay within touching distance, Gab in front because he has the best hearing. Brenda hears better than me, so she should bring up the rear, but I think she'll be better off in the middle, feeling protected. Besides, I want to have one of the weapons

GABRIEL

Never another night like that. I wound up firing at every sound, jumpy. But a few times there actually was something waiting in front of us, once something that wasn't a lizard. Big shaggy animal that stood up on its hind legs and reared over us, all teeth and claws and a dick the size of my arm. He was too dumb to know he was dead, and actually kept scrabbling toward us after I cut him off at the knees. If we'd gone a few steps farther before I fired he would have gotten at least me, maybe all of us. The crazer light was almost bright in the pitch blackness, a lurid strobe. I used up the last of one fuel cell and had to reload by touch.

At least we don't have to worry about the Plathys. Nothing remotely edible could make it through a night like that without energy weapons.

When I mentioned that to Maria, she said not to be too sure. They were tracking us on the jungle side before. Not the same, though. This jungle makes that one look like a park.

Dead tired but moving fast. We're looking for a pink granite outcropping. Fifty paces upstream from it there's a minor trail to the right; the dome clearing is about half a kilometer in. Can't be more than a few hours away.

BRENDA

There it is! The rock! Hard to…talk…running…

MARIA

Slow down! Careful! That's better. Not a sound now.

GABRIEL

Oh, no. Shit, no.

BRENDA

They…burned it?

GABRIEL

Spears—

MARIA

Take his weapon! Get to cover! Here!

BRENDA

I—oh!

MARIA

So...so this is how it ends. Gab died about ten minutes ago, in the first moment of the attack. A spear in the back of his head. Brenda was hit then too, a spear that went in her shoulder and came out her back. She lived for several minutes, though, and acquitted herself well when the Plathys charged. I think we killed them all, thirty-seven by my count. If there are any left in the jungle they are staying there for the time being.

They must have piled wood up around the dome and kept a bonfire going until the force field overloaded and collapsed. It wasn't engineered for that kind of punishment, I suppose. Obviously.

Little of use left in the ruins. Rations destroyed, fuel cells popped by the heat. There's a toolbox not badly harmed. Nothing around to repair with it, though. Maybe if I dug I could find some rations merely over-cooked. But I don't want to stay around to search. Doubt that I'll live long enough to have another meal, anyhow.

My fault. Eleven good people dead, and how many innocent savages, because I wasn't prudent. With that first abrupt life change, the frenzied breeding, I should have ordered us to tiptoe away. Another decade of satellite surveillance and we would have learned which times were safe to come in for close-up study. Now everything is a shambles.

Racial vanity is part of it, I guess, or my vanity. Thinking we could come naked into a heavily armed Stone Age culture and survive by our superior intelligence and advanced perspective. It worked before. But this place is not Obelobel.

I guess all I can do now is be sure a record survives. These teeth might not make it through a Plathy or lizard digestive system. I'll...I'll use the pliers from the tool kit. Leave the teeth here in the ruins. Buried enough so the Plathys can't find them easily. One hell of a prize to bring back from your Walk North.

I have only about a tenth charge left. Brenda used up all of the other before she died. Not enough to get out of the jungle, not even if it were all daylight. One woman alone doesn't have a bloody fucking chance on this world. I'll try the river. Maybe I can find a log that will float me down to the savannah. Then hike to the coast. If I can make it to the beach maybe I can stay alive there for a while. Sleep with one eye open. I don't know. Look for me there. But don't bother to look for too long. The pliers.

Sorry, Brenda....

Sorry...Gab. Sweet Gab. Still warm.

Now mine. One jerk. Some blood, some pain. *Tem se garlish. !ka.*

To: Ahmadou Masire, Coordinator
Selva Sector Recreational Facilities
Confederación Office Building, Suite 100
Bolivar 243 488 739
Selva

From: Federico Santesteban, Publicity Director
Office of Resources Allocation
Chimbarazo Interplanetario
Ecuador 3874658
Terra

Dr. Masire:

I hope you will find the enclosed transcript of some use. Your assistant, Sra. Videla, mentioned the possibility of a documentary cube show to generate interest in the hunting trips to Sanchrist IV. Seems to me that if you inject some romance into this you have a natural story: sacrifice, tragedy, brave kids battling against impossible odds.

We could save you some production costs by getting a few Plathys shipped to your studio via our xenological division on Perrin's World. They have a hundred or so there and keep their stock stable by cloning. You'll have to have somebody put together a grant proposal demonstrating that they'll be put to legitimate scholarly use. Garcia Belaunde at your Instituto Xenológico is a tame one, as you probably know. Have him talk to Leon Jawara at the PW Xenological Exchange Commission. He'll make sure you get the beasts at the right part of their life cycle. Otherwise they'd eat all of your actors.

I tried to pull some strings, but I'm afraid there's no way we can get you permission to take a crew onto the Plathy island itself. That's a xenological preserve now, isolated by a force field, the few remaining Plathys constantly monitored by flying bugs. You can shoot on the mainland, if your actors are as crazy as your hunters, or use the crater lake island. There are a few feral Plathys roaming there, though, so take precautions, no matter what the season. Use a restraining field if that's within your budget; otherwise, regrettably, the smartest thing would be to kill them on sight. Their behavior patterns become erratic if they're separated from family for more than a year.

The search party that followed up on Dr. Rubera's expedition could only find five of the tooth transmitters. There was no trace of Maria Rubera, or any other human remains.

A sad story but I think a useful one for your purpose. Gives your expeditions a dramatic historical context.

Let me know if I can be of further service. And by all means send us a copy of the cube, if you decide to go into production.

Your servant,
Federico Santesteban

TECHNICAL NOTE

If I were using "Seasons" as a "write something like this" example in a class, it could be illustrative of various things:

1. Multiple viewpoint. The story is told through the eyes of five different characters (though one's used only once) with a coda at the end from an ironically detached viewpoint. Actually, I'd call it a "rotating" viewpoint, since most of the story develops linearly, one character picking it up where the previous one stopped. (I wrote a "mosaic novel" called *The Coming* that uses this technique with dozens of characters.)
2. Classical dramatic structure. Novellas tend to mimic the structure of three-act plays. With "Seasons" this notion drove the plot of the story very consciously. I wanted to mimic Greek tragedy, but with a purely science-fictional approach—so how can you have tragedy in a universe where there are laws but no gods? My substitute for the tragic flaw, *hamartia*, is Maria's faith in scientific method—in anthropologic methodology, specifically. And natural law substitutes for the wrath of the gods; the aliens do nothing that's evil or even wrong.
3. Compactness. A hell of a lot goes on in "Seasons," in terms of both action and ideas, and this seems to characterize readable novellas. Irving Howe says:

"Whereas the short story writer tries to strike off a flash of insight and the novelist hopes to create the illusion of a self-sufficient world, the author of the short novel is frequently concerned with showing an arc of human conduct that has a certain symbolic significance. The short novel is a form that encourages the writer to struggle with profound philosophic or moral problems through a compact yet extended narrative."

It wouldn't be a bad use of a semester to give a student that quote and say "Write me one."

* * *

INTRODUCTION TO "THE MONSTER"

People talk about "voice" in writing, but they don't normally mean a literal voice. In the case of this story, it was a real man's voice, beautiful and haunting.

He was our tour bus driver in Montego Bay, Jamaica. His basso growl was wonderfully creepy; an island accent redolent of voodoo, zombies, witch doctors.

We drove past a cemetery, strangely decorated with festive paper streamers. "That be the graveyard," he said in his sepulchral voice. "Ain't nobody want to be dere. Ev'ybody gettin' dere."

* * *

THE MONSTER

Start at the beginning? Which beginning?

Okay, since you be from Outside, I give you the whole thing. Sit over there, be comfort. Smoke em if you got em.

They talk about these guys that come back from the Nam all fucked up and shit, and say they be like time bombs: they go along okay for years, then get a gun and just go crazy. But it don't go nothing like that for me. Even though there be the gun involved, this time. And an actual murder, this time.

First time I be in prison, after the court-martial, I try to tell them what it be and what they get me? Social workers and shrinks. Guy to be a shrink in a prison ain't be no good shrink, what they can make Outside, is the way I figure it, so at first I don't give them shit, but then I always get Discipline, so I figure what the hell and make up a story. You watch any TV you can make up a Nam story too.

So some of them don't fall for it, they go along with it for a while because this is what crazy people do, is make up stories, then they give up and another one come along and I start over with a different story. And sometime when I know for sure they don't believe, when they start to look at me like you look at a animal in the zoo, that's when I tell them the real true story. And that's when they smile, you know, and nod, and the new guy come in next. Because if anybody would make up a story like that one, he'd have to be crazy, right? But I swear to God it's true.

Right. The beginning.

219

I be a lurp in the Nam, which means Long Range Recon Patrol. You look in these magazines about the Nam and they make like the lurps be always heroes, brave boys go out and face Charlie alone, bring down the artillery on them and all, but it was not like that. You didn't want to be no lurp where we be, they make you be a fuckin lurp if they want to get rid of your ass, and that's the God's truth.

Now I can tell you right now that I don't give a flyin fuck for that U.S. Army and I don't like it even more when I be drafted, but I got to admit they be pretty smart, the way they do with us. Because we get off on that lurp shit. I mean we be one bunch of bad ass brothers and good ole boys and we did love that rock an roll, and God they give us rock an roll—fuck your M-16, we get real tommy guns with 100-round drum, usually one guy get your automatic grenade launcher, one guy carry that starlite scope, another guy the full demo bag. I mean we could of taken on the whole fuckin North Vietnam army. We could of killed fuckin Rambo.

Now I like to talk strange, though any time I want, I can talk like other people. Even Jamaican like my mama ain't understand me if I try. I be born in New York City, but at that time my mama be only three months there—when she speak her English it be island music, but the guy she live with, bringing me up, he be from Taiwan, so in between them I learn shitty English, same-same shitty Chinese. And live in Cuban neighborhood, *por la español* shitty.

He was one mean mother fuckin Chinese cab driver, slap shit out of me for twelve year, and then I take a kitchen knife and slap him back. He never come back for the ear. I think maybe he go off someplace and die, I don't give a shit anymore, but when I be drafted they find out I speak Chinese, send me to language school in California, and I be so dumb I believe them when they say this means no Nam for the boy: I stay home and translate for them tapes from the radio.

So they send me to the Nam anyhow, and I go a little wild. I hit everybody that outranks me. They put me in the hospital and I hit the doctor. They put me in the stockade and I hit the guards, the guards hit back, some more hospital. I figure sooner or later they got to kill me or let me out. But then one day this strac dude come in and tell me about the lurp shit. It sound all right, even though the dude say if I fuck up they can waste me and it's legal. By now I know they can do that shit right there in LBJ, Long Binh Jail, so what the fuck? In two days I'm in the jungle with three real bad ass dudes with a map and a compass and enough shit we could start our own war.

THE MONSTER

They give us these maps that never have no words on them, like names of places, just "TOWN POP 1000" and shit like that. They play it real cute, like we so dumb we don't know there be places outside of Vietnam, where no GIs can go. They keep all our ID in base camp, even the dog tags, and tell us not to be capture. Die first, they say, that shall be more pleasant. We laugh at that later, but I keep to myself the way I do feel. That the grave be one place we all be getting to, long road or short, and maybe the short road be less bumps, less trouble. Now I know from twenty years how true that be.

They don't tell us where the place be we leave from, after the slick drop us in, but we always sure as hell head west. Guy name Duke, mean honky but not dumb, he say all we be doin is harassment, bustin up supply lines comin down the Ho Chi Minh Trail, in Cambodia. It do look like that, long lines of gooks carryin ammo and shit, sometime on bicycles. We would set up some mine and some claymores and wait till the middle of the line be there, then pop the shit, then maybe waste a few with the grenade launcher and tommy guns, not too long so they ain't regroup and get us. Duke be taking a couple Polaroids and we go four different ways, meet a couple miles away, then sneak back to the LZ and call the slick. We go out maybe six time a month, maybe lose one guy a month. Me and Duke make it through all the way to the last one, that last one.

That time no different from the other times except they tell us try to blow a bridge up, not a big bridge like the movies, but one that hang off a mountain side, be hard to fix afterward. It also be hard to get to.

We lose one guy, new guy name of Winter, just tryin to get to the fuckin bridge. That be bad in a special kind of way. You get used to guys gettin shot or be wasted by frags and like that. But to fall like a hundred foot onto rocks be a different kind of bad. And it just break his back or something. He laying there and crying, tell all the world where we be, until Duke shut him up.

So it be just Duke and Cherry and me, the Chink. I am for goin back, no fuckin way they could blame us for that. But Duke crazy for action, always be crazy for killing, and Cherry would follow Duke anywhere, I think he a fag even then. Later I do know. When the Monster kill them.

This is where I usually feel the need to change. It's natural to adjust one's mode of discourse to a level appropriate to the subject at hand, is it not? To talk about this "Monster" requires addressing such concepts as disassociation and multiple personality, if only to discount them, and it would be awkward to speak of these things directly the way I normally speak, as Chink. This does not mean that there are two or several personalities resident within the sequestered hide of this disabled black veteran. It only means that I can speak in different ways. You could as well, if you grew up switching back and forth among Spanish, Chinese, and two flavors of English, chocolate and vanilla. It might also help if you had learned various Vietnamese dialects, and then spent the past twenty years in a succession of small rooms, mainly reading and writing. There still be the bad mother fucker in here. He simply uses appropriate language. The right tool for the job, or the right weapon.

Let me save us some time by demonstrating the logical weakness of some facile first order rationalizations that always seem to come up. One: that this whole Monster business is a bizarre lie I concocted and have stubbornly held on to for twenty years—which requires that it never have occurred to me that recanting it would result in much better treatment and, possibly, release. Two: that the Monster is some sort of psychological shield, or barrier, that I have erected between my "self" and the enormity of the crime I committed. That hardly holds up to inspection, since my job and life at that time comprised little more than a succession of pre-meditated cold-blooded murders. I didn't kill the two men, but if I had, it wouldn't have bothered me enough to require elaborate psychological defenses. Three: that I murdered Duke and Cherry because I was…upset at discovering them engaged in a homosexual act. I am and was indifferent toward that aberration, or hobby. Growing up in the ghetto and going directly from there to an army prison in Vietnam, I witnessed perversions for which you psychologists don't even have names.

Then of course there is the matter of the supposed eyewitness. It seemed particularly odious to me at the time, that my government would prefer the testimony of an erstwhile enemy soldier over one of its own. I see the process more clearly now, and realize that I was convicted before the court-martial was even convened.

The details? You know what a *hoi chan* was? You're too young. Well, *chieu hoi* is Vietnamese for "open arms"; if an enemy soldier came up to the barbed wire with his hands up, shouting *chieu hoi*, then in theory he would be welcomed into our loving, also open, arms and rehabilitated. Unless he was killed before people could figure out what he was saying. The rehabilitated ones were called *hoi chans*, and sometimes were used as translators and so forth.

Anyhow, this Vietnamese deserter's story was that he had been following us all day, staying out of sight, waiting for an opportunity to surrender.

I don't believe that for a second. Nobody moves that quietly, that fast, through unfamiliar jungle. Duke had been a professional hunting guide back in the World, and he would have heard any slightest movement.

What do I say happened? You must have read the transcript... I see. You want to check me for consistency.

I had sustained a small but deep wound in the calf, a fragment from a rifle grenade, I believe. I did elude capture, but the wound slowed me down.

We had blown the bridge at 1310, which was when the guards broke for lunch, and had agreed to rendezvous by 1430 near a large banyan tree about a mile from the base of the cliff. It was after 1500 when I got there, and I was worried. Winter had been carrying our only radio when he fell, and if I wasn't at the LZ with the other two, they would sensibly enough leave without me. I would be stranded, wounded, lost.

I was relieved to find them still waiting. In this sense I may *have* caused their deaths: if they had gone on, the Monster might have killed only me.

This is the only place where my story and that of the *hoi chan* are the same. They were indeed having sex. I waited under cover rather than interrupt them.

Yes, I know, this is where he testified I jumped them and did all those terrible things. Like *he* had been sitting off to one side, waiting for them to finish their business. What a bunch of bullshit.

What actually happened—what *actually* happened—was that I was hiding there behind some bamboo, waiting for them to finish so we could get on with it, when there was this sudden loud crashing in the woods on the other side of them, and bang. There was the Monster. It was bigger than any man, and black—not black like me, but glossy black, like shiny hair—and it just flat smashed into them, bashed them apart. Then it was on Cherry, I could hear bones crack like sticks. It bit him between the legs, and that was enough for me. I was gone. I heard a couple of short bursts from Duke's tommy gun, but I didn't go back to check it out. Just headed for the LZ as fast as my leg would let me.

So I made a big mistake. I lied. Wouldn't you? I'm supposed to tell them sorry, the rest of the squad got eaten by a werewolf? So while I'm waiting for the helicopter I make up this believable account of what happened at the bridge.

The slick comes and takes me back to the fire base, where the medics dress the wound and I debrief to the major there. They send me to Tuy Hoa, nice hospital on the beach, and I debrief again, to a bunch of captains and a bird colonel. They tell me I'm in for a Silver Star.

So I'm resting up there in the ward, reading a magazine, when in comes a couple of MPs and they grab me and haul me off to the stockade. Isn't that just like the army, to have a stockade in a hospital?

What has happened is that this gook, honorable *hoi chan* Nguyen Van Trong, has come out of the woodwork with his much more believable story. So I get railroaded and wind up in jail.

Come on now, it's all in the transcript. I'm tired of telling it. It upsets me.

Oh, all right. This Nguyen claims he was a guard at the bridge we blew up, and he'd been wanting to escape—they don't say "desert"—ever since they'd left Hanoi a few months before. Walking down the Ho Chi Minh Trail. So in the confusion after the blast, he runs away; he hears Duke and Cherry and follows them. Waiting for the right opportunity to go *chieu hoi*. I've told you how improbable that actually is.

So he's waiting in the woods while they blow each other and up walks me. I get the drop on them with my Thompson. I make Cherry tie Duke to the tree. Then I tie Cherry up, facing him. Then I castrate Cherry—with my *teeth*! You believe that? And then with my teeth and fingernails, I flay Duke, skin him alive, from the neck down, while he's watching Cherry die. Then for dessert, I bite off his cock, too. Then I cut them down and stroll away.

You got that? This Nguyen claims to have watched the whole thing, must have taken hours. Like he never had a chance to interrupt my little show. What, did I hang on to my weapon all the time I was nibbling away? Makes a lot of sense.

After I leave, he say he try to help the two men. Duke, he say, be still alive, but not worth much. Say he follow Duke's gestures and get the Polaroid out of his pack.

When those picture show up at the trial, I be a Had Daddy. Forget that his story ain't makin sense. Forget for Chris' sake that he be the fuckin *enemy*! Picture of Duke be still alive and his guts all hangin out, this god-awful look on his face, I could of been fuckin Sister Theresa and they wouldn't of listen to me.

[At this point the respondent was silent for more than a minute, apparently controlling rage, perhaps tears. When he continued speaking, it was with the cultured white man's accent again.]

I know you are constrained not to believe me, but in order to understand what happened over the next few years, you must accept as tentatively true the fantastic premises of my delusional system. Mainly, that's the reasonable assertion that I didn't mutilate my friends, and the unreasonable one that the Cambodian jungle hides at least one glossy black humanoid over seven feet tall, with the disposition of a barracuda.

If you accept that this Monster exists, then where does that leave Mr. Nguyen Van Trong? One possibility is that he saw the same thing I did, and lied for the same reason I initially did—because no one in his right mind would believe the truth—but his lie implicated me, I suppose for verisimilitude.

A second possibility is the creepy one that Nguyen was somehow allied with the Monster; in league with him.

The third possibility…is that they were the same.

If the second or the third were true, it would probably be a good policy for me never to cross tracks with Nguyen again, or at least never to meet him unarmed. From that, it followed that it would be a good precaution for me to find out what had happened to him after the trial.

A maximum-security mental institution is far from an ideal place from which to conduct research. But I had several things going for me. The main thing was that I was not, despite all evidence to the contrary, actually crazy. Another was that I could take advantage of people's pre-conceptions, which is to say prejudices: I can tune my language from a mildly accented Jamaican dialect to the almost-impenetrable patois that I hid behind while I was in the army. Since white people assume that the smarter you are, the more like them you sound, and since most of my keepers were white, I could control their perception of me pretty well. I was a dumb nigger who with their help was getting a little smarter.

Finally I wangled a work detail in the library. Run by a white lady who thought she was hardass but had a heart of purest tapioca. Loved to see us goof off so long as we were reading.

I was gentle and helpful and appreciative of her guidance. She let me read more and more, and of course I could take books back to my cell. There was no record of many of the books I checked out: computer books.

She was a nice woman but fortunately not free of prejudice. It never occurred to her that it might not be a good idea to leave her pet darky alone with the computer terminal.

Once I could handle the library's computer system, my Nguyen project started in earnest. Information networks are wonderful, and computerized ordering and billing is, for a thief, the best tool since the credit card. I could order any book in print—after all, I opened the boxes, shelved the new volumes, and typed up the catalog card for each book. If I wanted it to be cataloged.

Trying to find out what the Monster was, I read all I could find about extraterrestrials, werewolves, mutations; all that science fiction garbage. I read up on Southeast Asian religions and folktales. Psychology books, because Occam's razor can cut the person who's using it, and maybe I *was* crazy after all.

Nothing conclusive came out of any of it. I had seen the Monster for only a couple of seconds, but the quick impression was, of course, branded on my memory. The face was intelligent, perhaps I should say "sentient," but it was not at all human. Two eyes, okay, but no obvious nose or ears. Mouth too big and lots of teeth like a shark's. Long fingers with too many joints, and claws. No mythology or pathology that I read about produced anything like it.

The other part of my Nguyen project was successful. I used the computer to track him down, through my own court records and various documents that had been declassified through the Freedom of Information Act.

Not surprisingly, he had emigrated to the United States just before the fall of Saigon. By 1986 he had his own fish market in San Francisco. Pillar of the community, the bastard.

Eighteen years of exemplary behavior and I worked my way down to minimum security. It was a more comfortable and freer life, but I didn't see any real chance of parole. I probably couldn't even be paroled if I'd been white and had bitten the cocks off two *black* men. I might get a medal, but not a parole.

So I had to escape. It wasn't hard.

I assumed that they would alert Nguyen, and perhaps watch him or even guard him for a while. So for two years I stayed away from San Francisco, burying myself in a dirtpoor black neighborhood in Washington. I saved my pennies and purchased or contrived the tools I would need when I eventually confronted him.

Finally I boarded a Greyhound, crawled to San Francisco, and rested up a couple of days. Then for another couple of days I kept an intermittent watch on the fish market, to satisfy myself that Nguyen wasn't under guard.

He lived in a two-room apartment in the rear of the store. I popped the back door lock a half hour before closing and hid in the bedroom. When I heard him lock the front door, I walked in and pointed a .44 Magnum at his face.

That was the most tense moment for me. I more than half expected him to turn into the Monster. I had even gone to the trouble of casting my own bullets of silver, in case that superstition turned out to be true.

He asked me not to shoot and took out his wallet. Then he recognized me and clammed up.

I made him strip to his shorts and tied him down with duct tape to a wooden chair. I turned the television on fairly loud, since my homemade silencer was not perfect, and traded the Magnum for a .22 automatic. It made about as much noise as a flyswatter, each time I shot.

There are places where you can shoot a person even with a .22 and he will die quickly and without too much pain. There are other sites that are quite the opposite. Of course I concentrated on those, trying to make him talk. Each time I shot him I dressed the wound, so there would be a minimum of blood loss.

I first shot him during the evening news, and he lasted well into Johnny Carson, with a new bullet each half hour. He never said a word, or cried out. Just stared.

After he died, I waited a few hours, and nothing happened. So I walked to the police station and turned myself in. That's it.

So here we be now. I know it be life for me. Maybe it be that rubber room. I ain't care. This be the only place be safe. The Monster, he know. I can feel.

[This is the end of the transcript proper. The respondent did not seem agitated when the guards led him away. Consistent with his final words, he seemed relieved to be back in prison, which makes his subsequent suicide mystifying. The circumstances heighten the mystery, as the attached coroner's note indicates.]

State of California
Department of Corrections
Forensic Pathology Division
Glyn Malin, M.D., Ph.D.—Chief of Research

I have read about suicides that were characterized by sudden hysterical strength, including a man who had apparently choked himself to death by throttling (though I seem to recall that it was a heart attack that actually killed him). The case of Royce "Chink" Jackson is one I would not have believed if I had not seen the body myself.

The body is well muscled, but not unusually so; when I'd heard how he died I assumed he was a mesomorphic weight lifter type. Bones are hard to break.

Also, his fingernails are cut to the quick. It must have taken a burst of superhuman strength, to tear his own flesh without being able to dig in.

My first specialty was thoracic surgery, so I well know how physically difficult it is to get to the heart. It's hard to believe that a person could tear out his own. It's doubly hard to believe that someone could do it after having brutally castrated himself.

I do have to confirm that that is what happened. The corridor leading to his solitary confinement cell is under constant video surveillance. No one came or went from the time the door was shut behind him until breakfast time, when the body was discovered.

He did it to himself, and in total silence.

GM:wr

* * *

INTRODUCTION TO "THE HEMINGWAY HOAX"

For some reason I was not, unlike most people in my generation, overexposed to Ernest Hemingway in high school. I didn't study him as an undergraduate, either—majoring in physics and astronomy, to which he contributed little—and so when my first novel came out, I was amused when critics talked about the obvious influence Hemingway had had on my writing. My only exposure had been "The Old Man and the Sea," in junior high school, which I hadn't liked much.

The influence was secondary, but still strong. The postwar science fiction that I'd devoured since childhood was heavily influenced by Hemingway, as was most popular fiction of the time.

I put in the back of my mind that I'd better read some of this guy before somebody exposed my ignorance. After my first novel came out, Gay and I took a summer vacation in Europe, starving-student style. Our Spanish rail pass covered the ferry over to Morocco, and we couldn't resist *that*. I ran out of reading material in Marrakesh, and in the sun-baked souk found a table full of books. One of the few in English was *Fiesta*, the British title of Hemingway's first novel, which we call *The Sun Also Rises*.

I read it with admiration and an unusual degree of identification: like Jake Barnes, I was a young American fiction writer trying to deal with the horror of war, still recovering from a serious wounding. (Mine considerably less serious than Jake's loss of his most important digit.)

Over the next year and a half I sought out and read almost every word that Hemingway had published. I also read a lot of critical and biographical material, fascinated by the curious links between his work and his life. (Such links rarely exist in mine: I've never been to Mars or annihilated an entire planet.)

By pure coincidence, Gay and I went down to Key West, to do some astronomy and partying, the same week that the International Hemingway Society was meeting there. They were having a banquet in a nice hotel over the water, so we bought tickets and sat at a random table.

The other people who sat down there included Michael Reynolds, Jackson Bryer, Jim Nagel, and Scott Donaldson—all big-league Hemingway scholars. That I had read their books was not surprising, but that I had done it just as a reader (rather than an academic) and that I was a professional fiction writer, made me someone special. So after the banquet we hit the bars, which is what one does in Key West, and by the end of the weekend we were good friends, fated to meet again, year after year, as the conference moved from Paris to Pamplona to Petoskey and beyond.

One fascinating aspect of Hemingway's life is the "lost manuscripts," which his first wife famously left in a train station.

One of my students gave me a ride to the airport when I was headed for Australia, and while we were waiting in the bar I told him the story of the lost manuscripts, and how much they would be worth if somebody found them—and, since writers' minds work that way, how much money you could make if you successfully counterfeited them. He's probably the easiest writer in the American idiom to pastiche.

On the way back from the men's room, I had a flash of inspiration. You wouldn't have to risk all that inconvenient jail time if, instead of writing fake Hemingway stories yourself, you wrote a story about someone *else* doing it! The next day, I was sitting in a screened-in porch on an island in the Great Barrier Reef, using my typewriter to carry me back to the similar muggy heat in Key West.

THE HEMINGWAY HOAX

1. THE TORRENTS OF SPRING

Our story begins in a run-down bar in Key West, not so many years from now. The bar is not the one Hemingway drank at, nor yet the one that claims to be the one he drank at, because they are both too expensive and full of tourists. This bar, in a more interesting part of town, is a Cuban place. It is neither clean nor well-lighted, but has cold beer and good strong Cuban coffee. Its cheap prices and rascally charm are what bring together the scholar and the rogue.

Their first meeting would be of little significance to either at the time, though the scholar, John Baird, would never forget it. John Baird was not capable of forgetting anything.

Key West is lousy with writers, mostly poor writers, in one sense of that word or the other. Poor people did not interest our rogue, Sylvester Castlemaine, so at first he didn't take any special note of the man sitting in the corner scribbling on a yellow pad. Just another would-be writer, come down to see whether some of Papa's magic would rub off. Not worth the energy of a con.

But Castle's professional powers of observation caught at a detail or two and focused his attention. The man was wearing jeans and a faded flannel shirt, but his shoes were expensive Italian loafers. His beard had been trimmed by a barber. He was drinking Heineken. The pen he was scribbling with was a fat Mont Blanc Diplomat, two hundred bucks on the hoof, discounted. Castle got his cup of coffee and sat at a table two away from the writer.

233

He waited until the man paused, set the pen down, took a drink. "Writing a story?" Castle said.

The man blinked at him. "No...just an article." He put the cap on the pen with a crisp snap. "An article about stories. I'm a college professor."

"Publish or perish," Castle said.

The man relaxed a bit. "Too true." He riffled through the yellow pad. "This won't help much. It's not going anywhere."

"Tell you what...bet you a beer it's Hemingway or Tennessee Williams."

"Too easy." He signaled the bartender. "Dos cervezas. Hemingway, the early stories. You know his work?"

"Just a little. We had to read him in school—*The Old Man and the Fish*? And then I read a couple after I got down here." He moved over to the man's table. "Name's Castle."

"John Baird." Open, honest expression; not too promising. You can't con somebody unless he thinks he's conning you. "Teach up at Boston."

"I'm mostly fishing. Shrimp nowadays." Of course Castle didn't normally fish, not for things in the sea, but the shrimp part was true. He'd been reduced to heading shrimp on the Catalina for five dollars a bucket. "So what about these early stories?"

The bartender set down the two beers and gave Castle a weary look.

"Well...they don't exist." John Baird carefully poured the beer down the side of his glass. "They were stolen. Never published."

"So what can you write about them?"

"Indeed. That's what I've been asking myself." He took a sip of the beer and settled back. "Seventy-four years ago they were stolen. December 1922. That's really what got me working on them; thought I would do a paper, a monograph, for the seventy-fifth anniversary of the occasion."

It sounded less and less promising, but this was the first imported beer Castle had had in months. He slowly savored the bite of it.

"He and his first wife, Hadley, were living in Paris. You know about Hemingway's early life?"

"Huh uh. Paris?"

"He grew up in Oak Park, Illinois. That was kind of a prissy, self-satisfied suburb of Chicago."

"Yeah, I been there."

"He didn't like it. In his teens he sort of ran away from home, went down to Kansas City to work on a newspaper.

"World War I started, and like a lot of kids, Hemingway couldn't get into the army because of bad eyesight, so he joined the Red Cross and went off to drive ambulances in Italy. Take cigarettes and chocolate to the troops.

"That almost killed him. He was just doing his cigarettes-and-chocolate routine and an artillery round came in, killed the guy next to him, tore up another, riddled Hemingway with shrapnel. He claims then that he picked up the wounded guy and carried him back to the trench, in spite of being hit in the knee by a machine gun bullet."

"What do you mean, 'claims'?"

"You're too young to have been in Vietnam."

"Yeah."

"Good for you. I was hit in the knee by a machine gun bullet myself, and went down on my ass and didn't get up for five weeks. He didn't carry anybody one step."

"That's interesting."

"Well, he was always rewriting his life. We all do it. But it seemed to be a compulsion with him. That's one thing that makes Hemingway scholarship challenging."

Baird poured the rest of the beer into his glass. "Anyhow, he actually was the first American wounded in Italy, and they made a big deal over him. He went back to Oak Park a war hero. He had a certain amount of success with women."

"Or so he says?"

"Right, God knows. Anyhow, he met Hadley Richardson, an older woman but quite a number, and they had a steamy courtship and got married and said the hell with it, moved to Paris to live a sort of Bohemian life while Hemingway worked on perfecting his art. That part isn't bullshit. He worked diligently and he did become one of the best writers of his era. Which brings us to the lost manuscripts."

"Do tell."

"Hemingway was picking up a little extra money doing journalism. He'd gone to Switzerland to cover a peace conference for a news service. When it was over, he wired Hadley to come join him for some skiing.

"This is where it gets odd. On her own initiative, Hadley packed up all of Ernest's work. All of it. Not just the typescripts, but the handwritten first drafts and the carbons."

"That's like a Xerox?"

"Right. She packed them in an overnight bag, then packed her own suitcase. A porter at the train station, the Gare de Lyon, put them aboard for her. She left the train for a minute to find something to read—and when she came back, they were gone."

"Suitcase and all?"

"No, just the manuscripts. She and the porter searched up and down the train. But that was it. Somebody had seen the overnight bag sitting there and snatched it. Lost forever."

That did hold a glimmer of professional interest. "That's funny. You'd think they'd get a note then, like 'If you ever want to see your stories again, bring a million bucks to the Eiffel Tower' sort of thing."

"A few years later, that might have happened. It didn't take long for Hemingway to become famous. But at the time, only a few of the literary intelligentsia knew about him."

Castle shook his head in commiseration with the long-dead thief. "Guy who stole 'em probably didn't even read English. Dumped 'em in the river."

John Baird shivered visibly. "Undoubtedly. But people have never stopped looking for them. Maybe they'll show up in some attic someday."

"Could happen." Wheels turning.

"It's happened before in literature. Some of Boswell's diaries were recovered because a scholar recognized his handwriting on an old piece of paper a merchant used to wrap a fish. Hemingway's own last book, he put together from notes that had been lost for thirty years. They were in a couple of trunks in the basement of the Ritz, in Paris." He leaned forward, excited. "Then after he died, they found another batch of papers down here, in a back room in Sloppy Joe's. It could still happen."

Castle took a deep breath. "It could be made to happen, too."

"Made to happen?"

"Just speakin', you know, in theory. Like some guy who really knows Hemingway, suppose he makes up some stories that're like those old ones, finds some seventy-five-year-old paper and an old, what do you call them, not a word processor—"

"Typewriter."

"Whatever. Think he could pass 'em off for the real thing?"

"I don't know if he could fool me," Baird said, and tapped the side of his head. "I have a freak memory: eidetic, photographic. I have just about every word Hemingway ever wrote committed to memory." He looked slightly embarrassed. "Of course that doesn't make me an expert in the sense of being able to spot a phony. I just wouldn't have to refer to any texts."

"So take yourself, you know, or somebody else who spent all his life studyin' Hemingway. He puts all he's got into writin' these stories—he knows the people who are gonna be readin' 'em; knows what they're gonna look for. And he hires like an expert forger to make the pages look like they came out of Hemingway's machine. So could it work?"

Baird pursed his lips and for a moment looked professorial. Then he sort of laughed, one syllable through his nose. "Maybe it could. A man did a similar thing when I was a boy, counterfeiting the memoirs of Howard Hughes. He made millions."

"Millions?"

"Back when that was real money. Went to jail when they found out, of course."

"And the money was still there when he got out."

"Never read anything about it. I guess so."

"So the next question is, how much stuff are we talkin' about? How much was in that old overnight bag?"

"That depends on who you believe. There was half a novel and some poetry. The short stories, there might have been as few as eleven or as many as thirty."

"That'd take a long time to write."

"It would take forever. You couldn't just 'do' Hemingway; you'd have to figure out what the stories were about, then reconstruct his early style—do you know how many Hemingway scholars there are in the world?"

"Huh uh. Quite a few."

"Thousands. Maybe ten thousand academics who know enough to spot a careless fake."

Castle nodded, cogitating. "You'd have to be real careful. But then you wouldn't have to do all the short stories and poems, would you? You could say all you found was the part of the novel. Hell, you could sell that as a book."

The odd laugh again. "Sure you could. Be a fortune in it."

"How much? A million bucks?"

"A million...maybe. Well, sure. The last new Hemingway made at least that much, allowing for inflation. And he's more popular now."

Castle took a big gulp of beer and set his glass down decisively. "So what the hell are we waiting for?"

Baird's bland smile faded. "You're serious?"

2. IN OUR TIME

Got a ripple in the Hemingway channel.

Twenties again?

No, funny, this one's in the 1990s. See if you can track it down?

Sure. Go down to the armory first and—

Look—no bloodbaths this time. You solve one problem and start ten more.

Couldn't be helped. It's no tea party, twentieth century America.

Just use good judgment. That Ransom guy...

Manson. Right. That was a mistake.

3. A WAY YOU'LL NEVER BE

You can't cheat an honest man, as Sylvester Castlemaine well knew, but then again, it never hurts to find out just how honest a man is. John Baird refused his scheme, with good humor at first, but when Castle persisted, his refusal took on a sarcastic edge, maybe a tinge of outrage. He backed off and changed the subject, talking for a half hour about commercial fishing around Key West, and then said he had to run. He slipped his business card into John's shirt pocket on the way out. (Sylvester Castlemaine, Consultant, it claimed.)

John left the place soon, walking slowly through the afternoon heat. He was glad he hadn't brought the bicycle; it was pleasant to walk in the shade of the big aromatic trees, a slight breeze on his face from the Gulf side.

One could do it. One could. The problem divided itself into three parts: writing the novel fragment, forging the manuscript, and devising a suitable story about how one had uncovered the manuscript.

The writing part would be the hardest. Hemingway is easy enough to parody—one-fourth of the take-home final he gave in English 733 was to write a page of Hemingway pastiche, and some of his graduate students did a credible job—but parody was exactly what one would not want to do.

It had been a crucial period in Hemingway's development, those three years of apprenticeship the lost manuscripts represented. Two stories survived, and they were maddeningly dissimilar. "My Old Man," which had slipped down behind a drawer, was itself a pastiche, reading like pretty good Sherwood Anderson, but with an O. Henry twist at the end—very unlike the bleak understated quality that would distinguish the stories that were to make Hemingway's reputation. The other, "Up in Michigan," had been out in the mail at the time of the loss. It was a lot closer to Hemingway's ultimate style, a spare and, by the standards of the time, pornographic description of a woman's first sexual experience.

John riffled through the notes on the yellow pad, a talismanic gesture, since he could have remembered any page with little effort. But the sight of the words and the feel of the paper sometimes helped him think.

One would not do it, of course. Except perhaps as a mental exercise. Not to show to anybody. Certainly not to profit from.

You wouldn't want to use "My Old Man" as the model, certainly; no one would care to publish a pastiche of a pastiche of Anderson, now undeservedly obscure. So "Up in Michigan." And the first story he wrote after the loss, "Out of Season," would also be handy. That had a lot of the Hemingway strength.

You wouldn't want to tackle the novel fragment, of course, not just as an exercise, over a hundred pages....

Without thinking about it, John dropped into a familiar fugue state as he walked through the run-down neighborhood, his freak memory taking over while his body ambled along on autopilot. This is the way he usually remembered pages. He transported himself back to the Hemingway collection at the JFK Library in Boston, last November, snow swirling outside the big picture windows overlooking the harbor, the room so cold he was wearing coat and gloves and could see his breath. They didn't normally let you wear a coat up there, afraid you might squirrel away a page out of the manuscript collection, but they had to make an exception because the heat pump was down.

He was flipping through the much-thumbed Xerox of Carlos Baker's interview with Hadley, page 52: "Stolen suitcase," Baker asked; "lost novel?"

The typescript of her reply appeared in front of him, more clear than the cracked sidewalk his feet negotiated: "This novel was a knockout, about Nick, up north in Michigan—hunting, fishing, all sorts of experiences—stuff on the order of 'Big Two-Hearted River,' with more action. Girl experiences well done, too." With an enigmatic addition, evidently in Hadley's handwriting, "Girl experiences too well done."

That was interesting. John hadn't thought about that, since he'd been concentrating on the short stories. Too well done? There had been a lot of talk in the eighties about Hemingway's sexual ambiguity—*gender* ambiguity, actually—could Hadley have been upset, sixty years after the fact, remembering some confidence that Hemingway had revealed to the world in that novel; something girls knew that boys were not supposed to know? Playful pillow talk that was filed away for eventual literary exploitation?

He used his life that way. A good writer remembered everything and then forgot it when he sat down to write, and reinvented it so the writing would be more real than the memory. Experience was important, but imagination was more important.

Maybe I would be a better writer, John thought, if I could learn how to forget. For about the tenth time today, like any day, he regretted not having tried to succeed as a writer, while he still had the independent income. Teaching and research had fascinated him when he was younger, a rich boy's all-consuming hobbies, but the end of this fiscal year would be the end of the monthly checks from the trust fund. So the salary from Boston University wouldn't be mad money any more, but rent and groceries in a city suddenly expensive.

Yes, the writing would be the hard part. Then forging the manuscript, that wouldn't be easy. Any scholar would have access to copies of thousands of pages that Hemingway typed before and after the loss. Could one find the typewriter Hemingway had used? Then duplicate his idiosyncratic typing style—a moment's reflection put a sample in front of him, spaces before and after periods and commas....

He snapped out of the reverie as his right foot hit the first step on the back staircase up to their rented flat. He automatically stepped over the fifth step, the rotted one, and was thinking about a nice tall glass of iced tea as he opened the screen door.

"Scorpions!" his wife screamed, two feet from his face.

"What?"

"We have scorpions!" Lena grabbed his arm and hauled him to the kitchen.

"Look!" She pointed at the opaque plastic skylight. Three scorpions, each about six inches long, cast sharp silhouettes on the milky plastic. One was moving.

"My word."

"Your *word*!" She struck a familiar pose, hands on hips, and glared up at the creatures. "What are we going to do about it?"

"We could name them."

"John."

"I don't know." He opened the refrigerator. "Call the bug man."

"The bug man was just here yesterday. He probably flushed them out."

He poured a glass of cold tea and dumped two envelopes of artificial sweetener into it. "I'll talk to Julio about it. But you know they've been there all along. They're not bothering anybody."

"They're bothering the hell out of me!"

He smiled. "Okay. I'll talk to Julio." He looked into the oven. "Thought about dinner?"

"Anything you want to cook, sweetheart. I'll be damned if I'm going to stand there with three...poisonous...arthropods staring down at me."

"Poised to jump," John said, and looked up again. There were only two visible now, which made his skin crawl.

"Julio wasn't home when I first saw them. About an hour ago."

"I'll go check." John went downstairs and Julio, the landlord, was indeed home, but was not impressed by the problem. He agreed that it was probably the bug man, and they would probably go back to where they came from in a while, and gave John a flyswatter.

John left the flyswatter with Lena, admonishing her to take no prisoners, and walked a couple of blocks to a Chinese restaurant. He brought back a few boxes of takeout, and they sat in the living room and wielded chopsticks in silence, listening for the pitter-patter of tiny feet.

"Met a real live con man today." He put the business card on the coffee table between them.

"Consultant?" she read.

"He had a loony scheme about counterfeiting the missing stories." Lena knew more about the missing stories than ninety-eight percent of the people who Hemingway'ed for a living. John liked to think out loud.

"Ah, the stories," she said, preparing herself.

"Not a bad idea, actually, if one had a larcenous nature." He concentrated for a moment on the slippery Moo Goo Gai Pan. "Be millions of bucks in it."

He was bent over the box. She stared hard at his bald spot. "What exactly did he have in mind?"

"We didn't bother to think it through in any detail, actually. You go and find..." He got the slightly walleyed look that she knew meant he was reading a page of a book a thousand miles away. "Yes. A 1921 Corona portable, like the one Hadley gave him before they were married. Find some old paper. Type up the stories. Take them to Sotheby's. Spend money for the rest of your life. That's all there is to it."

"You left out jail."

"A mere detail. Also the writing of the stories. That could take weeks. Maybe you could get arrested first, write the stories in jail, and then sell them when you got out."

"You're weird, John."

"Well. I didn't give him any encouragement."

"Maybe you should've. A few million would come in handy next year."

"We'll get by."

"'We'll get by.' You keep saying that. How do you know? You've never had to 'get by.'"

"Okay, then. We won't get by." He scraped up the last of the fried rice. "We won't be able to make the rent and they'll throw us out on the street. We'll live in a cardboard box over a heating grate. You'll have to sell your body to keep me in cheap wine. But we'll be happy, dear." He looked up at her, mooning. "Poor but happy."

"Slap-happy." She looked at the card again. "How do you know he's a con man?"

"I don't know. Salesman type. Says he's in commercial fishing now, but he doesn't seem to like it much."

"He didn't say anything about any, you know, criminal stuff he'd done in the past?"

"Huh uh. I just got the impression that he didn't waste a lot of time mulling over ethics and morals." John held up the Mont Blanc pen. "He was staring at this, before he came over and introduced himself. I think he smelled money."

Lena stuck both chopsticks into the half-finished carton of boiled rice and set it down decisively. "Let's ask him over."

"He's a sleaze, Lena. You wouldn't like him."

"I've never met a real con man. It would be fun."

He looked into the darkened kitchen. "Will you cook something?"

She followed his gaze, expecting monsters. "If you stand guard."

4. ROMANCE IS DEAD
SUBTITLE
THE HELL IT IS

"Be a job an' a half," Castle said, mopping up residual spaghetti sauce with a piece of garlic bread. "It's not like your Howard Hughes guy, or Hitler's notebooks."

"You've been doing some research." John's voice was a little slurred. He'd bought a half gallon of Portuguese wine, the bottle wrapped in straw like cheap Chianti, the wine not quite that good. If you could get past the first couple of glasses, it was okay. It had been okay to John for some time now.

"Yeah, down to the library. The guys who did the Hitler notebooks, hell, nobody'd ever seen a real Hitler notebook; they just studied his handwriting in letters and such, then read up on what he did day after day. Same with the Howard Hughes, but that was even easier, because most of the time nobody knew what the hell Howard Hughes was doing anyhow. Just stayed locked up in that room."

"The Hughes forgery nearly worked, as I recall," John said. "If Hughes himself hadn't broken silence…"

"Ya gotta know that took balls. 'Scuse me, Lena." She waved a hand and laughed. "Try to get away with that while Hughes was still alive."

"How did the Hitler people screw up?" she asked.

"Funny thing about that one was how many people they fooled. Afterwards everybody said it was a really lousy fake. But you can bet that before the newspapers bid millions of dollars on it, they showed it to the best Hitlerologists they could find, and they all said it was real."

"Because they wanted it to be real," Lena said.

"Yeah. But one of the pages had some chemical in it that wouldn't be in paper before 1945. That was kinda dumb."

"People would want the Hemingway stories to be real," Lena said quietly, to John.

John's gaze stayed fixed on the center of the table, where a few strands of spaghetti lay cold and drying in a plastic bowl. "Wouldn't be honest."

"That's for sure," Castle said cheerily. "But it ain't exactly armed robbery, either."

"A gross misuse of intellectual…intellectual…"

"It's past your bedtime, John," Lena said. "We'll clean up." John nodded and pushed himself away from the table and walked heavily into the bedroom.

Lena didn't say anything until she heard the bedsprings creak. "He isn't always like this," she said quietly.

"Yeah. He don't act like no alky."

"It's been a hard year for him." She refilled her glass. "Me, too. Money."

"That's bad."

"Well, we knew it was coming. He tell you about the inheritance?" Castle leaned forward. "Huh uh."

"He was born pretty well off. Family had textile mills up in New Hampshire. John's grandparents died in an auto accident in the forties and the family sold off the mills—good timing, too. They wouldn't be worth much today.

"Then John's father and mother died in the sixties, while he was in college. The executors set up a trust fund that looked like it would keep him in pretty good shape forever. But he wasn't interested in money. He even joined the army, to see what it was like."

"Jesus."

"Afterwards, he carried a picket sign and marched against the war— you know, Vietnam.

"Then he finished his Ph.D. and started teaching. The trust fund must have been fifty times as much as his salary, when he started out. It was still ten times as much, a couple of years ago."

"Boy...howdy." Castle was doing mental arithmetic and algebra with variables like Porsches and fast boats.

"But he let his sisters take care of it. He let them reinvest the capital."

"They weren't too swift?"

"They were idiots! They took good solid blue-chip stocks and tax-free municipals, too 'boring' for them, and threw it all away gambling on commodities." She grimaced. "*Pork* bellies? I finally had John go to Chicago and come back with what was left of his money. There wasn't much."

"You ain't broke, though."

"Damned near. There's enough income to pay for insurance and eventually we'll be able to draw on an IRA. But the cash payments stop in two months. We'll have to live on John's salary. I suppose I'll get a job, too."

"What you ought to get is a typewriter."

Lena laughed and slouched back in her chair. "That would be something."

"You think he could do it? I mean if he would, do you think he could?"

"He's a good writer." She looked thoughtful. "He's had some stories published, you know, in the literary magazines. The ones that pay four or five free copies."

"Big deal."

She shrugged. "Pays off in the long run. Tenure. But I don't know whether being able to write a good literary story means that John could write a good Hemingway imitation."

"He knows enough, right?"

"Maybe he knows too much. He might be paralyzed by his own standards." She shook her head. "In some ways he's an absolute nut about Hemingway. Obsessed, I mean. It's not good for him."

"Maybe writing this stuff would get it out of his system."

She smiled at him. "You've got more angles than a protractor."

"Sorry; I didn't mean to—"

"No." She raised both hands. "Don't be sorry; I like it. I like you, Castle. John's a good man, but sometimes he's too good."

He poured them both more wine. "Nobody ever accused me of that."

"I suspect not." She paused. "Have you ever been in trouble with the police? Just curious."

"Why?"

"Just curious."

He laughed. "Nickel-and-dime stuff, when I was a kid. You know, jus' to see what you can get away with." He turned serious. "Then I pulled two months' hard time for somethin' I didn't do. Wasn't even in town when it happened."

"What was it?"

"Armed robbery. Then the guy came back an' hit the same goddamned store! I mean, he was one sharp cookie. He confessed to the first one and they let me go."

"Why did they accuse you in the first place?"

"Used to think it was somebody had it in for me. Like the clerk who fingered me." He took a sip of wine. "But hell. It was just dumb luck. And dumb cops. The guy was about my height, same color hair, we both lived in the neighborhood. Cops didn't want to waste a lot of time on it. Jus' chuck me in jail."

"So you do have a police record?"

"Huh uh. Girl from the ACLU made sure they wiped it clean. She wanted me to go after 'em for what? False arrest an' wrongful imprisonment. I just wanted to get out of town."

"It wasn't here?"

"Nah. Dayton, Ohio. Been here eight, nine years."

"That's good."

"Why the third degree?"

She leaned forward and patted the back of his hand. "Call it a job interview, Castle. I have a feeling we may be working together."

"Okay." He gave her a slow smile. "Anything else you want to know?"

5. THE DOCTOR AND THE DOCTOR'S WIFE

John trudged into the kitchen the next morning, ignored the coffeepot, and pulled a green bottle of beer out of the fridge. He looked up at the skylight. Four scorpions, none of them moving. Have to call the bug man today.

Red wine hangover, the worst kind. He was too old for this. Cheap red wine hangover. He eased himself into a soft chair and carefully poured the beer down the side of the glass. Not too much noise, please.

When you drink too much, you ought to take a couple of aspirin, and some vitamins, and all the water you can hold, before retiring. If you drink too much, of course, you don't remember to do that.

The shower turned off with a bass clunk of plumbing. John winced and took a long drink, which helped a little. When he heard the bathroom door open he called for Lena to bring the aspirin when she came out.

After a few minutes she brought it out and handed it to him. "And how is Dr. Baird today?"

"Dr. Baird needs a doctor. Or an undertaker." He shook out two aspirin and washed them down with the last of the beer. "Like your outfit."

She was wearing only a towel around her head. She simpered and struck a dancer's pose and spun daintily around. "Think it'll catch on?"

"Oh my yes." At thirty-five, she still had the trim model's figure that had caught his eye in the classroom, fifteen years before. A safe, light tan was uniform all over her body, thanks to liberal sunblock and the private sunbathing area on top of the house—private except for the helicopter that came low overhead every weekday at 1:15. She always tried to be there in time to wave at it. The pilot had such white teeth. She wondered how many sunbathers were on his route.

She undid the towel and rubbed her long blond hair vigorously. "Thought I'd cool off for a few minutes before I got dressed. Too much wine, eh?"

"Couldn't you tell from my sparkling repartee last night?" He leaned back, eyes closed, and rolled the cool glass back and forth on his forehead.

"Want another beer?"

"Yeah. Coffee'd be smarter, though."

"It's been sitting all night."

"Pay for my sins." He watched her swivel lightly into the kitchen and, more than ever before, felt the difference in their ages. Seventeen years; he was half again as old as she. A young man would say the hell with the hangover, go grab that luscious thing and carry her back to bed. The

246

organ that responded to this meditation was his stomach, though, and it responded very audibly.

"Some toast, too. Or do you want something fancier?"

"Toast would be fine." Why was she being so nice? Usually if he drank too much, he reaped the whirlwind in the morning.

"Ugh." She saw the scorpions. "Five of them now."

"I wonder how many it will hold before it comes crashing down. Scorpions everywhere, stunned. Then angry."

"I'm sure the bug man knows how to get rid of them."

"In Africa they claimed that if you light a ring of fire around them with gasoline or lighter fluid, they go crazy, run amok, stinging themselves to death in their frenzies. Maybe the bug man could do that."

"Castle and I came up with a plan last night. It's kinda screwy, but it might just work."

"Read that in a book called *Jungle Ways*. I was eight years old and believed every word of it."

"We figured out a way that it would be legal. Are you listening?"

"Uh huh. Let me have real sugar and some milk."

She poured some milk in a cup and put it in the microwave to warm. "Maybe we should talk about it later."

"Oh no. Hemingway forgery. You figured out a way to make it legal. Go ahead. I'm all ears."

"See, you tell the publisher first off what it is, that you wrote it and then had it typed up to look authentic."

"Sure, be a big market for that."

"In fact, there could be. You'd have to generate it, but it could happen." The toast sprang up and she brought it and two cups of coffee into the living room on a tray. "See, the bogus manuscript is only one part of a book."

"I don't get it." He tore the toast into strips, to dunk in the strong Cuban coffee.

"The rest of the book is in the nature of an exegesis of your own text."

"If that con man knows what exegesis is, then I can crack a safe."

"That part's my idea. You're really writing a book *about* Hemingway. You use your own text to illustrate various points—'I wrote it this way instead of that way because....'"

"It would be different," he conceded. "Perhaps the second most egotistical piece of Hemingway scholarship in history. A dubious distinction."

"You could write it tongue-in-cheek, though. It could be really amusing, as well as scholarly."

"God, we'd have to get an unlisted number, publishers calling us night and day. Movie producers. Might sell ten copies, if I bought nine."

"You really aren't getting it, John. You don't have a particle of larceny in your heart."

He put a hand on his heart and looked down. "Ventricles, auricles. My undying love for you, a little heartburn. No particles."

"See, you tell the publisher the truth...but the publisher doesn't have to tell the truth. Not until publication day."

"Okay. I still don't get it."

She took a delicate nibble of toast. "It goes like this. They print the bogus Hemingway up into a few copies of bogus bound galleys. Top secret."

"My exegesis carefully left off."

"That's the ticket. They send it out to a few selected scholars, along with Xeroxes of a few sample manuscript pages. All they say, in effect, is 'Does this seem authentic to you? Please keep it under your hat, for obvious reasons.' Then they sit back and collect blurbs."

"I can see the kind of blurbs they'd get from Scott or Mike or Jack, for instance. Some variation of 'What kind of idiot do you think I am?'"

"Those aren't the kind of people you send it to, dope! You send it to people who think they're experts, but aren't. Castle says this is how the Hitler thing almost worked—they knew better than to show it to historians in general. They showed it to a few people and didn't quote the ones who thought it was a fake. Surely you can come up with a list of people who would be easy to fool."

"Any scholar could. Be a different list for each one; I'd be on some of them."

"So they bring it out on April Fool's Day. You get the front page of the *New York Times Book Review*. *Publishers Weekly* does a story. Everybody wants to be in on the joke. Best-seller list, here we come."

"Yeah, sure, but you haven't thought it through." He leaned back, balancing the coffee cup on his slight potbelly. "What about the guys who give us the blurbs, those second-rate scholars? They're going to look pretty bad."

"We did think of that. No way they could sue, not if the letter accompanying the galleys is carefully written. It doesn't have to say—"

"I don't mean getting sued. I mean I don't want to be responsible for hurting other people's careers—maybe wrecking a career, if the person was too extravagant in his endorsement, and had people looking for things to use against him. You know departmental politics. People go down the chute for less serious crimes than making an ass of yourself and your institution in print."

She put her cup down with a clatter. "You're always thinking about other people. Why don't you think about yourself for a change?" She was on the verge of tears. "Think about *us*."

"All right, let's do that. What do you think would happen to my career at BU if I pissed off the wrong people with this exercise? How long do you think it would take me to make full professor? Do you think BU would make a full professor out of a man who uses his specialty to pull vicious practical jokes?"

"Just do me the favor of thinking about it. Cool down and weigh the pluses and minuses. If you did it with the right touch, your department would love it—and God, Harry wants to get rid of the chairmanship so bad he'd give it to an axe murderer. You know you'll make full professor about thirty seconds before Harry hands you the keys to the office and runs."

"True enough." He finished the coffee and stood up in a slow creak. "I'll give it some thought. Horizontally." He turned toward the bedroom.

"Want some company?"

He looked at her for a moment. "Indeed I do."

6. IN OUR TIME

Back already?

Need to find a meta-causal. One guy seems to be generating the danger flag in various timelines. John Baird, who's a scholar in some of them, a soldier in some, and a rich playboy in a few. He's always a Hemingway nut, though. He does something that starts off the ripples in '95, '96, '97; depending on which time line you're in— but I can't seem to get close to it. There's something odd about him, and it doesn't have to do with Hemingway specifically.

But he's definitely causing the eddy?

Has to be him.

All right. Find a meta-causal that all the doom lines have in common, and forget about the others. Then go talk to him.

There'll be resonance—

But who cares? Moot after A.D. 2006.

That's true. I'll hit all the doom lines at once, then: neutralize the meta-causal, then jump ahead and do some spot checks.

Good. And no killing this time.

I understand. But—

You're too close to 2006. Kill the wrong person, and the whole thing could unravel.

Well, there are differences of opinion. We would certainly feel it if the world failed to come to an end in those lines.

As you say, differences of opinion. My opinion is that you better not kill anybody or I'll send you back to patrol the fourteenth century again.

Understood. But I can't guarantee that I can neutralize the meta-causal without eliminating John Baird.

Fourteenth century. Some people love it. Others think it was nasty, brutish, and long.

7. A CLEAN, WELL-LIGHTED PLACE

Most of the sleuthing that makes up literary scholarship takes place in settings either neutral or unpleasant. Libraries' old stacks, attics metaphorical and actual; dust and silverfish, yellowed paper and fading ink. Books and letters that appear in card files but not on shelves.

Hemingway researchers have a haven outside of Boston, the Hemingway Collection at the University of Massachusetts's John F. Kennedy Library. It's a triangular room with one wall dominated by a picture window that looks over Boston Harbor to the sea. Comfortable easy chairs surround a coffee table, but John had never seen them in use; worktables under the picture window provided realistic room for computer and clutter. Skins from animals the Hemingways had dispatched in Africa snarled up from the floor, and one wall was dominated by Hemingway memorabilia and photographs. What made the room Nirvana, though, was row upon row of boxes containing tens of thousands of Xerox pages of Hemingway correspondence, manuscripts, clippings—everything from a boyhood shopping list to all extant versions of every short story and poem and novel.

John liked to get there early so he could claim one of the three computers. He snapped it on, inserted a CD, and typed in his code number. Then he keyed in the database index and started searching.

The more commonly requested items would appear on screen if you asked for them—whenever someone requested a physical copy of an item, an electronic copy automatically was sent into the database—but most of the things John needed were obscure, and he had to haul down the letter boxes and physically flip through them, just like some poor scholar inhabiting the first nine-tenths of the twentieth century.

Time disappeared for him as he abandoned his notes and followed lines of instinct, leaping from letter to manuscript to note to interview, doing what was in essence the opposite of the scholar's job: a scholar would normally be trying to find out what these stories had been about. John instead was trying to track down every reference that might restrict what he himself could write about, simulating the stories.

The most confining restriction was the one he'd first remembered, walking away from the bar where he'd met Castle. The one-paragraph answer that Hadley had given to Carlos Baker about the unfinished novel; that it was a Nick Adams story about hunting and fishing up in Michigan. John didn't know anything about hunting, and most of his fishing experience was limited to watching a bobber and hoping it wouldn't go down and break his train of thought.

There was the one story that Hemingway had left unpublished, "Boys and Girls Together," mostly clumsy self-parody. It covered the right period and the right activities, but using it as a source would be sensitive business, tiptoeing through a minefield. Anyone looking for a fake would go straight there. Of course John could go up to the Michigan woods and camp out, see things for himself and try to recreate them in the Hemingway style. Later, though. First order of business was to make sure there was nothing in this huge collection that would torpedo the whole project—some postcard where Hemingway said "You're going to like this novel because it has a big scene about cleaning fish."

The short stories would be less restricted in subject matter. According to Hemingway, they'd been about growing up in Oak Park and Michigan and the battlefields of Italy.

That made him stop and think. The one dramatic experience he shared with Hemingway was combat—fifty years later, to be sure, in Vietnam, but the basic situations couldn't have changed that much. Terror, heroism, cowardice. The guns and grenades were a little more streamlined, but they did the same things to people. Maybe do a World War I story as a finger exercise, see whether it would be realistic to try a longer growing-up-in-Michigan pastiche.

He made a note to himself about that on the computer, oblique enough not to be damning, and continued the eyestraining job of searching through Hadley's correspondence, trying to find some further reference to the lost novel—damn!

Writing to Ernest's mother, Hadley noted that "the taxi driver broke his typewriter" on the way to the Constantinople conference—did he get it fixed, or just chuck it? A quick check showed that the typeface of his manuscripts did indeed change after July 1924. So they'd never be able to find it. There were typewriters in Hemingway shrines in Key West, Billings, Schruns; the initial plan had been to find which was the old Corona, then locate an identical one and have Castle arrange a swap.

So they would fall back on Plan B. Castle had claimed to be good with mechanical things, and thought if they could find a 1921 Corona, he could tweak the keys around so they would produce a convincing manuscript— lowercase "s" a hair low, "e" a hair high, and so forth.

How he could be so sure of success without ever having seen the inside of a manual typewriter, John did not know. Nor did he have much confidence.

But it wouldn't have to be a perfect simulation, since they weren't out to fool the whole world, but just a few reviewers who would only see two or three Xeroxed pages. He could probably do a close enough job. John put it out of his mind and moved on to the next letter.

But it was an odd coincidence for him to think about Castle at that instant, since Castle was thinking about him. Or at least asking.

8. THE COMING MAN

"How was he when he was younger?"

"He never was younger." She laughed and rolled around inside the compass of his arms to face him. "Than you, I mean. He was in his mid-thirties when we met. You can't be much over twenty-five."

He kissed the end of her nose. "Thirty this year. But I still get carded sometimes."

"I'm a year older than you are. So you have to do anything I say."

"So far so good." He'd checked her wallet when she'd gone into the bathroom to insert the diaphragm, and knew she was thirty-five. "Break out the whips and chains now?"

"Not till next week. Work up to it slowly." She pulled away from him and mopped her front with the sheet. "You're good at being slow."

"I like being asked to come back."

"How 'bout tonight and tomorrow morning?"

"If you feed me lots of vitamins. How long you think he'll be up in Boston?"

"He's got a train ticket for Wednesday. But he said he might stay longer if he got onto something."

Castle laughed. "Or into something. Think he might have a girl up there? Some student like you used to be?"

"That would be funny. I guess it's not impossible." She covered her eyes with the back of her hand. "The wife is always the last to know."

They both laughed. "But I don't think so. He's a sweet guy but he's just not real sexy. I think his students see him as kind of a favorite uncle."

"You fell for him once."

"Uh huh. He had all of his current virtues plus a full head of hair, no potbelly—and, hm, what am I forgetting?"

"He was hung like an elephant?"

"No, I guess it was the millions of dollars. That can be pretty sexy."

9. WANDERINGS

It was a good thing John liked to nose around obscure neighborhoods shopping; you couldn't walk into any old K mart and pick up a 1921 Corona portable. In fact, you couldn't walk into any typewriter shop in Boston and find one, not any. Nowadays they all sold self-contained word processors, with a few dusty electrics in the back room. A few had fancy manual typewriters from Italy or Switzerland; it had been almost thirty years since the American manufacturers had made a machine that wrote without electronic help.

He had a little better luck with pawnshops. Lots of Smith-Coronas, a few L.C. Smiths, and two actual Coronas that might have been old enough. One had too large a typeface and the other, although the typeface was the same as Hemingway's, was missing a couple of letters: Th quick b own fox jump d ov th lazy dog. The challenge of writing a convincing Hemingway novel without using the letters "e" and "r" seemed daunting. He bought the machine anyhow, thinking they might ultimately have two or several broken ones that could be concatenated into one reliable machine.

The old pawnbroker rang up his purchase and made change and slammed the cash drawer shut. "Now you don't look to me like the kind of man who would hold it against a man who..." He shrugged. "Well, who sold you something and then suddenly remembered that there was a place with lots of those somethings?"

"Of course not. Business is business."

"I don't know the name of the guy or his shop; I think he calls it a museum. Up in Brunswick, Maine. He's got a thousand old typewriters. He buys, sells, trades. That's the only place I know of you might find one with the missing whatever-you-call-ems."

"Fonts." He put the antique typewriter under his arm—the handle was missing—and shook the old man's hand. "Thanks a lot. This might save me weeks."

With some difficulty John got together packing materials and shipped the machine to Key West, along with Xeroxes of a few dozen pages of Hemingway's typed copy and a note suggesting Castle see what he could do. Then he went to the library and found a Brunswick telephone directory. Under "Office Machines & Supplies" was listed Crazy Tom's Typewriter Museum and Sales Emporium. John rented a car and headed north.

The small town had rolled up its sidewalks by the time he got there. He drove past Crazy Tom's and pulled into the first motel. It had a neon VACANCY sign but the innkeeper had to be roused from a deep sleep. He took John's credit card number and directed him to Room 14 and pointedly turned on the NO sign. There were only two other cars in the motel lot.

John slept late and treated himself to a full "trucker's" breakfast at the local diner: two pork chops and eggs and hash browns. Then he worked off ten calories by walking to the shop.

Crazy Tom was younger than John had expected, thirtyish with an unruly shock of black hair. A manual typewriter lay upside down on an immaculate worktable, but most of the place was definitely maculate. Thousands of peanut shells littered the floor. Crazy Tom was eating them compulsively from a large wooden bowl. When he saw John standing in the doorway, he offered some. "Unsalted," he said. "Good for you."

John crunched his way over the peanut-shell carpet. The only light in the place was the bare bulb suspended over the worktable, though two unlit high-intensity lamps were clamped on either side of it. The walls were floor-to-ceiling gloomy shelves holding hundreds of typewriters, mostly black.

"Let me guess," the man said as John scooped up a handful of peanuts. "You're here about a typewriter."

"A specific one. A 1921 Corona portable."

"Ah." He closed his eyes in thought. "Hemingway. His first. Or I guess the first after he started writing. A '27 Corona, now, that'd be Faulkner."

"You get a lot of calls for them?"

"Couple times a year. People hear about this place and see if they can find one like the master used, whoever the master is to them. Sympathetic magic and all that. But you aren't a writer."

"I've had some stories published."

"Yeah, but you look too comfortable. You do something else. Teach school." He looked around in the gloom. "Corona Corona." Then he sang the six syllables to the tune of "Corina, Corina." He walked a few steps into the darkness and returned with a small machine and set it on the table. "Newer than 1920 because of the way it says 'Corona' here. Older than 1927 because of the tab setup." He found a piece of paper and a chair. "Go on, try it."

John typed out a few quick foxes and aids to one's party. The typeface was identical to the one on the machine Hadley had given Hemingway before they'd been married. The up-and-down displacements of the letters were different, of course, but Castle should be able to fix that once he'd practiced with the backup machine.

John cracked a peanut. "How much?"

"What you need it for?"

"Why is that important?"

"It's the only one I got. Rather rent it than sell it." He didn't look like he was lying, trying to push the price up. "A thousand to buy, a hundred a month to rent."

"Tell you what, then. I buy it, and if it doesn't bring me luck, you agree to buy it back at a pro ratum. My one thousand dollars minus ten percent per month."

Crazy Tom stuck out his hand. "Let's have a beer on it."

"Isn't it a little early for that?"

"Not if you eat peanuts all morning." He took two long-necked Budweisers from a cooler and set them on paper towels on the table. "So what kind of stuff you write?"

"Short stories and some poetry." The beer was good after the heavy greasy breakfast. "Nothing you would've seen unless you read magazines like *Iowa Review* and *Triquarterly*."

"Oh yeah. Foldouts of Gertrude Stein and H.D. I might've read your stuff."

"John Baird."

He shook his head. "Maybe. I'm no good with names."

"If you recognized my name from *The Iowa Review* you'd be the first person who ever had."

"I was right about the Hemingway connection?"

"Of course."

"But you don't write like Hemingway for no *Iowa Review*. Short declarative sentences, truly this truly that."

"No, you were right about the teaching, too. I teach Hemingway up at Boston University."

"So that's why the typewriter? Play show-and-tell with your students?"

"That, too. Mainly I want to write some on it and see how it feels."

From the back of the shop, a third person listened to the conversation with great interest. He, it, wasn't really a "person," though he could look like one: he had never been born and he would never die. But then he didn't really exist, not in the down-home pinch-yourself-ouch! way that you and I do.

In another way, he did *more* than exist, since he could slip back and forth between places you and I don't even have words for.

He was carrying a wand that could be calibrated for heart attack, stroke, or metastasized cancer on one end; the other end induced a kind of aphasia. He couldn't use it unless he materialized. He walked toward the two men, making no crunching sounds on the peanut shells because he weighed less than a thought. He studied John Baird's face from about a foot away.

"I guess it's a mystical thing, though I'm uncomfortable with that word. See whether I can get into his frame of mind."

"Funny thing," Crazy Tom said; "I never thought of him typing out his stories. He was always sitting in some café writing in notebooks, piling up saucers."

"You've read a lot about him?" That would be another reason not to try the forgery. This guy comes out of the woodwork and says "I sold John Baird a 1921 Corona portable."

"Hell, all I do is read. If I get two customers a day, one of 'em's a mistake and the other just wants directions. I've read all of Hemingway's fiction and most of the journalism and I think all of the poetry. Not just the *Querschnitt* period; the more interesting stuff."

The invisible man was puzzled. Quite obviously John Baird planned some sort of Hemingway forgery. But then he should be growing worried over this man's dangerous expertise. Instead, he was radiating relief.

What course of action, inaction? He could go back a few hours in time and steal this typewriter, though he would have to materialize for that, and it would cause suspicions. And Baird could find another. He could kill one or both of them, now or last week or next, but that would mean duty in the fourteenth century for more than forever—when you exist out of time, a century of unpleasantness is long enough for planets to form and die.

He wouldn't have been drawn to this meeting if it were not a strong causal nexus. There must be earlier ones, since John Baird did not just stroll down a back street in this little town and decide to change history by buying a typewriter. But the earlier ones must be too weak, or something was masking them.

Maybe it was a good timeplace to get John Baird alone and explain things to him. Then use the wand on him. But no, not until he knew exactly what he was preventing. With considerable effort of will and expenditure of something like energy, he froze time at this instant and traveled to a couple of hundred adjacent realities that were all in this same bundle of doomed timelines.

In most of them, Baird was here in Crazy Tom's Typewriter Museum and Sales Emporium. In some, he was in a similar place in New York. In two, he was back in the Hemingway collection. In one, John Baird didn't exist: the whole planet was a lifeless blasted cinder. He'd known about that timeline; it had been sort of a dry run.

"He did both," John then said in most of the timelines. "Sometimes typing, sometimes fountain pen or pencil. I've seen the rough draft of his first novel. Written out in a stack of seven French schoolkids' copybooks." He looked around, memory working. A red herring wouldn't hurt. He'd never come across a reference to any other specific Hemingway typewriter, but maybe this guy had. "You know what kind of machine he used in Key West or Havana?"

Crazy Tom pulled on his chin. "Nope. Bring me a sample of the typing, and I might be able to pin it down, though. And I'll keep an eye out—got a card?"

John took out a business card and his checkbook. "Take a check on a Boston bank?"

"Sure, I'd take one on a Tierra del Fuego bank. Who'd stiff you on a seventy-year-old typewriter?" Sylvester Castlemaine might, John thought. "I've had this business almost twenty years," Tom continued. "Not a single bounced check or bent plastic."

"Yeah," John said. "Why would a crook want an old typewriter?" The invisible man laughed and went away.

10. BANAL STORY

Dear Lena & Castle,

Typing this on the new/old machine to give you an idea about what has to be modified to mimic EH's:
abcdefghijklmnopqrstuvwxyz

ABCDEFGHIJKLMNOPQRSTUVWXYZ234567890,./ "#$%_&'()*?

Other mechanical things to think about--

1. Paper-- One thing that made people suspicious about the Hitler forgery is that experts know that old paper smells old. And of course there was that fatal chemical-composition error that clinched it.

As we discussed, my first thought was that one of us would have to go to Paris and nose around in old attics and so forth, trying to find either a stack of 75-year-old paper or an old blank book we could cut pages out of. But in the JFK Library collection I found out that EH actually did bring some American-made paper along with him. A lot of the rough draft of in our time--written in Paris a year or two after our "discovery"--was typed on the back of 6 X 7" stationery from his parents' vacation place in Windemere, Xerox enclosed. It should be pretty easy to duplicate on a hand press, and of course it will be a lot easier to find 75-year-old American paper. One complication, unfortunately, is that I haven't really seen the paper; only a Xerox of the pages. Have to come up with some pretext to either visit the vault or have a page brought up, so I can check the color of the ink, memorize the weight and deckle of the paper, check to see how the edges are cut...

I'm starting to sound like a real forger. In for a penny, though, in for a pound. One of the critics who's sent the fragment might want to see the actual document, and compare it with the existing Windemere pages.

2. Inks. This should not be a problem. Here's a recipe for typewriter ribbon ink from a 1918 book of commercial formulas:

8 oz. lampblack

4 oz. gum Arabic

1 quart methylated spirits

That last one is wood alcohol. The others ought to be available in Miami if you can't find them on the Rock.

Aging the ink on the paper gets a little tricky. I haven't been able to find anything about it in the libraries around here; no FORGERY FOR FUN & PROFIT. May check in New York before coming back.

(If we don't find anything, I'd suggest baking it for a few days at a temperature low enough not to greatly affect the paper, and then interleaving it with blank sheets of the old paper and pressing them together for a few days, to restore the old smell, and further absorb the residual ink solvents.)

Toyed with the idea of actually allowing the manuscript to mildew somewhat, but that might get out of hand and actually destroy some of it--or for all I know we'd be employing a species of mildew that doesn't speak French. Again, thinking like a true forger, which may be a waste of time and effort, but I have to admit is kind of fun. Playing cops and robbers at my age.

Well, I'll call tonight. Miss you, Lena.

Your partner in crime,

11. A DIVINE GESTURE

When John returned to his place in Boston, there was a message on his answering machine: "John, this is Nelson Van Nuys. Harry told me you were in town. I left something in your box at the office and I strongly suggest you take it before somebody else does. I'll be out of town for a week, but give me a call if you're here next Friday. You can take me and Doris out to dinner at Panache."

Panache was the most expensive restaurant in Cambridge. Interesting. John checked his watch. He hadn't planned to go to the office, but there was plenty of time to swing by on his way to returning the rental car. The train didn't leave for another four hours.

Van Nuys was a fellow Hemingway scholar and sometimes drinking buddy who taught at Brown. What had he brought ninety miles to deliver in person, rather than mail? He was probably just in town and dropped by. But it was worth checking.

No one but the secretary was in the office, noontime, for which John was obscurely relieved. In his box were three interdepartmental memos, a textbook catalog, and a brown cardboard box that sloshed when he picked it up. He took it all back to his office and closed the door.

The office made him feel a little weary, as usual. He wondered whether they would be shuffling people around again this year. The department liked to keep its professors in shape by having them haul tons of books and files up and down the corridor every couple of years.

He glanced at the memos and pitched them, irrelevant since he wasn't teaching in the summer, and put the catalog in his briefcase. Then he carefully opened the cardboard box.

It was a half-pint Jack Daniel's bottle, but it didn't have bourbon in it. A cloudy greenish liquid. John unscrewed the top and with the sharp Pernod tang the memory came back. He and Van Nuys had wasted half an afternoon in Paris years ago, trying to track down a source of true absinthe. So he had finally found some.

Absinthe. Nectar of the gods, ruination of several generations of French artists, students, workingmen—outlawed in 1915 for its addictive and hallucinogenic qualities. Where had Van Nuys found it?

He screwed the top back on tightly and put it back in the box and put the box in his briefcase. If its effect really was all that powerful, you probably wouldn't want to drive under its influence. In Boston traffic, of course, a little lane weaving and a few mild collisions would go unnoticed.

Once he was safely on the train, he'd try a shot or two of it. It couldn't be all that potent. Child of the sixties, John had taken LSD, psilocybin, ecstasy, and peyote, and remembered with complete accuracy the quality of each drug's hallucinations. The effects of absinthe wouldn't be nearly as extreme as its modern successors. But it was probably just as well to try it first in a place where unconsciousness or Steve Allen imitations or speaking in tongues would go unremarked.

He turned in the rental car and took a cab to South Station rather than juggle suitcase, briefcase, and typewriter through the subway system. Once there, he nursed a beer through an hour of the Yankees murdering the Red Sox, and then rented a cart to roll his burden down to track 3, where a smiling porter installed him aboard the *Silver Meteor*, its range newly extended from Boston to Miami.

He had loved the train since his boyhood in Washington. His mother hated flying and so they often clickety-clacked from place to place in the snug comfort of first-class compartments. Eidetic memory blunted his enjoyment of the modern Amtrak version. This compartment was as large as the ones he had read and done puzzles in, forty years before—amazing and delighting his mother with his proficiency in word games—but the smell of good old leather was gone, replaced by plastic, and the fittings that had been polished brass were chromed steel now. On the middle of the red plastic seat was a Hospitality Pak, a plastic box encased in plastic wrap that contained a wedge of indestructible "cheese food," as if cheese had to eat, a small plastic bottle of cheap California wine, a plastic glass to contain it, and an apple, possibly not plastic.

John hung up his coat and tie in the small closet provided beside where the bed would fold down, and for a few minutes he watched with interest as his fellow passengers and their accompaniment hurried or ambled to their cars. Mostly old people, of course. Enough young ones, John hoped, to keep the trains alive a few decades more.

"Mr. Baird?" John turned to face a black porter, who bowed slightly and favored him with a blinding smile of white and gold. "My name is George, and I will be at your service as far as Atlanta. Is everything satisfactory?"

"Doing fine. But if you could find me a glass made of glass and a couple of ice cubes, I might mention you in my will."

"One minute, sir." In fact, it took less than a minute. That was one aspect, John had to admit, that had improved in recent years: The service on Amtrak in the sixties and seventies had been right up there with Alcatraz and the Hanoi Hilton.

He closed and locked the compartment door and carefully poured about two ounces of the absinthe into the glass. Like Pernod, it turned milky on contact with the ice.

He swirled it around and breathed deeply. It did smell much like Pernod, but with an acrid tang that was probably oil of wormwood. An experimental sip: the wormwood didn't dominate the licorice flavor, but it was there.

"Thanks, Nelson," he whispered, and drank the whole thing in one cold fiery gulp. He set down the glass and the train began to move. For a weird moment that seemed hallucinatory, but it always did, the train starting off so smoothly and silently.

For about ten minutes he felt nothing unusual, as the train did its slow tour of Boston's least attractive backyards. The conductor who checked his ticket seemed like a normal human being, which could have been a hallucination.

John knew that some drugs, like amyl nitrite, hit with a swift slap, while others creep into your mind like careful infiltrators. This was the way of absinthe; all he felt was a slight alcohol buzz, and he was about to take another shot, when it subtly began.

There were *things* just at the periphery of his vision, odd things with substance, but somehow without shape, that of course moved away when he turned his head to look at them. At the same time a whispering began in his ears, just audible over the train noise, but not intelligible, as if in a language he had heard before but not understood. For some reason the effects were pleasant, though of course they could be frightening if a person were not expecting weirdness. He enjoyed the illusions for a few minutes, while the scenery outside mellowed into woodsy suburbs, and the visions and voices stopped rather suddenly.

He poured another ounce and this time diluted it with water. He remembered the sad woman in "Hills Like White Elephants" lamenting that everything new tasted like licorice, and allowed himself to wonder what Hemingway had been drinking when he wrote that curious story.

Chuckling at his own—what? Effrontery?—John took out the 1921 Corona and slipped a sheet of paper into it and balanced it on his knees. He had earlier thought of the first two lines of the WWI pastiche; he typed them down and kept going:

```
The dirt on the sides of the trenches was never com-
pletely dry in the morning. If Nick could find an old
newspaper he would put it between his chest and the dirt
when he went out to lean on the side of the trench and
wait for the light. First light was the best time. You
might have luck and see a muzzle flash. But patience was
better than luck. Wait to see a helmet or a head without
a helmet.
    Nick looked at the enemy line through a rectangular
box of wood that went through the trench at about ground
level. The other end of the box was covered by a square
of gauze the color of dirt. A person looking directly at
it might see the muzzle flash when Nick fired through
```

the box. But with luck, the flash would be the last thing he saw.

Nick had fired through the gauze six times, perhaps killing three enemy, and the gauze now had a ragged hole in the center.

Okay, John thought, he'd be able to see slightly better through the hole in the center but staring that way would reduce the effective field of view, so he would deliberately try to look to one side or the other. How to type that down in a simple way? Someone cleared his throat.

John looked up from the typewriter. Sitting across from him was Ernest Hemingway, the weathered, wise Hemingway of the famous Karsh photograph.

"I'm afraid you must not do that," Hemingway said.

John looked at the half-full glass of absinthe and looked back. Hemingway was still there. "Jesus Christ," he said.

"It isn't the absinthe." Hemingway's image rippled and he became the handsome teenager who had gone to war, the war John was writing about. "I am quite real. In a way, I am more real than you are." As it spoke it aged: the mustachioed leading-man-handsome Hemingway of the twenties; the slightly corpulent, still magnetic media hero of the thirties and forties; the beard turning white, the features hard and sad and then twisting with impotence and madness, and then a sudden loud report and the cranial vault exploding, the mahogany veneer of the wall splashed with blood and brains and imbedded chips of skull. There was a strong smell of cordite and blood. The almost-headless corpse shrugged, spreading its hands. "I can look like anyone I want." The mean disappeared and it became the young Hemingway again.

John slumped and stared

"This thing you just started must never be finished. This Hemingway pastiche. It will ruin something very important."

"What could it ruin? I'm not even planning to—"

"Your plans are immaterial. If you continue with this project, it will profoundly affect the future."

"You're from the future?"

"I'm from the future and the past and other temporalities that you can't comprehend. But all you need to know is that you must not write this Hemingway story. If you do, I or someone like me will have to kill you."

It gestured and a wand the size of a walking stick, half-black and half-white, appeared in its hand. It tapped John's knee with the white end. There was a slight tingle.

"Now you won't be able to tell anybody about me, or write anything about me down. If you try to talk about me, the memory will disappear—and reappear moments later, along with the knowledge that I will kill you if you don't cooperate." It turned into the bloody corpse again. "Understood?"

"Of course."

"If you behave, you will never have to see me again." It started to fade.

"Wait. What do you really look like?"

"This...." For a few seconds John stared at an ebony presence deeper than black, at once points and edges and surfaces and volume and hints of further dimensions. "You can't really see or know," a voice whispered inside his head. He reached into the blackness and jerked his hand back, rimed with frost and numb. The thing disappeared.

He stuck his hand under his armpit and feeling returned. That last apparition was the unsettling one. He had Hemingway's appearance at every age memorized, and had seen the corpse in his mind's eye often enough. A drug could conceivably have brought them all together and made up this fantastic demand—which might actually be nothing more than a reasonable side of his nature trying to make him stop wasting time on this silly project.

But that thing. His hand was back to normal. Maybe a drug could do that, too; make your hand feel freezing. LSD did more profound things than that. But not while arguing about a manuscript.

He considered the remaining absinthe. Maybe take another big blast of it and see whether ol' Ernie comes back again. Or no—there was a simpler way to check.

The bar was four rocking and rolling cars away, and bouncing his way from wall to window helped sober John up. When he got there, he had another twinge for the memories of the past. Stained Formica tables. No service; you had to go to a bar at the other end. Acrid with cigarette fumes. He remembered linen tablecloths and endless bottles of Coke with the names of cities from everywhere stamped on the bottom and, when his father came along with them, the rich sultry smoke of his Havanas. The fat Churchills from Punch that emphysema stopped just before Castro could. "A Coke, please." He wondered which depressed him more, the red can or the plastic cup with miniature ice cubes.

The test. It was not in his nature to talk to strangers on public conveyances. But this was necessary. There was a man sitting alone who looked about John's age, a Social Security-bound hippy with wire-rimmed John Lennon glasses, white hair down to his shoulders, bushy grey beard. He nodded when John sat down across from him, but didn't say anything. He sipped beer and looked blankly out at the gathering darkness.

"Excuse me," John said, "but I have a strange thing to ask you."

The man looked at him. "I don't mind strange things. But please don't try to sell me anything illegal."

"I wouldn't. It may have something to do with a drug, but it would be one I took."

"You do look odd. You tripping?"

"Doesn't feel like it. But I may have been...slipped something." He leaned back and rubbed his eyes. "I just talked to Ernest Hemingway."

"The writer?"

"In my roomette, yeah."

"Wow. He must be pretty old."

"He's dead! More than thirty years."

"Oh wow. Now that is something weird. What he say?"

"You know what a pastiche is?"

"French pastry?"

"No, it's when you copy...when you create an imitation of another person's writing. Hemingway's, in this case."

"Is that legal? I mean, with him dead and all."

"Sure it is, as long as you don't try to foist it off as Hemingway's real stuff."

"So what happened? He wanted to help you with it?"

"Actually, no...he said I'd better stop."

"Then you better stop. You don't fuck around with ghosts." He pointed at the old brass bracelet on John's wrist. "You in the 'Nam."

"Sixty-eight," John said. "Hue."

"Then you oughta know about ghosts. You don't fuck with ghosts."

"Yeah." What he'd thought was aloofness in the man's eyes, the set of his mouth, was aloneness, something slightly different. "You okay?"

"Oh yeah. Wasn't for a while, then I got my shit together." He looked out the window again, and said something weirdly like Hemingway: "I learned to take it a day at a time. The day you're in's the only day that's real. The past is shit and the future, hell, some day your future's gonna be that you got no future. So fuck it, you know? One day at a time."

John nodded. "What outfit were you in?"

"Like I say, man, the past is shit. No offense?"

"No, that's okay." He poured the rest of his Coke over the ice and stood up to go.

"You better talk to somebody about those ghosts. Some kinda shrink, you know? It's not that they're not real. But just you got to deal with 'em."

"Thanks. I will." John got a little more ice from the barman and negotiated his way down the lurching corridor back to his compartment, trying not to spill his drink while also juggling fantasy, reality, past, present, memory....

He opened the door and Hemingway was there, drinking his absinthe. He looked up with weary malice. "Am I going to have to kill you?"

What John did next would have surprised Castlemaine, who thought he was a nebbish. He closed the compartment door and sat down across from the apparition. "Maybe you can kill me and maybe you can't."

"Don't worry. I can."

"You said I wouldn't be able to talk to anyone about you. But I just walked down to the bar car and did."

"I know. That's why I came back."

"So if one of your powers doesn't work, maybe another doesn't. At any rate, if you kill me, you'll never find out what went wrong."

"That's very cute, but it doesn't work." It finished off the absinthe and then ran a finger around the rim of the glass, which refilled out of nowhere.

"You're making assumptions about causality that are necessarily naïve, because you can't perceive even half of the dimensions that you inhabit."

"Nevertheless, you haven't killed me yet."

"And assumptions about my 'psychology' that are absurd. I am no more a human being than you are a paramecium."

"I'll accept that. But I would make a deal with a paramecium if I thought I could gain an advantage from it."

"What could you possibly have to deal with, though?"

"I know something about myself that you evidently don't, that enables me to overcome your don't-talk restriction. Knowing that might be worth a great deal to you."

"Maybe something."

"What I would like in exchange is, of course, my life, and an explanation of why I must not do the Hemingway pastiche. Then I wouldn't do it."

"You wouldn't do it if I killed you, either."

John sipped his Coke and waited.

"All right. It goes something like this. There is not just one universe, but actually uncountable zillions of them. They're all roughly the same size and complexity as this one, and they're all going off in a zillion different directions, and it is one hell of a job to keep things straight."

"You do this by yourself? You're God?"

"There's not just one of me. In fact, it would be meaningless to assign a number to us, but I guess you could say that altogether, we are God... and the Devil, and the Cosmic Puppet Master, and the Grand Unification Theory, the Great Pumpkin and everything else. When we consider ourselves as a group, let me see, I guess a human translation of our name would be the Spatio-Temporal Adjustment Board."

"STAB?"

"I guess that is unfortunate. Anyhow, what STAB does is more the work of a scalpel than a knife." The Hemingway scratched its nose, leaving the absinthe suspended in midair. "Events are supposed to happen in certain ways, in certain sequences. You look at things happening and say cause and effect, or coincidence, or golly, that couldn't have happened in a million years—but you don't even have a clue. Don't even try to think about it. It's like an ant trying to figure out General Relativity."

"It wouldn't have a clue. Wouldn't know where to start."

The apparition gave him a sharp look and continued. "These universes come in bundles. Hundreds of them, thousands, that are pretty much the same. And they affect each other. Resonate with each other. When something goes wrong in one, it resonates and screws up all of them."

"You mean to say that if I write a Hemingway pastiche, hundreds of universes are going to go straight to hell?"

The apparition spread its hands and looked to the ceiling. "Nothing is simple. The only thing that's simple is that nothing is simple.

"I'm a sort of literature specialist. American literature of the nineteenth and twentieth centuries. Usually. Most of my timespace is taken up with guys like Hemingway, Teddy Roosevelt, Heinlein, Bierce. Crane, Spillane, Twain."

"Not William Dean Howells?"

"Not him or James or Carver or Coover or Cheever or any of those guys. If everybody gave me as little trouble as William Dean Howells, I could spend most of my timespace on a planet where the fishing was good."

"Masculine writers?" John said. "But not all hairy-chested macho types."

"I'll give you an A— on that one. They're writers who have an accumulating effect on the masculine side of the American national character. There's no one word for it, though it is a specific thing: individualistic, competence-worshiping, short-term optimism and long-term existentialism. 'There may be nothing after I die but I sure as hell will do the job right while I'm here, even though I'm surrounded by idiots.' You see the pattern?"

"Okay. And I see how Hemingway fits in. But how could writing a pastiche interfere with it?"

"That's a limitation I have. I don't know specifically. I do know that the accelerating revival of interest in Hemingway from the seventies through the nineties is vitally important. In the Soviet Union as well as the United States. For some reason, I can feel your pastiche interfering with it." He stretched out the absinthe glass into a yard-long amber crystal, and it changed into the black-and-white cane. The glass reappeared in the drink holder by the window. "Your turn."

"You won't kill me after you hear what I have to say?"

"No. Go ahead."

"Well...I have an absolutely eidetic memory. Everything I've ever seen—or smelled or tasted or heard or touched, or even dreamed—I can instantly recall.

"Every other memory freak I've read about was limited—numbers, dates, calendar tricks, historical details—and most of them were *idiots savants*. I have at least normal intelligence. But from the age of about three, I have never forgotten anything."

The Hemingway smiled congenially. "Thank you. That's exactly it." It fingered the black end of the cane, clicking something. "If you had the choice, would you rather die of a heart attack, stroke, or cancer?"

"That's it?" The Hemingway nodded. "Well, you're human enough to cheat. To lie."

"It's not something you could understand. Stroke?"

"It might not work."

"We're going to find out right now." He lowered the cane.

"Wait! What's death? Is there...anything I should do, anything you know?"

The rod stopped, poised an inch over John's knee. "I guess you just end. Is that so bad?"

"Compared to not ending, it's bad."

"That shows how little you know. I and the ones like me can never die. If you want something to occupy your last moment, your last thought, you might pity me."

John stared straight into his eyes. "Fuck you."

The cane dropped. A fireball exploded in his head.

12. MARRIAGE IS A DANGEROUS GAME

"We'll blackmail him." Castle and Lena were together in the big antique bathtub, in a sea of pink foam, her back against his chest.

"Sure," she said. "'If you don't let us pass this manuscript off as the real thing, we'll tell everybody you faked it.' Something wrong with that, but I can't quite put my finger on it."

"Here, I'll put mine on it."

She giggled. "Later. What do you mean, blackmail?"

"Got it all figured out. I've got this friend Pansy, she used to be a call girl. Been out of the game seven, eight years; still looks like a million bucks."

"Sure. We fix John up with this hooker—"

"Call girl isn't a hooker. We're talkin' class."

"In the first place, John wouldn't pay for sex. He did that in Vietnam and it still bothers him."

"Not talkin' about pay. Talkin' about fallin' in love. While she meanwhile fucks his eyeballs out."

"You have such a turn of phrase, Sylvester. Then while his eyeballs are out, you come in with a camera."

"Yeah, but you're about six steps ahead."

"Okay, step two; how do we get them together? Church social?"

"She moves in next door." There was another upstairs apartment, unoccupied. "You and me and Julio are conveniently somewhere else when she shows up with all these boxes and that big flight of stairs."

"Sure, John would help her. But that's his nature; he'd help her if she were an ugly old crone with leprosy. Carry a few boxes, sit down for a cup of coffee, maybe. But not jump into the sack."

"Okay, you know John." His voice dropped to a husky whisper and he cupped her breasts. "But I know men, and I know Pansy...and Pansy could give a hard-on to a corpse."

"Sure, and then fuck his eyeballs out. They'd come out easier."

"What?"

"Never mind. Go ahead."

"Well...look. Do you know what a call girl does?"

"I suppose you call her up and say you've got this eyeball problem."

"Enough with the eyeballs. What she does, she works for like an escort service. That part of it's legal. Guy comes into town, business or maybe on vacation, he calls up the service and they ask what kind of companion he'd like. If he says, like, give me some broad with a tight ass, can suck the chrome off a bumper hitch—the guy says like 'I'm sorry, sir, but this is not that kind of a service.' But mostly the customers are pretty hip to it, they say, oh, a pretty young blonde who likes to go dancing."

"Meanwhile they're thinking about bumper hitches and eyeballs."

"You got it. So it starts out just like a date, just the guy pays the escort service like twenty bucks for getting them together. Still no law broken."

"Now about one out of three, four times, that's it. The guy knows what's going on but he don't get up the nerve to ask, or he really doesn't know the score, and it's like a real dull date. I don't think that happened much with Pansy."

"In the normal course of things, though, the subject of bumper hitches comes up."

"Uh huh, but not from Pansy. The guy has to pop the question. That way if he's a cop it's, what, entrapment."

"Do you know whether Pansy ever got busted?"

"Naw. Mainly the cops just shake down the hookers, just want a blowjob anyhow. This town, half of 'em want a blowjob from guys.

"So they pop the question and Pansy blushes and says for you, I guess I could. Then, on the way to the motel or wherever she says, you know, I wouldn't ask this if we weren't really good friends, but I got to make a car payment by tomorrow, and I need like two hundred bucks before noon tomorrow?"

"And she takes MasterCard and VISA."

"No, but she sure as hell knows where every bank machine in town is. She even writes up an I.O.U." Castle laughed. "Told me a guy from Toledo's holdin' five grand of I.O.U.s from her."

"All right, but that's not John. She could suck the chrome off his eyeballs and he still wouldn't be interested in her if she didn't know Hemingway from hummingbirds."

Castle licked behind her ear, a weird gesture that made her shiver. "That's the trump card. Pansy reads like a son of a bitch. She's got like a thousand books. So this morning I called her up and asked about Hemingway."

"And?"

"She's read them all."

She nodded slowly. "Not bad, Sylvester. So we promote this love affair and sooner or later you catch them in the act. Threaten to tell me unless John accedes to a life of crime."

"Think it could work? He wouldn't say hell, go ahead and tell her?"

"Not if I do my part...starting tomorrow. I'm the best, sweetest, lovingest wife in this sexy town. Then in a couple of weeks Pansy comes into his life, and there he is, luckiest man alive. Best of both worlds. Until you accidentally catch them *in flagrante delicioso.*"

"So to keep both of you, he goes along with me."

"It might just do it. It might just." She slowly levered herself out of the water and smoothed the suds off her various assets.

"Nice."

"Bring me that bumper hitch, Sylvester. Hold on to your eyeballs."

13. IN ANOTHER COUNTRY

John woke up with a hangover of considerable dimension. The diluted glass of absinthe was still in the drink holder by the window. It was just past dawn, and a verdant forest rushed by outside. The rails made a steady hum; the car had a slight rocking that would have been pleasant to a person who felt well.

A porter knocked twice and inquired after Mr. Baird. "Come in," John said. A short white man, smiling, brought in coffee and Danish.

"What happened to George?"

"Pardon me, sir? George who?"

John rubbed his eyes. "Oh, of course. We must be past Atlanta."

"No, sir." The man's smile froze as his brain went into nutty-passenger mode. "We're at least two hours from Atlanta."

"George...is a tall black guy with gold teeth who—"

"Oh, you mean George Mason, sir. He does do this car, but he picks up the train in Atlanta, and works it to Miami and back. He hasn't had the northern leg since last year."

John nodded slowly and didn't ask what year it was. "I understand." He smiled up and read the man's name tag. "I'm sorry, Leonard. Not at my best in the morning." The man withdrew with polite haste.

Suppose that weird dream had not been a dream. The Hemingway creature had killed him—the memory of the stroke was awesomely strong and immediate—but all that death amounted to was slipping into another universe where George Mason was on a different shift. Or perhaps John had gone completely insane.

The second explanation seemed much more reasonable.

On the tray underneath the coffee, juice, and Danish was a copy of *USA Today*, a paper John normally avoided because, although it had its comic aspects, it didn't have any funnies. He checked the date, and it was

271

correct. The news stories were plausible—wars and rumors of war—so at least he hadn't slipped into a dimension where Martians ruled an enslaved Earth or Barry Manilow was president. He turned to the weather map and stopped dead.

Yesterday the country was in the middle of a heat wave that had lasted weeks. It apparently had ended overnight. The entry for Boston, yesterday, was "72/58/sh." But it hadn't rained and the temperature had been in the nineties.

He went back to the front page and began checking news stories. He didn't normally pay much attention to the news, though, and hadn't seen a paper in several days. They'd canceled their *Globe* delivery for the six weeks in Key West and he hadn't been interested enough to go seek out a newsstand.

There was no mention of the garbage collectors' strike in New York; he'd overheard a conversation about that yesterday. A long obituary for a rock star he was sure had died the year before.

An ad for DeSoto automobiles. That company had gone out of business when he was a teenager.

Bundles of universes, different from each other in small ways. Instead of dying, or maybe because of dying, he had slipped into another one. What would be waiting for him in Key West?

Maybe John Baird.

He set the tray down and hugged himself, trembling. Who or what was he in this universe? All of his memories, all of his personality, were from the one he had been born in. What happened to the John Baird that was born in this one? Was he an associate professor in American Literature at Boston University? Was he down in Key West wrestling with a paper to give at Nairobi—or working on a forgery? Or was he a Fitzgerald specialist snooping around the literary attics of St. Paul, Minnesota?

The truth came suddenly. Both John Bairds were in this compartment, in this body. And the body was slightly different.

He opened the door to the small washroom and looked in the mirror. His hair was a little shorter, less grey, beard better trimmed.

He was less paunchy and…something felt odd. There was feeling in his thigh. He lowered his pants and there was no scar where the sniper bullet had opened his leg and torn up the nerves there.

That was the touchstone. As he raised his shirt, the parallel memory flooded in. Puckered round scar on the abdomen; in this universe the sniper had hit a foot higher—and instead of the convalescent center in Cam Ranh Bay, the months of physical therapy and then back into the war, it had been peritonitis raging; surgery in Saigon and Tokyo and Walter Reed, and no more army.

But slowly they converged again. Amherst and U. Mass.—perversely using the G.I. Bill in spite of his access to millions—the doctorate on *The Sun Also Rises* and the instructorship at B.U., meeting Lena and virtuously waiting until after the semester to ask her out. Sex on the second date, and the third…but there they verged again. This John Baird hadn't gone back into combat to have his midsection sprayed with shrapnel from an American grenade that bounced off a tree; never had dozens of bits of metal cut out of his dick—and in the ensuing twenty-five years had made more use of it. Girlfriends and even one disastrous homosexual encounter with a stranger. As far as he knew, Lena was in the dark about this side of him; thought that he had remained faithful other than one incident seven years after they married. He knew of one affair she had had with a colleague, and suspected more.

The two Johns' personalities and histories merged, separate but one, like two vines from a common root, climbing a single support.

Schizophrenic but not insane.

John looked into the mirror and tried to address his new or his old self—John A, John B. There were no such people. There was suddenly a man who had existed in two separate universes and, in a way, it was no more profound than having lived in two separate houses.

The difference being that nobody else knows there is more than one house.

He moved over to the window and set his coffee in the holder, picked up the absinthe glass and sniffed it, considered pouring it down the drain, but then put it in the other holder, for possible future reference.

Posit this: is it more likely that there are bundles of parallel universes prevailed over by a Hemingway look-alike with a magic cane, or that John Baird was exposed to a drug that he had never experienced before and it had had an unusually disorienting effect?

He looked at the paper. He had not hallucinated two weeks of drought. The rock star had been dead for some time. He had not seen a DeSoto in twenty years, and that was a hard car to miss. Tail fins that had to be registered as lethal weapons.

But maybe if you take a person who remembers every trivial thing, and zap his brain with oil of wormwood, that is exactly the effect: perfectly recalled things that never actually happened.

The coffee tasted repulsive. John put on a fresh shirt and decided not to shave and headed for the bar car. He bought the last imported beer in the cooler and sat down across from the long-haired white-bearded man who had an earring that had escaped his notice before, or hadn't existed in the other universe.

The man was staring out at the forest greening by. "Morning," John said.

"How do." The man looked at him with no sign of recognition.

"Did we talk last night?"

He leaned forward. "What?"

"I mean did we sit in this car last night and talk about Hemingway and Vietnam and ghosts?"

He laughed. "You're on somethin', man. I been on this train since two in the mornin' and ain't said boo to nobody but the bartender."

"You were in Vietnam?"

"Yeah, but that's over; that's shit." He pointed at John's bracelet. "What, you got ghosts from over there?"

"I think maybe I have."

He was suddenly intense. "Take my advice, man; I been there. You got to go talk to somebody. Some shrink. Those ghosts ain't gonna go 'way by themselves.

"It's not that bad."

"It ain't the ones you killed." He wasn't listening. "Fuckin' dinks, they come back but they don't, you know, they just stand around." He looked at John and tears came so hard they actually spurted from his eyes. "It's your fuckin' friends, man, they all died and they come back now...." He took a deep breath and wiped his face. "They used to come back every night. That like you?" John shook his head, helpless, trapped by the man's grief. "Every fuckin' night, my old lady, finally she said you go to a shrink or go to hell." He fumbled with the button on his shirt pocket and took out a brown plastic prescription bottle and stared at the label. He shook out a capsule. "Take a swig?" John pushed the beer over to him. He washed the pill down without touching the bottle to his lips.

He sagged back against the window. "I musta not took the pill last night, sometimes I do that. Sorry." He smiled weakly. "One day at a time, you know? You get through the one day. Fuck the rest. Sorry." He leaned forward again suddenly and put his hand on John's wrist. "You come outa nowhere and I lay my fuckin' trip on you. You don' need it."

John covered the hand with his own. "Maybe I do need it. And maybe I didn't come out of nowhere." He stood up. "I will see somebody about the ghosts. Promise."

"You'll feel better. It's no fuckin' cure-all, but you'll feel better."

"Want the beer?"

He shook his head. "Not supposed to."

"Okay." John took the beer and they waved at each other and he started back.

He stopped in the vestibule between cars and stood in the rattling roar of it, looking out the window at the flashing green blur. He put his forehead against the cool glass and hid the blur behind the dark red of his eyelids.

Were there actually a zillion of those guys each going through a slightly different private hell? Something he rarely asked himself was "What would Ernest Hemingway have done in this situation?"

He'd probably have the sense to leave it to Milton.

14. THE DANGEROUS SUMMER

Castle and Lena met him at the station in Miami and they drove back to Key West in Castle's old pickup. The drone of the air conditioner held conversation to a minimum, but it kept them cool, at least from the knees down.

John didn't say anything about his encounter with the infinite, or transfinite, not wishing to bring back that fellow with the cane just yet. He did note that the two aspects of his personality hadn't quite become equal partners yet, and small details of this world kept surprising him. There was a monorail being built down to Pigeon Key, where Disney was digging an underwater park. Gasoline stations still sold Regular. Castle's car radio picked up TV as well as AM/FM, but sound only.

Lena sat between the two men and rubbed up against John affectionately. That would have been remarkable for John-one and somewhat unusual for John-two. It was a different Lena here, of course; one who had had more of a sex life with John, but there was something more than that, too. She was probably sleeping with Castle, he thought, and the extra attention was a conscious or unconscious compensation, or defense.

Castle seemed a little harder and more serious in this world than the last, not only from his terse moodiness in the pickup, but from recollections of parallel conversations. John wondered how shady he actually was, whether he'd been honest about his police record.

(He hadn't been. In this universe, when Lena had asked him whether he had ever been in trouble with the police, he'd answered a terse "no." In fact, he'd done eight hard years in Ohio for an armed robbery he hadn't committed—the real robber hadn't been so stupid, here—and he'd come out of prison bitter, angry, an actual criminal. Figuring the world owed him one, a week after getting out he stopped for a hitchhiker on a lonely country road, pulled a gun, walked him a few yards off the road into a field of high corn, and shot him point-blank at the base of the skull. It didn't look anything like the movies.)

(He drove off without touching the body, which a farmer's child found two days later. The victim turned out to be a college student who was on probation for dealing—all he'd really done was buy a kilo of green and make his money back by selling bags to his friends, and one enemy—so the papers said DRUG DEALER FOUND SLAIN IN GANGLAND-STYLE KILLING and the police pursued the matter with no enthusiasm. Castle was in Key West well before the farmer's child smelled the body, anyhow.)

As they rode along, whatever Lena had or hadn't done with Castle was less interesting to John than what *he* was planning to do with her. Half of his self had never experienced sex, as an adult, without the sensory handicaps engendered by scar tissue and severed nerves in the genitals, and he was looking forward to the experience with a relish that was obvious, at least to Lena. She encouraged him in not-so-subtle ways, and by the time they crossed the last bridge into Key West, he was ready to tell Castle to pull over at the first bush.

He left the typewriter in Castle's care and declined help with the luggage. By this time Lena was smiling at his obvious impatience; she was giggling by the time they were momentarily stalled by a truculent door key; laughed her delight as he carried her charging across the room to the couch, then clawing off a minimum of clothing and taking her with fierce haste, wordless, and keeping her on a breathless edge he drifted the rest of the clothes off her and carried her into the bedroom, where they made so much noise Julio banged on the ceiling with a broomstick.

They did quiet down eventually, and lay together in a puddle of mingled sweat, panting, watching the fan push the humid air around. "Guess we both get to sleep in the wet spot," John said.

"No complaints." She raised up on one elbow and traced a figure eight on his chest. "You're full of surprises tonight, Dr. Baird."

"Life is full of surprises."

"You should go away more often—or at least come back more often."

"It's all that Hemingway research. Makes a man out of you."

"You didn't learn this in a book," she said, gently taking his penis and pantomiming a certain motion.

"I did, though, an anthropology book." In another universe. "It's what they do in the Solomon Islands."

"Wisdom of Solomon," she said, lying back. After a pause: "They have anthropology books at JFK?"

"Uh, no." He remembered he didn't own that book in this universe. "Browsing at Wordsworth's."

"Hope you bought the book."

"Didn't have to." He gave her a long slow caress. "Memorized the good parts."

On the other side of town, six days later, she was in about the same position on Castle's bed, and even more exhausted.

"Aren't you overdoing the loving little wifey bit? It's been a week."

She exhaled audibly. "What a week."

"Missed you." He nuzzled her and made an unsubtle preparatory gesture.

"No, you don't." She rolled out of bed. "Once is plenty." She went to the mirror and ran a brush through her damp hair. "Besides, it's not me you missed. You missed *it*." She sat at the open window, improving the neighborhood's scenery. "It's gonna need a Teflon lining installed."

"Old boy's feelin' his oats?"

"Not feeling *his* anything. God, I don't know what's gotten into him. Four, five times a day; six."

"Screwed, blewed, and tattooed. You asked for it."

"As a matter of fact, I didn't. I haven't had a chance to start my little act. He got off that train with an erection, and he still has it. No woman would be safe around him. Nothing wet and concave would be safe."

"So does that mean it's a good time to bring in Pansy? Or is he so stuck on you he wouldn't even notice her?"

She scowled at the brush, picking hair out of it. "Actually, Castle, I was just about to ask you the same thing. Relying on your well-known expertise in animal behavior."

"Okay." He sat up. "I say we oughta go for it. If he's a walkin' talkin' hard-on like you say...Pansy'd pull him like a magnet. You'd have to be a fuckin' monk not to want Pansy."

"Like Rasputin."

"Like who?"

"Never mind." She went back to the brush. "I guess, I guess one problem is that I really am enjoying the attention. I guess I'm not too anxious to hand him over to this champion sexpot."

"Aw, Lena—"

"Really. I do love him in my way, Castle. I don't want to lose him over this scheme."

"You're not gonna lose him. Trust me. You catch him dickin' Pansy, get mad, forgive him. Hell, you'll have him wrapped around your finger."

"I guess. You make the competition sound pretty formidable."

"Don't worry. She's outa there the next day."

"Unless she winds up in love with him. That would be cute."

"He's almost twice her age. Besides, she's a whore. Whores don't fall in love."

"They're women, Castle. Women fall in love."

"Yeah, sure. Just like on TV."

She turned away from him; looked out the window. "You really know how to make a woman feel great, you know?"

"Come on." He crossed over and smoothed her hair. She turned around but didn't look up. "Don't run yourself down, Lena. You're still one hell of a piece of ass."

"Thanks." She smiled into his leer and grabbed him. "If you weren't such a poet, I'd trade you in for a vibrator."

15. IN PRAISE OF HIS MISTRESS

Pansy was indeed beautiful, even under normal conditions; delicate features, wasp waist combined with generous secondary sexual characteristics. The conditions under which John first saw her were calculated to maximize sexiness and vulnerability. Red nylon running shorts, tight and very short, and a white sleeveless T-shirt from a local bar that was stamped LAST HETEROSEXUAL IN KEY WEST—all clinging to her golden skin with a healthy sweat, the cloth made translucent enough to reveal no possibility of underwear.

John looked out the screen door and saw her at the other door, struggling with a heavy box while trying to make the key work. "Let me help you," he said through the screen, and stepped across the short landing to hold the box while she got the door open.

"You're too kind." John tried not to stare as he handed the box back. Pansy, of course, was relieved at his riveted attention. It had taken days to set up this operation, and would take more days to bring it to its climax, so to speak, and more days to get back to normal. But she did owe Castle a big favor and this guy seemed nice enough. Maybe she'd learn something about Hemingway in the process.

"More to come up?" John asked.

"Oh, I couldn't ask you to help. I can manage."

"It's okay. I was just goofing off for the rest of the day."

It turned out to be quite a job, even though there was only one load from a small rented truck. Most of the load was uniform and heavy boxes of books, carefully labeled LIT A-B, GEN REF, ENCY 1-12, and so forth. Most of her furniture, accordingly, was cinder blocks and boards, the standard student bookshelf arrangement.

John found out that despite a couple of dozen boxes marked LIT, Pansy hadn't majored in literature, but rather Special Education; during the school year, she taught third grade at a school for the retarded in Key Largo. She didn't tell him about the several years she'd spent as a call girl, but if she had, John might have seen a connection that Castle would never have made—that the driving force behind both of the jobs was the same, charity. The more or less easy forty dollars an hour for going on a date and then having sex was a factor, too, but she really did like making lonely men feel special, and had herself felt more like a social worker than a woman of easy virtue. And the hundreds of men who had fallen for her, for love or money, weren't responding only to her cheerleader's body. She had a sunny disposition and a natural, artless way of concentrating on a man that made him for a while the only man in the world.

John would not normally be an easy conquest. Twenty years of facing classrooms full of coeds had given him a certain wariness around attractive young women. He also had an impulse toward faithfulness, Lena having suddenly left town, her father ill. But he was still in the grip of the weird overweening horniness that had animated him since inheriting this new body and double-image personality. If Pansy had said "Let's do it," they would be doing it so soon that she would be wise to unwrap the condom before speaking. But she was being as indirect as her nature and mode of dress would allow.

"Do you and your wife always come down here for the summer?"

"We usually go somewhere. Boston's no fun in the heat."

"It must be wonderful in the fall."

And so forth. It felt odd for Pansy, probably the last time she would ever seduce a man for reasons other than personal interest. She wanted it to be perfect. She wanted John to have enough pleasure in her to compensate for the embarrassment of their "accidental" exposure, and whatever hassle his wife would put him through afterwards.

She was dying to know why Castle wanted him set up. How Castle ever met a quiet, kindly gentleman like John was a mystery, too—she had met some of Castle's friends, and they had other virtues.

Quiet and kindly, but horny. Whenever she contrived, in the course of their working together, to expose a nipple or a little beaver, he would turn around to adjust himself, and blush. More like a teenager, discovering his sexuality, than a middle-aged married man.

He was a pushover, but she didn't want to make it too easy. After they had finished putting the books up on shelves, she said thanks a million; I gotta go now, spending the night house-sitting up in Islamorada. You and your wife come over for dinner tomorrow? Oh, then come on over yourself. No, that's all right, I'm a big girl. Roast beef okay? See ya.

Driving away in the rented truck, Pansy didn't feel especially proud of herself. She was amused at John's sexiness and looking forward to trying it out. But she could read people pretty well, and sensed a core of deep sadness in John. Maybe it was from Vietnam; he hadn't mentioned it, but she knew what the bracelet meant.

Whatever the problem, maybe she'd have time to help him with it— before she had to turn around and add to it.

Maybe it would work out for the best. Maybe the problem was with his wife, and she'd leave, and he could start over....

Stop kidding yourself. Just lay the trap, catch him, deliver him. Castle was not the kind of man you want to disappoint.

16. FIESTA

She had baked the roast slowly with wine and fruit juice, along with dried apricots and apples plumped in port wine, seasoned with cinnamon and nutmeg and cardamom. Onions and large cubes of acorn squash simmered in the broth. She served new potatoes steamed with parsley and dressed Italian style, with garlicky olive oil and a splash of vinegar. Small Caesar salad and air-light *pan de agua*, the Cuban bread that made you forget every other kind of bread.

The way to a man's heart, her mother had contended, was through his stomach, and although she was accustomed to aiming rather lower, she thought it was probably a good approach for a longtime married man suddenly forced to fend for himself. That was exactly right for John. He was not much of a cook, but he was an accomplished eater.

He pushed the plate away after three helpings. "God, I'm such a pig. But that was irresistible."

"Thank you." She cleared the table slowly, accepting John's offer to help. "My mother's 'company' recipe. So you think Hadley might have just thrown the stories away, and made up the business about the train?"

"People have raised the possibility. There she was, eight years older than this handsome hubby—with half the women on the Left Bank after him, at least in her mind—and he's starting to get published, starting to build a reputation...."

"She was afraid he was going to 'grow away' from her? Or did they have that expression back then?"

"I think she was afraid he would start making money from his writing. She had an inheritance, a trust fund from her grandfather, that paid over two thousand a year. That was plenty to keep the two of them comfortable in Paris. Hemingway talked poor in those days, starving artist, but he lived pretty well."

"He probably resented it, too. Not making the money himself."

"That would be like him. Anyhow, if she chucked the stories to ensure his dependency, it backfired. He was still furious thirty years later—three wives later. He said the stuff had been 'fresh from the mint,' even if the writing wasn't so great, and he was never able to reclaim it."

She opened a cabinet and slid a bottle out of its burlap bag, and selected two small glasses. "Sherry?" He said why not? and they moved into the living room.

The living room was mysteriously devoid of chairs, so they had to sit together on the small couch. "You don't actually think she did it."

"No." John watched her pour the sherry. "From what I've read about her, she doesn't seem at all calculating. Just a sweet gal from St. Louis who fell in love with a cad."

"Cad. Funny old-fashioned word."

John shrugged. "Actually, he wasn't really a cad. I think he sincerely loved every one of his wives…at least until he married them."

They both laughed. "Of course it could have been something in between," Pansy said, "I mean, she didn't actually throw away the manuscripts, but she did leave them sitting out, begging to be stolen. Why did she leave the compartment?"

"That's one screwy aspect of it. Hadley herself never said, not on paper. Every biographer seems to come up with a different reason: she went to get a newspaper, she saw some people she recognized and stepped out to talk with them, wanted some exercise before the long trip…even Hemingway had two different versions—she went out to get a bottle of Evian water or to buy something to read. That one pissed him off, because she did have an overnight bag full of the best American writing since Mark Twain."

"How would you have felt?"

"Felt?"

"I mean, you say you've written stories, too. What if somebody, your wife, made a mistake and you lost everything?"

He looked thoughtful. "It's not the same. In the first place, it's just hobby with me. And I don't have that much that hasn't been published—when Hemingway lost it, he lost it for good. I could just go to a university library and make new copies of everything."

"So you haven't written much lately?"

"Not stories. Academic stuff."

"I'd love to read some of your stories."

"And I'd love to have you read them. But I don't have any here. I'll mail you some from Boston."

She nodded, staring at him with a curious intensity. "Oh hell," she said, and turned her back to him. "Would you help me with this?"

"What?"

"The zipper." She was wearing a clingy white summer dress. "Undo the zipper a little bit."

He slowly unzipped it a few inches. She did it the rest of the way, stood up and hooked her thumbs under the shoulder straps and shrugged. The dress slithered to the floor. She wasn't wearing anything else.

"You're blushing." Actually, he was doing a good imitation of a beached fish. She straddled him, sitting back lightly on his knees, legs wide, and started unbuttoning his shirt.

"Uh," he said.

"I just get impatient. You don't mind?"

"Uh…no?"

17. ON BEING SHOT AGAIN

John woke up happy but didn't open his eyes for nearly a minute, holding on to the erotic dream of the century. Then he opened one eye and saw it hadn't been a dream: the tousled bed in the strange room, unguents and sex toys on the nightstand, the smell of her hair on the other pillow. A noise from the kitchen; coffee and bacon smells.

He put on pants and went into the living room to pick up the shirt where it had dropped. "Good morning, Pansy."

"Morning, stranger." She was wearing a floppy terry cloth bathrobe with the sleeves rolled up to her elbows. She turned the bacon carefully with a fork. "Scrambled eggs okay?"

"Marvelous." He sat down at the small table and poured himself a cup of coffee. "I don't know what to say."

She smiled at him. "Don't say anything. It was nice."

"More than nice." He watched her precise motions behind the counter. She broke the eggs one-handed, two at a time, added a splash of water to the bowl, plucked some chives from a windowbox and chopped them with a small Chinese cleaver, rocking it in a staccato chatter; scraped them into the bowl, and followed them with a couple of grinds of pepper. She set the bacon out on a paper towel, with another towel to cover. Then she stirred the eggs briskly with the fork and set them aside. She picked up the big cast-iron frying pan and poured off a judicious amount of grease. Then she poured the egg mixture into the pan and studied it with alertness.

"Know what I think?" John said.

"Something profound?"

"Huh uh. I think I'm in a rubber room someplace, hallucinating the whole thing. And I hope they never cure me."

"I think you're a butterfly who's dreaming he's a man. I'm glad I'm in your dream." She slowly stirred and scraped the eggs with a spatula.

"You like older men?"

"One of them." She looked up, serious. "I like men who are considerate…and playful." She returned to the scraping. "Last couple of boyfriends I had were all dick and no heart. Kept to myself the last few months."

"Glad to be of service."

"You could rent yourself out as a service." She laughed. "You must have been impossible when you were younger."

"Different." Literally.

She ran hot water into a serving bowl, then returned to her egg stewardship. "I've been thinking."

"Yes?"

"The lost manuscript stuff we were talking about last night, all the different explanations." She divided the egg into four masses and turned each one. "Did you ever read any science fiction?"

"No. Vonnegut."

"The toast." She hurriedly put four pieces of bread in the toaster. "They write about alternate universes. Pretty much like our own, but different in one way or another. Important or trivial."

"What, uh, what silliness."

She laughed and poured the hot water out of the serving bowl, and dried it with a towel. "I guess maybe. But what if...what if all of those versions were equally true? In different universes. And for some reason they all came together here." She started to put the eggs into the bowl when there was a knock on the door.

It opened and Ernest Hemingway walked in. Dapper, just twenty, wearing the Italian army cape he'd brought back from the war. He pointed the black-and-white cane at Pansy. "Bingo."

She looked at John and then back at the Hemingway. She dropped the serving bowl; it clattered on the floor without breaking. Her knees buckled and she fainted dead away, executing a half turn as she fell so that the back of her head struck the wooden floor with a loud thump and the bathrobe drifted open from the waist down.

The Hemingway stared down at her frontal aspect. "Sometimes I wish I were human," it said. "Your pleasures are intense. Simple, but intense." It moved toward her with the cane.

John stood up. "If you kill her—"

"Oh?" It cocked an eyebrow at him. "What will you do?"

John took one step toward it and it waved the cane. A waist-high brick wall surmounted by needle-sharp spikes appeared between them. It gestured again and an impossible moat appeared, deep enough to reach down well into Julio's living room. It filled with water and a large croco-dile surfaced and rested its chin on the parquet floor, staring at John. It yawned teeth.

The Hemingway held up its cane. "The white end. It doesn't kill, remember?" The wall and moat disappeared and the cane touched Pansy lightly below the navel. She twitched minutely but continued to sleep. "She'll have a headache," it said. "And she'll be somewhat confused by the uncommunicatable memory of having seen me. But that will all fade, compared to the sudden tragedy of having her new lover die here, just sitting waiting for his breakfast."

"Do you enjoy this?"

"I love my work. It's all I have." It walked toward him, footfalls splashing as it crossed where the moat had been. "You have not personally helped, though. Not at all."

It sat down across from him and poured coffee into a mug that said ON THE SIXTH DAY GOD CREATED MAN—SHE MUST HAVE HAD PMS.

"When you kill me this time, do you think it will 'take'?"

"I don't know. It's never failed before." The toaster made a noise. "Toast?"

"Sure." Two pieces appeared on his plate; two on the Hemingway's. "Usually when you kill people they stay dead?"

"I don't kill that many people." It spread margarine on its toast, gestured, and marmalade appeared. "But when I do, yeah. They die all up and down the Omniverse, every timespace. All except you." He pointed toast at John's toast. "Go ahead. It's not poison."

"Not my idea of a last meal."

The Hemingway shrugged. "What would you like?"

"Forget it." He buttered the toast and piled marmalade on it, determined out of some odd impulse to act as if nothing unusual were happening. Breakfast with Hemingway, big deal.

He studied the apparition and noticed that it was somewhat translucent, almost like a traditional TV ghost. He could barely see a line that was the back of the chair, bisecting its chest below shoulder-blade level. Was this something new? There hadn't been too much light in the train; maybe he had just failed to notice it before.

"A penny for your thoughts."

He didn't say anything about seeing through it. "Has it occurred to you that maybe you're not *supposed* to kill me? That's why I came back?"

The Hemingway chuckled and admired its nails. "That's a nearly content-free assertion."

"Oh really." He bit into the toast. The marmalade was strong, pleasantly bitter.

"It presupposes a higher authority, unknown to me, that's watching over my behavior, and correcting me when I do wrong. Doesn't exist, sorry."

"That's the oldest one in the theologian's book." He set down the toast and kneaded his stomach; shouldn't eat something so strong first thing in the morning. "You can only *assert* the nonexistence of something; you can't prove it."

"What you mean is *you* can't." He held up the cane and looked at it. "The simplest explanation is that there's something wrong with the cane. There's no way I can test it; if I kill the wrong person, there's hell to pay up and down the Omniverse. But what I can do is kill you without the cane. See whether you come back again, some timespace."

Sharp, stabbing pains in his stomach now. "Bastard." Heart pounding slow and hard: shirt rustled in time to its spasms.

"Cyanide in the marmalade. Gives it a certain *frisson*, don't you think?"

He couldn't breathe. His heart pounded once, and stopped. Vicious pain in his left arm, then paralysis. From an inch away, he could just see the weave of the white tablecloth. It turned red and then black.

18. THE SUN ALSO RISES

From blackness to brilliance: the morning sun pouring through the window at a flat angle. He screwed up his face and blinked.

Suddenly smothered in terry cloth, between soft breasts. "John, John."

He put his elbow down to support himself, uncomfortable on the parquet floor, and looked up at Pansy. Her face was wet with tears. He cleared his throat. "What happened?"

"You, you started putting on your foot and...you just fell over. I thought..."

John looked down over his body, hard ropy muscle and deep tan under white body hair, the puckered bullet wound a little higher on the abdomen. Left leg ended in a stump just above the ankle.

Trying not to faint. His third past flooding back. Walking down a dirt road near Kontum, the sudden loud bang of the mine and he pitched forward, unbelievable pain, rolled over and saw his bloody boot yards away; grey, jagged shinbone sticking through the bloody smoking rag of his pant leg, bright crimson splashing on the dry dust, loud in the shocked silence; another bloodstain spreading between his legs, the deep mortal pain there—and he started to buck and scream and two men held him while the medic took off his belt and made a tourniquet and popped morphine through the cloth and unbuttoned his fly and slowly worked his pants down: penis torn by shrapnel, scrotum ripped open in a bright red flap of skin, bloody grey-blue egg of a testicle separating, rolling out. He fainted, then and now.

And woke up with her lips against his, her breath sweet in his lungs, his nostrils pinched painfully tight. He made a strangled noise and clutched her breast.

She cradled his head, panting, smiling through tears, and kissed him lightly on the forehead. "Will you stop fainting now?"

"Yeah. Don't worry." Her lips were trembling. He put a finger on them. "Just a longer night than I'm accustomed to. An overdose of happiness."

The happiest night of his life, maybe of three lives. Like coming back from the dead.

"Should I call a doctor?"

"No. I faint every now and then." Usually at the gym, from pushing too hard. He slipped his hand inside the terry cloth and covered her breast. "It's been...do you know how long it's been since I...did it? I mean...three times in one night?"

"About six hours." She smiled. "And you can say 'fuck.' I'm no schoolgirl."

"I'll say." The night had been an escalating progression of intimacies, gymnastics, accessories. "Had to wonder where a sweet girl like you learned all that."

She looked away, lips pursed, thoughtful. With a light fingertip she stroked the length of his penis and smiled when it started to uncurl. "At work."

"What?"

"I was a prostitute. That's where I learned the tricks. Practice makes perfect."

"Prostitute. Wow."

"Are you shocked? Outraged?"

"Just surprised." That was true. He respected the sorority and was grateful to it for having made Vietnam almost tolerable, an hour or so at a time. "But now you've got to do something really mean. I could never love a prostitute with a heart of gold."

"I'll give it some thought." She shifted. "Think you can stand up?"

"Sure." She stood and gave him her hand. He touched it but didn't pull; rose in a smooth practiced motion, then took one hop and sat down at the small table. He started strapping on his foot.

"I've read about those new ones," she said, "the permanent kind."

"Yeah; I've read about them, too. Computer interface, graft your nerves onto sensors." He shuddered. "No, thanks. No more surgery."

"Not worth it for the convenience?"

"Being able to wiggle my toes, have my foot itch? No. Besides, the VA won't pay for it." That startled John as he said it: here, he hadn't grown up rich. His father had spent all the mill money on a photocopy firm six months before Xerox came on the market. "You say you 'were' a prostitute. Not anymore?"

"No, that was the truth about teaching. Let's start this egg thing over." She picked up the bowl she had dropped in the other universe. "I gave up whoring about seven years ago." She picked up an egg, looked at it, set it down. She half turned and stared out the kitchen window. "I can't do this to you."

"You...can't do what?"

"Oh, lie. Keep lying." She went to the refrigerator. "Want a beer?"

"Lying? No, no thanks. What lying?"

She opened a beer, still not looking at him. "I like you, John. I really like you. But I didn't just...spontaneously fall into your arms." She took a healthy swig and started pouring some of the bottle into a glass.

"I don't understand."

She walked back, concentrating on pouring the beer, then sat down gracelessly. She took a deep breath and let it out, staring at his chest. "Castle put me up to it."

"Castle?"

She nodded. "Sylvester Castlemaine, boy wonder."

John sat back stunned. "But you said you don't do that anymore," he said without too much logic. "Do it for money."

"Not for money," she said in a flat, hurt voice.

"I should've known. A woman like you wouldn't want..." He made a gesture that dismissed his body from the waist down.

"You do all right. Don't feel sorry for yourself." Her face showed a pinch of regret for that, but she plowed on. "If it were just the obligation, once would have been enough. I wouldn't have had to fuck and suck all night long to win you over."

"No," he said, "that's true. Just the first moment, when you undressed. That was enough."

"I owe Castle a big favor. A friend of mine was going to be prosecuted for involving a minor in prostitution. It was a setup, pure and simple."

"She worked for the same outfit you did?"

"Yeah, but this was freelance. I think it was the escort service that set her up, sort of delivered her and the man in return for this or that."

She sipped at the beer. "Guy wanted a three-way. My friend had met this girl a couple of days before at the bar where she worked part-time... she looked old enough, said she was in the biz."

"She was neither?"

"God knows. Maybe she got caught as a juvie and made a deal. Anyhow, he'd just slipped it to her and suddenly cops comin' in the windows. Threw the book at him. 'Two inches, twenty years,' my friend said. He was a county commissioner somewhere, with enemies. Almost dragged my friend down with him. I'm *sorry*." Her voice was angry.

"Don't be," John said, almost a whisper. "It's understandable. Whatever happens, I've got last night."

She nodded. "So two of the cops who were going to testify got busted for possession, cocaine. The word came down and everybody remembered the woman was somebody else."

"So what did Castle want you to do? With me?"

"Oh, whatever comes natural—or *un*-natural, if that's what you wanted. And later be doing it at a certain time and place, where we'd be caught in the act."

"By Castle?"

"And his trusty little VCR. Then I guess he'd threaten to show it to your wife, or the university."

"I wonder. Lena...she knows I've had other women."

"But not lately."

"No. Not for years."

"It might be different now. She might be starting to feel, well, insecure."

"Any woman who looked at you would feel insecure."

She shrugged. "That could be part of it. Could it cost you your job, too?"

"I don't see how. It would be awkward, but it's not as if you were one of my students—and even that happens, without costing the guy his job." He laughed. "Poor old Larry. He had a student kiss and tell, and had to run the Speakers' Committee for four or five years. Got allergic to wine and cheese. But he made tenure."

"So what is it?" She leaned forward. "Are you an addict or something?"

"Addict?"

"I mean how come you even *know* Castle? He didn't pick your name out of a phone book and have me come seduce you, just to see what would happen."

"No, of course not."

"So? I confess, you confess."

John passed a hand over his face and pressed the other hand against his knee, bearing down to keep the foot from tapping. "You don't want to be involved."

"What do you call last night, Spin the Bottle? I'm *involved*!"

"Not the way I mean. It's illegal."

"Oh golly. Not really."

"Let me think." John picked up their dishes and limped back to the sink. He set them down there and fiddled with the straps and pad that connected the foot to his stump, then poured himself a cup of coffee and came back, not limping.

He sat down slowly and blew across the coffee. "What it is, is that *Castle* thinks there's a scam going on. He's wrong. I've taken steps to ensure that it couldn't work." His foot tapped twice.

"You think. You hope."

"No. I'm sure. Anyhow, I'm stringing Castle along because I need his expertise in a certain matter."

"'A certain matter,' yeah. Sounds wholesome."

"Actually, that part's not illegal."

"So tell me about it."

"Nope. Still might backfire."

She snorted. "You know what might *back*fire. Fucking with Castle."

"I can take care of him."

"You don't know. He may be more dangerous than you think he is."

"He talks a lot."

"You men." She took a drink and poured the rest of the bottle into the glass. "Look, I was at a party with him, couple of years ago. He was drunk, got into a little coke, started babbling."

"In vino veritas?"

"Yeah, and Coke is It. But he said he'd killed three people, strangers, just to see what it felt like. He liked it. I more than halfway believe him."

John looked at her silently for a moment, sorting out his new memories of Castle. "Well...he's got a mean streak. I don't know about murder. Certainly not over this thing."

"Which is?"

"You'll have to trust me. It's not because of Castle that I can't tell you." He remembered her one universe ago, lying helpless while the Hemingway lowered its cane onto her nakedness. "Trust me?"

She studied the top of the glass, running her finger around it. "Suppose I do. Then what?"

"Business as usual. You didn't tell me anything. Deliver me to Castle and his video camera; I'll try to put on a good show."

"And when he confronts you with it?"

"Depends on what he wants. He knows I don't have much money." John shrugged. "If it's unreasonable, he can go ahead and show the tape to Lena. She can live with it."

"And your department head?"

"He'd give me a medal."

19. IN OUR TIME

So it wasn't the cane. He ate enough cyanide to kill a horse, but evidently only in one universe.

You checked the next day in all the others?

All 119. He's still dead in the one where I killed him on the train—

That's encouraging.

—but there's no causal resonance in the others.

Oh, but there is some resonance. He remembered you in the universe where you poisoned him. Maybe in all of them.

That's impossible.

Once is impossible. Twice is a trend. A hundred and twenty means something is going on that we don't understand.

What I suggest—

No. You can't go back and kill them all one by one.

If the wand had worked the first time, they'd all be dead anyhow. There's no reason to think we'd cause more of an eddy by doing them one at a time.

It's not something to experiment with. As you well know.

I don't know how we're going to solve it otherwise.

Simple. Don't kill him. Talk to him again. He may be getting frightened, if he remembers both times he died.

Here's an idea. What if someone else killed him?

I don't know. If you just hired someone—made him a direct agent of your will—it wouldn't be any different from the cyanide. Maybe as a last resort. Talk to him again first.

All right. I'll try.

20. OF WOUNDS AND OTHER CAUSES

Although John found it difficult to concentrate, trying not to think about Pansy, this was the best time he would have for the foreseeable future to summon the Hemingway demon and try to do something about exorcising it. He didn't want either of the women around if the damned thing went on a killing spree again. They might just do as he did, and slip over into another reality—as unpleasant as that was, it was at least living—but the Hemingway had said otherwise. There was no reason to suspect it was not the truth.

Probably the best way to get the thing's attention was to resume work on the Hemingway pastiche. He decided to rewrite the first page to warm up, typing it out in Hemingway's style:

ALONG WITH YOUTH

1. Mitraigliatrice

The dirt on the side of the trench was never dry in the morning. If Fever could find a dry newspaper he could put it between his chest and the dirt when he went out to lean on the side of the trench and wait for the light .First light was the best time . You might have luck and see a muzzle flash to aim at . But patience was better than luck. Wait to see a helmet or a head without a helmet.

Fever looked at the enemy trench line through a rectangular box of wood that pushed through the trench wall at about ground level. The other end of the box was covered with a square of gauze the color of dirt. A man looking directly at it might see the muzzle flash when Fever fired through the box. But with luck, the flash would be the last thing he saw.

Fever had fired through the gauze six times. He'd potted at least three Austrians. Now the gauze had a ragged hole in the center. One bullet had come in the other way, an accident, and chiseled a deep gouge in the floor of the wooden box. Fever knew that he would be able to see the splinters sticking up before he could see any detail at the enemy trench line.

That would be maybe twenty minutes. Fever wanted a cigarette. There was plenty of time to go down in the bunker and light one. But it would fox his night vision. Better to wait.

Fever heard movement before he heard the voice. He picked up one of the grenades on the plank shelf to his left and his thumb felt the ring on the cotter pin. Someone was crawling in front of his position. Slow crawling but not too quiet. He slid his left forefinger through the ring and waited.

——Help me, came a strained whisper.

——Fever felt his shoulders tense. Of course many Austrians could speak Italian.

——I am wounded. Help me. I can go no farther.

——What is your name and unit, Fever whispered through the box.

——Jean-Franco Dante. Four forty-seventh.

That was the unit that had taken such a beating at the evening show.——At first light they will kill me.

——All right. But I'm coming over with a grenade in my hand. If you kill me, you die as well.

——I will commend this logic to your superior officer. Please hurry.

Fever slid his rifle into the wooden box and eased himself to the top of the trench. He took the grenade out of his pocket and carefully worked the pin out, the arming lever held secure. He kept the pin around his finger so he could replace it.

He inched his way down the slope, guided by the man's whispers. After a few minutes his probing hand found the man's shoulder.——Thank God. Make haste, now.

The soldier's feet were both shattered by a mine. He would have to be carried.

——Don't cry out, Fever said. This will hurt.

——No sound, the soldier said. And when Fever raised him up onto his back there was only a breath. But his canteen was loose. It fell on a rock and made a loud hollow sound.

Firecracker pop above them and the night was all glare and bobbing shadow. A big machine gun opened up rong, cararong, rong, rong. Fever headed for the parapet above as fast as he could but knew it was hopeless. He saw dirt spray twice to his right and then felt the thud of the bullet into the Italian, who said "Jesus" as if only annoyed, and they almost made it then but on the lip of the trench a hard snowball hit Fever behind the kneecap and they both went down in a tumble. They fell two yards to safety but the Italian was already dead.

Fever had sprained his wrist and hurt his nose falling and they hurt worse than the bullet. But he couldn't move his toes and he knew that must be bad. Then it started to hurt.

A rifleman closed the Italian's eyes and with the help of another clumsy one dragged Fever down the trench to the medical bunker. It hurt awfully and his shoe filled up with blood and he puked. They stopped to watch him puke and then dragged him the rest of the way.

The surgeon placed him between two kerosene lanterns. He removed the puttee and shoe and cut the bloody pants leg with a straight razor. He rolled Fever onto his stomach and had four men hold him down while he probed for the bullet. The pain was great but Fever was insulted enough by the four men not to cry out. He heard the bullet clink into a metal dish. It sounded like the canteen.

"That's a little too pat, don't you think?" John turned around and there was the Hemingway, reading over his shoulder. "'It sounded like the canteen,' indeed." Khaki army uniform covered with mud and splattered with bright blood. Blood dripped and pooled at its feet.

"So shoot me. Or whatever it's going to be this time. Maybe I'll rewrite the line in the next universe."

"You're going to run out soon. You only exist in eight more universes."

"Sure. And you've never lied to me." John turned back around and stared at the typewriter, tensed.

The Hemingway sighed. "Suppose we talk, instead."

"I'm listening."

The Hemingway walked past him toward the kitchen. "Want a beer?"

"Not while I'm working."

"Suit yourself." It limped into the kitchen, out of sight, and John heard it open the refrigerator and pry the top off of a beer. It came back out as the five-year-old Hemingway, dressed up in girl's clothing, both hands clutching an incongruous beer bottle. It set the bottle on the end table and crawled up onto the couch with childish clumsiness.

"Where's the cane?"

"I knew it wouldn't be necessary this time," it piped. "It occurs to me that there are better ways to deal with a man like you."

"Do tell." John smiled. "What is 'a man like me'? One on whom your cane for some reason doesn't work?"

"Actually, what I was thinking of was curiosity. That is supposedly what motivates scholars. You *are* a real scholar, not just a rich man seeking legitimacy?"

John looked away from the ancient eyes in the boy's face. "I've sometimes wondered myself. Why don't you cut to the chase, as we used to say. A few universes ago."

"I've done spot checks on your life through various universes," the child said. "You're always a Hemingway buff, though you don't always do it for a living."

"What else do I do?"

"It's probably not healthy for you to know. But all of you are drawn to the missing manuscripts at about this time, the seventy-fifth anniversary."

"I wonder why that would be."

The Hemingway waved the beer bottle in a disarmingly mature gesture. "The Omniverse is full of threads of coincidence like that. They have causal meaning in a dimension you can't deal with."

"Try me."

"In a way, that's what I want to propose. You will drop this dangerous project at once, and never resume it. In return, I will take you back in time, back to the Gare de Lyon on December 14, 1921."

"Where I will see what happens to the manuscripts."

Another shrug. "I will put you on Hadley's train, well before she said the manuscripts were stolen. You will be able to observe for an hour or so, without being seen. As you know, some people have theorized that there never was a thief; never was an overnight bag; that Hadley simply threw the writings away. If that's the case, you won't see anything dramatic. But the absence of the overnight bag would be powerful indirect proof."

John looked skeptical. "You've never gone to check it out for yourself?"

"If I had, I wouldn't be able to take you back. I can't exist twice in the same timespace, of course."

"How foolish of me. Of course."

"Is it a deal?"

John studied the apparition. The couch's plaid upholstery showed through its arms and legs. It did appear to become less substantial each time. "I don't know. Let me think about it a couple of days."

The child pulled on the beer bottle and it stretched into a long amber stick. It turned into the black-and-white cane. "We haven't tried cancer yet. That might be the one that works." It slipped off the couch and sidled toward John. "It does take longer and it hurts. It hurts 'awfully.'"

John got out of the chair. "You come near me with that and I'll drop kick you into next Tuesday."

The child shimmered and became Hemingway in his midforties, a big-gutted barroom brawler. "Sure you will, Champ." It held out the cane so that the tip was inches from John's chest. "See you around." It disappeared with a barely audible pop, and a slight breeze as air moved to fill its space.

John thought about that as he went to make a fresh cup of coffee. He wished he knew more about science. The thing obviously takes up space, since its disappearance caused a vacuum, but there was no denying that it was fading away.

Well, not fading. Just becoming more transparent. That might not affect its abilities. A glass door is as much of a door as an opaque one, if you try to walk through it.

He sat down on the couch, away from the manuscript so he could think without distraction. On the face of it, this offer by the Hemingway was an admission of defeat. An admission, at least, that it couldn't solve its problem by killing him over and over. That was comforting. He would just as soon not die again, except for the one time.

But maybe he should. That was a chilling thought. If he made the Hemingway kill him another dozen times, another hundred…what kind of strange creature would he become? A hundred overlapping autobiographies, all perfectly remembered? Surely the brain has a finite capacity for storing information; he'd "fill up," as Pansy said. Or maybe it wasn't finite, at least in his case—but that was logically absurd. There are only so many cells in a brain. Of course he might be "wired" in some way to the John Bairds in all the other universes he had inhabited.

And what would happen if he died in some natural way, not dispatched by an interdimensional assassin? Would he still slide into another identity? That was a lovely prospect: sooner or later he would be 130 years old, on his deathbed, dying every fraction of a second for the rest of eternity.

Or maybe the Hemingway wasn't lying, this time, and he had only eight lives left. In context, the possibility was reassuring.

The phone rang; for a change, John was grateful for the interruption. It was Lena, saying her father had come home from the hospital, much better, and she thought she could come on home day after tomorrow. Fine, John said, feeling a little wicked; I'll borrow a car and pick you up at the airport. Don't bother, Lena said; besides, she didn't have a flight number yet.

John didn't press it. If, as he assumed, Lena was in on the plot with Castle, she was probably here in Key West, or somewhere nearby. If she had to buy a ticket to and from Omaha to keep up her end of the ruse, the money would come out of John's pocket.

He hung up and, on impulse, dialed her parents' number. Her father answered. Putting on his professorial tone, he said he was Maxwell Perkins, Blue Cross claims adjuster, and he needed to know the exact date when Mr. Monaghan entered the hospital for this recent confinement. He said you must have the wrong guy; I haven't been inside a hospital in twenty years, knock on wood. Am I not speaking to John Franklin Monaghan? No, this is John *Frederick* Monaghan. Terribly sorry, natural mistake. That's okay; hope the other guy's okay, good-bye, good night, sir.

So tomorrow was going to be the big day with Pansy. To his knowledge, John hadn't been watched during sex for more than twenty years, and never by a disinterested, or at least dispassionate, observer. He hoped that knowing they were being spied upon wouldn't affect his performance. Or knowing that it would be the last time.

A profound helpless sadness settled over him. He knew that the last thing you should do, in a mood like this, was go out and get drunk. It was barely noon, anyhow. He took enough money out of his wallet for five martinis, hid the wallet under a couch cushion, and headed for Duval Street.

21. DYING, WELL OR BADLY

John had just about decided it was too early in the day to get drunk. He had polished off two martinis in Sloppy Joe's and then wandered uptown because the tourists were getting to him and a band was setting up, depressingly young and cheerful. He found a grubby bar he'd never noticed before, dark and smoky and hot. In the other universes it was a yuppie boutique. Three Social Security drunks were arguing politics almost loudly enough to drown out the game show on the television. It seemed to go well with the headache and sour stomach he'd reaped from the martinis and the walk in the sun. He got a beer and some peanuts and a couple of aspirin from the bartender, and sat in the farthest booth with a copy of the local classified ad newspaper. Somebody had obscurely carved FUCK ANARCHY into the tabletop.

Nobody else in this world knows what anarchy *is*, John thought, and the helpless anomie came back, intensified somewhat by drunken sentimentality. What he would give to go back to the first universe and undo this all by just not...

Would that be possible? The Hemingway was willing to take him back to 1921; why not back a few weeks? Where the hell was that son of a bitch when you needed him, it, whatever.

The Hemingway appeared in the booth opposite him, an Oak Park teenager smoking a cigarette. "I felt a kind of vibration from you. Ready to make your decision?"

"Can the people at the bar see you?"

"No. And don't worry about appearing to be talking to yourself. A lot of that goes on around here."

"Look. Why can't you just take me back to a couple of weeks before we met on the train, back in the first universe? I'll just..." The Hemingway was shaking its head slowly. "You can't."

"No. As I explained, you already exist there—"

"You said that *you* couldn't be in the same place twice. How do you know I can't?"

"How do you know you can't swallow that piano? You just can't."

"You thought I couldn't talk about you, either, you thought your stick would kill me. I'm not like normal people."

"Except in that alcohol does nothing for your judgment."

John ate a peanut thoughtfully. "Try this on for size. At 11:46 on June 3, a man named Sylvester Castlemaine sat down in Dos Hermosas and started talking with me about the lost manuscripts. The forgery would never have occurred to me if I hadn't talked to him. Why don't you go back and keep him from going into that cafe? Or just go back to 11:30 and kill him."

The Hemingway smiled maliciously. "You don't like him much."

"It's more fear than like or dislike." He rubbed his face hard, remembering. "Funny how things shift around. He was kind of likable the first time I met him. Then you killed me on the train and in the subsequent universe, he became colder, more serious. Then you killed me in Pansy's apartment and in this universe, he has turned mean. Dangerously mean, like a couple of men I knew in Vietnam. The ones who really love the killing. Like you, evidently."

It blew a chain of smoke rings before answering. "I don't 'love' killing, or anything else. I have a complex function and I fulfill it, because that is what I do. That sounds circular because of the limitations of human language.

"I can't go killing people right and left just to see what happens. When a person dies at the wrong time it takes forever to clean things up. Not that it wouldn't be worth it in your case. But I can tell you with certainty that killing Castlemaine would not affect the final outcome."

"How can you say that? He's responsible for the whole thing." John finished off most of his beer and the Hemingway touched the mug and it refilled. "Not poison."

"Wouldn't work," it said morosely. "I'd gladly kill Castlemaine any way you want—cancer of the penis is a possibility—if there was even a fighting chance that it would clear things up. The reason I know it wouldn't is that I am not in the least attracted to that meeting. There's no probability nexus associated with it, the way there was with your buying the Corona or starting the story on the train, or writing it down here. You may think that you would never have come up with the idea for the forgery on your own, but you're wrong."

"That's preposterous."

"Nope. There are universes in this bundle where Castle isn't involved. You may find that hard to believe, but your beliefs aren't important."

John nodded noncommittally and got his faraway remembering look. "You know...reviewing in my mind all the conversations we've had, all five of them, the only substantive reason you've given me not to write this pastiche, and I quote, is that 'I or someone like me will have to kill you.' Since that doesn't seem to be possible, why don't we try some other line of attack?"

It put out the cigarette by squeezing it between thumb and forefinger. There was a smell of burning flesh. "All right, try this: give it up or I'll kill Pansy. Then Lena."

"I've thought of that, and I'm gambling that you won't, or can't. You had a perfect opportunity a few days ago—maximum dramatic effect— and you didn't do it. Now you say it's an awfully complicated matter."

"You're willing to gamble with the lives of the people you love?"

"I'm gambling with a lot. Including them." He leaned forward. "Take me into the future instead of the past. Show me what will happen if I succeed with the Hemingway hoax. If I agree that it's terrible, I'll give it all up and become a plumber."

The old, wise Hemingway shook a shaggy head at him. "You're asking me to please fix it so you can swallow a piano. I can't. Even I can't go straight to the future and look around; I'm pretty much tied to your present and past until this matter is cleared up."

"One of the first things you said to me was that you were from the future. And the past. And 'other temporalities,' whatever the hell that means. You were lying then?"

"Not really." It sighed. "Let me force the analogy. Look at the piano."

John twisted half around. "Okay."

"You can't eat it—but after a fashion, I can." The piano suddenly transformed itself into a piano-shaped mountain of cold capsules, which immediately collapsed and rolled all over the floor. "Each capsule contains a pinch of sawdust or powdered ivory or metal, the whole piano in about a hundred thousand capsules. If I take one with each meal, I will indeed eat the piano, over the course of the next three hundred-some years. That's not a long time for me."

"That doesn't prove anything."

"It's not a *proof*; it's a demonstration." It reached down and picked up a capsule that was rolling by, and popped it into its mouth, "One down, 99,999 to go. So how many ways could I eat this piano?"

"Ways?"

"I mean I could have swallowed any of the hundred thousand first. Next I can choose any of the remaining 99,999. How many ways can—"

"That's easy. One hundred thousand factorial. A huge number."

"Go to the head of the class. It's ten to the godzillionth power. That represents the number of possible paths—the number of futures—leading to this one guaranteed, preordained event: my eating the piano. They are all different, but in terms of whether the piano gets eaten, their differences are trivial.

"On a larger scale, every possible trivial action that you or anybody else in this universe takes puts us into a slightly different future than would have otherwise existed. An overwhelming majority of actions, even seemingly significant ones, make no difference in the long run. All of the futures bend back to one central, unifying event—except for the ones that you're screwing up!"

"So what is this big event?"

"It's impossible for you to know. It's not important, anyhow." Actually, it would take a rather cosmic viewpoint to consider the event unimportant: the end of the world.

Or at least the end of life on Earth. Right now there were two earnest young politicians, in the United States and Russia, who on 11 August 2006 would be President and Premier of their countries. On that day, one would insult the other beyond forgiveness, and a button would be pushed, and then another button, and by the time the sun set on Moscow, or rose on Washington, there would be nothing left alive on the planet at all—from the bottom of the ocean to the top of the atmosphere—not a cockroach, not a paramecium, not a virus, and all because there are some things a man just doesn't have to take, not if he's a real man.

Hemingway wasn't the only writer who felt that way, but he was the one with the most influence on this generation. The apparition who wanted John dead or at least not typing didn't know exactly what effect his pastiche was going to have on Hemingway's influence, but it was going to be decisive and ultimately negative. It would prevent or at least delay the end of the world in a whole bundle of universes, which would put a zillion adjacent realities out of kilter, and there would be hell to pay all up and down the Omniverse. Many more people than six billion would die—and it's even possible that all of Reality would unravel, and collapse back to the Primordial Hiccup from whence it came.

"If it's not important, then why are you so hell-bent on keeping me from preventing it? I don't believe you."

"*Don't* believe me, then!" At an imperious gesture, all the capsules rolled back into the corner and reassembled into a piano, with a huge crashing chord. None of the barflies heard it. "I should think you'd cooperate with me just to prevent the unpleasantness of dying over and over."

John had the expression of a poker player whose opponent has inadvertently exposed his hole card. "You get used to it," he said. "And it occurs to me that sooner or later I'll wind up in a universe that I really like. This one doesn't have a hell of a lot to recommend it." His foot tapped twice and then twice again.

"No," the Hemingway said. "It will get worse each time."

"You can't know that. This has never happened before."

"True so far, isn't it?"

John considered it for a moment. "Some ways. Some ways not."

The Hemingway shrugged and stood up. "Well. Think about my offer." The cane appeared. "Happy cancer." It tapped him on the chest and disappeared.

The first sensation was utter tiredness, immobility. When he strained to move, pain slithered through his muscles and viscera, and stayed. He could hardly breathe, partly because his lungs weren't working and partly because there was something in the way. In the mirror beside the booth he looked down his throat and saw a large white mass, veined, pulsing. He sank back into the cushion and waited. He remembered the young wounded Hemingway writing his parents from the hospital with ghastly cheerfulness: "If I should have died it would have been very easy for me. Quite the easiest thing I ever did." I don't know, Ernie; maybe it gets harder with practice. He felt something tear open inside and hot stinging fluid trickled through his abdominal cavity. He wiped his face and a patch of necrotic skin came off with a terrible smell. His clothes tightened as his body swelled.

"Hey buddy, you okay?" The bartender came around in front of him and jumped. "Christ, Harry, punch nine-one-one!"

John gave a slight ineffectual wave. "No rush," he croaked.

The bartender cast his eyes to the ceiling. "Always on my shift?"

22. DEATH IN THE AFTERNOON

John woke up behind a Dumpster in an alley. It was high noon and the smell of fermenting garbage was revolting. He didn't feel too well in any case; as if he'd drunk far too much and passed out behind a Dumpster, which was exactly what had happened in this universe.

In this universe. He stood slowly to a quiet chorus of creaks and pops, brushed himself off, and staggered away from the malefic odor. Staggered, but not limping—he had both feet again, in this present. There was a hand-sized numb spot at the top of his left leg where a .51 caliber machine gun bullet had missed his balls by an inch and ended his career as a soldier.

And started it as a writer. He got to the sidewalk and stopped dead. This was the first universe where he wasn't a college professor. He taught occasionally—sometimes creative writing; sometimes Hemingway—but it was only a hobby now, and a nod toward respectability.

He rubbed his fringe of salt-and-pepper beard. It covered the bullet scar there on his chin. He ran his tongue along the metal teeth the army had installed thirty years ago. Jesus. Maybe it does get worse every time. Which was worse, losing a foot or getting your dick sprayed with shrapnel, numb from severed nerves, plus bullets in the leg and face and arm? If you knew there was a Pansy in your future, you would probably trade a foot for a whole dick. Though she had done wonders with what was left.

Remembering furiously, not watching where he was going, he let his feet guide him back to the oldster's bar where the Hemingway had showed him how to swallow a piano. He pushed through the door and the shock of air-conditioning brought him back to the present.

Ferns. Perfume. Lacy underthings. An epicene sales clerk sashayed toward him, managing to look worried and determined at the same time. His nose was pierced, decorated with a single diamond button. "Si-i-r," he said in a surprisingly deep voice, "may I *help* you?"

Crotchless panties. Marital aids. The bar had become a store called The French Connection. "Guess I took a wrong turn. Sorry." He started to back out.

The clerk smiled. "Don't be shy. Everybody needs *something* here."

The heat was almost pleasant in its heavy familiarity. John stopped at a convenience store for a six-pack of greenies and walked back home.

An interesting universe; much more of a divergence than the other had been. Reagan had survived the Hinckley assassination and actually went on to a second term. Bush was elected rather than succeeding to the presidency, and the country had not gone to war in Nicaragua. The Iran/Contra scandal nipped it in the bud.

The United States was actually cooperating with the Soviet Union in a flight to Mars. There were no DeSotos. Could there be a connection?

And in this universe he had actually met Ernest Hemingway.

Havana, 1952. John was eight years old. His father, a doctor in this universe, had taken a break from the New England winter to treat his family to a week in the tropics. John got a nice sunburn the first day, playing on the beach while his parents tried the casinos. The next day they made him stay indoors, which meant tagging along with his parents, looking at things that didn't fascinate eight-year-olds.

For lunch they went to La Florida, on the off chance that they might meet the famous Ernest Hemingway, who supposedly held court there when he was in Havana.

To John it was a huge dark cavern of a place, full of adult smells. Cigar smoke, rum, beer, stale urine. But Hemingway was indeed there, at the end of the long dark wood bar, laughing heartily with a table full of Cubans.

John was vaguely aware that his mother resembled some movie actress, but he couldn't have guessed that that would change his life. Hemingway glimpsed her and then stood up and was suddenly silent, mouth open. Then he laughed and waved a huge arm. "Come on over here, daughter."

The three of them rather timidly approached the table, John acutely aware of the careful inspection his mother was receiving from the silent Cubans. "Take a look, Mary," he said to the small blond woman knitting at the table. "The Kraut."

The woman nodded, smiling, and agreed that John's mother looked just like Marlene Dietrich ten years before. Hemingway invited them to sit down and have a drink, and they accepted with an air of genuine astonishment. He gravely shook John's hand, and spoke to him as he would to an adult. Then he shouted to the bartender in fast Spanish, and in a couple of minutes his parents had huge daiquiris and he had a Coke with a wedge of lime in it, tropical and grown-up. The waiter also brought a tray of boiled shrimp. Hemingway even ate the heads and tails, crunching loudly, which impressed John more than any Nobel Prize. Hemingway might have agreed, since he hadn't yet received one, and Faulkner had.

For more than an hour, two Cokes, John watched as his parents sat hypnotized in the aura of Hemingway's famous charm. He put them at ease with jokes and stories and questions—for the rest of his life John's father would relate how impressed he was with the sophistication of Hemingway's queries about cardiac medicine—but it was obvious even to a child that they were in awe, electrified by the man's presence.

Later that night John's father asked him what he thought of Mr. Hemingway. Forty-four years later, John of course remembered his exact reply: "He has fun all the time. I never saw a grown-up who plays like that."

Interesting. That meeting was where his eidetic memory started. He could remember a couple of days before it pretty well, because they had still been close to the surface. In other universes, he could remember back well before grade school. It gave him a strange feeling. All of the universes were different, but this was the first one where the differentness was so tightly connected to Hemingway.

He was flabby in this universe, fat over old, tired muscle, like Hemingway at his age, perhaps, and he felt a curious anxiety that he realized was a real *need* to have a drink. Not just desire, not thirst. If he didn't have a drink, something very very bad would happen. He knew that was irrational. Knowing didn't help.

John carefully mounted the stairs up to their apartment, stepping over the fifth one, also rotted in this universe. He put the beer in the refrigerator and took from the freezer a bottle of icy vodka—that was different—and poured himself a double shot and knocked it back, medicine drinking.

That spiked the hangover pretty well. He pried the top off a beer and carried it into the living room, thoughtful as the alcoholic glow radiated through his body. He sat down at the typewriter and picked up the air pistol, a fancy Belgian target model. He cocked it and, with a practiced two-handed grip, aimed at a paper target across the room. The pellet struck less than half an inch low.

All around the room the walls were pocked from where he'd fired at roaches, and once a scorpion. Very Hemingwayish, he thought; in fact, most of the ways he was different from the earlier incarnations of himself were in Hemingway's direction.

He spun a piece of paper into the typewriter and made a list:

```
        EH & me--

--both had doctor fathers

--both forced into music lessons

--in high school wrote derivative stuff that didn't show
promise

--Our war wounds were evidently similar in severity and loca-
tion. Maybe my groin one was worse; army doctor there said that
in Korea (and presumably WWI), without helicopter dustoff, I
would have been dead on the battlefield. (Having been wounded
in the kneecap and foot myself, I know that His story about
carrying the wounded guy on his back is unlikely. It was a
month before I could put any stress on the knee.) He mentioned
genital wounds, possibly similar to mine, in a letter to Bernard
Baruch, but there's nothing in the Red Cross report about them.
    But in both cases, being wounded and surviving was the
central experience of our youth. Touching death.

--We each wrote the first draft of our first novel in six
weeks (but his was better and more ambitious).
```

--Both had unusual critical success from the beginning.

--Both shy as youngsters and gregarious as adults.

--Always loved fishing and hiking and guns; I loved the bullfight from my first corrida, but may have been influenced by His books.

--Spain in general

--have better women than we deserve

--drink too much

--hypochondria

--accident proneness

--a tendency toward morbidity

--One difference. I will never stick a shotgun in my mouth and pull the trigger. Leaves too much of a mess.

He looked up at the sound of the cane tapping. The Hemingway was in the Karsh wise-old-man mode, but was nearly transparent in the bright light that streamed from the open door. "What do I have to do to get your attention?" it said. "Give you cancer again?"

"That was pretty unpleasant."

"Maybe it will be the last." It half sat on the arm of the couch and spun the cane around twice. "Today is a big day. Are we going to Paris?"

"What do you mean?"

"Something big happens today. In every universe where you're alive, this day glows with importance. I assume that means you've decided to go along with me. Stop writing this thing in exchange for the truth about the manuscripts."

As a matter of fact, he had been thinking just that. Life was confusing enough already, torn between his erotic love for Pansy and the more domestic, but still deep, feeling for Lena...writing the pastiche was kind of fun, but he did have his own fish to fry. Besides, he'd come to truly dislike

Castle, even before Pansy had told him about the setup. It would be fun to disappoint him.

"You're right. Let's go."

"First destroy the novel." In this universe, he'd completed seventy pages of the Up-in-Michigan novel.

"Sure." John picked up the stack of paper and threw it into the tiny fireplace. He lit it several places with a long barbecue match, and watched a month's work go up in smoke. It was only a symbolic gesture, anyhow; he could retype the thing from memory if he wanted to.

"So what do I do? Click my heels together three times and say 'There's no place like the Gare de Lyon'?"

"Just come closer."

John took three steps toward the Hemingway and suddenly fell up down sideways—

It was worse than dying. He was torn apart and scattered throughout space and time, being nowhere and everywhere, everywhen, being a screaming vacuum forever—

Grit crunched underfoot and coalsmoke was choking thick in the air. It was cold. Grey Paris skies glowered through the long skylights, through the complicated geometry of the black steel trusses that held up the high roof. Bustling crowds chattering French. A woman walked through John from behind. He pressed himself with his hands and felt real.

"They can't see us," the Hemingway said. "Not unless I will it."

"That was awful."

"I hoped you would hate it. That's how I spend most of my timespace. Come on." They walked past vendors selling paper packets of roasted chestnuts, bottles of wine, stacks of baguettes and cheeses. There were strange resonances as John remembered the various times he'd been here more than a half century in the future. It hadn't changed much.

"There she is." The Hemingway pointed. Hadley looked worn, tired, dowdy. She stumbled, trying to keep up with the porter who strode along with her two bags. John recalled that she was just recovering from a bad case of the grippe. She'd probably still be home in bed if Hemingway hadn't sent the telegram urging her to come to Lausanne because the skiing was so good, at Chamby.

"Are there universes where Hadley doesn't lose the manuscripts?"

"Plenty of them," the Hemingway said. "In some of them he doesn't sell 'My Old Man' next year, or anything else, and he throws all the stories away himself. He gives up fiction and becomes a staff writer for the

Toronto *Star*. Until the Spanish Civil War; he joins the Abraham Lincoln Battalion and is killed driving an ambulance. His only effect on American literature is one paragraph in *The Autobiography of Alice B. Toklas*."

"But in some, the stories actually do see print?"

"Sure, including the novel, which is usually called *Along With Youth*. There." Hadley was mounting the steps up into a passenger car. There was a microsecond of agonizing emptiness, and they materialized in the passageway in front of Hadley's compartment. She and the porter walked through them.

"*Merci*," she said, and handed the man a few sou. He made a face behind her back.

"*Along With Youth*?" John said.

"It's a pretty good book, sort of prefiguring *A Farewell To Arms*, but he does a lot better in universes where it's not published. *The Sun Also Rises* gets more attention."

Hadley stowed both the suitcase and the overnight bag under the seat. Then she frowned slightly, checked her wristwatch, and left the compartment, closing the door behind her.

"Interesting," the Hemingway said. "So she didn't leave it out in plain sight, begging to be stolen."

"Makes you wonder," John said. "This novel. Was it about World War I?"

"The trenches in Italy," the Hemingway said.

A young man stepped out of the shadows of the vestibule, looking in the direction Hadley took. Then he turned around and faced the two travelers from the future.

It was Ernest Hemingway. He smiled. "Close your mouth, John. You'll catch flies." He opened the door to the compartment, picked up the overnight bag, and carried it into the next car.

John recovered enough to chase after him. He had disappeared.

The Hemingway followed. "What *is* this?" John said "I thought you couldn't be in two timespaces at once."

"That wasn't me."

"It sure as hell wasn't the real Hemingway. He's in Lausanne with Lincoln Steffens."

"Maybe he is and maybe he isn't."

"He knew my *name*!"

"That he did." The Hemingway was getting fainter as John watched.

"Was he another one of you? Another STAB agent?"

"No. Not possible." It peered at John. "What's happening to you?"

Hadley burst into the car and ran right through them, shouting in French for the conductor. She was carrying a bottle of Evian water.

"Well," John said, "that's what—"

The Hemingway was gone. John just had time to think *Marooned in 1922?* when the railroad car and the Gare de Lyon dissolved in an inbursting cascade of black sparks and it was no easier to handle the second time, spread impossibly thin across all those light years and millennia, wondering whether it was going to last forever this time, realizing that it did anyhow, and coalescing with an impossibly painful *snap*:

Looking at the list in the typewriter. He reached for the Heineken; it was still cold. He set it back down. "God," he whispered. "I hope that's that."

The situation called for higher octane. He went to the freezer and took out the vodka. He sipped the gelid syrup straight from the bottle, and almost dropped it when out of the corner of his eye he saw the overnight bag.

He set the open bottle on the counter and sleepwalked over to the dining room table. It was the same bag, slightly beat-up, monogrammed EHR, Elizabeth Hadley Richardson. He opened it and inside was a thick stack of manila envelopes.

He took out the top one and took it and the vodka bottle back to his chair. His hands were shaking. He opened the folder and stared at the familiar typing.

ERNEST M. HEMINGWAY

ONE-EYE FOR MINE

Fever stood up. In the moon light he could xx see blood starting on his hands. His pants were torn at the knee and he knew it would be bleeding there too. He watched the lights of the caboose disppear in the trees where the track curved.

That lousy crut of a brakeman. He would get him xxxday some day.

Fever sxxxxxxx off the end of a tie and sat down to pick the cinders out of his hands and knee. He could use some water. The brakeman had his canteen.

He could smell a campfire. He wondered if it would be smart to go find it. He knew about the wolves, the human kind that lived along the rails and the disgusting things they liked. He wasn't afraid of them but you didn't look for trouble.

You don't have to look for trouble, his father would say. Trouble will find you. His father didn't tell him about wolves, though, ~~or about women.~~

There was a noise in the brush. Fever stood up and slipped his hand around the horn grip of the fat Buck clasp knife in his pocket.

* * *

The screen door creaked open and he looked up to see Pansy walk in with a strange expression on her face. Lena followed, looking even stranger. Her left eye was swollen shut and most of that side of her face was bruised blue and brown.

He stood up, shaking with the sudden collision of emotions. "What the hell—"

"Castle," Pansy said. "He got outta hand."

"Real talent for understatement." Lena's voice was tightly controlled but distorted.

"He went nuts. Slappin' Lena around. Then he started to rummage around in a closet, rave about a shotgun, and we split."

"I'll call the police."

"We've already been there," Lena said. "It's all over."

"Of course. We can't work with—"

"No, I mean he's a *criminal*. He's wanted in Mississippi for second-degree murder. They went to arrest him, hold him for extradition. So no more Hemingway hoax."

"What Hemingway?" Pansy said.

"We'll tell you all about it," Lena said, and pointed at the bottle. "A little early, don't you think? You could at least get us a couple of glasses."

John went into the kitchen, almost floating with vodka buzz and anxious confusion. "What do you want with it?" Pansy said oh-jay and Lena said ice. Then Lena screamed.

He turned around and there was Castle standing in the door, grinning. He had a pistol in his right hand and a sawed-off shotgun in his left.

"You cunts," he said. "You fuckin' cunts. Go to the fuckin' cops."

There was a butcher knife in the drawer next to the refrigerator, but he didn't think Castle would stand idly by and let him rummage for it.

Nothing else that might serve as a weapon, except the air pistol. Castle knew that it wouldn't do much damage.

He looked at John. "You three're gonna be my hostages. We're gettin' outta here, lose 'em up in the Everglades. They'll have a make on my pickup, though."

"We don't have a car," John said.

"I *know* that, asshole! There's a Hertz right down on One. You go rent one and don't try nothin' cute. I so much as *smell* a cop, I blow these two cunts away."

He turned back to the women and grinned crookedly, talking hard-guy through his teeth. "Like I did those two they sent, the spic and the nigger. They said somethin' about comin' back with a warrant to look for the shotgun and I was just bein' as nice as could be, I said hell, come on in, don't need no warrant. I got nothin' to hide, and when they come in I take the pistol from the nigger and kill the spic with it and shoot the nigger in the balls. You shoulda heard him. Some nigger. Took four more rounds to shut him up."

Wonder if that means the pistol is empty, John thought. He had Pansy's orange juice in his hand. It was an old-fashioned Smith & Wesson .357 Magnum six-shot, but from this angle he couldn't tell whether it had been reloaded. He could try to blind Castle with the orange juice.

He stepped toward him. "What kind of car do you want?"

"Just a *car*, damn it. Big enough." A siren whooped about a block away. Castle looked wary. "Bitch. You told 'em where you'd be."

"No," Lena pleaded. "We didn't tell them anything."

"Don't do anything stupid," John said.

Two more sirens, closer. "I'll show you *stupid!*" He raised the pistols toward Lena. John dashed the orange juice in his face.

It wasn't really like slow motion. It was just that John didn't miss any of it. Castle growled and swung around and in the cylinder's chambers John saw five copper-jacketed slugs. He reached for the gun and the first shot shattered his hand, blowing off two fingers, and struck the right side of his chest. The explosion was deafening and the shock of the bullet was like being hit simultaneously in the hand and chest with baseball bats. He rocked, still on his feet, and coughed blood spatter on Castle's face. He fired again, and the second slug hit him on the other side of the chest, this time spinning him half around. Was somebody screaming? Hemingway said it felt like an icy snowball, and that was pretty close, except for the inside part, your body saying Well, time to close up shop. There was a terrible familiar radiating pain in the center of his chest, and John realized that he was having a totally superfluous heart attack. He pushed off from the dinette and staggered toward Castle again. He made a grab for the shotgun and Castle emptied both barrels into his abdomen. He dropped to his knees and then fell over on his side. He couldn't feel anything. Things started to go dim and red. Was this going to be the last time?

Castle cracked the shotgun and the two spent shells flew up in an arc over his shoulder. He took two more out of his shirt pocket and dropped one. When he bent over to pick it up, Pansy leaped past him. In a swift motion that was almost graceful—it came to John that he had probably practiced it over and over, acting out fantasies—he slipped both shells into their chambers and closed the gun with a flip of the wrist. The screen door was stuck. Pansy was straining at the knob with both hands. Castle put the muzzles up to the base of her skull and pulled one trigger. Most of her head covered the screen or went through the hole the blast made. The crown of her skull, a bloody bowl, bounced off two walls and went spinning into the kitchen. Her body did a spastic little dance and folded, streaming.

Lena was suddenly on his back, clawing at his face. He spun and slammed her against the wall. She wilted like a rag doll and he hit her hard with the pistol on the way down. She unrolled at his feet, out cold, and with his mouth wide open laughing silently he lowered the shotgun and blasted her point-blank in the crotch. Her body jackknifed and John tried with all his will not to die but blackness crowded in and the last thing he saw was that evil grin as Castle reloaded again, peering out the window, presumably at the police.

It wasn't the terrible sense of being spread infinitesimally thin over an infinity of pain and darkness; things had just gone black, like closing your eyes. If this is death, John thought, there's not much to it.

But it changed. There was a little bit of pale light, some vague figures, and then colors bled into the scene, and after a moment of disorientation he realized he was still in the apartment, but apparently floating up by the ceiling. Lena was conscious again, barely, twitching, staring at the river of blood that pumped from between her legs. Pansy looked unreal, headless but untouched from the neck down, lying in a relaxed, improbable posture like a knocked-over department store dummy, blood still spurting from a neck artery out through the screen door.

His own body was a mess, the abdomen completely excavated by buckshot. Inside the huge wound, behind the torn coils of intestine, the shreds of fat and gristle, the blood, the shit, he could see sharp splintered knuckles of backbone. Maybe it hadn't hurt so much because the spinal cord had been severed in the blast.

He had time to be a little shocked at himself for not feeling more. Of course most of the people he'd known who had died did die this way, in loud spatters of blood and brains. Even after thirty years of the occasional polite heart attack or stroke carrying off friend or acquaintance, most of the dead people he knew had died in the jungle.

He had been a hero there, in this universe. That would have surprised his sergeants in the original one. Congressional Medal of Honor, so-called, which hadn't hurt the sales of his first book. Knocked out the NVA machine gun emplacement with their own satchel charge, then hauled the machine gun around and wiped out their mortar and command squads. He managed it all with bullet wounds in the face and triceps. Of course without the bullet wounds he wouldn't have lost his cool and charged the machine gun emplacement, but that wasn't noted in the citation.

A pity there was no way to trade the medals in—melt them down into one big fat bullet and use it to waste that crazy motherfucker who was ignoring the three people he'd just killed, laughing like a hyena while he shouted obscenities at the police gathering down below.

Castle fires a shot through the lower window and then ducks and a spray of automatic weapon fire shatters the upper window, filling the air with a spray of glass; bullets and glass fly painlessly through John where he's floating and he hears them spatter into the ceiling and suddenly everything is white with plaster dust—it starts to clear and he is much closer to his body, drawing down closer and closer; he merges with it and there's an instant of blackness and he's looking out through human eyes again.

A dull noise and he looked up to see hundreds of shards of glass leap up from the floor and fly to the window; plaster dust in billows sucked up into bullet holes in the ceiling, which then disappeared.

The top windowpane reformed as Castle uncrouched, pointed the shotgun, then jerked forward as a blossom of yellow flame and white smoke rolled back into the barrel.

His hand was whole, the fingers restored. He looked down and saw rivulets of blood running back into the hole in his abdomen, then individual drops; then it closed and the clothing restored itself; then one of the holes in his chest closed up and then the other.

The clothing was unfamiliar. A tweed jacket in this weather? His hands had turned old, liver spots forming as he watched. Slow like a plant growing, slow like the moon turning, thinking slowly too, he reached up and felt the beard, and could see out of the corner of his eye that it was white and long. He was too fat, and a belt buckle bit painfully into his belly. He sucked in and pried out and looked at the buckle, yes, it was old brass and said GOTT MIT UNS, the buckle he'd taken from a dead German so long ago. The buckle Hemingway had taken.

John got to one knee. He watched fascinated as the stream of blood gushed back into Lena's womb, disappearing as Castle grinning jammed the barrels in between her legs, flinched, and did a complicated dance in reverse (while Pansy's decapitated body writhed around and jerked upright); Lena, sliding up off the floor, leaped up between the man's back and the wall, then fell off and ran backwards as he flipped the shotgun up to the back of Pansy's neck and seeming gallons of blood and tissue came flying from every direction to assemble themselves into the lovely head and face, distorted in terror as she jerked awkwardly at the door and then ran backwards, past Castle as he did a graceful pirouette, unloading the gun and placing one shell on the floor, which flipped up to his pocket as he stood and put the other one there.

John stood up and walked through some thick resistance toward Castle. Was it *time* resisting him? Everything else was still moving in reverse: Two empty shotgun shells sailed across the room to snick into the weapon's chambers; Castle snapped it shut and wheeled to face John—

But John wasn't where he was supposed to be. As the shotgun swung around, John grabbed the barrels—hot!—and pulled the pistol out of Castle's waistband. He lost his grip on the shotgun barrels just as he jammed the pistol against Castle's heart and fired. A spray of blood from all over the other side of the room converged on Castle's back and John felt the recoil sting of the Magnum just as the shotgun muzzle cracked hard against his teeth, mouthful of searing heat then blackness forever, back in the featureless infinite timespace hell that the Hemingway had taken him to, forever, but in the next instant, a new kind of twitch, a twist…

23. THE TIME EXCHANGED

What does that mean, you "lost" him?

We were in the railroad car in the Gare de Lyon, in the normal observation mode. This entity that looked like Hemingway walked up, greeted us, took the manuscripts, and disappeared.

Just like that.

No. He went into the next car. John Baird ran after him. Maybe that was my mistake. I translated instead of running.

That's when you lost him.

Both of them. Baird disappeared, too. Then Hadley came running in—

Don't confuse me with Hadleys. You checked the adjacent universes.

All of them, yes. I think they're all right.

Think?

Well…I can't quite get to that moment. When I disappeared. It's as if I were still there for several more seconds, so I'm excluded.

And John Baird is still there?

Not by the time I can insert myself. Just Hadley running around—

No Hadleys. No Hadleys. So naturally you went back to 1996.

Of course. But there is a period of several minutes there from which I'm excluded as well. When I can finally insert myself, John Baird is dead.

Ah.

In every doom line, he and Castlemaine have killed each other. John is lying there with his head blown off, Castle next to him with his heart torn out from a point-blank pistol shot, with two very distraught women screaming while police pile in through the door. And this.

The overnight bag with the stories.

I don't think anybody noticed it. With Baird dead, I could spot-check the women's futures; neither of them mentions the bag. So perhaps the mission is accomplished.

Well, Reality is still here. So far. But the connection between Baird and this Hemingway entity is disturbing. That Baird is able to return to 1996 without your help is *very* disturbing. He has obviously taken on some of your characteristics, your abilities, which is why you're excluded from the last several minutes of his life.

I've never heard of that happening before.

It never has. I think that John Baird is no more human than you and I.

Is?

I suspect he's still around somewhen.

24. ISLANDS IN THE STREAM

and the unending lightless desert of pain becomes suddenly one small bright spark and then everything is dark red and a taste, a bitter taste, Hoppe's No. 9 gun oil and the twin barrels of the fine Boss pigeon gun cold and oily on his tongue and biting hard against the roof of his mouth; the dark red is light on the other side of his eyelids, sting of pain before he bumps a tooth and opens his eyes and mouth and lowers the gun and with shaking hands unloads—no, *dis*-loads—both barrels and walks backwards, shuffling in the slippers, slumping, stopping to stare out into the Idaho morning dark, helpless tears coursing up from the snarled white beard, walking backwards down the stairs with the shotgun heavily cradled in his elbow, backing into the storeroom and replacing it in the rack, then back up the stairs and slowly put the keys there in plain sight on the kitchen windowsill, a bit of mercy from Miss Mary, then sit and stare at the cold bad coffee as it warms back to one acid sip—

A tiny part of the mind saying *wait! I am John Baird it is 1996*

and back to a spiritless shower, numb to the needle spray, and cramped constipation and a sleep of no ease; an evening with Mary and George Brown tiptoeing around the blackest of black-ass worse and worse each day, only one thing to look forward to

got to throw out an anchor

faster now, walking through the Ketchum woods like a jerky cartoon in reverse, fucking FBI and IRS behind every tree, because you sent Ezra that money, felt sorry for him because he was crazy, what a fucking joke, should have finished the *Cantos* and shot himself.

effect preceding cause but I can read or hear scraps of thought somehow speeding to a blur now, driving in reverse hundreds of miles per hour back from Ketchum to Minnesota, the Mayo Clinic, holding the madness in while you talk to the shrink, promise not to hurt myself have to go home and write if I'm going to beat this, figuring what he wants to hear, then the rubber mouthpiece and smell of your own hair and flesh slightly burnt by the electrodes then deep total blackness

sharp stabs of thought sometimes stretching

hospital days blur by in reverse, cold chrome and starch white, a couple of mouthfuls of claret a day to wash down the pills that seem to make it worse and worse

what will happen to me when he's born?

When they came back from Spain was when he agreed to the Mayo Clinic, still all beat-up from the plane crashes six years before in Africa, liver and spleen shot to hell, brain, too, nerves, can't write or can't stop: all day on one damned sentence for the Kennedy book but a hundred thousand fast words, pure shit, for the bullfight article. Paris book okay but stuck. Great to find the trunks in the Ritz but none of the stuff Hadley lost.

Here it stops. A frozen tableau:

Afternoon light slanting in through the tall cloudy windows of the Cambon bar, where he had liberated, would liberate, the hotel in August 1944. A good large American-style martini gulped too fast in the excitement. The two small trunks unpacked and laid out item by item. Hundreds of pages of notes that would become the Paris book. But nothing before '23, of course. *the manuscripts* The novel and the stories and the poems still gone. One moment nailed down with the juniper sting of the martini and then time crawling rolling flying backwards again—

no control?

Months blurring by, Madrid Riviera Venice feeling sick and busted up, the plane wrecks like a quick one-two punch brain and body, blurry sick even before them at the Finca Vigia, can't get a fucking thing done after the Nobel Prize, journalists day and night, the prize bad luck and bullshit anyhow but need the $35,000

damn, had to shoot Willie, cat since the boat-time before the war, but winged a burglar too, same gun, just after the Pulitzer, now that was all right

slowing down again—Havana—the Floridita—

Even Mary having a good time, and the Basque jai alai players, too, though they don't know much English, most of them, interesting couple of civilians, the doctor and the Kraut look-alike, but there's something about the boy that makes it hard to take my eyes off him, looks like someone I guess, another round of Papa Dobles, that boy, what is it about him? and then the first round, with lunch, and things speeding up to a blur again.

out on the Gulf a lot, enjoying the triumph of *The Old Man and the Sea,* the easy good-paying work of providing fishing footage for the movie, and then back into 1951, the worst year of his life that far, weeks of grudging conciliation, uncontrollable anger, and black-ass depression from the poisonous critical slime that followed *Across the River,* bastards gunning for him, Harold Ross dead, mother Grace dead, son Gregory a dope addict hip-deep into the dianetics horseshit, Charlie Scribner dead but first declaring undying love for that asshole Jones

most of the forties an anxious blur, Cuba Italy Cuba France Cuba China found Mary kicked Martha out, thousand pages on the fucking *Eden* book wouldn't come together Bronze Star better than Pulitzer

Martha a chrome-plated bitch in Europe but war is swell otherwise, liberating the Ritz, grenades rifles pistols and bomb runs with the RAF,

China boring compared to it and the Q-ship runs off Cuba, hell, maybe the bitch was right for once, just kid stuff and booze

marrying the bitch was the end of my belle epoch, easy to see from here, the thirties all sunshine Key West Spain Key West Africa Key West, good hard writing with Pauline holding down the store, good woman but sorry I had to

sorry I had to divorce

stopping

Walking Paris streets after midnight:

I was never going to throw back at her losing the manuscripts. Told Steffens that would be like blaming a human for the weather, or death. These things happen. Nor say anything about what I did the night after I found out she really had lost them. But this one time we got to shouting and I think I hurt her. Why the hell did she have to bring the carbons what the hell did she think carbons were for stupid stupid stupid and she crying and she giving me hell about Pauline Jesus any woman who could fuck up Paris for you could fuck up a royal flush

it slows down around the manuscripts or me—

golden years the mid-twenties everything clicks Paris Vorarlburg Paris Schruns Paris Pamplona Paris Madrid Paris Lausanne

couldn't believe she actually

most of a novel dozens of poems stories sketches—*contes*, Kitty called them by God woman you show me your *conte* and I'll show you mine

so drunk that night I know better than to drink that much absinthe so drunk I was half crawling going up the stairs to the apartment I saw weird I saw God I saw *I saw myself standing there on the fourth landing with Hadley's goddamn bag*

I waited almost an hour, that seemed like no time or all time, and when he, when I, when he came crashing up the stairs he blinked twice, then I walked through me groping, shook my head without looking back and managed to get the door unlocked

flying back through the dead winter French countryside, standing in the bar car fighting hopelessness to Hadley crying so hard she can't get out what was wrong with Steffens standing gaping like a fish in a bowl

twisting again, painlessly inside out, I suppose through various dimensions, seeing the man's life as one complex chord of beauty and purpose and ugliness and chaos, my life on one side of the Möbius strip consistent through its fading forty-year span, starting, *starting*, here:

the handsome young man sits on the floor of the apartment holding himself, rocking racked with sobs, one short manuscript crumpled in front of him, the room a mess with drawers pulled out, their contents scattered on the floor, it's like losing an arm a leg (a foot a testicle), it's like losing your youth and along with youth

with a roar he stands up, eyes closed fists clenched, wipes his face dry and stomps over to the window

breathes deeply until he's breathing normally

strides across the room, kicking a brassiere out of his way

stands with his hand on the knob and thinks this:

life can break you but you can grow back strong at the broken places

and goes out slamming the door behind him, somewhat conscious of having been present at his own birth.

With no effort I find myself standing earlier that day in the vestibule of a train. Hadley is walking away, tired, looking for a vendor. I turn and confront two aspects of myself.

"Close your mouth, John. You'll catch flies."

They both stand paralyzed while I slide open the door and pull the overnight bag from under the seat. I walk away and the universe begins to tingle and sparkle.

I spend forever in the black void between timespaces. I am growing to enjoy it.

I appear in John Baird's apartment and set down the bag. I look at the empty chair in front of the old typewriter, the green beer bottle sweating cold next to it, and John Baird appears, looking dazed, and I have business elsewhere, elsewhen. A train to catch. I'll come back for the bag in twelve minutes or a few millennia, after the bloodbath that gives birth to us all

25. A MOVEABLE FEAST

He wrote the last line and set down the pencil and read over the last page sitting on his hands for warmth. He could see his breath. Celebrate the end with a little heat.

He unwrapped the bundle of twigs and banked them around the pile of coals in the brazier. Crazy way to heat a room, but it's France. He cupped both hands behind the stack and blew gently. The coals glowed red and then orange and with the third breath the twigs smoldered and a small yellow flame popped up. He held his hands over the fire, rubbing the stiffness out of his fingers, enjoying the smell of the birch as it cracked and spit.

He put a fresh sheet and carbon into the typewriter and looked at his penciled notes. Final draft? Worth a try:

```
Ernest M. Hemingway,
74 rue da Cardinal Lemoine,
Paris, France


              ))UP IN MICHIGAN))


    Jim Gilmore came to Horton's Bay from Canada . He bought
the blacksmith shop from old man Hortom
```

Shit, a typo. He flinched suddenly, as if struck, and shook his head to clear it. What a strange sensation to come out of nowhere. A sudden cold stab of grief. But larger somehow than grief for a person.

Grief for everybody, maybe. For being human.

From a typo?

He went to the window and opened it in spite of the cold. He filled his lungs with the cold damp air and looked around the familiar orange-and-grey mosaic of chimney pots and tiled roofs under the dirty winter Paris sky.

He shuddered and eased the window back down and returned to the heat of the brazier. He had felt it before, exactly that huge and terrible feeling. But where?

For the life of him he couldn't remember.

INTRODUCTION TO "GRAVES"

This story comes from a macabre experience I had in Vietnam. I was a demolition engineer, temporarily in charge of a squad with a kind of scary assignment. A bunch of artillery pieces were being airlifted into place on a hill, and the hill had lots of trees for the enemy to hide behind. Our job was to place explosives at the base of each tree in about a half an acre, and wire them all together, and then pop them all at once— the Big Bang Theory of lumberjacking.

The forest smelled to high heaven, the sickly-sweet smell of rotting flesh. We found two bodies side by side, a North Vietnamese lieutenant and private—scouts, we supposed—who had been killed by a random artillery round a couple of days before. The lieutenant had been decapitated; his head had rolled a few yards away, empty sockets staring up at the jungle canopy.

One of the guys snapped and gave the head a kick. Another one, giggling, kicked it hard, and in a couple of seconds they were all running or trying to run on the slippery sloping ground, hooting with hysterical laughter, kicking the poor guy's skull around in a macabre game of pick-up soccer.

I implored them to stop and be civilized, though the command surely had the word "fucking" in it once or twice, and they ignored me. I was not a born leader, and they were not all that good at following orders.

They were also in the grip of something primal; something that was more about their own mortality than the lieutenant's. A few months later, all but me and one other would have lost life or limbs. Maybe they felt it.

GRAVES

I have this persistent sleep disorder that makes life difficult for me, but still I want to keep it. Boy, do I want to keep it. It goes back twenty years, to Vietnam. To Graves.

Dead bodies turn from bad to worse real fast in the jungle. You've got a few hours before rigor mortis makes them hard to handle, hard to stuff in a bag. By that time they start to turn greenish, if they started out white or yellow, where you can see the skin. It's mostly bugs by then, usually ants. Then they go to black and start to smell.

They swell up and burst.

You'd think the ants and roaches and beetles and millipedes would make short work of them after that, but they don't. Just when they get to looking and smelling the worst, the bugs sort of lose interest, get fastidious, send out for pizza. Except for the flies. Laying eggs.

The funny thing is, unless some big animal got to it and tore it up, even after a week or so, you've still got something more than a skeleton, even a sort of a face. No eyes, though. Every now and then we'd get one like that. Not too often, since soldiers don't usually die alone and sit there for that long, but sometimes. We called them dry ones. Still damp underneath, of course, and inside, but kind of like a sunburned mummy otherwise.

You tell people what you do at Graves Registration "Graves," and it sounds like about the worst job the army has to offer. It isn't. You just stand there all day and open body bags, figure out which parts maybe belong to which dog tag, not that it's usually that important, sew them up more or less with a big needle, account for all the wallets and jewelry, steal the dope out of their pockets, box them up, seal the casket, do the paperwork. When you have enough boxes, you truck them out to the airfield. The first week maybe is pretty bad. But after a hundred or so, after you get used to the smell and the godawful feel of them, you get to thinking that opening a body bag is a lot better than winding up inside one. They put Graves in safe places.

Since I'd had a couple years of college, pre-med, I got some of the more interesting jobs. Captain French, who was the pathologist actually in charge of the outfit, always took me with him out into the field when he had to examine a corpse *in situ*, which only happened maybe once a month. I got to wear a .45 in a shoulder holster, tough guy. Never fired it, never got shot at, except the one time.

That was a hell of a time. It's funny what gets to you, stays with you.

Usually when we had an *in situ* it was a forensic matter, like an officer they suspected had been fragged or otherwise terminated by his own men. We'd take pictures and interview some people and then Frenchy would bring the stiff back for autopsy, see whether the bullets were American or Vietnamese. (Not that that would be conclusive either way. The Viet Cong stole our weapons and our guys used the North Vietnamese AK-47s, when we could get our hands on them. More reliable than the M-16 and a better cartridge for killing. Both sides proved that over and over.) Usually Frenchy would send a report up to Division, and that would be it. Once he had to testify at a court-martial. The kid was guilty but just got life. The officer was a real prick.

Anyhow we got the call to come look at this *in situ* corpse about five in the afternoon. Frenchy tried to put it off until the next day, since if it got dark we'd have to spend the night. The guy he was talking to was a major, though, and obviously proud of it, so it was no use arguing. I threw some C's and beer and a couple canteens into two rucksacks that already had blankets and air mattresses tied on the bottom. Box of .45 ammo and a couple hand grenades. Went and got a jeep while Frenchy got his stuff together and made sure Doc Carter was sober enough to count the stiffs as they came in. (Doc Carter was the one supposed to be in charge, but he didn't much care for the work.)

Drove us out to the pad and, lo and behold, there was a chopper waiting, blades idling. Should of started to smell a rat then. We don't get real high priority, and it's not easy to get a chopper to go anywhere so close to sundown. They even helped us stow our gear. Up, up, and away.

GRAVES

I never flew enough in helicopters to make it routine. Kontum looked almost pretty in the low sun, golden red. I had to sit between two flamethrowers, though, which didn't make me feel too secure. The door gunner was smoking. The flamethrower tanks were stenciled NO SMOKING.

We went fast and low out toward the mountains to the west. I was hoping we'd wind up at one of the big fire bases up there, figuring I'd sleep better with a few hundred men around. But no such luck. When the chopper started to slow down, the blades' whir deepening to a whuck-whuck-whuck, there was no clearing as far as the eye could see. Thick jungle canopy everywhere. Then a wisp of purple smoke showed us a helicopter-sized hole in the leaves. The pilot brought us down an inch at a time, nicking twigs. I was very much aware of the flamethrowers. If he clipped a large branch we'd be so much pot roast.

When we touched down, four guys in a big hurry unloaded our gear and the flamethrowers and a couple cases of ammo. They put two wounded guys and one client on board and shooed the helicopter away. Yeah, it would sort of broadcast your position. One of them told us to wait, he'd go get the major.

"I don't like this at all," Frenchy said.

"Me neither," I said. "Let's go home."

"Any outfit that's got a major and two flamethrowers is planning to fight a real war." He pulled his .45 out and looked at it as if he'd never seen one before. "Which end of this do you think the bullets come out of?"

"Shit," I advised, and rummaged through the rucksack for a beer. I gave Frenchy one and he put it in his side pocket.

A machine gun opened up off to our right. Frenchy and I grabbed the dirt. Three grenade blasts. Somebody yelled for them to cut that out. Guy yelled back he thought he saw something. Machine gun started up again. We tried to get a little lower.

Up walks this old guy, thirties, looking annoyed. The major.

"You men get up. What's wrong with you? He was playin' games."

Frenchy got up, dusting himself off. We had the only clean fatigues in twenty miles. "Captain French, Graves Registration."

"Oh," he said, not visibly impressed. "Secure your gear and follow me." He drifted off like a mighty ship of the jungle. Frenchy rolled his eyes and we hoisted our rucksack and followed him. I wasn't sure whether "secure your gear" meant bring your stuff or leave it behind, but Budweiser could get to be a real collectors' item in the boonies, and there were a lot of collectors out here.

We walked too far. I mean a couple hundred yards. That meant they were really spread out thin. I didn't look forward to spending the night. The goddamned machine gun started up again. The major looked annoyed and shouted "Sergeant, will you please control your men?" and the sergeant told the machine gunner to shut the fuck up and the machine gunner told the sergeant there was a fuckin' gook out there, and then somebody popped a big one, like a claymore, and then everybody was shooting every which way. Frenchy and I got real horizontal. I heard a bullet whip by over my head. The major was leaning against a tree looking bored, shouting "Cease firing, cease firing!" The shooting dwindled down like popcorn getting done. The major looked over at us and said, "Come on. While there's still light." He led us into a small clearing, elephant grass pretty well trampled down. I guess everybody had had his turn to look at the corpse.

It wasn't a real gruesome body, as bodies go, but it was odd-looking, even for a dry one. Moldy like someone had dusted flour over it. Naked and probably male, though all the soft parts were gone. Tall; a Montagnard rather than an ethnic Vietnamese. Emaciated, dry skin taut over ribs. Probably old, though it doesn't take long for these people to get old. Lying on its back, mouth wide-open, a familiar posture. Empty eye sockets staring skyward. Arms flung out in supplication, loosely, long past rigor mortis.

Teeth chipped and filed to points, probably some Montagnard tribal custom. I'd never seen it before, but we didn't "do" many natives.

Frenchy knelt down and reached for it, then stopped. "Checked for booby traps?"

"No," the major said. "Figure that's your job." Frenchy looked at me with an expression that said it was my job.

Both officers stood back a respectful distance while I felt under the corpse. Sometimes they pull the pin on a hand grenade and slip it under the body so that the body's weight keeps the arming lever in place. You turn it over and *Tomato Surprise!*

I always worry less about a hand grenade than about the various weird serpents and bugs that might enjoy living underneath a decomposing corpse. Vietnam has its share of snakes and scorpions and mega-pedes.

I was lucky this time; nothing but maggots. I flicked them off my hand and watched the major turn a little green. People are funny. What does he think is going to happen to him when he dies? Everything has to eat. And he was sure as hell going to die if he didn't start keeping his head down. I remember that thought, but didn't think of it then as a prophecy.

They came over. "What do you make of it, Doctor?"

"I don't think we can cure him." Frenchy was getting annoyed at this cherry bomb. "What else do you want to know?"

"Isn't it a little...*odd* to find something like this in the middle of nowhere?"

"Naw. Country's full of corpses." He knelt down and studied the face, wiggling the head by its chin. "We keep it up, you'll be able to walk from the Mekong to the DMZ without stepping on anything but corpses."

"But he's been castrated!"

"Birds." He toed the body over, busy white crawlers running from the light. "Just some old geezer who walked out into the woods naked and fell over dead. Could happen back in the World. Old people do funny things."

"I thought maybe he'd been tortured or something."

"God knows. It could happen." The body eased back into its original position with a creepy creaking sound, like leather. Its mouth had closed halfway. "If you want to put torture in your report, your body count, I'll initial it."

"What do you mean by that, Captain?"

"Exactly what I said." He kept staring at the major while he flipped a cigarette into his mouth and fired it up. Nonfilter Camels; you'd think a guy who worked with corpses all day long would be less anxious to turn into one. "I'm just trying to get along."

"You believe I want you to falsify—"

Now "falsify" is a strange word for a last word. The enemy had set up a heavy machine gun on the other side of the clearing, and we were the closest targets. A round struck the major in the small of his back, we found on later examination. At the time, it was just an explosion of blood and guts and he went down with his legs flopping every which way, barfing, then loud death rattle. Frenchy was on the ground in a ball holding his left hand, going "Shit shit shit." He'd lost the last joint of his little finger. Painful but not serious enough, as it turned out, to get him back to the World.

I myself was horizontal and aspiring to be subterranean. I managed to get my pistol out and cocked, but realized I didn't want to do anything that might draw attention to us. The machine gun was spraying back and forth over us at about knee height. Maybe they couldn't see us; maybe they thought we were dead. I was scared shitless.

"Frenchy," I stage-whispered, "we've got to get outa here." He was trying to wrap his finger up in a standard first-aid-pack gauze bandage, much too large. "Get back to the trees."

"After you, asshole. We wouldn't get halfway." He worked his pistol out of the holster but couldn't cock it, his left hand clamping the bandage and slippery with blood. I armed it for him and handed it back. "These are going to do a hell of a lot of good. How are you with grenades?"

"Shit. How you think I wound up in Graves?" In basic training they'd put me on KP whenever they went out for live grenade practice. In school I was always the last person when they chose up sides for baseball, for the same reason, though to my knowledge a baseball wouldn't kill you if you couldn't throw it far enough. "I couldn't get one halfway there." The tree line was about sixty yards away.

"Neither could I, with this hand." He was a lefty.

Behind us came the "poink" sound of a sixty-millimeter mortar, and in a couple of seconds there was a gray-smoke explosion between us and the tree line. The machine gun stopped and somebody behind us yelled, "Add twenty!"

At the tree line we could hear some shouting in Vietnamese and a clanking of metal. "They're gonna bug out," Frenchy said. "Let's di-di."

We got up and ran and somebody did fire a couple of bursts at us, probably an AK-47, but he missed, and then there was a series of poinks and a series of explosions pretty close to where the gun had been.

We rushed back to the LZ and found the command group, about the time the firing started up again. There was a first lieutenant in charge, and when things slowed down enough for us to tell him what had happened to the major, he expressed neither surprise nor grief. The man had been an observer from Battalion and had assumed command when their captain was killed that morning. He'd take our word for it that the guy was dead—that was one thing we were trained observers in—and not send a squad out for him until the fighting had died down and it was light again.

We inherited the major's' hole, which was nice and deep, and in his rucksack found a dozen cans and jars of real food and a flask of scotch. So as the battle raged through the night, we munched paté on Ritz crackers, pickled herring in sour cream sauce, little Polish sausages on party rye with real French mustard. We drank all the scotch and saved the beer for breakfast.

For hours the lieutenant called in for artillery and air support, but to no avail. Later we found out that the enemy had launched coordinated attacks on all the local airfields and Special Forces camps, and every camp that held POWs. We were much lower priority.

Then about three in the morning, Snoopy came over. Snoopy was a big C-130 cargo plane that carried nothing but ammunition and gatling guns; they said it could fly over a football field and put a round into every square inch. Anyhow, it saturated the perimeter with fire and the enemy stopped shooting. Frenchy and I went to sleep.

At first light we went out to help round up the KIAs. There were only four dead, counting the major, but the major was an astounding sight, at least in context.

He looked sort of like a cadaver left over from a teaching autopsy. His shirt had been opened and his pants pulled down to his thighs, and the entire thoracic and abdominal cavities had been ripped open and emptied of everything soft, everything from esophagus to testicles, rib cage like blood-streaked fingers sticking rigid out of sagging skin, and there wasn't a sign of the guts anywhere, just a lot of dried blood.

Nobody had heard anything. There was a machine gun position not twenty yards away, and they'd been straining their ears all night. All they'd heard was flies.

Maybe an animal feeding very quietly. The body hadn't been opened with a scalpel or a knife; the skin had been torn by teeth or claws—but seemingly systematically, throat to balls.

And the dry one was gone. Him with the pointed teeth.

There is a rational explanation. Modern warfare is partly mind-fuck, and we aren't the only ones who do it, dropping unlucky cards, invoking magic and superstition. The Vietnamese knew how squeamish Americans were, and would mutilate bodies in clever ways. They could also move very quietly. The dry one? They might have spirited him away just to fuck with us. Show what they could do under our noses.

And as for the dry one's odd mummified appearance, the mold, there might be an explanation. I found out that the Montagnards in that area don't bury their dead; they put them in a coffin made from a hollowed-out log and leave them above ground. So maybe he was just the victim of a grave robber. I thought the nearest village was miles away, like twenty miles, but I could have been wrong. Or the body could have been carried that distance for some obscure purpose—maybe the VC set it out on the trail to make the Americans stop in a good place to be ambushed.

That's probably it. But for twenty years now, several nights a week, I wake up sweating with a terrible image in my mind. I've gone out with a flashlight and there it is, the dry one, scooping steaming entrails from the major's body, tearing them with its sharp teeth, staring into my light with black empty sockets, unconcerned. I reach for my pistol, and it's never there. The creature stands up, shiny with blood, and takes a step toward me—for a year or so that was it; I would wake up. Then it was two steps, and then three. After twenty years it has covered half the distance, and its dripping hands are rising from its sides.

The doctor gives me tranquilizers. I don't take them. They might help me stay asleep.

INTRODUCTION TO "NONE SO BLIND"

For several years I had a note pinned to my bulletin board at MIT, asking "Why aren't all blind people geniuses?" The reasoning behind that question, and the story that follows, is that a large fraction of the brain is given over to the visual cortex. A blind person doesn't use it, so why doesn't the brain rewire those 300 million neurons for some other function, like enhancing intellect?

If the brain won't do it by itself, perhaps neurosurgery could help it along.

I glanced at the note with that idea for some years, not sure whether I had a novel, a short story, or a poem. Ultimately what I *did* have was a contract for a book of short stories, so I did a little research and jumped into it.

In the years between writing the note and writing the story, I'd learned a little bit about blind people. At the time, we lived in Daytona Beach, Florida, which had a regional center for the Library of Congress collection of "talking tapes" for the blind. They asked me to come down and record some of my books (the three or four that hadn't already been recorded), which I was glad to do. My wife and I recorded other stuff there for years, until we moved away—she was valuable to them because she's bilingual; I was useful not only for my own books, but because I could read texts in advanced science and mathematics. (Try to imagine a person without training trying to read a differential equation out loud!) I also did Greek tragedy and oddball stuff like knitting instructions, confession magazines, and a text on how to be a fire chief. All grist for the storyteller's mill, of course.

We got to know a few blind people there, but Amy here is modeled after a black teenager I met at a science fiction convention, born blind, who apparently knew more about science and literature than I did.

NONE SO BLIND

I t all started when Cletus Jefferson asked himself "Why aren't all blind people geniuses?" Cletus was only thirteen at the time, but it was a good question, and he would work on it for fourteen more years, and then change the world forever.

Young Jefferson was a polymath, an autodidact, a nerd literally without peer. He had a chemistry set, a microscope, a telescope, and several computers, some of them bought with paper route money. Most of his income was from education, though: teaching his classmates not to draw to inside straights.

Not even nerds, not even nerds who are poker players nonpareil, not even nerdish poker players who can do differential equations in their heads, are immune to Cupid's darts and the sudden storm of testosterone that will accompany those missiles at the age of thirteen. Cletus knew that he was ugly and his mother dressed him funny. He was also short and pudgy and could not throw a ball in any direction. None of this bothered him until his ductless glands started cooking up chemicals that weren't in his chemistry set.

So Cletus started combing his hair and wearing clothes that mismatched according to fashion, but he was still short and pudgy and irregular of feature. He was also the youngest person in his school, even though he was a senior—and the only black person there, which was a factor in Virginia in 1994.

Now if love were sensible, if the sexual impulse was ever tempered by logic, you would expect that Cletus, being Cletus, would assess his situation and go off in search of someone homely. But of course he didn't. He just jingled and clanked down through the Pachinko machine of adolescence, being rejected, at first glance, by every Mary and Judy and Jenny and Veronica in Known Space, going from the ravishing to the beautiful to the pretty to the cute to the plain to the "great personality," until the irresistible force of statistics brought him finally into contact with Amy Linderbaum, who could not reject him at first glance because she was blind.

The other kids thought it was more than amusing. Besides being blind, Amy was about twice as tall as Cletus and, to be kind, equally irregular of feature. She was accompanied by a guide dog who looked remarkably like Cletus, short and black and pudgy. Everybody was polite to her because she was blind and rich, but she was a new transfer student and didn't have any actual friends.

So along came Cletus, to whom Cupid had dealt only slings and arrows, and what might otherwise have been merely an opposites-attract sort of romance became an emotional and intellectual union that, in the next century, would power a social tsunami that would irreversibly transform the human condition. But first there was the violin.

Her classmates had sensed that Amy was some kind of nerd herself, as classmates will, but they hadn't figured out what kind yet. She was pretty fast with a computer, but you could chalk that up to being blind and actually needing the damned thing. She wasn't fanatical about it, nor about science or math or history or Star Trek or student government, so what the hell kind of nerd was she? It turns out that she was a music nerd, but at the time was too painfully shy to demonstrate it.

All Cletus cared about, initially, was that she lacked those pesky Y-chromosomes and didn't recoil from him: in the Venn diagram of the human race, she was the only member of that particular set. When he found out that she was actually smart as well, having read more books than most of her classmates put together, romance began to smolder in a deep and permanent place. That was even before the violin.

Amy liked it that Cletus didn't play with her dog and was straightforward in his curiosity about what it was like to be blind. She could assess people pretty well from their voices: after one sentence, she knew that he was young, black, shy, nerdly, and not from Virginia. She could tell from his inflection that either he was unattractive or he thought he was. She was six years older than him and white and twice his size, but otherwise they matched up pretty well, and they started keeping company in a big way.

Among the few things that Cletus did not know anything about was music. That the other kids wasted their time memorizing the words to inane Top 40 songs was proof of intellectual dysfunction if not actual lunacy. Furthermore, his parents had always been fanatical devotees of opera. A universe bounded on one end by puerile mumblings about unrequited love and on the other end by foreigners screaming in agony was not a universe that Cletus desired to explore. Until Amy picked up her violin.

They talked constantly. They sat together at lunch and met between classes. When the weather was good, they sat outside before and after school and talked. Amy asked her chauffeur to please be ten or fifteen minutes late picking her up.

So after about three weeks' worth of the fullness of time, Amy asked Cletus to come over to her house for dinner. He was a little hesitant, knowing that her parents were rich, but he was also curious about that lifestyle and, face it, was smitten enough that he would have walked off a cliff if she asked him nicely. He even used some computer money to buy a nice suit, a symptom that caused his mother to grope for the Valium.

The dinner at first was awkward. Cletus was bewildered by the arsenal of silverware and all the different kinds of food that didn't look or taste like food. But he had known it was going to be a test, and he always did well on tests, even when he had to figure out the rules as he went along.

Amy had told him that her father was a self-made millionaire; his fortune had come from a set of patents in solid-state electronics. Cletus had therefore spent a Saturday at the university library, first searching patents, and then reading selected texts, and he was ready at least for the father. It worked very well. Over soup, the four of them talked about computers. Over the calimari cocktail, Cletus and Mr. Linderbaum had it narrowed down to specific operating systems and partitioning schemata. With the beef Wellington, Cletus and "Call-me-Lindy" were talking quantum electrodynamics; with the salad they were on an electron cloud somewhere, and by the time the nuts were served, the two nuts at that end of the table were talking in Boolean algebra while Amy and her mother exchanged knowing sighs and hummed snatches of Gilbert and Sullivan.

By the time they retired to the music room for coffee, Lindy liked Cletus very much, and the feeling was mutual, but Cletus didn't know how much he liked Amy, *really* liked her, until she picked up the violin.

It wasn't a Strad—she was promised one if and when she graduated from Julliard—but it had cost more than the Lamborghini in the garage, and she was not only worth it, but equal to it. She picked it up and tuned it quietly while her mother sat down at an electronic keyboard next to the grand piano, set it to "harp," and began the simple arpeggio that a music-ally sophisticated person would recognize as the introduction to the violin showpiece "Méditation" from Massenet's *Thaïs*.

Cletus had turned a deaf ear to opera for all his short life, so he didn't know the back-story of transformation and transcending love behind this intermezzo, but he did know that his girlfriend had lost her sight at the age of five, and the next year—the year he was born!—was given her first violin. For thirteen years she had been using it to say what she would not say with her voice, perhaps to see what she could not see with her eyes, and on the deceptively simple romantic matrix that Massenet built to present the beautiful courtesan Thaïs gloriously reborn as the bride of Christ, Amy forgave her godless universe for taking her sight, and praised it for what she was given in return, and she said this in a language that even Cletus could understand. He didn't cry very much, never had, but by the last high, wavering note he was weeping into his hands, and he knew that if she wanted him, she could have him forever, and oddly enough, considering his age and what eventually happened, he was right.

He would learn to play the violin before he had his first doctorate, and during a lifetime of remarkable amity they would play together for ten thousand hours, but all of that would come after the big idea. The big idea—"Why aren't all blind people geniuses?"—was planted that very night, but it didn't start to sprout for another week.

Like most thirteen-year-olds, Cletus was fascinated by the human body, his own and others, but his study was more systematic than others' and, atypically, the organ that interested him most was the brain.

The brain isn't very much like a computer, although it doesn't do a bad job, considering that it's built by unskilled labor and programmed more by pure chance than anything else. One thing computers do a lot better than brains, though, is what Cletus and Lindy had been talking about over their little squids in tomato sauce: partitioning.

Think of the computer as a big meadow of green pastureland, instead of a little dark box full of number-clogged things that are expensive to replace, and that pastureland is presided over by a wise old magic shep-herd who is not called a macroprogram. The shepherd stands on a hill and looks out over the pastureland, which is full of sheep and goats and cows. They aren't all in one homogeneous mass, of course, since the cows would step on the lambs and kids and the goats would make everybody nervous, leaping and butting, so there are *partitions* of barbed wire that keep all the species separate and happy.

This is a frenetic sort of meadow, though, with cows and goats and sheep coming in and going out all the time, moving at about 3×10^8 meters per second, and if the partitions were all of the same size, it would be a disaster, because sometimes there are no sheep at all, but lots of cows, who would be jammed in there hip to hip and miserable. But the shepherd, being wise, knows ahead of time how much space to allot to the various creatures and, being magic, can move barbed wire quickly without hurting himself or the animals. So each partition winds up marking a comfortable-sized space for each use. Your computer does that, too, but instead of barbed wire you see little rectangles or windows or file folders, depending on your computer's religion.

The brain has its own partitions, in a sense. Cletus knew that certain physical areas of the brain were associated with certain mental abilities, but it wasn't a simple matter of "music appreciation goes over there; long division in that corner." The brain is mushier than that. For instance, there are pretty well defined partitions associated with linguistic functions, areas named after French and German brain people. If one of those areas is destroyed, by stroke or bullet or flung frying pan, the stricken person may lose the ability—reading or speaking or writing coherently—associated with the lost area.

That's interesting, but what is more interesting is that the lost ability sometimes comes back over time. Okay, you say, so the brain grew back—but it doesn't! You're born with all the brain cells you'll ever have. (Ask any child.) What evidently happens is that some other part of the brain has been sitting around as a kind of backup, and after a while the wiring gets rewired and hooked into that backup. The afflicted person can say his name, and then his wife's name, and then "frying pan," and before you know it he's complaining about hospital food and calling a divorce lawyer.

So on that evidence, it would appear that the brain has a shepherd like the computer-meadow has, moving partitions around, but alas, no. Most of the time when some part of the brain ceases to function, that's the end of it. There may be acres and acres of fertile ground lying fallow right next door, but nobody in charge to make use of it—at least not consistently. The fact that it sometimes *did* work is what made Cletus ask "Why aren't all blind people geniuses?"

Of course there have always been great thinkers and writers and composers who were blind (and in the twentieth century, some painters to whom eyesight was irrelevant), and many of them, like Amy with her violin, felt that their talent was a compensating gift. Cletus wondered whether there might be a literal truth to that, in the microanatomy of the brain. It didn't happen every time, or else all blind people *would* be geniuses. Perhaps it happened occasionally, through a mechanism like the one that helped people recover from strokes. Perhaps it could be made to happen.

Cletus had been offered scholarships at both Harvard and MIT, but he opted for Columbia, in order to be near Amy while she was studying at Julliard. Columbia reluctantly allowed him a triple major in physiology, electrical engineering, and cognitive science, and he surprised everybody who knew him by doing only moderately well. The reason, it turned out, was that he was treating undergraduate work as a diversion at best; a necessary evil at worst. He was racing ahead of his studies in the areas that were important to him.

If he had paid more attention in trivial classes like history, like philosophy, things might have turned out differently. If he had paid attention to literature, he might have read the story of Pandora.

Our own story now descends into the dark recesses of the brain. For the next ten years the main part of the story, which we will try to ignore after this paragraph, will involve Cletus doing disturbing intellectual tasks like cutting up dead brains, learning how to pronounce cholecystokinin, and sawing holes in people's skulls and poking around inside with live electrodes.

In the other part of the story, Amy also learned how to pronounce cholecystokinin, for the same reason that Cletus learned how to play the violin. Their love grew and mellowed, and at the age of nineteen, between his first doctorate and his M.D., Cletus paused long enough for them to be married and have a whirlwind honeymoon in Paris, where Cletus divided his time between the musky charms of his beloved and the sterile cubicles of Institute Marey, learning how squids learn things, which was by serotonin pushing adenylate cyclase to catalyze the synthesis of cyclic adenosine monophosphate in just the right place, but that's actually the main part of the story, which we have been trying to ignore, because it gets pretty gruesome.

They returned to New York, where Cletus spent eight years becoming a pretty good neurosurgeon. In his spare time he tucked away a doctorate in electrical engineering. Things began to converge.

At the age of thirteen, Cletus had noted that the brain used more cells collecting, handling, and storing visual images than it used for all the other senses combined. "Why aren't all blind people geniuses?" was just a specific case of the broader assertion, "The brain doesn't know how to make use of what it's got." His investigations over the next fourteen years were more subtle and complex than that initial question and statement, but he did wind up coming right back around to them.

Because the key to the whole thing was the visual cortex.

When a baritone saxophone player has to transpose sheet music from cello, he (few women are drawn to the instrument) merely pretends that the music is written in treble clef rather than bass, eyeballs it up an octave, and then plays without the octave key pressed down. It's so simple a child could do it, if a child wanted to play such a huge, ungainly instrument. As his eye dances along the little fence posts of notes, his fingers automatically perform a one-to-one transformation that is the theoretical equivalent of adding and subtracting octaves, fifths, and thirds, but all of the actual mental work is done when he looks up in the top right corner of the first page and says, "Aw hell. Cello again." Cello parts aren't that interesting to saxophonists.

But the eye is the key, and the visual cortex is the lock. When blind Amy "sight-reads" for the violin, she has to stop playing and feel the Braille notes with her left hand. (Years of keeping the instrument in place while she does this has made her neck muscles so strong that she can crack a walnut between her chin and shoulder.) The visual cortex is not involved, of course; she "hears" the mute notes of a phrase with her fingertips, temporarily memorizing them, and then plays them over and over until she can add that phrase to the rest of the piece.

Like most blind musicians, Amy had a very good "ear"; it actually took her less time to memorize music by listening to it repeatedly, rather than reading, even with fairly complex pieces. (She used Braille nevertheless for serious work, so she could isolate the composer's intent from the performer's or conductor's phrasing decisions.)

She didn't really miss being able to sight-read in a conventional way. She wasn't even sure what it would be like, since she had never seen sheet music before she lost her sight, and in fact had only a vague idea of what a printed page of writing looked like.

So when her father came to her in her thirty-third year and offered to buy her the chance of a limited gift of sight, she didn't immediately jump at it. It was expensive and risky and grossly deforming: implanting miniaturized video cameras in her eye sockets and wiring them up to stimulate her dormant optic nerves. What if it made her only half-blind, but also blunted her musical ability? She knew how other people read music, at least in theory, but after a quarter century of doing without the skill, she wasn't sure that it would do much for her. It might make her tighten up.

Besides, most of her concerts were done as charities to benefit organizations for the blind or for special education. Her father argued that she would be even more effective in those venues as a recovered blind person. Still she resisted.

Cletus said he was cautiously for it. He said he had reviewed the literature and talked to the Swiss team who had successfully done the implants on dogs and primates. He said he didn't think she would be harmed by it even if the experiment failed. What he didn't say to Amy or Lindy or anybody was the grisly Frankensteinian truth: that he was himself behind the experiment; that it had nothing to do with restoring sight; that the little video cameras would never even be hooked up. They were just an excuse for surgically removing her eyeballs.

Now a normal person would have extreme feelings about popping out somebody's eyeballs for the sake of science, and even more extreme feelings on learning that it was a husband wanting to do it to his wife. Of course Cletus was far from being normal in any respect. To his way of thinking, those eyeballs were useless vestigial appendages that blocked surgical access to the optic nerves, which would be his conduits through the brain to the visual cortex. *Physical* conduits, through which incredibly tiny surgical instruments would be threaded. But we have promised not to investigate that part of the story in detail.

The end result was not grisly at all. Amy finally agreed to go to Geneva, and Cletus and his surgical team (all as skilled as they were unethical) put her through three twenty-hour days of painstaking but painless microsurgery, and when they took the bandages off and adjusted a thousand-dollar wig (for they'd had to go in behind as well as through the eye sockets), she actually looked more attractive than when they had started. That was partly because her actual hair had always been a disaster. And now she had glass baby-blues instead of the rather scary opalescence of her natural eyes. No Buck Rogers TV cameras peering out at the world.

He told her father that that part of the experiment hadn't worked, and the six Swiss scientists who had been hired for the purpose agreed.

"They're lying," Amy said. "They never intended to restore my sight. The sole intent of the operations was to subvert the normal functions of the visual cortex in such a way as to give me access to the unused parts of my brain." She faced the sound of her husband's breathing, her blue eyes looking beyond him. "You have succeeded beyond your expectations."

Amy had known this as soon as the fog of drugs from the last operation had lifted. Her mind started making connections, and those connections made connections, and so on at a geometrical rate of growth. By the time they had finished putting her wig on, she had reconstructed the entire microsurgical procedure from her limited readings and conversations with Cletus. She had suggestions as to improving it, and was eager to go under and submit herself to further refinement.

As to her feelings about Cletus, in less time than it takes to read about it, she had gone from horror to hate to understanding to renewed love, and finally to an emotional condition beyond the ability of any merely natural language to express. Fortunately, the lovers did have Boolean algebra and propositional calculus at their disposal.

Cletus was one of the few people in the world she *could* love, or even talk to one-on-one, without condescending. His IQ was so high that its number would be meaningless. Compared to her, though, he was slow, and barely literate. It was not a situation he would tolerate for long.

The rest is history, as they say, and anthropology, as those of us left who read with our eyes must recognize every minute of every day. Cletus was the second person to have the operation done, and he had to accomplish it while on the run from medical ethics people and their policemen. There were four the next year, though, and twenty the year after that, and then two thousand and twenty thousand. Within a decade, people with purely intellectual occupations had no choice, or one choice: lose your eyes or lose your job. By then the "secondsight" operation was totally automated, totally safe.

It's still illegal in most countries, including the United States, but who is kidding whom? If your department chairman is secondsighted and you are not, do you think you'll get tenure? You can't even hold a conversation with a creature whose synapses fire six times as fast as yours, with whole encyclopedias of information instantly available. You are, like me, an intellectual throwback.

You may have an excuse, being a painter, an architect, a naturalist, or a trainer of guide dogs. Maybe you can't come up with the money for the operation, but that's a weak excuse, since it's trivially easy to get a loan against future earnings. Maybe there's a good physical reason for you not to lie down on that table and open your eyes for the last time.

I know Cletus and Amy through music. I was her keyboard professor once, at Julliard, though now, of course, I'm not smart enough to teach her anything. They come to hear me play sometimes, in this run-down bar with its band of ageing firstsight musicians. Our music must seem boring, obvious, but they do us the favor of not joining in.

Amy was an innocent bystander in this sudden evolutionary explosion. And Cletus was, arguably, blinded by love.

The rest of us have to choose which kind of blindness to endure.

INTRODUCTION TO "FOR WHITE HILL"

Gregory Benford asked me to write a story for his anthology *Far Futures*, the basic thrust of which was to set realistic sf stories at least a thousand years in the future.

I decided to write a love story, and secretly structure it after one of the oldest and most mysterious love stories in literature: Shakespeare's Sonnet 14—"Shall I compare thee to a summer's day?" This story's ending recalls "So long lives this, and this gives life to thee."

Shakespeare isn't mentioned, although there are hints throughout the story—not the least of which is that the story has a sonnet structure, with fourteen parts, each based on a line from that poem. I disguised that by dividing the sections with symbols from a made-up number system, which is fourteen-based.

The 1609 edition of Shakespeare's sonnets cites one "W. H." as their "onlie begetter." His W. H. was probably a guy, but times change.

FOR WHITE HILL

●

I am writing this memoir in the language of England, an ancient land of Earth, whose tales and songs White Hill valued. She was fascinated by human culture in the days before machines — not just thinking machines, but working ones; when things got done by the straining muscles of humans and animals.

Neither of us was born on Earth. Not many people were, in those days. It was a desert planet then, ravaged in the twelfth year of what they would call the Last War. When we met, that war had been going for over four hundred years, and had moved out of Sol Space altogether, or so we thought.

Some cultures had other names for the conflict. My parent, who fought the century before I did, always called it the Extermination, and their name for the enemy was "roach," or at least that's as close as English allows. We called the enemy an approximation of their own word for themselves, Fwndyri, which was uglier to us. I still have no love for them, but have no reason to make the effort. It would be easier to love a roach. At least we have a common ancestor. And we accompanied one another into space.

One mixed blessing we got from the war was a loose form of interstellar government, the Council of Worlds. There had been individual treaties before, but an overall organization had always seemed unlikely, since no two inhabited systems are less than three light-years apart, and several of them are over fifty. You can't defeat Einstein; that makes more than a century between "How are you?" and "Fine."

The Council of Worlds was headquartered on Earth, an unlikely and unlovely place, if centrally located. There were fewer than ten thousand people living on the blighted planet then, an odd mix of politicians, religious extremists, and academics, mostly. Almost all of them under glass. Tourists flowed through the domed-over ruins, but not many stayed long. The planet was still very dangerous over all of its unprotected surface, since the Fwndyri had thoroughly seeded it with nanophages. Those were sub-microscopic constructs that sought out concentrations of human DNA. Once under the skin, they would reproduce at a geometric rate, deconstructing the body, cell by cell, building new nanophages. A person might complain of a headache and lie down, and a few hours later there would be nothing but a dry skeleton, lying in dust. When the humans were all dead, they mutated and went after DNA in general, and sterilized the world.

White Hill and I were "bred" for immunity to the nanophages. Our DNA winds backwards, as was the case with many people born or created after that stage of the war. So we could actually go through the elaborate airlocks and step out onto the blasted surface unprotected.

I didn't like her at first. We were competitors, and aliens to one another.

When I worked through the final airlock cycle, for my first moment on the actual surface of Earth, she was waiting outside, sitting in meditation on a large flat rock that shimmered in the heat. One had to admit she was beautiful in a startling way, clad only in a glistening pattern of blue and green body paint. Everything else around was grey and black, including the hardpacked talcum that had once been a mighty jungle, Brazil. The dome behind me was a mirror of grey and black and cobalt sky.

"Welcome home," she said. "You're Water Man."

She inflected it properly, which surprised me. "You're from Petros?"

"Of course not." She spread her arms and looked down at her body. Our women always cover at least one of their breasts, let alone their genitals. "Galan, an island on Seldene. I've studied your cultures, a little language."

"You don't dress like that on Seldene, either." Not anywhere I'd been on the planet.

"Only at the beach. It's so warm here." I had to agree. Before I came out, they'd told me it was the hottest autumn on record. I took off my robe and folded it and left it by the door, with the sealed food box they had given me. I joined her on the rock, which was tilted away from the sun and reasonably cool.

She had a slight fragrance of lavender, perhaps from the body paint. We touched hands. "My name is White Hill. Zephyr-meadow-torrent."

"Where are the others?" I asked. Twenty-nine artists had been invited; one from each inhabited world. The people who had met me inside said I was the nineteenth to show up.

"Most of them traveling. Going from dome to dome for inspiration."

"You've already been around?"

"No." She reached down with her toe and scraped a curved line on the hard-baked ground. "All the story's here, anywhere. It isn't really about history or culture."

Her open posture would have been shockingly sexual at home, but this was not home. "Did you visit my world when you were studying it?"

"No, no money, at the time. I did get there a few years ago." She smiled at me. "It was almost as beautiful as I'd imagined it." She said three words in Petrosian. You couldn't say it precisely in English, which doesn't have a palindromic mood: *Dreams feed art and art feeds dreams.*

"When you came to Seldene I was young, too young to study with you. I've learned a lot from your sculpture, though."

"How young can you be?" To earn this honor, I did not say.

"In Earth years, about seventy awake. More than one-forty-five in time-squeeze."

I struggled with the arithmetic. Petros and Seldene were 22 light-years apart; that's about 45 years' squeeze. Earth is, what, a little less than 40 light-years from her planet. That leaves enough gone time for someplace about 25 light-years from Petros, and back.

She tapped me on the knee, and I flinched. "Don't overheat your brain. I made a triangle; went to ThetaKent after your world."

"Really? When I was there?"

"No, I missed you by less than a year. I was disappointed. You were why I went." She made a palindrome in my language: *Predator becomes prey becomes predator?* "So here we are. Perhaps I can still learn from you."

I didn't much care for her tone of voice, but I said the obvious: "I'm more likely to learn from you."

"Oh, I don't think so." She smiled in a measured way. "You don't have much to learn."

Or much I could, or would, learn. "Have you been down to the water?"

"Once." She slid off the rock and dusted herself, spanking. "It's interesting. Doesn't look real." I picked up the food box and followed her down a sort of path that led us into low ruins. She drank some of my water, apologetic; hers was hot enough to brew tea.

"First body?" I asked.

"I'm not tired of it yet." She gave me a sideways look, amused. "You must be on your fourth or fifth."

"I go through a dozen a year." She laughed. "Actually, it's still my second. I hung on to the first too long."

"I read about that, the accident. That must have been horrible."

"Comes with the medium. I should take up the flute." I had been making a "controlled" fracture in a large boulder and set off the charges prematurely, by dropping the detonator. Part of the huge rock rolled over onto me, crushing my body from the hips down. It was a remote area, and by the time help arrived I had been dead for several minutes, from pain as much as anything else. "It affected all of my work, of course. I can't even look at some of the things I did the first few years I had this body."

"They are hard to look at," she said. "Not to say they aren't well-done, and beautiful, in their way."

"As what is not? In its way." We came to the first building ruins and stopped. "Not all of this is weathering. Even in four hundred years." If you studied the rubble, you could reconstruct part of the design. Primitive but sturdy, concrete reinforced with composite rods. "Somebody came in here with heavy equipment or explosives. They never actually fought on Earth, I thought."

"They say not." She picked up an irregular brick with a rod through it. "Rage, I suppose. Once people knew that no one was going to live."

"It's hard to imagine." The records are chaotic. Evidently the first people died two or three days after the nanophages were introduced, and no one on Earth was alive a week later. "Not hard to understand, though. The need to break something." I remembered the inchoate anger I felt as I squirmed there helpless, dying from *sculpture*, of all things. Anger at the rocks, the fates. Not at my own inattention and clumsiness.

"They had a poem about that," she said. "'Rage, rage against the dying of the light.'"

"Somebody actually wrote something during the nanoplague?"

"Oh no. A thousand years before. Twelve hundred." She squatted suddenly and brushed at a fragment that had two letters on it. "I wonder if this was some sort of official building. Or a shrine or church." She pointed along the curved row of shattered bricks that spilled into the street. "That looks like it was some kind of decoration, a gable over the entrance." She tiptoed through the rubble toward the far end of the arc, studying what was written on the faceup pieces. The posture, standing on the balls of her feet, made her slim body even more attractive, as she must have known. My own body began to respond in a way inappropriate for a man more than three times her age. Foolish, even though that particular part is not so old. I willed it down before she could see.

"It's a language I don't know," she said. "Not Portuguese; looks like Latin. A Christian church, probably, Catholic."

"They used water in their religion," I remembered. "Is that why it's close to the sea?"

"They were everywhere: sea, mountains, orbit. They got to Petros?"

"We still have some. I've never met one, but they have a church in New Haven."

"As who doesn't?" She pointed up a road. "Come on. The beach is just over the rise here."

I could smell it before I saw it. It wasn't an ocean smell; it was dry, slightly choking.

We turned a corner and I stood staring. "It's a deep blue farther out," she said, "and so clear you can see hundreds of metras down." Here the water was thick and brown, the surf foaming heavily like a giant's chocolate drink, mud piled in baked windrows along the beach. "This used to be soil?"

She nodded. "There's a huge river that cuts this continent in half, the Amazon. When the plants died, there was nothing to hold the soil in place." She tugged me forward. "Do you swim? Come on."

"Swim in *that*? It's filthy."

"No, it's perfectly sterile. Besides, I have to pee." Well, I couldn't argue with that. I left the box on a high fragment of fallen wall and followed her. When we got to the beach, she broke into a run. I walked slowly and watched her gracile body, instead, and waded into the slippery heavy surf. When it was deep enough to swim, I plowed my way out to where she was bobbing. The water was too hot to be pleasant, and breathing was somewhat difficult. Carbon dioxide, I supposed, with a tang of halogen.

We floated together for a while, comparing this soup to bodies of water on our planets and ThetaKent. It was tiring, more from the water's heat and bad air than exertion, so we swam back in.

●●

We dried in the blistering sun for a few minutes and then took the food box and moved to the shade of a beachside ruin. Two walls had fallen in together, to make a sort of concrete tent.

We could have been a couple of precivilization aboriginals, painted with dirt, our hair baked into stringy mats. She looked odd but still had a kind of formal beauty, the dusty mud residue turning her into a primitive sculpture, impossibly accurate and mobile. Dark rivulets of sweat drew painterly accent lines along her face and body. If only she were a model, rather than an artist. Hold that pose while I go back for my brushes.

We shared the small bottles of cold wine and water and ate bread and cheese and fruit. I put a piece on the ground for the nanophages. We watched it in silence for some minutes, while nothing happened. "It probably takes hours or days," she finally said.

"I suppose we should hope so," I said. "Let us digest the food before the creatures get to it."

"Oh, that's not a problem. They just attack the bonds between amino acids that make up proteins. For you and me, they're nothing more than an aid to digestion."

How reassuring. "But a source of some discomfort when we go back in, I was told."

She grimaced. "The purging. I did it once, and decided my next outing would be a long one. The treatment's the same for a day or a year."

"So how long has it been this time?"

"Just a day and a half. I came out to be your welcoming committee."

"I'm flattered."

She laughed. "It was their idea, actually. They wanted someone out here to 'temper' the experience for you. They weren't sure how well traveled you were, how easily affected by...strangeness." She shrugged. "Earthlings. I told them I knew of four planets you'd been to."

"They weren't impressed?"

"They said well, you know, he's famous and wealthy. His experiences on these planets might have been very comfortable." We could both laugh at that. "I told them how comfortable ThetaKent is."

"Well, it doesn't have nanophages."

"Or anything else. That was a long year for me. You didn't even stay a year."

"No. I suppose we would have met, if I had."

"Your agent said you were going to be there two years."

I poured us both some wine. "She should have told me you were coming. Maybe I could have endured it until the next ship out."

"How gallant." She looked into the wine without drinking. "You famous and wealthy people don't have to endure ThetaKent. I had to agree to one year's indentureship to help pay for my triangle ticket."

"You were an actual slave?"

"More like a wife, actually. The head of a township, a widower, financed me in exchange for giving his children some culture. Language, art, music. Every now and then he asked me to his chambers. For his own kind of culture."

"My word. You had to...*lie* with him? That was in the contract?"

"Oh, I didn't have to, but it kept him friendly." She held up a thumb and forefinger. "It was hardly noticeable."

I covered my smile with a hand, and probably blushed under the mud.

"I'm not embarrassing you?" she said. "From your work, I'd think that was impossible."

I had to laugh. "That work is in reaction to my culture's values. I can't take a pill and stop being a Petrosian."

White Hill smiled, tolerantly. "A Petrosian woman wouldn't put up with an arrangement like that?"

"Our women are still women. Some actually would like it, secretly. Most would claim they'd rather die, or kill the man."

"But they wouldn't actually *do* it. Trade their body for a ticket?" She sat down in a single smooth dancer's motion, her legs open, facing me. The clay between her legs parted, sudden pink.

"I wouldn't put it so bluntly." I swallowed, watching her watching me. "But no, they wouldn't. Not if they were planning to return."

"Of course no one from a civilized planet would want to stay on ThetaKent. Shocking place."

I had to move the conversation onto safer grounds. "Your arms don't spend all day shoving big rocks around. What do you normally work in?"

"Various mediums." She switched to my language. "Sometimes I shove little rocks around." That was a pun for testicles. "I like painting, but my reputation is mainly from light and sound sculpture. I wanted to do something with the water here, internal illumination of the surf, but they say that's not possible. They can't isolate part of the ocean. I can have a pool, but no waves, no tides."

"Understandable." Earth's scientists had found a way to rid the surface of the nanoplague. Before they reterraformed the Earth, though, they wanted to isolate an area, a "park of memory," as a reminder of the Sterilization and these centuries of waste, and brought artists from every world to interpret, inside the park, what they had seen here.

Every world except Earth. Art on Earth had been about little else for a long time.

Setting up the contest had taken decades. A contest representative went to each of the settled worlds, according to a strict timetable. Announcement of the competition was delayed on the nearer worlds so that each artist would arrive on Earth at approximately the same time.

The Earth representatives chose which artists would be asked, and no one refused. Even the ones who didn't win the contest were guaranteed an honorarium equal to twice what they would have earned during that time at home, in their best year of record.

The value of the prize itself was so large as to be meaningless to a normal person. I'm a wealthy man on a planet where wealth is not rare, and just the interest that the prize would earn would support me and a half dozen more. If someone from ThetaKent or Laxor won the prize, they would probably have more real usable wealth than their governments. If they were smart, they wouldn't return home.

The artists had to agree on an area for the park, which was limited to a hundred square kaymetras. If they couldn't agree, which seemed almost inevitable to me, the contest committee would listen to arguments and rule.

Most of the chosen artists were people like me, accustomed to working on a monumental scale. The one from Laxor was a composer, though, and there were two conventional muralists, paint and mosaic. White Hill's work was by its nature evanescent. She could always set something up that would be repeated, like a fountain cycle. She might have more imagination than that, though.

"Maybe it's just as well we didn't meet in a master-student relationship," I said. "I don't know the first thing about the techniques of your medium."

"It's not technique." She looked thoughtful, remembering. "That's not why I wanted to study with you, back then. I was willing to push rocks around, or anything, if it could give me an avenue, an insight into how you did what you did." She folded her arms over her chest, and dust fell. "Ever since my parents took me to see Gaudí Mountain, when I was ten."

That was an early work, but I was still satisfied with it. The city council of Tresling, a prosperous coastal city, hired me to "do something with" an unusable steep island that stuck up in the middle of their harbor. I melted it judiciously, in homage to an Earthling artist.

"Now, though, if you'd forgive me…well, I find it hard to look at. It's alien, obtrusive."

"You don't have to apologize for having an opinion." Of course it looked alien; it was meant to evoke *Spain!* "What would you do with it?"

She stood up and walked to where a window used to be, and leaned on the stone sill, looking at the ruins that hid the sea. "I don't know. I'm even less familiar with your tools." She scraped at the edge of the sill with a piece of rubble. "It's funny: earth, air, fire, and water. You're earth and fire, and I'm the other two."

I have used water, of course. The Gaudí is framed by water. But it was an interesting observation. "What do you do, I mean for a living? Is it related to your water and air?"

"No. Except insofar as everything is related." There are no artists on Seldene, in the sense of doing it for a living. Everybody indulges in some sort of art or music, as part of "wholeness," but a person who only did art would be considered a parasite. I was not comfortable there.

She faced me, leaning. "I work at the Northport Mental Health Center. Cognitive science, a combination of research and…is there a word here? *Jaturnary.* 'Empathetic therapy,' I guess."

I nodded. "We say *jådr-ny*. You plug yourself into mental patients?"

"I share their emotional states. Sometimes I do some good, talking to them afterwards. Not often."

"It's not done on Petrosia," I said, unnecessarily.

"Not legally, you mean."

I nodded. "If it worked, people say, it might be legal."

"'People say.' What do you say?" I started to make a noncommittal gesture. "Tell me the truth?"

"All I know is what I learned in school. It was tried but failed spectacularly. It hurt both the therapists and the patients."

"That was more than a century ago. The science is much more highly developed now."

I decided not to push her on it. The fact is that drug therapy is spectacularly successful, and it *is* a science, unlike *jådr-ny*. Seldene is backward in some surprising ways.

I joined her at the window. "Have you looked around for a site yet?"

She shrugged. "I think my presentation will work anywhere. At least that's guided my thinking. I'll have water, air, and light, wherever the other artists and the committee decide to put us." She scraped at the ground with a toenail. "And this stuff. They call it 'loss.' What's left of what was living."

"I suppose it's not everywhere, though. They might put us in a place that used to be a desert."

"They might. But there will be water and air; they were willing to guarantee that."

"I don't suppose they have to guarantee rock," I said.

"I don't know. What would you do if they did put us in a desert, nothing but sand?"

"Bring little rocks." I used my own language; the pun also meant courage.

She started to say something, but we were suddenly in deeper shadow. We both stepped through the tumbled wall, out into the open. A black line of cloud had moved up rapidly from inland.

She shook her head. "Let's get to the shelter. Better hurry."

We trotted back along the path toward the Amazonia dome city. There was a low concrete structure behind the rock where I first met her. The warm breeze became a howling gale of sour steam before we got there, driving bullets of hot rain. A metal door opened automatically on our approach and slid shut behind us. "I got caught in one yesterday," she said, panting. "It's no fun, even under cover. Stinks."

We were in an unadorned anteroom that had protective clothing on wall pegs. I followed her into a large room furnished with simple chairs and tables, and up a winding stair to an observation bubble.

"Wish we could see the ocean from here," she said. It was dramatic enough. Wavering sheets of water marched across the blasted landscape, strobed every few seconds by lightning flashes. The tunic I'd left outside swooped in flapping circles off to the sea.

It was gone in a couple of seconds. "You don't get another one, you know. You'll have to meet everyone naked as a baby."

"A dirty one at that. How undignified."

"Come on." She caught my wrist and tugged. "Water is my specialty, after all."

The large hot bath was doubly comfortable for having a view of the tempest outside. I'm not at ease with communal bathing—I was married for fifty years and never bathed with my wife—but it seemed natural enough after wandering around together naked on an alien planet, swimming in its mud-puddle sea. I hoped I could trust her not to urinate in the tub. (If I mentioned it, she would probably turn scientific and tell me that a healthy person's urine is sterile. I know that. But there is a time and a receptacle for everything.)

On Seldene, I knew, an unattached man and woman in this situation would probably have had sex even if they were only casual acquaintances, let alone fellow artists. She was considerate enough not to make any overtures, or perhaps (I thought at the time) not greatly stimulated by the sight of muscular men. In the shower before bathing, she offered to scrub my back, but I left it at that. I helped her strip off the body paint from her back. It was a nice back to study, pronounced lumbar dimples, small waist. Under more restrained circumstances, it might have been I who made an overture. But one does not ask a woman when refusal would be awkward.

Talking while we bathed, I learned that some of her people, when they become wealthy enough to retire, choose to work on their art full-time, but they're considered eccentric, even outcasts, egotists. White Hill expected one of them to be chosen for the contest, and wasn't even going to apply. But the Earthling judge saw one of her installations and tracked her down.

She also talked about her practical work in dealing with personality disorders and cognitive defects. There was some distress in her voice when she described that to me. Plugging into hurt minds, sharing their pain or blankness for hours. I didn't feel I knew her well enough to bring up the aspect that most interested me, a kind of ontological prurience: what is it like to actually *be* another person; how much of her, or him, do you take away? If you do it often enough, how can you know which parts of you are the original you?

And she would be plugged in to more than one person at once, at times, the theory being that people with similar disorders could help each other, swarming around in the therapy room of her brain. She would fade into the background, more or less unable to interfere, and later analyze how they had interacted.

She had had one particularly unsettling experience, where through a planetwide network, she had interconnected more than a hundred congenitally retarded people. She said it was like a painless death. By the time half of them had plugged in, she had felt herself fade and wink out. Then she was reborn with the suddenness of a slap. She had been dead for about ten hours.

But only connected for seven. It had taken technicians three hours to pry her out of a persistent catatonia. With more people, or a longer period, she might have been lost forever. There was no lasting harm, but the experiment was never repeated.

It was worth it, she said, for the patients' inchoate happiness afterwards. It was like a regular person being given supernatural powers for half a day—powers so far beyond human experience that there was no way to talk about them, but the memory of it was worth the frustration.

After we got out of the tub, she showed me to our wardrobe room: hundreds of white robes, identical except for size. We dressed and made tea and sat upstairs, watching the storm rage. It hardly looked like an inhabitable planet outside. The lightning had intensified so that it crackled incessantly, a jagged insane dance in every direction. The rain had frozen to white gravel somehow. I asked the building, and it said that the stuff was called *granizo* or, in English, hail. For a while it fell too fast to melt, accumulating in white piles that turned translucent.

Staring at the desolation, White Hill said something that I thought was uncharacteristically modest. "This is too big and terrible a thing. I feel like an interloper. They've lived through centuries of this, and now they want *us* to explain it to them?"

I didn't have to remind her of what the contest committee had said, that their own arts had become stylized, stunned into a grieving conformity. "Maybe not to *explain*—maybe they're assuming we'll fail, but hope to find a new direction from our failures. That's what that oldest woman, Norita, implied."

White Hill shook her head. "Wasn't she a ray of sunshine? I think they dragged her out of the grave as a way of keeping us all outside the dome."

"Well, she was quite effective on me. I could have spent a few days investigating Amazonia, but not with her as a native guide." Norita was about as close as anyone could get to being an actual native. She was the last survivor of the Five Families, the couple of dozen Earthlings who, among those who were offworld at the time of the nanoplague, were willing to come back after robots constructed the isolation domes.

In terms of social hierarchy, she was the most powerful person on Earth, at least on the actual planet. The class system was complex and nearly opaque to outsiders, but being a descendant of the Five Families was a prerequisite for the highest class. Money or political power would not get you in, although most of the other social classes seemed associated with wealth or the lack of it. Not that there were any actual poor people on Earth; the basic birth dole was equivalent to an upper-middle-class income on Petros.

The nearly instantaneous destruction of ten billion people did not destroy their fortunes. Most of the Earth's significant wealth had been of-planet, anyhow, at the time of the Sterilization. Suddenly it was concentrated into the hands of fewer than two thousand people.

Actually, I couldn't understand why anyone would have come back. You'd have to be pretty sentimental about your roots to be willing to spend the rest of your life cooped up under a dome, surrounded by instant death. The salaries and amenities offered were substantial, with bonuses for earthborn workers, but it still doesn't sound like much of a bargain. The ships that brought the Five Families and the other original workers to Earth left loaded down with sterilized artifacts, not to return for exactly one hundred years.

Norita seemed like a familiar type to me, since I come from a culture also rigidly bound by class. "Old money, but not much of it" sums up the situation. She wanted to be admired for the accident of her birth and the dubious blessing of a torpid longevity, rather than any actual accomplishment. I didn't have to travel 33 light-years to enjoy that kind of company.

"Did she keep you away from everybody?" White Hill said.

"Interposed herself. No one could act naturally when she was around, and the old dragon was never *not* around. You'd think a person her age would need a little sleep."

"'She lives on the blood of infants,' we say."

There was a phone chime, and White Hill said *"Bono"* as I said *"Châ."* Long habits. Then we said Earth's *"Hola"* simultaneously.

The old dragon herself appeared. "I'm glad you found shelter." Had she been eavesdropping? No way to tell from her tone or posture. "An administrator has asked permission to visit with you."

What if we said no? White Hill nodded, which means yes on Earth. "Granted," I said.

"Very well. He will be there shortly." She disappeared. I suppose the oldest person on a planet can justify not saying hello or good-bye. Only so much time left, after all.

"A physical visit?" I said to White Hill. "Through this weather?"

She shrugged. "Earthlings."

After a minute there was a "ding" sound in the anteroom, and we walked down to see an unexpected door open. What I'd thought was a hall closet was an airlock. He'd evidently come underground.

Young and nervous and moving awkwardly in plastic. He shook our hands in an odd way. Of course we were swimming in deadly poison. "My name is Warm Dawn. Zephyr-boulder-brook."

"Are we cousins through Zephyr?" White Hill asked.

He nodded quickly. "An honor, my lady. Both of my parents are Seldenian, my gene-mother from your Galan."

A look passed over her that was pure disbelieving chauvinism: *Why would anybody leave Seldene's forests, farms, and meadows for this sterile death trap?* Of course she knew the answer. The major import and export, the only crop, on Earth, was money.

"I wanted to help both of you with your planning. Are you going to travel at all, before you start?"

White Hill made a noncommittal gesture. "There are some places for me to see," I said. "The Pyramids, Chicago, Rome. Maybe a dozen places, twice that many days." I looked at her. "Would you care to join me?"

She looked straight at me, wheels turning. "It sounds interesting."

The man took us to a viewscreen in the great room and we spent an hour or so going over routes and making reservations. Travel was normally by underground vehicle, from dome to dome, and if we ventured outside unprotected, we would of course have to go through the purging before we were allowed to continue. Some people need a day or more to recover from that, so we should put that into the schedule, if we didn't want to be hobbled, like him, with plastic.

Most of the places I wanted to see were safely under glass, even some of the Pyramids, which surprised me. Some, like Ankgor Wat, were not only unprotected but difficult of access. I had to arrange for a flyer to cover the thousand kaymetras, and schedule a purge. White Hill said she would wander through Hanoi, instead.

I didn't sleep well that night, waking often from fantastic dreams, the nanobeasts grown large and aggressive. White Hill was in some of the dreams, posturing sexually.

By the next morning the storm had gone away, so we crossed over to Amazonia, and I learned firsthand why one might rather sit in a hotel room with a nice book than go to Ankgor Wat, or anywhere that required a purge. The external part of the purging was unpleasant enough, even with pain medication, all the epidermis stripped and regrown. The inside part was beyond description, as the nanophages could be hiding out anywhere. Every opening into the body had to be vacuumed out, including the sense organs. I was not awake for that part, where the robots most gently clean out your eye sockets, but my eyes hurt and my ears rang for days. They warned me to sit down the first time I urinated, which was good advice, since I nearly passed out from the burning pain.

White Hill and I had a quiet supper of restorative gruel together, and then crept off to sleep for half a day. She was full of pep the next morning, and I pretended to be at least sentient, as we wandered through the city making preparations for the trip.

After a couple of hours I protested that she was obviously trying to do in one of her competitors; stop and let an old man sit down for a minute.

We found a bar that specialized in stimulants. She had tea and I had bhan, a murky warm drink served in a large nut shell, coconut. It tasted woody and bitter, but was restorative.

"It's not age," she said. "The purging seems a lot easier the second time you do it. I could hardly move, all the next day, the first time."

Interesting that she didn't mention that earlier. "Did they tell you it would get easier?"

She nodded, then caught herself and wagged her chin horizontally, Earth style. "Not a word. I think they enjoy our discomfort."

"Or like to keep us off guard. Keeps them in control." She made the little kissing sound that's Lortian for agreement and reached for a lemon wedge to squeeze into her tea. The world seemed to slow slightly, I guess from whatever was in the bhan, and I found myself cataloging her body microscopically. A crescent of white scar tissue on the back of a knuckle, fine hair on her forearm, almost white, her shoulders and breasts moving in counterpoised pairs, silk rustling, as she reached forward and back and squeezed the lemon, sharp citrus smell and the tip of her tongue between her thin lips, mouth slightly large. Chameleon hazel eyes, dark green now because of the decorative ivy wall behind her.

"What are you staring at?"

"Sorry, just thinking."

"Thinking." She stared at me in return, measuring. "Your people are good at that."

After we'd bought the travel necessities we had the packages sent to our quarters and wandered aimlessly. The city was comfortable, but had little of interest in terms of architecture or history, oddly dull for a planet's administrative center. There was an obvious social purpose for its bland-ness—by statute, nobody was *from* Amazonia; nobody could be born there or claim citizenship. Most of the planet's wealth and power came there to work, electronically if not physically, but it went home to some other place.

A certain amount of that wealth was from interstellar commerce, but it was nothing like the old days, before the war. Earth had been a hub, a central authority that could demand its tithe or more from any transaction between planets. In the period between the Sterilization and Earth's token rehabitation, the other planets made their own arrangements with one another, in pairs and groups. But most of the fortunes that had been born on Earth returned here.

So Amazonia was bland as cheap bread, but there was more wealth under its dome than on any two other planets combined. Big money seeks out the company of its own, for purposes of reproduction.

Two other artists had come in, from Auer and Shwa, and once they were ready, we set out to explore the world by subway. The first stop that was interesting was the Grand Canyon, a natural wonder whose desolate beauty was unaffected by the Sterilization.

We were amused by the guide there, a curious little woman who rattled on about the Great Rift Valley on Mars, a nearby planet where she was born. White Hill had a lightbox, and while the Martian lady droned on we sketched the fantastic colors, necessarily loose and abstract because our fingers were clumsy in clinging plastic.

We toured Chicago, like the Grand Canyon, wrapped in plastic. It was a large city that had been leveled in a local war. It lay in ruins for many years, and then, famously, was rebuilt as a single huge structure from those ruins. There's a childish or drunken ad hoc quality to it, a scarcity of right angles, a crazy-quilt mixture of materials. Areas of stunning imaginative brilliance next to juryrigged junk. And everywhere bones, the skeletons of ten million people, lying where they fell. I asked what had happened to the bones in the old city outside of Amazonia. The guide said he'd never been there, but he supposed that the sight of them upset the politicians, so they had them cleaned up. "Can you imagine this place without the bones?" he asked. It would be nice if I could.

The other remnants of cities in that country were less interesting, if no less depressing. We flew over the east coast, which was essentially one continuous metropolis for thousands of kaymetras, like our coast from New Haven to Stargate, rendered in sterile ruins.

The first place I visited unprotected was Giza, the Great Pyramids. White Hill decided to come with me, though she had to be wrapped up in a shapeless cloth robe, her face veiled, because of local religious law. It seemed to me ridiculous, a transparent tourism ploy. How many believers in that old religion could have been offplanet when the Earth died? But every female was obliged at the tube exit to go into a big hall and be fitted with a *chador* robe and veil before a man could be allowed to look at her.

(We wondered whether the purging would be done completely by women. The technicians would certainly see a lot of her uncovered during that excruciation.)

They warned us it was unseasonably hot outside. Almost too hot to breathe, actually, during the day. We accomplished most of our sightseeing around dusk or dawn, spending most of the day in air-conditioned shelters.

Because of our special status, White Hill and I were allowed to visit the Pyramids alone, in the dark of the morning. We climbed up the largest one and watched the sun mount over desert haze. It was a singular time for both of us, edifying but something more.

Coming back down, we were treated to a sandstorm, *khamsin*, which actually might have done the first stage of purging if we had been allowed to take off our clothes. It explained why all the bones lying around looked so much older than the ones in Chicago; they normally had ten or twelve of these sandblasting storms every year. Lately, with the heat wave, the *khamsin* came weekly or even more often.

Raised more than five thousand years ago, the Pyramids were the oldest monumental structures on the planet. They actually held as much fascination for White Hill as for me. Thousands of men moved millions of huge blocks of stone, with nothing but muscle and ingenuity. Some of the stones were mined a thousand kaymetras away, and floated up the river on barges.

I could build a similar structure, even larger, for my contest entry, by giving machines the right instructions. It would be a complicated business, but easily done within the two-year deadline. Of course there would be no point to it. That some anonymous engineer had done the same thing within the lifetime of a king, without recourse to machines—I agreed with White Hill: that was an actual marvel.

We spent a couple of days outside, traveling by surface hoppers from monument to monument, but none was as impressive. I suppose I should have realized that and saved Giza for last.

We met another of the artists at the Sphinx, Lo Tan-Six, from Pao. I had seen his work on both Pao and ThetaKent, and admitted there was something to be admired there. He worked in stone, too, but was more interested in pure geometric forms than I was. I think stone fights form, or imposes its own tensions on the artist's wishes.

I liked him well enough, though, in spite of this and other differences, and we traveled together for a while. He suggested we not go through the purging here, but have our things sent on to Rome, because we'd want to be outside there, too. There was a daily hop from Alexandria to Rome, an airship that had a section reserved for those of us who could eat and breathe nanophages.

As soon as she was inside the coolness of the ship, White Hill shed the *chador* and veil and stuffed them under the seat. "Breathe," she said, stretching. Her white bodysuit was a little less revealing than paint.

Her directness and undisguised sexuality made me catch my breath. The tiny crease of punctuation that her vulva made in the bodysuit would have her jailed on some parts of my planet, not to mention the part of this one we'd just left. The costume was innocent and natural and, I think, completely calculated.

Lo studied her with an interested detachment. He was neuter, an option that was available on Petros, too, but one I've never really understood. He claimed that sex took too much time and energy from his art. I think his lack of gender took something else away from it.

We flew about an hour over the impossibly blue sea. There were a few sterile islands, but otherwise it was as plain as spilled ink. We descended over the ashes of Italy and landed on a pad on one of the hills overlooking the ancient city. The ship mated to an airlock so the normal-DNA people could go down to a tube that would whisk them into Rome. We could call for transportation or walk, and opted for the exercise. It was baking hot here, too, but not as bad as Egypt.

White Hill was polite with Lo, but obviously wished he'd disappear. He and I chattered a little too much about rocks and cements, explosives and lasers. And his asexuality diminished her interest in him—as, perhaps, my polite detachment increased her interest in me. The muralist from Shwa, to complete the spectrum, was after her like a puppy in its first heat, which I think amused her for two days. They'd had a private conversation in Chicago, and he'd kept his distance since, but still admired her from afar. As we walked down toward the Roman gates, he kept a careful twenty paces behind, trying to contemplate things besides White Hill's walk.

Inside the gate we stopped short, stunned in spite of knowing what to expect. It had a formal name, but everybody just called it Òssi, the Bones.

FOR WHITE HILL

An order of Catholic clergy had spent more than two centuries building, by hand, a wall of bones completely around the city. It was twice the
height of a man, varnished dark amber. There were repetitive patterns of
femurs and rib cages and stacks of curving spines, and at eye level, a row
of skulls, uninterrupted, kaymetra after kaymetra.

This was where we parted. Lo was determined to walk completely
around the circle of death, and the other two went with him. White
Hill and I could do it in our imaginations. I still creaked from climbing
the pyramid.

Prior to the ascent of Christianity here, they had huge spectacles,
displays of martial skill where many of the participants were killed, for
punishment of wrongdoing or just to entertain the masses. The two large
amphitheaters where these displays went on were inside the Bones but
not under the dome, so we walked around them. The Circus Maximus
had a terrible dignity to it, little more than a long depression in the
ground with a few eroded monuments left standing. The size and age of
it were enough; your mind's eye supplied the rest. The smaller one, the
Colosseum, was overdone, with robots in period costumes and ferocious
mechanical animals re-creating the old scenes, lots of too-bright blood
spurting. Stones and bones would do.

I'd thought about spending another day outside, but the shelter's air-
conditioning had failed, and it was literally uninhabitable. So I braced
myself and headed for the torture chamber. But as White Hill had said, the
purging was more bearable the second time. You know that it's going to end.

Rome inside was interesting, many ages of archeology and history
stacked around in no particular order. I enjoyed wandering from place to
place with her, building a kind of organization out of the chaos. We were
both more interested in inspiration than education, though, so I doubt
that the three days we spent there left us with anything like a coherent
picture of that tenacious empire and the millennia that followed it.

A long time later she would surprise me by reciting the names of the
Roman emperors in order. She'd always had a trick memory, a talent for
retaining trivia, ever since she was old enough to read. Growing up different
that way must have been a factor in swaying her toward cognitive science.

We saw some ancient cinema and then returned to our quarters to
pack for continuing on to Greece, which I was anticipating with pleasure. But it didn't happen. We had a message waiting: ALL MUST RETURN
IMMEDIATELY TO AMAZONIA. CONTEST PROFOUNDLY CHANGED.

Lives, it turned out, profoundly changed. The war was back.

▲

We met in a majestic amphitheater, the twenty-nine artists dwarfed by the size of it, huddled front row center. A few Amazonian officials sat behind a table on the stage, silent. They all looked detached, or stunned, brooding.

We hadn't been told anything except that it was a matter of "dire and immediate importance." We assumed it had to do with the contest, naturally, and were prepared for the worst: it had been called off; we had to go home.

The old crone Norita appeared, "We must confess to carelessness," she said. "The unseasonable warmth in both hemispheres, it isn't something that has happened, ever since the Sterilization. We looked for atmospheric causes here, and found something that seemed to explain it. But we didn't make the connection with what was happening in the other half of the world.

"It's not the atmosphere. It's the Sun. Somehow the Fwndyri have found a way to make its luminosity increase. It's been going on for half a year. If it continues, and we find no way to reverse it, the surface of the planet will be uninhabitable in a few years.

"I'm afraid that most of you are going to be stranded on Earth, at least for the time being. The Council of Worlds has exercised its emergency powers and commandeered every vessel capable of interstellar transport. Those who have sufficient power or the proper connections will be able to escape. The rest will have to stay with us and face…whatever our fate is going to be."

I saw no reason not to be blunt. "Can money do it? How much would a ticket out cost?"

That would have been a gaffe on my planet, but Norita didn't blink. "I know for certain that two hundred million marks is not enough. I also know that some people have bought 'tickets,' as you say, but I don't know how much they paid, or to whom."

If I liquidated everything I owned, I might be able to come up with three hundred million, but I hadn't brought that kind of liquidity with me; just a box of rare jewelry, worth perhaps forty million. Most of my wealth was thirty-three years away, from the point of view of an earth-bound investor. I could sign that over to someone, but by the time they got to Petra, the government or my family might have seized it, and they would have nothing save the prospect of a legal battle in a foreign culture.

Norita introduced Skylha Sygoda, an astrophysicist. He was pale and sweating. "We have analyzed the solar spectrum over the past six months.

If I hadn't known that each spectrum was from the same star, I would have said it was a systematic and subtle demonstration of the micro-stages of stellar evolution in the late main sequence."

"Could you express that in some human language?" someone said.

Sygoda spread his hands. "They've found a way to age the Sun. In the normal course of things, we would expect the Sun to brighten about six percent each billion years. At the current rate, it's more like one percent per year."

"So in a hundred years," White Hill said, "it will be twice as bright?"

"If it continues at this rate. We don't know."

A stocky woman I recognized as !Oona Something, from Jua-nguvi, wrestled with the language: "To how long, then? Before this Earth is uninhabitable?"

"Well, in point of fact, it's uninhabitable now, except for people like you. We could survive inside these domes for a long time, if it were just a matter of the outside getting hotter and hotter. For those of you able to withstand the nanophages, it will probably be too hot within a decade, here; longer near the poles. But the weather is likely to become very violent, too.

"And it may not be a matter of a simple increase in heat. In the case of normal evolution, the Sun would eventually expand, becoming a red giant. It would take many billions of years, but the Earth would not survive. The surface of the Sun would actually extend out to touch us.

"If the Fwndyri were speeding up time somehow, locally, and the Sun were actually *evolving* at this incredible rate, we would suffer that fate in about thirty years. But it would be impossible. They would have to have a way to magically extract the hydrogen from the Sun's core."

"Wait," I said. "You don't know what they're doing now, to make it brighten. I wouldn't say anything's impossible."

"Water Man," Norita said, "if that happens, we shall simply die, all of us, at once. There is no need to plan for it. We do need to plan for less extreme exigencies." There was an uncomfortable silence.

"What can we do?" White Hill said. "We artists?"

"There's no reason not to continue with the project, though I think you may wish to do it inside. There's no shortage of space. Are any of you trained in astrophysics, or anything having to do with stellar evolution and the like?" No one was. "You may still have some ideas that will be useful to the specialists. We will keep you informed."

Most of the artists stayed in Amazonia, for the amenities if not to avoid purging, but four of us went back to the outside habitat. Denli om

Cord, the composer from Luxor, joined Lo and White Hill and me. We could have used the tunnel airlock, to avoid the midday heat, but Denli hadn't seen the beach, and I suppose we all had an impulse to see the Sun with our new knowledge. In this new light, as they say.

White Hill and Denli went swimming while Lo and I poked around the ruins. We had since learned that the destruction here had been methodical, a grim resolve to leave the enemy nothing of value. Both of us were scouting for raw material, of course. After a short while we sat in the hot shade, wishing we had brought water.

We talked about that and about art. Not about the Sun dying, or us dying, in a few decades. The women's laughter drifted to us over the rush of the muddy surf. There was a sad hysteria to it.

"Have you had sex with her?" he asked conversationally.

"What a question. No."

He tugged on his lip, staring out over the water. "I try to keep these things straight. It seems to me that you desire her, from the way you look at her, and she seems cordial to you, and is after all from Seldene. My interest is academic, of course."

"You've never done sex? I mean before."

"Of course, as a child." The implication of that was obvious.

"It becomes more complicated with practice."

"I suppose it could. Although Seldenians seem to treat it as casually as...conversation." He used the Seldenian word, which is the same as for intercourse.

"White Hill is reasonably sophisticated," I said. "She isn't bound by her culture's freedoms." The two women ran out of the water, arms around each other's waists, laughing. It was an interesting contrast; Denli was almost as large as me, and about as feminine. They saw us and waved toward the path back through the ruins.

We got up to follow them. "I suppose I don't understand your restraint," Lo said. "Is it your own culture? Your age?"

"Not age. Perhaps my culture encourages self-control."

He laughed. "That's an understatement."

"Not that I'm a slave to Petrosian propriety. My work is outlawed in several states, at home."

"You're proud of that."

I shrugged. "It reflects on them, not me." We followed the women down the path, an interesting study in contrasts, one pair nimble and naked except for a film of drying mud, the other pacing evenly in monkish robes. They were already showering when Lo and I entered the cool shelter, momentarily blinded by shade.

We made cool drinks and, after a quick shower, joined them in the communal bath. Lo was not anatomically different from a sexual male, which I found obscurely disturbing. Wouldn't it bother you to be constantly reminded of what you had lost? Renounced, I suppose Lo would say, and accuse me of being parochial about plumbing.

I had made the drinks with guava juice and ron, neither of which we have on Petrosia. A little too sweet, but pleasant. The alcohol loosened tongues.

Denli regarded me with deep black eyes. "You're rich, Water Man. Are you rich enough to escape?"

"No. If I had brought all my money with me, perhaps."

"Some do," White Hill said. "I did."

"I would too," Lo said, "coming from Seldene. No offense intended."

"Wheels turn," she admitted. "Five or six new governments before I get back. *Would* have gotten back."

We were all silent for a long moment. "It's not real yet," White Hill said, her voice flat. "We're going to die here?"

"We were going to die somewhere," Denli said. "Maybe not so soon."

"And not on Earth," Lo said. "It's like a long preview of Hell." Denli looked at him quizzically. "That's where Christians go when they die. If they were bad."

"They send their bodies to Earth?" We managed not to smile. Actually, most of my people knew as little as hers, about Earth. Seldene and Luxor, though relatively poor, had centuries' more history than Petros, and kept closer ties to the central planet. The Home Planet, they would say. Homey as a blast furnace.

By tacit consensus, we didn't dwell on death anymore that day. When artists get together they tend to wax enthusiastic about materials and tools, the mechanical lore of their trades. We talked about the ways we worked at home, the things we were able to bring with us, the improvisations we could effect with Earthling materials. (Critics talk about art, we say; artists talk about brushes.) Three other artists joined us, two sculptors and a weathershaper, and we all wound up in the large sunny studio drawing and painting. White Hill and I found sticks of charcoal and did studies of each other drawing each other.

While we were comparing them, she quietly asked "Do you sleep lightly?"

"I can. What did you have in mind?"

"Oh, looking at the ruins by starlight. The moon goes down about three. I thought we might watch it set together." Her expression was so open as to be enigmatic.

Two more artists had joined us by dinnertime, which proceeded with a kind of forced jollity. A lot of ron was consumed. White Hill cautioned me against overindulgence. They had the same liquor, called "rum," on Seldene, and it had a reputation for going down easily but causing storms. There was no legal distilled liquor on my planet.

I had two drinks of it, and retired when people started singing in various languages. I did sleep lightly, though, and was almost awake when White Hill tapped. I could hear two or three people still up, murmuring in the bath. We slipped out quietly.

It was almost cool. The quarter-phase moon was near the horizon, a dim orange, but it gave us enough light to pick our way down the path. It was warmer in the ruins, the tumbled stone still radiating the day's heat. We walked through to the beach, where it was cooler again. White Hill spread the blanket she had brought, and we stretched out and looked up at the stars.

As is always true with a new world, most of the constellations were familiar, with a few bright stars added or subtracted. Neither of our home stars was significant, as dim here as Earth's Sol is from home. She identified the brightest star overhead as AlphaKent; there was a brighter one on the horizon, but neither of us knew what it was.

We compared names of the constellations we recognized. Some of hers were the same as Earth's names, like Scorpio, which we call the Insect. It was about halfway up the sky, prominent, imbedded in the galaxy's glow. We both call the brightest star there Antares. The Executioner, which had set perhaps an hour earlier, they call Orion. We had the same meaningless names for its brightest stars, Betelgeuse and Rigel.

"For a sculptor, you know a lot about astronomy," she said. "When I visited your city, there was too much light to see stars at night."

"You can see a few from my place. I'm out at Lake Påchlå, about a hundred kaymetras inland."

"I know. I called you."

"I wasn't home?"

"No; you were supposedly on ThetaKent."

"That's right, you told me. Our paths crossed in space. And you became that burgher's slave wife." I put my hand on her arm. "Sorry I forgot. A lot has gone on. Was he awful?"

She laughed into the darkness. "He offered me a lot to stay."

"I can imagine."

She half turned, one breast soft against my arm, and ran a finger up my leg. "Why tax your imagination?"

I wasn't expecially in the mood, but my body was. The robes rustled off easily, their only virtue.

The moon was down now, and I could see only a dim outline of her in the starlight. It was strange to make love deprived of that sense. You would think the absence of it would amplify the others, but I can't say that it did, except that her heartbeat seemed very strong on the heel of my hand. Her breath was sweet with mint, and the smell and taste of her body were agreeable; in fact, there was nothing about her body that I would have cared to change, inside or out, but nevertheless, our progress became difficult after a couple of minutes, and by mute agreement we slowed and stopped. We lay joined together for some time before she spoke.

"The timing is all wrong. I'm sorry." She drew her face across my arm, and I felt tears. "I was just trying not to think about things."

"It's all right. The sand doesn't help, either." We had gotten a little bit inside, rubbing.

We talked for a while and then drowsed together. When the sky began to lighten, a hot wind from below the horizon woke us up. We went back to the shelter.

Everyone was asleep. We went to shower off the sand, and she was amused to see my interest in her quicken. "Let's take that downstairs," she whispered, and I followed her down to her room.

The memory of the earlier incapability was there, but it was not greatly inhibiting. Being able to see her made the act more familiar, and besides, she was very pleasant to see, from whatever angle. I was able to withhold myself only once, and so the interlude was shorter than either of us would have desired.

We slept together on her narrow bed. Or she slept, rather, while I watched the bar of sunlight grow on the opposite wall and thought about how everything had changed.

They couldn't really say we had thirty years to live, since they had no idea what the enemy was doing. It might be three hundred; it might be less than one—but even with bodyswitch that was always true, as it was in the old days: sooner or later something would go wrong and you would die. That I might die at the same instant as ten thousand other people and a planet full of history—that was interesting. But as the room filled with light, and I studied her quiet repose, I found her more interesting than that.

I was old enough to be immune to infatuation. Something deep had been growing since Egypt, maybe before. On top of the pyramid, the rising Sun dim in the mist, we had sat with our shoulders touching, watching the ancient forms appear below, and I felt a surge of numinism mixed oddly with content. She looked at me—I could only see her eyes—and we didn't have to say anything about the moment.

And now this. I was sure, without words, that she would share this, too. Whatever "this" was. England's versatile language, like mine and hers, is strangely hobbled by having the one word, love, stand for such a multiplicity of feelings.

Perhaps that lack reveals a truth, that no one love is like any other. There are other truths that you might forget, or ignore, distracted by the growth of love. In Petrosian there is a saying in the palindromic mood that always carries a sardonic, or at least ironic, inflection: "Happiness presages disaster presages happiness." So if you die happy, it means you were happy when you died. Good timing or bad?

!Oona M'vua had a room next to White Hill, and she was glad to switch with me, an operation that took about three minutes but was good for a much longer period of talk among the other artists. Lo was smugly amused, which in my temporary generosity of spirit I forgave.

Once we were adjacent, we found the button that made the wall slide away and pushed the two beds together under her window. I'm afraid we were antisocial for a couple of days. It had been some time since either of us had had a lover. And I had never had one like her, literally, out of the dozens. She said that was because I had never been involved with a Seldenian, and I tactfully agreed, banishing five perfectly good memories to amnesia.

It's true that Seldenian women, and men as well, are better schooled than those of us from normal planets, in the techniques and subtleties of sexual expression. Part of "wholeness," which I suppose is a weak pun in English. It kept Lo, and not only him, from taking White Hill seriously as an artist: the fact that a Seldenian, to be "whole," must necessarily treat art as an everyday activity, usually subordinate to affairs of the heart, of the body. Or at least on the same level, which is the point.

The reality is that it is all one to them. What makes Seldenians so alien is that their need for balance in life dissolves hierarchy: this piece of art is valuable, and so is this orgasm, and so is this crumb of bread. The bread crumb connects to the artwork through the artist's metabolism, which connects to orgasm. Then through a fluid and automatic mixture of logic, metaphor, and rhetoric, the bread crumb links to soil, sunlight, nuclear fusion, the beginning and end of the universe. Any intelligent person can map out chains like that, but to White Hill it was automatic, drilled into her with her first nouns and verbs: *Everything is important. Nothing matters. Change the world but stay relaxed.*

I could never come around to her way of thinking. But then I was married for fifty Petrosian years to a woman who had stranger beliefs. (The marriage as a social contract actually lasted fifty-seven years; at the half-century mark we took a vacation from each other, and I never saw her again.) White Hill's worldview gave her an equanimity I had to envy. But my art needed unbalance and tension the way hers needed harmony and resolution.

By the fourth day most of the artists had joined us in the shelter. Maybe they grew tired of wandering through the bureaucracy. More likely, they were anxious about their competitors' progress.

White Hill was drawing designs on large sheets of buff paper and taping them up on our walls. She worked on her feet, bare feet, pacing from diagram to diagram, changing and rearranging. I worked directly inside a shaping box, an invention White Hill had heard of but had never seen. It's a cube of light a little less than a metra wide. Inside is an image of a sculpture—or a rock or a lump of clay—that you can feel as well as see. You can mold it with your hands or work with finer instruments for cutting, scraping, chipping. It records your progress constantly, so it's easy to take chances; you can always run it back to an earlier stage.

I spent a few hours every other day cruising in a flyer with Lo and a couple of other sculptors, looking for native materials. We were severely constrained by the decision to put the Memory Park inside, since everything we used had to be small enough to fit through the airlock and purging rooms. You could work with large pieces, but you would have to slice them up and reassemble them, the individual chunks no bigger than two-by-two-by-three metra.

We tried to stay congenial and fair during these expeditions. Ideally, you would spot a piece, and we would land by it or hover over it long enough to tag it with your ID; in a day or two the robots would deliver it to your "holding area" outside the shelter. If more than one person wanted the piece, which happened as often as not, a decision had to be made before it was tagged. There was a lot of arguing and trading and Solomon-style splitting, which usually satisfied the requirements of something other than art.

The quality of light was changing for the worse. Earthling planetary engineers were spewing bright dust into the upper atmosphere, to reflect back solar heat. (They modified the nanophage-eating machinery for the purpose. That was also designed to fill the atmosphere full of dust, but at a lower level—and each grain of *that* dust had a tiny chemical brain.) It made the night sky progressively less interesting. I was glad White Hill had chosen to initiate our connection under the stars. It would be some time before we saw them again, if ever.

And it looked like "daylight" was going to be a uniform overcast for the duration of the contest. Without the dynamic of moving sunlight to continually change the appearance of my piece, I had to discard a whole family of first approaches to its design. I was starting to think along the lines of something irrational-looking; something the brain would reject as impossible. The way we mentally veer away from unthinkable things like the Sterilization, and our proximate future.

We had divided into two groups, and jokingly but seriously referred to one another as "originalists" and "realists." We originalists were continuing our projects on the basis of the charter's rules: a memorial to the tragedy and its aftermath, a stark sterile reminder in the midst of life. The realists took into account new developments, including the fact that there would probably never be any "midst of life" and, possibly, no audience, after thirty years.

I thought that was excessive. There was plenty of pathos in the original assignment. Adding another, impasto, layer of pathos along with irony and the artist's fear of personal death...well, we were doing art, not literature. I sincerely hoped their pieces would be fatally muddled by complexity.

If you asked White Hill which group she belonged to, she would of course say, "Both." I had no idea what form her project was going to take; we had agreed early on to surprise one another, and not impede each other with suggestions. I couldn't decipher even one-tenth of her diagrams. I speak Seldenian pretty well, but have never mastered the pictographs beyond the usual travelers' vocabulary. And much of what she was scribbling on the buff sheets of paper was in no language I recognized, an arcane technical symbology.

We talked about other things. Even about the future, as lovers will. Our most probable future was simultaneous death by fire, but it was calming and harmless to make "what if?" plans, in case our hosts somehow were able to find a way around that fate. We did have a choice of many possible futures, if we indeed had more than one. White Hill had never had access to wealth before. She didn't want to live lavishly, but the idea of being able to explore all the planets excited her.

Of course she had never tried living lavishly. I hoped one day to study her reaction to it, which would be strange. Out of the box of valuables I'd brought along, I gave her a necklace, a traditional beginning-love gift on Petros. It was a network of perfect emeralds and rubies laced in gold.

She examined it closely. "How much is this worth?"

"A million marks, more or less." She started to hand it back. "Please keep it. Money has no value here, no meaning."

She was at a loss for words, which was rare enough. "I understand the gesture. But you can't expect me to value this the way you do."

"I wouldn't expect that."

"Suppose I lose it? I might just set it down somewhere."

"I know. I'll still have given it to you."

She nodded and laughed. "All right. You people are strange." She slipped the necklace on, still latched, wiggling it over her ears. The colors glowed warm and cold against her olive skin.

She kissed me, a feather, and rushed out of our room wordlessly. She passed right by a mirror without looking at it.

After a couple of hours I went to find her. Lo said he'd seen her go out the door with a lot of water. At the beach I found her footprints marching straight west to the horizon.

She was gone for two days. I was working outside when she came back, wearing nothing but the necklace. There was another necklace in her hand: she had cut off her right braid and interwoven a complex pattern of gold and silver wire into a closed loop. She slipped it over my head and pecked me on the lips and headed for the shelter. When I started to follow she stopped me with a tired gesture. "Let me sleep, eat, wash." Her voice was a hoarse whisper. "Come to me after dark."

I sat down, leaning back against a good rock, and thought about very little, touching her braid and smelling it. When it was too dark to see my feet, I went in, and she was waiting.

I spent a lot of time outside, at least in the early morning and late afternoon, studying my accumulation of rocks and ruins. I had images of every piece in my shaping box's memory, but it was easier to visualize some aspects of the project if I could walk around the elements and touch them.

Inspiration is where you find it. We'd played with an orrery in the museum in Rome, a miniature solar system that had been built of clockwork centuries before the Information Age. There was a wistful, humorous, kind of comfort in its jerky regularity.

My mental processes always turn things inside out. Find the terror and hopelessness in that comfort. I had in mind a massive but delicately balanced assemblage that would be viewed by small groups; their presence would cause it to teeter and turn ponderously. It would seem both fragile and huge (though of course the fragility would be an illusion), like the ecosystem that the Fwndyri so abruptly destroyed.

The assemblage would be mounted in such a way that it would seem always in danger of toppling off its base, but hidden weights would make that impossible. The sound of the rolling weights ought to produce a nice anxiety. Whenever a part tapped the floor, the tap would be amplified into a hollow boom.

If the viewers stood absolutely still, it would swing to a halt. As they left, they would disturb it again. I hoped it would disturb them as well.

The large technical problem was measuring the distribution of mass in each of my motley pieces. That would have been easy at home; I could rent a magnetic resonance densitometer to map their insides. There was no such thing on this planet (so rich in things I had no use for!), so I had to make do with a pair of robots and a knife-edge. And then start hollowing the pieces out asymmetrically, so that once set in motion, the assemblage would tend to rotate.

I had a large number of rocks and artifacts to choose from, and was tempted to use no unifying principle at all, other than the unstable balance of the thing. Boulders and pieces of old statues and fossil machinery. The models I made of such a random collection were ambiguous, though. It was hard to tell whether they would look ominous or ludicrous, built to scale. A symbol of helplessness before an implacable enemy? Or a lurching, crashing junkpile. I decided to take a reasonably conservative approach, dignity rather than daring. After all, the audience would be Earthlings and, if the planet survived, tourists with more money than sophistication. Not my usual jury.

I was able to scavenge twenty long bars of shiny black monofiber, which would be the spokes of my irregular wheel. That would give it some unity of composition: make a cross with four similar chunks of granite at the ordinal points, and a larger chunk at the center. Then build up a web inside, monofiber lines linking bits of this and that.

Some of the people were moving their materials inside Amazonia, to work in the area marked off for the park. White Hill and I decided to stay outside. She said her project was portable, at this stage, and mine would be easy to disassemble and move.

After a couple of weeks, only fifteen artists remained with the project, inside Amazonia or out in the shelter. The others had either quit, surrendering to the passive depression that seemed to be Earth's new norm, or, in one case, committed suicide. The two from Wolf and Mijhøven opted for coldsleep, which might be deferred suicide. About one person in three slept through it; one in three came out with some kind of treatable mental disorder. The others went mad and died soon after reawakening, unable or unwilling to live.

Coldsleep wasn't done on Petrosia, although some Petrosians went to other worlds to indulge in it as a risky kind of time travel. Sleep until whatever's wrong with the world has changed. Some people even did it for financial speculation: buy up objects of art or antiques, and sleep for a century or more while their value increases. Of course their value might not increase significantly, or they might be stolen or co-opted by family or government.

But if you can make enough money to buy a ticket to another planet, why not hold off until you had enough to go to a really *distant* one? Let time dilation compress the years. I could make a triangle from Petrosia to Skaal to Mijhøven and back, and more than 120 years would pass, while I lived through only three, with no danger to my mind. And I could take my objects of art along with me.

White Hill had worked with coldsleep veterans, or victims. None of them had been motivated by profit, given her planet's institutionalized anti-materialism, so most of them had been suffering from some psychological ill before they slept. It was rare for them to come out of the "treatment" improved, but they did come into a world where people like White Hill could at least attend them in their madness, perhaps guide them out.

I'd been to three times as many worlds as she. But she had been to stranger places.

The terraformers did their job too well. The days grew cooler and cooler, and some nights snow fell. The snow on the ground persisted into mornings for a while, and then through noon, and finally it began to pile up. Those of us who wanted to work outside had to improvise cold-weather clothing.

I liked working in the cold, although all I did was direct robots. I grew up in a small town south of New Haven, where winter was long and intense. At some level I associated snow and ice with the exciting pleasures that waited for us after school. I was to have my fill of it, though.

It was obvious I had to work fast, faster than I'd originally planned, because of the increasing cold. I wanted to have everything put together and working before I disassembled it and pushed it through the airlock. The robots weren't made for cold weather, unfortunately. They had bad traction on the ice, and sometimes their joints would seize up. One of them complained constantly, but of course it was the best worker, too, so I couldn't just turn it off and let it disappear under the drifts, an idea that tempted me.

White Hill often came out for a few minutes to stand and watch me and the robots struggle with the icy heavy boulders, machinery, and statuary. We took walks along the seashore that became shorter as the weather worsened. The last walk was a disaster.

We had just gotten to the beach when a sudden storm came up with a sandblast wind so violent that it blew us off our feet. We crawled back to the partial protection of the ruins and huddled together, the wind screaming so loudly that we had to shout to hear each other. The storm continued to mount and, in our terror, we decided to run for the shelter. White Hill slipped on some ice and suffered a horrible injury, a jagged piece of metal slashing her face diagonally from forehead to chin, blinding her left eye and tearing off part of her nose. Pearly bone showed through, cracked, at eyebrow, cheek, and chin. She rose up to one elbow and fell slack.

I carried her the rest of the way, immensely glad for the physical strength that made it possible. By the time we got inside she was unconscious and my white coat was a scarlet flag of blood.

A plastic-clad doctor came through immediately and did what she could to get White Hill out of immediate danger. But there was a problem with more sophisticated treatment. They couldn't bring the equipment out to our shelter, and White Hill wouldn't survive the stress of purging unless she had had a chance to heal for a while. Besides the facial wound, she had a broken elbow and collarbone and two cracked ribs.

For a week or so she was always in pain or numb. I sat with her, numb myself, her face a terrible puffed caricature of its former beauty, the wound glued up with plaskin the color of putty. Split skin of her eyelid slack over the empty socket.

The mirror wasn't visible from her bed, and she didn't ask for one, but whenever I looked away from her, her working hand came up to touch and catalogue the damage. We both knew how fortunate she was to be alive at all, and especially in an era and situation where the damage could all be repaired, given time and a little luck. But it was still a terrible thing to live with, an awful memory to keep reliving.

When she was more herself, able to talk through her ripped and pasted mouth, it was difficult for me to keep my composure. She had considerable philosophical, I suppose you could say spiritual, resources, but she was so profoundly stunned that she couldn't follow a line of reasoning very far, and usually wound up sobbing in frustration.

Sometimes I cried with her, although Petrosian men don't cry except in response to music. I had been a soldier once and had seen my ration of injury and death, and I always felt the experience had hardened me, to my detriment. But my friends who had been wounded or killed were just friends, and all of us lived then with the certainty that every day could be anybody's last one. To have the woman you love senselessly mutilated by an accident of weather was emotionally more arduous than losing a dozen companions to the steady erosion of war, a different kind of weather.

I asked her whether she wanted to forget our earlier agreement and talk about our projects. She said no; she was still working on hers, in a way, and she still wanted it to be a surprise. I did manage to distract her, playing with the shaping box. We made cartoonish representations of Lo and old Norita, and combined them in impossible sexual geometries. We shared a limited kind of sex ourselves, finally.

The doctor pronounced her well enough to be taken apart, and both of us were scourged and reappeared on the other side. White Hill was already in surgery when I woke up; there had been no reason to revive her before beginning the restorative processes.

I spent two days wandering through the blandness of Amazonia, jungle laced through concrete, quartering the huge place on foot. Most areas seemed catatonic. A few were boisterous with end-of-the-world hysteria. I checked on her progress so often that they eventually assigned a robot to call me up every hour, whether or not there was any change.

On the third day I was allowed to see her, in her sleep. She was pale but seemed completely restored. I watched her for an hour, perhaps more, when her eyes suddenly opened. The new one was blue, not green, for some reason. She didn't focus on me.

"Dreams feed art," she whispered in Petrosian; "and art feeds dreams." She closed her eyes and slept again.

▲■

She didn't want to go back out. She had lived all her life in the tropics, even the year she spent in bondage, and the idea of returning to the ice that had slashed her was more than repugnant. Inside Amazonia it was always summer, now, the authorities trying to keep everyone happy with heat and light and jungle flowers.

I went back out to gather her things. Ten large sheets of buff paper I unstuck from our walls and stacked and rolled. The necklace, and the satchel of rare coins she had brought from Seldene, all her worldly wealth.

I considered wrapping up my own project, giving the robots instructions for its dismantling and transport, so that I could just go back inside with her and stay. But that would be chancy. I wanted to see the thing work once before I took it apart.

So I went through the purging again, although it wasn't strictly necessary; I could have sent her things through without hand-carrying them. But I wanted to make sure she was on her feet before I left her for several weeks.

She was not on her feet, but she was dancing. When I recovered from the purging, which now took only half a day, I went to her hospital room, and they referred me to our new quarters, a three-room dwelling in a place called Plaza de Artistes. There were two beds in the bedroom, one a fancy medical one, but that was worlds better than trying to find privacy in a hospital.

There was a note floating in the air over the bed saying she had gone to a party in the common room. I found her in a gossamer wheelchair, teaching a hand dance to Denli om Cord, while a harpist and flautist from two different worlds tried to settle on a mutual key.

She was in good spirits. Denli remembered an engagement, and I wheeled White Hill out onto a balcony that overlooked a lake full of sleeping birds, some perhaps real.

It was hot outside, always hot. There was a mist of perspiration on her face, partly from the light exercise of the dance, I supposed. In the light from below, the mist gave her face a sculpted appearance, unsparing sharpness, and there was no sign left of the surgery.

"I'll be out of the chair tomorrow," she said, "at least ten minutes at a time." She laughed, "*Stop* that!"

"Stop what?"

"Looking at me like that."

I was still staring at her face. "It's just...I suppose it's such a relief."

"I know." She rubbed my hand. "They showed me pictures, of before. You looked at that for so many days?"

"I saw you."

She pressed my hand to her face. The new skin was taut but soft, like a baby's. "Take me downstairs?"

▲▲

It's hard to describe, especially in light of later developments, disintegrations, but that night of fragile lovemaking marked a permanent change in the way we linked, or at least the way I was linked to her: I've been married twice, long and short, and have been in some kind of love a hundred times. But no woman has ever owned me before.

This is something we do to ourselves. I've had enough women who *tried* to possess me, but always was able to back or circle away, in literal preservation of self. I always felt that life was too long for one woman.

Certainly part of it is that life is not so long anymore. A larger part of it was the run through the screaming storm, her life streaming out of her, and my stewardship, or at least companionship, afterwards, during her slow transformation back into health and physical beauty. The core of her had never changed, though, the stubborn serenity that I came to realize, that warm night, had finally infected me as well.

The bed was a firm narrow slab, cooler than the dark air heavy with the scent of Earth flowers. I helped her onto the bed (which instantly conformed to her) but from then on it was she who cared for me, saying that was all she wanted, all she really had strength for. When I tried to reverse that, she reminded me of a holiday palindrome that has sexual overtones in both our languages: Giving is taking is giving.

▲ ▲ ●

We spent a couple of weeks as close as two people can be. I was her lover and also her nurse, as she slowly strengthened. When she was able to spend most of her day in normal pursuits, free of the wheelchair or "intelligent" bed (with which we had made a threesome, at times uneasy), she urged me to go back outside and finish up. She was ready to concentrate on her own project, too. Impatient to do art again, a good sign.

I would not have left so soon if I had known what her project involved. But that might not have changed anything.

As soon as I stepped outside, I knew it was going to take longer than planned. I had known from the inside monitors how cold it was going to be, and how many ceemetras of ice had accumulated, but I didn't really *know* how bad it was until I was standing there, looking at my piles of materials locked in opaque glaze. A good thing I'd left the robots inside the shelter, and a good thing I had left a few hand tools outside. The door was buried under two metras of snow and ice. I sculpted myself a passageway, an application of artistic skills I'd never foreseen.

I debated calling White Hill and telling her that I would be longer than expected. We had agreed not to interrupt each other, though, and it was likely she'd started working as soon as I left.

The robots were like a bad comedy team, but I could only be amused by them for an hour or so at a time. It was so cold that the water vapor from my breath froze into an icy sheath on my beard and moustache. Breathing was painful; deep breathing probably dangerous.

So most of the time, I monitored them from inside the shelter. I had the place to myself; everyone else long since gone into the dome. When I wasn't working I drank too much, something I had not done regularly in centuries.

It was obvious that I wasn't going to make a working model. Delicate balance was impossible in the shifting gale. But the robots and I had our hands full, and other grasping appendages engaged, just dismantling the various pieces and moving them through the lock. It was unexciting but painstaking work. We did all the laser cuts inside the shelter, allowing the rock to come up to room temperature so it didn't spall or shatter. The air-conditioning wasn't quite equal to the challenge, and neither were the cleaning robots, so after a while it was like living in a foundry: everywhere a kind of greasy slickness of rock dust, the air dry and metallic.

So it was with no regret that I followed the last slice into the airlock myself, even looking forward to the scourging if White Hill was on the other side.

She wasn't. A number of other people were missing, too. She left this note behind:

> I knew from the day we were called back here what my new piece would have to be, and I knew I had to keep it from you, to spare you sadness. And to save you the frustration of trying to talk me out of it.
>
> As you may know by now, scientists have determined that the Fwndyri indeed have sped up the Sun's evolution somehow. It will continue to warm, until in thirty or forty years there will be an explosion called the "helium flash." The Sun will become a red giant, and the Earth will be incinerated.
>
> There are no starships left, but there is one avenue of escape. A kind of escape.
>
> Parked in high orbit there is a huge interplanetary transport that was used in the terraforming of Mars. It's a couple of centuries older than you, but like yourself it has been excellently preserved. We are going to ride it out to a distance sufficient to survive the Sun's catastrophe, and there remain until the situation improves, or does not.
>
> This is where I enter the picture. For our survival to be meaningful in this thousand-year war, we have to resort to coldsleep. And for a large number of people to survive centuries of coldsleep, they need my jaturnary skills. Alone, in the ice, they would go slowly mad. Connected through the matrix of my mind, they will have a sense of community, and may come out of it intact.
>
> I will be gone, of course. I will be by the time you read this. Not dead, but immersed in service. I could not be revived if this were only a hundred people for a hundred days. This will be a thousand, perhaps for a thousand years.
>
> No one else on Earth can do jaturnary, and there is neither time nor equipment for me to transfer my ability to anyone. Even if there were, I'm not sure I would trust anyone else's skill. So I am gone.
>
> My only loss is losing you. Do I have to elaborate on that?
>
> You can come if you want. In order to use the transport, I had to agree that the survivors be chosen in accordance with the Earth's strict class system—starting with dear Norita, and from that pinnacle, on

down—but they were willing to make exceptions for all of the visiting artists. You have until mid-Deciembre to decide; the ship leaves Januar first.

If I know you at all, I know you would rather stay behind and die. Perhaps the prospect of living "in" me could move you past your fear of coldsleep; your aversion to jaturnary. If not, not.

I love you more than life. But this is more than that. Are we what we are?

W.H.

The last sentence is a palindrome in her language, not mine, that I believe has some significance beyond the obvious.

I did think about it for some time. Weighing a quick death, or even a slow one, against spending centuries locked frozen in a tiny room with Norita and her ilk. Chattering on at the speed of synapse, and me unable to not listen.

I have always valued quiet, and the eternity of it that I face is no more dreadful than the eternity of quiet that preceded my birth.

If White Hill were to be at the other end of those centuries of torture, I know I could tolerate the excruciation. But she was dead now, at least in the sense that I would never see her again.

Another woman might have tried to give me a false hope, the possibility that in some remote future the process of *jaturnary* would be advanced to the point where her personality could be recovered. But she knew how unlikely that would be even if teams of scientists could be found to work on it, and years could be found for them to work in. It would be like unscrambling an egg.

Maybe I would even do it, though, if there were just some chance that, when I was released from that din of garrulous bondage, there would be something like a real world, a world where I could function as an artist. But I don't think there will even be a world where I can function as a man.

There probably won't be any humanity at all, soon enough. What they did to the Sun they could do to all of our stars, one assumes. They win the war, the Extermination, as my parent called it. Wrong side exterminated.

Of course the Fwndyri might not find White Hill and her charges. Even if they do find them, they might leave them preserved as an object of study.

The prospect of living on eternally under those circumstances, even if there were some growth to compensate for the immobility and the company, holds no appeal.

■ ●

What I did in the time remaining before mid-Deciembre was write this account. Then I had it translated by a xenolinguist into a form that she said could be decoded by any creature sufficiently similar to humanity to make any sense of the story. Even the Fwndyri, perhaps. They're human enough to want to wipe out a competing species.

I'm looking at the preliminary sheets now, English down the left side and a jumble of dots, squares, and triangles down the right. Both sides would have looked equally strange to me a few years ago.

White Hill's story will be conjoined to a standard book that starts out with basic mathematical principles, in dots and squares and triangles, and moves from that into physics, chemistry, biology. Can you go from biology to the human heart? I have to hope so. If this is read by alien eyes, long after the last human breath is stilled, I hope it's not utter gibberish.

■

So I will take this final sheet down to the translator and then deliver the whole thing to the woman who is going to transfer it to permanent sheets of platinum, which will be put in a prominent place aboard the transport. They could last a million years, or ten million, or more. After the Sun is a cinder, and the ship is a frozen block enclosing a thousand bits of frozen flesh, she will live on in this small way.

So now my work is done. I'm going outside, to the quiet.

INTRODUCTION TO "CIVIL DISOBEDIENCE"

Ernest Lilley was putting together an anthology of stories set in Washington, D.C., and he knew I'd grown up there, so asked me for one. I was not happy with the Bush administration, either of them, so I was not going to write a happy story.

The proximate reason for writing this particular tale was the administration's blithe dismissal of warnings from mainstream British scientists that catastrophic flooding from global warming could be in our immediate future. Fortunately, the government immediately responded to the scientists' warnings, and everything is fine now. (And I have a big boat in my back yard.)

CIVIL DISOBEDIENCE

I'm old enough to remember when the Beltway was a highway, not a dike. Even then, there were miles that had to be elevated over low places that periodically flooded.

We lived in suburban Maryland when I was a child. I remember seeing on television the pictures of downtown Washington after Hurricane Hilda, with the Washington Monument and the Capitol and the Lincoln Memorial all isolated islands. My brother and I helped our parents stack sandbags around our Bethesda house, but the water rose over them. Good thing the house had two stories.

That was when they built the George W. Bush Dam to regulate the flow of the Potomac, after Hilda. (My grandfather kept mumbling, "Bush Dam...Damn Bush.) That really was the beginning of the end for the UniParty, a symbol for all that went wrong afterwards.

The politicos claimed they didn't cause the water to rise—it was supposed to be a slow process, hundreds or even thousands of years before a greenhouse crisis. I guess they built the dam just in case they were wrong.

Then there were three hurricanes in four weeks, and they all made it this far north, so the dam closed up tight—and people in flooded Maryland and Virginia could look over the Beltway dike and see low-and-dry Washington, and sort of resent what their tax dollars had bought. Maybe what happened was inevitable.

Over the next decade, the dikes also went up around New York, Boston, Philadelphia, and Miami. The Hamptons, Cape Cod. Temporary at first, but soon enough, as the water rose, bricked into permanence. While suburbs and less wealthy coastal towns from Maine to Florida simply drowned.

By the time the water got to rooftop level, of course all those towns were deserted, their inhabitants relocated inland, into Rehab camps if they couldn't afford anything else. We spent a couple of years in the Rockville one, until Dad had saved enough to get into an apartment in Frederick. It was about as big as a matchbox, but by then we two boys had gone off to college and trade school.

I was an autodidact without too much respect for authority, so I said the hell with college and became a SCUBA instructor, a job with a future. That was after I'd been in the Navy for one year, and the Navy brig for one week. Long enough in the service to learn some underwater demolition, and that's on my website, which brought me to the attention of Homeland Security, about a day and a half after the Bush Dam blew.

Actually, I'm surprised it took them that long. Most of my income for several years had been from Soggy Suburbs, diving tours of the drowned suburbs of Washington. People mostly come back to see what's become of the family manse, now that fish have moved in, and it does not generate goodwill toward the government. They've tried to shut me down a couple of times, but I have lawyers from both the ACLU and the Better Business Bureau on my side.

I returned to my dock with a boatload of tourists—only four, in the bitter January cold—and found a couple of suits and a couple of cops waiting, along with a Homeland Security helicopter. They had a federal warrant to bring me in for questioning.

It was an interesting ride. I'm used to seeing the 'burbs underwater, of course, but it was strange to fly over what had become an inland sea, inside the Beltway dike. The dam demolition had been a pretty thorough job, and in less than a day, it became as deep inside the Beltway as outside. They can fill up the collapsed part and pump the water out, but it will take a long time.

(The guy who did it called it "civil disobedience" rather than terrorism, which I thought was a stretch. But he did time the charges so that the flooding was gradual, and no one but looters drowned.)

Since I was a suspected terrorist, I lost the protection of the courts, not to mention the ACLU and the Better Business Bureau. They didn't haul out the cattle prods, but they did lock me in a small room for twenty-four hours, saying, "We'll get to you."

It could have been worse. It was a hotel room, not a jail, but there was nothing to read or eat, no TV or phone. They took my shoulder bag with the book I was reading and my computer and cell.

I guess they thought that would scare me. It just made me angry, and then resigned. I hadn't really done anything, but since when did that matter, with the UniParty. And not doing anything was not the same as not knowing anything.

The smell of mildew was pervasive, and the carpet was squishy. When we landed on the roof, it looked like about four stories were above the waterline. I couldn't see anything from the room; the window was painted over with white paint from the outside.

Exactly twenty-four hours after they had brought me in, one of the suits entered through the hotel-room door, leaving a guard outside.

"What do you need a cop for?"

He gave me a look. "Full employment." He sat down on the couch. "First of all, where were you—"

"I get food, you get answers."

"You have that backward." He looked at the back of his hand. "Answers, then food. Can you prove where you were when the dam was sabotaged?"

"No, and neither can you."

"What do you mean by that?"

"Food."

Yet another look. He stood up without a word and knocked twice on the door. The guard opened it, and he left.

A few minutes later I tried knocking, myself. No result. But the man did come back eventually, bearing a ham sandwich on a Best Western plate.

I peeled back the white bread and looked at it. "What if I don't eat ham?"

"You left a package of sliced ham in your refrigerator on K Street. You ordered a ham sandwich at Denny's for lunch on the twenty-eighth of November. I checked while they were making the sandwich."

Now *that* was scary, considering where my refrigerator was now. I tore into the sandwich even though it was probably full of truth serum. "If you know so much about me," I said between bites, "then you must know where I was at any given time."

"You said that neither you nor I could say where we were when the dam blew."

"No...you asked where I was when it was *sabotaged*. That could have been a week or a year before the actual explosions. The saboteurs were probably back in Albania or Alabama or wherever by then."

"So where were you when it blew?"

"At my girlfriend's place. It rattled the dishes and a picture fell off the wall."

"That's the tree house she's squatting in, out in Wheaton?"

"Home sweet home, yeah. Her original apartment is kind of damp. She paid a premium for ground floor. Wrong side of the Beltway."

"So we only have her word for where you were."

"And mine, yes. What, you don't have surveillance cameras out in Treetown yet?"

"None that show her place."

I guess it was my turn to respond, or react. I finished the sandwich instead, slowly, while he watched. He took the plate, I suppose so I couldn't Frisbee it at his head, take his keys and gun, subdue the guard, steal the helicopter, and go blow up the New York dike. Instead I posited: "If the saboteurs could have been anyplace in the world when it blew, what difference does it make where I was?"

"You weren't in town. It looks like you knew something was going to happen."

"Really."

"Yes, *really*. We got a warrant, and a Navy SEAL forensic team searched your apartment."

"Are my goldfish all right? Water's kind of cold."

"It's interesting what's missing. Not just toiletries and clothes, but boxes of books and pictures from the walls. Your computer system, not portable. All the paper having to do with your business. Your pistol and its registration. You moved them with four cab rides between your apartment and the Sligo dock, all two days before the Flood."

"So I moved in with my girlfriend. It happens."

"Not so conveniently."

I tried to look confused. "That's why you're on my case. I'm one of the dozens, hundreds, of people who moved out of D.C. that day or the next?"

"You're the only one with underwater demolition training. On that alone, we could haul you down to Cuba and throw away the key."

"Come on—"

"And you were already on a watch list for your attitude. The things you've said to customers."

"The apartment was too expensive, so I got back my deposit and moved out. My girlfriend—"

"A week before the first of the month."

"Sure. It was——"

"In a blizzard."

"Yeah, it was snowing. No problem. Or the cabbie's problem, not mine. We wanted to have Christmas together."

"For Christmas, you just sort of boated through twelve miles of blizzard. By compass, for the fun of it."

"Oh, bullshit. I just kept the Beltway to my left for ten-some miles and turned right at the half-submerged Chevron sign. Then about a hundred yards to a flagpole, bear left, and so forth. I've done it a hundred times. You try it with a compass. I want to watch."

He nodded without changing expression. "One of the things we lost when the dam blew was a really delicate sniffing machine. It can tell whether you've been anywhere near high explosives recently. The closest one's in our New York office."

"Let's go. I haven't touched anything like that since the Navy. Four or five years ago." I'd been in the same house with some, but I hadn't touched it.

He stood up very smoothly, one flex, not touching the arm of the couch. I wouldn't want to get into anything physical with him. "Get your coat."

I got it from the musty closet and shook it out, shedding molecules of mold and plastic explosive. How sensitive was that machine, really?

He knocked twice, and the cop took us to an open elevator. The buttons under 4 were covered with duct tape. The cop used a cylindrical fire department key to start it. "Roof?"

"Right."

"Where's my stuff?" I said. "I don't want to leave it here."

"We're not going anywhere." He buttoned up his coat and I zipped mine up. We got out of the elevator into a glassed-in waiting area and went out onto the roof. There was no helicopter on the pad. Not too cold, high twenties with no wind, and the air smelled really good, almost like the ocean.

I followed him over to the edge. There was water all the way to where the horizon was lost in bright afternoon haze, the tops of a few building rising like artificial islands in a science-fiction world. Behind us, the Beltway, with almost no traffic.

"It's quiet," I said. Faint rustle of ice slurry below us. I peered over the rusty guardrail and saw it rolling along the building wall.

"They said 'Power to the People.' This isn't power to anybody. It's like the country's been beheaded."

I didn't say that if you're ugly enough, extreme cosmetic surgery could help. I might be in enough trouble already.

"Whoever did this didn't think it through. It's not just the government, the bureaucracy. It's the country's history. Our connection to the past; our identity as America."

That was something Hugh was always on about. The way they wrap themselves in the flag and pretend to be the inheritors of a grand democratic tradition. While they're really alchemists, turning the public trust into gold.

"Hugh Oliver," he said, startling me.

"What about Hugh?"

"He disappeared the same time you did."

"What, like I disappeared? I left a forwarding address."

"Your parents' address."

"They knew where I was."

"So did we. But we've lost Mr. Oliver. Perhaps you know where to find him?"

"Huh-uh. We're not that close."

"Funny." He took a pair of small binoculars out of his coat pocket and switched them on. The stabilizers hummed as he scanned along the horizon. Still looking at nothing, he said, "A surveillance camera saw you go into a coffeehouse in Georgetown with him last Wednesday. The Lean Bean."

Oh shit. "Yeah, I remember that. So?"

"The camera didn't show either of you coming out. You're not still there, so you must have left through the service entrance."

"He was parked in the alley out back."

"Not in his own car. It had a tracer."

"So I'm not my brother's car's keeper. It must have been somebody else's. What did he—"

"Or a rental?"

That much, I could give up. "Not a rental. It was clapped-out and full of junk."

"You didn't recognize it?"

I shook my head. Actually, I'd assumed it was Hugh's. "Why did you have a tracer on his car?"

"What did you talk about?"

"Business. How bad it is." Hugh's a diver; not much winter work. Idle hands do the devil's work, I guess. "We just had a cup of coffee, and he drove me home."

"And what did you do when you got home?"

"What? I don't know. Made dinner."

He put the binoculars down on the railing and pulled out a little sound recorder. "This is what you did."

It was a recording of me phoning my landlord, saying I'd found a cheaper place and would be moving out before Christmas.

"That was at six twenty-five," he said. "When you got home from the coffeehouse, you must have gone straight to the phone."

I had, of course. "No. But I guess it was the same day. That Wednesday."

He picked up the binoculars again and scanned the middle distance. "It's okay, Johnson."

The big man slammed me against the guardrail, hard, then tipped me over and grabbed my ankles. I was gasping, coughing, trying not to vomit, dangling fifty feet over the icy water.

"Johnson is strong, but he can't hold on to you forever. I think it's time for you to talk."

"You can't. . .you can't do this!"

"I guess you have about a minute," he said, looking at his watch. "Can you hold on a minute?" I could see Johnson nod, his upside-down smile.

"Let me put it to you this way. If you can tell us where Hugh Oliver went, you live. If you can't, you have this little accident. It doesn't matter whether it's because you don't know, or because you refuse to tell. You'll just fall."

My throat had snapped shut, paralyzed. "I—"

"You'll either drown or freeze. Neither one is particularly painful. That bothers me a little. But I can't tell you how little guilt I will feel."

Not the truth! "Mexico. Drove to Mexico."

"No, we have cameras at every crossing, with face recognition."

"He knew that!"

"Can you let go of one ankle?" He nodded and did, and I dropped a sickening foot. "Mexico returns terrorists to us. He must have known that, too."

"He was going to Europe from there. Speaks French." *Quebec.*

He shrugged and made a motion with his head. The big man grabbed the other ankle and hauled me back. My chin snapped against the railing, and my shoulder and forehead hit hard on the gravel.

"Yeah, Europe. You're lying, but I think you do know where he is. I can send you to a place where they get answers." He rubbed his hands together and blew on them. "Maybe I'll go along with you. It's warm down there."

Cuba. Point of no return.

My stomach fell. Even if I knew nothing about Hugh, I knew too much about them.

They couldn't let me live now. They'll pull out their answers and bury me in Guantanamo.

Johnson picked me up roughly. I kicked him in the shin, tore loose, ran three steps, and tried to vault over the edge. My hurt shoulder collapsed, and I cartwheeled clumsily into space.

Civil disobedience. What would the water feel like?

Scalding. Then nothing.

INTRODUCTION TO "FOUR SHORT NOVELS"

This is another "thousand years in the future" story, but its genesis was more specific than "For White Hill." The French publisher Flammarion asked Robert Silverberg to put together an anthology of stories called *Destination 3001*, and he asked me for one.

The deadline wasn't for a year or so, and so I decided to sit on it for awhile, trusting that sooner or later something would hatch.

I don't often know exactly when a story idea occurs to me, but in this case I do: I was doing a pretty serious bicycle ride, "interval training," going up hills faster than one would normally, trying to get to the top before cranking down into granny gears. The structure of the story came to me in one hyperoxygenated flash. By the time I finished the last hill, I knew what the first and last sections were going to be, and roughly what would go in between. As soon as I got home, I scribbled down some notes about it.

I couldn't write the story right away, because I was pushing a novel deadline (*The Coming*), trying to finish it before flying off to the World Science Fiction Convention in Australia.

Finished the novel and got through the whirlwind convention, and settled down to relax for awhile on the edge of the Great Barrier Reef, snorkeling and sunbathing with a bunch of friends united in our admiration of science fiction, topless sunbathers, and Australian beer. Some indomitable Puritan tropism made me take out my notebook in the mornings and finish this story.

FOUR SHORT NOVELS

REMEMBRANCE OF THINGS PAST

Eventually it came to pass that no one ever had to die, unless they ran out of money. When you started to feel the little aches and twinges that meant your body was running down, you just got in line at Immortality, Incorporated, and handed them your credit card. As long as you had at least a million bucks—and eventually everybody did—they would reset you to whatever age you liked.

One way people made money was by swapping knowledge around. Skills could be transferred with a technology spun off from the immortality process. You could spend a few decades becoming a great concert pianist, and then put your ability up for sale. There was no shortage of people with two million dollars who would trade one million to be their village's Van Cliburn. In the sale of your ability, you would lose it, but you could buy it back a few decades or centuries later.

For many people this became the game of life—becoming temporarily a genius, selling your genius for youth, and then clawing your way up in some other field, to buy back the passion that had rescued you first from the grave. Enjoy it a few years, sell it again, and so on ad infinitum. Or *finitum*, if you just once made a wrong career move, and wound up old and poor and bereft of skill. That happened less and less often, of course, Darwinism inverted: the un-survival of the least fit.

It wasn't just a matter of swapping around your piano-playing and brain surgery, of course. People with the existential wherewithal to enjoy century after century of life tended to grow and improve with age. A person could look like a barely pubescent teenybopper, and yet be able to out-Socrates Socrates in the wisdom department. People were getting used to seeing acne and *gravitas* on the same face.

Enter Jutel Dicuth, the paragon of his age, a raging polymath. He could paint and sculpt and play six instruments. He could write formal poetry with his left hand while solving differential equations with his right. He could write formal poetry *about* differential equations! He was an Olympic-class gymnast and also held the world record for the javelin throw. He had earned doctorates in anthropology, art history, slipstream physics, and fly-tying.

He sold it all.

Immensely wealthy but bereft of any useful ability, Jutel Dicuth set up a trust fund for himself that would produce a million dollars every year. It also provided a generous salary for an attendant. He had Immortality, Incorporated, set him back to the apparent age of one year, and keep resetting him once a year.

In a world where there were no children—where would you put them?—he was the only infant. He was the only person with no useful skills and, eventually, the only one alive who did not have nearly a thousand years of memory.

In a world that had outgrown the old religions—why would you need them?—he became like unto a god. People came from everywhere to listen to his random babbling and try to find a conduit to the state of blissful innocence buried under the weight of their wisdom.

It was inevitable that someone would see a profit in this. A consortium with a name we would translate as Blank Slate offered to "dicuth" anyone who had a certain large sum of what passed for money, and maintain them for as long as they wanted. At first people were slightly outraged, because it was a kind of sacrilege, or were slightly amused, because it was such a transparent scheme to gather what passed for wealth.

Sooner or later, though, everyone tried it. Most who tried it for one year went back for ten or a hundred, or, eventually, forever. After some centuries, permanent dicuths began to outnumber humans—though those humans were not anything you would recognize as people, crushed as they were by nearly a thousand years of wisdom and experience. And jealous of those who had given up.

On 31 December, A.D. 3000, the last "normal" person surrendered his loneliness for dicuth bliss. The world was populated completely by total innocents, tended by patient machines.

It lasted a long time. Then one by one, the machines broke down.

CRIME AND PUNISHMENT

Eventually it came to pass that no one ever had to die, unless they were so horrible that society had to dispose of them. Other than the occasional horrible person, the world was in an idyllic state, everyone living as long as they wanted to, doing what they wanted to do.

This is how things got back to normal.

People gained immortality by making copies of themselves, farlies, which were kept in safe places and updated periodically. So if you got run over by a truck or hit by a meteorite, your farlie would sense this and automatically pop out and take over, after prudently making a farlie of itself. Upon that temporary death, you would lose only the weeks or months that had gone by since your last update.

That made it difficult to deal with criminals. If someone was so horrible that society had to hang or shoot or electrocute or inject him to death, his farlie would crop up somewhere, still bad to the bone, make a farlie of itself, and go off on another rampage. If you put him in jail for the rest of his life, he would eventually die, but then his evil farlie would leap out, full of youthful vigor and nasty intent.

Ultimately, if society felt you were too horrible to live, it would take preemptive action: check out your farlie and destroy it first. If it could be found. Really bad people became adept at hiding their farlies. Inevitably, people who were really good at being really bad became master criminals. It was that, or die forever. There were only a few dozen of them, but they moved through the world like neutrinos: effortless, unstoppable, invisible.

One of them was a man named Bad Billy Beerbreath. He started the ultimate crime wave.

There were Farlie Centers where you would go to update your farlie— one hundred of them, all over the world—and that's where almost everybody kept their farlies stored. But you could actually put a farlie anywhere, if you got together enough liquid nitrogen and terabytes of storage and kept them in a cool dry place out of direct sunlight.

Most people didn't know this; in fact, it was forbidden knowledge. Nobody knew how to make Farlie Centers anymore, either. They were all built during the lifetime of Joan Farlie, who had wandered off with the blueprints after deciding not to make a copy of himself, himself.

Bad Billy Beerbreath decided to make it his business to trash Farlie Centers. In its way, this was worse than murder, because if a client died before he or she found out about it, and hadn't been able to make a new farlie (which took weeks)—he or she would die for real, kaput, out of the picture. It was a crime beyond crime. Just thinking about this gave Bad Billy an acute pleasure akin to a hundred orgasms.

Because there were a hundred Bad Billy Beerbreaths.

In preparation for his crime wave, Bad Billy had spent years making a hundred farlies of himself, and he stored them in cool dry places out of direct sunlight, all around the world. On 13 May 2999, all but one of those farlies jump-started itself and went out to destroy the nearest Farlie Center.

By noon, GMT, police and militia all over the world had captured or killed or subdued every copy (but one) of Bad Billy, but by noon every single Farlie Center in the world had been leveled, save the one in Akron, Ohio.

The only people left who had farlies were people who had a reason to keep them in a secret place. Master criminals like Billy. Pals of Billy. They all were waiting at Akron, and held off the authorities for months, by making farlie after farlie of themselves, like broomsticks in a Disney cartoon, sending most of them out to die, or "die," defending the place, until there were so many of them the walls were bulging. Then they sent out word that they wanted to negotiate, and during the lull that promise produced, they fled en masse, destroying the last Farlie Center behind them.

They were a powerful force, a hundred thousand hardened criminals united in their contempt for people like you and me, and in their loyalty to Bad Billy Beerbreath. Somewhat giddy, not to say insane, in their triumph after having destroyed every Farlie Center, they went on to destroy every jail and prison and courthouse. That did cut their numbers down considerably, since most of them only had ten or twenty farlies tucked away, but it also reduced drastically the number of police, not to mention the number of people willing to take up policing as a profession, since once somebody killed you twice, you had to stay dead.

By New Year's Eve, A.D. 3000, the criminals were in charge of the whole world.

Again.

WAR AND PEACE

Eventually it came to pass that no one ever had to die, unless they wanted to, or could be talked into it. That made it very hard to fight wars, and a larger and larger part of every nation's military budget was given over to psychological operations directed toward their own people: *dulce et decorum est* just wasn't convincing enough anymore.

There were two elements to this sales job. One was to romanticize the image of the soldier as heroic defender of the blah blah blah. That was not too hard; they'd been doing that since Homer. The other was more subtle: convince people that every individual life was essentially worthless—your own and also the lives of the people you would eventually be killing.

That was a hard job, but the science of advertising, more than a millennium after Madison Avenue, was equal to it, through the person of a genius named Manny O'Malley. The pitch was subtle, and hard for a person to understand who hasn't lived for centuries, but shorn of Manny's incomprehensible humor and appeal to subtle pleasures that had no name until the thirtieth century, it boiled down to this:

A thousand years ago, they seduced people into soldiering with the slogan, "Be all that you can be." But you have *been* all you can be. The only thing left worth being is *not* being.

Everybody else is in the same boat, O'Malley convinced them. In the process of giving yourself the precious gift of nonexistence, share it with many others.

It's hard for us to understand. But then we would be hard for them to understand, with all this remorseless getting and spending laying waste our years.

Wars were all fought in Death Valley, with primitive hand weapons, and the United States grew wealthy renting the place out, until it inevitably found itself fighting a series of wars *for* Death Valley, during one of which O'Malley himself finally died, charging a phalanx of no-longer-immortal pikemen on his robotic horse, waving a broken sword. His final words were, famously, "Oh, shit."

Death Valley eventually wound up in the hands of the Bertelsmann Corporation, which ultimately ruled the world. But by that time, Manny's advertising had been so effective that no one cared. Everybody was in uniform, lining up to do their bit for Bertelsmann.

Even the advertising scientists. Even the high management of Bertelsmann.

There was a worldwide referendum, utilizing something indistinguishable from telepathy, where everybody agreed to change the name of the planet to Death Valley, and on the eve of the new century, A.D. 3000, have at each other.

Thus O'Malley's ultimate ad campaign achieved the ultimate victory: a world that consumed itself.

THE WAY OF ALL FLESH

Eventually it came to pass that no one ever had to die, so long as just one person loved them. The process that provided immortality was fueled that way.

Almost everybody can find someone to love him or her, at least for a little while, and if and when that someone says good-bye, most people can clean up their act enough to find yet another.

But every now and then you find a specimen who is so unlovable that he can't even get a hungry dog to take a biscuit from his hand. Babies take one look at him and get the colic. Women cross their legs as he passes by. Ardent homosexuals drop their collective gaze. Old people desperate for company feign sleep.

The most extreme such specimen was Custer Tralia. Custer came out of the womb with teeth, and bit the doctor. In grade school he broke up the love-training sessions with highly toxic farts. He celebrated puberty by not washing for a year. All through middle school and high school, he made loving couples into enemies by spreading clever vicious lies. He formed a Masturbation Club and didn't allow anybody else to join. In his graduation yearbook, he was unanimously voted "The One Least Likely to Survive, If We Have Anything to Do with It."

In college, he became truly reckless. When everybody else was feeling the first whiff of mortality and frantically seducing in self-defense, Custer declared that he hated women almost as much as he hated men, and he reveled in his freedom from love, his superior detachment from the cloying crowd. Death was nothing compared to the hell of dependency. When, at the beginning of his junior year, he had to declare what his profession was going to be, he wrote down "hermit" for first, second, and third choices.

The world was getting pretty damned crowded, though, since a lot of people loved each other so much they turned out copy after copy of themselves. The only place Custer could go and be truly alone was the Australian outback. He had a helicopter drop him there with a big water tank and crates of food. They said they'd check back in a year, and Custer said don't bother. If you've decided not to live forever, a few years or decades one way or the other doesn't make much difference.

He found peace among the wallabies and dingoes. A kangaroo began to follow him around, and he accepted it as a pet, sharing his rehydrated KFC and fish and chips with it.

Life was a pleasantly sterile and objectless quest. Custer and his kangaroo quartered the outback, turning over rocks just to bother the things underneath. The kangaroo was loyal, which was a liability; but at least it couldn't talk, and its attachment to Custer was transparently selfish, so they got along. He taught it how to beg, and, by not rewarding it, taught it how to whimper.

One day, like Robinson Crusoe, he found footprints. Unlike Robinson Crusoe, he hastened in the opposite direction.

But the footprinter had been watching him for some time, and outsmarted him. Knowing he would be gone all day, she had started miles away, walking backwards by his camp, and knew that his instinct for hermitage would lead him directly, perversely, back into her cave.

Parky Gumma had decided to become a hermit, too, after she read about Custer's audacious gesture. But after about a year she wanted a bath, and wanted to have her so she wouldn't die, in that order. So under the wheeling Milky Way, on the eve of the thirty-first century, she stalked backwards to her cave and squandered a month's worth of water sluicing her body, which was unremarkable except for the fact that it was clean and the only female one in two hundred thousand square miles.

Parky left herself unclothed and squeaky clean, carefully perched on a camp stool, waiting for Custer's curiosity and misanthropy to lead him back to her keep. He crept in a couple of hours after sunrise.

She stood up and spread her arms, and his pet kangaroo boinged away in terror. Custer himself was paralyzed by a mixture of conflicting impulses. He had seen pictures of naked women, but never one actually in the flesh, and honestly didn't know what to do.

Parky showed him.

The rest is the unmaking of history. That Parky had admired him and followed him into the desert was even more endearing than the slip and slide that she demonstrated for him after she washed him up. But that was revolutionary, too. Custer had to admit that a year or a century or a millennium of that would be better than keeling over and having dingos tear up your corpse and spread your bones over the uncaring sands.

So this is Custer's story, and ours. He never did get around to liking baths, so you couldn't say that love conquers all. But it could still conquer death.

INTRODUCTION TO "ANGEL OF LIGHT"

This was an oddball story on several levels. It started with a request from Australian editor Damien Broderick for a Christmas story for *Cosmos* magazine. My family does celebrate Christmas, because what's not to like about peace and brotherhood and presents—but I'm an atheist and was pretty sure Damien was, too. I queried him about that and he responded with a word rate that put me in a religious frame of mind.

I'd been thinking about the place of Islam in the future of the United States, and had read a little about it (*The Infidel's Guide to Islam* or something) and with too little humility, I made up the hybrid religion Chrislam, which I didn't know had already been invented. Please don't write me any angry letters about how wrong I've gotten it, or if you do, please make them interesting.

ANGEL OF LIGHT

It began innocently enough Christmas-time and no money. I went down into the cellar and searched deeply for something to give the children. Something they wouldn't have already found during their *hajjes* down there.

On a high shelf, behind bundles of sticks waiting for the cold, I could just see an old wooden chest, pushed far back into a corner. I dropped some of the bundles on to the floor and pushed the others out of the way, and with some difficulty slid the chest to the edge of the shelf. From the thick layer of dust on top, I assumed it was from my father's time or before.

I had a warning thought: Don't open it. Call the authorities.

But just above the lock was engraved the name John Billings Washington. John Washington was my father's slave name, I think the Billings middle name was his father's. The box probably went back to the 20th century.

The lock was rusted tight, but the hasp was loose. I got down from the ladder and found a large screwdriver that I could use to pry it open.

I slid the chest out and balanced it on my shoulder, and carefully stepped down, the ladder creaking. I set it on the workbench and hung one lantern from the rafter over it, and set the other on a stack of scrap wood beside.

The screaming that the screws made, coming out of the hardwood, was so loud that it was almost funny, considering that I supposedly was working in secret. But Miriam was pumping out chords on the organ, singing along with Fatimah, rehearsing for the Christmas service. I could have fired a pistol and no one would have heard it.

The hasp swung free and the top lifted easily, with a sigh of brass. Musty smell and something else. Gun oil. A grey cloth bundle on top was heavy. Of course it held a gun.

It's not unusual to find guns left over from the old times; there were so many. Ammunition was rare, though. This one had two heavy magazines.

I recognised it from news and history pictures, an Uzi, invented and used by the old infidel state Israel. I set it down and wiped my hands.

It would not be a good Christmas present. Perhaps for Eid ul-Adha, for Ibriham, when he is old enough to decide whether he is to be called. A Jewish weapon, he would laugh. I could ask the imam whether to cleanse it and how.

There were three cardboard folders under the gun, once held together with rubber bands, which were just sticky lines now. They were full of useless documents about land and banking.

Underneath them, I caught a glimpse of something that looked like pornography. I looked away immediately, closed my eyes, and asked Muhammad and Jesus for strength. Then I took it out and put it in the light.

It was in a plastic bag that had stamped on it 'nitrogen seal.' What a strange word, a tech word from the old times.

The book inside had the most amazing picture on the front. A man and a woman, both white, embracing. But the woman is terrified. The man seems only resolute, as he fires a strange pistol at a thing like a giant squid, green as a plant. The woman's head is uncovered, and at first she seems naked, but in fact her clothes are simply transparent, like some dancers'. The book is called *Thrilling Wonder Stories*, and is dated "Summer 1944." That would be 1365, more than a hundred years before Chrislam.

I leafed through the book, fascinated in spite of its carnal and infidel nature. Most of it seemed to be tales—not religious parables or folk tales, but lies that were made up at the time, for entertainment. Perhaps there was moral instruction as well. Many of the pictures did show men in situations that were physically or morally dangerous.

The first story, "The Giant Runt," seemed at first sacrilegious; it was about a man furious with God for having created him shorter than normal men. But then a magical machine makes everyone else tiny, and his sudden superiority turns him into a monster. But he sees an opportunity for moral action and redeems himself. The machine is destroyed, the world is normal again, and God rewards him with love.

Nadia, my second wife, came to the door at the top of the stairs and asked whether I needed help with anything. "No," I said. "Don't wait up. I have something to study here. A man thing." I shouldn't have said that. She would be down here after the morning prayer, as soon as I left for work.

I looked at the woman on the cover of the book, so exposed and vulnerable. Perhaps I should destroy it before Nadia or Miriam were exposed to it. A present for Ibriham? No; he would like it, but it would lead him away from proper thought.

I put both lanterns on the table, with the book between them, for maximum light. The paper was brown and the ink faded. I turned the crumbling pages with care, although I would probably burn the book before dawn. First I would read as much of it as I could. I composed my mind with prayer, reciting the Prophet's *hadith* about the duty of learning.

In 1365 a war was raging all around the world, and various pages took note of this. I think this was only a year or two before America used nuclear weapons the first time, though I found no mention of them. (There were several exhortations to "buy bonds," which at first I misread as bombs. Bonds are financial instruments of some kind.) There were short pieces, evidently presented as truth, about science being used against the enemies of America. The ones that were not presented as true were more interesting, though harder to understand.

Much of the content was religious. "Horatius at the Bridge" was about a madman who could find the 'soul' of a bridge and bring it down with the notes from a flute. "Terror in the Dust" and "The Devouring Tide" described scientists who were destroyed because they tried to play God—the first by giving intelligence to ants and then treating them as if he were an almighty deity, and the second, grandly, by attempting to create a new universe, with himself as Allah. The last short story, "God of Light," had a machine that was obviously Shaytan, trying to tempt the humans into following it into destruction.

The language was crude and at times bizarre, though of course part of that was just a reflection of the technological culture those writers and readers endured together. Life is simpler and more pure now, at least on this side of the city walls. The Kafir may still have books like this.

That gave me an idea. Perhaps this sort of thing would be rare and sought after in their world. I shouldn't accept Kafir money—though people do, often enough—but perhaps I could trade it for something more appropriate for a Christmas gift. Barter could be done without an intermediary, too, and frankly I was not eager for my imam to know that I had this questionable book in my possession.

Things are less rigid now, but I sharply remember the day, more than 40 years ago, when my father had to burn all of his books. We carried box after box of them to the parking lot in front of the church, where they were drenched with gasoline and set afire. The smell of gasoline, rare now, always brings that back.

He was allowed to keep two books, a *New Koran* and a *New Bible*. When a surprise search party later found an old *Q'ran* in his study, he had to spend a week, naked, in a cage in that same spot—the jumble of fractured concrete in the middle of the church parking lot—with nothing but water, except a piece of bread the last day.

(It was an old piece of bread, rock-hard and mouldy. I remember how he thanked the imam, carefully brushed off the mould, and managed to stay dignified, gnawing at it with his strong side teeth.)

He told them he kept the old book because of the beauty of the writing, but I knew his feelings went deeper than that: he thought the *Q'ran* in any language other than Arabic was just a book, not holy. As a boy of five, I was secretly overjoyed that I could stop memorising the *Q'ran* in Arabic; it was hard enough in English.

I agree with him now, and ever since it was legal again, I've spent my Sundays trying to cram the Arabic into my grey head. With God's grace I might live long enough to learn it all. Having long ago memorised the English version helps make up for my slow brain.

I put the old book back in its nitrogen seal bag and took it up to bed with me, dropping off a bundle of sticks by the stove on the way. I checked on both children and both wives; all were sleeping soundly. With a prayer of thanks for this strange discovery, I joined Nadia and dreamed of a strange future that had not come to pass.

The next day was market day. I left Nadia with the children and Fatimah and I went down to the medina for the week's supplies.

It really is more a woman's work than a man's, and normally I enjoy watching Fatimah go through the rituals of inspection and barter—the mock arguments and grudging agreement that comprise the morning's entertainment for customer and merchant alike. But this time I left her in the food part of the medina with the cart, while I went over to the antiques section.

You don't see many Kafir in the produce part of the medina, but there are always plenty wandering through the crafts and antiques section, I suppose looking for curiosities and bargains. Things that are everyday to us are exotic to them, and vice versa.

It was two large tents, connected by a canvas breezeway under which merchants were roasting meats and nuts and selling drinks for dollars or dirhams. I got a small cup of sweet coffee, redolent of honey and cardamom, for two dirhams, and sipped it standing there, enjoying the crowd.

Both tents had similar assortments of useful and worthless things, but one was for dollar transactions and the other was for dirhams and barter. The dollar purchases had to go through an imam, who would extract a fee for handling the money, and pay the merchant what was left, converting into dirham. There were easily three times as many merchants and customers in the dirham-and-barter tent, the Kafir looking for bargains and the sellers for surprises, as much as for doing business. It was festive there, too, a lot of chatter and laughing over the rattle and whine of an amateur band of drummers and fiddlers. People who think we are aloof from infidels, or hate them, should spend an hour here.

Those who did this regularly had tables they rented by the day or month; we amateurs just sat on the ground with our wares on display I walked around and didn't see anyone I knew, so finally just sat next to a table where a man and a woman were selling books. I laid out a square of newspaper in front of me and set the *Thrilling Wonder Stories* on it.

The woman looked down at it with interest. "What kind of a magazine is that?"

Magazine, I'd forgotten that word. "I don't know. Strange tales, most of them religious."

"It's 'science fiction,'" the man said. "They used to do that, predict what the future would be like."

"Used to? We still do that."

He shrugged. "Not that way. Not as fiction."

"I wouldn't let a child see that," the woman said.

"I don't think the artist was a good Muslim," I said, and they both chuckled. They wished me luck with finding a buyer, but didn't make an offer themselves.

Over the next hour, five or six people looked at the magazine and asked questions, most of which I couldn't answer. The imam in charge of the tent came over and gave me a long silent look. I looked right back at him and asked him how business was.

Fatimah came by, the cart loaded with groceries. I offered to wheel it home if she would sit with the magazine. She covered her face and giggled. More realistically, I said I could push the cart home when I was done, if she would take the perishables now. She said no, she'd take it all after she'd done a turn around the tent. That cost me 20 dirham; she found a set of wooden spoons for the kitchen. They were freshly made by a fellow who had set up shop in the opposite corner, running a child-powered lathe, his sons taking turns striding on a treadmill attached by a series of creaking pulleys to the axis of the tool. People may have bought his wares more out of curiosity and pity for his sons than because of the workmanship.

I almost sold the magazine to a fat old man who had lost both ears, I suppose in the war. He offered 50 dirham, but while I was trying to bargain the price up, his ancient crone of a wife charged up and physically hauled him away, shrieking. If he'd had an ear, she would have pulled him by it. The bookseller started to offer his sympathies, but then both of them doubled over in laughter, and I had to join them.

As it turned out, the loss of that sale was a good thing. But first I had to endure my trial.

A barefoot man who looked as if he'd been fasting all year picked up the magazine and leafed through it carefully, mumbling. I knew he was trouble. I'd seen him around, begging and haranguing. He was white, which normally is not a problem with me. But white people who choose to live inside the walls are often types who would not be welcome at home, wherever that might be.

He proceeded to berate me for being a bad Muslim—not hearing my correction, that I belonged to Chrislam—and, starting with the licentious cover and working his way through the inside illustrations and advertisements to the last story, which actually had God's name in the title, he said that even a bad Muslim would have no choice but to burn it on the spot.

I would have gladly burned it if I could burn it under *him*, but I was saved from making that decision by the imam. Drawn by the commotion, he stamped over and began to question the man, in a voice as shrill as his own, on matters of doctrine. The man's Arabic was no better than his diet, and he slunk away in mid-diatribe. I thanked the imam and he left with a slight smile.

Then a wave of silence unrolled across the room like a heavy blanket, I looked to the tent entrance and there were four men: Abdullah Zaragosa, our chief imam, some white man in a business suit, and two policemen in uniform, seriously armed. In between them was an alien, one of those odd creatures visiting from Arcturus.

I had never seen one, though I had heard them described on the radio. I looked around and was sad not to see Fatimah; she would hate having missed this.

It was much taller than the tallest human; it had a short torso but a giraffe-like neck. Its head was something like a bird's, one large eye on either side. It cocked its head this way and that, looking around, and then dropped down to say something to the imam.

They all walked directly toward me, the alien rippling on six legs. Cameras clicked; I hadn't brought one. The imam asked if I was Ahmed Abd al-kareem, and I said yes, in a voice that squeaked.

"Our visitor heard of your magazine. May we inspect it?" I nodded, not trusting my voice, and handed it to him, but the white man took it.

He showed the cover to the alien. "This is what we expected you to look like."

"Sorry to disappoint," it said in a voice that sounded like it came from a cave. It took the magazine in an ugly hand, too many fingers and warts that moved, and inspected it with first one eye, and then the other.

It held the magazine up and pointed to it, with a smaller hand. "I would like to buy this."

"I—I can't take white people's money. Only dirhams or, or trade."

"Barter," it said, surprising me. "That is when people exchange things of unequal value, and both think they have gotten the better deal."

The imam looked like he was trying to swallow a pill. "That's true enough," I said. "At best, they both do get better deals, by their own reckoning."

"Here, then." It reached into a pocket or a pouch—I couldn't tell whether it was wearing clothes—and brought out a ball of light.

It held out the light to a point midway between us, and let go. It floated in the air. "The light will stay wherever you put it."

It shimmered a brilliant blue, with fringes of rainbow colours. "How long will it last?"

"Longer than you."

It was one of the most beautiful things I had ever seen. I touched it with my finger—it felt cool, and tingled—and pushed it a few inches. It stayed where I moved it.

"It's a deal, sir. Thank you."

"*Shukran,*" it said, and they moved on down the line of tables.

I don't think it bought anything else. But it might have. I kept looking away from it, back into the light.

The imams and the white scientists all want to take the light away to study it. Eventually, I will loan it out.

For now, though, it is a Christmas gift to my son and daughter. The faithful, and the merely curious, come to look at it, and wonder. But it stays in my house.

In Chrislam, as in old Islam, angels are not humanlike creatures with robes and wings. They are *male'ikah*, beings of pure light.

They look wonderful on the top of a tree.

INTRODUCTION TO "THE MARS GIRL"

When I wrote the first line of this story I had no idea that I was embarking on a six-year project. The story grew into a novel that grew into a trilogy (*Marsbound*, *Starbound*, and *Earthbound*), which I hope is the best long thing I've written.

Gardner Dozois and Jack Dann had asked me to write a story for their anthology *Escape from Earth*, which had an attractive premise. Most sf readers my age (and somewhat older and younger) grew up on the Robert Heinlein "young adult" novels—though that particular classification didn't exist at the time—like *Rocket Jockey*, *Farmer in the Sky*, and *Podkayne of Mars*. Gardner wanted long stories, novellas, written in that vein, though with a modern lack of restrictions on subject matter and expression.

Getting paid to reinvent Heinlein was irresistible. For research I revisited Podkayne, I guess with the question in my mind, "How would I write this differently?" I didn't know it would take till 2012 to completely answer the question.

THE MARS GIRL

1. GOODBYE, COOL WORLD

The space elevator is the only elevator in the world with barf bags. My brother Card pointed that out. He notices things like that; I noticed the bathroom. One bathroom, for forty-some people. Locked in an elevator for two weeks. It's not as big as it looks in the advertisements.

It wasn't too bad, actually, once we started going up. Nothing like the old-fashioned way of getting into orbit, strapped to a million pounds of high explosive. We lost weight slowly during the week it took us to get to the Orbit Hilton, where we were weightless. We dropped off a dozen or so rich tourists there (and spent a couple of hours and no money, looking around) and then continued crawling up the Elevator for another week, to where our Mars ship the *John Carter* was parked, waiting.

The newsies called it "Kids in Space," hand me a barf bag. The Mars colony had like seventy-five people, aged from the early thirties to the late sixties, and they wanted to add some young people. They set up a lottery among scientists and engineers with children age nine and older, and my parents were among the nine couples chosen, so they dragged me (Carmen Dula) and Card along.

Card thought it was wonderful, and I'll admit I thought it was spec, too, at the time. So Card and I got to spend a year of Saturday mornings training to take the test—just us; there was no test for parents. Adults make it or they don't, depending on things like education. Our parents have enough education for any dozen normal people.

These tests were basically to make *us* seem normal, or at least normal enough not to go detroit locked up in a sardine can with twenty-nine other people for six months.

So here's the billion-dollar question: Did any of the kids aboard pass the tests just because they actually were normal? Or did all of them also give up a year of Saturdays so they could learn how to hide their homicidal tendencies from the testers?

And the trillion-dollar question is "What was I *thinking*?" We had to stay on Mars a minimum of five years. I would be twenty-one, having pissed away my precious teenage years on a rusty airless rock.

So anyhow. Going aboard the good ship *John Carter* were seven boys and seven girls, along with their eighteen parents and one sort of attractive pilot, Paul Santos, not quite twice my age.

I just turned sixteen but am starting college. Which I'll attend by virtual reality and email. No wicked fraternity parties, no experimenting with drugs and sex and finding out how much beer you can hold before overflowing. Maybe this whole Mars thing was a ruse my parents made up to keep me off campus. My education was going to be so incomplete!

The living area of the *John Carter* was huge, compared to the Elevator. We had separate areas for study and exercise and meals, and a sleeping floor away from the parents, as long as we behaved. I roomed with my best friends aboard, Elspeth and Kaimei, from Israel and California.

We spent the first couple of hours strapped in, up in the lander on top of the ship. Most of the speed we needed for getting to Mars was "free"— when we left the high orbit at the end of the Space Elevator, we were like a stone thrown from an old-fashioned sling, or a bit of mud flung from a bicycle tire. Two weeks of relatively slow crawling built up into one big boost, from the orbit of Earth to the orbit of Mars.

We started out strapped in because there were course corrections, all automatic. The ship studied our progress and then pointed in different directions and made small bursts of thrust, which Paul studied but didn't correct. Then we unstrapped and floated back to the artificial gravity of the rotating living area.

It would take six months to get to Mars, most of it schoolwork and exercising. I started class at the University of Maryland in the second week.

I was not the most popular girl in my classes—I wasn't *in* class at all, of course, except as a face in a cube. As we moved away from Earth and the time delay grew longer, it became impossible for me to respond in real time to what was going on. So if I had questions to ask, I had to time it so I was asking them at the beginning of class the next day.

That's a prescription for making yourself a tiresome know-it-all bitch. I had all day to think about the questions and look stuff up. So I was always thoughtful and relevant and a tiresome know-it-all bitch. Of course it didn't help at all that I was younger than everybody else and a brave pioneer headed for another planet. The novelty of that wore off real fast.

Card wasn't having any such problems. But he already knew most of his classmates, some of them since grade school, and was more social anyhow. I've always been the youngest in my class, and the brain.

It's not as if anybody had forced me into the situation. I was bored as hell in grade school and middle school, and when I was given the option of testing out of a grade and skipping ahead, I did it, three times. Not a big problem when you're eight and ten and twelve. It *is* a problem when you're barely sixteen and everybody else is "college age," at least by the calendar.

I'm also a little behind them socially, or a lot behind. I had male friends but didn't date much. Still a virgin, technically, and when I'm around older kids feel like I'm wearing a sign proclaiming that fact.

That raised an interesting possibility. I never could see myself still a virgin at twenty-one. I might wind up being the first girl to lose it on Mars—or on any other planet at all. Maybe some day they'd put up a plaque: "In this storage room on such-and-such a date..."

About a month out, we developed a little problem, that we hoped wouldn't kill everybody more or less slowly. The ship started losing air, slowly but surely. We found out it was leaking out of the lander, but couldn't find the leak. So we just closed the airlock between the lander and the living quarters.

Paul was not happy about that, having to run things away from his pilot's console, using a laptop. But it wasn't like he had to steer around asteroids or anything.

The six months actually went by pretty fast. You might think that being locked up in a space ship would drive people crazy, but in fact it seemed to drive them sane, even the youngest. The idea of "Spaceship Earth" is such an old cliché that Granddad makes a face at it. But being constantly aware that we were isolated, surrounded by space, did seem to make us more considerate of one another. So if Earth is just a bigger ship, why couldn't they learn to be as virtuous as we are? Maybe they don't choose their crew carefully enough.

Anyhow, Mars became the brightest star, and then a little circle, and then a planet. We pumped air back into the lander and left our home there in orbit. Some people took pills as they strapped in. I wasn't that smart.

2. DOWN TO MARS

Someday, maybe before I'm dead, Mars will have its own Space Elevator, but until then people have to get down there the old-fashioned way, in space-shuttle mode. It's like the difference between taking an elevator from the top floor of a building, or jumping off with an umbrella and a prayer. Fast and terrifying.

We'd lived with the lander as part of our home for weeks, and then as a mysterious kind of threatening presence, airless and waiting. Most of us weren't eager to go into it.

Before we'd made our second orbit of Mars, Paul opened the inner door, prepared to crack the airlock, and said, "Let's go."

We'd been warned, so we were bundled up against the sudden temperature drop when the airlock opened, and were not surprised that our ears popped painfully. But then we had to take our little metal suitcases and float through the airlock to go strap into our assigned seats, and try not to shit while we dropped like a rock to our doom.

From my studies I knew that the lander loses velocity by essentially trading speed for heat—hitting the thin Martian atmosphere at a drastic angle so the ship heats up to cherry red. What the diagrams in the physical science book don't show is the toothrattling vibration, the bucking and gut-wrenching wobble. If I'm never that scared again in my life I'll be really happy.

All of the violence stopped abruptly when the lander decided to become a glider, I guess a few hundred miles from the landing strip. I wished we had windows like a regular airplane, but then realized that might be asking for a heart attack. It was scary enough just to squint at Paul's two-foot-wide screen as the ground rose up to meet us, too steep and fast to believe.

We landed on skis, grating and rumbling along the rocky ground. They'd moved all the big rocks out of our way, but we felt every one of the small ones. Paul had warned us to keep our tongues away from our teeth, which was a good thing. It could be awkward, starting out life on a new planet unable to speak because you've bitten off your tongue.

We hadn't put on the Mars suits for the flight down; they were too bulky to fit in the close-ranked seats—and I guess there wasn't any disaster scenario where we would still be alive and need them. So the first order of the day was to get dressed for our new planet.

We'd tested them several times, but Paul wanted to be super-cautious the first time they were actually exposed to the Martian near-vacuum. The airlock would only hold two people at once, so we went out one at a time, with Paul observing us, ready to toss us back inside if trouble developed.

We unpacked the suits from storage under the deck and sorted them out. One for each person and two blobby general-purpose ones.

We were to leave in reverse alphabetical order, which was no fun, since it made our family dead last. The lander had never felt particularly claustrophobic before, but now it was like a tiny tin can, the sardines slowly exiting one by one.

At least we could see out, via the pilot's screen. He'd set the camera on the base, where all seventy-five people had gathered to watch us land, or crash. That led to some morbid speculation on Card's part. What if we'd crash-landed into them? I guess we'd be just as likely to crash into the base behind them. I'd rather be standing outside with a space suit on, too.

We'd seen pictures of the base a million times, not to mention endless diagrams and descriptions of how everything worked, but it was kind of exciting to see it in real time, to actually be here. The farm part looked bigger than I'd pictured it, I guess because the people standing around gave it scale. Of course the people lived underneath, staying out of the radiation.

It was interesting to have actual gravity. I said it felt different and Mom agreed, with a scientific explanation. Residual centripetal blah blah blah. I'll just call it real gravity, as opposed to the manufactured kind. Organic gravity.

A lot of people undressed on the spot and got into their Mars suits. I didn't see any point in standing around for an hour in the thing. I'm also a little shy, in a selective way. I waited until Paul was on the other side of the airlock before I revealed my unvoluptuous figure and barely necessary bra. Which I'd have to take off anyhow, for the skinsuit part of the Mars suit.

That part was like a lightweight body stocking. It fastened up the front with a gecko strip and then you pushed a button on your wrist and something electrical happened and it clasped your body like a big rubber glove. It could be sexy-looking if your body was. Most people looked like big gray cartoons, the men with a little more detail than I wanted to see.

The outer part of the Mars suit was more like lightweight armor, kind of loose and clanky when you put it on, but it also did an electrical thing when you zipped up, and fit more closely. Then clumsy boots and gloves and a helmet, all airtight. The joints would sigh when you moved your arms or legs or bent at the waist.

Card's suit had a place for an extension at the waist, since he could grow as much as a foot taller while we were here. Mine didn't have any such refinement, though the chest part was optimistically roomy.

Since we did follow strict anti-alphabetical order, Card got the distinction of being the last one out, and I was next to last. I got in the airlock with Paul, and he checked my oxygen tank and the seals on my helmet, gloves, and boots. Then he pumped most of the air out, watching the clock, and asked me to count even numbers backward from thirty. (I asked him whether he had an obsession with backward lists.) He smiled at me through the helmet and kept his hand on my shoulder as the rest of the air pumped out and the door silently swung open.

The sky was brighter than I'd expected, and the ground darker. "Welcome to Mars," Paul said on the suit radio, sounding really far away.

We walked down a metal ramp to the sandy rock-strewn ground. I stepped onto another planet.

How many people had ever done that?

Everything was suddenly different. This was the most real thing I'd ever done.

They could talk until they were blue in the face about how special this was, brave new frontier, leaving the cradle of Earth, whatever, and it's finally just words. When I felt the crunch of Martian soil under my boot it was suddenly all very plain and wonderful. I remembered an old cube—a movie—of one of the first guys on the Moon, jumping around like a little kid, and I jumped myself, and again, way high.

"Careful!" came Paul's voice over the radio. "Get used to it first."

"Okay, okay." While I walked, feather light, toward the other airlock, I tried to figure out how many people had actually done it, set foot on another world. A little more than a hundred, in all of history. And me one of them, now.

There were four people waiting at the airlock door; everyone else had gone inside. I looked around at the rusty desert and stifled the urge to run off and explore—I mean, for more than three months we hadn't been able to go more than a few dozen feet in any direction, and here was a whole new world. But there would be time. Soon!

Mother was blinking away tears, unable to touch her face behind the helmet, crying with happiness. The dream of her lifetime. I hugged her, which felt strange, both of us swaddled in insulation. Our helmets clicked together and for a moment I heard her laugh.

While Paul went back to get Card, I just looked around. I'd spent hours there in virtual, of course, but that was fake. This was hard-edged and strange, even fearsome in a way. A desert with rocks. Yellow sky of air so thin it would kill you in a breath.

When Card got to the ground, he jumped higher than I had. Paul grabbed him by the arm and walked him over.

The airlock held four people. Paul and the two strangers gestured for us to go in when the door opened. It closed automatically behind us and a red light throbbed for about a minute. I could hear the muffled clicking of a pump. Then a green light and the inside door sighed open.

We stepped into the greenhouse, a dense couple of acres of grain and vegetables and dwarf fruit trees. A woman in shorts and a T-shirt motioned for us to take off our helmets.

She introduced herself as Emily. "I keep track of the airlock and suits," she said. "Follow me and we'll get you square."

Feeling overdressed, we clanked down a metal spiral stair to a room full of shelves and boxes, the walls unpainted rock. One block of metal shelves was obviously for our crew, names written on bright new tape under shelves that held folded Mars suits and the titanium suitcases.

"Just come on through to the mess hall after you're dressed," she said. "Place isn't big enough to get lost. Not yet." They planned to more than double the underground living area while we were here.

I helped Mother out of her suit and she helped me. I needed a shower and some clean clothes. My jumpsuit was wrinkled and damp with old sweat, fear sweat from the landing. I didn't smell like a petunia myself. But we were all in the same boat.

Paul and the two other men in Mars suits were rattling down the stairs as we headed for the mess hall. The top half of the corridor was smooth plastic that radiated uniform dim light, like the tubes that had linked the Space Elevator to the Hilton and the *John Carter*. The bottom half was numbered storage drawers.

I knew what to expect of the mess hall and the other rooms; the colony was a series of inflated half-cylinders inside a large irregular tunnel, a natural pipe through an ancient lava flow. Someday the whole thing would be closed off and filled with air like the part we'd just left, but for the time being everyone lived and worked in the reinforced balloons.

It all seemed pretty huge after living in a space ship. I don't suppose it would be that imposing if you went there directly from a town or a city on Earth.

The mess hall wasn't designed for everyone to crowd in there at once. Most of the colonists were standing around at the far end. There were two dining tables with plenty of empty chairs for us new people. We sat down, I guess all of us feeling a little awkward. Everybody sort of staring and nodding. We hadn't seen a stranger since the Hilton—but then none of these Martians had seen a new person since the last ship, fifteen months before.

I looked through the crowd and immediately picked out Oz. He gave me a little wave and I returned it.

The room had two large false windows, like the ones on the ship, looking out onto the desert. I assumed they were real-time. Nothing was moving, but then all the life on the planet was presumably right here.

You could see our lander sitting at the end of a mile-long plowed groove. I wondered whether Paul had cut it too close, stopping a couple of hundred feet away. He'd said the landing was mostly automatic, but I didn't see him let go of the joystick.

There was a carafe of water on the table, and some glasses. I poured half a glass, careful not to spill any, feeling everybody's eyes on me. Water was precious here, at least for the time being.

When Paul and the other two came into the room, an older woman stepped forward. Like many of them, men and women, she was wearing a belted robe made of some filmy material. She was pale and bony.

"Welcome to Mars. Of course I've spoken with most of you. I'm Dargo Solingen, current general administrator.

"The first couple of ares"—Martian days—"you are here, just settle in and get used to your new home. Explore and ask questions. We've assigned temporary living and working spaces to everyone, a compromise between the wish list you sent a couple of weeks ago and…reality." She shrugged. "It will be a little tight until the new module is in place. We will start on that as soon as the ship is unloaded."

She almost smiled, though it looked like she didn't have much practice with it. "It is strange to see children. It will be an interesting social experiment."

"One you don't quite approve of?" Dr. Jefferson said.

"You may as well know that I don't. But I was not consulted."

"Dr. Solingen," a woman behind her said in a tone of warning.

"I guess none of you were," he said. "It was an Earth decision."

Oz stepped forward. "We were polled. Most of us were very much in favor."

The woman who had cautioned Solingen joined him. "A hundred percent of the permanent party. Those of us who are not returning to Earth." She was either pregnant or the only fat person in the room. Looking more carefully, I saw one other woman who appeared to be pregnant.

You'd think that would have been on the news. Maybe it was, and I missed it, not likely. Mother and I exchanged significant glances. Something was going on.

3. MOVING IN

It turned out to be nothing more mysterious than a desire for privacy on the women's part, and everybody's desire to keep Earth out of their hair. When the first child was born, the Earth press would be all over them. Until then, there was no need for anyone to know the blessed event was nigh. So they asked that we not mention the pregnancies when writing or talking to home.

I shared a small room with Elspeth and Kaimei—an air mattress on the floor and a bunk bed. We agreed to rotate, so everyone would have an actual bed two-thirds of the time.

There was only one desk, with a small screen and a clunky keyboard and an old VR helmet with a big dent on the side. The timing for that worked out okay, since Elspeth had classes seven hours before Eastern time, and Kaimei three hours later. We drew up a chart and taped it to the wall. The only conflict was my physical science class versus Kaimei's History of Tao and Buddhism. Mine was mostly equations on the board, so I used the screen and let her have the helmet.

Our lives were pretty regimented the first couple of weeks, because we had to coordinate classes with the work roster here, and leave a little time for eating and sleeping.

Everybody was impatient to get the new module set up, but it wasn't just a matter of unloading and inflating it. First there was a light exoskeleton of spindly metal rods that became rigid when they were all pulled together. Then floorboards to bear the weight of the things and people inside. Then the connection to the existing base, through an improvised airlock until they were sure the module wouldn't leak.

I enjoyed working on that, at first outdoors, unloading the ship and sorting and pre-assembling some parts; then later, down in the lava cave, attaching the new to the old. I got used to working in the Mars suit and using the "dog," a wheeled machine about the size of a large dog. It carried backup oxygen and power.

About half the time, though, my work roster put me inside, helping the younger ones do their lessons and avoid boredom. "Mentoring," they called it, to make it sound more important than babysitting.

One day, though, while I was just getting off work detail, Paul came up and asked whether I'd like to go exploring with him. What, skip math? I got fresh oxygen and helped him check out one of the dogs and we went for a walk.

The surface of Mars might look pretty boring to an outsider, but it's not at all. It must be the same if you live in a desert on Earth: you pretty much have the space around your home memorized, every little mound and rock—and when you venture out it's "Wow! A different rock!"

He took me off to the left of Telegraph Hill, walking at a pretty good pace. The base was below the horizon in less than ten minutes. We were still in radio contact as long as we could see the antenna on top of the hill, and if we wanted to go farther, the dog had a collapsible booster antenna that went up ten meters, which we could leave behind as a relay.

We didn't need it for that, but Paul clicked it up into place when we came to the edge of a somewhat deep crater he wanted to climb into.

"Be really careful," he said. "We have to leave the dog behind. If we both were to fall and be injured, we'd be in deep shit."

I followed him, watching carefully as we picked our way to the top. Once there, he turned around and pointed.

It's hard to really say how strange the sight was. We weren't that high up, but you could see the curvature of the horizon. To the right of Telegraph Hill, the gleam of the greenhouse roof. The dog behind us looked tiny but unnaturally clear, in the near vacuum.

Paul was carrying a white bag, now a little rust-streaked from the dust. He pulled out a photo-map of the crater, unfolded it, and showed it to me. There were about twenty X's, starting on the top of the crater rim, where we must have been standing, then down the incline, and across the crater floor to its central peak.

"Dust collecting," he said. "How's your oxygen?"

I chinned the readout button. "Three hours forty minutes."

"That should be plenty. Now you don't have to go down if you—"

"I do! Let's go!"

"Okay. Follow me." I didn't tell him that my impatience wasn't all excitement, but partly anxiety at having to talk and pee at the same time. Peeing standing up, into a diaper, trying desperately not to fart. "Funny as a fart in a space suit" probably goes back to the beginning of space flight, but there's nothing real funny about it in reality. I'd taken two anti-gas tablets before I came out, and they seemed to still be working.

Keeping your footing was a little harder, going downhill. Paul had the map folded over so it only showed the path down the crater wall; every thirty or forty steps he would fish through the bag and take out a pre-labeled plastic vial, and scrape a sample of dirt into it.

On the floor of the crater I felt a little shiver of fear at our isolation. Looking back the way we'd come, though, I could see the tip of the dog's antenna.

The dust was deeper than I'd seen anyplace else, I guess because the crater walls kept out the wind. Paul took two samples as we walked toward the central peak.

"You better stay down here, Carmen. I won't be long." The peak was steep, and he scrambled up it like a monkey. I wanted to yell "Be careful," but kept my mouth shut.

Looking up at him, the sun behind me, I could see Earth gleaming blue in the ochre sky. How long had it been since I thought of Earth, other than "the place where school is"? I guess I hadn't been here long enough to feel homesickness. Nostalgia for Earth—crowded place with lots of gravity and heat.

It might be the first time I seriously thought about staying. In five years I'd be twenty-one and Paul would still be under forty. I didn't feel romantic about him, but I liked him and he was funny. That would put us way ahead of a lot of marriages I'd observed.

Romance was for movies and books, anyhow. When actual people you know started acting that way, they were so ridiculous.

But then how did I really feel about Paul? Up there being heroic and competent and, admit it, sexy.

Turn down the heat, girl. He's only twelve years younger than your father, probably sterile from radiation, too. I didn't think I wanted children, but it would be nice to have the option.

He collected his samples and tossed the bag down. It drifted slowly, rotating, and landed about ten feet away. I was enough of a Martian to be surprised to hear a click when it landed, the soles of my boots picking the noise up, conducted through the rock of the crater floor.

He worked his way down slowly, which was a relief. I was holding the sample bag; he took it and I followed him back the way we had come.

At the top of the crater wall, he stopped and looked back. "Can't see it from here," he said. "I'll show you."

"What?"

"My greatest triumph," he said, and started down. "You'll be impressed."

He didn't offer any further explanation on the ground. He picked up the dog's handle and proceeded to walk around to the other side of the crater.

It was a dumbo, an unpiloted supply vehicle. Its rear end was tilted up, the nose down in a small crater.

"I brought her in like that. I was not the most popular man on Mars." As we approached it, I could see the ragged hole someone had cut in the side with a torch or a laser. "Landed it right on the bay door, too."

"Wow. I'm glad you weren't hurt."

He laughed. "It was remote control; I landed it from a console inside the base. Harder than being aboard, actually." We turned around and headed back to the base.

"It was a judgment call. There was a lot of variable wind, and it was yawing back and forth." He made a hand motion like a fish swimming. "I was sort of trying not to hit the base or Telegraph Hill. But I overdid it."

"People could understand that."

"Understanding isn't forgiving. Everybody had to stop their science and become pack animals." I could see the expression on Solingen's face, having to do labor, and smiled.

She really had something against me. I had to do twice as much babysitting as Elspeth or Kaimei—and when I suggested that the boys ought to do it, too, she said that "personnel allocation" was *her* job, thank you. And when my person got allocated to an outside job, it would be something boring and repetitive, like taking inventory of supplies. (That was especially useful, in case there were Martians sneaking in at night to steal nuts and bolts.)

When we got back, I went straight to the console and found a blinking note from the Dragon herself, noting that I had missed math class, saying she wanted a copy of my homework. Did she monitor anybody else's VR attendance?

I'd had the class recorded, of course, the super-exciting chain rule for differentiation. I fell asleep twice, hard to do in VR, and had to start over.

Then I had a problem set with fifty chains to differentiate. Wrap me in chains and throw me in the differential dungeon, but I had to sleep. I got the air mattress partly inflated and flopped onto it without undressing.

Not delivering my homework like a good little girl got me into a special corner of Dargo Hell. I had to turn over my notes and homework in maths every day to Ana Sitral, who obviously didn't have time for checking it. She must have done something to piss off the Dragon herself.

Then I had to take on over half of the mentoring hours that Kaimei and Elspeth had been covering, and was not allowed any outside time. I had been selfish, Dargo said, tiring myself out on a silly lark, using up resources that might be needed for real work. So I had the temerity to suggest that part of my real work was getting to know Mars, and she really blew up about that. It was not up to me to make up my own training schedule.

Okay, part of it was that she didn't like kids. But part was also that she didn't like *me*, and wouldn't if I was a hundred years old. She didn't bother to hide that from anybody. I complained to Mother and she didn't disagree, but said I had to learn to work with people like that. Especially here, where there wasn't much choice.

I didn't bother complaining to Dad. He would make a Growth Experience out of it. I should try to see the world her way. Sorry, Dad. If I saw the world her way and thought about Carmen Dula, wouldn't that be self-loathing? That would not be a positive growth experience.

4. FISH OUT OF WATER

After a month, I was able to put a Mars suit on again, but I didn't go up to the surface. There was plenty of work down below, inside the lava tube that protected the base from cosmic and solar radiation.

There's plenty of water on Mars, but most of it is in the wrong place. If it was on or near the surface, it had to be at the north or south pole. We couldn't put bases there, because they were in total darkness a lot of the time, and we needed solar power.

But there was a huge lake hidden more than a kilometer below the base. It was the easiest one to get to on all of Mars, we learned from some kind of satellite radar, which was why the base was put here. One of the things we'd brought on the *John Carter* was a drilling system designed to tap it. (The drills that came with the first ship and the third broke, though, the famous Mars Luck.)

I worked with the team that set the drill up, nothing more challenging than fetch-and-carry, but a lot better than trying to mentor kids when you wanted to slap them instead.

For a while we could hear the drill, a faint sandpapery sound that was conducted through the rock. Then it was quiet, and most of us forgot about it. A few weeks later, though, it was Sagan 12th, which from then on would be Water Day.

We put on Mars suits and then walked down between the wall of the lava tube and the base's exterior wall. It was kind of creepy, just suit lights, less than a meter between the cold rock and the inflated plastic you weren't supposed to touch.

Then there was light ahead, and we came out into swirling madness—it was a blizzard! The drill had struck water and sent it up under pressure, several liters a minute. When it hit the cold vacuum it exploded into snow.

It was ankle-deep in places, but of course it wouldn't last; the vacuum would evaporate it eventually. But people were already working with lengths of pipe, getting ready to fill the waiting tanks up in the hydroponics farm. One of them had already been dubbed the swimming pool. And that's how the trouble started.

I got on the work detail that hooked the water supply up to the new pump. That was to go in two stages: emergency and "maintenance."

The emergency stage worked on the reasonable assumption that the pump wasn't going to last very long. So we wanted to save every drop of water we could, while it still did work.

This was the "water boy" stage. We had collapsible insulated water containers that held fifty liters each. That's 110 pounds on Earth, about my own weight, awkward but not too heavy to handle on Mars.

All ten of the older kids spent a couple of hours on duty, a couple off, doing water boy. We had wheelbarrows, three of them, so it wasn't too tiring. You fill the thing with water, which takes eight minutes, then turn off the valve and get away fast, so not too much pressure builds up before the next person takes over. Then trundle the wheelbarrow around to the airlock, leave it there, and carry or drag the water bag across the farm to the storage tanks. Dump in the water—a slurry of ice by then—and go back to the pump with your wheelbarrow.

The work was boring as dust, and would drive you insane if you didn't have music. I started out being virtuous, listening to classical pieces that went along with a book on the history of music. But as the days droned by, I listened to more and more city and even sag.

You didn't have to be a math whiz to see that it was going to take three weeks at this rate to fill the first tank, which was two meters tall and eight meters wide, bigger than some backyard pools in Florida.

The water didn't stay icy; they warmed it up to above room temperature. We all must have fantasized about diving in there and paddling around. Elspeth and Kaimei and I even planned for it.

There was no sense in asking permission from the Dragon. What we were going to do was coordinate our showers so we'd all be squeaky clean—so nobody could say we were contaminating the water supply—and come in the same time, off shift, and see whether we could get away with a little skinny-dip. Or see how long we could do it before somebody stopped us.

Jordan Westling, Barry's inventor dad, seemed to be in charge of that team. We always got along pretty well. He was old but always had a twinkle in his eye.

He and I were alone by the tank while he fiddled with some tubing and gauges. I lifted the water bag with a groan and poured it in.

"This ought to be the last day you have to do that," he said. "We should be on line in a few hours."

"Wow." I stepped up on a box and looked at the water level. It was more than half full, with a layer of red sediment at the bottom. "Dr. Westling... what would happen if somebody went swimming in this?"

He didn't look up from the gauge. "I suppose if somebody washed up first and didn't pee in the pool, nobody would have to know. It's not exactly distilled water. Not that I would endorse such an activity."

When I went back to the water point I touched helmets with Kaimei—that way you can talk without using the suit radio, which is probably monitored—and we agreed we'd do it at 02:15, just after the end of the next shift. She'd pass the word on to Elspeth, who came on at midnight. That would give her time to have a quick shower and smuggle a towel up to the tank.

I got off at 10 and VR'ed a class on Spinoza, better than any sleeping pill. I barely stayed awake long enough to set the alarm for 1:30.

Two and a half hours' sleep was plenty. I awoke with eager anticipation and, alone in the room, put on a robe and slippers and quietly made my way to the shower.

Kaimei had already bathed, and was sitting outside the shower with a reader. I took my two-liter shower and, while I was drying, Elspeth came in from work, wearing skinsuit and socks.

After she showered, the three of us tiptoed past the work/study area—a couple of people were working there, but a hanging partition kept them from being distracted by passersby.

The mess hall was deserted. We went up through the changing room and the airlock foyer and slipped into the farm.

There were only dim maintenance lights at this hour. We padded our way to the swimming pool tank—and heard whispered voices!

Oscar Jefferson, Barry Westling, and my idiot brother had beat us to it!

"Hey girls," Oscar said. "Look—we're out of a job." A faucet in the side was gurgling out a narrow stream.

"My father said we could quit," Barry said, "so we thought we'd take a swim to celebrate."

"You didn't tell him," I said.

"Do we look like idiots?" No, they looked like naked boys. "Come on in. The water's not too cold."

I looked at the other two girls and they shrugged okay. Space ships and Mars bases don't give you a lot of room for modesty.

I sort of liked the way Barry looked at me anyhow, when I stepped out of my robe and slippers. When Kaimei undressed, his look might have been a little more intense.

I stepped up on the box and had one leg over the edge of the tank when the lights snapped on full.

"Caught you!" Dargo Solingen marched down the aisle between the tomatoes and the squash. "I *knew* you'd do this." She looked at me, one foot on the box and the other dangling in space. "And I know exactly who the ringleader is."

She stood with her hands on her hips, studying. Elspeth was only half undressed, but the rest of us were obviously ready for some teenaged sex orgy. "Get out, now. Get dressed and come to my office at 0800. We will have a disciplinary hearing." She stomped back to the door and snapped off the bright lights on her way out.

"I'll tell her it wasn't you," Card said. "We just kind of all decided when Barry's dad said the thing was working."

"She won't believe you," I said, stepping down. "She's been after my ass all along."

"Who wouldn't be?" Barry said, studying the subject. He was such a born romantic.

All of our parents were crowded into the Dragon's office at 0800. That was not good. My parents both were working the shift from 2100 to 0400, and needed their sleep. The parents were on one side of the room, and we were on the other, separated by a large video screen.

Without any preamble, Dargo Solingin made the charge: "Last night your children went for a swim in the new Water Tank One. Tests on the water reveal traces of coliform bacteria, so it cannot be used for human consumption without boiling or some other form of sterilization."

"It was only going to be used for hydroponics," Dr. Westling said.

"You can't say that for certain. At any rate, it was an act of extreme irresponsibility, and one that you encouraged." She pointed a hand control at the video screen and clicked. I saw myself talking to him.

"What would happen if somebody went swimming in this?" He answered that nobody would have to know—not that he would endorse such a thing. He was restraining a smile.

"You're secretly recording me?" he said incredulously.

"Not you. Her."

"She didn't do it!" Card blurted out. "It was my idea."

"You will speak when spoken to," she said coldly. "Your loyalty to your sister is touching, but misplaced." She clicked again, and there was a picture of me and Kaimei at the water point, touching helmets.

"Tonight has to be skinny-dipping night. Dr Westling says they'll be on line in a few hours. Let's make it 0215, right after Elspeth gets off." You could hear Kaimei's faint agreement.

"You had my daughter's suit bugged?" my father said.

"Not really. I just disabled the OFF switch on her suit communicator."

"That is so...so illegal. On Earth they'd throw you out of court and then—"

"This isn't Earth. And on Mars, there is nothing more important than water. As you would appreciate if you had lived here as long as I have." Oh, sure. I think you could live longer without water than without air.

"Besides, it was improper for the boys and girls to be together naked. Even if they hadn't planned any sexual misbehavior—"

"Oh, please," I said. "Excuse me for speaking out of turn, Dr. Solingen, but there was nothing like that. We didn't even know the boys would be there."

"Really. The timing was remarkable, then. And you weren't acting surprised about them when I turned on the lights. Nor modest." Card was squirming, and put up his hand, but the Dragon ignored it. She turned to the parents. "I want to discuss with you what punishment might be appropriate."

"Twenty laps a day in the pool," Dr. Westling said, almost snarling. He didn't like her anyhow, I'd noticed, and spying on him apparently had been the straw that broke the camel's back. "They're just kids, for Chris'sake."

"You're going to say they didn't mean any harm. They have to learn that Mars doesn't recognize that as an excuse.

"An appropriate punishment, I think, would start with not allowing them to bathe for a month. I would also reduce the amount of water they be allowed to drink, but that is difficult to control. And I wouldn't want to endanger their health." God, she is so All Heart.

"For that month, I would also deny them recreational use of the cube and VR, and no exploring on the surface. Double that for the instigator, Ms. Dula"—and she turned back to face us—"and her brother as well, if he insists on sharing the responsibility."

"I *do*!" he snapped.

"Very well. Two months for both of you."

"It seems harsh," Kaimei's father said. "Kaimei told me that the girls did take the precaution of showering before entering the water."

"Intent means nothing. The bacteria are there."

"Harmless to plants," Dr. Westling repeated.

She looked at him for a long second. "Your dissent is noted. Are there any other objections to this punishment?"

"Not the punishment," my mother said, "but Dr. Dula and I both object to the means of acquiring evidence."

"I am perfectly willing to stand on review for that." The oldtimers would probably go along with her. The new ones might still be infected by the Bill of Rights, or the laws of Russia and France and Israel.

There were no other objections, so she reminded the parents that they would be responsible for monitoring our VR and cube use, but even more, she would rely on our sense of honor.

What were we supposed to be "honoring," though? The now old-fashioned sanctity of water? Her right to spy on us? In fact, her unlimited authority?

I would find a way to get back at her.

5. NIGHTWALK

After one day of steaming over it, I'd had enough. I don't know when I made the decision, or whether it even *was* a decision, rather than a kind of sleepwalking. It was sometime before three in the morning. I was still feeling so angry and embarrassed I couldn't get to sleep.

So I got up and started down the corridor to the mess hall, nibble on something. But I walked on past.

It looked like no one else was up. Just dim safety lights. I wound up in the dressing room and realized what I was doing.

Paul had shown me how to prop a pencil in the inner door so that the airlock chime wouldn't go off. With that disabled, a person could actually go outside alone, undetected. I could just be by myself for an hour or two, then sneak back in.

And did I ever want to be by myself.

I went through the dress-up procedure as quietly as possible. Then before I took a step toward the airlock, I visualized myself doing a safety check on another person and did it methodically on myself. It would be so pathetic to die out there, breaking the rules.

I went up the stairs silently as a thief. Well, I *was* a thief. What could they do, deport me?

For safety's sake, I decided to take a dog, even though it would slow me down a bit. I actually hesitated, and tested carrying two extra oxygen bottles by themselves, but that was awkward. *Better safe than sorry*, I said to myself in Mother's voice, and ground my teeth while saying it. But going out without a dog and dying would be pathetic. Arch-criminals are evil, not pathetic.

The evacuating pump sounded loud, though I knew you could hardly hear it in the changing room. It rattled off into silence, then the red light glowed green and the door swung open into darkness.

I stepped out, pulling the dog, and the door slid shut behind it.

I decided not to turn on the suit light, and stood there for several minutes while my eyes adjusted. Walking at night just by starlight—you couldn't do that any other place I've lived. It wouldn't be dangerous if I was careful. Besides, if I turned on a light, someone could see me from the mess hall window.

The nearby rocks gave me my bearings, and I started out toward Telegraph Hill. On the other side I'd be invisible from the base, and vice versa—alone for the first time in almost a year. Earth year.

Seeing the familiar rock field in this ghostly half-light brought back some of the mystery and excitement of the first couple of days. The landing and my first excursion with Paul.

If he knew I was doing this—well, he might approve, secretly. He wasn't much of a rule guy, except for safety.

Thinking that, my foot turned on a small rock and I staggered, getting my balance back. Keep your eyes on the ground while you're walking. It would be, what is the word I'm looking for, *pathetic* to trip and break your helmet out here.

It took me less than a half hour to get to the base of Telegraph Hill. It wasn't all that steep, but the dog's traction wasn't really up to it. A truly adventurous person would leave the dog behind and climb to the top with her suit air alone, and although I do like adventure, I'm also afflicted with pathetico-phobia. The dog and I could go around the mountain rather than over it. I decided to walk in a straight line for one hour, see how far I could get, and walk back.

That was my big mistake. One of them, anyhow. If I'd just gone to the top, taken a picture, and headed straight back, I might have gotten away with it.

I wasn't totally stupid. I didn't go into the hill's "radio shadow," and I cranked the dog's radio antenna up all the way, since I was headed for the horizon, and knew that any small depression in the ground could hide me from the colony's radio transceiver.

The wind picked up a little. I couldn't feel or hear it, of course, but the sky showed it. Jupiter was just rising, and its bright pale yellow light had a halo, and was slightly dimmed, by the dust in the air. I remembered Dad pointing out Jupiter, and then Mars, the morning we left Florida, and had a delicious shiver at the thought that I was standing on that little point of light now.

The area immediately around the colony was as well explored as any place on Mars, but I knew from rock-hounding with Paul that you could find new stuff just a couple hundred meters from the airlock door. I went four or five kilometers, and found something really new.

I had been going for 57 minutes, about to turn back, and was looking for a soft rock that I could mark with an X or something—maybe scratch SURRENDER, PUNY EARTHLINGS on it, though I suspected people would figure out who had done it.

There was no noise. Just a suddenly weightless feeling, and I was falling through a hole in the ground—I'd broken through something like a thin sheet of ice. But there was nothing underneath it!

I was able to turn on the suit light as I tumbled down, but all I saw was a glimpse of the dog spinning around beside and then above me.

It seemed like a long time, but I guess I didn't fall for more than a few seconds. I hit hard on my left foot and heard the sickening sound of a bone cracking, just an instant before the pain hit me.

I lay still, bright red sparks fading from my vision while the pain amped up and up. Trying to think, not scream.

My ankle was probably broken, and at least one rib on the left side. I breathed deeply, listening—Paul told me about how he had broken a rib in a car wreck, and he could tell by the sound that it had punctured his lung. This did hurt, but didn't sound different—and then I realized I was lucky to be breathing at all. The helmet and suit were intact.

But would I be able to keep breathing long enough to be rescued?

The suit light was out. I clicked the switch over and over, and nothing happened. If I could find the dog, and if it was intact, I'd have an extra sixteen hours of oxygen. Otherwise, I probably had two, two and a half hours.

I didn't suppose the radio would do any good, underground, but I tried it anyway. Yelled into it for a minute and then listened. Nothing.

These suits ought to have some sort of beeper to trace people with. But then I guess nobody else ever wandered off and disappeared.

It was about four. How long before someone woke up and noticed I was gone? How long before someone got worried enough to check, and see that the suit and dog were missing?

I tried to stand and it wasn't possible. The pain was intolerable and the bone made an ominous sound. I couldn't help crying but stopped after a minute. Pathetic.

Had to find the dog, with its oxygen and power. I stretched out and patted the ground back and forth, and scrabbled around in a circle, feeling for it.

It wasn't anywhere nearby. But how far could it have rolled after it hit?

I had to be careful, not just crawl off in some random direction and get lost. I remembered feeling a large, kind of pointy, rock off to my left— good thing I hadn't landed on it—and could use it as a reference point.

I found it and moved up so my feet were touching it. Visualizing an old-fashioned clock with me as the hour hand, I went off in the 12:00 direction, measuring four body lengths inchworm style. Then crawled back to the pointy rock and did the same thing in the opposite, 6:00, direction. Nothing there, nor at 9:00 or 3:00, and I tried not to panic.

In my mind's eye I could see the areas where I hadn't been able to reach, the angles midway between 12:00 and 3:00, 3:00 and 6:00, and so on. I went back to the pointy rock and started over. On the second try, my hand touched one of the dog's wheels, and I smiled in spite of my situation.

It was lying on its side. I uprighted it and felt for the switch that would turn on its light. When it came on, I was looking straight into it and it dazzled me blind.

Facing away from it, after a couple of minutes I could see some of where I was. I'd fallen into a large underground cavern, maybe shaped like a dome, though I couldn't see as far as the top. I guessed it was part of a lava tube that was almost open to the surface, worn so thin that it couldn't support my weight.

Maybe it joined up with the lava tube that we lived in! But even if it did, and even if I knew which direction to go, I couldn't crawl the four kilometers back. I tried to ignore the pain and do the math, anyhow—sixteen hours of oxygen, four kilometers, that means creeping 250 meters per hour, dragging the dog along behind me...no way. Better to hope they would track me down here.

What were the chances of that? Maybe the dog's tracks, or my boot prints? Only in dusty places, if the wind didn't cover them up before dawn.

If they searched at night, the dog's light might help. How close would a person have to come to the hole, to see it? Close enough to crash through and join me?

And would the dog's power supply last long enough to shine all night and again tomorrow night? It wouldn't have to last any longer than that.

The ankle was hurting less, but that was because of numbness. My hands and feet were getting cold. Was that a suit malfunction, or just because I was stretched out on this cold cave floor. Where the sun had never shined.

With a start, I realized the coldness could mean that my suit was losing power—it should automatically warm up the gloves and boots. I opened my mouth wide and with my chin pressed the switch that ought to project a technical readout in front of my eyes, with "power remaining," and nothing came up.

Well, the dog obviously had power to spare. I unreeled the recharge cable and plugged its jack into my LSU.

Nothing happened.

I chinned the switch over and over. Nothing.

Maybe it was just the readout display that was broken; I was getting power but it wasn't registering. Trying not to panic, I wiggled the jack, unplugged and replugged it. Still nothing.

I was breathing, though; that part worked. I unrolled the umbilical hose from the dog and pushed the fitting into the bottom of the LSU. It made a loud pop and a sudden breeze of cold oxygen blew around my neck and chin.

So at least I wouldn't die of that. I would be frozen solid before I ran out of air; how comforting. Acid rush of panic in my throat; I choked it back and sucked on the water tube until the nausea was gone.

Which made me think about the other end, and I clamped up. I was not going to fill the suit's emergency diaper with shit and piss before I died. Though the people who deal with dead people probably have seen that before. And it would be frozen solid, so what's the difference. Inside the body or outside.

I stopped crying long enough to turn on the radio and say goodbye to people, and apologize for my stupidity. Though it's unlikely that anyone would ever hear it. Unless there was some kind of secret recorder in the suit, thanks to the Dragon, and someone stumbled on it years from now.

I wished I had Dad's zen. If Dad were in this situation he would just accept it, and wait to leave his body.

I tipped the dog up on end, so its light shone directly up toward the hole I'd fallen through, still too high up to see.

I couldn't feel my feet or hands anymore and was growing heavy-lidded. I'd read that freezing to death was the least painful way to go, and one of my last coherent thoughts was "Who came back to tell them?"

Then I hallucinated an angel, wearing red, surrounded by an ethereal bubble. He was incredibly ugly.

6. ANGEL IN HELL

I woke up in some pain, ankle throbbing and hands and feet burning. I was lying on a huge inflated pillow. The air was thick and muggy and it was dark. A yellow light was bobbing toward me, growing brighter. I heard lots of feet.

It was a flashlight, or rather a lightstick like you wear nightdancing, and the person holding it…wasn't a person. It was the red angel from my dream.

Maybe I was still dreaming. I was naked, which sometimes happens in my dreams. The dog was sitting a few feet away. My broken ankle was splinted between two pieces of what felt like wood. On Mars?

This angel had too many legs, like four, sticking out from under the red tunic thing. His head, if that's what it was, looked like a potato that had gone really bad. Soft and wrinkled and covered with eyes. Maybe they *were* eyes, lots of them, or antennae. Like fat hairs that moved around. He was almost as big as a small horse. He seemed to have two regular-sized arms and two little ones. For an angel, he smelled a lot like tuna fish.

I should have been terrified, naked in front of this monster, but he definitely was the one who had saved me from freezing to death. Or he was dressed like that one.

"Are you real?" I said. "Or am I still dreaming, or dead?"

He made some kind of noise, sort of like a bullfrog with teeth chattering. Then he whistled and the lights came on, dim but enough to see around. The unreality of it made me dizzy.

I was taking it far too calmly, maybe because I couldn't think of a thing to do. Either I was in the middle of some complicated dream, or this is what happens to you after you die, or I was completely insane, or, least likely of all, I'd been rescued by a Martian.

But a Martian wouldn't breathe oxygen, not this thick. He wouldn't have wood for making splints. Though this one might know something about ankles, having so many of them.

"You don't speak English, do you?"

He responded with a long speech that sounded kind of threatening. Maybe it was about food animals not being allowed to talk.

I was in a circular room, a little too small for both me and Big Red, with a round wall that seemed to be several layers of plastic sheeting. He had come in through slits in the plastic. The polished stone floor was warm. The high ceiling looked like the floor, but there were four bluish lights imbedded in it, that looked like cheap plastic decorations.

It felt like a hospital room, and maybe it was one. The pillow was big enough for one like him to lie down on it.

On a stone pedestal over by the dog was a pitcher and a glass made of something that looked like obsidian. He poured me a glass of something and brought it over.

His hand, also potato-brown, had four long fingers without nails, and lots of little joints. The fingers were all the same length and it looked like any one of them could be the thumb. The small hands were miniature versions of the big ones.

The stuff in the glass didn't smell like anything and tasted like water, so I drank it down in a couple of greedy gulps.

He took the glass back and refilled it. When he handed it to me, he pointed into it with a small hand, and said, "Ar." Sort of like a pirate.

I pointed and said, "Water?" He answered with a sound like "war," with a lot of extra R's.

He set down the glass and brought me a plate with something that looked remarkably like a mushroom. No, thanks. I read that story.

(For a mad moment I wondered whether that could be it—I *had* eaten, or ingested, something that caused all this, and it was one big dope dream. But the pain was too real.)

He picked the thing up delicately and a mouth opened up in his neck, broad black teeth set in grisly red. He took a small nibble and replaced it on the plate. I shook my head no, though that could mean yes in Martian. Or some mortal insult.

How long could I go without eating? A week, I supposed, but my stomach growled at the thought.

He heard the growling and pointed helpfully to a hole in the floor. That took care of one question, but not quite yet, pal. We've hardly been introduced, and I don't even let my *brother* watch me do that.

I touched my chest and said "Carmen." Then I pointed at his chest, if that's what it was.

He touched his chest and said "Harn." Well, that was a start.

"No," I took his hand— dry, raspy skin—and brought it over to touch my chest. "Car-men," I said slowly. Me Jane, you Tarzan, or Mr. Potato Head.

"Harn," he repeated, which wasn't a bad Carmen if you couldn't pronounce C or M. Then he took my hand gently and placed it between his two small arms and made a sputtering sound no human could do, at least with the mouth. He let go but I kept my hand there and said, "Red. I'll call you Red."

"Reh," he said, and repeated it. It gave me a shiver. I was communicating with an alien. Someone put up a plaque! But he turned abruptly and left.

I took advantage of being alone and hopped over to the hole and used it, not as easy as that sounds. I needed to find something to use as a crutch. This wasn't exactly Wal-Mart, though. I drank some water and hopped back to the pillow and flopped down.

My hands and feet hurt a little less. They were red, like bad sunburn, which I supposed was the first stage of frostbite. I could have lost some fingers and toes—not that it would matter much to me, with lungs full of ice.

I looked around. Was I inside of Mars or was this some kind of a space ship? You wouldn't make a space ship out of stone. We had to be underground, but this stone didn't look at all like the petrified lava of the colony's tunnel. And it was warm, which had to be electrical or something. The lights and plastic sheets looked pretty high-tech, but everything else was kind of basic—a hole in the floor? (I hoped it wasn't somebody else's ceiling!)

I mentally reviewed why there can't be higher forms of life on Mars, least of all technological life: No artifacts—we've mapped every inch of it, and anything that looked artificial turned out to be natural. Of course there's nothing to breathe, though I seemed to be breathing. Same thing with water. And temperature.

There are plenty of microscopic organisms living underground, but how could they evolve into big bozos like Red? What is there on Mars for a big animal to eat? Rocks?

Red was coming back with his lightstick, followed by someone only half his size, wearing bright lime green. Smoother skin, like a more fresh potato. I decided she was female and called her Green. Just for the time being; I might have it backward. They had seen me naked, but I hadn't seen them—and wasn't eager to, actually. They were scary enough this way.

Green was carrying a plastic bag with things inside that clicked softly together. She set the bag down carefully and exchanged a few noises with Red.

First she took out a dish that looked like pottery, and from a plastic bag shook out something that looked like an herb, or pot. It started smoking immediately, and she thrust it toward me. I sniffed it; it was pleasant, like mint or menthol. She made a gesture with her two small hands, a kind of shooing motion, that I interpreted to mean "breathe more deeply," and I did.

She took the dish away and brought two transparent disks, like big lenses, out of the bag and handed one to me. While I held it, she pressed the other one against my forehead, then chest, then the side of my leg. She gently lifted up the foot with the broken ankle, and pressed it against the sole. Then she did the other foot. She put the lenses back in her bag and stood motionless, staring at me like a doctor or scientist.

I thought, okay, this is where the alien sticks a tube up your ass, but she must have left her tube back at the office.

She and Red conferred for a while, making gestures with their small arms while they made noises like porpoises and machinery. Then she reached into the bag and pulled out a small metal tube, which caused me to cringe away, but she gave it a snap with her wrist and it ratcheted out to about six feet long. She mimicked using it as a cane, which looked really strange, like a spider missing four legs, and handed it to me, saying "Harn."

Guess that was my name now. The stick felt lighter than aluminum, but when I used it to lever myself up, it was rigid and strong.

She reached into her bag of tricks and brought out a thing like her tunic, somewhat thicker and softer and colored gray. There was a hole in it for my head, but no sleeves or other complications. I put it on gratefully and draped it around so I could use the stick. It was agreeably warm.

Red stepped ahead and, with a rippling gesture of all four hands, indicated "Follow me." I did, with Green coming behind me.

It was a strange sensation, going through the slits in those plastic sheets, or whatever they were. It was like they were alive, millions of feathery fingers clasping you and then letting go all at once, to close behind you with a snap.

When I went through the first one, it was noticeably cooler, and cooler still after the second one, and my ears popped. After the fourth one, it felt close to freezing, though the floor was still warm, and the air was noticeably thin; I was almost panting, and could see my breath.

We stepped into a huge dark cavern. Rows of dim lights at about knee level marked off paths. The lights were all blue, but each path had its own kind of blue, different in shade or intensity. Meet me at the corner of bright turquoise and dim aquamarine.

I tried to remember our route, left at this shade and then right at *this* one, but I was not sure how useful the knowledge would be. What, I was going to escape? Hold my breath and run back to the base?

We went through a single sheet into a large area, at least as well lit as my hospital room, and almost as warm. It had a kind of barnyard smell, not unpleasant. There were things that had to be plants all around, like broccoli but brown and gray with some yellow, sitting in water that you could hear was flowing. A little mist hung near the ground, and my face felt damp. It was a hydroponic farm like ours, but without greens or the bright colors of tomatoes and peppers and citrus fruits.

Green leaned over and picked something that looked like a cigar, or something less polite, and offered it to me. I waved it away; she broke it in two and gave half to Red.

I couldn't tell how big the place was, probably acres. So where were all the people it was set up to feed?

I got a partial answer when we passed through another sheet, into a brighter room about the size of the new pod we'd brought on the *John Carter*. There were about twenty of the aliens arranged along two walls, standing at tables or in front of things like data screens, but made of metal rather than plastic. There weren't any chairs; I supposed quadrupeds don't need them.

They all began to move toward me, making strange noises, of course. If I'd brought one of them into a room, humans would have done the same thing, but nevertheless I felt frightened and helpless. When I shrank back, Red put a protective arm in front of me and said a couple of bullfrog syllables. They all stopped about ten feet away.

Green talked to them more softly, gesturing toward me. Then they stepped forward in an orderly way, by colors—two in tan, three in green, two in blue, and so forth—each standing quietly in front of me for a few seconds. I wondered if the color signified rank. None of the others wore red, and none were as big as Big Red. Maybe he was the alpha male, or the only female, like bees.

What were they doing? Just getting a closer look, or taking turns trying to destroy me with thought waves?

After that presentation, Red gestured for me to come over and look at the largest metal screen.

Interesting. It was a panorama of our greenhouse and the other parts of the colony that were above ground. The picture might have been from the top of Telegraph Hill. Just as I noticed that there were a lot of people standing around—too many for a normal work party—the *John Carter* came sliding into view, a rooster tail of red dust fountaining out behind her. A lot of the people jumped up and down and waved.

Then the screen went black for a few seconds, and a green rectangle opened slowly…it was the airlock light at night, as the door slid open. I was looking at myself, just a little while ago, coming out and pulling the dog behind me.

The camera must have been like those flying bugs that Homeland Security spies use. I certainly hadn't seen anything.

When the door closed, the picture changed to a ghostly blue, like moonlight on Earth. It followed me for a minute or so. Stumbling and then staring at the ground as I walked more cautiously.

440

Then it switched to another location, and I knew what was coming. The ground collapsed and the dog and I disappeared in a cloud of dust, which the wind swept away in an instant.

The bug, or whatever it was, drifted down through the hole to hover over me as I writhed around in pain. A row of glowing symbols appeared at the bottom of the screen. There was a burst of white light when I found the dog and switched it on.

Then Big Red floated down—this was obviously the speeded-up version—wearing several layers of that wall plastic, it seemed; riding a thing that looked like a metal sawhorse with two sidecars. He put me in one and the dog in the other. Then he floated back up.

Then they skipped all the way to me lying on that pillow, naked and unlovely, in an embarrassing posture—I blushed, as if any of them cared—and then moved in close to my ankle, which was blue and swollen. Then a solid holo of a human skeleton, obviously mine, in the same position. The image moved in the same way as before. The fracture line glowed red, and then my foot, below the break, shifted slightly. The line glowed blue and disappeared.

Just then I noticed it wasn't hurting anymore.

Green stepped over and gently took the staff away from me. I put weight on the foot and it felt as good as new.

"How could you do that?" I said, not expecting an answer. No matter how good they were at healing themselves, how could they apply that to a human skeleton?

Well, a human vet could treat a broken bone in an animal she'd never seen before. But it wouldn't heal in a matter of hours.

Two of the amber ones brought out my skinsuit and Mars suit, and put them at my feet.

Red pointed at me and then tapped on the screen, which again showed the surface parts of the colony. You could hardly see them for the dust, though; there was a strong storm blowing.

He made an up-and-down gesture with his small arms, and then his large ones, obviously meaning "Get dressed."

So with about a million potato eyes watching, I took off the tunic and got into the skinsuit. The diaper was missing, which made it feel kind of baggy. They must have thrown it away—or analyzed it, ugh.

The creatures stared in silence while I zipped that up and then climbed and wiggled into the Mars suit. I secured the boots and gloves and then clamped the helmet into place, and automatically chinned the switch for an oxygen and power readout, but of course it was still broken. I guess that would be asking too much—you fixed my ankle but you can't fix a foogly space suit? What kind of Martians *are* you?"

It was obvious I wasn't getting any air from the backpack, though. I'd need the dog's backup supply.

I unshipped the helmet and faced Green, and made an exaggerated pantomime of breathing in and out. She didn't react. Hell, they probably breathed by osmosis or something.

I turned to Red and crouched over, patting the air at the level of the dog. "Dog," I said, and pointed back the way we'd come.

He leaned over and mimicked my gesture, and said, "Nog." Pretty close. Then he turned to the crowd and croaked out a speech, which I think had both "Harn" and "nog" in it.

He must have understood, at least partly, because he made that four-armed "come along" motion at me, and went back to the place where we'd entered. I went through the plastic and looked back. Green was leading four others, it looked like one of each color, following us.

Red leading us, we all went back along what seemed the same path we'd used coming over. I counted my steps, so that when I told people about it I'd have at least one actual concrete number. The hydroponic room, or at least the part we cut through, was 185 steps wide; then it was another 204 steps from there to the "hospital" room. I get about 80 centimeters to a step, so the trip covered more than 300 meters, allowing for a little dog-leg in the middle. Of course it might go on for miles in every direction, but at least it was no smaller than that.

We went into the little room and they watched while I unreeled the umbilical and plugged it in. The cool air coming through the neck fitting was more than a relief. I put my helmet back on. Green stepped forward and did a pretty good imitation of my breathing pantomime.

I sort of didn't want to go. I was looking forward to coming back, and learning how to communicate with Red and Green. We had other people more qualified, though. I should have listened to Mother when she got after me to take a language in school. If I'd known this was going to happen, I would have taken Chinese and Latin and Body Noises.

The others stood away from the plastic and Red gestured for me to follow. I pulled the dog along through the four plastic layers; this time we turned sharply to the right and started walking up a gently sloping ramp.

After a few minutes I could look down and get a sense of how large this place was. There was the edge of a lake—an immense amount of water even if it was only a few inches deep. From above, the buildings looked like domes of clay, or just dirt, with no windows, just the pale blue light that filtered through the door layers.

There were squares of different sizes and shades that were probably crops like the mushrooms and cigars, and one large square had trees that looked like six-foot-tall broccoli, which could explain the wooden splints.

We came to a level place, brightly lit, that had shelves full of bundles of the plastic stuff. Red walked straight to one shelf and pulled off a bundle. It was his Mars suit. Bending over at a strange angle, bobbing, he slid his feet into four opaque things like thick socks. His two large arms went into sleeves, ending in mittens. Then the whole thing seemed to come alive, and ripple up and over him, sealing together and then inflating. It didn't have anything that looked like an oxygen tank, but air was coming from somewhere.

He gestured for me to follow and we went toward a dark corner. He hesitated there, and held out his hand to me. I took it, and we staggered slowly through dozens of layers of the stuff, toward a dim light.

It was obviously like a gradual airlock. We stopped at another flat area, which had one of the blue lights, and rested for a few minutes. Then he led me through another long series of layers, where it became completely dark—without him leading me, I might have gotten turned around—and then it lightened slightly, the light pink this time.

When we came out, we were on the floor of a cave; the light was coming from a circle of Martian sky. When my eyes adjusted, I could see there was a smooth ramp leading uphill to the cave entrance.

I'd never seen the sky that color. We were looking up through a serious dust storm.

Red pulled a dust-covered sheet off his sawhorse-shaped vehicle. I helped him put the dog into one of the bowl-like sidecars, and I got in the other. There were two things like stubby handlebars in front, but no other controls that I could see.

He backed onto the thing, straddling it, and we rose off the ground a foot or so, and smoothly started forward.

The glide up the ramp was smooth. I expected to be buffeted around by the dust storm, but as impressive as it looked, it didn't have much power. My umbilical tube did flap around in the wind, which made me nervous. If it snapped, a failsafe would close off the tube so I wouldn't immediately die. But I'd use up the air in the suit pretty fast.

I couldn't see more than ten or twenty feet in any direction, but Red, I hoped, could see farther. He was moving very fast. Of course, he was unlikely to hit another vehicle, or a tree.

I settled down into the bowl—there wasn't anything to see—and was fairly comfortable. I amused myself by imagining the reaction of Dargo Solingen and Mother and Dad when I showed up with an actual Martian.

It felt like an hour or more before he slowed down and we hit the ground and skidded to a stop. He got off his perch laboriously and came around to the dog's side. I got out to help him lift it and was knocked off balance by a gust. Four legs were a definite advantage here.

He watched while I got the umbilical untangled and then pointed me in the direction we were headed. Then he made a shooing motion.

"You have to come with me," I said, uselessly, and tried to translate it into arm motions. He pointed and shooed again, and then backed on to the sawhorse and took off in a slow U-turn.

I started to panic. What if I went in the wrong direction? I could miss the base by twenty feet and just keep walking on into the desert.

I took a few deep breaths. The dog was pointed in the right direction. I picked up its handle and looked straight ahead as far as I could see, through the swirling gloom. I saw a rock, directly ahead, and walked to it. Then another rock, maybe ten feet away. After the fourth rock, I looked up and saw I'd almost run into the airlock door. I leaned on the big red button and the door slid open immediately. It closed behind the dog and the red light on the ceiling started blinking. It turned green and the inside door opened on a wide-eyed Emily.

"Carmen! You found your way back!"

"Well, um…not really…"

"Got to call the search party!" She bounded down the stairs yelling for Howard.

I wondered how long they'd been searching for me. I would be in shit up to my chin.

I put the dog back in its place—there was only one other parked there, so three were out looking for me. Or my body.

Card came running in when I was half out of my skinsuit. "Sis!" He grabbed me and hugged me, which was moderately embarrassing. "We thought you were—"

"Yeah, okay. Let me get dressed? Before the shit hits the fan?" He let me turn around and step out of the skinsuit and into my coverall.

"What, you went out for a walk and got lost in that dust storm?"

For a long moment, I thought of saying yes. Who was going to believe my story? I looked at the clock and saw that it was 1900. If it was the same day, seventeen hours had passed. I *could* have wandered around that long without running out of air.

"How long have I been gone?"

"You can't remember? All foogly day, man. Were you derilious?"

"Delirious." I kneaded my brow and rubbed my face hard with both hands. "Let me wait and tell it all when Mother and Dad get here."

"That'll be hours! They're out looking for you."

"Oh, that's great. Who else?"

"I think it was Paul the pilot."

"Well," said a voice behind me. "You decided to come back after all."

It was Dargo Solingen. There was a quaver of emotion in her voice that I'd never heard. I think anger.

"I'm sorry," I said. "I don't know what I was thinking."

"I don't think you were thinking at *all*. You were being a foolish *girl*, and you put more lives than your own into danger."

About a dozen people were behind her. "Dargo," Dr. Jefferson said. "She's back, she's alive. Let's give her a little rest."

"Has she given *us* any rest?" she barked.

"I'm *sorry*! I'll do anything—"

"You will? Isn't that pretty. What do you propose to do?"

Dr. Estrada put a hand on her shoulder. "Please let me talk to her." Oh, good, a shrink. I needed a xenologist. But she would listen better than Solingen.

"Oh...do what you want. I'll deal with her later." She turned and walked through the small crowd.

Some people gathered around me and I tried not to cry. I wouldn't want her to think she had made me cry. But there were plenty of shoulders and arms for me to hide my eyes in.

"Carmen." Dr. Estrada touched my forearm. "We ought to talk before your parents get back."

"Okay." A dress rehearsal. I followed her down to the middle of A.

She had a large room to herself, but it was her office as well as quarters. "Lie down here," she indicated her single bunk, "and just try to relax. Begin at the beginning."

"The beginning isn't very interesting. Dargo Solingen embarrassed me in front of everybody. Not the first time, either. Sometimes I feel like I'm her little project. Let's drive Carmen crazy."

"So in going outside like that, you were getting back at her? Getting even in some way?"

"I didn't think of it that way. I just had to get out, and that was the only way."

"Maybe not, Carmen. We can work on ways to get away without physically leaving."

"Like Dad's zen thing, okay. But what I did, or why, isn't really important. It's what I *found!*"

"So what did you find?"

"Life. Intelligent life. They saved me." I could hear my voice and even I didn't believe it.

"Hmm," she said. "Go on."

"I'd walked four kilometers or so and was about to turn around and go back. But I stepped on a place that wouldn't support my weight. Me and the dog. We fell through. At least ten meters, maybe twenty."

"And you weren't hurt?"

"I *was!* I heard my ankle break. I broke a rib, maybe more than one, here."

She pressed the area, gently. "But you're walking."

"They fixed...I'm getting ahead of myself."

"So you fell through and broke your ankle?"

"Then I spent a long time finding the dog. My suit light went out when I hit the ground. But finally I found it, found the dog, and got my umbilical plugged in."

"So you had plenty of oxygen."

"But I was freezing. The circuit to my gloves and boots wasn't working. I really thought that was it."

"But you survived."

"I was rescued. I was passing out and this, uh, this *Martian* came floating down, I saw him in the dog's light. Then everything went black and I woke up—"

"Carmen! You have to see that this was a dream. A hallucination."

"Then how did I get here?"

Her mouth set in a stubborn line. "You were very lucky. You wandered around in the storm and came back here."

"But there *was* no storm when I left! Just a little wind. The storm came up while I was...well, I was underground. Where the Martians live."

"You've been through so much, Carmen..."

"This was *not* a dream!" I tried to stay calm. "Look. You can check the air left in the tanks. My suit and the dog. There will be *hours* unaccounted for. I was breathing the Martians' air."

"Carmen…be reasonable…"

"No, *you* be reasonable. I'm not saying anything more until—" There was one knock on the door and Mother burst in, followed by Dad.

"My baby," she said. When did she ever call me that? She hugged me so hard I could barely breathe. "You found your way back."

"Mother…I was just telling Dr. Estrada…I didn't find my way back. I was brought."

"She had a dream about Martians. A hallucination."

"*No!* Would you just listen?"

Dad sat down cross-legged, looking up at me. "Start at the beginning, honey."

I did. I took a deep breath and started with taking the suit and the dog and going out to be alone. Falling and breaking my ankle. Waking up in the little hospital room. Red and Green and the others. Seeing the base on their screen. Being healed and brought back.

There was an uncomfortable silence after I finished. "If it wasn't for the dust storm," Dad said, "it would be easy to verify your…your account. Nobody could see you from here, though, and the satellites won't show anything, either."

"Maybe that's why he was in a rush to bring me back. If they'd waited for the storm to clear, they'd be exposed."

"Why would they be afraid of that?" Dr. Estrada asked.

"Well, I don't know. But I guess it's obvious that they don't want anything to do with us—"

"Except to rescue a lost girl," Mother said.

"Is that so hard to believe? I mean, I couldn't say three words to them, but I could tell they were good-hearted."

"It just sounds so fantastic," Dad said. "How would you feel in our position? By far the easiest explanation is that you were under extreme stress and—"

"*No!* Dad, do you really think I would do that? Come up with some elaborate lie?" I could see on his face that he did indeed. Maybe not a lie, but a fantasy. "There's objective proof. Look at the dog. It has a huge dent where it hit the ground in the cave."

"Maybe so; I haven't seen it," he said. "But being devil's advocate, aren't there many other ways that could have happened?"

"What about the *air*? The air in the dog! I didn't use enough of it to have been out so long."

He nodded. "That would be compelling. Did you dock it?"

Oh hell. "Yes. I wasn't thinking I'd have to *prove* anything." When you dock the dog it automatically starts to refill air and power. "There must be a record. How much oxygen a dog takes on when it recharges."

They all looked at each other. "Not that I know of," Dad said. "But you don't need that. Let's just do an MRI of your ankle. That'll tell if it was recently broken."

"But they *fixed* it. The break might not show."

"It will show," Dr. Estrada said. "Unless there was some kind of… magic involved."

Mother's face was getting red. "Would you both leave? I need to talk to Carmen alone." They both nodded and went out.

Mother watched the door close. "I know you aren't lying. You've never been good at that."

"Thanks," I said. Thanks for nothing.

"But it was a stupid thing to do, going off like that, and you know it."

"I do, I *do*! And I'm sorry for all the trouble I—"

"But look. I'm a scientist, and so is your dad, after a fashion, and so is almost everybody else who's going to hear this story today. You see what I'm saying?"

"Yeah, I think so. They're going to be skeptical."

"Of course they are. They don't get paid for believing things. They get paid for questioning them."

"And you, Mother. Do you believe me?"

She stared at me with a fierce intensity I'd never seen before in my life. "Look. Whatever happened to you, I believe one hundred percent that you're telling the truth. You're telling the truth about what you remember, what you believe happened."

"But I might be nuts."

"Well, wouldn't you say so? If I came in with your story? You'd say 'Mom's getting old.' Wouldn't you?"

"Yeah, maybe I would."

"And to prove that I wasn't crazy, I would take you out and show you something that couldn't be explained any other way. You know what they say about extraordinary claims?"

"They require extraordinary evidence."

"That's right. Once the storm calms down, you and I are going out to where you say…to where you fell through to the cave." She put her hand on the back of my head and rubbed my hair. "I so much want to believe you. For my sake as well as yours. To find life here."

7. THE DRAGON LADY

Mother wanted to call a general assembly, so I could tell everybody the complete story, all at once, but Dargo Solingen wouldn't allow it. She said that children do stunts like this to draw attention to themselves, and she wasn't going to reward me with an audience. Of course she's an expert about children, never having had any herself. Good thing. They'd be monsters.

So it was like the whisper game, where you sit in a circle and whisper a sentence to the person next to you, and she whispers it to the next, and so on. When it gets back to you, it's all wrong, sometimes in a funny way.

This was not particularly funny. People would ask if I was really going around on the surface without a Mars suit, or think the Martians stripped me naked and interrogated me, or they broke my ankle on purpose. I put a detailed account on my website, but a lot of people would rather talk than read.

The MRI didn't help much, except for people who wanted to believe I was lying. Dr. Jefferson said it looked like an old childhood injury, long ago healed. Mother was with me at the time, and she told him she was absolutely sure I'd never broken that ankle. To people like Dargo Solingen that was a big thing, so I'd lied about that, too. I think we won Dr. Jefferson over, though he was inclined to believe me, anyhow. So did most of the people who came over on the *John Carter* with us. They were willing to believe in Martians before they'd believe I would make up something like that.

Dad didn't want to talk about it, but Mother was fascinated. I went to talk with her at the lab after dinner (she and two others were keeping a 24-hour watch on an experiment). "I don't see how they could be actual Martians," she said, "in the sense that we're Earthlings. I mean, if they evolved here as oxygen-water creatures similar to us, then that was three billion years ago. And, as you said, a large animal isn't going to evolve alone, without any other animals. Nor will it suddenly appear, without smaller, simpler animals preceding it. So they must be like us."

"From Earth?"

She laughed. "I don't think so. None of the eight-limbed creatures on Earth has very high technology. I think they have to have come from yet another planet. Unless we're completely wrong about areology, about the history of conditions on this planet, they can't have come from here."

"What if they used to live on the surface?" I said. "Then moved underground as the planet dried up and lost its air?"

She shook her head. "The time scale. No species more complicated than a bacterium has survived for billions of years."

"None on Earth," I said.

"Touché," she laughed. A bell chimed and she went to the other side of the room and looked inside an aquarium, or terrarium. Or ares-arium, here, I suppose. She looked at the things growing inside and typed some numbers onto her clipboard.

"So they went underground three billion years ago with the technology to duplicate what sounds like a high-altitude Earth environment. And stayed that way for three billion years." She shook her head. "It's not likely. And I still want to know where the fossils are. Maybe they dug them all up and destroyed them, just to confuse us?"

"But it's not like we've looked everywhere. Paul says it may be that life wasn't distributed uniformly, and we just haven't found any of the islands where things lived. The dinosaurs or whatever."

"Well, you know it didn't work that way on Earth. Fossils everywhere, from the bottom of the sea to the top of the Himalayas. Crocodile fossils in Antarctica."

"Okay. That's Earth."

"It's all we have. Coffee?" I said no and she poured herself half a cup. "You're right that it's weak to generalize from one example. Paul could very well be right, too; there's no evidence one way or the other.

"But look. We know all about one form of life on Mars: you and me and the others. We have to live in an artificial bubble that contains an alien environment, maintained by high technology, because we *are* the aliens here. So you stumble on eight-legged potato people who also live in a bubble that contains an alien environment, evidently maintained by high technology. The simplest explanation is that they're aliens, too. Alien to Mars."

"Yeah, I don't disagree. I know about Occam's Razor."

She smiled at that. "What's fascinating to me, one of many things, is that you spent hours in that environment and felt no ill effects. Their planet's very earthlike."

"What if it *was* Earth?"

That stopped her. "Wouldn't we have noticed?"

"I mean a long time ago. What if they lived only on mountain tops, and developed high technology thousands and thousands of years ago. Then they all left."

"It's an idea," she said. "But it's hard to believe that every one of them would be willing and able to leave—and that there would be no trace of their civilization, ten or even a hundred thousand years later. And where are their genetic precursors? The eight-legged equivalent of apes?"

"You don't really believe me."

"Well, I do; I do," she said seriously. "I just don't think there's an easy explanation."

"Like Dargo Solingen's? The Figment of Imagination Theory?"

"Especially that. People don't have complex consistent hallucinations; they're *called* hallucinations because they're fantastic, dreamlike.

"Besides, I saw the dog; you couldn't have put that dent in it with a lead-lined baseball bat. And she can't explain the damage to your Mars suit, either, without positing that you leaped off the side of a cliff just to give yourself an alibi." She was getting worked up. "And I'm your *mother*, even if I'm not a model one. I would goddamn remember if you had ever broken your ankle! That healed hairline fracture is enough proof for me—and for Dr. Jefferson and Dr. Milius and anybody else in this goddamned hole who didn't convict you before you opened your mouth."

"You've been a good mother," I said.

She suddenly sat up and hugged me across the table. "Not so good. Or you wouldn't have done this."

She sat down and rubbed my hand. "But if you hadn't done it—" She laughed. "—how long would it have been before we stumbled on these aliens? They're watching us, but they're not all that eager to have us see them."

The window on the wall was a greenboard of differential equations. She clicked on her clipboard and it became a real-time window. The storm was still blowing, but it had thinned out enough so I could see a vague outline of Telegraph Hill.

"Maybe tomorrow we'll be able to go out and take a look. If Paul's free, he'd probably like to come along; nobody knows the local real estate better than him."

I stood up. "I can hardly wait. But I *will* wait, promise."

"Good. Once is enough." She smiled up at me. "Get some rest. Probably a long day tomorrow."

Actually, I was up past midnight catching up on schoolwork, or not quite catching up. My brain wouldn't settle down enough to worry about Kant and his Categorical Imperative. Not with aliens out there waiting to be contacted.

8. BAD COUGH

Paul was free until 1400, so right after breakfast we suited up and equipped a dog with extra oxygen and climbing gear. He'd done a lot of climbing and caving on both Earth and Mars. If we found the hole—*when* we found the hole—he was going to approach it roped up, so if he broke through the way I did, he wouldn't fall far or fast.

I'd awakened early with a slight cough, but felt okay. I got some cough suppressant pills from the first-aid locker, chewed one and put two in my helmet's tongue-operated pill cache.

We went through the airlock and weren't surprised to see that the storm had covered all my tracks, and everyone else's—including Red's; I was hoping that his sawhorse thing might have gouged out a distinctive mark when it stopped.

We still had a good chance of finding the hole, thanks to the MPS built into the suit and its inertial compass. I'd started counting steps, going west, when I set out from Telegraph Hill, and was close to five thousand when I fell through. That's about four kilometers, maybe an hour's walk in the daytime.

"So we're probably being watched," Mother said, and waved to the invisible camera. "Hey there, Mr. Red! Hello, Dr. Green! We're bringing back your patient with the insurance forms."

I waved, too, both arms. Paul put up both his hands palm out, showing he wasn't armed. Though what it would mean to a four-armed creature, I wasn't sure.

No welcoming party appeared, so we went to the right of Telegraph Hill and started walking and counting. A lot of the terrain looked familiar. Several times I had us move to the left or right when I was sure I had been closer to a given formation.

We walked a half-kilometer or so past Paul's wrecked dumbo. I hadn't seen it in the dark.

Suddenly I noticed something. "Wait! Paul! I think it's just ahead of you." I hadn't realized it, walking in the dark, but what seemed to be a simple rise in the ground was actually rounded, like an overturned shallow bowl.

"Like a little lava dome, maybe," he said. "That's where you fell through." He pointed at something I couldn't quite see from my angle and height. "Big enough for you and the dog, anyhow."

He unloaded his mountaineering stuff from the dog, then took a hammer and pounded into the ground a long piton, which is like a spearpoint with a hole for the rope. Then he did another one about a foot away. He passed an end of the rope through both of them and tied it off.

He pulled on the rope with all his weight. "Carmen, Laura, help me test this." We did and it still held. He looped most of the rope over his shoulder and took a couple of turns under his arms, and then clamped it through a metal thing he called a crab. It's supposed to keep you from falling too fast, even if you let go.

"This probably isn't all necessary," he said, "since I'm just taking a look down. But better safe than dead." He backed up the slight incline, checking over his shoulder, and then got on his knees to approach the hole.

I held my breath as he took out a big flashlight and leaned over the edge. I didn't hear mother breathing, either.

"Okay!" he said. "There's the side reflector that broke off your dog. I've got a good picture."

"Good," I tried to say, but it came out as a cough. Then another cough, and then several, harder and harder. I felt faint and sat down and tried to stay calm. Eyes closed, shallow breathing.

When I opened my eyes, I saw specks of blood on the inside of my helmet. I could taste it inside my mouth and on my lips. "Mother, I'm sick."

She saw the blood and kneeled down next to me. "Breathe. Can you breathe?"

"Yes, I don't think it's the suit." She was checking the oxygen fitting and meter on the back.

"How long have you felt sick?"

"Not long…well, *now* I do. I had a little cough this morning."

"And didn't tell anybody."

"No, I took a pill and it was all right."

"I can see how all right it was. Do you think you can stand?"

I nodded and got to my feet, wobbling a little. She held on to my arm. Then Paul came up and held the other.

"I can just see the antenna on Telegraph Hill," he said. "I'll call for the jeep."

"No, don't," I pleaded. "I don't want to give the Dragon the satisfaction."

Mother gave a nervous laugh. "This is way beyond that, sweetheart. Blood in your lungs? What if I let you walk back and you dropped dead?"

"I'm not going to *die*." But saying that gave me a horrible chill. Then I coughed a bright red string onto my faceplate. Mother eased me back down, and awkwardly sat with my helmet in her lap while Paul shouted "Mayday!" over the radio.

"Where did they come up with that word?" I asked Mother.

"Easy to understand on a radio, I guess. 'Mo' dough' would work just as well." I heard the click as her glove touched my helmet. Trying to smooth my hair.

I didn't cry. Embarrassing to admit, but I guess I felt kind of important, dying and all. Dargo Solingen would feel like shit for doubting me. Though the cause-and-effect link there wasn't too clear.

I lay there trying not to cough for maybe twenty minutes before the jeep pulled up, driven by Dad. One big happy family. He and mother lifted me into the back and Paul took over the driving, leaving the dog and his climbing stuff behind.

It was a fast and rough ride back. I got into another coughing spasm and spattered more blood and goop on the faceplate.

Mother and Dad carried me into the airlock like a sack of grain or something, and then were all over each other trying to get me out of the Mars suit. At least they left the skinsuit on while they hurried me through the corridor and mess area to Dr. Jefferson's aid station.

He asked my parents to step outside, set me on the examination table, and stripped off the top of the skinsuit, to listen to my breathing with a stethoscope. He shook his head.

"Carmen, it sure sounds as if you've got something in your lungs. But when I heard you were coming in with this, I looked at the whole-body MRI we took yesterday, and there's nothing there." He clicked on his clipboard and asked the window for my MRI, and there I was in all my transparent glory.

"Better take another one." He pulled the top up over my shoulders. "You don't have to take anything off; just lie down here." The act of lying down made me cough sharply, but I caught it in my palm.

He took a tissue and gently wiped my hand, and looked at the blood. "Damn," he said quietly. "You aren't a smoker. I mean on Earth."

"Just twice. Once tobacco and once pot. Just one time each."

He nodded. "Now take a really deep breath and try to hold it." He took the MRI wand and passed it back and forth over my upper body. "Okay. You can breathe now.

"New picture," he said to the window. Then he was quiet for too long. "Oh my. What…what could that be?"

I looked, and there were black shapes in both of my lungs, about the size of golf balls. "What is…what are they?"

He shook his head. "Not cancer, not an infection, this fast. Bronchitis wouldn't show up black, anyhow. Better call Earth." He looked at me with concern and something else, maybe puzzlement. "Let's get you into bed in the next room, and I'll give you a sedative. Stop the coughing. And then maybe I'll take a look inside."

"Inside?"

"Brachioscopy, put a little camera down there. You won't feel anything."

In fact, I didn't feel anything until I woke up several hours later Mother was sitting by the bed, her hand on my forehead.

"My nose…the inside of my nose feels funny."

"That's where the tube went in. The brachioscope."

"Oh, yuck. Did he find anything?"

She hesitated. "It's…not from Earth. They snipped off some of it and took it to the lab. It's not…it doesn't have DNA."

"I've got a Martian disease?"

"Mars, or wherever your potato people are from. Not Earth, anyhow; everything alive on Earth has DNA."

I prodded where it ached, under my ribs. "It's not organic?"

"Well, it is. Carbon, hydrogen, oxygen. Nitrogen, phosphorus, sulfur—it has amino acids and proteins and even something like RNA. But that's as far as it goes."

That sounded bad enough. "So they're going to have to operate? On both of my lungs?"

She made a little noise and I looked up and saw her wiping her eyes. "What is it? Mother?"

"It's not that simple. The little piece they snipped off, it had to go straight into the glove box, the environmental isolation unit. That's the procedure we have for any Martian life we discover, because we don't know what effect it might have on human life. In your case…"

"In my case, it's already attacked a human."

"That's right. And they can't operate on you in the glove box."

"So they're just going to leave it there?"

"No. But Dr. Jefferson can't operate until he can work in a place that's environmentally isolated from the rest of the base. They're working on it now, turning the far end of Unit B into a little self-contained hospital. You'll move in there tomorrow or the next day, and he'll take out the stuff. Two operations."

"Two?"

"The first lung has to be working before he opens the second. On Earth, he could put you on a heart/lung machine, I guess, and work on both. But not here."

I felt suddenly cold and clammy and I must have turned pale. "It's not that bad," Mother said quickly. "He doesn't have to open you up; he'll be working through a small hole in your side. It's called thorascopy. Like when I had my knee operated on, and I was just in and out. And he'll have the best surgeons on Earth looking over his shoulder, advising him."

With a half-hour delay, I thought. What if their advice was "No— don't do *that*!" Oops.

I thought of an old bad joke: Politicians cover their mistakes with money; cooks cover their mistakes with mayonnaise; doctors cover theirs with dirt. I could be the first person ever buried on Mars, what an honor.

"Wait," I said. "Maybe *they* could help."

"The Earth doctors? Sure—"

"No! I mean the aliens."

"Honey, they couldn't—"

"They fixed my ankle just like that, didn't they?"

"Well, evidently they did. But that's sort of a mechanical thing. They wouldn't have to know any internal medicine..."

"But it wasn't medicine at all, not like we know it. Those big lenses, the smoking herbs. It was kind of mumbo-jumbo, but it worked!"

There was one loud rap on the door, and Dr. Jefferson opened it and stepped inside, looking agitated. "Laura, Carmen—things have gone from bad to worse. The Parienza kids started coughing blood; they've got it. So I put my boy through the MRI, and he's got a mass in one of his lungs, too.

"Look, I have to operate on the Parienzas first; they're young and this is hitting them harder..."

"That's okay," I said. By all means, get some practice on someone else first.

"Laura, I want you to assist me in the surgery along with Selene." Dr. Milius. "So far, this is only infecting the children. If it gets into the general population, if *I* get it—"

"Alf! I'm not a surgeon—I'm not even a doctor!"

"If Selene and I get this and die, you are a doctor. You are *the* doctor. You at least know how to use a scalpel."

"Cutting up animals that are already dead!"

"Just…calm down. The machine's not that complicated. It's a standard waldo interface, and you have real-rime MRI to show you where you're going."

"Can you hear yourself talking, Alphonzo? I'm just a biologist."

There was a long moment of silence while he looked at her. "Just come and pay attention. You might have to do Carmen."

"All right," Mother said. She looked grim. "Now?"

He nodded. "Selene's preparing them. I'm going to operate on Murray while she watches and assists; then she'll do Roberta while I observe. Maybe an hour and a half each."

"What can I do?" I said.

"Just stay put and try to rest," he said. "We'll get to you in three or four hours. Don't worry…you won't feel anything." Then he and mother were gone.

Won't feel anything? I was already feeling pretty crappy. I get pissed off and go for a walk and bring back the Plague from Outer Space?

I touched the window and said "Window outside." It was almost completely dark, just a faint line of red showing the horizon. The dust storm was over.

The whole plan crystallized then. I guess I'd been thinking of parts of it since I knew I'd be alone for a while.

I just zipped up my skinsuit and walked. The main corridor was almost deserted, people running along on urgent errands. Nobody was thinking of going outside—no one but me.

If the aliens had had a picture of me leaving the base at two in the morning, before, then they probably were watching us all the time. I could signal them. Send a message to Red.

I searched around for pencil to disable the airlock buzzer. Even while I was doing it, I wondered whether I was acting sanely. Was I just trying to escape being operated on? Mother used to say "Do something, even if it's wrong." There didn't seem to be anything else to do other than sit around and watch things go from bad to worse.

If the aliens were watching, I could make Red understand how serious it was. Whether he and Green could do anything, I didn't know. But what else was there? Things were happening too fast.

I didn't run into anyone until I was almost there. Then I nearly collided with Card as he stepped out of the Pod A bathroom.

"What you doing over here?" he said. "I thought you were supposed to be in sick bay."

"No, I'm just—" Of course I started coughing. "Let me by, all right?"

"No! What are you up to?"

"Look, microbe. I don't have time to explain." I pushed by him. "Every second counts."

"You're going outside again! What are you, crazy?"

"Look, look, look—for once in your life, don't be a..." I had a moment of desperate inspiration, and grabbed him by the shoulders. "Card, listen. I need you. You have to trust me."

"What, this is about your crazy Martian story?"

"I can prove it's not crazy, but you have to come help me."

"Help you with what?"

"Just suit up and step outside with me. I think they'll come if I signal them, and they might be able to help us."

He was hesitant. I knew he only half believed me—but at least he did half believe me. "What? What do you want me to do outside?"

"I just want you to stand in the door, so the airlock can't close. That way no grown-up can come out and froog the deal."

That did make him smile. "So what you want is for me to be in as deep shit as you are."

"Exactly! Are you up for it?"

"You are so easy to see through, you know? You could be a window."

"Yeah, yeah. Are you with me?"

He glanced toward the changing room, and then back down the hall. "Let's go."

We must have gotten me into my suit in ninety seconds flat. It took him an extra minute because he had to strip and wiggle into the skinsuit first. I kept my eye on the changing room door, but I didn't have any idea what I would say if someone walked in. We're playing doctor?

My faceplate was still spattered with dried blood, which was part of the vague plan: I assumed they would know that the blood meant trouble, and their bug camera, or whatever it was, would be on me as soon as I stepped outside. I had a powerful flashlight, and would turn that on my face, with no other lights. Then wave my arms, jump around, whatever.

We rushed through the safety check and I put two fresh oxygen bottles into the dog I'd bashed up. Disabled the buzzer, and we crowded into the airlock, closed it and cycled it.

We'd agreed not to use the radio. Card signaled for me to touch helmets. "How long?"

"An hour, anyhow." I could walk past Telegraph Hill by then.

"Okay. Watch where you step, clumsy." I hit his arm.

The door opened and I stepped out into the darkness. Card put one foot out on the sand and leaned back against the door. He pantomimed looking at his watch.

I closed my eyes and pointed the light at my face. Bright red through my eyelids; I knew I'd be dazzled blind for a while after I stopped. So after I'd given them a minute of the bloody faceplate I just stood in one place and shined the light out over the plain, waving it around in fast circles, which I hoped would mean "Help!"

I wasn't sure how long it had taken Red to bring me from their habitat level to the cave where he was parked, and then on to here. Maybe two hours? I hadn't been tracking too well. Without a dust storm it might be faster. I pulled on the dog and headed toward the right of Telegraph Hill.

The last thing I expected to happen was this: I hadn't walked twenty yards when Red came zooming up on his weird vehicle and stopped in a great spray of dust.

Card broke radio silence with a justifiable *"Holy shit!"*

Red helped me put the dog on one side and I got into the other and we were off. I looked back and waved at Card, and he waved back. The base shrank really fast and slipped under the horizon.

I looked forward for a moment and then turned away. It was just a little too scary, screaming along a few inches over the ground, missing boulders by a hair. The steering must have been automatic. Or maybe Red had inhuman reflexes. Nothing else about him was all that human.

Except the need to come back and help. He must have been waiting nearby.

It seemed no more than ten or twelve minutes before the thing slowed down and drifted into the slanted cave I remembered. Maybe he had taken a roundabout way before, to hide the fact that they were so close.

We got out the dog and I followed him back down the way we had come a couple of days before. I had to stop twice with coughing fits, and by the time we got to the place where he shed his Mars suit, there was a scary amount of blood.

An odd thing to think, but I wondered whether he would take my body back if I died here. Why should I care?

We went on down, and at the level where the lake was visible, Green was waiting, along with two small ones dressed in white. We went together down to the dark floor and followed blue lines back to what seemed to be the same hospital room where I'd first awakened after the accident.

I slumped down on the pillow, feeling completely drained and about to barf. I unshipped my helmet and took a cautious breath. It smelled like a cold mushroom farm, exactly what I expected.

Red handed me a glass of water and I took it gratefully. Then he picked up my helmet with his two large arms and did a curiously human thing with a small one: he wiped a bit of blood off the inside with one finger, and then lifted it to his mouth to taste it.

"Wait!" I said. "That could be poison to you!"

He set the helmet down. "How nice of you to be concerned," he said, in a voice like a British cube actor.

I just shook my head. After a few seconds I was able to say "What?"

"Many of us can speak English," Green said, "or other of your languages. We've been listening to your radio, television, and cube for two hundred years."

"But...before...you..."

"That was to protect ourselves," Red said. "When we saw you had hurt yourself and I had to bring you here, it was decided that no one would speak a human language in your presence. We are not ready to make contact with humans. You are a dangerous violent race that tends to destroy what it doesn't understand."

"Not all of us," I said.

"We know that. We were considering various courses of action when we found out you were ill."

"We monitor your colony's communications with Earth," one of the white ones said, "and saw immediately what was happening to you. We all have that breathing fungus soon after we're born. But with us it isn't serious. We have an herb that cures it permanently."

"So...you can fix it?"

Red spread out all four hands. "We are so different from you, in chemistry and biology. The treatment might help you. It might kill you."

"But this crap is sure to kill me if we don't do anything!"

The other white-clad one spoke up. "We don't know. I am called Rezlan, and I am…of a class that studies your people. A scientist, or philosopher.

"The fungus would certainly kill you if it continued to grow. It would fill up your lungs and you couldn't breathe. But we don't know; it never happens to us. Your body may learn to adapt to it, and it would be… illegal? Immoral, improper…for us to experiment on you. If you were to die…I don't know how to say it. Impossible."

"The cure for your ankle was different," Green said. "There was no risk to your life."

I coughed and stared at the spatter of blood on my palm. "But if you don't treat me, and I die? Won't that be the same thing?"

All four of them made a strange buzzing sound. Red patted my shoulder. "Carmen, that's a wonderful joke. 'The same thing.'" He buzzed again, and so did the others.

"Wait," I said, "I'm going to *die* and it's funny?"

"No no no," Green said. "Dying itself isn't funny." Red put his large hands on his potato head and wuggled it back and forth, and the others buzzed.

Red tapped his head three times, which set them off again. A natural comedian. "If you have to explain a joke, it isn't funny."

I started to cry, and he took my hand in his small scaly one and patted it. "We are so different. What is funny…is how we here are caught. We don't have a choice. We have to treat you even though we don't know what the outcome will be." He buzzed softly. "But that's not funny to you."

"*No!*" I tried not to wail. "I can see this part. There's a paradox. You might kill me, trying to help me."

"And that's not funny to you?"

"No, not really. Not at all, really."

"Would it be funny if it was somebody else?"

"Funny? *No!*"

"What if it was your worst enemy. Would that make you smile?"

"No. I don't have any enemies that bad."

He said something that made the others buzz. I gritted my teeth and tried not to cry. My whole chest hurt, like both lungs held a burning ton of crud, and here I was trying not to barf in front of a bunch of potato-head aliens. "Red. Even if I don't get the joke. Could you do the treatment before I foogly die?"

"Oh, Carmen. It's being prepared. This is…it's a way of dealing with difficult things. We joke. You would say laughing instead of crying." He turned around, evidently looking back the way we had come, though it's hard to tell which way a potato is looking. "It is taking too long, which is part of why we have to laugh. When we have children, it's all at one time, and so they all need the treatment at the same time, a few hundred days later, after they bud. We're trying to grow…it's like trying to find a vegetable out of season? We have to make it grow when it doesn't want to. And make enough for the other younglings in your colony."

"The adults don't get it?"

He did a kind of shrug. "We don't. Or rather, we only get it once, as children. Do you know about whooping cough and measles?"

"What-sels?"

"Measels and whooping cough used to be diseases humans got as children. Before your parents' parents were born. We heard about them on the radio, and they reminded us of this."

A new green-clad small one came through the plastic sheets, holding a stone bowl. She and Red exchanged a few whistles and scrapes. "If you are like us when we are small," he said, "this will make you excrete in every way. So you may want to undress."

How wonderful. Here comes Carmen, the shitting pissing farting burping barfing human sideshow. Don't forget snot and earwax. I got out of the Mars suit and unzipped the skinsuit and stepped out of that. I was cold, and every orifice clenched up tight. "Okay. Let's go."

Red held my right arm with his two large ones, and Green did the same on the left. Not a good sign. The new green one spit into the bowl, and it started to smoke.

She brought the smoking herb under my nose and I tried to get away, but Red and Green held me fast. It was the worst-smelling crap you could ever imagine. I barfed through mouth and nose and then started retching and coughing explosively, horribly, like a cat with a hair ball. It did bring up the two fungus things, like furry rotten fruit. I would've barfed again if there had been anything left in my stomach, but I decided to pass out instead.

9. INVASION FROM EARTH

I half woke up, I don't know how much later, with Red tugging gently on my arm. "Carmen," he said, "do you live now? There is a problem."

I grunted something that meant yes, I am alive, but no, I'm not sure I want to be. My throat felt like someone had pulled something scratchy and dead up through it. "Sleep," I said, but he picked me up and started carrying me like a child.

"There are humans from Earth here," he said, speeding up to a run. "They do not understand. They're wrecking everything." He blew through the plastic sheets into the dark hall.

"Red...it's hard to breathe here." He didn't respond, just ran faster, a rippling horse gait. His own breath was coming hard, like sheets of paper being ripped. "Red. I need...suit. Oxygen."

"As we do." We were suddenly in the middle of a crowd—hundreds of them in various sizes and colors—surging up the ramp toward the surface. He said three short words over and over, very loud, and the crowd stopped moving and parted to let us through.

When we went through the next set of doors I could hear air whistling out. On the other side my ears popped with a painful *crack* and I felt cold, colder than I ever had been. "What's happening?"

"Your...humans...have a...thing." He was wheezing before each word. "A tool...that...tears...through."

He set me down gently on the cold rock floor. I shuddered out of control, teeth chattering. No air. Lungs full of nothing but pain. The world was going white. I was starting to die but instead of praying or something I just noticed that the hairs in my nose had frozen and were making a crinkly sound when I tried to breathe.

Red was putting on the plastic layers that made up his Mars suit. He picked me up and I cried out in startled pain—the skin on my right forearm and breast and hip had frozen to the rock—and he held me close with three arms while the fourth did something to seal the plastic. Then he held me with all four arms and crooned something reassuring to weird creatures from another planet. He smelled like a mushroom you wouldn't eat, but I could breathe again.

I was bleeding some from the ripped skin and my lungs and throat still didn't want to work, and I was being hugged to death by a nightmarish singing monster, so rather than put up with it all my body just passed out again.

I woke up to my father fighting with Red, with me in between. Red was trying to hold on to me with his small arms while my father was going after him with some sort of pipe, and he was defending himself with the large arms. "No!" I screamed. "Dad! No!"

Of course he couldn't hear anything in the vacuum, but I guess anyone can lip-read the word "no." He stepped back with an expression on his face that I had never seen. Anguish, I suppose, or rage. Well, here was his daughter, naked and bleeding, in the many arms of a gruesome alien, looking way too much like a movie poster from a century ago.

Taka Wu and Mike Silverman were carrying a spalling laser. "Red," I said, "watch out for the guys with the machine."

"I know," he said, "We've seen you use it underground. That's how they tore up the first set of doors. We can't let them use it again."

It was an interesting standoff. Four big aliens in their plasticwrap suits. My father and mother and nine other humans in Mars suits, armed with tomato stakes and shovels and one laser, the humans looking kind of pissed off and frightened. The Martians probably were, too. A good thing we hadn't brought any guns to this planet.

Red whispered. "Can you make them leave the machine and follow us?"

"I don't know…they're scared." I mouthed "Mother, Dad," and pointed back the way we had come. "Fol-low us," I said with slow exaggeration. Confined as I was, I couldn't make any sweeping gestures, but I jabbed one forefinger back the way we had come.

Dad stepped forward slowly, his hands palm out. Mother started to follow him. Red shifted me around and held out his hand and my father took it, and held his other one out for mother. She took it and we went crabwise through the dark layers of the second airlock. Then the third and the fourth, and we were on the slope overlooking the lake.

The crowd of aliens we'd left behind was still there, perhaps a daunting sight for mother and Dad. But they held on, and the crowd parted to let us through.

I noticed ice was forming on the edge of the lake. Were we going to kill them all?

"Pardon," Red muttered, and held me so hard I couldn't breathe, while he wiggled out of his suit and left it on the ground, then set me down gently.

It was like walking on ice—on *dry* ice—and my breath came out in plumes. But he and I walked together along the blue line paths, followed by my parents, down to the sanctuary of the white room. Green was waiting there with my skinsuit. I gratefully pulled it on and zipped up. "Boots?"

"Boots," she said, and went back the way we'd come.

"Are you all right?" Red asked.

My father had his helmet off. "These things speak English?"

Red sort of shrugged. "And Chinese, in my case. We've been eaves-dropping on you since you discovered radio."

My father fainted dead away.

Green produced this thing that looked like a gray cabbage and held it by Dad's face. I had a vague memory of it being used on me, sort of like an oxygen source. He came around in a minute or so.

"Are you actually Martians?" Mother said. "You can't be."

Red nodded in a jerky way. "We are Martians only the same way you are. We live here. But we came from somewhere else."

"Where?" Dad croaked.

"No time for that. You have to talk to your people. We're losing air and heat, and have to repair the door. Then we have to treat your children. Carmen was near death."

Dad got to his knees and stood up, then stooped to pick up his helmet. "You know how to fix it? The laser damage."

"It knows how to repair itself. But it's like a wound in the body. We have to use stitches or glue to close the hole. Then it grows back."

"So you just need for us to not interfere."

"And help, by showing where the damage is."

He started to put his helmet on. "What about Carmen?"

"Yeah Where's my suit?"

Red faced me. I realized you could tell that by the little black mouth slit. "You're very weak. You should stay here."

"But—"

"No time to argue. Stay here till we return." All of them but Green went bustling through the airlock.

"So," I said to her. "I guess I'm a hostage."

"My English no good," she said. "Parlez-vous Français?" I said no. "Nihongo hanasu koto ga dekimasu?"

Probably Japanese, or maybe Martian. "No, sorry." I sat down and waited for the air to run out.

10. ZEN FOR MORONS

Green put a kind of black fibrous poultice on the places where my skin had burned off from the icy ground, and the pain stopped immediately. That raised a big question I couldn't ask, having neglected both French and Japanese in school. But help was on its way.

While I was getting dressed after Green had finished her poulticing, another green one showed up.

"Hello," it said. "I was asked here because I know English. Some English."

"I—I'm glad to meet you. I'm Carmen."

"I know. And you want me to say my name. But you couldn't say it yourself. So give me a name."

"Um…Robin Hood?"

"I am Robin Hood, then. I am pleased to meet you."

I couldn't think of any pleasantries, so I dove right in: "How come your medicine works for us? My mother says we're unrelated at the most basic level, DNA."

"Am I 'DNA' now? I thought I was Robin Hood."

This was not going to be easy. "No. Yes. You're Robin Hood. Why does your medicine work on humans?"

"I don't understand. Why shouldn't it? It's medicine."

So much for the Enigmatic Superior Aliens theory. "Look. You know what a molecule is?"

"I know the word. Very small. Too small to see." He took his big head in two large-arm hands and wiggled it, the way Red did when he was agitated. "Forgive me. Science is not my…there is no word. I can't know science. I don't think any of us can, really. But especially not me."

I gestured at everything. "Then where did *this* all come from? It didn't just *happen*."

"That's right. It didn't happen. It's always been this way."

I needed a scientist and they sent me a philosopher. Not too bright, either. "Can you ask her?" I pointed to Green. "How can her medicine work, when we're chemically so different?"

"She's not a 'her.' Sometimes she is, and sometimes she's a 'he.' Right now she's a 'what.'"

"Okay. Would you please ask it?"

They exchanged a long series of wheedly-poot-rasp sounds.

"It's something like this," Robin Hood said. "Curing takes intelligence. With Earth humans, the intelligence comes along with the doctor, or scientists. With us, it's in the medicine." He touched the stuff on my breast, which made me jump. "It knows you are different, and works on you differently. It works on the very smallest level."

"Nanotechnology," I said.

"Maybe smaller than that," he said. "As small as chemistry. Intelligent molecules."

"You do know about nanotechnology?"

"Only from TV and the cube." He spidered over to the bed. "Please sit. You make me nervous, balanced there on two legs."

I obliged him. "This is how different we are, Carmen. You know when nanotechnology was discovered."

"End of the twentieth century sometime."

"There's no such knowledge for us. This medicine has always been. Like the living doors that keep the air in. Like the things that make the air, concentrate the oxygen. Somebody made them, but that was so long ago, it was before history. Before we came to Mars."

"Where *did* you come from? When?"

"We would call it Earth, though it's not your Earth, of course. Really far away, really long ago." He paused. "More than ten thousand ares."

A hundred centuries before the Pyramids. "But that's not long enough ago for Mars to be inhabitable. Mars was Mars a million ares ago."

He made an almost human gesture, all four hands palms up. "It could be much longer. At ten thousand ares, history becomes mystery. Our far-away Earth could be a myth. There aren't any space ships lying around.

"What deepens the mystery is that we could never live on Mars, on the surface, but we *could* live on Earth, your Earth. So why were we brought many light years and left on the wrong planet?"

I thought about what Red had said. "Maybe because we're too dangerous."

"That's a theory. Or it might have been dinosaurs. They looked pretty dangerous."

11. SUFFER THE LITTLE CHILDREN

The damage from the laser was repaired in a few hours, and I was bundled back to the colony to be rayed and poked and prodded and interviewed by doctors and scientists. They couldn't find anything wrong with me, human or alien in origin.

"The treatment they gave you sounds like primitive armwaving," Dr. Jefferson said. "The fact that they don't know why it works is scary."

"They don't know why *anything* works over there. It sounds like it's all hand-me-down science from thousands of years ago."

He nodded and frowned. "You're the only data point we have. If the disease were less serious, I'd introduce it to the kids one at a time, and monitor their progress. But there's no time."

Rather than try to take a bunch of sick children over there, they invited the aliens to come to us. It was Red and Green, logically, with Robin Hood and an amber one following closely behind. I was outside, waiting for them, and escorted Red through the airlock.

Half the adults in the colony seemed crowded into the changing room for a first look at the aliens. There was a lot of whispered conversation while Red worked his way out of his suit.

"It's hot," he said. "The oxygen makes me dizzy. This is less than Earth, though?"

"Slightly less," Dr. Jefferson said. He was in the front of the crowd. "Like living on a mountain."

"It smells strange. But not bad. I can smell your hydroponics."

"Where are children?" Green said as soon as she was out of the suit. "No time talk." She held out her bag of herbs and chemicals and shook it.

The children had been prepared with the idea that these "Martians" were our friends, and had a way to cure them. There were pictures of them and their cave. But a picture of an eightlegged potato-head monstrosity isn't nearly as distressing as the real thing—especially to a room full of children who are terribly ill with something no one can explain (but which they suspect is Martian in origin). So their reaction when Dr. Jefferson walked in with Dargo Solingen and Green was predictable—screaming and crying and, from the ambulatory ones, escape attempts. Of course the doors were locked, with people like me spying in through the windows, looking in on the chaos.

Everybody loves Dr. Jefferson, and almost everybody is afraid of Dargo Solingen, and eventually the combination worked. Green just quietly stood there like Exhibit A, which helped. It takes a while not to think of giant spiders when you see them walk.

They had talked about the possibility of sedating the children, to make the experience less traumatic, but the only data they had about the treatment was my description, and they were afraid that if the children were too relaxed, they wouldn't cough forcefully enough to expel all the crap. Without sedation, the experience might haunt them for the rest of their lives, but at least they would *have* lives.

They wanted to keep the children isolated, and both adults would have to stay in there for a while after the treatment, to make sure they hadn't caught it, unlikely as that seemed.

So the only thing between the child being treated and the ones who were waiting for it was a sheet suspended from the ceiling, and after the first one, they all had heard what they were in for. It was done in age order, youngest to oldest, and at first there was some undignified running around, grabbing the victims and dragging them behind the sheet, where they volubly did the hairball performance.

But the children all seemed to sleep peacefully after the thing was over, which calmed most of the others—if they were like me, they hadn't been sleeping much. Card, one of the oldest, who had to wait the longest, pretended to be unconcerned and sleep before the treatment. I know how brave that was of him; he doesn't handle being sick well. As if I did.

The rest of us were mostly crowded into the mess hall, talking with Red and Robin Hood. The other one asked that we call him Fly in Amber, and said that it was his job to remember, so he wouldn't be saying much.

Red said that his job, his function, was hard to describe in human terms. He was sort of like a mayor, a local leader or organizer. He also did things that called for a lot of strength.

Robin Hood said he was being modest; for forty ares he had been a respected leader. When their surveillance device showed that I was in danger of dying, they all looked to Red to make the decision and then act on it.

"It was not a hard decision," he said. "Ever since you landed, we knew that a confrontation was inevitable. I took this opportunity to initiate it, so it would be on our terms. I couldn't know that Carmen would catch this thing, which you call a disease, and bring it back home with her."

"You don't call it a disease?" one of the scientists asked.

"No…I guess in your terms it might be called a 'phase,' a developmental phase. You go from being a young child to being an older child. For us, it's unpleasant but not life-threatening."

"It doesn't make sense," the xenologist Howard Jain said. "It's like a human teenager who has acne, transmitting it to a trout. Or even more extreme than that—the trout at least has DNA."

"And you and the trout have a common ancestor," Robin Hood said. "We have no idea what we might have evolved from."

"Did you get the idea of evolution from us?" he asked.

"No, not as a practical matter. We've been cross-breeding plants for a long time. But Darwinism, yes, from you. From your television programs back in the twentieth century."

"Wait," my father said. "How did you build a television receiver in the first place?"

There was a pause, and then Red spoke: "We didn't. It's always been there."

"What?"

"It's a room full of metal spheres, about as tall as I am. They started making noises in the early twentieth century..."

"Those like me remembered them all," Fly in Amber said, "though they were just noises at first."

"...and we knew the signals were from Earth, because we only got them when Earth was in the sky. Then the spheres started showing pictures in mid-century, which gave us visual clues for decoding human language. Then when the cube was developed, they started displaying in three dimensions."

"How long is 'always'?" Howard Jain asked. "How far back does your history go?"

"We don't have history in your sense," Fly in Amber said. "Your history is a record of conflict and change. We have neither, in the normal course of things. A meteorite damaged an outlying area of our home 4,359 ares ago. Otherwise, not much has happened until your radio started talking."

"You have explored Mars more than we have," Robin Hood said, "with your satellites and rovers, and much of what we know about the planet, we got from you. You put your base in this area because of the large frozen lake underground; we assume that's why we were put here, too. But that memory is long gone."

"Some of us have a theory," Red said, "that the memory was somehow suppressed, deliberately erased. What you don't know you can't tell."

"You can't erase a memory," Fly in Amber said.

"*We* can't. The ones who put us here obviously could do many things we can't do."

"You are not a memory expert. I am."

Red's complexion changed slightly, darkening. It probably wasn't the first time they'd had this argument. "One thing I do remember is the 1950s, when television started."

"You're that old!" Jain said.

"Yes, though I was young then. That was during the war between Russia and the United States, the Cold War."

"You have told us this before," Robin Hood said. "Not all of us agree."

Red pushed on. "The United States had an electronic network it called the 'Distant Early Warning System,' set up so they would know ahead of time, if Russian bombers were on their way." He paused. "I think that's what we are."

"Warning whom?" Jain said.

"Whoever put us here. We're on Mars instead of Earth because they didn't want you to know about us until you had space flight."

"Until we posed a threat to them," Dad said.

"That's a very human thought." Red paused. "Not to be insulting. But it could also be that they didn't want to influence your development too early. Or it could be that there was no profit in contacting you until you had evolved to this point."

"We wouldn't be any threat to them," Jain said. "If they could come here and set up the underground city we saw, thousands and thousands of years ago, it's hard to imagine what they could do now."

The uncomfortable silence was broken by Maria Rodriguez, who came down from the quarantine area. "They're done now. It looks like all the kids are okay." She looked around at all the serious faces. "I said they're okay. Crisis over."

Actually, it had just begun.

12. THE MARS GIRL

Which is how I became an ambassador to the Martians. Everybody knows they didn't evolve on Mars, but what else are you going to call them?

Red, whose real name is Twenty-one Leader Leader Lifter Leader, suggested that I would be a natural choice as a go-between. I was the first human to meet them, and the fact that they risked exposure by saving my life would help humans accept their good intentions.

On Earth, there was a crash program to orbit a space station, Little Mars, that duplicated the living conditions they were used to. Before my five-year residence on Mars was over, I was taken back there with Red and three other Martians, along with Howard Jain, who would be coordinating research.

Nobody wanted to bring them all the way down to Earth quite yet. A worldwide epidemic of the lung crap wouldn't improve relations, and nobody could say whether they might harbor something even more unpleasant.

So I'm sort of a lab animal, under quarantine and constant medical monitoring, maybe for life. But I'm also an ambassador, the human side-kick for Red and the others. Leaders come up from Earth to make symbolic gestures of friendship, even though it's obviously more about fear than brotherhood. When the Others show up, we want to have a good report card from the Martians.

That will be decades or centuries or even millennia—unless they've figured a way around the speed-of-light speed limit. I'm pretty confident they have. So I might meet them.

A couple of days a week, the Elevator comes up and I meet all kinds of presidents and secretariats and so forth, though there's always a pane of glass between us. More interesting is talking with the scientists and other thinkers who vie for one-week residences here, in the five Spartan rooms the Mars Institute maintains. Sometimes rich people come over from the Hilton to gawk. They pay.

The rest of the time, I spend with Red and the others, trying to learn their language—me, who chickened out of French—and teach them about humans. Meanwhile exercise two hours a day in the thin cold air and Martian gravity, and study for my degrees in xenology. I'll be writing the book some day. Not "a" book. The book.

Every now and then some silly tabloid magazine or show will do the "poor little Mars Girl" routine, about how isolated I am in this goldfish bowl hovering over the Earth, never to have anything like a normal life.

But everybody on Mars is under the same quarantine as I am; everybody who's been exposed to the Martians. I could go back some day and kick Dargo Solingen out of office. Marry some old space pilot.

Who wants a normal life, anyhow?

INTRODUCTION TO "SLEEPING DOGS"

I think it was Paul Simon who said that if you asked him to write a song about a woman in a red dress sitting alone smoking in a bar, he could do it right away, but if you asked him to just write a song, he'd be stuck.

So that was my problem: "just write a story." Elizabeth Anne Hull asked me to contribute an original story for *Gateways*, a festschrift in honor of Frederik Pohl. Just a science fiction story; no other restrictions except that it should of course be wonderful.

So starting with just a blank sheet of paper, I began free-associating in a circle, and filled a large page with thoughts and quotes.

I threw away easily 95 percent of the meandering diagram, but one quotation gave me the core of my story—"Soldiers are citizens of death's grey land, drawing no dividend from time's tomorrows." That's the first line of Siegfried Sassoon's great poem "Dreamers."

Perhaps it's a literary crime of some significance, to take a dramatic statement of thirteen words, which pound home like nails into a soldier's coffin—and expand it into a science-fiction novella. I think Sassoon would forgive me for making a living.

SLEEPING DOGS

The cab took my eyeprint and the door swung open. I was glad to get out. No driver to care how rough the ride was, on a road that wouldn't even be called a road on Earth. The place had gone downhill in the thirty years I'd been away.

Low gravity and low oxygen. My heart was going too fast. I stood for a moment, concentrating, and brought it down to a hundred, then ninety. The air had more sulfur sting than I remembered. It seemed a lot warmer than I remembered that summer, too, but then if I could remember it all I wouldn't have to be here. My missing finger throbbed.

Six identical buildings on the block, half-cylinders of stained pale green plastic. I walked up the dirt path to number 3: Offworld Affairs and Confederación Liaison. I almost ran into the door when it didn't open. Pushed and pulled and it reluctantly let me inside.

It was a little cooler and less sulfurous. I went to the second door on the right, Travel Documents and Permissions, and went in.

"You don't knock on Earth?" A cadaverous tall man, skin too white and hair too black.

"Actually, no," I said, "not public buildings. But I apologize for my ignorance."

He looked at a monitor built into his desk. "You would be Flann Spivey, from Japan on Earth. You don't look Japanese."

"I'm Irish," I said. "I work for a Japanese company, Ichiban Imaging."

He touched a word on the screen. "Means number one. Best, or first?"

"Both, I think."

"Papers." I laid out two passports and a folder of travel documents. He spent several minutes inspecting them carefully. Then he slipped them into a primitive scanning machine, which flipped through them one by one, page by page.

He finally handed them back. "When you were here twenty-nine Earth years ago, there were only eight countries on Seca, representing two competing powers. Now there are 79 countries, two of them off-planet, in a political situation that's…impossible to describe simply. Most of the other 78 countries are more comfortable than Spaceport. Nicer."

"So I was told. I'm not here for comfort, though." There weren't many planets where they put their spaceports in nice places.

He nodded slowly as he selected two forms from a drawer. "So what does a 'thanatopic counselor' do?"

"I prepare people for dying." For living completely, actually, before they leave.

"Curious." He smiled. "It pays well?"

"Adequately."

He handed me the forms. "I've never seen a poor person come through that door. Take these down the hall to Immunization."

"I've had all the shots."

"All that the Confederación requires. Seca has a couple of special tests for returning veterans. Of the Consolidation War."

"Of course. The nanobiota. But I was tested before they let me return to Earth."

He shrugged. "Rules. What do you tell them?"

"Tell?"

"The people who are going to die. We just sort of let it catch up with us. Avoid it as long as possible, but…"

"That's a way." I took the forms. "Not the only way."

I had the door partly open when he cleared his throat. "Dr. Spivey? If you don't have any plans, I would be pleased to have midmeal with you."

Interesting. "Sure. I don't know how long this will take…"

"Ten minims, fifteen. I'll call us a floater, so we don't have to endure the road."

The blood and saliva samples took less time than filling out the forms. When I went back outside, the floater was humming down and Braz Nitian was watching it land from the walkway.

It was a fast two-minute hop to the center of town, the last thirty seconds disconcerting free fall. The place he'd chosen was Kaffee Rembrandt, a rough-hewn place with a low ceiling and guttering oil lamps in pursuit of a 16th-century ambience, somewhat diluted by the fact that the dozens of Rembrandt reproductions glowed with apparently sourceless illumination.

A busty waitress in period flounce showed us to a small table, dwarfed by a large self-portrait of the artist posed as "Prodigal Son with a Whore."

I'd never seen an actual flagon, a metal container with a hinged top. It appeared to hold enough wine to support a meal and some conversation.

I ordered a plate of braised vegetables, following conservative dietary advice—the odd proteins in Seca's animals and fish might lay me low with a xeno-allergy. Among the things I didn't remember about my previous time here was whether our rations had included any native flesh or fish. But even if I'd safely eaten them thirty years ago, the Hartford doctor said, I could have a protein allergy now, since an older digestive system might not completely break down those alien proteins into safe amino acids.

Braz had gone to college on Earth, UCLA, an expensive proposition that obligated him to work for the government for ten years (which would be fourteen Earth years). He had degrees in mathematics and macroeconomics, neither of which he used in his office job. He taught three nights a week and wrote papers that nine or ten people read and disagreed with.

"So how did you become a thanatopic counselor? Something you always wanted to be when you grew up?"

"Yeah, after cowboy and pirate."

He smiled. "I never saw a cowboy on Earth."

"Pirates tracked them down and made them walk the plank. Actually, I was an accountant when I joined the military, and then started out in pre-med after I was discharged, but switched over to psychology and moved into studying veterans."

"Natural enough. Know thyself."

"Literally." Find thyself, I thought. "You get a lot of us coming through?"

"Well, not so many, not from Earth or other foreign planets. Being a veteran doesn't correlate well with wealth."

"That's for sure." And a trip from Earth to Seca and back costs as much as a big house.

"I imagine that treating veterans doesn't generate a lot of money, either." Eyebrows lifting.

"A life of crime does." I smiled and he laughed politely. "But most of the veterans I do see are well off. Almost nobody with a normal life span needs my services. They're mostly for people who've lived some centuries, and you couldn't do that without wealth."

"They get tired of life?"

"Not the way you or I could become tired of a game, or a relationship. It's something deeper than running out of novelty. People with that little imagination don't need me. They can stop existing for the price of a bullet or a rope—or a painless prescription, where I come from."

"Not legal here," he said neutrally.

"I know. I'm not enthusiastic about it, myself."

"You'd have more customers?"

I shrugged. "You never know." The waitress brought us our first plates, grilled fungi on a stick for me. Braz had a bowl of small animals with tails, deep-fried. Finger food; you hold them by the tail and dip them into a pungent yellow sauce.

It was much better than I'd expected; the fungi were threaded onto a stick of some aromatic wood like laurel; she brought a small glass of a lavender-colored drink, tasting like dry sherry, to go with them.

"So it's not about getting bored?" he asked. "That's how you normally see it. In books, on the cube…"

"Maybe the reality isn't dramatic enough. Or too complicated to tell as a simple drama.

"You live a few hundred years, at least on Earth, you slowly leave your native culture behind. You're an immortal—culturally true if not literally—and your non-immortal friends and family and business associates die off. The longer you live, the deeper you go into the immortal community."

"There must be some nonconformists."

"'Mavericks,' the cowboys used to say."

"Before the pirates did them in."

"Right. There aren't many mavericks past their first century of life extension. The people you grew up with are either fellow immortals or dead. Together, the survivors form a society that's unusually cohesive. So when someone decides to leave, decides to stop living, the arrangements are complex and may involve hundreds of people.

"That's where I come in, the practical part of my job: I'm a kind of overall estate manager. They all have significant wealth; few have any living relatives closer than great-great-grandchildren."

"You help them split up their fortunes?"

"It's more interesting than that. The custom for centuries has been to put together a legacy, so called, that is a complex and personal aesthetic expression. To simply die, and let the lawyers sort it out, would trivialize your life as well as your death. It's my job to make sure that the legacy is a meaningful and permanent extension of the person's life.

"Sometimes a physical monument is involved; more often a financial one, through endowments and sponsorships. Which is what brings me here."

Our main courses came; Braz had a kind of eel, bright green with black antennae, apparently raw, but my braised vegetables were reassuringly familiar.

"So one of your clients is financing something here on Seca?"

"Financing me, actually. It's partly a gift; we get along well. But it's part of a pattern of similar bequests to non-immortals, to give us back lost memories."

"How lost?"

"It was a military program, to counteract the stress of combat. They called the drug aqualethe. Have you heard of it?"

He shook his head. "Water of what?"

"It's a linguistic mangling, or mingling. Latin and Greek. Lethe was a river in Hell; a spirit drank from it to forget his old life, so he could be reincarnated.

"A pretty accurate name. It basically disconnects your long-term memory as a way of diverting combat stress, so called post-traumatic stress disorder."

"It worked?"

"Too well. I spent eight months here as a soldier, when I was in my early twenties. I don't remember anything specific between the voyage here and the voyage back."

"It was a horrible war. Short but harsh. Maybe you don't want the memory back. 'Let sleeping dogs lie,' we say here."

"We say that, too. But for me...well, you could say it's a professional handicap. Though actually it goes deeper.

"Part of what I do with my clients is a mix of meditation and dialogue. I try to help them form a coherent tapestry of their lives, the good and the bad, as a basic grounding for their legacy. The fact that I could never do

479

that for myself hinders me as a counselor. Especially when the client, like this one, had his own combat experiences to deal with."

"He's, um, dead now?"

"Oh, no. Like many of them, he's in no particular hurry. He just wants to be ready."

"How old is he?"

"Three hundred and ninety Earth years. Aiming for four centuries, he thinks."

Braz sawed away at his eel and looked thoughtful, "I can't imagine. I mean, I sort of understand when a normal man gets so old he gives up. Their hold on life becomes weak, and they let go. But your man is presumably fit and sane."

"More than I, I think."

"So why four hundred years rather than five? Or three? Why not try for a thousand? That's what I would do, if I were that rich."

"So would I. At least that's how I feel now. My patron says he felt that way when he was mortal. But he can't really articulate what happened to slowly change his attitude.

"He says it would be like trying to explain married love to a babe just learning to talk. The babe thinks it knows what love is, and can apply the word to its own circumstances. But it doesn't have the vocabulary or life experience to approach the larger meaning."

"An odd comparison, marriage," he said, delicately separating the black antennae from the head. "You can become unmarried. But not undead."

"The babe wouldn't know about divorce. Maybe there is a level of analogy there."

"We don't know what death is?"

"Perhaps not as well as they."

I liked Braz and needed to hire a guide; he had some leave coming and could use the side income. His Spanish was good, and that was rare on Secas; they spoke a kind of patchwork of Portuguese and English. If I'd studied it thirty years before, I'd retained none.

The therapy to counteract aqualethe was a mixture of brain chemistry and environment. Simply put, the long-term memories were not destroyed by aqualethe, but the connection to them had been weakened. There was a regimen of twenty pills I had to take twice daily, and I had to take them in surroundings that would jog my memory.

That meant going back to some ugly territory.

There were no direct flights to Serraro, the mountainous desert where my platoon had been sent to deal with a situation now buried in secrecy, perhaps shame. We could get within a hundred kilometers of it, an oasis town called Console Verde. I made arrangements to rent a general-purpose vehicle there, a jépe.

After Braz and I made those arrangements, I got a note from some Chief of Internal Security saying that my activities were of questionable legality, and I should report to his office at 0900 tomorrow to defend my actions. We were in the airport, fortunately, when I got the message, and we jumped on a flight that was leaving in twenty minutes, paying cash. Impossible on Earth.

I told Braz I would buy us a couple of changes of clothing and such at the Oasis, and we got on the jet with nothing but our papers, my medications, and the clothes on our backs—and my purse, providentially stuffed with the paper notes they use instead of plastic. (I'd learned that the exchange rate was much better on Earth, and was carrying half a year's salary in those notes.)

The flight wasn't even suborbital, and took four hours to go about a tenth of the planet's circumference. We slept most of the way; it didn't take me twenty minutes to tell him everything I had been able to find out about that two-thirds year that was taken from me.

Serraro is not exactly a bastion of freedom of information under the best of circumstances, and that was a period in their history that many would just as soon forget.

It was not a poor country. The desert was rich in the rare earths that interstellar jumps required. There had been lots of small mines around the countryside (no farms) and only one city of any size. That was Novo B, short for Novo Brasil, and it was still not the safest spot in the Confederación. Not on our itinerary.

My platoon had begun its work in Console Verde as part of a force of one thousand. When we returned to that oasis, there were barely six hundred of us left. But the country had been "unified." Where there had been 78 mines there now was one, Preciosa, and no one wanted to talk about how that happened.

The official history says that the consolidation of those 78 mines was a model of self-determinism, the independent miners banding together for strength and bargaining power. There was some resistance, even some outlaw guerilla action. But the authorities—I among them, evidently—got things under control in less than a year.

Travel and residence records had all been destroyed by a powerful explosion blamed on the guerillas, but in the next census, Serarro had lost thirty-five percent of its population. Perhaps they walked away.

We stood out as foreigners in our business suits; most men who were not in uniform wore a plain loose white robe. I went immediately into a shop next to the airport and bought two of them, and two sidearms. Braz hadn't fired a pistol in years, but he had to agree he would look conspicuous here without one.

We stood out anyway, pale and tall. The men here were all sunburned and most wore long braided black hair. Our presence couldn't be kept secret; I wondered how long it would be before that Chief of Internal Security caught up with me. I was hoping it was just routine harassment, and they wouldn't follow us here.

There was only one room at the small inn, but Braz didn't mind sharing. In fact, he suggested we pass the time with sex, which caught me off guard. I told him men don't routinely do that on Earth, at least not the place and time I came from. He accepted that with a nod.

I asked the innkeeper whether the town had a library, and he said no, but I could try the schoolhouse on the other side of town. Braz was napping, so I left a note and took off on my own, confident in my ability to turn right and go to the end of the road.

Although I'd been many places on Earth, the only time I'd been in space was that eight-month tour here. So I kept my eyes open for "alien" details.

Seca had a Drake index of 0.95, which by rule of thumb meant that only five percent of it was more harsh than the worst the Earth had to offer. The equatorial desert, I supposed. We were in what would have been a temperate latitude on Earth, and I was sweating freely in the dry heat.

The people here were only five generations away from Earth, but some genetic drift was apparent. No more profound than you would find on some islands and other isolated communities on Earth. But I didn't see a single blonde or red-head in the short, solidly built population here.

The men wore scowls as well as guns. The women, brighter colors and a neutral distant expression.

Some of the men, mostly younger, wore a dagger as well as a sidearm. I wondered whether there was some kind of code duello that I would have to watch out for. Probably *not* wearing a dagger would protect you from that.

Aside from a pawn shop, with three balls, and a tavern with bright signs announcing berbesa and bino, most of the shops were not identified. I supposed that in a small isolated town, everybody knew where everything was.

Two men stopped together, blocking the sidewalk. One of them touched his pistol and said something incomprehensible, loudly.

"From Earth," I said, in unexcited Confederaciôn Spanish. "*Soy de la Tierra.*" They looked at each other and went by me. I tried to ignore the crawling feeling in the middle of my back.

I reflected on my lack of soldierly instincts. Should I have touched my gun as well? Probably not. If they'd started shooting, what should I do? Hurl my 60-year-old body to the ground, roll over with the pistol in my hand, and aim for the chest?

"Two in the chest, then one in the head," I remembered from crime drama. But I didn't remember anything that basic from having been a soldier. My training on Earth had mainly been calisthenics and harassment. Endless hours of parade-ground drill. Weapons training would come later, they said. The only thing "later" meant to me was months later, slowly regaining my identity on the trip back to Earth.

By the time I'd gotten off the ship, I seemed to have all my memories back through basic training, and the lift ride up to the troop carrier. We had 1.5-gee acceleration to the Oort portal, but somewhere along there I lost my memory, and didn't get it back till the return trip. Then they dropped me on Earth—me and the other survivors—with a big check and a leather case full of medals. Plus a smaller check, every month, for my lost finger.

I knew I was approaching the school by the small tide of children running in my direction, about fifty of them, ranging from seven or eight to about twelve, in Earth years.

The school house was small, three or four rooms. A grey-bearded man marched, stepped out and I hailed him. We established that we had English in common and I asked whether the school had a library. He said yes, and it would be open for two hours yet. "Mostly children's books, of course. What are you interested in?"

"History," I said. "Recent. The Consolidation War."

"Ah. Follow me." He led me through a dusty playground, to the rear of the school. "You were a Confederaciôn soldier?'

"I guess that's obvious."

He paused with his hand on the doorknob. "You know to be careful?" I said I did. "Don't go out at night alone. Your size is like a beacon." He opened the door and said, "Suela? A traveler is looking for a history book."

The room was high-ceilinged and cool, with thick stone walls and plenty of light from the uniform glow of the ceiling. An elderly woman with white hair taking paper books from a cart and re-shelving them.

"Pardon my poor English," she said, with an accent better than mine. "But what do you want in a paper book that you can't as easily download?"

"I was curious to see what children are taught about the Consolidation War."

"The same truth as everyone," she said with a wry expression, and stepped over to another shelf. "Here..." she read titles, "this is the only one in English. I can't let you take it away, but you're welcome to read it here."

I thanked her and took the book to an adult-sized table and chair at the other end of the room. Most of the study area was scaled down. A girl of seven or eight stared at me.

I didn't know, really, what I expected to find in the book. It had four pages on the Consolidation and Preciosa, and in broad outline there was not much surprising. A coalition of mines decided that the Confederación wasn't paying enough for dysprosium, and they got most of the others to go along with the scheme of hiding the stuff and holding out for a fair price—what the book called profiteering and restraint of trade. Preciosa was the biggest mine, and they made a separate deal with the Confederación, guaranteeing a low price, freezing all their competitors out. Which led to war.

Seca—actually Preciosa—asked for support from the Confederación, and the war became interstellar.

The book said that most of the war took place far from population centers, in the bleak high desert where the mines were. Here.

It struck me that I hadn't noticed many old buildings, older than about thirty years. I remembered a quote from a twentieth-century American war: "We had to destroy the village in order to save it."

The elderly librarian sat down across from me. She had a soft voice. "You were here as a soldier. But you don't remember anything about it."

"That's true. That's exactly it."

"There are those of us who do remember."

I pushed the book a couple of inches toward her. "Is any of this true?"

She turned the book around and scanned the pages it was open to, and shook her head with a grim smile. "Even children know better. What do you think the Confederación is?"

I thought for a moment. "At one level, it's a loose federation of 48 or 49 planets with a charter protecting the rights of humans and non-humans, and with trade rules that encourage fairness and transparency. At another level, it's the Hartford Corporation, the wealthiest enterprise in human history. Which can do anything it wants, presumably."

"And on a personal level? What is it to you?"

"It's an organization that gave me a job when jobs were scarce. Security specialist. Although I wasn't a 'specialist' in any sense of the word. A generalist, so called."

"A mercenary."

"Not so called. Nothing immoral or illegal."

"But they took your memory of it away. So it could have been either, or both."

"Could have been," I admitted. "I'm going to find out. Do you know about the therapy that counteracts aqualethe?"

"No...it gives you your memories back?"

"So they say. I'm going to drive down into Serarro tomorrow, and see what happens. You take the pills in the place you want to remember."

"Do me a favor," she said, sliding the book back, "and yourself, perhaps. Take the pills here, too."

"I will. We had a headquarters here. I must have at least passed through."

"Look for me in the crowd, welcoming you. You were all so exotic and handsome. I was a girl, just ten."

Ten here would be fourteen on Earth. This old lady was younger than me. No juve treatments. "I don't think the memories will be that detailed. I'll look for you, though."

She patted my hand and smiled. "You do that."

Blaz was still sleeping when I got back to the inn. Six time zones to adjust to; might as well let him sleep. My body was still on meaningless starship time, but I've never had much trouble adjusting. My counseling job is a constant whirl of time zones.

I quietly slipped into the other bunk and put some Handel in my earbuds to drown out his snoring.

The inn didn't have any vegetables for breakfast, so I had a couple of eggs that I hoped had come from a bird, and a large dry flavorless cracker. Our jepé arrived at 8:30 and I went out to pay the substantial deposit and inspect it. Guaranteed bulletproof except for the windows, nice to know.

I took the first leg of driving, since I'd be taking the memory drug later, and the label had the sensible advice *Do Not Operate Machinery While Hallucinating.* Words to live by.

The city, such as it was, didn't dwindle off into suburbs. It's an oasis, and where the green stopped, the houses stopped.

I drove very cautiously at first. My car in LA is restricted to autopilot, and it had been several years since I was last behind a steering wheel. A little exhilarating.

After about thirty kilometers, the road suddenly got very rough. Braz suggested that we'd left the state of Console Verde and had entered Pretorocha, whose tax base wouldn't pay for a shovel. I gave the wheel to him after a slow hour, when we got to the first pile of tailings. Time to take the first twenty pills.

I didn't really know what to expect. I knew the unsupervised use of the aqualethe remedy was discouraged, because some people had extreme reactions. I'd given Braz an emergency poke of sedative to administer to me if I really lost control.

Rubble and craters. Black grit over everything. Building ruins that hadn't weathered much; this place didn't have much weather. Hot and dry in the summer, slightly less hot and more dry in the winter. We drove around and around and absolutely nothing happened. After two hours, the minimum wait, I swallowed another twenty.

Pretorocha was where they said I'd lost my finger, and it was where the most Confederación casualties had been recorded. Was it possible that the drug just didn't work on me?

What was more likely, if I properly understood the literature, was one of two things: one, the place had changed so much that my recovering memory didn't pick up any specifics; two, that I'd never actually been here.

That second didn't seem possible. I'd left a finger here, and the Confederacíon verified that; it had been paying for the lost digit for thirty years.

The first explanation? Pictures of the battle looked about as bleak as this blasted landscape. Maybe I was missing something basic, like a smell or the summer heat. But the literature said the drug required visual stimuli.

"Maybe it doesn't work as well on some as on others," Braz said. "Or maybe you got a bad batch. How long do we keep driving around?"

I had six tubes of pills left. The drug was in my system for sure: cold sweat, shortness of breath, ocular pressure. "Hell, I guess we've seen enough. Take a pee break and head back."

Standing by the side of the road there, under the low hot sun, urinating into black ash, somehow I knew for certain that I'd never been there before. A hellish place like this would burn itself into your subconscious.

But aqualethe was strong. Maybe too strong for the remedy to counter.

I took the wheel for the trip back to Console Verde. The air-conditioning had only two settings, frigid and off. We agreed to turn it off and open the non-bulletproof windows to the waning heat.

There was a kind of lunar beauty to the place. That would have made an impression on me back then. When I was still a poet. An odd thing to remember. Something did happen that year to end that. Maybe I lost it with the music, with the finger.

When the road got better I let Braz take over. I was out of practice with traffic, and they drove on the wrong side of the road anyhow.

The feeling hit me when the first buildings rose up out of the rock. My throat. Not like choking; a gentler pressure, like tightening a necktie.

Everything shimmered and glowed. *This* was where I'd been. This side of the city.

"Braz...it's happening. Go slow." He pulled over to the left and I heard warning lights go click-click-click.

"You weren't...down there at all? You were here?"

"I don't know! Maybe. I don't know." It was coming on stronger and stronger. Like seeing double, but with all your body. "Get into the right lane." It was getting hard to see, a brilliant fog. "What is that big building?"

"Doesn't have a name," he said. "Confederación sigil over the parking lot."

"Go there...go there...I'm losing it, Braz."

"Maybe you're finding it."

The car was fading around me, and I seemed to drift forward and up. Through the wall of the building. Down a corridor. Through a closed door. Into an office.

I was sitting there, a young me. Coal black beard, neatly trimmed. Dress uniform. All my fingers.

Most of the wall behind me was taken up by a glowing spreadsheet. I knew what it represented.

Two long tables flanked my work station. They were covered with old ledgers and folders full of paper correspondence and records.

My job was to steal the planet from its rightful owners—but not the whole planet. Just the TREO rights, Total Rare Earth Oxides.

There was not much else on the planet of any commercial interest to the Confederación. When they found a tachyon nexus, they went off in search of dysprosium nearby, necessary for getting back to where you came from, or continuing farther out. Automated probes had found a convenient source in a mercurian planet close to the nexus star Poucoyellow. But after a few thousand pioneers had staked homestead claims on Seca, someone stumbled on a mother lode of dysprosium and other rare earths in the sterile hell of Serarro.

It was the most concentrated source of dysprosium ever found, on any planet, easily a thousand times the output of Earth's mines.

The natives knew what they had their hands on, and they were cagey. They quietly passed a law that required all mineral rights to be deeded on paper; no electronic record. For years, 78 mines sold two percent of the dysprosium they dug up, and stockpiled the rest—as much as the Confederación could muster from two dozen other planets. Once they had hoarded enough, they could absolutely corner the market.

But they only had one customer.

Routine satellite mapping gave them away; the gamma ray signature of monazite-allenite stuck out like a flag. The Confederación deduced what was going on, and trained a few people like me to go in and remedy the situation, along with enough soldiers to supply the fog of war.

While the economy was going crazy, dealing with war, I was quietly buying up small shares in the rare earth mines, through hundreds of fictitious proxies.

When we had voting control of 51 percent of the planet's dysprosium, and thus its price, the soldiers did an about-face and went home, first stopping at the infirmary for a shot of aqualethe.

I was a problem, evidently. Aqualethe erased the memory of trauma, but I hadn't experienced any. All I had done was push numbers around, and occasionally forge signatures.

So one day three big men wearing black hoods kicked in my door and took me to a basement somewhere. They beat me monotonously for hours, wearing thick gloves, not breaking bones or rupturing organs. I was blindfolded and handcuffed, sealed up in a universe of constant pain.

Then they took off the blindfold and handcuffs and those three men held my arm and hand while a fourth used heavy bolt-cutters to snip off the ring finger of my left hand, making sure I watched. Then they dressed the stump and gave me a shot.

I woke up approaching Earth, with medals and money and no memory. And one less finger.

Woke again on my bunk at the inn. Braz sitting there with a carafe of *melán*, what they had at the inn instead of coffee. "Are you coming to?" he said quietly. "I helped you up the stairs." Dawn light at the window. "It was pretty bad?"

"It was …not what I expected." I levered myself upright and accepted a cup. "I wasn't really a soldier. In uniform, but just a clerk. Or a con man." I sketched out the story for him.

"So they actually chopped off your finger? I mean, beat you senseless and then snipped it off?"

I squeezed the short stump gingerly. "So the drug would work.

"I played guitar, before. So I spent a year or so working out alternative fingerings, formations, without the third finger. Didn't really work."

I took a sip. It was like kava, a bitter alkaloid. "So I changed careers."

"You were going to be a singer?"

"No. Classical guitar. So I went back to university instead, pre-med and then psychology and philosophy. Got an easy doctorate in Generalist Studies. And became this modern version of the boatman, ferryman… Charon—the one who takes people to the other side."

"So what are you going to do? With the truth."

"Spread it around, I guess. Make people mad."

He rocked back in his chair. "Who?"

"What do you mean? Everybody."

"Everybody?" He shook his head. "Your story's interesting, and your part in it is dramatic and sad, but there's not a bit of it that would surprise anyone over the age of twenty. Everyone knows what the war was really about.

"It's even more cynical and manipulative than I thought, but you know? That won't make people mad. When it's the government, especially the Confederación, people just nod and say, 'more of the same.'"

"Same old, we say. Same old shit."

"They settled death and damage claims generously; rebuilt the town. And it was half a lifetime ago, our lifetimes. Only the old remember, and most of them don't care anymore."

That shouldn't have surprised me; I've been too close to it. Too close to my own loss, small compared to others'.

I sipped at the horrible stuff and put it back down. "I should do something. I can't just sit on this."

"But you can. Maybe you should."

I made a dismissive gesture and he leaned forward and continued with force. "Look, Spivey. I'm not just a backsystem hick—or I am, but I'm a hick with a rusty doctorate in macroeconomics—and you're not seeing or thinking clearly. About the war and the Confederación. Let the drugs dry out before you do something that you might regret."

"That's pretty dramatic."

"Well, the situation you're in is *melo*dramatic! You want to go back to Earth and say you have proof that the Confederación used you to subvert the will of a planet, to the tune of more than a thousand dead and a trillion hartfords of real estate, then tortured and mutilated you in order to blank out your memory of it?"

"Well? That's what happened."

He got up. "You think about it for awhile. Think about the next thing that's going to happen." He left and closed the door quietly behind him.

I didn't have to think too long. He was right.

Before I came to Seca, of course I searched every resource for verifiable information about the war. That there was so little should have set off an alarm in my head.

It's a wonderful thing to be able to travel from star to star, collecting exotic memories. But you have no choice of carrier. To take your memories back to Earth, you have to rely on the Confederación.

And if those memories are unpleasant, or just inconvenient…they can fix that for you.

Over and over.

INTRODUCTION TO "COMPLETE SENTENCE"

MIT's journal *Technology Review* asked me to write a short-short story, under a thousand words. I have a sentimental attachment to MIT—have taught there in the fall since 1983—so I would have written the story even if they hadn't offered, let me see (counting up on fingers) exactly ten times the word rate of a science fiction magazine.

I also sent it to the experts at *Writers Digest* magazine, along with an entry fee, for their annual short-short story writing contest. They took my paper clip and didn't even give it an honorable mention.

Of course I wouldn't have included it in this collection if I shared that low opinion. I value brevity and drama. Sometimes a story does have to be long. Sometimes it should be sudden as a slap.

COMPLETE SENTENCE

The cell was spotless white and too bright and smelled of chlorine bleach.

"So I've had it, is what you're saying." Charlie Draper sat absolutely still on the cell bunk. "I didn't kill Maggie. You know that better than anybody."

His lawyer nodded slowly and looked at him with no expression. She was beautiful, and that sometimes helped with a jury, though evidently not this time. "We've appealed, of course." Her voice was a fraction of a second out of synch with her mouth. "It's automatic."

"And meaningless. I'll be out before they open the envelope."

"Well." She stepped over to the small window and looked down at the sea. "We went over the pluses and minuses before you opted for virtual punishment."

"So I serve a hundred years in one day—"

"Less than a day. Overnight."

"—and then sometime down the pike some other jury decides I'm innocent, or at least not guilty, and then what? They give me back the hundred years I sat here?"

He was just talking, of course; he knew the answer. There might be compensation for wrongful imprisonment. A day's worth, though, or a century? Nobody had yet been granted it; virtual sentencing was too new.

"You have to leave now, counselor," a disembodied voice said. She nodded, opened her mouth to say something, and disappeared.

That startled him. "It's already started?"

493

The door rattled open, and an unshaven trusty in an orange jumpsuit shambled in with a tray. Behind him was a beefy guard with a shotgun.

"What's with the gun?" he said to the trusty. "This isn't real; I can't escape."

"Don't answer him," the guard said. "You'll wind up in solitary, too."

"Oh, bullshit. Neither of you are real people."

The guard stepped forward, reversed the weapon, and thumped him hard on the sternum. "Not real?" He hit the wall behind him and slid to the floor, trying to breathe, pain radiating from the center of his chest.

✺

As the cell walls and Draper faded, a nurse gently wiggled the helmet until it came off her head. It was like a light bicycle helmet, white. With a warm gloved hand, she helped her sit up on the gurney.

She looked over at Draper, lying on the gurney next to hers. His black helmet was more complicated, a thick cable and lots of small wires. The same blue hospital gown as she was wearing. But he had a catheter, and there was a light black cable around his chest, hardly a restraint, held in place by a small lock with a tag she had signed.

The nurse set her white helmet down carefully on a table. "You don't want to drive or anything for a couple of hours." She had a sour expression, lips pursed.

"No problem. I have Autocar."

She nodded microscopically. *Rich bitch.* "Take you where your things are."

"Okay. Thank you." As she scrunched off the gurney, the gown slid open, and she reached back to hold it closed, feeling silly. Followed the woman as she stalked through the door. "I take it you don't approve."

"No, ma'am. He serves less than one day for murdering his wife."

"A, he didn't murder her, and B, it will feel like a hundred years."

"That's what they say." She turned with eyes narrowing. "They all say they didn't do it. And they say it feels like a long time. What would you expect them to say? 'I beat the system and was in and out in a day'? Here."

As soon as the door clicked shut, she opened the locker and lifted out her neatly folded suit, the charcoal grey one she had appeared to be wearing in the cell a few minutes before.

✸

The blow had knocked the wind out of him. By the time he got his voice back, they were gone.

The tray had a paper plate with something like cold oatmeal on it. He picked up the plastic spoon and tasted the stuff. Grits. They must have known he hated grits.

"They didn't say anything about solitary. What, I'm going to sit here like this for a hundred years?" No answer.

He carried the plate over to the barred window. It was open to the outside. A fall of perhaps a hundred feet to an ocean surface. He could hear faint surf but, leaning forward, couldn't see the shore, even with the cold metal bars pressing against his forehead. The air smelled of seaweed, totally convincing.

He folded the paper plate and threw it out between the bars. The grits sprayed out and the plate dipped and twirled realistically, and fell out of sight.

He studied the waves. Were they too regular? That would expose their virtuality. He had heard that if you could convince yourself that it wasn't real—completely convince your body that this wasn't happening—the time might slip quickly away in meditation. Time might disappear.

But it was hard to ignore the throbbing in his chest. And there were realistic irregularities in the waves. In the trough between two waves, a line of pelicans skimmed along with careless grace.

Maybe the illusion was only maintained at that level when he was concentrating. He closed his eyes and tried to think of nothing.

Zen trick: four plain tiles. Make each one disappear. The nothing that is left is just as real. Exactly as real. After a while, he opened his eyes again.

The pelicans came back. Did that mean anything?

Maybe he shouldn't have thrown away the grits. You probably get hungry in virtual reality. But you couldn't starve to death, not overnight. No matter how long it seemed.

He gave the iron bar a jerk. It squeaked.

He tugged on it twice, and it seemed to move a fraction of a millimeter each time. Was that possible? He looked closely, and indeed the hole the bar was seated in had slightly enlarged. He could wiggle it.

"Trusty?" he shouted. Nothing. He walked to the steel door and shouted through the little hole. "Hey! Your goddamn jail's already falling apart!" He peered through the small peephole. Nothing but darkness.

He sniffed at the hole, and it smelled of drilled metal. "Hey! I know you're out there!"

But what did he really know?

✺

She popped her umbrella against the afternoon shower and was almost to the parking place when a young man came running out. "Ms. Hartley!" He was waving a piece of paper. "Ms. Hartley!" She stepped toward him and let him get under the umbrella.

"Your objection was approved. You can bring him out any time!"

She glanced at her watch. He'd only been in VR for about twenty minutes, counting the time she'd spent dressing. "Let's go!" Two months passing each minute.

Security at the courthouse door took an agonizing five minutes. But the young man raced on ahead to make sure the room was ready.

She crashed through a door and rushed up the single flight of stairs rather than wait for the elevator. The sour-faced woman was blocking the entrance to the VR room.

"Get out of the way. Every second, he spends a day in that awful cell."

"You know this won't work if he doesn't believe in his own innocence. If he blames himself in any way."

"He wasn't even *there* when his wife was murdered!" The woman's eyes searched the lawyer's face. "Look! I've been a defense attorney for eighteen years. I know when someone's lying to me. *He didn't kill her!*"

She pushed on in and the young man was standing by a chair, next to the gurney that Charlie Draper lay on, holding the white helmet. "Here. You don't have to lie down. Just put this on."

✺

Crappy system can't even make an illusion that works.

He went back to the iron bar and rotated it squeaking in its concrete socket, and gave it a good rattle. Concrete dust sifted down. He seized it in both hands and gave it all he had. "Bitch!" He squeezed it as hard as he had Maggie's neck, and jerked, with the strength that had snapped it and killed her.

The bar came free in his hands. A piece of concrete fell to the floor with a solid thunk."You call this a..."

496

A large crack crawled up and down from floor to ceiling. With a loud growl, half the wall tilted and fell piecemeal into the sea."Wait." A fine powder was drifting down. He looked up to see the ceiling disappear. "No." All four walls crumbled into gravel and showered to the sea.

❋

When they took the helmet off her, there was an older man, dressed like a doctor, standing there.

"It's a temporary thing," he said. "He's resisting coming out of it. For some reason."

"I didn't go to the cell. I didn't go anywhere," she said, peering inside the helmet. "It was all just white, and white noise, static."

"You're out of the circuit. The electronics do test out. But he's not letting you making contact."

She looked into her client's vacant eyes. She touched his cheek gently and he didn't respond. "Has this happened before?"

"Not with people who know and trust each other. But we'll get through to him."

"Meanwhile…every ten hours is a hundred years?"

"That's a safe assumption." The doctor opened the manila folder in his hand and looked at the single piece of paper within. "He signed a waiver—"

"I know. I was there." She lifted her client's hand and let it drop back onto the sheet. "He's a…social kind of guy. I hope he's not too lonely."

❋

There was only the floor and the iron door. He touched the door and it fell away. It turned end over end once, and slid flawlessly into the water, like an Olympic diver.

Above him, a perfect cloudless sky that somehow had no sun. Below, the waves marched from one horizon to the opposite. A line of pelicans appeared.

He tried to throw himself into the water, but he hit something soft and invisible, and fell gently back.

He screamed until he was hoarse. Then he tried to sleep. But the noise of the waves kept him awake.

497